Mr. Myombekere and His Wife Bugonoka, Their Son Ntulanalwo and Daughter Bulihwali:

THE STORY OF AN ANCIENT AFRICAN COMMUNITY

Anicet Kitereza

Translated from the original Kikerewe novel
with an introduction and notes by Gabriel Ruhumbika

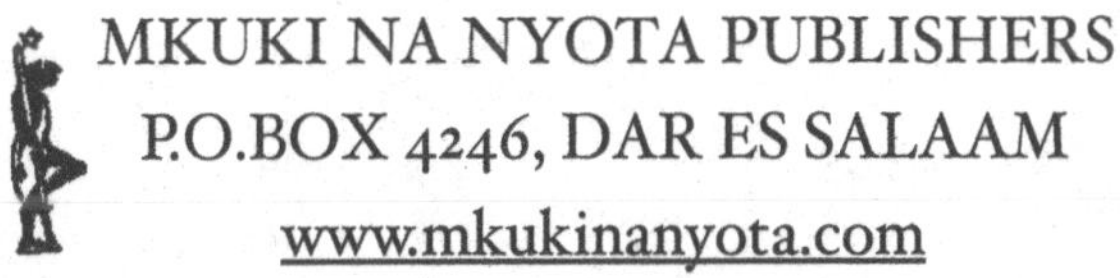

MKUKI NA NYOTA PUBLISHERS
P.O.BOX 4246, DAR ES SALAAM
www.mkukinanyota.com

Mkuki na Nyota Publishers,
P.O. Box 4246, Dar es salaam, Tanzania.
www.mkukinanyota.com

Published by Mkuki na Nyota *Publishers 2002*

Copyright © Translation and Notes: Gabriel Ruhumbika 2002
Cover picture: The author and his wife by Walter Bgoya
Cover Design: Petra's Maridadi

ISBN 9976 686 382

Contents

ACKNOWLEDGMENTS

I wrote this English translation of Aniceti Kitereza's Kikerewe novel *Myombekere na Bugonoka na Ntulanalwo na Bulihwali* with the help of a grant from the American National Endowment for the Humanities, and my thanks go first to the agency for the assistance, without which my work would probably have not taken off. I would also like to thank the University of Georgia for having made it possible for me to carry out further research for my annotations and Introduction to supplement what I was able to accomplish by the NHE grant; and Dr. Ronald Bogue, the university's former Head of the Comparative Literature Department, for his encouragement and support.

I also owe thanks to the Western Africanist scholars and their Tanzanian colleagues who made possible the publication of the author's Swahili translation of his work, especially the late American professor, Dr. Gerald W. Hartwig, his wife Dr. Charlotte (Shoonie) Hartwig and Walter Bgoya then at the Tanzania Publishing House (TPH) and publisher of this English translation. The only other edition of the novel published so far is a German translation based on the Swahili translation, and there is no doubt in my mind that my translation too, though based on the original Kikerewe text, owes its existence to the fact that in 1980 TPH published the Swahili translation which finally brought to light this great African work of art.

I would also like to thank my cousin Rev. Father Alexander Mugonya, the heir to the estate of our late paternal uncle Aniceti Kitereza, for giving me permission to translate and publish this English translation of the author's still unpublished original Kikerewe text, and for making available to me the author's personal correspondence and other documents, including his notes on his novel. He also made available to me the diary the author kept over several decades, which gave me invaluable insight into the life of the extraordinary human being and great artist that he was and furthered my understanding and appreciation of his work.

Lastly, I very much doubt whether I would have completed this translation had my wife Resty not done everything she could to make it possible for me to devote to my work every free moment I had. Throughout the many years that this work took, there isn't a single one of our children, our daughter Kutina and our three sons Michael Lukumbuzya, Kaseza and Ibanda, who did not ask me the same question over and over again: "Dad, when will you finish writing your book?" I would, therefore, like to end by sincerely thanking my wife for seeing me through my work with such loving support and our children for their years of patience and understanding.

Gabriel Ruhumbika

INTRODUCTION

In 1945, Aniceti Kitereza wrote the novel *Myombekere na Bugonoka na Ntulanalwo na Bulihwali* in his native language, Kikerewe. *Mr. Myombekere and His Wife Bugonoka, Their Son Ntulanalwo and Daughter Bulihwali: The Story of an Ancient African Community* is my translation of this novel that portrays the traditional social and cultural life of the people inhabiting Ukerewe[1] in northern Tanzania.

At the beginning of the seventeenth century, the Basilanga-Bahinda clan founded the African kingdom of Ukerewe. Kitereza belonged to this clan. The kingdom comprised Ukerewe Island (494 sq. km.), the surrounding twenty-five minor islands with a total area of approximately fifty square kilometers, all situated in the southern part of Lake Nyanza, now more commonly called Lake Victoria, and Mwibara or "Mainland" Ukerewe, a peninsula adjacent to the main island.

The German colonial administration conducted the first census of the kingdom in 1907, showing a total population of forty five thousand people. Of those, thirty thousand lived on Ukerewe Island, two thousand lived on the minor islands, and thirteen thousand on the sparsely populated Mwibara or Mainland Ukerewe. (Hurel 1911, 62-65) (Machunda 1988, 12).

By the time Kitereza wrote his novel, the population of Ukerewe had almost trebled (Tanganyika Government Blue Book Statistics 1949). In addition to an increase in the population, other important demographic changes had also occurred. The Wakerewe now counted for only thirty percent of the population. The Wajita, on the other hand, had increased from what the British-American explorer Henry M. Stanley reported as a small enclave living on the south coast of the main island just before the beginning of white colonial rule (Stanley 250) to account for forty percent of the population (Moffett 185).[2] The remaining population consisted of Waruri and other Wajita-related people from Musoma area north of Mwibara peninsula, and the Wakara from neighboring Ukara Island.

European colonization brought untold changes that threatened the disappearance of Kikerewe society, language and social values. Drawing on the Kikerewe culture of story-telling, Kitereza reached the conclusion that he could best preserve Kikerewe traditions by writing a novel about his people's actual way of life, as it used to be. In this way, he could preserve all the important things that he wanted remembered. In 1940 he began writing, in Kikerewe, his novel about the way of life of the pre-colonial Kikerewe community before the colonial white man took his people's kingdom. Kitereza wrote:

"I finished writing this book on February 13th, 1945, a book I wrote out of my deeply felt desire to preserve the Customs and Way of Life of our Ancestors, such as they actually lived them in the days of yore, when our people dressed in skins of cows and goats and slept on beddings of hides of cows and goats and sheep, all expertly treated and turned into soft clothing materials which folded nicely and were comfortable to wear and to sleep on...

In those days, when men helped each other to perform their duties they acted out of the spirit of real cooperation, with honestly cheerful hearts, speaking in beautiful language as they pointed out to each other how to perform their tasks well... Likewise the women helped each other perform their tasks their hearts overflowing with happiness amidst abundance of laughter... and on their way back home from such cooperative work they would be signing joyful songs all the time, to which they added the ringing of ululation...

I felt I had a duty to write about that way of life of our ancestors, which was characterized by their spirit of cooperation in all their daily tasks and by the friendly visits they paid each other and their neighborly palavers in which they discussed sensible matters in orderly sessions, holding counsel and following accepted ways of correcting whoever had erred and bringing him or her back to proper human behavior. I felt I had to write about how our elders respected their *abakama* (kings) and their *abakungu* (village headman), how people knew how to discipline their children and how children knew how to respect and honor their parents.

Fearing this great way of life of our ancestors and the principles that governed them would one day disappear and be completely forgotten, I felt I had to write them down, otherwise further generations of our people would lose their rightful *Heritage* of the customs and traditions of their ancestors. The prospect of such a loss filled me with great pity for the generations of our people to come, and so I looked for the best way of telling them how their ancestors lived... That's why I decided to write this story... It was obvious to me that writing this book in a story form would *attract* (attract in English in parenthesis), make people want to read the book more. But, above all, I wanted this to be a way of preserving the language of our ancestors, by showing the reader how beautifully they spoke to each other, whether it was in their neighborly conversations during palavers in each other's homes or simply in the casual exchange of greetings between even total strangers who chanced to meet on the roads, who too would always politely exchange with each other greetings and news of wherever they were coming from and inform each other of where they were going."

The novel completed, Kitereza discovered that it was very difficult indeed to find a publisher for an epic written in the African language of a tiny tribe.[3] European colonial masters who, generally, believed that nothing worthwhile could be written in an African language compounded the difficulties, making it virtually impossible. For almost a quarter century that was the fate of Kitereza's manuscript and grand ambition. An American Africanist scholar, Gerald Hartwig, who came across the author while doing research in Ukerewe in 1968 , suggested that Kitereza translate his work into Kiswahili to improve its chances of being published. In 1961 Tanganyika (renamed Tanzania in 1964) attained independence and since then Kiswahili had became the national language of the country, besides being the lingua franca of the rest of East Africa and parts of Central Africa.

The Kikerewe author, however, was now an old man and partially paralyzed by rheumatism for more than a decade. In addition, he felt unsure about his ability to translate his novel from Kikerewe into Swahili. More fundamentally, translating his novel into Kiswahili meant losing a very important part of its significance: the preservation of his people's language. Despite the concerns, he realized he had no choice if his work were to ever be published. And so he painstakingly wrote down with his aching rheumatic hands the Swahili translation of his voluminous manuscript in his neat calligraphy, completing it in 1969.

Once completed, his Swahili translation also remained unpublished for more than a decade. Even in independent Tanzania, with Swahili as the national language, finding a publisher for such a lengthy book remained an enormous challenge. All over the continent the publishing industry remains monopolized by Western multinationals and their local subsidiaries, whose main interest is selling textbooks to African schools, colleges and universities, where the medium of instruction, generally, continues to be the languages of Africa's former colonial masters. Even in independent Swahili speaking Tanzania, the medium of instruction in post primary education, the level at which the novel would best be appreciated, is English. It was not until 1981 that the Tanzania Publishing House finally published the novel, thanks to Mr. Walter Bgoya, the Managing Director of the company at the time, who made the publication of Kitereza's work his one-man mission. Unfortunately Kitereza himself was not there to witness the great event for which he had been waiting for decades. Two weeks before the printed books arrived in Dar es Salaam, Tanzania's capital, Kitereza had died at the age of eighty-five.

The Author

By the time Kitereza was born in 1896, Ukerewe was already under the German colonial thumb. From December 1884 to January 1885, the great nations of Europe had met in Berlin and decided to end their scramble for Africa by dividing up the continent among them. Today's mainland Tanzania became part of German East Africa. At the time, Kitereza's paternal uncle, Lukonge, was the *Omukama,* or king, of Ukerewe, having succeeded Kitereza's grandfather, *Omukama* Machunda, who ruled Ukerewe from 1825 to 1867.

In 1895, just one year before Kitereza's birth, the Germans arrived in the Ukerewe Kingdom to claim it as their own. Kitereza's uncle, *Omukama* Lukonge, resisted them fiercely, but the Germans deposed, exiled, and imprisoned him. Prince Mukaka, the paternal first cousin, replaced Lukonge (Mukaka was considered Lukonge's younger brother in the Kikerewe extended-family tradition).

Kitereza was born in 1896 to Miss Muchuma[4] and her husband Malindima. In 1901 when Kitereza was a young boy of five, his father died of smallpox. Kitereza and his mother then went to live at the court of the *Omukama* Mukaka, who brought up Kitereza as one of his own children.

Determined to learn the secrets of the white man's power and knowledge, Mukaka sent his sons and the sons of his close relatives to study with white missionaries at the Roman Catholic Mission School in nearby Kagunguli village. In contrast, other kings and traditional rulers elsewhere in the colony sent the sons of their slaves and servants to school in place of their own sons to avoid the contamination of the white man's religion and education. Kitereza began schooling at Kagunguli Mission in 1905. There he was baptized and given the Christian name of Aniceti.

Two years later, in 1907, King Mukaka died and was succeeded by his son Ruhumbika. Ruhumbika proved to be equally eager to learn about the white man's economy and education, and so he continued sending children of family members to the school at Kagunguli Mission and the German colonial administration school in Mwanza. He also converted to Christianity and took the Christian name of Gabriel. With support and encouragement from Ruhumbika, Kitereza left Kagunguli in 1909 to pursue further schooling at the Rubya Roman Catholic Seminary in today's Kagera region near the Ugandan border.

Kitereza studied at the Rubya Seminary for ten years advancing to senior seminary and mastering Latin, the medium of instruction in Roman Catholic seminaries. He learned Greek, a requirement of the classical education of the seminary as well as German, the language of the colonial masters. Kitereza also learned Kiswahili, the African language used as the lingua franca by Arab traders, slavers, and the coastal middlemen. After German defeat in World War I, the Germans lost their overseas colonies and German East Africa was divided and Rwanda and Burundi were given to the Belgians while Tanganyika was given to the British. Kitereza also learned English. In addition to the languages, he studied theology and philosophy as part of his Roman Catholic priesthood training.

In 1919, Kitereza left Rubya Seminary, returned to Ukerewe and married Anna Katura, the daughter of a non-Mkerewe man, a Mnyamwezi from far off Tabora who served as a cook for the white Kagunguli missionaries. In Ukerewe, Kitereza worked for some time as a catechist for the Kagunguli missionaries before finding employment at Mwanza Rice Mill in the provincial capital of the area, Mwanza, as a clerk and purchaser for the company, buying rice from the farmers in Ukerewe and neighboring Ukara Island. Even though his job was based in Mwanza, he was able to continue essentially living in Ukerewe Island.

In 1928, Kitereza left amicably Mwanza Rice Mill due to his employer's financial problems and began working for another Mwanza crop purchasing firm, East Africa Rice Mills Ltd. He continued to work at that firm until the outbreak of World War II put an end to normal economic activity in the area. This time, when Kitereza moved back to Ukerewe, he returned for good.

Upon his arrival in Ukerewe, the white fathers of Kagunguli Mission once again hired Kitereza. At the mission he served as a clerk and translator, charged with translating in Kikerewe the Bible, Prayerbook, the Catechism and other religious writings. He was also responsible for teaching the white missionaries the Kikerewe language, customs, and traditions as well as advising on other African matters. The parish priest, the French Canadian Fr. Simard who employed him commented about Kitereza:

"I wanted him beside me so that he could help me take good care of my books, but above all so that he could initiate me into the secrets of the language of the natives and help me become well versed in the customs and traditions of the country. With his knowledge of Latin, German, English, and several African languages, he was an invaluable help to me at the beginning of my missionary life, above all with regard to composing the first dictionary ever written in Kikerewe, the language of Ukerewe."

By 1939, Kitereza had grown painfully aware of the impact of colonialism and the changes it wrought on Kikerewe society from a socio-economic perspective as well as how it robbed people's confidence in themselves, undermining traditional values, culture, and living norms. These changes had been visibly building since Kitereza's youth.

After becoming *Omukama* back in 1907, Kitereza's cousin Gabriel Ruhumbika began promoting the white man's economy in Ukerewe by encouraging cultivation of two important cash crops, rice and cotton. Ruhumbika set the example by extensively farming his own crops. He also grew sugar cane, processed it, and marketed the brown sugar successfully. He looked for ways to open up his land to rapidly increased cash crop cultivation, but found he could only do so by inviting settlers from surrounding mainland tribes. Most Wakerewe remained too attached to their life in the old settled areas by the lakeshore to open up new lands in the interior. And so the immigrants came, and with them, still more changes.

Once the settlers arrived, they began to clear the thick forest wilderness of Ukerewe to turn it into cropland. Within a decade or two, the entire *ekituntu*, the dense forest that Kitereza describes in his novel, virtually became a thing of the past. Only the thick equatorial rain forest of Rubya in the extreme northwest of the island remained, and only because it had been made a government reserve forest. As Kitereza tells us in his novel, elephants, including the giant elephant *enkaranga* of his story, formerly abounded in the forests of the island. Throughout the 19th century, Ukerewe had been an important source of elephant tusks for trade destined for Arab traders. By the time that Kitereza began writing his novel, no habitat remained for the elephants (the last elephant was killed in 1928).

As the lands were cleared, production of cash crops increased. By 1911, Fr. Hurel of Kagunguli Mission wrote that Ukerewe Island was the leading producer of rice for the entire German colony of East Africa (Hurel 1911, 93). When *Omukama* Ruhumbika died in 1938, Ukerewe was not only a leading producer of rice but also of cotton, a far more lucrative cash crop. Ukerewe also supplied sweet potatoes, bananas, oranges, mangoes, other fruits, and fish to the growing population of Mwanza and other towns in the Lake Province.

Despite their agricultural successes, Kitereza notes that these "developments" fundamentally changed Ukerewe. The influx of outside tribes changed the demographics of the Ukerewe Kingdom, introducing different customs and traditions. The people's relationship to the land altered in Ukerewe as more intensive agriculture became the norm and the traditional ways for earning a living changed. Communal relationships changed as the population quickly grew.

Kitereza understood that the changes from the arrival of the new tribes and the social upheavals brought about by the European colonization threatened the extinction of the old Ukerewe way of life, so he began to chronicle his people's customs and traditions.

At first, Kitereza began this task by simply writing down what he felt were memorable things about his people, supplementing what he knew by communicating with male and female elders who were known as authorities on Kikerewe matters. He also contacted his people's traditional historians, *abanzuzi* (Hartwig 1976, 18). The result was a number of manuscripts written in the Kikerewe language: *Kikerewe Stories, Kikerewe Proverbs and Sayings, The History of Ukerewe,* and *Ethics and Correct Behavior Among the Wakerewe.*5

Kitereza was, however, a great lover of literature. In Kikerewe society, story telling was an essential part of bringing up children and an important educational medium. It is notable that among the things Kitereza felt needed to be remembered for posterity among the Wakerewe were their stories, proverbs, and sayings. Later, he arrived at the conclusion that he could best achieve his objective by writing a story about his people's actual way of life, such as it used to be, in which all those things he wanted remembered would find a natural place. This led in turn to his epic novel, *Myombekere na Bugonoka na Ntulanalwo na Buliwhali*.

Kitereza displayed enormous foresight in identifying the different threats to the Ukerewe traditional way of life. From the time that the novel was completed to the time it was published, other forces altered even further the traditional Ukerewe society. In some respects, one may argue the impact from Tanzania's independence had no less profound an effect on Kitereza's Ukerewe society than European colonialism. For during British colonialism, the colonial masters supported Ukerewe's traditional ruling structure to better serve colonial interests, as they did everywhere with their so-called "Indirect Rule" policy. Shortly after independence in 1961, Tanzania's first president Julius Nyerere issued a simple decree that abolished all traditional rule throughout the country.

Other political events also adversely impacted on Ukerewe. In 1965, the Tanzanian national government dismembered the old Ukerewe Kingdom by separating Mwibara (Mainland) Ukerewe from Ukerewe District. Mainland Ukerewe then became part of Bunda District. Ukerewe suffered further changes when, in the early 1970s, President Julius Nyerere implement his *Ujamaa* or "extended-family" socialism, moving people into collective villages. In already overcrowded Ukerewe, this policy created enormous social upheavals; people were forced out of their homes and uprooted from their progressive and enterprising communities. As the people were moved into makeshift shacks with virtually no planning or infrastructure, the community's accomplishments disappeared overnight and the standard of living plummeted.

For the construction of their collective-village shacks, the ruling Party's *Mgambo* (People's militia) forced the people of Ukerewe to cut down literally every tree which was still standing and uproot all grass for thatch. The Ukerewe people helplessly looked on as their old homes and buildings fell into ruin, their lands were allotted to strangers by the national government, and burial grounds were turned into crop fields. Kitereza, who was now a sick, paralyzed old man, found himself forced to move from his homestead into a one-room shack which his wife, Anna, equally aged and very frail had hastily put up with the help of compassionate relatives and strangers in one of those collective settlements. In that destruction, even Kitale Mountain, the burial grounds of the author's ancestors, the Kings of Ukerewe, was not spared: its sacred woods were cleared by the builders of

Ujamaa dwellings, and the *Abasita*, guardians of the royal burial grounds who had lived for centuries at the foot of the lakeside mountain were ordered to move to the nearest collective village.

By the time Kitereza died in 1981, he was aware that the people of his tribe were a disappearing minority in what remained of Ukerewe. Sadly, the children for whom he had written his epic novel were abandoning the Kikerewe language for Kiswahili, the language of the new nation.[6]

His diary reveals that up to his death, Kitereza remained a devout Christian and served as an active and influential member of his Roman Catholic community. After he was too ill to attend church on Sundays, he continued to pay his church dues punctually and to make other contributions. He also continued to write Kikerewe prayers and songs for special occasions for the congregation. Even after Tanzania adopted Kiswahili as the national language, people in Ukerewe continued to recite and sing many of the Kikerewe prayers and songs that Kitereza had translated or composed.

During his life, Kitereza also served as an elder frequently consulted by relatives, neighbors, and the official counsel for Ukerewe District on traditional matters and customary law. He proved himself to be an invaluable authority in matters like traditional land ownership, inheritance, divorce, and other marriage-related issues.

In reviewing Kitereza's diary, personal correspondence, and other documents, it is clear that Kitereza lived a generous life. Even when he suffered from the paralyzing effects of severe rheumatism, he punctually responded to every letter sent to him. The abundant correspondence shows that the children and grand children of his brothers, sisters, and cousins considered him a parent and grandparent, although he was himself childless.

Kitereza's wife Anna had given birth to four children, all of whom died in infancy. After that, she conceived no more children. In Kitereza's polygamous society, childbearing and parenting gave human existence meaning. Men, especially from the author's Basilanga-Bahinda ruling clan, were expected to have at least two or three wives. Other considerations, such as one's religion or how many children had already been fathered, were secondary. Without any children, Kitereza was under enormous psychological and social pressure to marry another wife to give him a chance for posterity. Remarkably, Kitereza withstood this pressure for more than sixty years. Anna died in 1980, as Kitereza's one and only wife.

Kitereza's diary reveals a man who was very closely attached to his wife. For example, there is one entry during the years when Kitereza was bedridden from rheumatism. He notes that Anna had gone to pay condolences to their relatives some distance away and, as custom required, she had to pass a night at the home of their bereaved relatives. The author's entry ends: "And me? Nothing but loneliness!!!" Given their love for each other, it is no surprise that Kitereza did not survive a year beyond his wife's death.

The Story of Mr. Myombekere and His Wife Bugonoka, Ntulanalwo na Bulihwali

Mr. Myombekere and His Wife Bugonoka, Ntulanalwo and Bulihwali is set in Ukerewe, in pre-colonial times. In their oral history, the rulers of Ukerewe claim that the founder of their dynasty, Katobaha I of Ukerewe, was the son of a Muhinda (pl. Bahinda) hunter named Kankombya who originated from Kisenyi, to the north of what was to become Mwibara, "Mainland" of Ukerewe kingdom.[7] While on a hunting expedition, Kankombya trekked until he reached the court of *omukama* of Ihangiro, a kingdom on the west side of the lake, where, because of his great hunting and warring skills, he became a favorite of the king. The King gave him a royal maid for a wife, by whom he had a son, Katobaha. Katobaha grew up to become an even more famous hunter and warrior than his father. Eventually the king of Ihangiro viewed Katobaha as a threat to his power, and conspired to kill him. Learning of the conspiracy, Katobaha escaped with his mother and a group of faithful followers in a fleet of eighty boats, carrying with them their weapons, their fishing tools and some banana plants. Katobaha and his party first landed at Iramba on the north of Mwibara peninsula before finally going to Ukerewe Island. Both on the peninsula and in the island they introduced to the indigenous people the banana plant, their superior fishing methods and the boat building skills from which their clan name Basilanga comes. *Ku-silanga* is Kikerewe for "to make a perfect water vessel."

There are other versions of the origin of Basilanga-Bahinda of Ukerewe, the most convincing being the one according to the oral history of the Wazinza[8] people who inhabit present day Geita, Sengerema and Biharamulo districts in North West Tanzania. That version claims Katobaha I of Ukerewe to have been the great-grandson of Katobaha I of

Uzinza. His father Kabambo was the grandson of Katobaha of Uzinza and it is he who extended the rule of the Bahinda as far as Karagwe on the Tanzania Uganda border in addition to the three districts mentioned above. He put his son Katobaha as ruler of Ukerewe (Betbeder 1971, 744) (see appendixes II and III).

Kitereza set his novel in an undifferentiated pre-European, pre-colonial past in Ukerewe where even the few known historical events follow the dictates of his fictional story. These events are not necessarily recounted chronologically or as they actually occurred. As mentioned earlier, the threatened extinction of pre-colonial Ukerewe culture and way of life is what motivated Kitereza to write his epic novel. Kitereza himself defined the objective of his novel, as follows:

"I then looked for a way in which I could clearly communicate to the reader the beautiful customs and way of life of our people of yore, who dressed in skins of cows and goats but were healthy people with comely physiques who fed on *obitwa*[9] of the nutritious *obubele* millet. I, therefore, decided to explore what the life of a human being is really all about, from birth to old age and death...

With that in mind, I pondered the reality of the people of this Ukerewe land of ours, and it became clear to me that the one thing, which every person, male or female, deplores most, is being childless. With that realization, I decided I can best write my book by writing the story of a married couple whose marriage starts off being tested by a long period of barrenness. I decided to make the marriage monogamous, so that I can best show the ordeal the husband went through on account of his one barren wife."

The novel begins with the account of how Myombekere's love for his wife, Bugonoka, is tested by the greatest misfortune in Ukerewe--barrenness. Withstanding the trials by their failure to have children, the couple's marriage is not only saved but they emerge from their ordeal as their community's exemplary couple. Their actions bear daily testimony to their great and true love for each other. Finally, the Creator rewards them with the greatest gift that can be bestowed--the gift of human life. The trial and redemption is the cornerstone of Part I of the novel.

In Part I of the novel, Kitereza demonstrates his powerful convictions that love in marriage is the cornerstone of the family, the community, and of the human race. He fervently believes that this love must prevail over any and all obstacles. Frequently, he sees this love betrayed by men who are not "man enough" to withstand or to ward off the meddling of relatives and the public. In a communal society based on extended family, this is no easy task. Kitereza tells us a story within the story of "How Men and Women Came to Live Together", which constitutes Chapter XIII of the novel. Kitereza implies that men took advantage of the kindly and trusting nature of women to deprive them of their equal rights, treating them as "dogs."

Unlike Kitereza and Anna, Myombekere and Bugonoka triumph over their barrenness and bear children, a boy and a girl. Kitereza chose to give his characters children of both sexes. The story was meant to explore all aspects of Kikerewe society from birth to death, including both female and male experiences and perspectives. In Kikerewe society, a young man's maturation is achieved by his *myombekere,* his "founding and managing a household," marrying and starting a new family. A young woman's maturation is achieved by getting married and becoming a mother. It is procreation and the building of a new family that lead to fulfillment and strengthening of the extended family and tribe. It is also only in marriage that man and woman are strong enough to face up to the ever-present trials of life, the "*(obuzune) bugonoka*", "(misfortune) strikes unannounced." Hence, the names are derived for the two main characters and the novel's title, the husband *Myombekere* and his wife *Bugonoka.*

Fittingly, Part II of the novel starts with the birth of Myombekere and Bugonoka's first child, the son Ntulanalwo. The son's name means "death is my eternal companion." This is followed by the birth of their second and last child, the daughter Bulihwali, a name signifying "When will suffering ever end!" Since death and suffering are inseparable from human existence, they are important features of Kitereza's story. The characters must engage in a daily struggle to survive and search for happiness against the overriding interests and concerns of their community: their extended family, their clan and tribe. This corresponds to their neighborhood, their village and kingdom; sacred religious beliefs, healers, seers, oracles, ancestral spirits, witchcraft, and even miracles.

Kitereza depicts a loving and humane people to whom kindred and community come before the individual, a moral and ethical people who seek religious guidance in every aspect of their individual and communal life and adhere scrupulously to the social values of their particular culture.

For Kitereza's people, everyone was supposed to strive to love each other and to appreciate the virtues in other people quietly. Love, like the appreciation of the good in others, was not something that is publicly displayed but quietly shown by deeds. Regarding sexual love, everything touching on sex and the love between a man and a woman were strictly forbidden outside of the privacy of the two lovers. That is why in Kitereza's novel we find Bugonoka in Chapter XVI referring to three argumentative neighbors as "disgusting," "monsters," and "male creatures gone mad," when she discovers that in a palaver they had with her husband in the couple's home, they touched on the forbidden subject. She reminds her husband:

"*Aa! hee!* Myombekere! I should think that matters of a man and a woman are only meant for the two, and that's how it was meant to be, everything in its proper place. For that same reason, I don't know matters of men, that is, even though I know them from being a married woman I cannot recount them to my fellow women that way; never!"

In Ukerewe culture, even to this day, people find it phony and crude for one to say, "I love you!" to a person as a way of expressing one's love for him or her. For a verbal declaration to be appropriate, it must be justified by a special occasion and in accordance with proper etiquette.

We find, in Chapter IX, Myombekere making such a proper declaration of love for his wife. Myombekere's relatives had given her such a hard time for being a barren woman that her parents had taken her away from him intent on ending their marriage. On the day his wife finally returns to his home, Myombekere held a long party with dance, music, and banana beer for her and for those who had accompanied him to bring her back from the in-laws. He chose to sing for his audience the song of a childless woman who lost her much-loved husband. He poured his heart into his music until he was overcome with emotion and called out to Bugonoka:

"'Bugonoka, where are you!' 'Yes, Sir, my husband!' his wife answered and at once came forward and raised both her husband's hands in the air to congratulate him while ululating for him: '*Ililili!* Long live my husband! To which Myombekere replied, 'The same to you, my beloved, my fellow traveler, my inseparable life companion till death!'"

While there are some similarities drawn from his life, this is not an autobiographical novel. For Kitereza, the objective of his work was too important for his story to be limited to his personal life. For instance, in spite of his devotion to Roman Catholicism, he writes about the African religion of his people not as a Christian, but as a Mkerewe of the past. He conveys how the Wakerewe practiced, believed, doubted and questioned their religious beliefs. As a result, the author's Christian religion and the white men who brought it and colonial rule are completely absent from the novel.

Professor Gerald Hartwig and his wife Charlotte, the two Western Africanists who knew the author in person and who, more than anybody else, brought Kitereza's novel and the author to the attention of other international scholars, are correct when they comment:

"Completely unaffected by post-World War II influences, Kitereza does not write in the genre of most other contemporary African writers. He is not seeking identification; he fights no battles, voices no protest... His goal is to preserve tradition before it is erased by time. His intended audience: the Kerebe" (Gerald and Charlotte Hartwig 1970, 20).

The Significance of Kitereza's work in African Literature

The Wakerewe are part of a much larger community of linguistically and culturally related people. To quote the American Professor Gerald Hartwig: "The Kerebe were distinctive in their district a century ago: they represented a rather isolated extension of the awe-inspiring interlacustrine culture zone found on the other (western) side of the lake" (ix-x). Bantu speaking parts of the Great Lakes region include southern Uganda, Burundi, Rwanda, part of eastern Democratic Republic of Congo, part of western Kenya, in addition to northwestern Tanzania (Ogot 1984, 498-524). As already seen, Kitereza's Basilanga-Bahinda clan who founded Ukerewe Kingdom were part of the Wahaya-Wazinza people of that interlacustrine Bantu community.

In Africa today, Bantu-speaking Africa spreads over half of sub-Saharan African beyond the Great Lakes region described above. The area includes Cameroon and Gabon on the Atlantic coast stretching eastward through the Central African Republic, Democratic Republic of Congo, and Uganda all the way to the Indian Ocean coast of Kenya and Tanzania. Bantu-speaking Africa then extends south, all the way to the southernmost tip of South Africa, including the Comoro Islands and parts of Madagascar in the Indian Ocean (Werner 1919,3) (Johnson 1919, 1-38) (Lwanga-Lunyiigo and Vansina 1988, 140) (Bryan 1959).

Kitereza's novel, therefore, is not only "a mine of ethnographical, historical, and scientific information about pre-colonial Bukerebe and its people" (Mulokozi 1985, 179), but also the detailed story of the past and culture of an important branch of the Bantu Africans and, consequently, a story of significance for the entire African people.

Although Bantu languages have been studied for more than 150 years, no similar systematic study of Bantu cultures has ever been carried out. The failure to analyze these cultures is most probably because the social researchers in African have until very recently been Western Africanists and their African protégées who did not accept that African cultures were "culture" at all (Okpewho 1992, 17).   Kitereza's intimate and exhaustive portrayal of his Kikerewe pre-colonial community may serve as an invaluable point of departure.

Even forty years after the independence of African countries, the African writer almost everywhere still writes in the languages of the former European colonial masters. These languages are spoken and understood by only a very tiny minority of the African people, excluding most people without good formal education. Except in Tanzania where Swahili was adopted as an official national language, the African writer is still faced with the double handicap of having to write in a foreign language and of being unable to communicate with most of his or her potential readers.

But change may be coming. Newly found respect for African languages and literature is emerging. African writers are beginning to hear the call for the use of African languages. Enlightened African writers, intellectuals, and even politicians are beginning to realize that African literature can only blossom through the use of African languages. Kitereza's Kikerewe epic was an important pioneer work heralding the needed change.

The author's accomplishments are even more remarkable considering that the novel was written in his native language in 1945, at the height of colonialism. All over Africa, black people lived their colonial experience as a conquered and humiliated people. Aside from the economic impact and social upheaval addressed above, colonialism deeply wounded the confidence people had in themselves. Colonial masters tried to convince Africans to believe that they were a primitive and savage people without history and culture, including literature. The colonial masters dismissed traditional religions and frowned upon African languages. The material civilization of the colonial master so overwhelmed African people that many Africans came to believe the dehumanizing effort.

Compounding the problem, the first to succumb to Western dehumanization were African leaders who received colonial educations in towns and cities where they were cut off from their tribal base and pre-colonial way of life. Without the local leadership, the appreciation of local ways, rites, customs and traditions gradually declined and resulted in the neglect of traditional practices and cultural identity.

Other external influences, frequently accompanying colonialism, also served to upset social stability and peace. In Tanzania, competing Christian and Islamic efforts to convert African peoples to their religions have disrupted traditional religious harmony. While these two religions disagree on many things, they both attempt to discredit and denigrate traditional African religions, which they consider "animist" and "paganism". Africa seems to have reached a point where proper direction in the religious life is no longer only a spiritual issue. The consequences may be seen in the self-destruction, civil strife, wars, and suffering resulting from religious conflicts in so many countries on the continent.

In a post-colonial Tanzania and Africa desperately in need of cultural, spiritual, and moral direction, Kitereza's story takes on larger significance. The African people of the past with their religion and moral principles that Kitereza shows us were culturally conscious, ethical, community-minded and deeply humane. Kitereza's novel is therefore a work of art that can play an important role in the African people's effort to re-evaluate their past, cure their wounded humanity, and chart paths for their cultural future. Professor Manfred Prinz of Heinrich-Heine University, Düsseldorf, Germany states in *Research in African Literatures:*

"The originality of Kitereza's novel derives from its depiction of the African world with its intrinsic logic and its capacity to foster communal solidarity. He dispenses with any reference to European, colonial influence because the viability and enduring values of African culture speak for themselves. The African worldview is not contrasted with rationalism and European modernity, for the society of Bugonoka and Myombekere incorporates both forms of thought, and Kitereza portrays them not as polar opposites, but as fundamental constituents of the human condition." (Prinz 1993) (Translation from German by Richard Bjornson).

Or as the American professor Gerald Hartwig states: "To seek and find and then share the secrets of life in a bygone era, to discover 'those things loved and those things despised' became his goals" and enabled him to write a story of universal significance, because: "It concerns common people, those whose daily unglorified existence and beliefs must be respected because their fundamental concerns are also ours" (Hartwig 1976, 3-4).

Kitereza's novel is significant for more than its content. It also adds to a new style of African literature, for Kitereza adopted an innovative storyteller style. Rather than merely transcribing African oral stories or imitating traditional African literature (Scheub 1985, 34), Kitereza used the old art form to create a new kind of work. He narrated his story like a traditional African storyteller employing an array of oral-tradition conventions to create a work that depicts better-defined characters than conventional oral stories and seeks to explore in depth human and social experiences.

It is this innovative style, which, more than anything else, makes his work both an important African contribution to world literature and a milestone in the growth of modern African literature.

Translating Kitereza into English

This is the first and only complete translation of Kitereza's great work into English. It is not, however, the first attempt to translate the original story into a European language. The first such attempt was by a French-Canadian missionary, Fr. Almas Simard in 1952. The result of that project, but even more telling, the comment he made about the work itself, are evidence of the racist prejudice, "the sociological bias" that Okpewho wrote about in his important publication on African oral literature. According to him, two major problems that can distort research findings on Africa by Western Africanists and limit the usefulness of their publications are, "Inadequate understanding of the language by the foreign scholar" and "the sociological bias of the whole research project" (Okpewho 1992, 12). Father Simard, the author's employer at Kagunguli Mission above, in 1952 took the original manuscript of Kitereza's work with him to Canada while on vacation so as to continue looking for a publisher for it and also to try and translate it into French during his vacation. He did not come back to Ukerewe as he had hoped as he suddenly died in his native Canada, but not before he had completed his French translation of Kitereza's work.

What Fr. Simard did to Kitereza's work appears to suggest that even where linguistic problems have been overcome, the sociological bias alone can still remain a real barrier. There is no doubt that Fr. Simard was fluent in Kikerewe language. In addition to that he was the one person who encouraged the Kikerewe author to write the novel, which on completion he found good and important enough to want to translate into his native French. Judging from what he wrote about Kitereza, there can also be no doubt that he regarded him highly both as an author and a scholar. Yet despite that high regard for Kitereza he still was incapable of transcending the white man's biased views of Africa and the Africans. This is what Fr. Simard himself tells us about his French translation in the "Translator's Preface":

"In the author's indigenous language the volume is no doubt twice as thick as this one, since I have left out many unnecessary repetitions which don't add anything of interest to the story and since I have also been obliged to strike out certain details which would have shocked the minds and sensitivity of civilized people" (Simard c. 1952).

Rev. Fr. Simard's translation of Kitereza work is in fact a selective summary of Kikerewe customs and traditions and the episodes in which they occur, a manuscript of about a third the length of the original work and with twenty-five chapters instead of the thirty-eight of the novel. Kitereza's great story was turned it into a censored manual of the customs and traditions of a "primitive" people (*"nègres"*) palatable to the "civilized" world!

Better but still problematic, was the translation into German by Professor J. G. Möhlig, an Africanist scholar of the University of Cologne. As I do not read German, I cannot make any judgment on the quality of the translation. However, it was based on the author's Swahili translation, whose shortcomings, compared to his original Kikerewe work, are admitted by the author himself in the text of the translation:

"We find it impossible to translate here everything as we should, because of our ignorance of how to say in Swahili each and everything and as beautifully as it is said (in Kikerewe) in the original text of *Myombekere na Bugonoka etc.*" (Kitereza 1980, 165).

Additionally, and even more to the point, the German translator admits in the Epilogue of his translation that he lacked the experience and felt unequal to the task of translating a literary text of an African language: "As an oralist, I have had to deal quite often with the problems of translation too. But my translation was always concerned with the problems of meaning and never with the problems of style or aesthetics. I had therefore to venture here into a linguistic field in which I never worked before." As a result, he informs his reader, he decided that his translation would concern itself primarily with "the concrete meaning (sense)" and not with "the literary form" and "the importance associated with it." Needless to say, whatever its other merits, a translation with such a limited objective cannot be a fair translation of a work of art like Kitereza's novel, in which language usage and conventions with all their nuances are of paramount importance.

There is yet another point the German translator makes which I think should be mentioned here: "Translating is always at the same time interpretation. Consciously or unconsciously, therefore, the wording of the present German text may have been influenced by my subjective understanding of the aims and goals which Kitereza wanted to express in his work." We cannot but agree with German professor that in order to interpret and translate a text well it is crucial for the translator to read the author's aims and goals correctly.

The question which we are therefore bound to ask is to what extent did the difficulties of dealing with Kitereza's Swahili combined with the unavoidable errors the German translator himself calls his "possible false interpretations" affect his translation? Translations of reviews in the German Press were on the whole favorable and the translator must be commended for bringing the work to the attention of a large European audience. Nevertheless one cannot but be disturbed by the fact that he chose to give his translation "exotic" titles in no way justified by the story of the African author. He has named Part I of the novel *Die Kinder der Regenmacher*, "*Children of the Rainmaker*", which is puzzling, since not only are there no such characters in the novel, but the belief that there exists human beings with power to make rain is one we see questioned in Kitereza's novel. Our consternation becomes even greater when he titled Part II *Der Schlangentöter*, "The Snake-slayer", again an "exotic" title whose justification the reader will search for in vain in the novel, because it is based on blowing out of all proportion a single incident in the story. The translator himself has, in fact, been candid enough to admit in his epilogue that not only did he want to "facilitate understanding of the cultural context" of the novel, but he also wanted to "preserve its *exotic character* in the German text" (emphasis added). An exotic character is the last thing Kitereza, as well as those who take his work as seriously as it deserves, would have associated with his moving story of the human condition of his African people – clearly another "sociological bias." The cover picture of the German publication, two pathetic looking Africans, hardly the robust characters in the novel is further proof of the "sociological bias" that pervades the perspectives of European writers and scholars on and about Africans and our cultures.

In translating this novel into English, I brought to it my skills as a native Kikerewe speaker, an African literary scholar, and a writer in English, Kiswahili, and other Bantu languages. My experience may be of interest to others embarking on work of similar nature in their own languages.

Until recently, Western scholars usually dismissed African languages as primitive and incapable of expressing abstract thought or elevated discourse. Western Africanists are now realizing and admitting that not only are these African languages as complete as any of their Western languages, but that they at times express exact and subtle meanings more easily than European languages. In Bantu languages, for example, their exceptional tonality and intricate tone patterns not only make them very melodious languages but, more importantly, enable them to express with the same word or phrase a multiplicity of meaning (Johnson 1919, 6) (Ashton 1947, 11-34, 70-81, 110-117). In addition, their noun-class-based syntax makes possible very compressed language structure, which cannot be replicated in English. What the German translator says on the difficulty of dealing with that feature of a Bantu languages is equally true of English and it was a problem I had to address. He writes of Bantu languages, to which Swahili and Kikerewe belong:

"According to their structural type, they are class-languages characterized by a strict formal concordance between syntactically dependent elements of the sentence. As a result, the reader or hearer can always recognize the syntactical relationship even in a complex passage. Compared to Bantu languages, the German language possesses much fewer possibilities of expressing syntactic coherence. It is, therefore, quite impossible to imitate the structure of the (Swahili) text" (Möhlig 1991, 311-330.) (Translation from German here and above by Rev. Fr. Cyprian Tirumanywa).

Additionally, the fact that Kitereza wrote the novel for a very restricted community further complicated the task of translating his text. The author shared a stock of common references and allusions with his small tribe of Wakerewe people. Often the mention of a first phrase or word from a proverb or a saying would trigger the audience's understanding of the remaining entire context.

All this meant that I had to fill in a lot of the understood or implied references, occasionally even at the expense of the artistic quality of the passage. For example, it is the compressed form and familiar brief references that make proverbs so memorable. Parables tend to lose their effectiveness when fully explained. With Kitereza's wit-loving Wakerewe people delighting in these references, it is easy to understand why the translator faced difficulty providing full explanations to non-Wakerewe readers.

Kitereza also makes very frequent use of ideophones or, to borrow Okpewho's definition, "ideas in sound." Many Bantu linguists and other Africanists have pointed out the very important role this device plays in a Bantu language. In Kitereza's novel they are everywhere because they are an important feature of commonly used Kikerewe. A Mkerewe would, for example, signify a person's hard fall with the onomatopoeic *pu*! But if the hard fall has been caused by somebody or something, then the speaker could signal that fact by *ligiti*!, the ideophone for falling down completely. For a defeated person in a wrestling match, one might hear *gingiri*! the onomatopoeia for thunder to signify the resounding fall. The person who arrives suddenly and unexpectedly in another person's home is said to have arrived *bwaa*!, the ideophone for sudden and pervasive invasion like a spreading water spill engulfing a person before he or she knows it. The sighting of a person who simply appears as if from nowhere is signified by *kigi*!, the ideophone for sighting something suddenly as it if were an apparition. Eating and finishing food completely is signified by *fu*! or for emphasis, *fu fu fu*!

In the absence of equivalent parts of speech in English, these important features of the Kikerewe language could not be directly translated without sacrificing essential quality of Kitereza's language and style. I have, therefore, retained the ideophones and followed them by their implied meanings. I had, however, to leave out ideophones that, like puns, depend on both the sound and meaning of the other words in a sentence or phrase.

I could not eliminate the stylistic elements of Kitereza's novel where the story is told as if it were performed in front of a live audience. Kitereza, for example, constantly uses phrases like "from here to there," "this way," "like this," because he is telling the story as if in front of an attentive audience, demonstrating what he is describing. I have therefore left these characteristics of his particular style in the text.

For the same reason, I have left in the text the numerous repetitions, another important characteristic of Kitereza's oral narrative style, well aware that some of my readers may at first find them unnecessary and intrusive. I agree with Okpewho who says that to cut out repetitions from a piece of oral literature, as most Western transcribers intent on "meaning" alone have done, is to deprive it of "one of the most fundamental characteristic features of oral literature." (71-78). Similarly, Richard Lattimore, in the Introduction to his 1951 translation of Homer's *Iliad*, first notes that the *Iliad* is essentially an oral composition, intended to be read aloud, not ready silently. Lattimore then says of repetitions in the epic poem, "Such repeats are frequent in Homer. Even the casual reader will notice them, but only the careful student will find a pattern of repetition so pervasive that it creates an essential texture of language without which Homer would not be Homer." (Lattimore 1951, 37-38).

In Kitereza's novel this is also true to a certain extent. We find all three kinds of repetitions Lattimore observes in Homer, namely repetitions of "an entire passage, often of considerable length," those which are a "few lines" long, and finally, "single line" repetitions. As Lattimore correctly observes, in oral traditions there is a "principle" that "a thing once said in the right way should be said again the *same* way when occasion demands." In Kitereza's novel when characters meet they "greet each other properly, exchange news of each other until they are done and finished," over and over again. The same is true with the procedures women observe when providing men with food at mealtimes. These repetitions are quite common in Part I of the novel, but in Part II, Kitereza gradually cuts down on their use until he almost drops them altogether, especially the long ones, because they seemed to have served their purpose.

The reader of this translation will soon appreciate these repetitions as an essential part of the author's style. I am likewise convinced the reader will easily accept and enjoy the other characteristics of oral literature in the text, such as the narrative digressions. The most outstanding of such digressions are two stories within the story, namely the story of "How Men and Women Came to Live Together," an entire chapter meant to drive home the injustice and inhumanity of men to women. The other story describes a great hunter who killed a leopard, recounted to instruct young men on the price of fame. The reader will further enjoy the many "asides" in which Kitereza confides in his reader what only the two of them are supposed to know.

I combined paragraphs and divided others where I felt changed paragraphing was appropriate in English. My punctuation had to be guided by what I felt were the demands of correct English grammar and usage, which were frequently different from the oral style of Kitereza's African language narrative.

Apart from the compositional changes, which are always part of the translation process, I have followed the original Kikerewe text very closely. The only notable exception is that I have numbered the chapters of Part I and Part II continuously. The original Kikerewe text Part II begins with a second Chapter I. This change in the English translation follows the example of the author in his own published Kiswahili translation of the novel. In the Kiswahili translation, the Table of Contents shows Part II beginning with a new Chapter I. The actual text of Part II, however, uses continuous numbering from Part I. Continuous numbering of the chapters for Parts I and II is called for by the very structure of the novel. Not only are the two parts integral sections of a single story, but the same two characters dominate both Parts I and II. Myombekere and his wife Bugonoka who are the main characters in Part I, are also the main characters for more than three-quarters of Part II. Only near the end do they cede their place to their son Ntulanalwo and daughter Bulihwali who continue and conclude their parents' story.

My annotations have all been put at the end of the chapters. They are intended for the African Literature and African Studies student, researchers, or other Africanists as well as the curious general reader who wants to be taken deeper into Kitereza's world of the African past. Kitereza himself sought information from the elders of Ukerewe of those days to complement his personal knowledge of the culture and past of his people. With support from the American National Endowment for the Humanities and the University of Georgia, I managed to travel to Tanzania and Ukerewe to carry out research. I am glad to say, I was able to find surviving Wakerewe elders who supplied me with needed information or with whom I compared knowledge so that I could annotate Kitereza's work accurately. I have made sure the text is clearly understandable throughout even without the annotations in question, so the reader does not have to consult with the notes to enjoy the story.

And with that, I leave you to Kitereza and the story of *Mr. Myombekere and His Wife Bugonoka, Their Son Ntulanalwo and Daughter Bulihwali: The Story of an Ancient African Community.*

Gabriel Ruhumbika

NOTES

1. The Swahili forms of this word and its derivatives will be used here rather than the Kikerewe ones. Therefore, the kingdom will be called "Ukerewe" the language "Ukerewe," and the people "Wakerewe" (singular "Mkerewe") rather than "Bukerebe," "Kiberebe" and Bakerebe (singular "Mkerebe") respectively.

2. Tanganyika Territory British colonial government Blue Book Statistics cited above show the population of Ukerewe, according to 1948 census, to be 112,000, out of whom approximately 34,000 were Wakerewe, 45,000 Wajita, and the rest were Wakara and other Wajita-related people. The same records show that at the same time Majita, the homeland of the Wajita, had 26,000 inhabitants. In other words there were already twice as many Wajita in Ukerewe as there were in their land of origin. The homeland of Wakerewe had already also become the land of Wajita and other Wajita-related people.

3. Because of the negative connotations"civilized" white people have given the term "tribe", some African scholars find it objectionable and prefer to use "ethnic group" instead. To me these African intellectuals should find that substitute even more objectionable, given the fact that "ethnic" also means "heathen" or "pagan", leave alone the fact that even in its accepted usage, such as we find in the US, "ethnic group" is an inadequate designation, if not a misnomer, for those traditional units of African society. Native Americans, for example, are said to be an ethnic group, though they belong to many tribes, or "nationalities", for those who prefer that term. I therefore prefer "tribe" a term which, irrespective of what the West may choose to think, Africans all over the continent who speak European languages use to name with nothing but   pride and wholesome connotations those ancient communities of their people. See also my article "The African Language policy of Development: African National Languages" In *Reseach in African Literatures* 23.1 (1992): 74.

4. Wakerewe women continued to be known by their maiden names after they were married.

5. I have been able to trace only one of these manuscripts: *Kikerewe Stories.* On my last visit to the author in Ukerewe just before he died in 1981, he told me he had lost all his manuscripts. White missionaries and some other visiting Western reseachers borrowed the material but never returned it. Kitereza asked that I help him to locate them. I finally located *Engani za Bukerebe (Kikerewe Stories)* at the Documentation Center of the Canadian White

Fathers in Montreal, Canada. The archivists were kind enough to send me a photocopy of these 145 wonderful stories in addition to a copy of the original manuscript of Kitereza's novel. I used this copy of Kitereza's novel for my English translation of *Mr. Myombekere and His Wife Bugonoka, Their Son Ntulanalwo and Daughter Bulihwali: The Story of an Ancient African Community.* I located another copy of the stories at Mwanza Roman Catholic Cathedral. That copy, fortunately enough, has the Table of Contents page written in Kitereza's own unmistakable calligraphy, proving incontestably that the stories were written and collected by Kitereza, not by a white missionary as the typed cover of the stories indicates. I continue to search for Kitereza's other lost manuscripts. Those who read them say that they are also important writings.

6. These is no doubt that some of the changes seen in independent Tanzania were not only inevitable but should be welcomed in general. Some of these developments present a more promising future for coming generations of the people of Ukerewe and Tanzania, though they come with some cost. The spread and growth of Kiswahili in post independence Tanzania comes at the expense of the more than 100 indigenous language found in the country, but it is necessary to have a national language. It is also proof that with both enlightened leadership and social will to put national interests above all others, it is possible to see the development of African national languages, which, as is the case in Tanzania, can play an important role in the consolidation of African nation states.

7. For the succession of Bahinda and the Ukerewe dynasty see Appendices to the Introduction I and II after Cited works.

8. As in the case of Ukerewe above, the Swahili versions of Buzinza and its derivatives, "Uzinza" (the country) "Wazinza" (the people), will be used here most of the times instead of "Buzinza" and Bazinza" respectively.

9. *Obwita,* called *Ugali* in Swahili, which the British colonialists termed "stiff-porridge, is made from a mixture of flour and boiling water.

Part I

MR. MYOMBEKERE AND HIS WIFE BUGONOKA

Chapter I

MYOMBEKERE'S WIFE BUGONOKA IS TAKEN AWAY FROM HIM BY HER PARENTS

Mr. Myombekere married his wife Bugonoka[1] when both of them were still unmarried youths.[2] They lived together for one year and in their second year of marriage Bugonoka conceived her first child. She carried the pregnancy for four months, then in the fifth month she aborted what would have been a baby boy. When she resumed her monthly periods, she conceived a child the second time. This time she carried the pregnancy for six months before giving birth prematurely to a seven-month old baby girl. The tiny infant lived only for one day and on the following day died.

After that Myombekere's wife did not conceive again and the couple lived for many years without issue.

That is why Myombekere's relatives burned with resentment against his wife and felt he should divorce her and told him so: "Son, you, a man in the prime of your life, have really decided to spend your entire life with this barren and completely dried up wife of yours, so that when you are dead and buried that will be the end of you for ever! What do you think the Resurrection of human beings means on this earth, if not procreation and leaving behind your own self when you die? Where would you yourself have come from if your father and mother had not brought you into this world? You know very well that a man is never sterile, is never in need of fertility drugs: the only fertility drug a male person ever needs is the bow and arrow of his manhood.[3] If you court another woman and marry again, such a real man as you cannot remain for long without children."

"What, exactly, do you want me to do?" Myombekere answered back his relatives.

"Our only wish for you is that you divorce your wife and court and marry another woman, because if you remain stuck with this one you are doomed to die without issue," they retorted.

What Myombekere's relatives were saying against his wife leaked out and slowly spread and kept on spreading until finally those words reached her parents.

When Myombekere's father-in-law, whose name was Namwero, and mother-in-law, who was called Nkwanzi, heard all that, they became very angry and talked of going to take away their child from him. And indeed on the following day Bugonoka's parents were on their way to Myombekere's home, walking as fast as they could, for it was a considerable distance away and the couple wanted to arrive at their destination early during the day so that they could return home the same day.

While on their way, husband and wife began asking each other questions: "By the way, when we arrive at our son-in-law's home, what can we say that will so get at him and his relatives that they will be left with no option but to give us our daughter?" Nkwanzi asked her husband.

"There must indeed be something wrong with you women! How can a simple thing like this appear a problem to you! For, my wife, let's face it, isn't it obvious that the ordeal to which our in-laws have subjected our child Bugonoka means they want to get rid of her, as if she were some heavy faggot of wood they were carrying and are now dying to throw down! Indeed what they have done to her amounts to rejecting her and casting her away in broad daylight. As a matter of fact all this happened only because your daughter is a shameless creature. I wish I could say it is because she is still too young, but I can't, for she can't be too young if she is old enough to be a mother, and she would be having two children now, had it not been for the death of her child and the loss of her other pregnancy. But, alas! there she is, your dear daughter, forcing herself on people, so dumb and blind to everything around her that all the insults they are heaping on her leave her completely unaffected! Had she been a person of solid character like I know you are, she would have left that home a long time ago. In fact we would have already returned to our son-in-law the bride-price he gave us for her, and would already have even married her to another suitor, and for so long that her bride's new house would by now be an old building. And is this, my dear wife, supposed to be the problem you can't handle! Why don't you women ever ponder matters in your heads first before voicing your worries!

"However, you are right, in that when we arrive in our son-in-law's home we will remain quiet and calm for a while, to give our in-laws time to receive our weapons[4] and offer us chairs and to allow ourselves time to sit down and exchange greetings with them properly, acting as if we were completely unaware of their wrongdoing. We can't jump on them before we have even sat down, as if we were some mannerless Abakwaya.[5] And since you will be received by your daughter and be alone with her in her house, you will be the one to give her a taste of the bad news first. Tell her: `What has brought your father and I here is to take you away from this home, because we have heard so many ugly things said against you here that your father and I cannot stand it any longer. But then I don't need to go into details, since you yourself are the one who knows more about it all. All I can say is that what we have heard makes it clear that your husband's people no longer want any bit of you. Can it be true that you're such a shameless creature that you are incapable of knowing when you are no longer wanted! Are we to understand that you are waiting for your ritual horn and kitchen tray[6] to be thrown out of your house before you know you are unwanted! And so we have come for you and we will not leave this home without you.'

"When you finish telling her that then call me and say: `Namwero, are we not going back home! Are we passing the night here!' It is then that I will call my in-laws together and tell them whatever I will tell them, short and to the point, before we are homeward bound again. So, where is that overwhelming problem on which we will waste our time as if we were some supplicants begging for a favor?"

They had been wading through the water of the rivers they had to cross and through dew-soaked grass in the footpaths they took at that early morning hour in the season of the year when dew forms thickest on grass and when they got close to where their son-in-law lived each one of them went behind a near-by thicket to answer nature's call, to first pay the toll that wet and cold early morning journey demanded from their bodies. They entered the gate of their son-in-law's home at the time of the morning sun at which milk curdles. A little girl, a niece of Myombekere he was bringing up in his home, was playing on top of a platform for drying kitchen utensils and spotted them when they were still in the fenced cattle trail, just before reaching the gate of the home compound and cried out: "I win! I am the first to see our visitors!"

Myombekere looked up towards the gate of his home and saw that the visitor was none other than his father-in-law and got up and hurried to meet him. However he had made only a couple of steps when he saw his mother-in-law too! So he had to withdraw,[7] walking backwards, and, likewise, his mother-in-law stood still for a while near the kitchen utensils platform, where the visiting couple had now reached. Myombekere then called aloud his wife, who was in their house washing and preparing for cooking sweet potatoes she had just brought home from their water-side fields:[8] "Bugonoka!"

"Yes!" his wife answered.

"Bring us some seats, and come and relieve our visitors of their weapons." He had to call on his wife to hurry and bring seats to their visitors and relieve them of their weapons because, to begin with, that morning a calf belonging to relatives of his had died of some disease in his home and since waking up he was busy stewing the calf's meat before drying it over fire to preserve it for the owners. His hands were therefore full of meat-fat and barbecue soot and he wouldn't dare soil his father-in-law's weapons by receiving them himself. Then he had run into his mother-in-law and the Wakerewe customs demand that parents-in-law and their children-in-law of the opposite sex avoid each other: the mother-in-law avoids her son-in-law and likewise the son-in-law avoids his mother-in-law. There is no greater sign of respect than that among the Wakerewe.

On coming out of her house Bugonoka saw that the visitors her husband wanted her to receive were his father and mother. She relieved her father of his weapons and also invited her mother into the house, since her son-in-law had already withdrawn by going back to the distant corner of his home compound where his barbecue was and was no longer in her way. The barbecue was near *itoma* tree and Bugonoka in no time brought a chair for her father and placed it under the shade of the tree so that he could sit near his son-in-law's place of work.

Her father sat down and then asked her, "Can I have some water to drink?" His daughter went inside the house and opened the drinking water pot, took a cup[9] for drinking water and beat its mouth against her hand to make sure it was free of dirt and dust and then drew water with it and brought it outside for him. Before giving him the water, she got down on a carefully bent knee and offered him a drink of water with both her hands to show her deep respect for him and her father received it. It was a calabash cup of the most special kind, one which rarely left the remote nook of the rack where it was   hung and which was always kept nicely scented and whose very appearance proclaimed it foreign to unpleasant smells. He drank the water without a pause: *gutiguti gutiguti...!* and then stopped and poured on the ground what was left in the calabash while at the same time breathing out a deep sigh of relief, "*Yehuu!*"

His daughter was surprised and queried him: "Father, what makes you drink water this way!"

To which her father responded, "What indeed, my child! We were drinking banana beer almost the entire night at our place, plus the early morning cold and wetness through which we traveled seem to have had the better of me!"

Only then did Bugonoka greet her father and only then did her husband too greet him, very politely: "How have you been, Sir!"

"I have been well, my son!"

Myombekere and his father-in-law then exchanged news of their respective homes and neighborhoods until they were done and finished. Then they talked of some diverse matters and, after a while, Myombekere went to greet his mother-in-law, who was already inside the house. When he got to the porch of the door of his house, he squatted down behind the door wall, on the left side, so that his mother-in-law would not be able to see him from where he knew she would be seated, by the hearth in the inner room, where the Wakerewe always seated their special visitors so that when a visitor got tired of sitting he or she could stretch a bit on a bed, since that was also the sleeping room.[10] While thus squatting, he greeted his mother-in-law in a voice full of humility: "Did you pass the night well, mother-in-law?"

His mother-in-law answered him, "We passed a good night, my son!"[11]

Then the two of them went on to exchange news of each other's home and neighborhood at some length, but without ever setting eyes on each other, conversing only by responding to each other's voice but never casting a glance at each other. When Myombekere finished greeting his mother-in-law and exchanging news with her, he got up and went to rejoin his father-in-law at the place of his task of stewing and smoking meat his visitors found him preoccupied with.

Inside the house Bugonoka got busy preparing something to eat for her visitors, amidst an intimate mother-and-daughter talk with her mother.

At one moment they would whisper as if meaning to keep those outside the house from hearing what they were talking about, and at another they would let go their voices, throwing to the winds all restraint, Bugonoka's voice ringing out with laughter. Outside Myombekere and his father in-law could only wonder what was going on in that house! After some time Myombekere, by way of sounding out his wife on where she had got with preparing food for their visitors, called out to her: "Bugonoka!"

His wife answered at once with a sweet and cheerful voice, "Yes, Sir!"

To which her husband rejoined by asking her, "How are you doing in there?"

"Just as you'd want me to do!" she reassured him.

Son-in-law and father-in-law had just resumed their talk, with Myombekere facing his father-in-law and his back turned on his barbecue, when all of a sudden a huge dog with its greedy eyes all over the meat appeared from nowhere and snatched a piece of meat from the barbecue, the tongue of the cow, and ran away at full speed with it, closely pursued by Myombekere in that very instant. Before the dog got past the gate of his household, Myombekere threw at it a piece of wood he had grabbed and hit it really hard in the ribs: "*Bwe!*" it cried out in pain and dropped the meat but kept on running, lamely, and he retrieved the meat and brought it back to the barbecue. He continued fuming and hurling at the greedy dog a few insults, even though it was already long gone and was nowhere to be seen: "Go! You are lucky, you abominable creature! You incurable thief!"

His father-in-law said, "I see! You have a stealing dog?"

To which Myombekere responded, "Don't even ask, father-in-law, it is simply terrible! We no longer know what to do in the entire neighborhood; it never allows us a moment of peace! It can even steal food from pots cooking on fire and drink milk from containers hoisted up in hangers! We have tried our best to convince its owner to kill it but all he does is to listen to us and then do nothing! Ah! That is not a dog to keep in a person's home!"

Shortly after the dog incident, Bugonoka brought water, warmed slightly, in a small pot, for her father and her husband to wash their hands before eating. Following her behind was the little girl of their home, carrying a cup of drinking water. When Bugonoka got near his father's legs, she knelt down, got hold of a washbasin:,[2] dusted and wiped it clean and then welcomed her husband and her father to eat by telling them: "Will you come this way!" and poured warm water into the washbasin. The little girl then handed her the calabash of drinking water, which she received while remaining in the same kneeling position, with the respect of a Mkerewe woman serving food to her menfolk. When the men finished washing their hands, she removed the washbasin and put it away, before giving her father drinking water so that he could rinse his mouth and then passing it to her husband, who likewise rinsed his mouth and spit out the water and she took back the cup of water and placed it on a ground pad.[13] In no time she was back in the house and out again with a dish of *obwita*[14] and a pot of relish, covered by a bowl,[15] just as the bowl of *obwita* too was covered over by yet another bowl, still new-looking, to keep flies from fouling the food. She knelt down again next to the feet of her father and her husband and then uncovered *obwita* and put away the cover and immediately placed the food in front of the men, a nicely kneaded and rounded dish with a well-pointed head, and followed that by placing in front of them a pot of relish and a plate[16] on which to serve the relish, which was minced dried meat seasoned the Kikerewe way, with some rock[17] salt and enough butter to see your reflection in its broth! The real good old Kikerewe cuisine!

With that she finished serving her father and her husband and went back to the house to attend to her mother and serve her food too, which she would eat with the little girl for company.

When the men finished eating, Myombekere called his wife to come and take away the food utensils.

Bugonoka returned the utensils to the house, and her mother also finished eating and everything was well and fine and a bit of time passed, and then Nkwanzi, from inside the house where she was seated beside her daughter, called out to her husband outside and said: "Hello, Namwero! Are we passing the night here today!" just as it had been agreed between her and her husband while on their way, and her husband answered her: "Oh, no! We are going back."

As soon as Myombekere and his father-in-law moved away from the place they were sitting while eating, Namwero told his son-in-law, "Could you please tell your wife to come here! I have something I want to tell both of you!"

Myombekere called his wife as requested: "Bugonoka, you are wanted here!"

She came accompanied by her mother and the two of them sat down under the shade of a grain store.[18] The sun was now almost directly above their heads.

It was then that Namwero told his son-in-law the following: "My son-in-law, today I have come here to take away your wife. I will not leave her behind. We are doing so because words have reached us at our home that your very own sisters and brothers have been coming to pick a quarrel with her in your own home here, saying to her: `Go away from here, you wretched female! You too dare call yourself a woman! Indeed! What kind of a woman is one who can't bear children? What is more, you are not fit to be the wife of our Myombekere, such a splendid man! You will end by making our brother die without issue!' That is what has brought us here; because having children is the will of God. Our daughter too wanted children very much. It is only the One-Who-Takes-Away who denied her children, when she herself was dying with longing for them. And since it is our child who is the source of this human decay, this barrenness, let us take her away, so that she can suffer while in the hands of us to whom she belongs."

Myombekere's mother-in-law added the following: "Yes, indeed! For that's what the Mkerewe means by the saying: `Whatever remains unsold goes back to the owner', and by the saying: `Ugly to other mothers but beautiful to its mother.'"

Myombekere begged and pleaded with his father-in-law and mother-in-law to no avail: "Could you, please, forgive me: the first fault never ends a marriage; because my wife and I love each other, and we have always loved each other. Even if my relatives decide they don't want her any more, as long as we who are concerned love each other and all is well between us nothing else matters!"

To which his in-laws answered: "It matters a lot, because a mere woman should not cause a rift between you and your blood relatives, make you their enemy, to such an extent that they don't greet you any more, all that on account of a woman. Whether you like it or not, people would not understand such a thing!"

That settled, Bugonoka's parents told her, "Go into the house and take out your tiny tray[19] without loss of time, so that we can be on our way back home, for we don't want to travel in the night".

Their daughter got up, at the same time calling her husband, "Please come with me!" Once inside the house, she nicely stowed away all her possessions she considered of value and then fetched her *enkorongo*[20] ritual horn and her kitchen tray. When she emerged from her house with those two articles, she went to her parents and they at once left with her to go back to their home.

Myombekere had already brought out of the house his father-in-law's weapons and he escorted his wife and her parents for same distance, a rather short one, with a heart full of sadness, almost to the point of shading tears, for his in-laws were taking away his wife whom he loved and who still loved him, and then he bid farewell his father-in-law, "Good-bye, father-in-law." "Good-bye, Son," his father-in-law answered, and he said to his mother-in-law, "May you pass a good night, mother-in-law!" to which his mother-in-law replied, "Thank you, son." Then it was the turn of his wife to say good-bye to him, nicely: "Good-bye, dear. Stay well," to which he answered as best as he could: "Thank you. Go in peace."

With that husband and wife turned their backs on each other: the husband to take back to his home his misery, his wife to tag after her parents. Once alone with her parents, Bugonoka recounted to them in details the very many other insults she had endured from her brothers-in-law and sisters-in-laws.

Chapter I

NOTES

1. The title of the novel in Kikerewe is *Myombekere na Bugonoka na Ntulanalwo na Bulihwali*, the names of the father, mother, son and daughter, the four main characters of the story, *"na"* being the conjunction "and". Myombekere's wife Bugonoka is known by her name through out the novel because Wakerewe women retain their maiden names after marriage.

   The Wakerewe have normally two types of names: the "hereditary" name and the "baby-sitters' name", the name given to a child at birth to reflect some particular circumstance surrounding that child's birth or to carry a wish or a guiding principle for the child. Both types of names usually have male and female forms or equivalents. Like the given name, the hereditary name too is personal to each child, because it is chosen from a large stock of names of the child's paternal and maternal ancestors of the same gender, so that there are no family names or surnames as such. Hence the significance in the novel of *kwetonda*, reciting ones family lineages to each other by way of introduction whenever strangers meet. Whichever of the two names proves more popular during childhood usually becomes the one name by which that person is mainly known.

   All Kikerewe names usually have meaning, although some "inherited" names have eventually lost their original meaning and become just names recognized for being particular to a given clan. A list of Kikerewe names used in the novel together with their meaning is found at the end of this translation, because obviously in many cases Kitereza chose them because of their particular meaning.

   The following is the meaning of the names of the four title characters of the story: *Myombekere*, the name of the father of the family, means, as a noun, "The lifestyle of a household", and, as an imperative form of the verb *ku-yombeka*, "to build", it also means "Build a house or household for (her)"; *Bugonoka,* the name of his wife, is the short form of the Kikerewe saying "*Obuzune bugonoka* ", "misfortune strikes unannounced (spares nobody)", an encouragement to live on and strive to be happy in spite of whatever adversities one may encountered in life; *Ntulanalwo,* the name of the couple's son, means "Death is my inseparable companion"; and the name of the couple's daughter, *Bulihwali,* is the short form of "*obuzune bulihwali!*", "When will suffering ever end!"

2. *Kwalurana* in Kikerewe: The wedding of an unmarried young man and a

maiden. In polygamous Kikerewe society such marriages were highly valued, especially by the bride's relatives, since the young girl could easily have been married off to a man much older than herself, or even to an old man, and with several wives to boot.

3.　Male potency was believed to be the proof of male fertility, so that only an impotent man was thought of as "barren". Bow-and-arrow was the symbol of manhood the bridegroom carried on his wedding day, and the expression "a man's fertility drug is his bow" means that any man who can marry and consummate marriage, or shoot his manhood into a woman, to extend the bow-and-arrow symbol, can have children.

4.　The Kikerewe text has in parenthesis: "because men in those times carried weapons whenever they traveled, whether on a long trip or simply going to pay a social visit".

5.　"Abakwaya" is the Wakerewe's pejorative name for Bajita or Wajita, recent immigrants to Ukerewe (see Introduction), a mainland people who speak a different language and have different customs and traditions, whom the insular and very reserved Wakerewe tended to find too aggressive and boisterous to the extent of considering them uncouth and vulgar.

6.　*Olugali:* Circular basin or tray of water-tight woven grass, usually about two feet in diameter at the rim, a multi-purpose woman's household utensil. On getting married, the bride brought with her into her husband's home a ritual horn of an animal, *ihembe*, from her family's ritual paraphernalia and *olugali.* The horn stood for her people's religious obligations and rites and *olugali* for her right to her own house and kitchen in her husband's household. In the case of a divorce, those were the two items which the wife took out of her husband's house in the presence of her father or his representative to signify the end of their marriage. She would then come for the rest of her belongings at her convenience later.

7.　A mother-in-law and her son-in-law were not allowed by Kikerewe custom to be near each other or to have their eyes meet.

8.　The Wakerewe had two types of crop fields (*ensambu*): *ensambu zy'olugulu*, "upland fields", in which they grew their main crops of millets, cassava and sweet potatoes during the planting or rain season, and *amasanga*, "water-side fields" along the lakeshore and in river valleys, in which they planted mainly sweet potatoes and some greens (later on rice was added on) when   crops were off-season in the upland fields.

9.　*Omutaho:* Calabash container with a long slender handle used as a cup for drawing and drinking water

10.   With a porch at the door. The house was usually divided into two parts: the front-room, where the grinding-stone and the milk-churn were located and which served as the sitting room, called *omwalilo*, "the stretching floor", since there too was where beds were usually made for visitors who stayed for the night, and *omukugiro* or inner-room, in which the kitchen was situated and which was also the bedroom. Only intimate visitors, especially female ones, of the mistress of the house, like Bugonoka's mother here, would therefore be received in the inner-room, which was sometimes further divided so as to form a smaller additional bed-room called *oluhongore*, "the secluded room."

11.   The Wakerewe have a very elaborate system of greeting each other for which there is simply no English equivalent. To begin with, they consider greetings so important that a person cannot greet people collectively but has to address an individual salutation to each person in a group of people and if they are too many then to greet as many of them as he or she can. Then the greetings themselves are different, and very much so, depending on whether the two individuals are peers or a senior and a junior according ranking by age, gender, blood, clan or in-law kinship. Blood and clan kinship ranks always take precedence over age and gender and any other considerations of seniority, so that, for example, a little girl who is a cousin of an old man's mother is his mother's "sister" in their extended family relationship and therefore is greeted by the man with the salutation of respect with which he greets his real mother and other female senior relatives of his, any female cousin of a man's mother-in-law is considered another "mother-in-law" of that man and greeted by him as such irrespective of her age, the paternal aunt of a man's wife is greeted by that man as if she were male and his real father-in-law, a little boy who is a cousin of a man's father is that man's "younger father" and greeted by the man as if he were his real father, and so on.

On top of that, all those numerous different salutations are mostly conventional words and phrases with no other independent meaning in the language, so that the English equivalents used here like "Good morning!", "Good evening!" and "How are you!" in Kikerewe would be considered not the greetings themselves but follow-ups to greetings or "exchanging news" of each other's welfare.

12.   *Olusabuzyo* or *isabuzyo* (plural *ensabuzyo* or *amasabuzyo*): Wooden trough-like washbasin in which men washed their hands before a meal, a word whose primary meaning is the "bail" of a water vessel, a similarly shaped wooden water container, only much lighter and more bowl-like, from the verb

kusabula, "to bail" water from a water vessel. Another version of *olusabazyo* is a wooden container for drinking banana beer, which is like a bail with a well defined rectangular rim, from whose four corners beer is drunk.

13. *Engata*: Ringed cushion or pad, usually made of strips of dry banana stem fiber (or cloth), on which to station things on the ground and on which to place loads carried on the head (mostly by women) or shoulders (by men).

14. *Obwita*: : Dish of food, nicknamed "stiff porridge" by the British during their colonial rule of East Africa, made by cooking flour in hot water, the Wakerewe's staple meal, eaten with meat, fish, green vegetables, beans or peas as relish. The dish, called *ugali* in Swahili, in its different varieties is found practically all over Black Africa.

15. *Ekibo* (plural *ebibo*): Bowl-like water-tight container made of woven grass the way *olugali* above is crafted and used mainly for serving *obwita* in.

16. *Olunanga* (plural *enanga*): Plate, which was usually wooden and mounted on a stand cut out of the same piece of hard wood, and shaped like a soup plate.

17. *Lunzebe*:   Rock salt, as opposed to "ash salt", the poor man's substitute for rock salt. Kitereza in his note for his Swahili translation of the novel describes it as: "salt obtained from the island of Namasanze". The salt, which has long been supplanted by "European" common salt, is now used only for medicinal purposes and is known as *omwonu gw'*Abagaya, "Jaluo salt," most likely because when the former local source was exhausted the new source became the Jaluo traders from the north of Ukerewe on the Tanzania-Kenya border.

18 . *Ekitala*:   Kikerewe grain store, a round structure shaped like a hut with a movable thatched roof, made of twigs, vines or tree-climbers and mounted on a short platform. A typical Kikerewe home had at least one *ekitala*.

19. *Akagali*: Diminutive form of *olugali* (see note 6 above), used here by Bugonoka's parents to show how unappreciated the symbol of her marriage was by her husband and his relatives.

20. *Enkorongo*: A large antelope whose horns were sometimes used instead of the horns of cows as ritual horns and cups for drinking medicines, and hence, by extension, a "ritual horn".

Chapter II

BUGONOKA RETURNS TO HER PARENTS' HEARTH, HER HUSBAND GOES TO WOO HER BACK

Bugonoka returned to her parent's home to live as a divorced woman; which meant that back in her own home her husband became an adult man living without a wife.

So her husband Myombekere went here and there and everywhere among his relatives looking for a female relative of his who could come and live in his home and cook for him. Myombekere also owned cattle, and so he also had to get somebody who would look after his livestock on the days he would be forced to go away from home in the changed circumstances of his life.

In the meanwhile his life of a man without a wife proved to be very painful existence for him: at times he would spend an entire day going from the home of one relative of his to that of another, or even wandering through the homes of people in no way related to him at all, uninvited and unexpected, looking for something to eat. That beggar's life for an adult able-bodied human being proved simply too painful for him to bear, and as a result there were days when from morning till evening he ate nothing at all, or all he ate was a piece of raw cassava he had chewed, or whatever he had manage to roast by rummaging in the courtyard fireplace of his home.[1] And there were others when he passed the night on an empty stomach. His cows gave milk, but he was missing his wife so much that from the time she was taken away from him he could no longer stand the taste of milk. As you know, in this Ukerewe of ours, women are the foundation of people's homes and without a woman a man's home is a house without a roof. Once a man is married, he can never be a normal person again without a wife: for there is no greater shame for a man than for him to have to perform women duties like grinding flour, cooking, picking greens and drawing water. However hungry he might be, he would rather sleep with an empty stomach than face the spectacle of a cooking pot of relish boiling between his legs!

Finally, after some time, his relatives too felt sorry for him and gave him someone to cook for him, a divorced female relative of his, and also a boy grown enough to help him look after his cattle.

But Myombekere's misery did not end with his finding someone to cook for him and a herder for his cattle. Not in the least. The pain in his heart raged on, because he missed his wife Bugonoka very much. It was not until about two months had passed that he even remembered his relatives had told him they wanted to see him court and marry another woman. That night he could not sleep. He was tormented by thoughts throughout the night, thoughts which had started their onslaught on him when he took his cow-skin bed sheet and looked for a stick[2] to dust it with ready to go to bed. That night he thought long and deep and asked himself a lot of questions and said to himself: "What wretched existence for a man to sleep alone in his bed, with no woman to hold in his arms, a woman with whom to exchange the secrets of their hearts, a man at my age, when he is a properly created male person? What then is the purpose of my existence on earth? What do I want in life then, if I am a man without a wife?"

By that time there was no longer a single relative of his, male or female, or a single friend, who came to see him who spoke to him of anything else other than that he should court another woman and remarry. Especially his neighbors, who, as days went by, finally said many derogatory things about him, that there was something seriously wrong with him, that he was actually insane, capable of taking off his clothes in public, for choosing to remain an adult man without a wife. He finally could no longer bear it and decided to do something about his intolerable situation, except he kept that resolution to himself. But then when he finally wanted to begin looking for another woman to marry, he felt he should first go to his wife's parents to try and woo back his wife Bugonoka. And that is what he did.

At the home of his wife's parents he was received by his wife Bugonoka herself. She relieved him of his weapons, a bow and arrows, and took them into the house and then brought him a chair outside. He sat down and they greeted each other and exchanged news at some length. That done, Myombekere asked his wife: "It appears my father-in-law and mother-in-law are not at home?"

"My father, when he woke up this morning, went to look for fish in his *olubigo*[3] fish trap, but he's finished with that and has already come back. Now he has gone to work on a trunk of a tree he felled yesterday in his farm-lands yonder. I hear he wants to make a boat from it. As to my mother, she has gone to sun cassava[4] on our drying rock[5] and should be back any minute now." They had hardly finished talking about her when Myombekere's mother-in-law called her daughter: "Bugonoka! Bugonoka *wuu*!"

"Yes, mother!"

"Bring me a broom; I forgot to bring one with me."

Because her daughter had been in the middle of talking with her husband, she did not catch well what it was her mother wanted her to do and so she asked her, "What did you say, mother?"

Her mother answered her back in a voice meant to reach far: "I said: `Bring me a broom for sweeping this sand off the rock!'. Can't you hear me! Are you talking with somebody?"

"All right!"

She went into the house at once and fetched a broom and took it to her mother at the food-drying rock. When she got there, her mother asked her, "Who is there, with whom you are talking so excitedly?"

"I am talking with my husband Myombekere. He has just arrived, just as you left home to bring your cassava here."

"And where did he say he is coming from?"

"I wish I knew! I too haven't been with him long enough to ask him where he is coming from. All I know is that he has just arrived, bow and arrow in hand."

"Well, what about giving me a hand by sweeping off this sand, my dear! I wish I knew whose kids these are who are so determined to put our drying rock out of use! Can you do that before you return to your visitor, to keep him company, lest he feels neglected? Because, to be honest, he is still your husband, and I can't pretend I don't know it; otherwise, why haven't you brought home another suitor?"

Her daughter burst our laughing, happily. She swept the food drying-stone and then returned home to her husband, who she found gone to pass water in her father's banana plantation. When he came back, they chatted a bit and then Bugonoka went inside the house to grind flour. Before long, Bugonoka's mother came back, and on entering the home she told his son-in-law, "Son, could you please make way so that I can pass!" Her son-in-law withdrew out of the way and his mother-in-law passed and went into her house. Only then did they greet each other and exchange news. His mother-in-law asked Myombekere, "Son, where are you coming from? And what brings you our way?" To which her son in-law answered by saying he had come from his home to visit them and see how they were doing.

After talking with his mother-in-law for a bit, Myombekere asked his wife, "By the way, Bugonoka, where did you say my father-in-law was working on a tree trunk?" His wife left her work at the grinding-stone to come and show him where her father was. They had hardly walked any distance when she pointed out her father by a finger and said, "There he is!"

Her husband rejoined: "That's right! Let me go and greet him."

Bugonoka went back home to continue with her work of grinding flour and preparing food for her husband.

Myombekere greeted his father-in-law and the two men exchanged news with each other courteously. Then, without waste of time, he took an ax and helped his father-in-law cut branches off the trunk of the tree he had felled for making a boat big enough for fishing with *amahongora*,[6] but not before his father-in-law had tried to dissuade him from doing so. On seeing his son-in-law tighten his clothes and get hold of an ax in a businesslike manner ready to attack the tree, Namwero had protested: "Leave it alone, son-in-law. You are a visitor here; you don't have to do that!" "Let me help you, father-in-law; you are working at a real men's job!" Myombekere had answered and Namwero could find no answer to that. When he finished helping him cut the branches off, he helped him turn the felled tree around.

They had just managed to do that when a child from Namwero's home arrived to call them: "I have been sent to tell you to come home with me!" They left for home, carrying with them their axes, and found food ready for them.

As soon as they sat down Bugonoka came outside to fetch the chair on which her husband was sitting and said to him as she did so, "Please, come inside this house!"[7]

In Namwero's home there was, besides his own house, another house of sorts, the bachelor's hut[8] of Bugonoka's brother Lweganwa, who was away from home on a hippopotamus hunting expedition as a rower for the hippopotamus hunters.[9] It was in Lweganwa's bachelor's hut that Bugonoka, accompanied by a little boy, another brother of hers, took her husband. She first brought some warm water for washing hands and poured it into a washbasin,[10] then she went back to her parent's house for drinking water and some hand leaves.[11] Myombekere washed his hands, followed by his little brother-in-law, then Bugonoka removed the washbasin and gave her husband the calabash of drinking water and he rinsed his mouth and his wife received back the water from him and placed it on a ground pad,[12] and then she gave him some soft tree leaves and he wiped his hands dry: she did not want him to eat with water dripping into his food. That done, at once she brought *obwita*[13] and a pot of relish and placed in front of her husband the dish of *obwita* first, as a woman is supposed to do when serving food to men, before putting in front of him the pot of relish with a plate[14] on which to put relish for the little boy[15] eating with him for company. Before going back to her mother inside the house ready to serve food to her father, who was seated outside in the shade of *omulumba*[16] tree, she first confided to her husband something: "This boy really gobbles relish! Put his share on the plate; only then can he temper his appetite for relish." After alerting her husband thus, she added, addressing her little brother: "Don't gobble the visitor's relish; temper your appetite!" and the child answered, "All right!" The relish with which the visiting son-in-law ate his food was *emamba*[17] of the sweetest kind, a female one replete with fish-eggs and fats which Namwero had caught in his *olubigo* that morning. It was Nkwanzi who had prepared it with great culinary skill, the way a Mkerewe woman prepares food for her son-in-law. No wonder Bugonoka was such a great cook! A woman is a great cook or a poor one depending on what she learnt from her mother's kitchen! And it was from her mother than Bugonoka had learnt to be such a wonderful cook of every kind of food and every kind of relish, be it fish, meat or greens! It was from her mother too that she learned her mastery of grinding grain so that her flour was always soft to perfection. And she always had flour in store. She was not the type of woman who goes to the grinding-stone whenever a visitor calls. And so, in Bugonoka's home, a hungry visitor got attended to and given something to eat at once. She was also friends with her hoe, a real hard worker, and, as a result, hunger and famine were things unknown to her house: she had in store every kind of food to last her until the following harvest and it was to her that people in all sorts of need went for help. Not only that, she was also good at all the other women callings, like weaving grass-made household utensils such as bowls[18] and trays[19] and making *ebiyanzi*, *ebisusi*, cups[20] and other calabash containers from gourds.

Bugonoka then went to give food to her father. Her mother had prepared two nicely kneaded dishes of *obwita*, one for her son-in-law and the other one for her husband, and also put aside a third cut of food for her daughter and herself. Women normally did not eat with men, and, of course, it was unthinkable for Bugonoka's mother to eat with her son-in-law.

Their meal over Myombekere told his little brother-in-law to call his sister to come and take away the utensils. Bugonoka did so and then brought fresh warm water and poured it into the washbasin; and when her husband finished washing his hands she handed him water for rinsing his mouth and for drinking. Her husband rinsed his mouth and drank some water and then asked her, "Is father-in-law still eating?"

"Yes, but he too will soon be through. Is there something you want to see him about?"

"Yes, there is", Myombekere answered.

Shortly after that Namwero also finished eating and washed his hands and Bugonoka went back into his brother's bachelor hut to inform her husband of that and to take his chair for him so that he could come outside and sit by his father-in-law for a chat.

Myombekere sat down by his father-in-law and settled and then chatted with him about other matters altogether. Only after a while did he finally touch on the subject of wooing back his wife: "Father-in-law, what has brought me here is to throw myself at your feet and ask you to give me back my wife, so that I can go back with her, so that we can live together again the way you intended it to be when you gave her to me in wedding. Too much time has already passed: this is now the second month I am living a wretched life, all alone at home, an adult man at my age, as if I don't have a wife! Whatever I may have done, our people said: `A single fault never ends a marriage.'"

His father-in-law responded: "Living such a wretched life is simply your choice: why don't you court another woman and marry? There are plenty of women everywhere and you have the daughters of the entire

Ukerewe to choose from! If you look, you will find the beautiful woman who will please all your relatives, one who bears children who stay alive. For the truth is, I never refused you a wife. You know very well that you came to court my daughter, pleaded with me, and I accepted you without reserve and gave you a wife. As to taking her away from you, there too you know I didn't do so out of spite. I saw wrongdoing on your part and on the part of your brothers and sisters. Can you imagine how much your mother-in-law and I were disturbed by what we heard! Imagine an outsider being the bearer of such bad news to us, from your place all the way to here, such a stranger being the person to tell us that Bugonoka had suffered a lot, to tell us how it was being said that her husband and his brothers and sisters all no longer wanted any bit of her, to the extent that your relatives had decided never to come to your home anymore as long as she remained there, and all that simply because she bears children who die! One would think she was the witch who killed them when those who died were her very own children, who died in spite of her loving them! Is it not true that losing pregnancies happens to all women in the world? How is it then that my daughter was treated like a woman to whom this had happened for the first time on earth, when what happened to her is a misfortune which spares nobody! Why was my daughter treated as if she had the most deadly womb-rot on earth! In fact it has taken me so long before bringing her to your home for divorce and returning to you the bride-price you gave us for her simply because her brother is away from home on an expedition with hippopotamus hunters, but, with the blessings of the heavens, should he return home well and sound, on the day he comes back is the very day you should expect me to invade your home with each and everything you gave me as my daughter's bride-price, with not a single item missing."

Myombekere's mother-in-law heard her husband say to their son-in-law words which were meant to wound and hurt him and she too decided not to spare him and said: "If I had my way, Bugonoka should have remarried by now. Why should his bride-price be an issue when we have it! My understanding is that a problem arises and becomes a suit in court only when the bride-price to be returned is no longer there! How then can bride-price which is still intact disgrace a person! As to Bugonoka going back to his place, that is something I am opposed to. One even wonders whether there isn't something very wrong with this silly wife of his! If she had any sense in her, wouldn't she realize what is happening! Since she came here, two entire months have come and gone and yet not a single person has been here to woo her back, be it a brother or sister of her husband! What then are her grounds for saying: `They love me, where I was married!' In fact, even though cases of women marrying themselves off to men against their people's wishes are not unheard of, they are never like this one. A woman marries a man against her people's wishes only when she knows and sees that she is loved. Not otherwise. It is indeed my opinion that what has brought our son-in-law here today is not to woo back his wife but what people call to escort her back to her parents' home and make sure she arrived. May be he has even married another woman already, for anything we know, since we don't live with him!"

When his father-in-law and mother-in-law finished talking to him that way, sadly Myombekere responded to them: "My father-in-law and my mother-in-law, I have come here to woo back my wife, and I have nothing to do with those other matters of escorting her back home and wanting back the bride-price I gave you for her. And that's the truth, because you took away from me my wife whom I love and who loves me. As to her losing pregnancies time and time again, she can't be the only one to blame. May be the bad luck is mine, I am the one who was cursed by the Sun[21] with: `You will die an adult man without issue!' so that even if I married a lot of wives, if God continues to will that I get no children, all I will have is the meaningless pride of being a man with many wives. I am not the first childless man in the world: the likes of me abound. I am therefore entreating you, my parents, to become real parents to me again as you did once when you gave me your daughter for a wife, by giving her back to me. That is all."

His mother-in-law spoke out and said: "If you are capable of saying such nice things, what kept you for so long from coming to see how your wife was doing? You know very well that when we came to take her away her womb had just lost a living thing!"[22]

"What kept me away this long are the problems of a single person's home, and livestock, which people in this Ukerewe of ours think a person should have and of which I too keep a few heads in my home. To go away from home and leave your cows lowing on their tethers the whole day, with nobody to take them out to pasture, is something people would not understand. You see me here today because very recently my relatives finally pitied my plight and gave me a herder. Only then did it become possible for me to leave home and come here."

When the discussion ended, Myombekere asked to be given his

weapons so that he could go back to his home and on hearing that his wife went to look for a more fitting robe in which to escort her husband. Then Myombekere said good-bye to his father-in-law and mother-in-law and left escorted by his wife alone.

They had not gone very far when his wife said, "Here, take your bow! I am going back home. I have to go to the lake, because the drinking-water pot happens to be empty today."

Her husband said, "What about escorting me on a little further, darling, to the shade of that tree yonder, before you go back?" Bugonoka hesitated at first before agreeing to do so and leading the way again, with her husband following behind.[23] When they got to the tree in question, *ikombayaga*, they sat down under its shade. That is when the husband reiterated to his wife the purpose of his journey and wooed her back and told her: "Look at me now, going back home a sad person this way, retracing my journey all alone and looking so ridiculous. Indeed, what can I do? For it appears things have taken a really bad turn, and very much so, since both your parents seem to have made up their minds to take you away from me. Really, my dear wife, we were so happily married, you caring for whatever mattered to me and I too caring for whatever mattered to you! Are you too really willing to go along with your parents and cast me away, just like that?"

His wife silently stared at him first before answering: "So you think I no longer love you? So, in your way of looking at things, you would like to see me return to you on my own, just like that, by just bursting through the gate of your home, before you know I love you very much?"

"Yes. For what is there to be ashamed of? You will be coming back to your own home. What are you afraid of? You won't be some uninvited guest gate-crashing into some other person's home! Secondly, it can't be said that you left me to come to your parents' home because we had quarreled, or because I had beaten you and hurt you or had angered you by insulting you in some unbearable way so that you can't come back to me on your own. So that's how you women are! You are completely incapable of pity! Because if you had any pity in you you would by now be saying to yourself, `My husband surely has already suffered this way and that way!' See what has happened to you! Just by staying at your parents' home for some time you have become like an unwed woman, unattached[24] in every way, so that even what I am talking to you about at this very moment is wasted breath, with none of it getting to you, because your mind is somewhere else!"

"So, according to you, only the wife who leaves because of a quarrel or because she had been beaten by her husband needs to be wooed back! Don't you think that your relatives insulted me really badly? But, in spite of that, I personally don't think much of it: those you have to contend with are my parents, the two people who gave me to you. Those are the ones who found the insults I was subjected to unbearable. They would, in fact, have already married me off to another man by now, if I had not told them: `But even if you marry me off to another husband, will the first duty of my new husband be to look for the cure of my womb for me so that I can become a wholesome woman? If that is not the case, how is it that all the time I have been here I haven't seen you make any attempt to look for a healer for me? I remember somebody came here and told you that what causes the loss of my pregnancies and the death of my children are the two diseases of *ihuzi* and *endokaloki*,[25] to which you replied: If that is the case, we'll take her to medicine men to cure her of the diseases.' That is what appears to be holding them back."

"Since your parents came to take you away I too have been quietly inquiring among people here and there regarding that issue, until I came across a medicine man who told me: `How can I treat you if you are not with your wife? Go and come back with her and only then can I prepare my herbs for you. As to whether I will heal her or not, that is the work of the Sun!'"

They parted at that and Myombekere retraced his way back to his home.

On his journey back home Myombekere was consumed by thoughts, thoughts of being a man without a wife, a mature male person who is condemned to make his own bed, who is a lonely being with no child to send on this and that errand of his, a child to do things for.

It was at that moment that he came across a certain woman on the road and the two of them greeted each other and exchange news at some length until they knew where each one of them lived and whether they were married or not.

Myombekere found himself courting the woman there and then and saying to her: "Madam, as soon as I saw you my heart began feasting on you! And, as you see me here, I am debating with myself how I should start telling you what I want to tell you. But I find I have no choice but to tell you, even if you find what I will say to be mere nonsense, for the truth of the matter is, I can keep it inside me no longer. What is more, as our elders said: 'When what you have is really yours and you didn't steal it you run no danger of having your arm broken for it!'"

The woman answered him back: "Just go ahead and tell me what is bothering you. For all I know, you may ask me to give you what I don't have or to tell you what I don't know!"

Myombekere replied by declaring to her his intentions as openly as he could right away: "What I want to speak to you about, Madam, is that I would like to court you with a view to our becoming life companions. For that is how it was meant to be since the beginning of time, for us men to initiate courtship. As our elders once said: 'A woman is like the men's fish *emamba* in the sea, to be got only by he who plunges his fishing-spear in the waters.'"

The woman too liked what she heard, however what she said in answer was: "And what if we hadn't met here by chance? Where would you have seen me?" To which our man responded, "Well, we men were created to be vagabonds, always on the road and in people's homes in search of women, until death! When you meet the woman the Sun has destined to be one with you, even if it is on a public road like this one, you should court her, for, as our ancestors put it: ' You pay homage to the throne wherever the king[26] happens to be.'" The woman laughed. Our man pursued the matter further by adding: "For, as you know, people say: `One who ventures out finds something, the stay-at-home grows a swollen tummy.' We have met on a public road, it is true, and certainly a human being is not something you pick up on a road: a man gets a woman to marry from her parents' home, from her father and mother. But, in most cases, before that he usually would have met her somewhere else first, learnt something about her, found out whether she is married or not. Sometimes a woman may not be married and yet she may be already bespoken to a suitor and you have no way of knowing it unless somebody tells you or you find out for yourself. And that is the way things are with you and me, since we are lucky to have met we can find out all about ourselves, where each one of us lives, what are our clans, and all the important things people need to know in such matters. So, let me ask you again: `Are you unattached?'"

"Yes, it is true I am free, only my former husband has not yet divorced me, although I have already been living with my parents for four whole months and by the next new moon it will be five months since he wanted no more of me.

"Please! Since when does a man reject a woman! Just say you want no more of him?"

"My husband has yet to divorce me and I don't want to hide the truth from you when you know our Kikerewe customs as well as I do. It is now that I hear my brother talk about taking me to his home for the divorce. Most likely that will be after the next new moon, and only then will I be free to invite home suitors."

"That husband of yours, were you his first wife and he your first husband? Did you bring human beings into this world with him? What is his clan?'

"Yes, he was my first husband and I his first wife, and we had children together, two of whom survived, a boy and a girl -- they are people living on this earth and so I can't hide them, even if I wanted to. The boy was my first born; and he is now a grown-up child. If my husband's people were wealthy, I could say this year they would give him a woman to marry. After he was born, when I got pregnant again I gave birth to a girl. Those are my too surviving children. Regarding those who died, the pregnancy which followed the girl ended in the premature birth of an eight-month baby, already a human being. We put the tiny thing in a washbasin for incubation, as is done in such cases. All the same, because it came into this world not intended to stay, its life was extinguished after only a few nights. Because the woman who loses a child does not take long before conceiving again,[27] as soon as I resumed my monthly periods I became pregnant again. I carried my precious load for about three months and during that third month it developed complications and I lost it. And after that, alas, we remained a couple with no further luck up to this day! Then after a time the other wives of my husband, for no reason, claimed they were afraid something bad was going to happen to them and said: 'We have been accused of witchcraft. It is being said that we are the ones who killed the children of our co-wife.' Then, on account of that problem of their own creation, my co-wives took off in anger and went to their parents' homes to summon their relatives so that we could go to a diviner to find out the truth. When their people assembled, since at that time my father was still alive, I went to call him and he too came, accompanied by my brother. And then when we all went to the diviner together to know the truth, my husband's other wives were indeed revealed to be the culprits. So my father and my brother had no choice but to take me away from my husband after telling me: `You can no longer stay here, because these witches are after you by a well-planned attack. As you can see, they have began by attacking the issues of your womb, and, now that you have become barren, we don't want them, since the malice of their kind of people knows no limit, to go after your very person and leave us altogether empty-handed, for, as our ancestors said: What eats the hair on the head is after the brain!' There now, that is how my people took me away from my husband. For, let you be my judge, how could I have acted differently? Should I have remained with my husband at the risk of losing my life?

"Oh! certainly not! You could only remain if those co-wives of yours were mere victims of other people's unfounded accusations of witchcraft, were being called creatures of the night unjustly, the way we all fear each other and all the time attribute to other people witchcraft. But that's not what we are talking about here: you went to find out the truth from a seer and the diviner exposed their evil deeds in broad daylight! Oh, no! In such a situation you couldn't have dared to stay, however courageous you are in facing death, for, as our people say, prevention is better than cure!"

"As to my husband's clan, his people are the ...eee... please help me out! What is happening to me today, that I can't even remember my husband's people ... shame on me! ... Say, what is the clan of people with power to ward off the locust plague?"

"The Abayango."

"Yes! Abayango. That's it! That is the clan of my husband's people."

Our man resorted to spearing the ground with one end of his bow, his head drooping, before saying: "Oh, I see! They must be relatives of these other Abayango who reside in our locality."

"Yes, indeed. Those are my fathers-in-law, you see. They and my real father-in-law are children of the same father, they are half-brothers. My father-in-law is a child of a wife of one house and the man you have mentioned a child of the wife of the other house, but children of one and the same master of a household, paternal brothers, and so people of one and the same clan."[28]

The man was stunned and dropped his head, as if somebody had hit him in the face and he was bleeding from the nose, before responding: "Oh, I see! Now I see why our people of yore said: `Before you kill each other know each other's clans and relatives!'"[29] He was simply dumbfounded and shook his head in disbelief and said: "*Uu!* What a turn of events! It appears it is taboo for us to marry, since your husband's people are our greatest *abagurwe*[30] joking-mates. As a matter of fact, regarding their power to ward off locusts, they never want to hear it mentioned, so that even we, their *abagurwe*, usually remind them of it only by taking advantage of our joking relationship and even then not without forcing matters a bit. Should somebody else pester then with it the way we do, my goodness, there would be real trouble!"

The woman was likewise rendered speechless and said, "It is a bad situation, indeed! The taboo of *abagurwe*! May be if it were the taboo of which people say: `The taboo of the maternal nephew and niece washes off!' That is the kind of taboo which can be cleansed so as to allow people to marry. But never that of *abagurwe*. Clan joking-mates marrying would be knowingly swallowing the hook of calamity's bait!" [31]

When that issue was concluded, when it became clear to both of them that there had come to light a great interdiction which made it impossible for them to marry, they said good-bye to each other and parted in opposite directions, the man going his way and the woman hers. But, as they traveled to their different destinations, the man appeared to be walking with the matter still weighing much more heavily on his mind than it did on the woman's, for he had not been flirting with her but courting her in earnest, with the intention of really marrying her, had such a formidable taboo not come in between them.

Myombekere retraced his way back home speaking to himself in undertones like a madman: he was a hunter who had struck a prize game only to lose it again.

Chapter II

NOTES

1. *Ekikome* or *ekome*: Open-air fireplace situated in the compound of a home, the place where men sat in the evening and ate their dinner at night, an important family gathering place, especially for the men and their male children. Cassava and sweet potatoes roast well in the hot ashes of *ekikome* fire, but, among the Wakerewe, unless intended as provisions for a journey, such food was all right only for children, because a man with a home was supposed to eat properly cooked meals.

2. *Akakoromyo*: Short thick stick for beating dust out of cow-skins and goat-skins which were used as bed sheets.

3. *Olubigo*: Permanent structure built in the shallow waters of the lake for catching fish, consisting of fences of reeds on wooden support with a series of catch chambers.

4. *Obutaga*: Dried cassava before it is ground or pounded into flour. The Wakerewe prepared cassava for grinding into flour by peeling cassava roots, slicing them and then sunning the slices until they were partly dry before dampening them by spraying them with water and then covering them until they molded, after which the slices were scraped clean of the mold and dried again.

5. *Olukiri*: The surface of a large granite rock used as a floor on which to sun food items which need drying and on which grain was threshed. Many Kikerewe homes were built near these important stone floors, which were often shared by a number of homes in a neighborhood. The alternative was what in the novel are referred to as the unsatisfactory earthen threshing floors, like that of Myombekere's home, of hardened soil plastered over with cow-dung and then left to dry, whose grain tended to have a lot of sand in it.

6. *Amahongora*, plural for *ihongora*: Fish traps made of trellised large vines or tree-climbers and twigs of trees instead of splits of papyruses and *amabingo* canes which were normally used for making the fish-trapping baskets, whose general name is *emigono* (singular *omugono*). *Amahongora* or larger and stronger *emigono* were used for catching big fish in deep sea waters.

7. A son-in-law is a very special visitor to the parents of his wife, and so he is always served his visitor's meal inside a house, whereas, in general, Wakerewe men took their meals outside in their homestead compounds.

8. *Endaro*: "Bachelor's house", literally "camp". On reaching puberty, a male

child was required by Kikerewe custom to build with his own hands *endaro* in his parents home, both a test of his manhood and for his independence, since an unmarried young man's hut was out of bounds to his parents.

9.   *Abanyaga*: Hippopotamus hunters. Hippopotamus hunting in Ukerewe was normally exclusively by members of a society of initiates called *abanyaga*, who hunted the aquatic animals in the lake with harpoons in huge and thick-framed boats.

10.   *Olusabuzyo*: See note 12 of Chapter I.

11.   *Ebibabi* or *ebitutu*: Tree leaves, usually the large and soft ones with absorbent surfaces, used for toilet purposes and for drying kitchen utensils.

12.   *Engata*: See note 13 of Chapter I.

13.   *Obwita*: See note 14 of Chapter I.

14.   *Olunanga*: See note 16 of Chapter I.

15.   Often men ate men-only relish straight from the pot, especially when none of the relish was intended to be left over, and here too Myombekere would do so, after his young companion has been served his share.

16.   *Omulumba*: Large evergreen tree with an abundance of foliage commonly planted in Kikerewe homes as a shade tree.

17.   *Emanba*: Type of catfish which, unlike other catfishes, has scales and one of the relishes which were taboo to the Wakerewe women. The other kinds of fish adult Wakerewe women, that is those who had reached the age of puberty, did not eat we come across in the in the novel are *embete, enkuyu, enzegere, ebigugu* and *enkorobondo*. Wakerewe women did not also eat goat meat, mutton, wild game, chicken, including eggs, and all fowls, big and small.

18.   *Ebibo* (plural for *ekibo*): See note 15 of Chapter I.

19.   *Engali,* plural for   *olugali*:   See note 6 of Chapter I.

20.   *Ebiyanzi, ebisusi, emitaho*: Names for different calabash containers: *ebiyanzi*, singular *ekiyanzi*: a large calabash used for churning milk; *ebisusi*, singular *ekisusii*: calabashes for carrying and storing water; *emitaho* singular *omutaho*: calabash with a handle for drawing and drinking water with (see note 9 of Chapter I). The other calabash containers with special use we come across in the novel are: *ekizanda* (plural *ebizanda*), for drinking milk with, *engunda*, for storing and drinking banana bear, *isayayi* (plural of *amasayayi*), a calabash bowl, *enchuma* or *oluchuma*, a small calabash for carrying liquid butter as a ritual ointment during wedding ceremonies, *embilikira*, a cover for the mouths of the *ebizanda* of milk.

21.   *Izoba*: The "Sun", Wakerewe's way of naming Providence; *Izoba* was also one of the attributes of *omukama* (king) of Ukerewe.

22.   Kitereza, in his preoccupation with building the mother-in-law's case against Myombekere, forgets the beginning of his story where Bugonoka is said to have lived for a long time without conceiving again after one abortion followed by the loss of her prematurely born child, which was what led to the relatives of her husband saying bad things about her which angered her parents and made them come to take her away.

23.   The Wakerewe always traveled in Indian-files, in which ones position was to a certain extent determined by his or her relationship to his or her fellow-travelers. A wife always walked in front of her husband and, in general, the young ones preceded their elders, except that, unless they were still little girls, women always walked behind their male relatives, since it would be considered unbecoming and improper for an adult man to watch from behind how his adult female relative walks.

24.   *Omusimbe*: A "free woman". In Kikerewe society the term is used for an unmarried adult woman, whether divorced, widowed or a spinster, who is not bound by customary parental or spousal restrictions.

25.   In his Swahili translation of his novel Kitereza defines *ihuzi* as "worms which kill a woman's eggs in her womb" and *endokaloki* as "worms which destroy the young head and brain of the foetus."

26.   *Omukama*: The king; the hereditary male sovereign and head of the tribe of the Wakerewe. People greeted him by kneeling down (men on one knee and women on both their knees) and raising their hands to him with palms joined together and hailing him by reciting some of his kingly attributes, which he answered by "Greetings!" in the case of women and acknowledged only by a simple grunt "Mn!" in the case of men.

27.   In the case of the mother of a child who lived, among the Wakerewe she was supposed to refrain from having sex until she weaned her child, after suckling it for at least a year, so that there was always a gap of a least two years between any two children of a mother born one after the other. It was believed a mother bearing another child too soon could harm her nursing child, a risk which husbands too could not take. As a result, until recently, that spaced childbirth was the norm with Kikerewe mothers.

28.   The Wakerewe are a patrilineal people, and since family relationships are within an extended family, the woman's father-in-law and the man living in Myombekere's village are not actually half-brothers but the descendants of such half-brothers, otherwise the woman would have described them simply as brothers with the same father and different mothers.

29.   See note 1 of Chapter I on the importance to Wakerewe of "*kwetonda*",

reciting ones family lineages when strangers introduce themselves to each other.

30. *Abagurwe* (singular *omugurwe*): Joking-mates. Customary joking relationship between clans, which existed only between very few clans, in Ukerewe carried with it almost unlimited license regarding what a person could say or do to his or her clan joking-mate and, perhaps because of that fact, it was taboo for people to marry from a clan of their *abagurwe*. Since the woman was married in the clan in which Myombekere can't marry, she too had for ever become part of that taboo and Myombekere couldn't marry her, even after her impending divorce.

31. Death, barrenness, contracting an incurable disease were the kind of punishment by which it was believed the heavens smote those who broke serious taboos, who were sometimes punished together with their relatives or through them.

Chapter III

MYOMBEKERE FINDS FELONY CHARGES AWAITING HIM AT HOME: HIS CATTLE HAD GRAZED ANOTHER PERSON'S CROPS

Myombekere arrived home in the evening, after the sun had completely disappeared from the sky. He ran into the boy who was staying at his home, the one he had brought to help him herd his cattle, as the boy was about to shut the gate of his homestead for the night.[1] On seeing Myombekere, the boy relieved him of his bow and took it inside the house and placed it on its hanger, but the wrong way up, while Myombekere himself remained behind to close the gate. When he too finally went into the house, the first thing he did was to ask the child, "Where could you have put my bow and the arrows?"

"I put the bow on its hanger and stuck the arrows over there, in the loops on the middle wall".

Myombekere could not see, for it was already dark in the house, and so searched for the bow by feeling for its hanger on the wall with his hands until he found it. Then, by touching his weapon, he discovered it was hung upside-down, the cord-entwined end facing up and, of reprimanding the boy, said to him, "Is this how to position a bow, the end with the cord spiral facing up! Have you ever seen such a thing?" Then he hung it correctly first before putting away the arrows in a quiver, after which he took a chair and sat down and exchanged greetings with the woman who had come to cook for him.

It was not until much later that the woman informed him of what had befallen them on that day by telling him, "We back here spent the day taking care of our cattle, but we have committed a felony."

"What kind of felony?"

"We have grazed our cattle in people's crops."

"Which crops?"

"The crops belong to that man they call ... What is his name again? Oh, me! I have lost his name, but I know it, it sounds like Ntama, or something like that!"

"Where abouts were you grazing the cattle?"

"Ee..! yonder, near the mangroves."

"You seem to have grazed Ntamba's crop?"

"Yes, that's him! *Aa*! To tell the truth that man wanted to end the lives of both of us today! This is what happened: When the sun was past noon and beginning to descend, the cows, which we had already driven down to the lake and watered, lazied about, huddled and rested; and as soon as they rested I left to came home, saying to myself, `Let me go home and drink some water and fetch some more for drinking here, and also see whether everything is all right back there and move the calves and tether them in fresh pasture and water them, lest they go thirsty the whole day, and also find out whether he who has gone to woo back his wife has returned.'

"And so home I came and my companion remained out there keeping an eye on the cattle. Here at home I drank some water, watered the calves, moved them from where I had tethered them in the morning, put some drinking water in a small calabash and got on my way back, all ignorant of anything else.

"As I got to the clearance yonder, I heard an alarm being raised, voices shouting: `Beat it really hard, and let you and its master kill each other, if you must, for the creature has wronged you!' And on looking to my right this way, what do I see but that very man Ntamba racing after this child here, the child ahead, the man hard by behind, a huge stick clasped in his hands, intent on killing the child, the child praying for his legs not to let him down! This child here passed me first as he raced on and when he was gone by from here to there I shouted after him and said, `What do you mean running home this way?  Who is going to heard the cattle you are leaving behind?'  Before the child could say a single word, Ntamba was already by me. When he came to me with his heavy stick raised, as if to beat me too with it, I said to him, `What is wrong with you! Why do you want to kill some other people's child!' And there and then, all furious, he answered me by insulting my mother: `What is wrong with me of *nyoko*![2] Other people's child of *nyoko*! Aren't you the female creature living at Myombekere's? Should I beat you instead of him, you wretch, so that Myombekere can come and fight me to death! Indeed you better come with me, so that you can witness how your cows have razed to the ground my entire millet crop! Whatever the case, today you've had it, you wretched creatures, you simply will have to compensate me for my millet!'

"Apparently when the man saw that some two or three of our cows had entered his farm, he thought of nothing else except to go in search of whoever was in charge of the cattle and found this child sitting down and resting under the shade of a bush and at once fell on him, belaboring him with twigs of trees: *pu! pu! pu!...* with one hand while holding him with the other one! The child cried and cried until he could cry no more. When the twigs he had were all used up and he went looking for more, the child managed to tear himself from the grip of his hand and ran for his life and he chased after him, after picking up a huge stick with which to finish him off. That was when he came by me and we went back together, the child following us behind. By the time we got back to the crop field, the whole herd had drifted into the farm and we fell to driving the cows out. He left us still doing that and ran to the village headman's[3] home to lodge a complaint against us.

"We drove home cattle from the pastures at sunset, and after our neighbors had taken away their cows from the herd we brought ours home.[4]

"That's how this misfortune befell us. But that fellow is crazy, and an opium smoker to boot, otherwise he wouldn't be so raving mad! That's how this boy got as badly beaten as you see him. When you arrived, I had just finished boiling hot water with which to massage the sprains and swellings he has all over his body as I said to myself: 'The stick is like a taboo and kills long after the deed.'"

Myombekere, where he was, was greatly disturbed by what he heard. And so, after a long silence, he said: "Let him be! He is lucky I was away! Even now it is only because it is already dark; if there was still a bit of twilight I would've already gone to his home to ask him for a full explanation why he beat this boy like this. What's more, the monster is bragging for nothing, because he does not even own a single cow in that herd he keeps in his home: it is all other people's property! But he is a lucky dog, and so let him be! It will soon be another day like this one and we will hear whatever people will have to say on the matter."

When they finished discussing the incident the unmarried woman[5] of Myombekere's home went to massage with hot water the wounded young boy, after which she brought some water outside to Myombekere for him to wash his hands before milking cows, and when she was over with attending to Myombekere milking cows she went to prepare dinner.

During dinner the woman as well as Myombekere himself tried their best to wake up the young boy, who had gone to rest, so that he could take his dinner but the boy refused to eat and said, "No, I don't feel like eating."

Myombekere pleaded with him a bit more, "Are you hurting too much! Has pain from that beating become serious sickness! But, even so, please eat something, son!" and still the boy replied, "No, I can't. I feel cold, and also I have no appetite."

After dinner, Myombekere and the woman of his home too retired for the night until the following day.

The following day early in the morning Myombekere woke up the boy: "Wake up and come outside, please. I want to see how Ntamba beat you."

Kagufwa, as the boy was called, woke up and went outside walking unsteadily due to having just woke up from sleep. He first disappeared behind the house to pass water and then came back and stood in the courtyard close to the house, where Myombekere was and Myombekere examined his whole body and saw that Ntamba had beaten him very badly indeed and bruises of sticks covered his entire body! He asked the boy, "Please tell me, are you still feeling cold, and are you still hurting much!"

"No, I stopped feeling cold during the night; and, as to pain, I am no longer hurting much. The only pain which I still feel now is that of sprains all over my body, from the kicks he was stamping me with, that's all. But now, if things continue this way, I'll be fine."

When it became a warm and bright morning sun, the woman who was cooking for Myombekere boiled water once more and when the water was hot enough she told Kagufwa to go behind the house so that she could massage him again, removed the big pot of hot water from the kitchen cooking-stones and strained and carried it behind the house, came back to the house and fetched a door shutter[6] and laid it down, before going to look for the softest tree leaves[7] she could find and, using the leaves, massaged with hot water the boy as he lay stretched on the door-shutter and kneaded him thoroughly with hot water all over his wounded body. Whenever she came to a place where he hurt, the boy would cry out in pain: `*Yai*! you are killing me!' to which his masseuse would reply: "Courage, son! Let me save you, for the monster who did this to you wanted to kill you! How could anybody beat so cruelly some other people's dear child as if he were beating a witch or witch doctor who had killed a relative of his?"

Kagufwa remained behind the house drying up, and when he was dry he came to the courtyard and sat down to warm himself in the mild morning sun. The woman of Myombekere's home turned to preparing breakfast. Before the food was even ready, what should Myombekere see at the gate of his home but the envoy of the village headman! On arriving at the gate, the village headman's envoy called out: "People of this home! Is Myombekere at home or not!?"

Myombekere answered, "We are here, Sir; and where else do you think he could have already gone this early in the morning?"

"I was thinking that perhaps, since he is a man without a wife, he's already long gone this early to court a woman to marry, for anything I know! For, indeed, why should a bachelor stay put in one place like a man tied onto a wife!"

The caller arrived and Myombekere handed him a chair to sit on and he accepted the invitation, after which they exchanged greetings and the boy Kagufwa too greeted the headman's envoy.

"Is there somebody else I should greet in the house?" the headman's messenger asked.

"Yes, there is."

"Is the person a man or a woman?"

"A woman, not a man."

Having found out that, the envoy exchanged greetings with her: "Good morning, Madam!"

The person inside the house answered, "Good morning, Sir." And they went on to ask further news of each other, as all people do whenever they exchange greetings.

It was after that that the village headman's envoy informed Myombekere of his mission: "My dear man, I happen to be an envoy. I have been sent to you by the village headman to summon you to his place.

I understand you are to defend yourself against Ntamba, who lodged a complaint against you with the headman yesterday and said: `Myombekere has grazed his cattle in my millet crop; he let into the crop the whole communal herd he was in charge of on his neighborhood herding day of duty and the cows wiped clean my entire crop!' That is what our village headman has sent me here for. And my instructions are that you leave with me now, because I understand in the afternoon the headman has to go and pay his respects to some relatives of his among whom a death has occurred. He has not yet gone to condole them and so the visit is a debt he has to pay. And so I can't stay much longer, and you too should hurry up and come before people begin wondering and ask: `Why did you leave him behind when, as an envoy sent to summon a culprit, you were supposed to come back with the offender!'"

As the man was about to leave, Myombekere invited him to have something to eat first: "They are preparing something to eat inside that house. What is more, you should witness how badly Ntamba beat my child who was grazing the cows. I too have just seen him, since I wasn't here yesterday. I was away attending to what you spoke of to me, courting back my wife, and I came back here in the evening after sunset, when it was almost dark night."

The man, who was already on his feet, sat down again and called Kagufwa and said, "Come near, son, and let me look at you." Kagufwa did as he was told and when he was near enough the man examined him well and then exclaimed loudly: "*Uu!* What a really evil man this Ntamba must be! Even if a person has wronged you by grazing his cows in your crops, that is no reason to beat him to the extent of tearing him up this way! Even if it is a child of your own who has wronged you and you mean to teach him a lesson, you cannot do this to him! This being the case, bring him with you; let him be present too and let's hear what people will say about this. My goodness!"

The headman's messenger had just finished examining the boy when the men outside were given water to wash their hands, for the woman who was cooking food inside the house was ready to serve them breakfast, and she quickly brought from the house what she had prepared for them, which was *obwita*[8] with a pot of meat for relish, and the three men took their meal.

When they finished eating, Myombekere called their cook and said, "Come and take away your things!"

The woman came and removed the utensils to take them back into the house, but when she realized they didn't finish *obwita* she exclaimed and said, "So you didn't eat! The food is still all here! Was it badly prepared or what?"

Myombekere answered her back jokingly: "It appears your food was uncooked. Cook again for us, well prepared *obwita* this time!" and they all laughed.

The woman then went on to say, "I said so because Kagufwa slept on an empty stomach last night, he could not eat his dinner. It appears that man who beat him was kicking him everywhere, even in the stomach, so I was saying so because, since we massaged his belly with hot water last night as well as this morning, I was thinking that perhaps by now he would be able to stand better a bit of food."

And so when Myombekere finished milking his cows for the morning, he informed his household cook that he and Kagufwa were accompanying the envoy of their village headman to go and answer charges of grazing their cattle in another person's crop, and that she should drive their cattle to the person whose turn it was that day to herd for their neighborhood.

Myombekere and his companions arrived in the headman's home to find Ntamba already there, seated and waiting for them. Present were also some dignitaries who had come to pay the headman a visit and to present him with some banana beer.9 The three of them had just sat down for a little while, after exchanging greetings with the village headman and the people present, including that Ntamba fellow himself, when the headman called his son: "Lubona!" Because his son did not answer quickly enough, he called him the second time: "Lubona!"

His son answered: "Yes, Sir!"

His father rejoined, "Come here!"

Lubona came and the village headman got up and left the gathering of people and stood aside, some distance away, with his son and whispered something in his son's ear. His son left the place running and disappeared into his father's house as his father on his part came back to the gathering of people he had just left and sat down again. On the part of the young man who had disappeared into the house, all the other men could hear from outside was: *duduli! duduli!* between him and his mother, together with the sound of calabashes knocking against each other: *gongoro! gongoro!* Before long he emerged straining under the weight of a pot of beer. When Lubona was about to bring the pot of beer to where the people were gathered, his father made him a sign with his hand and followed it with: "Take it to that better tree shade over there. You want to roast us in this sun as if we were lizards!" With that everybody deserted that place to go and gather again where the delicious drink had been taken.

By the time people formed another gathering, the young man had gone back inside the house to look for a small   cup[10]   for drawing beer from the pot and a beer drinking bowl[11]   for serving the beer. When he returned, it was again to him that the duty of serving the beer was assigned. And so he removed the cover of strips of dry banana stem fiber from the beer pot, and then called his mother in the house and said to her, "Please, bring your calabash bowl so that we can give you your poison[12] share!"

His mother brought a calabash bowl[13] and people received it and handed it over to her son, who put into it two or so measures of the tiny cup for drawing beer and again a man received the bowl and passed the beer to the young man's mother.

On the mother's part, when she looked into the container she was dissatisfied with what she had been given and called back her son and told him: "Is this all you give me from such a huge pot! What's more, I am not alone. Your wife and the other women will want some too!" And so people received back from her the bowl and gave it to Lubona and he dropped in some three more tiny cupfuls of the beer and somebody handed it back to her. The person who had received the beer wanted to give it to her without drinking a bit from it and Lubona's mother told him, "You have to drink a bit first before giving it to me. It should not be said I passed beer by your mouth without giving you some! Unless of course you know it is poisoned and you are afraid of dying!"

Those present supported her and said, "May be that's it! Otherwise, what is he afraid of?"

After Lubona gave his mother her "poison" share of the beer as Kikerewe custom dictates, he began serving beer to people in an orderly manner. For the first round, he filled the wooden bowl with beer and raised it to give to his own father, the village headman.

On seeing that the men gathered there voiced their protest and said, "No! That's not right. Since when did you see in Ukerewe a village headman or a prince being the first persons to drink from a pot of beer? What type of an adult are you?"

And so that first measure of beer was given to an old man in the gathering. The old man drank until near the bottom of the drinking bowl and a man seated beside him told him, "Don't kill yourself with beer! Leave some for me!" and the old man took the beer from his mouth breathing out noisily: "*Fuu!*" and adding, "*Aa!* The dog who pressed this beer from the banana fruit is a really great dog!" Everybody burst out laughing, although the man who brewed the beer and had personally come to offer it as a present to the village headman was still in the audience. But even he did not get angry at being so insulted, because that is a real time-honored Kikerewe custom, that is what all Wakerewe say when they want to praise a person who has brewed great banana beer. Then the person who had asked the old man for some beer drank and finish it off.

The second bowl, full to the brim, that Lubona drew from the pot he offered to his father, the village headman. The person who was next to the server received from him the beer and took it to the headman and knelt down and raised his hands to give their village head the beer. Before receiving it, the village headman said, "I should not pass beer by your mouth without giving you some; lead the way for me." The man sucked in the beer until he breathed out to catch his breath and then took in another draught before passing the drink to the headman. The village headman too took a long suck at the beer, then he gave the remainder of his share to somebody he chose to recognize.

After that the server went around and served beer to the entire group of men. When each and everyone had been served, only then, as the Kikerewe customs demands, did Lubona feel free to serve himself his own measure and only then did he too have a drink. When the server too had drunk his turn, the village headman told his son to pause for some time and serve no more beer.

Chapter III

NOTES

1. One of the early white missionaries in Ukerewe describes a typical Kikerewe homestead as follows:

   "In Ukerewe everybody lives wherever he pleases, usually in the middle of his property or, sometimes, in a corner of his banana plantation (*rutoke*). There his courtyard is enclosed in a fence (*orugo*), and that's his home (*eka*), without an immediate neighbor.

   "The cottages are enclosed in a hedge of euphorbias (*makukuru, makoni*) which has only two gates, one for livestock and the other one for people. The first gate (*orukondo*) is a crude gap made through the thick growth of euphorbias which is closed as best as it can be by a shutter of thorn-shrubs or planks hardly properly shaped; the other gate (*ilembo*), on the contrary, is set up in a remarkable way. Across two long perches made of stacks of trees and mounted on posts planted in the ground lies a thick and heavy movable board (*rusonzyo*); the hinges, or rather the hinge, is on top of that frame instead of being on the side, so that when the gate is open the board is hanging over the heads of the passers. In the morning at sunrise that trapdoor is raised and immobilized with the help of a pole planted in the ground in the middle of the entrance.

   "Inside that courtyard the huts are arranged in a circle all along the euphorbia hedge, leaving an empty space in the center, big or small depending on the wealth and importance of the owner" P. Eugene Hurel, "*Religion et Vie domestique de Bakerewe*," *Anthropos* 6 (1911): 276.

2. *Nyoko*: "*Noko*" means "your mother", and "*nyoko!*" is the insult to ones mother, regarded the strongest possible insult to a person.

3. *Omukungu* (plural *abakungu*): The village headman and representative of the *omukama* (king) in a village, who was usually a prince or relative or friend of the king.

4. Herding cattle was usually a communal activity for all the homes in a neighborhood with many enough cows to need herding. The homes in a "herding neighborhood" took turns to herd the cattle of the entire group, for rounds of duty of usually two days each, thus freeing the people of the other homes to attend to their other activities until their turn of duty came.

5. *Omusimbe*: See note 24 of Chapter II.

6. *Ihara*: Movable house door shutter usually made of stalks of slender sugarcane-like *amabingo* canes or papyrus stalks attached to stick ribs. The

structure was also used as a bed-top and a stretcher, among other things.

7.   *Ebibabi* or *ebitutu*: See note 11 of Chapter II.

8.   *Obwita*: Staple dish of a Kikerewe meal. See note 14 of Chapter 1. Breakfast used to be a very substantial meal among the Wakerewe.

9.   Whenever a man brewed beer in the village, he sent a pot of the banana beer to the village headman as dues. In turn, each village headman and his people paid periodical visits to *omukam's* palace with pots of banana beer and other presents, usually grain, goats or cows, their dues to their king. Private individuals who were capable of it too did take presents to their king directly as a way of paying their homage to him, as we see Myombekere and his neighbor and friend Kanwaketa do in the novel.

10.   *Omutaho*: See note 9 of Chapter 1.

11.   *Olusabuzyo*: Here a wooden container for drinking banana beer with. See note 12 of Chapter I.

12.   *Obulogo*: "Poison." Whoever offered beer to people had to taste it first; and since this pot of beer was coming from the house of Lubona's mother she was entitled to her " poison-tasting" share.

13.   *Isayayi*: See note 20 of Chapter II.

Chapter IV

MYOMBEKERE IS SUED IN THE VILLAGE COURT BY NTAMBA

The village headman[1] then addressed the people who had gathered in his home as follows: "Ladies and gentlemen, the pot of banana beer is the boon companion of conversation,[2] so I simply have to interrupt this happy company.

"Yesterday afternoon, sometime before sunset, I was seated here, in this home of mine, relaxing and chatting with my wives under that tree over there, when all of a sudden Ntamba arrived before me: *bwaa!*[3] soaked with sweat from head to foot, panting and out of breath like a man locked in a bodily combat. The women of this home wanted to give him a seat but he objected: `Are you inviting me to sit down!' `Well?' they queried. `No, I am not sitting down. I am here to fetch the village headman to come and witness how Myombekere's cows have destroyed my millet crop.' Hearing that, I asked him, `Did you, by any chance, leave the guilty man at the farm?' 'No, it wasn't him,' he answered, "It was a boy who stays in his home I found with the cows, having already let the whole herd graze my millet. And when I saw that, I decided to give him a beating, to make him cry out so that his master could hear him and come to his rescue and face me in a battle of life and death. Even at this very moment I left them driving the cattle out of my farm, that is that boy and a certain woman, who also stays at Myombekere's home.'

"On my part, seeing that it was already too late to hold court, I told him, `Go home now, and come back tomorrow morning. I will have sent someone to summon here Myombekere.' And so here they are, both of them have already arrived. I now want each one of them to state his side of the matter before you so that you can form an opinion of their case. That's why I had to interrupt your pleasant palaver by reminding you that conversation over a pot of beer never ends."

On hearing that the people present, now glib-tongued after a sip of the banana beer, took up what their village headman had said and agreed with him and said, "That's it, our headman; you've done the right thing. We all would like to hear what each of them has to say, because fair judgement can only come from the voice of many."

The village headman told the plaintiff to speak first: "Ntamba, go first, because you are the one who lodged a complaint against Myombekere for having grazed his cows in your millet crop."

Ntamba was about to stand up when people stopped him and said, "No, speak like a man: you can still be heard even if you speak while seated," hearing which he tested his voice first, by clearing his throat of a trifle cough with some bravado, before bursting out in full voice and saying: "Hear me, our village headman, and all you noble[4] people present. I am suing Myombekere for grazing his cattle in my millet crop.

"Yesterday, towards evening, I left my home saying to myself: `Let me go and take a look at my millet, because since we finished weeding it I haven't been back to see how the crop's doing.'  And so I went.  When I neared the farm, on casting my glance that way I saw three cows which looked as if they were in my farm! I exclaimed: `Who can that be who grazes cows on millet instead of grass!   Is he or she someone who never eats earth food and lives on milk alone?' That's how I wondered in my mind. But when I got near enough, I discovered that it was not a matter of some three cows but an entire herd that had been let loose into my farm! I said nothing more except to look for the herder and I had hardly rounded a bush when I saw a person seated under the shade of trees! *Aa*! I said nothing and approached him. When I got where he was I asked him, `What are you doing?'"

"I am herding cattle."

"Where do you live?"

"In Myombekere's home."

"And where is Myombekere himself?"

"He is not here."

"On hearing that I completely lost my temper and angrily told him, `Is this the way you herd cows, by letting them graze other people's crops?' When he tried to get up and run away, I lunged and caught him up in the air like this and told him, `So that's it! Well, you won't get away from me that easily! It is true you are a young man and can run faster than I, but since I already have my hands on you let me give you a beating, you useless creature, for having destroyed my crop with your cows this way!' With that I jerked and pulled him to a thicket nearby, from which I tore some twigs with which I thrashed him around the shoulders, the back and on his bottom. I saw him begin to cry out hard, to which I said: `Good! May be that will bring out your lord and master quickly so that he and I can battle each other to death.' After that I released him from my grip. He then ran away as if to go to their home and I chased after him. At that moment I had already picked up a piece of wood, which I was holding high up this way in my two hands as I ran after him. To say the truth, if it were not for the fact that I came across the women who stays at Myombekere's home, who told me that she too was looking after the cows and I came back to the herd of cattle with her, I would have pursued the boy right to their home, to his lord and master, to find out whether he was the one who sent him to graze his cows in my food crops. So, since I came across that women first, she was the one I took to see the damage their cattle had done to my crops. Since my anger continued to mount, I left them still driving their cows from my millet farm and ran here to the village headman's home to lodge a complaint against the culprits, because their destruction of my millet caused me unbearable pain! That's why I ran to those in charge of judging people's disputes and said, `Please judge us, for this is a case where we alone cannot settle our differences.' That's all I have to say, my headman and all you great and noble people who have gathered here."

Myombekere then stated what he had to say as follows: "As for me, my headman and you great and noble people present here, I was not at home yesterday. I left very early in the morning to go and court back my wife and did not come back home until in the evening, after dark. That is when I met the news that misfortune had befallen us, that our cows had grazed other people's crops, Ntamba's millet. I was further told: `That man wanted to kill one of us! Ntamba beat this child until he tired of beating him, and he was beating him with thorny twigs, accompanying that by kicking the boy in the stomach.' And indeed as a result of that the child was so sick he couldn't eat at night. Here he is in person before you; let him stand up and show you how severely Ntamba beat him."

Kagufwa stood up, and people looked at him. Everybody exclaimed with shock, even the women who were inside the houses came out to see for themselves and they too couldn't believe what they saw and exclaimed: "What! How can anybody beat another person's child this badly simply because cows had grazed in his crop! He meant to kill him!"

Myombekere went on to say: "All the same I don't intend to deny the fact that I have wronged him, because my cows grazed in his farm. However, cows straying into people's crops is something which happens all the time, even when the herders are adults. Secondly, we are all farmers here and we have all dealt with herders, children and adults alike, whose cows grazed our crops, but most of the time we simply do nothing to them, or at most we simply exchange strong words with them over the incident and the matter ends there. But this time this man Ntamba finds that two or three cows have strayed into his millet farm and, instead of driving them out first before looking for the herder as he should have done, he right away pounces on my child and flogs him this way and stamps on him and kicks him in the stomach so brutally! In addition to that, he then drives into his own millet crop the entire herd of cattle! What can this mean? Is it greed for compensation! Very well. Even if it was compensation he was after, he should not have beaten my child so brutally! Where has he ever seen such behavior! As a matter of fact he was lucky I was away; for had I been present one of us would have ended up a dead man. And that is all I want to tell you, our village headman and all you great noble people assembled here. Judge us. What is done cannot be undone, and committing felonies is the curse of all men."

With that the village headman said to the people assembled: "There you are, ladies and gentlemen, judge these two quickly so that we can attend to other matters."

And so a man stood up and said the following: "In this case, where Myombekere is accused of grazing his cows in Ntamba's millet crop, in my view Myombekere is guilty as accused. He should therefore pay five goats to Ntamba. He should have paid six goats, but since Ntamba too is guilty of beating Myombekere's boy so badly, let him be denied the sixth goat which would otherwise be due him, as his punishment for beating the boy. That, ladies and gentlemen, is how I see this case."

A woman stood up from the women side of the gathering and, on her part, found this to say: "It is true that it is customary for a person found guilty of grazing his livestock in another person's crop to pay six fine items, but, in this particular suit brought here by Ntamba against Myombekere, my opinion is as follows: the plaintiff Ntamba is more guilty and is the one who should be fined and made to pay one fine item as judgement fee[5] to the village headman, you great noble people gathered here, for having brought his suit to this court when he should have known that he too wronged the defendant.   On top of that, his crime of beating Myombekere's boy clears Myombekere from the obligation to pay him the five goats mentioned by the man who has just spoken. In my opinion, the crime of grazing cattle in crops and that of beating the child should cancel out each other and let both parties be losers, let the man whose millet crop was grazed and the culprit whose child was beaten both receive no compensation. For the truth of the matter is that Ntamba, by beating this child so brutally and pounding him with kicks in the stomach, was nothing but a killer and a person who had decided to take the law into his own hands instead of bringing his plaint to court for judgement. As a matter of fact this little boy should thank his swift limbs, without which he would have been a dead man there and then. Look at how swollen all over his body the child still is even now! How can anyone speak of paying Ntamba five goats in a situation like this! If what Ntamba did isn't a crime, what is? This is how this matter appears to me, my headman and all you noble people seated here. May be others see the matter differently; so let them tell us how they feel about it."

A certain old man also joined in, and, without standing up, said: "I have been around this world for quite a while. At my age, I have seen quite a few things, including herdsmen guilty of grazing their livestock in other people's crops as well as the reactions of those whose crops they grazed, those who sought compensation as well as those who didn't. I have seen them all. But with this Ntamba fellow here, I have scrutinized and thoroughly searched the inside of his being and all I could find there was nothing but a greedy person lusting after Myombekere's property under the guise of compensation! What's more, I have found him to be the man in the story `Fool-who-courts-his-own-death',[6] because if he weren't, on finding Myombekere's cows in his farm, and it does not matter how many were already in, he should have first quietly driven the cows from his millet crop before looking for the herder, wherever he was, to tell him how his cattle had grazed his millet and show him the cows he had driven out of the farm in evidence. And had the herder tried to deny it, he could have said to him: `Follow me and I will show you the destruction your cattle wrought on my crop.' And since it was something which happened in broad daylight, those who had witnessed what had happened would certainly have testified to the truth of the matter. But since he decided to take the law into his own hands and beat this boy, he has killed his own case, as this woman rightly pointed out. What remains for him to do is to pay to the village headman the judgement fee and let the matter rest at that. There can simply be no comparison between the felony of grazing one's livestock in another person's crop and murder. That is my opinion of this matter, my headman and you the public who have assembled here in such great numbers."7

Following that, there was a consensus among the people gathered, who all   said: "That's right, old man, for if what he wanted was compensation he shouldn't have beaten this boy. And so, since he beat this boy to the point of almost killing him, let him be a loser too. For indeed his crime of wanting to kill a human being is infinitely greater than the wrongdoing of grazing cattle in another person's crops."

After that Ntamba could find nothing to say. He became a lost man with nowhere to turn. The village headman then asked him the following question: "And indeed, Ntamba, had you killed this boy, would you have all the same come here to sue Myombekere?"

"My headman, please don't ask me such things! I don't know anything anymore, because I was only acting under the pain of seeing my millet destroyed by cattle. What is more, I don't have much else to say on the matter. Moreover our people say: `There is no dishonor in losing a case in the king's Bukindo'.8 If you are ready to pronounce judgement, please do your duty."

The village headman rang out a shrill whistle with his mouth to call for silence and when quiet was restored he went directly to the heart of the matter and said, "I am adding my voice to the voices of our very noble and gentle people assembled here by saying that Ntamba you have lost your case: because it is the many who judge a case. And what killed your case was your decision to take the law into your own hands by beating to the point of death Myombekere's child. And you would indeed have killed this child, had his swift limbs not saved him. You are therefore to pay judgement fee, which is one he-goat. And we are not giving you until tomorrow or the day after tomorrow to do so: we want you to bring the goat here this very moment. And you too Myombekere should learn to graze your livestock well: when you herd your cattle near people's crops you should keep good watch over your animals! And so, you Ntamba, get up quickly and go and bring here the judgement fee before this assembly disperses."

On hearing that Ntamba stood up and said to the beer server, Lubona, "Please, give me a tiny share of the beer before I go, in case by the time I am back there should be nothing left but an empty pot." The beer server drew from the pot one tiny cupful for him and Ntamba drank the beer, finished and handed back the beer drinking bowl[9] to those next him and then off he went to fetch payment for his fine. After that begging for beer became the only language everybody left behind at the pot of banana beer spoke: "Please, give me some! Please, give me some!..."

Before people knew it, Ntamba was back, accompanied by his son, both of them panting and sweating, dragging along a he-goat. When he got to the headman he stopped, and so did his son, who was the one holding the goat, and then the father said, "My headman, this is the goat I found. I don't have better than this in my stock."

The village headman answered, "Go and tether it on that tree over there," and then turned to the people present and asked them: "What do you say, ladies and gentlemen! Is this goat satisfactory as judgement fee?"

The people answered him back and said, "For us, since we have seen the goat, we feel the issue is settled. If it is your pleasure to give us the goat, please do so and let us slaughter it."

The village headman then told son Lubona, "Finish distributing the beer" and his son distributed the beer until it was all gone. That done, the headman said, "The young men present take the goat behind the household compound and slaughter it."

At once some young men shot off after the goat and fell to strangling it by the mouth and nose[10] and twisting its neck backwards and kicking it in the stomach. And since they were already tipsy, by the time they got to where they were supposed to slaughter the goat it was already dead. In no time they had skinned it bare. As to the eaters of raw meat,[11] the men, they were already restless with gluttony, to the extent that even the elders had moved near the animal being slaughtered so that they too could eat some raw meat and asked the young men slaughtering the goat to give them some to eat, to which the young men responded, "You want raw meat before we have even began to cut up the carcass!" and their elders rejoined, "Disembowel it quickly, so that we can eat some raw meat, will you!

As soon as those butchering the goat cut open its belly, the greedy pack of men began looking for the parts of the entrails good for eating raw so that they could savor some morsels of raw meat without having to wait for the entire carcass to be cut up first.

When the men had asked for a taste of raw meat before the carcass of the goat had even been disemboweled those butchering the animal had reminded those gluttons that they could not get at the entrails, parts of which are the only meat eaten raw, before the carcass was cut open, to which the other men had responded by telling the young men to stab the dead animal's stomach at once so that they could have their raw meat without further ado, because to the Wakerewe men, as the saying goes: "Raw meat is worth a man dying for!" And then an old man present had said: "I see! You seem to forget that it is not merely a question of having to disembowel the animal and get to the entrails, but that there is a taboo which forbids the eating of raw meat before completing cutting and removing the limbs of the carcass! He who does not know of this taboo yet should take the trouble to inquire from those who know and they will inform him of its origin."

And so those slaughtering the animal removed its limbs first before disemboweling it and immediately it was disemboweled the men were all up to get a piece of the stomach and the liver, scrambling for raw meat parts to the point of almost cutting each other with knives, after which they ate raw pieces of the liver and the stomach of the goat by first squeezing onto the meat drops of the animal's bile to season it with bile bitterness.

In that very instant some men had collected firewood and made a fire near the place of slaughter. When the fire was properly lit, they took both slabs of the ribs of the goat and put the two chunks of meat onto the fire so that they could eat roast goat meat. Fortunately the headman was there to restrains them, otherwise left alone they would have barbecued the entire goat. The headman however couldn't let them do that, because he wanted some of the meat cooked for them as relish with which to eat *obwita.*[12]

When those slaughtering the animal finished cutting up the carcass, the village headman   called one of his wives and told her to bring to the men outside a pot in which to cook the meat,[13] and she did so. Another wife of his brought from her house water for washing the entrails, the intestines and the stomach, that is what was left of those parts after the raw-meat eaters had taken away their share, as well as the parts of the entrails which are never eaten raw in Ukerewe. Some men split logs for firewood, others erected cooking-stones for cooking the meat out there in the courtyard, while yet others cut into smaller pieces ready for cooking the share of goat meat their village headman had given them, which was one leg, the two arms, the head, the back and the kidneys. That was the meat the men cooked. As to the village headman himself, the meat which was put aside for his home was just the remaining leg, plus the chest and the tongue, and nothing else. But had that gathering of men had their wish he wouldn't have had even that, because their intention was to cook the entire goat and get enough meat with which to cleanse their throats of the banana beer!

The male cooks then got busy with feeding firewood to the fire to get the meat ready quickly, since meat cooked by men is not supposed to cook for a long time! And in no time they were calling out to the women inside the houses and saying: "Put *obwita* pots on your cooking-stones, our meat is ready!" Some men tried to voice their protest by exclaiming: "That meat is still raw!" and another man got back at them really strongly and said, speaking at the top of his voice, "Women, please do as you are told! Put *obwita* pots on your cooking-stones and don't mind the people who want to cook our meat into pulp as if we have no teeth! Let he who has no teeth eat none of the meat and make do with broth! Meat meant for men shouldn't be over-cooked. Never!"

As soon as the women finished cooking *obwita*, they told the men to get seated in a circle and be served food. The men went under the shade of another tree and formed a circle and settled down, and when they were all properly seated the women brought for them water and dishes of *obwita* and plates[14] for serving the meat on and for drinking broth. Ntamba and his son too were still in the village headman's home and they too took their places in the meal circle with the other men. The meat server looked for a really nice piece of meat, one fit to serve the village headman, and dished it out of the pot and put it on a select plate, then took the plate and placed it in front of the headman and those who were seated beside him. Only then did he serve the rest of men seated in the large meal circle: the one to whom he gave a bare bone would growl and he to whom he handed a piece of steak would be stared at by envious eyes! When he had served each and everyone only then did he too sit down, there inside the meal circle, to eat.

At the end of the meal the meat server took hold of the pot in which the meat had been cooked and poured broth on the plates for people to drink and the men drank broth and finished and called the women: "Come and save us from your utensils!"

The men hadn't finished washing their hands when a pack of dogs were all over their legs fighting each other over the bones as the men shouted at them: "Go away! Go away, you disorderly creatures!" But it was the men who gave way, some of them before they had even washed their hands so that they had to go and do so somewhere else.

After eating Ntamba asked the village headman to give him the skin of his goat,[15] but the headmen refused and, instead, gave it to the old man who spoke out on how that case should be settled, and so Ntamba continued being a loser. He and his relatives were therefore only left to console themselves with reviling Myombekere in his absence saying: "The wicked creature! He goes out and intentionally grazes his cows in our millet crop and then pays nothing, and, instead, Ntamba, the person whose crops were destroyed, ends up being the one who paid the fine of a goat as judgement fee, as if he were the one guilty of a felony! That creature cannot be an ordinary mortal, he must have some hidden powers, he must be some witch doctor incarnate!"

The business of the day concluded, people said good-bye to their village headman and returned to their homes. As soon as Myombekeres got home his female relative come to cook for him welcomed him back and then asked him, "How did it go!" and Myombekere answered, "It went well: I made that Ntamba fellow eat the dust of the earth in our court wrestling match. He couldn't remain on his feet for a single moment! His case was rejected by all present, including your fellow womenfolk, for his having beaten this child like a murderer this way."

The women rejoined, "Now I see! That's why the headman's messenger insisted, `You must come with him!' Had people in the court not seen the condition of the child with their own eyes, Ntamba could have won."

Chapter IV

NOTES

1. *Omukungu*:   See note 3 of Chapter III.

2. Banana beer was a very important drink for the Wakerewe and no worthwhile occasion or social function was deemed complete without it.

3. *Bwaa!* : Ideophone for arriving suddenly and unexpectedly.

4. *Enfura*: Person or persons of noble birth. When the term, or its emphatic form *mafura* used here, was applied to ordinary citizens it was a polite term of address meant to compliment people on their nobility of character, hence its frequent use by speakers in this formal setting of a court hearing. Etiquette and good breeding were qualities the Wakerewe prized very highly in a person (see Fr. Eugene Hurel quoted in the Introduction on the subject).

5. *Endamuro*: Judgement (or court) expenses, a fee in valuable goods paid by the party which lost the case to the village headman for the community, in addition to the fine imposed, if any.

6. *Masirugetegwire*: "Fools-who-court-their-own-death", name of a character in a Kikerewe folk story.

7. Court cases were judged by the public, consisting of ones neighbors and whoever had assembled at the village headman's during the hearing, with the village headman delivering whatever emerged as the verdict and imposing whatever customary penalty for the offense was proposed by "the voice of the many". Bigger cases went to *omukama's* (king's) court, to be judged in the same way, but usually with the king's courtiers acting as the spokesmen of the gathered people.

8. Bukindo: The palace and residence of the *omukama* (king), also the name of the village in which the palace was situated. In the saying it means the "*omukama's* courts", including those of his representatives in the villages, the village headmen.

9. *Olusabazyo*:   Here a wooden container for drinking banana beer with. See note 12 of Chapter I.

10. Traditionally, the Wakerewe killed goats, and even cows, by strangling them.

11. *Obubisi*: Meat eaten raw. Only Wakerewe men ate raw meat and the meat eaten raw was, as seen in the novel, some select parts of the entrails, which were usually seasoned with the animal's bile before they were eaten.

12. *Obwita:*   See note 14 of Chapter I.

13. During public celebrations and other occasions involving preparing food for many people where a goat or cow had been slaughtered men cooked their

own share of the meat outside in the compound of the home.

14. *Enanga*, plural for *olunanga*:   See note 16 of Chapter I.

15. Skins of goats and cows were the main clothing material and hence were valuable property.

Chapter V

MYOMBEKERE GOES TO WOO BACK HIS WIFE THE SECOND TIME

After a number of days had passed since Myombekere went to his wife's parents to woo her back, he thought of going there again for the same purpose. And on the very day that thought kept him awake all night long, he was on his way to the home of his in-laws at the first cockcrow of early morning.

It was during the season of heavy rains and he was still on his way, had covered a considerable distance but was still far away from his in-laws' village, when heavy rain announced its approach with repeated bouts of thunder and lightning. And so he walked as fast as his legs could carry him to try and escape the downpour from a sky which was thundering so threateningly. Realizing that where he was there were no homes anywhere nearby, he broke into a trot but, because it was not yet daylight, he could not run fast, since he ran while afraid all the time of falling into ditches and porcupine holes. He had been running for quite a while when rain said: "What I am sparing you for!" and it poured down buckets, real heavy rain, foaming rain amidst a raging storm shaking the skies! Myombekere on his part kept up his trot until he could run no more and just walked and got soaked until he could take it no more! And yet going back home was out of question, given how far he had come, and where he was going too was still some real distance away! And so there he was, stuck in the middle, with nowhere to go! But, in spite of it all, the man did not give up or slacken his pace but kept on forging ahead until finally he sighted people's homes, and on seeing homes while that heavy rain continued to pour down relentlessly, with no sign of intending to slacken, he picked one of them and went there to seek shelter, his eyes all red, his head already pounding from the downpour.

In the home he had picked he found in the house some people warming themselves by the fire while others were lying down covered with skins, for the house was leaking. He too went straight to the fire, to warm himself up, since he was all met and dying of cold, and then greeted the people he found there, exchanged greetings with those who greeted him back and let be those who did not, for he too knew there were people who were not allowed to utter a word when it was raining, especially in a thunderstorm like that one.

As it happened, that home was the home of a rain-maker, and when he had time to look around he saw a person busying himself in his rain charm pots[1] in the house, dressed in tatters of bits and ends of skins and loudly haranguing the heavens and proclaiming his self-praises to his heart's content.[2] Myombekere was completely nonplussed and found himself with wide-open mouth staring at the busy man who was not afraid of bragging about himself that way in the midst of such an ominous downpour! When he had time to reflect on what was going on, he said to himself: "So far I had seen nothing in this world! Today I have chanced on the real powerful of this earth, a person who when he speaks even the heavens listen and listen well!" As Myombekere finished reflecting that way the rain as well as the storm began to relent. At that very instant lightning flashed: *myee!* followed at once with the rumble of thunder: *gingiri,* and everybody in the house was thrown to the ground: *ligiti!.*[3]

Apparently when that mighty lightening flashed: *myee!* even the rain-maker busy in his rain charm pots was taken from there and dumped at the fireplace with the rest of the people! Much later, when people regained their senses, is when those who had been sitting on chairs realized they too were now in dust on the floor! And that was when Myombekere, on casting a glance to look at the man who was bragging and singing his praises and haranguing the heavens found that, lo and behold! the man of mighty powers was no longer at work in the nook of his special function but he too was busy dusting himself clean after his fall, like everybody else! Myombekere exclaimed to himself without uttering a word: `Wasn't this the very same man who was talking to raging rain like I don't know what, and he too has received the same deal as we the weaklings of the earth whose bodies bear no trace of a rain medicine incision!'4

When that rain finally stopped and the sky cleared, the rain-maker was the first person to open the door and take a look outside to see how heavy the downpour had been and as soon as he got outside, on turning his eyes towards his cattle's kraal, he saw that lightning had killed three of his cows! He exclaimed really loud and said, "*Eee!* My father!5 What is happening in this home today! This has never been seen here before! I have lived here a long time and never before had I seen anything like this! This must be something new, wouldn't you say! Oh, me! You too who are in those other houses of this household come out, come and witness this!"

Those in the other houses came out and everybody went to the kraal to have a closer look and found that indeed three animals were all stiff dead and everyone exclaimed with great surprise.

At that point Myombekere left the house to continue with his journey, leaving behind him the people of that home exploding with anger against him in his absence and saying: "It was that creature who took shelter from the rain in this house who is responsible for all this! He must be some thief, one of those creatures who live on stealing other people's property! It is the creature himself who should have been struck dead by thunderbolt,6 the monster, instead of wrecking destruction on our cows this way!" That's how the rain-maker and his people reviled Myombekere as soon as he left, adding, "And such creatures will never stop crashing into people's homes to take shelter from rain while knowing fully well they are thieving monsters! As a matter of fact he is lucky this home happened to be a fortified one. If it had been an ordinary home, without potent protection, it is he who'd have died and not the cows. Not at all!" And one of them added: "You can in fact say that had he been on the road just a bit longer before coming here that is where that thunderbolt would have struck and killed him there and then."

Myombekere could not seen the sun in the overcast sky and was therefore under the impression that it was still early in the morning and not the advanced time of the day it actually was and traveled under the shade of that clouded sky until he finally arrived at his in-law's home.

As soon as he arrived and finished exchanging greetings with his father-in-law and mother-in-law and his wife Bugonoka, his brother-in-law Lweganwa also came out of his bachelor house to meet him and the two exchanged greetings. It was Lweganwa who relieved him of his weapons and gave him a seat and he sat down. Once settled, his in-laws asked him, "Where did you pass to come here in all this rain!"

"I came wading through it as best as I could; and it really poured on me, until I could take no more! In fact I was lucky in that I found an excellent place for shelter, because there was a fire going in the house where I took shelter. Only there was one small incident which wanted to kill us all."

"And what was that?"

He then told his in-laws how the house in which he took shelter was a rain-maker's house, how he had found the rain-maker himself busy at work in his rain charm pots in that very house, dressed in rags of skins and hides, how he was carrying on with lauding himself and haranguing the heavens whenever he heard the sky rumble. Then he told them how thunderbolt wanted to kill them, how all those who were in that house, without exception, were thrown to the ground when lightning struck, how even that rain-maker himself was roughly thrown down by the fireplace in the inner part of the house, after being lifted from the milk-churn corner of the front room where he was busying himself heatedly among his rain maker's pots, how that thunderbolt, even though it spared them, did strike and kill three cows in the rain-maker's kraal.

On hearing that his brother-in-law got hold of Myombekere's arm and raised it up and said, "So glad to see you, brother-in-law! You were indeed at death's door!" His wife Bugonoka and his mother-in-law and father-in-law also said, "Yes, indeed! That was a narrow escape! You could indeed have been killed! What is more the accursed rain of these recent years has taken to pouring down with wanton malice. Rain of the past was more restrained, not like the rain of these days."

Myombekere then said, "From this day I don't believe in rain-makers anymore! Not after what I witnessed! Nobody will be able to take me in again by claiming that rain-makers exist, people who speak to the heavens and make the skies do their bidding. Not a chance! For the truth of the matter is that when I arrived at this rain-makers home and heard and saw him so busy haranguing the heavens and singing his self-praises I said to myself: 'To this day I had only heard people speak of rain-makers but had never seen one myself, but today I am lucky to have actually come across one in action, a genuine rain-maker, with the power to make the heavens let fall their water in the way it has poured on me and soaked me so thoroughly!' And then, right there, before that thought had even left my mind, I saw all of us piled on the ground, in the home of the same rain-maker, the rain-maker himself among us, his cows too killed as if they belonged to an ordinary household, the home of one of us the weaklings of the earth, the know-nothing people! Today my eyes have been opened, wide and clear. So these rain-makers never have the power to command and be obeyed by the heavens! Never at all!"

His father-in-law answered him back and said: "Well! Not exactly. Rain-makers do exist indeed. Only their power to make rain differs with each individual rain-maker. And, in addition, they also work against each other. For example, son-in-law, if we take the one you have told us about, even if he knows how to make rain, some other rain-maker could have worked against him. Have you never heard the expression `we are all equal is only a manner of speaking?' The one who has more than you is not your equal!"

"That, father-in-law, is certainly true, I must admit. But, all the same, starting today for me rain-makers' power has become something very difficult to believe. What is more, a rain-maker who will ever get from me something of value by way of payment, *aa! ee!* that would be a very lucky one! A very lucky one indeed!"

Lweganwa asked him the: "And so this appears incomprehensible to you?"

"Yes, brother-in-law, I find it incomprehensible."

"If the events you witnessed today pose such a problem to you, what then of the medicine men and women who use charms and all sorts of medicines, do you believe in such people at all?"

"I believe in those because I see them treat people and cure them, make them wholesome again. I see even people who had been overwhelmed by some health complication resort to medicine men and women and find one who manages to lift their complication and cure them, and that is the basis of my faith in them. But the likes of this rain-maker I just saw, no!"

They then dropped that subject. The sun at that moment finally peeped through the clouds and, on turning their eyes to the sky, they were all surprise to see that it was already past noon and a late afternoon sun! Myombekere then turned to chatting with Lweganwa by first asking him, "By the way, brother-in-law, when did you come back?"

"Since I arrived this night which is falling will be the fifth night I will pass at home."

"And so, how was the sea?"

"Well, the sea was fine, thank heavens, since all of us who sailed came back well and sound. We also got a bit of what we had gone to sea for, it is true, but that we all came back alive is what matters most. For, as Omukwaya[7] trader once sang: "As to trade, I traded nothing. But it doesn't matter, because I brought home a song of joy." On hearing that none of the other men could resist laughing.

They were still on that issue when Bugonoka called her brother and said to him: "Would you please take your brother-in-law to your house."

The two brothers-in-law got up. Myombekere was about to carry the chair on which he was sitting when Lweganywa said, "No, brother-in-law, let me carry the chair for you. You can only do that if I am not at home, or if the only person at home is your mother-in-law. But not when I am here, me, your brother-in-law. Please don't, my dear fellow, lest I give you grounds for reproaching my sister whenever you are reminding each other of how important it is for people to help each other, to love each other, to understand each other and to count on each other in times of need by telling her: `How is it then that in your parents' home I always carry my own seat into your brother's bachelor house!'"

As soon as they were seated inside Lwegananwa's bachelor house, Bugonoka brought warm water in a small pot and poured it into a washbasin[8] and then told her brother to put a finger in the water to find out whether it was too hot and needed to be tempered with a bit of cold water. She then gave her husband soft tree leaves[9] with which to wipe dry his hands before going back to the house to fetch food. She brought a dish of *obwita*[10] in a bowl[11] covered over with another bowl, accompanied by a little girl who was following behind with a big pot of hippopotamus meat, which she put down and then went back to the house to fetch a plate[12] on which to serve the meat and from which to drink broth. The little girl brought the plate and Bugonoka received it from her and placed it between Lweganwa's legs, since he was the one who would dish meat from the impressive pot. After serving her husband and her brother, she went back into her parents' house to attend to serving her father, who had remained seated outside under the shade of a tree. By that time the sun had finally fully come out of its cover of clouds and, *aa*! my goodness! what a hot sun it had become all of a sudden! You know, you too, how a sun which has just appeared from under the clouds all at once bursts into a hot sun and it is not as if I am speaking to a person who has never seen such a sun!

Lweganwa then dished out of the pot hippopotamus meat and piled it high on the plate, then took the plate and placed it in between Myombekere's legs and said to him the customary words of inviting visitors to eat: "Try and take a bite if you can, brother-in-law. We in these parts have never been famous for worthwhile food!"

"That is how it is everywhere, brother-in-law. In fact you over here are still doing fairly well, since, here we are, you even have men's food."[13]

"Had I not ventured out and come back with this paltry excuse for going to sea, we too wouldn't have dared to retain a visitor for a meal for lack of relish.

And with that they fell to eating, while at the same time pursuing their lively chat, because when they were called inside for food Myombekere was still asking his brother-in-law about his sea trip, how their expedition had been and how they had fared in their hippopotamus hunting. It was while they were eating that Lweganwa told him in details how their hunt had been and of the meat they brought home. He went on, "I left here as a rower for the hippopotamus hunters and that continued to be my work once we got to their hunting place. And, once there, when the men started hunting the animals, they killed hippopotamuses like never before! Among the five hunters I was with there wasn't a single one who did not kill his own animal. And let me tell you, brother-in-law, the way those people eat food out there in the wilderness is something else! All the time I used to hear people say: `Do you want to eat food like a hippopotamus hunter?' and this time I saw with my own eyes what that means: the meat piled on this plate is nothing to what one hippopotamus hunter eats before he catches breath like a watering cow and before he's eaten his fill, after which he pours down a huge plate of broth! Yes indeed! Those men know how to feed themselves well! And, what's more, they are a courageous lot. Very courageous indeed! When one of them harpoons a hippopotamus and the harpoon is securely lodged in the animal, that's the time to witness their courage, when they are pitted against the ferocious struggle of a hippopotamus fighting for its life. *Aa! hii!* brother-in-law, if you are not a bold man you will run away saying to yourself, `This, for heaven's sake, is not a battle to fight!' *Aa*! But with them the hippopotamus simply has no chance. None at all!

"As to the buyers of hippopotamus meat, there are always plenty of them, some offering for barter bracelets and iron hoes and waist bead-strings. And as to those who come with food, it's simply incredible! You see those carrying huge bowls of flour, the size of *emigero* of the Wasukuma[14] people, you see those with large carrying baskets full of cassava and sweet potatoes. *Ee! aa! we!* The hunter who smoke-dries meat does so only because he wants to and not because he couldn't sell all his fresh meat. Believe me, you find among those buyers a single person going in for the entire hind limb plus the whole arm of the carcass of a hippopotamus, in which case he would have come prepared like a real man, complete with his own porters. Such buyers come and select the parts they want and pay for them sometimes even before the carcass has been cut up, and as soon as they get their hefty parts they heave them to some secluded spot, from where they cut them up with their own knives and divide the meat and put it into their porters' containers. There are others who tie their hefty meat chunks on shoulder poles and carry it off to their homes that way, for in those parts of the world hippopotamus meat is something everybody eats, women included. The women in those countries are not like our women here, who are simply too finicky. No, those women eat each and everything which comes their way, just like their men. Now, when you realize it was the meat of an entire hippopotamus carcass which was bought out in a single day then you imagine and say to yourself, `Tomorrow, may be even the day after tomorrow, if these hippopotamus hunters[15] were to kill another one there wouldn't be any buyers for the meat at all.' But no! Even if on the following day they bring tumbling down another one, you will inevitably find among the buyers people you saw buying the meat of the carcass of the day before! As to what I brought home with me, brother-in-law, I don't intend to hide it from you. Here it is: I brought back one *ekitukuru*[16] of *obubele*[17] millet so big it takes a real man just to lift it from the ground, ten bracelets, and likewise ten iron hoes. And so, since I am not yet married, I am thinking of using my Wazinza hoes[18] for bride-price when I get married. As to chunks of dried meat, I brought two oversize carrying baskets[19] of the meat, in addition to which I was given three pots of hippopotamus oil. Those are the goods I brought home. By the way, I should not forget, I also came with two cow-skins and five goat-skins."

Myombekere said, "Well done! That was a worthwhile trip. Really worthwhile! And that's why our ancestors said: `Show us what you have is said to those returning from venturing out.' Had you not ventured out, where would you have got all that!"

That over, Myombekere moved on to pleading his case to his brother-in-law under the guise of wanting to know what was going on by saying to him: "I am well too, my brother-in-law, except I have suffered a lot because of being alone at home, for, my brother-in-law, a home since the beginning of time was meant to be the dwelling place of two people, of a man and his wife, and was never meant for a man alone the way mine is now; not at all! I came here to woo back my wife and found that my wife and I still love each other; so that, apparently, it is my father-in-law and mother-in-law who are bent on taking her from me. I am saying this because they spoke to me very angrily, regretting you were away, otherwise maybe that would have been the day they would have really taken her away from me forever."

"Me too when I came back and found your wife still here, that was the first thing I asked my parents by saying to them: `Can it be that Bugonoka has never gone back to her home, or has she just come back to see you again yesterday?' And they answered me back: `I think that means you love your brother-in-law very much?' I said, `Yes, and why do you ask?' And they answered: `Well, we see that you would like him to have his wife back. As for us, yes, we intended to take her away from him. For what else can we do, since her husband will not take her to medicine men and women. When we realized that he won't do that, our conclusion could only be that he does not love your sister. Is it really possible for anyone to already count Bugonoka, at her young age, among barren women?' On my part I then told them: `And why don't you, who know where such healers are, put her on the road and take her to them. After all, she is your child, it is you who brought her into this world.' In that very instant I heard your wife also say, `That's right, dear brother! They are indeed the ones who brought me into this world and yet now they want my husband to be the only one responsible for me. You have failed to do anything to help me and now you want to wash your hands of me and throw me over to him, as if he were the one who gave me life!' On hearing that her parents said, `Oh, I see! So that's it! Bugonoka loves her husband, so that all we are saying on our part is a waste of time! Well, well! Does this then mean that if our son-in-law was to come here today you would be willing to go back with him?' `Yes, I love him; because you are the ones who gave me to him; I did not marry myself off on my own. And also, yes, should he come for me I could go back with him. For how long has it been since I came here? Hasn't it been a very long time? And how is it that I haven't seen you make even the slightest attempt to look for those medicine men and women for me? You are quite right, my brother! What you said needed to be said.' And then, after some time, I asked my parents the following: `By the way, why do you want to take from my brother-in-law his wife? On what grounds, when Bugonoka and her husband still love each other?'  And they answered: `Because the relatives of our son-in-law no longer love her. How can she continue staying with her husband when her brothers-in-law and sisters-in-law don't love her anymore, when to them she is a barren woman?' Then I said, `But are those relatives of his the ones she is married to or is she Myombekere's wife? `What is that supposed to mean! She is married to our son-in-law, the one we gave her to in marriage.' `There you are', I said. `You acknowledge she is married to your son-in-law, to whom you yourselves married her. And why should you now blame that son-in-law of yours for wrongdoing of which he is innocent? What's more, aren't you the same Wakerewe who said a single fault never ends a marriage! What is this then?' Then I saw them think of what I had said for quite a while and, much later, I heard my father answer me back and say, `In that case, let her do whatever she pleases. When our son-in-law comes here again, we will find something to tell him, that is if he still loves his wife the way she loves him.' And since that day I have never heard them say another word on the issue, to tell you the truth. May be today, now that you are here, they will say something."

After some time Myombekere stopped eating and Lweganwa asked him, "Why aren't you eating, brother-in-law? What is happening?"

"I've eaten enough, my brother-in-law, because the human stomach, though it can drive a person to steal, happens to be a tiny little thing."

Lweganwa called aloud Bugonoka to come and take away the food utensils, "Come and take these things."

His sister came out of the house again with the small pot of warm water and found her brother had already put aside the utensils. She at once knelt down and poured out of the washbasin the old water and replaced it with fresh warm water and remained in that kneeling position until her husband and his brother had finished washing their hands, and then took a cup[20] of drinking water and passed it to her husband and he drunk some water and rinsed his mouth before passing the water to his brother-in-law, who passed it back to his sister when he too was finished with it. Only then did she get up from her kneeling position and take the utensils into the house, one at a time, aided by the little girl with whom she had served the food. In the meanwhile Myombekere was drying his hands with tree leaves and when he finished he gave the used leaves too to the women.

Myombekere and his brother-in-law kept on chatting for some time until Namwero too finished eating, since he had been served after them. When Myombekere saw that his father-in-law had finished eating, he told Lweganwa, "Let's go outside, brother-in-law, so that I can warm myself in the sun a bit, because that rain really poured down on me; even now my head feels as if I am about to have a bit of headache."

They went and sat near Namwero and Myombekere once more spoke words of wooing back his wife Bugonoka. He first coughed very slightly this way: *koho*! to clear his throat, so that he could speak to his father-in-law words of wooing back his wife with a clear voice and humbly, and then began by saying, "My father-in-law, I have come back to you saying to myself: `Let me go to my father-in-law and beg him to forgive me for the fault I committed, for which he had to take away my wife from me. Because, the first time I came here, I saw that you were very angry, and, when I went back to my home, I too realized how justified you were in being angry with me on account of my relatives having mumbled words without head or tail when they should know they never have any sense in them, the wretched lot! Imagine their causing me all these problems I don't merit, their causing my father-in-law to take away my wife, with whom we have always loved each other, their pouring dirt into our love, just like that! And since for them they still eat their fill and their life goes on as usual, they don't remember a thing of all that; not at all. I suffer all alone the misery they have caused me. Even with those sisters of mine themselves who said the things which put me into this trouble, there isn't a single one of them who has ever come to visit me in my misery. Not a single one. Not a single one of them has ever remembered to say, `Let me send him this bit of flour or this bit of sweet potatoes or cassava in this tiny basket!' No! My father-in-law, I am yet to see such a sister of mine in my home ever since my wife left me and came here. That's what has brought me in front of you, my father-in-law, so that I can raise my empty hands to you in the hope that you will have mercy on me and give me back my wife, so that we can live together again in harmony as we had been living since we got married. Because our ancestors said: `The parent never vomits, however disgusting the child.'"

As Myombekere was pouring out words of his misery to his father-in-law to convince him to give him back his wife his mother-in-law was seated by the door of their house with cocked ears, she too following what their son-in-law was telling her husband. And so was Bugonoka.

Myombekere then added the following to what he had said: "You yourself can bear witness: even after the misfortune which befell my home I haven't seen a single relative of mine come to find out how I fared. Not a single one!"

From inside the house his mother-in-law, on hearing him speak of a misfortune, directed her voice at him and asked, "What sort of misfortune befell you, my son?"

"It was the felony of grazing cattle in people's crops, my mother-in-law."

And on hearing that Bugonoka anxiously asked him, "Who committed the felony?"

"I did?"

"Whose crops did you graze?"

"Ntamba's."

Myombekere then told them in great details how his cattle grazed the man's crop, how he was sued and how he won, because of Ntamba beating his boy like a murderer. Then he said, "These days when Ntamba and I meet we don't greet each other, we simply brush shoulders as we pass by each other and silently move on, each one his own way! To all of which I say: `Please yourself, Ntamba, since your enmity alone doesn't make of me an ostracized person or drive me in any way out of my home.' At some future day, when he comes to his senses on his own and decides to greet me again, we will start exchanging greetings once more, because, on my side too, since the child of my relative healed, I won't harbor a grudge against him. But it is Ntamba's relatives who insist on hating me body and soul and keep on reviling me for supposedly grazing my cattle in their millet crop and then refusing to pay them compensation! Where have you ever seen the like of that, a person volunteering to compensate somebody against whom he won a court judgement! That is also why I could not return here sooner, because the child who was beaten was still sick and I had to take him to the lake and immerse him in cold water early in morning and late in evening, daily, massage him with sand and cold lake water, amidst his loud cries of pain, which I wouldn't heed lest I fail to administer the needed treatment. And when he finally healed completely and was strong enough to look after livestock again I said to myself, `No, I can't wait any longer; let me drop in on them today.' Then while on the way it poured buckets on me. I am inclined to think that it is that rain which has given me this headache. In fact at this very moment it is as if I am being invaded by a bit of cold as well."

When Myombekere and his hosts chanced to look up in the sky again they found the descending sun already near the horizon and they all exclaimed their surprise and said, "A cloudy sun never delays to set; before you know it, it is already nighttime!"

Then Namwero told Myombekere: "What I want to say to you, son-in-law, is that you appease[21] me with six pots of banana beer. And so the day you bring me the banana beer will be the day you will return to your home with your wife. Because you and I are both married men, both of us are husbands of other people's daughters. Also we all know the suffering of a married man, a man who has built a home of his own, when forced to live without a wife."

Myombekere raised his joined hands to his father-in-law and said, "Your praises, my father-in-law! When a parent says: `I am hungry' to his or her child, it is always an honor to the child.

That matter concluded, Lweganwa took Myombekere back to his bachelor's house. Bugonoka too came to the house, to dust a cow-skin bed sheet for her husband to lie on and he at once lay down and stretched himself on the cow-skin and listened to the cold which was invading his body and giving him a pounding head.

Chapter V

NOTES

1.   *Ebigemero*: A rain-maker's charm pots.

2.   *Kwikorobozya*: Proclaiming ones self-praises or, as used here, haranguing the heavens by a healer, diviner or any other person with supernatural powers.

3.   *Myee! gingiri! ligiti*! *Myee*! and *ligiti*! ideophones, the first one for the blinding flash of lightning and the second for falling down completely; *gingiri*! onomatopoeia for the rumble of thunder (and for falling down "resoundingly").

4.   Initiation rites which conferred supernatural powers on people normally involved rubbing potent medicines into their bodies through incisions, which usually left behind permanent marks on the recipients.

5.   *Tata*!: My father! an interjection.

6.   The Wakerewe believed one of the things which could happen to thieves as their punishment was being struck by lightning.

7.   Omukwaya: See note 5 of Chapter I.

8.   *Olusabuzyo*: See note 12 of Chapter I.

9.   *Ebibabi* or *ebitutu*: See note 11 of Chapter II.

10.   *Obwita*: See note 14 of Chapter I.

11.   *Ekibo*: See note 15 of Chapter I.

12.   *Olunanga*: See note 16 of Chapter I.

13.   Hippopotamus meat and all other game meat was among the relishes which adult Wakerewe women did not eat. See note 17 of Chapter II.

14.   Abagwe: Here Wakerewe's name for Wasukuma; also the name of the clan of the king-makers of Ukerewe, also called Abasita, who were also the guardians of the burial grounds of the kings at the foot of the lakeside Kitale Mountain (see Introduction). *Emigero*, plural for *omugero*: Very large *ekibo* above.

15.   *Abanyaga*: See note 9 of Chapter II.

16.   *Ekitukuru* (plural *ebitukuru*): Wickerwork basket for carrying things like flour and grain and the container in which women usually carried presents of food and other provisions, so that, by extension, the word in plural also means "presents".

17.   *Obubele:* Small-grained millet, formerly the main food crop of the Wakerewe and considered more nutritious than cassava, a root-crop easier to grow, in that it is semi-perennial, does not involve bird watching and survives drought better, which eventually supplanted the millet in importance before replacing it altogether so that today the millet is hardly grown at all in

Ukerewe, a fact which led to a dietary change among his people Kitereza seems to regret (see Introduction).

18. Wazinza hoes: Heart-shaped and spiked hoes, planted in the hoe handle by the spike. Abarongo clan of the Wazinza mainland cousins of the Wakerewe (see Introduction) were the main ironsmiths of the entire southern lake region and it was from Uzinza that Ukerewe obtained most of its hoes and other ironwares. Hoes were among the things of value the Wakerewe paid as bride-price to the bride's parents and to date there still has to be included a hoe or two, now of the "European type", in a   typical Kikerewe   bride-price, even though   for purely traditional reasons, since hoes have become very readily available and are certainly no longer counted as valuables..

19. *Engega* (singular *olugega*): Baskets made of trellised splits of slender sugarcane-like *amabingo* canes or papyruses, the most commonly used baskets for carrying and storing things.

20. *Omutaho*: See note 9 of Chapter I.

21. *Kuzogora*: To make amends for an offense against a customary obligation by paying an appeasement fine, which was for men usually in terms of pots of banana beer, though a goat or even a cow could be demanded if the offense in question was very serious, and for women usually in terms of baskets of grain or flour.

Chapter VI

MYOMBEKERE PASSES A NIGHT AT HIS IN-LAWS' WHILE WOOING HIS WIFE BACK

Later on that day Lweganwa went to the lake to bathe and to see whether there was any catch in their *olubigo*[1] fish trap. At the lake he took off his clothes and went into the water with his fishing spear to look for fish in *olubigo*'s catch chambers. In the first chamber he stirred the water with the spear, only to find not a single fish in that one. He proceeded to the second chamber, where again he passed his fishing-spear through the water and on stirring the water there he found one tilapia, of *ensendera*[2] kind. He took his hand basket[3] and drew the fish out of the water with it, killed the fish and tossed it onto sand on the beach. From there he went on to the third catch-chamber and likewise stirred the water of the chamber and in that one too he found a single tilapia, this time the big *engonogono*,   fished that one too out of the water with his small basket, killed it and again tossed that one too onto the beach sand. With that he come out of *olubigo*, bathed in the lake and after taking a thorough bath went to scale his fish and disemboweled and cleaned them.   Then he stringed his catch on a papyrus strand, dipped the fish into the water of the lake to wash off their fish-blood and the scales still clinging on them, put on his clothes and tied the fish on his fishing-spear and left for home.

He had walked only for a little while and was still by the lakeshore when he saw a boat of *abagonzo*[4] fishermen landing and went to them. He found some acquaintances of his among the fishermen just landed and when those friends of his took out their part of the catch, they gave him a present of one *embete*,[5] and he disemboweled the big fish and cut it into several chunks. He had to tie that fish on a separate part of his fishing-spear, because it is a men's fish and couldn't be mixed with fish which women too eat. That done, he said good-bye to the fishermen and left to take home the booty of his venturing out for the day as the setting sun was just about to disappear from the sky.

On arriving home he took the fish he had brought from the lake and placed them in a shrine hut,[6] where they stayed for a little while before the women of their home came to fetch them and took them into the house ready for cooking. Then he was out again, to fetch home the cows from the pastures. He brought their cattle home and barricaded them in the kraal, except for the milk cows, which he tethered on pegs erected outside the kraal. Then he went inside his house to his brother-in-law, whom he found covered from head to foot with a cow-skin bed sheet and tried to wake him, "Brother-in-law!" "*Di!* " no answer. He called him the second time, "Brother-in-law!"

Only then did he respond: "Yes, Sir!"

Lweganwa approached him and asked him, "Is your head still paining you?"

"It appears it is getting a bit better, brother-in-law."

"What about your feeling cold?"

"That too has now subsided, may be because I have sweated a bit. Why don't you come and see for yourself, my brother-in-law?" Lweganwa uncovered his head and found that indeed he was dripping with sweat, a lot of sweat, and on touching him he found that his fever was subsiding. Before long Bugonoka also came to the house, with a big pot of hot water, which she put down at the door before coming inside to her husband. Lweganwa then left the house and went to make fire at the courtyard fireplace.[7] Once in the house, Bugonoka went to her husband and began feeling him by touching his forehead, his neck and his chest with the palm of her hand to see how bad his fever was and then asked him in a low voice, "Is your head still paining you?"

"It is getting a bit better. I think, if things continue this way, I am on my way to recovering. Now I no longer even feel cold."

"It appears you also did sweat a lot?"

"Yes, I did. It is my brother-in-law who has just woke me up and found me still perspiring from the fever. It is when he woke me that I too realized

I had been sweating."

Bugonoka then came outside and took the hot water behind her brother's house and then went to fetch a movable door-shutter on which her husband would take a bath, before going back to the house to tell him to go behind the house and bathe, and Myombekere came out, with Bugonoka following. Once outside he took off his clothes and sat on the reeds door-shutter and his wife brought the hot water near him and drew some of it with a calabash and began pouring it on him until he had a thorough bath, with his wife rubbing and massaging him in the back and all over his body with the toilet leaves she had brought with her until she finished bathing him and Myombekere put on his clothes again. Bugonoka then fetched a chair for her husband and placed it at their courtyard fireplace, where her brother had already set the fire going, and her husband sat down, in the company of his father-in-law and brother-in-law. She then went to take away from behind the house the pot and the other things she had taken there for her husband's bath and, that done, went into her parent's house to join her mother.

As soon as Lweganwa saw gadflies disappear with the coming of night, he called aloud Bugonoka in the house and told her, "Please bring water so that we can begin milking cows!" Bugonoka was up at once, drew water from a pot with a cup[8] and brought the water outside, looked for a washbasin[9] and poured the water into it and Lweganwa washed his hands ready for milking cows.

While her brother was washing his hands, Bugonoka quickly untethered a calf and then returned into the house to fetch *ekisahi*,[10] coming back in no time with the wooden milk container and rejoining her brother, as he on his part got hold of a cow-leg tether.[11] He had to hurry up and tether the legs of the cow and begin milking before the calf which had been let loose to go to its mother had sucked all the milk. As soon as Lweganwa tethered the legs of the cow, he began directing with his hand the sucking of its calf, making it push and pull at its mother's teats until the mother had let milk flow freely and its teats had filled out, then he put out a hand to Bugonoka and she handed him *ekisahi*. Bugonoka then held the calf and kept it near its mother's mouth so that the milk cow would continue calling its calf and licking it with its tongue as it was being milked. Lweganwa milked the cow while whistling a song all the time, with now and then breaking off to whistle to the cow a call for calm, to make the cow stand still and let its milk flow freely.

After a while Lweganwa told his sister to release the calf to come and suck again until its mother would chew its cud. Bugonoka let go the calf and again it sucked its mother's milk with Lweganwa directing its sucking as before, making it pull and push at its mothers teats. In the meanwhile Bugonoka on her part got hold of *ekisahi* of milk and quickly took the milk into the house, where she poured it into a milk pot[12] and came back in a jiffy, gave back *ekisahi* to Lweganwa and then held the cow's calf once more, because the cow being milked was their spotless black cow which had enough milk to fill that wooden milk container twice each milking. Lweganwa milked the cow the second time and filled yet another *ekisahi* and then stopped, so as to leave the cow some milk for its calf. His sister received that milk too and took it into the house, and then told her mother to put onto the fire the pot for preparing *obwita*[13] and her mother did so.

Bugonoka delayed a bit coming back from the house and Lweganwa called her aloud and said, "You over there! What are you doing in the house? Come and untether the calf of Brown-and-white !" The brown cow with white spots in question was calling out for its calf and mooing loudly, as on his part its milker whistled to it to try and calm it down. When Lweganwa saw that his sister still remained in the house instead of coming to untether the calf, he finally shouted at her rather angrily: "If you have refused to come and untether the calves, I won't milk the cows anymore! You'll come and milk them yourself, if that's what you want!"

"I'm coming. I had to attend to something first, but I'm now through." And in that instant she had untethered the calf of the brown-and-white cow, which went to its mother at full trot, with Bugonoka following behind. By that time beside the cow to be milked next Lweganwa had already been driven to quarreling and talking to himself and saying: "Now I see! Because you women never milk cows,[14] because all you do is drink the milk, you don't know at all the hardships of a milker, what it feels like to remain squatting for so long under a cow's udder! So just give me that *ekisahi* so that I can milk the cows, and then you can go back to fooling about that way after!"

His sister handed him *ekisahi* and then quickly went to the other side to hold the calf. Because that cow did not need milking with a break and then continuing after it had chewed cud, since it had very little milk, was in fact still being milked at all only as a way of helping it gradually stop producing milk, the milker too did not take long at it and in no time he had given back to Bugonoka the milk container, which was still half full.

Bugonoka this time passed by the calf of the red cow, the one next in line to be milked, and untethered it first, just in case she delayed in the house again and risked another reprimand from his brother, and then took the milk into the house. But this time she wasted no time before coming back to join Lweganwa at the red cow he was about to milk, where she remained only for a little while before Lweganwa asked her to give him *ekisahi*, as Bugonoka on her part pulled away the calf and held it near the mouth of its mother, before she too folded her robe and squatted down. Because that cow had large and heavy teats, when Lweganwa was milking it its milk was zooming in *ekisahi* so that even from a distance what one heard was: *vuu!* and not: *chorwe, chorwe!* or even: *chororwe!* That red cow had enough milk for one container and a near full second one. When Lweganwa milked the cow and filled *ekisahi*, he told Bugonoka to release the calf to come and suck again so that the cow could chew cud and she let go the calf and quickly received *ekisahi* of milk and hurried to take the milk into the house.

In no time she had brought back *ekisahi* and given it to Lweganwa and once again Lweganwa was making the milk of the red cow zoom in the wooden container. When he estimated that there was left in the cow's udder only enough milk for the calf, just enough for it not to starve, since it hadn't begun eating grass, he stopped, untethered the mother cow's legs, got out from under its udder and handed to his sister the partly full container of milk he had. They kept some cats in the home, and so Bugonoka passed by the huge broken pot in which the cats were given milk and poured in it some for them and they at once lapped it in with their tongues and finished what she poured in for them the first time and she poured in some more for them before taking into the house what was left in *ekisahi*.

Then she came out of the house again to take all the calves away from their mothers lest they develop swollen mouth-glands or end up with diarrhea from over-sucking. She securely tethered the calves on pegs and returned to the house, where she found water in *obwita* pot already boiling and at once put flour into the pot and prepared food. *Obwita* ready, she dished it out of the pot and divided it up, putting the women's share in a separate bowl[15] and the men's in the men's bowl[16] and pressing the men's dish and nicely rounding and shaping it and pointing its top. While she was still busy properly shaping the men's *obwita* and cleaning the remains of food from the pot and cooking spoon,[17] her mother put on the fire another pot and warmed up water for the men to wash their hands with. In no time she was ready and the men outside at the courtyard fireplace were served dinner

Namwero told Lweganwa to hurry up and serve relish so that their son-in-law could eat[18] and get out of the chilly nighttime draft, lest he should fall sick again. Lweganwa served them hippopotamus meat first, by taking out of the pot a big piece of the meat and depositing it on a plate,[19] and they started eating. After they had been eating for some time, Lweganwa got hold of another pot of relish, which had been brought later, and took another plate and served on it fish, *embete*, and placed the plate in between his brother-in-law's legs and told him, "Don't forget to try this one too, brother-in-law, and see what it tastes like!"

His father asked him, "What kind of fish is that?"

"It is *embete*, a present from the *abagonzo* fishermen I came across at the lake when I dropped in to see our *olubigo* trap," his son answered.

Myombekere answered back Lweganwa's invitation by saying, "Brother-in-law, I can eat no more, because I ate so much of the meal we were served during daytime that even now my stomach is still bulging. I must stop lest I burst."

"With people like you your stomachs have already shrunk, I am sure. Do, at least, eat some of the fish without *obwita*."[20]

"No thank you, because food is not like beer. It is with beer that you see a person, even when he's already as drunk as can be, on seeing a pot of beer being brought ask for some more: `Give me too a bit of beer, gentlemen!' which, given his condition, leaves you wondering and saying to yourself, `Where will this man put the beer he is asking for, even if he gets it, drunk as he already is?' And if he is given the beer you would indeed see him get hold of the bowlful and pour down his throat all of it to the last drop! But with food, my brother-in-law, once you have eaten your fill and have satisfied your appetite even when you see other people eating you say to yourself, `What can they be eating? Can they really find whatever they are eating appetizing!'"

Myombekere remained seated in his place waiting for his father-in-law and his brother-in-law to finish eating before he could wash his hands. Even if he had been an ordinary visitor and not a guest of his in-laws, people to whom he owed special respect, he wouldn't have washed his hands before his hosts had finished eating, because a person who stopped eating before others couldn't wash his or her hands or leave the meal round before all the others had also stopped eating. Never! Anybody doing that was considered a really ill-mannered person and a person with no respect for others. As it was, it was his father-in-law who washed his hands first. When Namwero too stopped eating, Lweganwa removed and put aside the food utensils and called aloud Bugonoka and told her, "Please come and take away your utensils!" After she had taken the utensils into the house Namwero too called her and said, "Hurry and finish putting away the utensils and go and make a fire in Lweganwa's bachelor's house, where you will sleep with your husband, so that our in-law can get away from this chill."

The men were still seated outside, talking about this and that, when they saw Bugonoka pass by with embers on grass and carrying some firewood for starting a fire with. When she got near his brother's bachelor house, the embers on the grass burst into flame and she threw the fire down, covered it with the rest of the grass she was holding and blew on the flame and extinguished it. Then she picked up the embers and placed them on grass again and put out the few embers which remained on the ground by stepping on them and grinding them in the soil with her foot. She then looked around for some dry twigs with which to set burning the firewood she had and went into the house and started a fire until it flamed, put on the flame the dry twigs first and then placed firewood on top of the twigs.

When the fire was going properly she dusted the cow-skin which was spread on Lweganwa's bed and then went to the courtyard fireplace and told her husband, "Get up, let's go into the house."

Myombekere got up, said good-night to his father-in-law and brother-in-law and mother-in-law, then Bugonoka took his seat and led the way to her brother's bachelor house and he followed behind. She got to a place where there was a rock in the way and, since it was a dark night, alerted her husband of it: "Walk carefully, there is a stone in the way. Don't stumble on it and hurt your toes."

"Where is it?"

"Here it is."

"*Uu!* Yes, indeed! I can see! If a person comes by walking without paying attention this stone can wipe off his or her toes, completely! *Aa! hee!* this rock is where it shouldn't be: in the middle of the way!"

Once in the house, wife blew on the fire to make it blaze so that they could go to bed in the light, after which husband asked wife a question: "And where will my brother-in-law sleep tonight?"

"You forget he is a young man! Who knows where he will go! My guess is that he's already gone to his friends in the homes of the neighborhood to sleep in their bachelors' houses; especially since there was talk of a dance tonight, at Kabigo's home, he can't still be anywhere near here, he must have already left for the dance. Did you want him?"

"Well, no. I just wanted to know; even though, it is true, I also needed him."

"What for?"

"I want him to take me outside to help myself, because I can hear worms rumbling in this belly of mine. If I go to bed without going to relieve myself I will not pass a comfortable night."

"Let me go and fetch a hoe from my parent's house, since the household gate is already shut and it would be so much trouble to go into the bush. What is more, my father doesn't like the habit of people going into the bush after the home gate has been closed for the night. So let me bring a hoe and then I will dig a hole for you somewhere behind this house so that you can relieve yourself."

Bugonoka thought of how best to ask for a hoe from her parents' house after they had already retired for the night, and so when she got to the house she called out, "Hello, in there!" In the house people were still talking and they did not hear her, and so she called out again, this time with: "Barongo!"

Barongo answered, with some alarm in her voice: "Yes! Did I hear somebody call me outside?"

Bugonoka said, "Yes. It's me. I need a hoe, pass me one, I have stomachache and I need to dig a hole." She was ashamed to say that it was her husband who wanted to shit so she had to pretend it was herself who wanted to go. She had to speak in riddles, as it were. Inside the house hoes were piled together in one place and Barongo noisily knocked them against each other before she could disengage one and bring it to Bugonoka, who left being escorted by her mother's words: "Keep it with you there in that house of yours. Don't come to wake us up and make us open doors for you again. Avoid the trouble of having to come all this way again, should your stomach continue to trouble you during the night."

"All right", her daughter answered.

Bugonoka got back to the door of Lweganwa's bachelor house and called out to her husband, speaking in riddles again, "Come and escort me this way behind the house, where I want to dig a hole, my stomach is troubling me and I am afraid to go there alone in this dark night."

Myombekere got up and joined his wife outside and the two went behind Lweganwa's bachelor house and wife dug a hole into the ground for husband to shit in,　husband squatted over the hole as his wife on her part went to the fence of their home and cut from its hedge soft tree leaves[21] for her husband to clean himself with and came back and gave them to him. The husband finished relieving himself and got away from the hole and quickly his wife took the hoe and covered the hole with soil and the two went back to the house.

Back in the house they found the fire still going well and warmed their legs and feet on it to dry the dew-wet sand and rain mud they had stepped in while outside before dusting themselves. Myombekere took off his cow-skin robe he was wearing and gave it to his wife and she hung it on the house bulkhead as he himself climbed onto the bed and lay down. Quickly, Bugonoka came and unfolded *enkanda*[22] and covered her husband. On her part, because she was wearing a lot of *obunerere,*[23] she went back to the fire to dry the piles of fine wire ornaments on her legs and then shook soil out of them to make sure she didn't carry it with her to their bed and spread sand all over it. When she too was done with cleaning and dusting her *obunerere*, she left the fireside, after she had taken out of the fire the long pieces of firewood and put them out by sticking their burning ends in the ground, as a precaution lest they should burn on during the night and risk the fire spreading out and burning down the house. The fire well contained, she took off her clothes and she too hung them on the house bulkhead, cleaned her feet by rubbing them against each other and dusting them thoroughly on a wooden block[24] on the ground at the lower end of the bed. Then she climbed on the bed and lay down on the woman side[25] of the bed and covered herself with the same *enkanda* with which her husband was covered and settled in bed.

After she had been in bed for a while, Bugonoka told her husband, "Move to your side a little, I don't feel comfortable yet this side, or is the bed perhaps too little for the two of us?"

"That wouldn't surprise me, since it is a bachelor's bed, meant for one person."

"Even a bachelor needs a bigger bed. What when he brings in a woman, doesn't it then become a bed for two?"

"Yes, may be when you look at it that way."

"Even if it is not that, what about his fellow young men who sometimes come to sleep here on their way from dancing at night, are those not people with whom he shares the bed?"

"I see! They are people, all right. But do men ever need much space on a bed?"

"And why do we women need a lot of space?"

"Well, for many reasons".

"Which ones?"

"You need more space because you are more substantial, and also because of the ornaments you wear, like the strings of fairly large beads you wear around your waists, and the abundant *obunerere* on your wrists and ankles, and the bracelets on your arms, and all the different kinds of charms you wear around your neck, and the like. That's why you take up a lot of space in bed. And we men, do we ever have any of that?" Bugonoka laughed. With that they then moved on to talk a bit of other matters of mutual interest.

Only after a while did Myombekere talk to his wife of matters dear to his heart, revealing to her the suffering he had experienced as a man alone since she left him. He told her how living in a home alone is like living in a bush, because, after getting used to a home of two, when one of the two leaves to go to some place and spends there a month or more the one left behind is as if he or she is living in a jungle, especially at night. And he went on to say, "Especially with us men the situation is really unbearable. Possibly matters are a bit better with you women, because, as you can see, when you women are the ones left alone in the house you cook, fetch and bring drinking water in the house, fill the house with the sound of the grinding-stone, make a fire in it everyday. Such things make the house sound cheerful and keep it warm at least, so that you are left only with the misery of not having a companion to talk with at night, assuming you women too feel that need like us men. But what we men suffer when left alone in the house goes much further than that. Allow me to enumerate for you what happens with us, during daytime to start with. There is the shame which prevents a man from placing a pot on the cooking-stones, the shame of a man grinding flour on the grinding-stone, the shame which keeps a man from going to the water-side fields to dig up and bring home sweet potatoes, even when there is food in the fields, the shame of a man having to pick green vegetables, like *empwani, omususa, omugobe, omuyobyo, omusaga*[26] and all the other greens, because if a man did such things it would only be an act of desperation, by which he brings on himself nothing but censure and much contempt, making people say of him, `Whom are you speaking about? So and so! Oh, that one! The man in between whose legs the cooking pot has been boiling for so long! You speak of such a man as if he were a normal human being! May be you have run out of matters to talk about, in which case it were much better you kept quiet rather than talk about the like of him.' And then at nighttime there is this: the shame of a married man making ready his own bed for going to bed. Especially that one, which is perhaps the hardest to bear. And the lack of someone to talk with, being all alone in the house with so many things going through your mind until you can't sleep a wink, even if you resort to taking as much tobacco as you can! Nothing would help you sleep! Indeed, my wife, we men suffer a lot once married and then your wife, who should never leave you her husband, deserts you and leaves you really all alone, does something which is completely wrong like that to you! My father-in-law on his part has spoken of banana beer for appeasement, but maybe he is bluffing, maybe when I've brought the beer he will still retain you, having perhaps found something else to say?"

"What else could that be, when he himself is the one who has said so! What's more, he is an elder and couldn't do such a thing."

"Maybe he will change his mind, my dear wife?"

"No, I don't think so, because banana beer is what he said he wanted even before you came, when his son came back and wanted to know whether I had never left, had never gone back to my home all that time. So, what other reason can he find for wanting to retain me here?"

"I can't wait for daybreak! It is true I have no banana plantation, but as soon as I get home I will go everywhere to people with banana plantations, wherever I can, and get whoever will take pity of me to give me something, even if it is a single bunch it will still help, until I have enough and I can bring him the beer. *Aa!* what sort of life is this! For how much longer can this go on before I die from the misery of a bachelor's life?"

And after a while the nephew of death sleep took them both, since there is no way to guard against sleep! And when it dawned, around the first cockcrow Myombekere woke up and awoke his wife. When she too woke up, he told her, "I want to be on my way and see how things are over there in my home; for, look, the first cockcrow has gone!"

"No, you can't do that! You must wait until daybreak before you go lest it rains on you again like yesterday. What's more, the country has become too dangerous these days."

He heeded his wife's advice and pulled *enkanda* over his jaw again and fell asleep. When it was finally daybreak, still very early morning, Bugonoka woke up and went to her parents house and they opened the door for her. Once in the house, she knelt down on the floor of the fore-room, near where Barongo was sleeping, and greeted her father and mother. Then she took an empty water pot, and so did Barongo, and the two of them went to the lake to draw water. The early morning birds began twittering when they were already at the lake, washing their faces. They washed their hands and their faces, then took off their clothes and laid them on the beach sand and took their pots and waded into the lake to draw water, filled their pots, and came and stood their pots of water in the sand of the beach and then went back into the lake to bathe. They bathed, scrubbed clean the soles of their feet and brushed their teeth with very fine lake-bottom sand to get rid of food films from their teeth lest they stain their teeth and give their mouths a bad smell, and then came out of the water and put on their clothes again, placed their pots of water on their heads and returned home.

They poured water into the big drinking-water pot and Bugonoka went to see whether there was fire in the kitchen fireplace and found none, the fire having all died out during the night. Her mother asked her, "What are you looking for, Bugonoka?"

"I was digging for fire in the fireplace here, mother dear, but I have found none; it appears to have died out."

"Why don't you fetch some from the courtyard fireplace? Is there none there too?"

"I haven't been there yet."

Then her father asked her, "Is it likely to rain today too?"

"When we woke up to go to the lake the sky then was heavy with clouds, but now they have cleared, so perhaps it will be sunny."

Bugonoka came out of the house and went near a grain store,[27] where she gathered some dry grass from the ground before going to the courtyard fireplace, in which she found the fire still live, took out some embers, grabbed some fire wood on her way back and went to start a fire in her parents' house. When the fire was going, she took from a hanger a pot of relish and examined it, then drew from the water pot a tiny bit of water and dripped it into the pot before placing the pot on the cooking-stones. That done, she told her sister[28] Barongo, whose mother and her mother were children of the same man and the same women, Bugonoka's mother being the older and Barongo's mother her immediate younger sister, "Could you please come, sister, and look after this pot for me while I bring our visitor water for washing his face, so that I can hurry back and prepare for him something to eat and let him start on his way back before it gets too hot. In fact he wanted to leave at cockcrow, had I not stopped him and told him, `No, you can't, lest it rains on you like it did yesterday and makes you sick again." On hearing that her father asked her, "By the way, is our son-in-law's headache better this morning? What about his cold, has it left him?" To which his daughter replied, "The cold has stopped and the headache too has subsided."

Barongo got up and went to look after the pot on the cooking-stones, and Bugonoka took a calabash from the utensils rack and drew some water from the drinking-water pot and took it to her husband for washing his face, as her mother left her bed and got ready to skim milk. She went to her husband and awoke him and he dressed and got out of the house and went behind the house to pass water, and from there he went straight to wish his father-in-law a good-day: "Good-morning, my father-in-law! How did you pass the night?"

"Good-morning, son; we slept well. Did that headache and that cold of yours subside a bit?"

"I am recovered, and the cold has left me."

Then he greeted his mother-in-law: "Did you sleep well, mother-in-law?"

"We slept well, son. Are your illnesses getting any better?"

"I am recovered, mother-in-law."

Then he greeted his sister-in-law Barongo: "Greetings, sister-in-law!"

"Greetings!"

"Greetings, you the foundation of my home!"[29]

"Greetings!"

"Greetings, my dear one!"

"Greetings!"

"Greetings, you whose saliva is butter for seasoning my *omugobe* greens!"

"Greetings!" and with that his sister-in-law laughed: *kwekwekwe!*

Myombekere went back to his brother-in-law's bachelor house to join his wife, who gave him at once a seat and he sat down. She then poured some water for him in a washbasin and put it near him and he washed his hands first. His wife handed him a piece of grass with which to clean dirt from under his fingernails. When he finished, she slowly poured water into the cup of his right hand and her husband washed his face, cleaning dirt from his eyes and flipping it away with the fingernail of one of his little fingers, which he had let grow really long. He washed his legs as well and when he finished his wife took the washbasin, poured away the water her husband had used, laid it on the ground overturned, and then left to go back to her parents house to cook something for him.

Just as Bugonoka was coming out of her brother's bachelor house, she ran into Lweganwa himself coming back from wherever he had passed the night, and they exchanged greetings. Lweganwa went to greet his brother-in-law first. After the two chatted a bit, he said, "Let me first go and greet the old man before I come back to chat," and he left and went to bid his father and his mother and his other sister, Barongo, good-morning and they all exchanged greetings with him. Shortly after that, Bugonoka told him, "Go to the other house, to eat with your brother-in-law and keep him company," and he went and rejoined Myombekere.

Bugonoka brought them food, which was *obwita* with hippopotamus meat for relish. Seeing that, Lweganwa told his sister, "Could you bring my *embete* for me, or didn't you warm it up?"

"It is warmed up," she answered.

While they were eating, Myombekere queried his brother-in-law and said, "It seems today you are determined to leave all the meat to me! Otherwise, how is it I haven't seen you take a bite from this plate?"

"It looks as if I am beginning to lose appetite for hippopotamus meat as a result of having eaten so much of it during our hunting expedition. It is true I still can eat the meat, but when there is some other relish besides it, like now, I tend to rather shun it. But you too should taste what we have on this other plate, because last night you didn't eat any of the fish, saying you were already full."

Myombekere took a piece of the fish and on putting it into his mouth found it really appetizing. They ate their fill and Lweganwa called aloud Bugonoka and said, "Come and save us, please, we have reached the end of our appetites." Bugonoka came with warm water, as the women of that home were wont to do. When the brothers-in-law had finished washing their hands, Bugonoka took *ekizanda*[30] of milk, churned it around with her hands and handed it to her husband. Her husband receive it, put it to his mouth and drank the milk non-stop, and then paused and wanted to pass the milk to Lweganwa but Bugonoka stopped him and said, "No, you must drink on. Even if you can drink it all, please go ahead and give yourself the strength you need for the journey, because it is such a long one." To which Lweganwa too agreed and said, "Yes indeed! Drink on, brother-in-law, or is the milk perhaps not to your taste because it has just been skimmed and hadn't settled?" Myombekere took in another draught of the milk, but even then he had to surrender, because it was a large *ekizanda* and with plenty of milk in it. He gave up trying to finish the milk and passed it to his brother-in-law and said, "No, brother-in-law, this is enough. I shouldn't eat like a person who has never seen food and harm myself, because eating until you are so full that the worms inside your stomach have no room to play in can't be right." Lweganwa too drank his fill and handed back *ekizanda* of milk to his sister and told Myombekere: "*Aa! hee!* brother in law, to finish so much milk one would need the appetite of a hippopotamus hunter, for since witnessing their gluttony I would say food which a hippopotamus hunter can't finish must be something to marvel at indeed!"

Myombekere rested a bit after eating and washing his hands until his hands dried and were no longer sticky with water and then took out his snuff wrapped in a piece of dry banana stem fiber and inhaled until the snuff got into him properly and he blew it out of his nose. That done, he told his brother-in-law to give him his weapons and Lweganwa went to fetch them from his parents' house. His parents asked him what he wanted and he answered, "Our in-law says he wants to start on his way back home." His father then said, "Give him six chunks of hippopotamus meat from over there and tie them onto his spear for him, for somebody to stew for him at his place." Lweganwa's mother said, "Rather than tie the meat on his spear for him, why not let him carry it in Lweganwa's small carrying basket[31] here. He can bring it back with him when he comes next."

Lweganwa shot off to cut some banana leaves from their banana plantation and was back in no time and gave them to Bugonoka. His sister first laid at the bottom of the small basket a fresh banana leaf before placing into the basket the six chunks of meat, to which she added a seventh, then she took another banana leaf and covered the meat, and Lweganwa brought a carrying stick and tied the basket on one end of the stick. Then Myombekere's hosts came out of the house to see off their son-in-law. Myombekere said good-bye to his father-in-law and his mother-in-law: "Stay well," to which the two of them answered at the same time, "Thank you, you too. Have a safe journey, and give our greetings to the people of your home."

"I will, thank you."

Lweganwa led the way, carrying his brother-in-law's weapons, and Myombekere's sister-in-law, Barongo, escorted him too, carrying the basket of dried hippopotamus meat.   When they had gone some distance, Lweganwa gave Myombekere's spear to his sister Bugonoka and said, "Take this spear, if you two want to continue escorting him. I must go back now, brother-in-law. Have a safe journey and greetings to the people of your home."

"Good-bye and thank you, brother-in-law. You too stay well."

"Thank you."

Lweganwa was already on his way back when he remembered he forgot to tell Myombekere not to forget to bring back his basket soon, to come with it when he came to see them again, and called out to him from that far, "Brother-in-law, *wowe*!" Bugonoka told her husband, "I think that is your brother-in-law calling you." Myombekere answered back: "Yes, Sir!" Lweganwa then said, "What I am reminding you of is: Don't forget to bring back that small basket. When you come again, bring it with you, please!" "All right!" Myombekere answered.

Then Myombekere asked his wife, "To be so concerned about his basked, is he about to go to sea again?"

"No, may be he simply needs it, because it is the one with which he goes to angle *enembe*,[32] but otherwise to go to sea again in that sense and be away from home he is not about to do that. What's more, his wedding is also approaching: the courting among the bride's relatives has been completed[33] and we were only waiting for his return. My guess is that may be this very day father will pay his fellow parents-in-law a visit to inform them that his son is back from the sea so that if they intend to give him a daughter-in-law they would let him know whatever it is they want to tell him."

Bugonoka and Barongo escorted him for just a little longer and then they too said good-bye to him. Bugonoka told her husband: "Good-bye, have a safe journey and remember whenever you eat to put aside something for me."

Myombekere rejoined, "I will. And you too stay well and don't eat anything without putting aside something for me." Everybody laughed.

Barongo said, "Here is your load, brother-in-law. Have a safe journey and greet your empty bed for me!"

"Thanks; only you are being unfair, my sister-in-law."

"How I am being unfair to you? Or maybe you are already married? I should have bid you good-bye by saying: 'Greetings to your wife!'"

"Get married! Oh, my dear, you speak of getting a wife as if it is catching fish by the basketfuls!"

"Well, aren't you a Mkerewe?"

"That I am, it is true, but why do you ask?"

"*Aa!* Isn't that exactly what Wakerewe men of yore said, that women are like fish, to be caught by the basketfuls?" and they all laughed again. Then Barongo added, "That's only a sister-in-law's joke. Just hurry up and bring us the dear old banana beer so that we can soak ourselves in it and forget our miseries for a while."

"And when are you going back to your home?"

"With me I am waiting to know what will be decided concerning Lweganwa's wedding before I go and then come back to help with preparations for the wedding."

"Well, when you go back greet your husband for me."

"I will, thank you."

They parted and Bugonoka and her sister went back home and Myombekere started on his return journey.

Chapter VI

NOTES

1. *Olubigo*:   See note 3 of Chapter II.
2. *Esendera*, and *engonogono* : Types of *ensato,* the lake fish tilapia. *Ensendera,* named after a small bird of that name, is the small type, caught mainly during the rain season, and *engonogono* is the bigger and more delicious type. *Ensato* is fish Wakerewe consider the best.
3. *Ekisanzo*: Very small trellised basket, *olugega* (see note 19 of Chapter V), here used for drawing fish out of the catch-chambers of *olubigo* fish trap.
4. *Abagonzo*: Fishermen who fish with *emigonzo* (singular *omugonzo)*: Fishing device consisting of a row of large hooks attached to a rope and used   for catching large fish far out in the deep waters of the sea.
5. *Embete*: See note 17 of Chapter II.
6. *Amazu g'abakekuru*: Literally "old women's houses", the ancestral shrines Wakerewe heads of households built in their homes, which were miniature forms of the houses in which they lived, and of which each household had at least one. Fish brought home from the sea was put in a shrine hut first before it was taken out by the women of the home for cooking.
7. *Ekikome*: See note 1 of Chapter II.
8. *Omutaho:* See note 9 of chapter I.
9. *Olusabuzyo*: See note 12 of Chapter I.
10. *Ekisahi* (plural *ebisahi*): Wooden milk container, with a capacity of one to two gallons, mounted on a stand with several round legs, each small enough for a person to grip and hold the container in one hand, used exclusively as a milk receptacle when milking cows (the Wakerewe don't milk goats or sheep).
11. *Embohera*: Short rope for tying together the hind legs of a milk cow to keep it from moving while it is being milked.
12. *Olwabya*: "The milk pot", a large cooking pot used exclusively for storing fresh milk.
13. *Obwita*: See note 14 of Chapter I.
14. The Wakerewe had some fairly strict division of labor between men and women and milking cows was a men's job, and so was herding and taking care of livestock in general, so that the woman in Myombekere's home helping a boy to herd Myombekere's cattle is meant to emphasize the hardship and disruption of normal life that household was experiencing since the departure of Myombekere's wife Bugonoka. Other jobs women were not supposed to do included hunting, fishing, sailing, clearing new land for crop fields, clearing

brush and undergrowth from fallow crop fields ready for hoeing and planting, and building houses. In return, as seen in the story, it was considered a real misfortune for a man to have to cook and do house-keeping jobs and cultivate certain types of crops, like greens and vegetables, considered women crops.

15. *Ekibo*: See note 15 of Chapter I.

16. *Ekibo cha baseza*: Men's *ekibo*, which differed from the women's in that it was decorated, by patterns of usually blue or black and red in a white background, while the women's *ekibo* was plain white.

17. *Omwiko*: Large wooden cooking spoon.

18. Visitors were served food alone, with another person eating with them only to keep them company, only during the one meal of welcoming them, after which they took their meals with the rest of host family, according to their gender, since Wakerewe men and women ate separately, except in the very rare cases of the man who lived all alone with his wife, in which case the couple ate together.

19. *Olunanga*:   See note 16 of Chapter I.

20. To eat relish, whether meat or fish or vegetables, without the dish it was supposed to accompany was *kumira endiro*, "to gobble relish", considered gluttonous, especially in an adult male, hence the special invitation by Lweganwa to his visiting brother-in-law to eat a bit of that "men's" fish alone, without eating *obwita* with it.

21. *Ebitutu* or *ebibabi*: See note 11 of Chapter II.

22. *Enkanda*: Cow-skin which has been treated and turned into very soft material for wear or a quilt made from pieces of such cow-skins. *Enkanda* is also the name of a women dance, sometimes called *lwakalera*, performed at weddings, in which women drum on rolls of rawhide and play maracas to the tune of traditional wedding songs.

23. *Enerere or obunerere:* Bracelets and anklets of very fine iron or brass wire worn in bundles by women on legs and arms as ornaments.

24. *Isingiro*: Block of wood which was kept by the bedside for people to clean their feet on before going to bed, since Wakerewe normally walked barefooted so that their feet always needed such dusting before they went to bed.

25. Among the Wakerewe a woman lies on the man's right-hand side when he is lying on his back, so that when they face each other lying on their sides the man's left arm would encircle her waist and the right arm of the women would encircle his waist in what is called *kufumbatana*, "intimate embracing", the position in which they make love.

26. Names of the different kinds of greens.

27. *Ekitala*:   See note 18 of Chapter I.

28. Among the Wakerewe the term "cousin" implies very distant blood relationship, so that,   within the extended family,   cousins, paternal and maternal alike, up to   several degrees removed are regarded as real brothers and sisters.

29. Brothers-in-law have a joking relationship with their sisters-in-law and greet each other by such conventional formulas of mock gallantry, on which some improvisations may be added, as part of that joking relationship, which also applies to in-laws and their peers-in-law of the same sex, though to a less extent and without the mock gallantry. See note 11 of Chapter I.

30. *Ekizanda*: See note 20 of Chapter II.

31. *Olugega*: See note 19 of Chapter V.

32. *Enembe*: Medium size scaleless oily fish, very soft and delicious when cooked.

33. Courtship among the Wakerewe, as we see in the novel when Myombekere courts a maid for his son Ntulanalwo, involves the bridegroom's parents, in addition to obtaining the consent of the bride's parents, wooing the consent of all the maternal and paternal relatives of the bride her father and mother choose to recognize.

Chapter VII

MYOMBEKERE BREWS BANANA BEER FOR APPEASING HIS WIFE'S PARENTS

The afternoon sun was beginning to descend in the sky when Myombekere arrived back home. The woman who was cooking for him, who was a niece of his, was on her way back home from watering the calves and on seeing her uncle she put down the water-calabashes she was carrying and went to relieve him of his spear and the things he had brought with him and took them into the house. The little boy Kagufwa quickly brought him a chair and put it under the shade of a tree and Myombekere sat down and the two greeted each other. Then his niece too came and knelt down and greeted her uncle, "Good day,[1] Sir! How was your day? How is Bugonoka, and your father-in-law, and your mother-in-law? Has your brother-in-law come back home from his seafaring task?"

"Good day! I am fine. Bugonoka is fine too, and she sends you her very warm greetings, and so do my father-in-law and mother-in-law. Yes, my brother-in-law is already back, but very recently, just a few days ago. What is new with you here?"

"There's nothing new, everything is fine. What about Bugonoka, are her parents still bent on retaining her?"

"They are still retaining her, except this time I have brought back a good word from them and here it is: It appears my father-in-law wants me to appease him with six pots of banana beer and the day I send the appeasement beer will be the day I will come back with my wife. The only problem is how to get bananas these days, especially given how difficult people with banana plantations have become! They no longer just help you out, without your giving them something in payment! In my desperation, I will may be try and see whether I can barter my big he-goat, the black one with a white head spot. For what else can I do?"

"I agree with you. That's not a bad idea, because your property is meant to serve you. As our elders said: `What saves the buffalo from brush fire is its thick hide,'  and again they said: `Women are the end of men's property.' And indeed, of what use is property to you as a man if you are not married? Who knows you? Aren't you good for nothing in spite of your property, however wealthy you may be? Spend it all, if you must, if doing so will give you a wife, make you build a home of your own and settle. That is the beautiful life for which everybody strives. Even if the Creator has not willed to bless you with children like other people, you will still enjoy your life with your wife in your home, where a relative of yours can visit you and have a drink of water, rather than remain without a wife this way, when you are an adult man."

And so the following day early in the morning Myombekere put his goat on a tether and went to hawk it for bananas. In the home where he made his first call, he found only the mistress of the home, with her husband away. He exchanged greetings with the woman, who offered him a seat, which he refused and said, "You offer me a seat as if I can sit down?"

"Why not?"

"I am a hawker: I am hawking this goat of mine in exchange for bananas. Is the master of the home present by any chance?"

"Yes and no. The home has a master but he is away from home. He went to the Mainland,[2] where he was called on an emergency. A messenger came and told him: `Your sister is fighting for her life. You may be lucky and find her still alive or you may not.' And he has been gone for two nights, this night will be his third night away from home. And we here, women alone in a home, are lost as to the course of action to take. Did he find his sister still breathing? Is she already dead? We have no way of finding out. However, even if you had found him at home, he wouldn't have been in position to produce enough bunches of banana to barter for a goat. No, because he harvested some a very short while ago and not enough time has passed for others to mature. May be you should try some other homes; since you too have something of value you cannot fail to find the barter you want."

Myombekere went from one home to another with his goat. Whenever he tagged it along on its tether for a long time and it got tired of walking and tried to lie down he would lift it and put it on his shoulders and walk on and when he too got tired of carrying it he would put it down and it would walk along again. He hawked his goat for a fairly long time, now running into empty homes, now into homes whose masters were present but unable to provide what he wanted, until he became really worried and said to himself: "What I am going to do if I fail to get the bananas I need, poor me! My father-in-law wants nothing but banana beer! Today I've had it!" Finally he came to a home where the master of the home was present together with many other people and he was offered a seat and declined it: "Thanks for the chair, but I am a hawker. I would like to barter this goat for bananas." When those present saw the goat in question, they all taunted the master of that home to buy it and said to him: "There is a goat, buy it, because you have the bananas and you shouldn't let go this chance to buy a goat as if you don't. What is more, this is a really fat goat, and with such a beautiful skin that if a wife of yours is dressed in a robe made of it she would look great indeed!"

The master of that home said, "Maybe Myombekere is just bluffing when in fact he is on his way to the home of his friend Nkwesi to ask him to rear the goat for him?" To which the owner of the goat replied, "No, I am not on my way to entrusting the goat to another person. I am indeed in need of bananas."

The owner of the bananas got up and went inside a house to fetch a billhook and, accompanied by Myombekere and the people present, led the way and they all went into his banana plantation. Once in the plantation, they first counted the banana bunches still on their stems and found more than sixty had matured enough for pressing into beer juice. Then they got to bargaining the amount of bananas to exchange for a goat, how many bunches of banana was the heifer of a goat worth and how many a mother goat, and what was the right number for an ordinary he-goat and for a steer. And when they had bargained to the end, the people who were witnessing the deal then said that Myombekere's goat should be exchanged for twenty bunches of bananas, because it was an excellent goat, and that they were appraising it that high because it was not only fat but had a beautiful skin as well. On hearing that the owner of the bananas gave his last offer of the bargain by saying: "That being the case, let me add some five more bunches for him, because I need the goat for the courtship of one of my brothers, our very last born, the one our mother was still carrying in her womb when our father died. He is the one on whose account I've been making courtship rounds everywhere in people's homes, and now his courtship has come to a head and we are about to take the bride-price to our in-laws. That's why I want to buy this goat." Myombekere was likewise satisfied. And so he was given the billhook and he cut down his bunches of bananas from the first to the last and the owner of the bananas took possession of his goat in exchange.

Before leaving that home Myombekere gathered his bunches of bananas in one heap, and then got on his way, straight to the home of that friend of his, Nkwesi, who lived in that neighborhood. He found his friend at home and they exchanged greetings. Myombekere then told his friend that his wife was still gone, living at her parents' home, where he had come from wooing her back the previous day, that his father-in-law had told him to give him six pots of banana beer in appeasement, and that he had come that way to look for bananas, that he had come with a goat which he was hawking for the bananas and that he had bartered the goat in Bituro's home for twenty-five bunches of bananas. Then he went on to plead his case to his friend, to ask for some more help from him: "And now look! Can some miserable twenty bunches of bananas alone yield six pots of beer!"

Nkwesi answered him: "If beer is all the parents of your wife asked from you, that shouldn't worry you, my brother, because I have a banana plantation. So, if that is what they want and nothing else, we will make the beer and you will take it to them and they will drink it." Myombekere found himself digging into the earth of the ground with the big toe of his foot out of joy on hearing what his friend said.

After a little while Nkwesi took him into his banana plantation to look for the bananas, and they found what they wanted, counted the bunches of bananas ready for harvesting and got twenty five. When they went around the declining part of the plantation, which the owner had already counted out and neglected, they found there an additional three. With that Nkwesi told Myombekere, "On the day you decide to harvest them, even if I am not at home, just cut them down, all those we were lucky to find. Myombekere sincerely thanked his friend and said, "This is great, my dear friend! You can't imagine what a great thing you have done for me. I can't imagine what can ever poison our great friendship, unless of course it is the proverbial sweet plug of tobacco concealed behind the ear our elders of yore spoke of, may be that!" Nkwesi laughed. Myombekere went on: "Did you say on the day I decide to harvest the bananas? That day for me is today, because even with the bunches I bought with the goat I cut the bananas down before I left that home to come here. I would like to cut all the bananas the same day so that they can all ripen together. As a matter of fact, I will bring those other bunches here as well and hole them all together for ripening here and nowhere else. This type of work is best done in a home where you are no stranger. Let me indeed go home and fetch my billhook."

Nkwesi said, "Stay where you are; I'll bring you a billhook. I would have called the women and told them to bring us one, but at this time of the day they are busy cooking; we shouldn't disturb them." Nkwesi went and fetched a billhook and the two friends cut down the bunches of bananas. Then they carried the bananas and put them beside a ripening pit.[3] Myombekere also brought near the pit a pile of green banana leaves, ready for covering the bananas with in the pit the following day. He had just finished doing that when the wives of Nkwesi sent for them to come and eat lunch.

In Nkwesi's home, after eating, Myombekere pleaded with Nkwesi's wives, the whole gang of four, together with the three boys of the home, to give him a hand in bringing his bananas from the distant home to their home and they agreed and said, "Our brother-in-law,[4] how can we refuse an invitation to eat! Get up and let's go. How many bunches are there, by the way?"

"Not many; it is a mere twenty-five."

"Only that! Can't you and your friend and these three children finish the job alone and leave us in peace?"

Myombekere answered back Nkwesi's wives by pleading with them, "Please, let's go! `Save me from my deep waters that I may be around to save you from your shallow ones.'"

And everybody got up. Nkwesi fetched two carrying poles and gave one to two of his three sons who were a bit grown up and counted his third son, who was still too young, on the side of the female carriers, took the other carrying pole for himself and Myombekere and they all left to fetch the bunches of bananas.

At the heap of bananas, they saw that all of them were bunches which needed a real man just to lift from the ground! And so they strained to carry them. For the four women and Nkwesi's youngest son, Myombekere and Nkwesi selected bunches of the size they could carry one each and the four women made head pads for themselves and for the little boy with strips of dry banana fiber and the five light carriers were given a hand by the others and placed their bunches onto their heads. Then the two big boys tied four bunches on their carrying pole and Myombekere and Nkwesi tied six on theirs and they all got on their way back. By the time they put down their loads by the ripening pit, they were all covered in quite a bit of sweat. When they counted what they had brought, they found that they had carried fifteen bunches in that one trip. And so they went back for the remaining ten. When they got back, the five light carriers took one bunch each, the two young men put on their shoulders their carrying pole with two bunches on it and Myombekere and Nkwesi carried three bunches on their shoulder pole and the whole pile of bananas was cleaned off the ground: *fu*! On putting down their load of bananas by the ripening pit this time the women joked with Myombekere by asking him, "Are there still some left for us to go back for?" To which Myombekere replied, "Where would I get them from, poor me!" When they counted what they had brought and what Nkwesi had given him, it was found he had altogether fifty-three bunches.

Myombekere jumped into the ripening pit and said, "Could someone bring me a small hoe and a washbasin?[5] I want to clean out this pit so that it will stay dry overnight. That way all I have to do when I come tomorrow in the afternoon is to warm it up with a bit of fire before enclosing in the bananas for ripening."

The boys brought him what he needed to do his work and he cleaned out the pit and finished. Then he got out and his hosts escorted him and he went back to his home.

The following day, after lunch, when he estimated that by the time he got to Nkwesi's it would be the right time for holing his bananas, he stood up, took his walking stick and got on his way. He got to Nkwesi's home at the time of the scorching overhead noon sun. His friend Nkwesi saw him coming and went to meet him when he was still at the gate of the household and relieved him of his walking stick. They got home and he welcomed him, gave him a seat and he sat down. Nkwesi called out to his wives in their houses and said, "Do you, by any chance, have one tiny sweet potato left to give to this visitor here?"

"That's what we too are asking ourselves, as a matter of fact," his wives answered.

Myombekere said, "I left after eating in my home too."

Nkwesi responded, "The visitor who didn't eat in your home to you hasn't eaten." In that very moment one of Nkwesi's wives, the usual succorer of the visitors of that home from hunger, who was also the master's favorite wife, brought water outside and gave it to Myombekere to wash his hands. Then his sister-in-law gave him a cup of drinking water and he rinsed his mouth. That wife of Nkwesi then brought him sweet potatoes which had been peeled before cooking, accompanied by *ekizanda*[6] of skimmed milk, after which his friends other three wives also brought him some food: this one some four bits of sweet potatoes, the other one some six, the other yet some two, until Myombekere, all alone, was surrounded by quite a collection of food and all he could do was pinch bits of it here and there, leaving the rest untouched. He then called his friend's wives to come and fetch their utensils and he washed his hands. After that he asked Nkwesi for some *ekilangi*[7] tobacco, and it was brought and given to him and he poured it down his nostrils and let it get into him and then blew it out. It was a solution of really fiery tobacco and it intoxicated him to the extent of making him ask for water to drink. It was not until that *ekilangi* wore out of him that he felt his body regain strength. Then, on looking up in the sky, he saw that the sun had reached the time for him to enclose his bananas in the ripening pit and he asked Nkwesi, "Don't you think it's now the right time of the afternoon to cover the bananas in the pit"?

"Yes indeed, this is the time."

The two men got up, took a billhook for cutting banana stems to put on top of the ripening pit, a hoe and embers and went into the banana plantation. Once at the pit, first they gathered dry grass and threw it inside the pit and then started a fire with the embers and threw it into the pit too and the dry grass in there caught fire and flamed. Whenever the flame in the pit was about to die down, Myombekere would throw in some more dry grass and it would light up again. Finally his companion told him, "That's enough. That much firing should do."

"It's all right, let me fire it properly, it was so full of water, otherwise there is danger of the bananas not ripening well."

"If your hand is bad at ripening bananas, then I should call one of my sons to come and do the holing for you. He has an excellent hand for the job. Even if he holes bananas which have just been freshly cut that very day, it is very rare indeed that you'd end up with half-ripe bananas."

Nkwesi went home to call that son of his to come and hole the bananas for his friend while Myombekere remained at the ripening pit scattering about the fire inside the pit so that it would die out quickly, trimming fiber from banana stems, and cutting green banana leaves with which to cover the banana stem logs on top of the pit after the fruits have been holed.

He was still thus preoccupied when the young man arrived and he and Myombekere got busy and began holing the bananas. The young man, from above, first stood banana leaves in the pit and lined the round wall of the pit with the leaves until he had covered it completely. Then he dropped into the pit, his clothes well tightened, ready for hard work and Myombekere from above passed him more banana leaves, this time the green ones as well as some dry ones, as the young man inside the pit directed him to do. When all the inside of the ripening pit had been completely covered with green and dry banana leaves, from bottom to top, Myombekere then passed the young man the bananas and the young man holing the fruits carefully arranged banana bunches in the pit as only his skillful hands knew how. As he was doing that, he told Myombekere, "When you came across bird nests in the rows of bananas on bunches, please remove them: the fruits don't look good when they ripen with bird nests in them." When they finished holing the bananas, Myombekere carefully covered the pit by folding green banana leaves on top of the bananas. Then the two men placed logs of banana stems across the pit opening, covered the logs with more green banana leaves and then covered everything with soil. That done, they lifted one side of the pit cover and stuffed in the opening dry banana leaves before replacing the cover. And after that the young man in charge of holing made a fire and lit the dry banana leaves leading to the fruits inside the hole, quickly grabbed some pieces of green banana leaves in his two hands and using the leaves as bellows vigorously worked on the fire until he was dripping with sweat.

When he judged enough smoke had circulated in the pit, he stopped, covered the fire with the green banana leaves he was using as bellows and extinguished it, got up, took a hole and quickly in turn covered the green leaves with soil to prevent smoke from escaping from the hole and causing the fruits to ripen poorly. That done, Myombekere brought a young shoot of a banana tuber and gave it to his friend Nkwesi's son and the young man crushed the shoot in his hands, passed the crushed shoot under both soles of his feet and then placed it on top of the ripening pit.[8] The three men then took everything they had brought with them and headed for Nkwesi's home.

Back in Nkwesi's home Myombekere asked for his walking stick at once and said good-bye to his friend's wives. Nkwesi escorted him, but hadn't gone far when he gave him his walking stick and said to him, "Here is your walking stick so that you can walk alone and hurry up, otherwise it would be night before you get home." Myombekere took his walking stick and parted with his friend and went back home.

The bananas stayed in the ripening pit the first night and the second night, and on the third day Nkwesi removed the pit cover.[9] On the forth day Myombekere came to cut grass[10] for use in the press and went back home. The following day, at cockcrow, he was up, loaded with an empty beer pot and some fermentation flour[11] for brewing the beer, because that was the fifth day since holing the fruits, hence the brewing day. By the time the men Nkwesi had asked to come and help Myombekere press his bananas arrived, Myombekere at the ripening pit had already single-handedly finished unholing the ripe bananas, had plucked fruits from their bunches and loaded them into the press dugout[12] and had began pressing the bananas mixed with grass and the fruits were already yielding juice. Shortly after the helping men arrived, Myombekere came out of the dugout, and its load of bananas he was working on was turned over. Then he went in again and worked on for just a little longer and came out once more and a press platform[13] was placed on top of the dugout and the six press-men stepped onto the platform and the heaping man, who was none other than Myombekere himself, went to work, putting a sizable mound of the mash of banana and grass from the dugout under the feet of each man on top of the platform and replenishing the heaps as soon as those they were trampling were pressed dry.

And so the men on the platform kept on pressing banana juice out of the piles of grass-and-banana pulp with their feet as the heaping man supplied them with yet some more of the mash. All his bunches of banana had ripened well, each and every one of them. Out of the lot, he had taken a single bunch and given it to his friend Nkwesi's family, the people who had helped him to carry the bananas. Those were the only people who tasted his ripe bananas fruits and not another single soul! He was equally stingy with his *ensanki*,[14] refusing to give any of it to whoever came to ask for some, so that only the press-men chewed a bit of the sweet mash and not a single other soul! Myombekere felt he had to be that strict with both his ripe bananas and *ensanki* because he was afraid of failing to produce enough banana juice for the pots of beer he had to send to his in-laws as their appeasement. It was for that reason also that he had decided to personally stamp into mash his own bananas as well as to be his own mash-heaping hand, thus cutting down the number of people entitled to some ripe bananas and *ensanki* for chewing, not to mention the beer itself, all of which would have contributed to his falling short, according to the calculation he had worked out in his mind.

The men had been working on the press for some time when they were invaded by bees. Myombekere ran to fetch fire from Nkwesi's home, came and started a fire on both sides of the press dugout and then put some wet remains of pressed *ensaki* on the fire. At once a cloud of smoke engulfed the legs of the press-men, from time to time rising and covering them completely, making them sniffle madly, not to mention their blowing of their noses, while the bees on their part remained undaunted in their quest for the sweetness they had come for and kept on swarming around their legs, so that the press-men were trampling some as they worked at the same time as the bees too continued to attack them.

At lunch time Nkwesi's wives brought food to the men at the banana press, which was sweet potatoes and cassava and several *ebizanda* of skimmed milk. The men got off press platform and sat down to eat. It was while they were eating that those press-men put to test Myombekere's generosity by telling him, "No, dear man, give us a taste of the banana juice! It is true we have milk, and we all know that nothing goes better with sweet potatoes than milk, that the two are like mother and daughter, but, all the same, we would like you to give us some banana juice to take with our food, because that juice too agrees greatly with sweet potatoes."

Myombekere pondered the matter over and said to himself: "Indeed, if I don't give these men some banana juice and I tell them to just make do with milk, to begin with I will disgrace myself. Secondly, I will give myself a bad name, so that one day or another should I be in need, should a bush fall on me, as the saying goes, nobody would come to my aid. So let me give them some, irrespective of what I feel about the matter, because, as our ancestors said: 'One who dies working dies eating.'" Having come to that conclusion, he got up and took a large empty calabash and drew the juice and gave the men the calabashful of banana juice, and again he dished out of the dugout another large calabashful and gave it to a son of Nkwesi to take to Nkwesi's wives and that day the wives of his friend too ate their lunch of sweet potatoes and cassava with banana juice.

After lunch the press-men told Myombekere to draw the juice and he did so and got out of the dugout six pots for that first fruit loading. The press-men said, "What a high yield of juice for your bananas! This is because they were all perfectly ripe and yet not overripe and because most of them were of the juicy type, and hence the high yield. Had they been mostly of the stuffy kind, we would have ended up with more suspension than juice." Myombekere replied with, "Let's wait and see."

As Myombekere was drawing juice all his press-men one after another went off into the bush to relieve themselves a bit after their heavy lunch, now that they were having a break to let food settle down, at the same time as those who used *ekilangi* took some and snuff users likewise indulged themselves. After the men had taken their tobacco and blown their noses, they climbed on the dugout platform again to press the second and last fruit loading. Again Myombekere was in charge of piling the mash of grass and banana pulp under the feet of the press-men. Just as the sun was beginning to descend in the sky, the men got off the press, their work on the second loading also done. That second loading was bigger than the first one and when Myombekere drew the juice he filled seven pots plus a rather large calabash, so that altogether he had thirteen pots and a big calabash.

He was overjoyed. Now all that was left was to hope that the juice would not spoil, that the beer would come out right, that it would not fail to ferment or yield bad beer by taking too long to ferment. On seeing the yield of their labor, the press-men exclaimed: "Well, well! So, if you really want beer you simply can't afford to be too generous with your ripe bananas and your *ensanki* mesh, because there won't be much juice left for the beer! That is the truth we have just witnessed!"

Then the men got hold of the pots of banana juice and carried them one after the other to Nkwesi's home and poured the juice into the fermentation dugout[15] in the house of Nkwesi's favorite wife, poured in all the pots to the very last one, and then put fermentation flour into the juice and completed their work and went to the lake to bathe and from there went back to their homes.

As soon as his helpers left, Myombekere covered the fermentation dugout with green banana leaves, then took the pots outside and put them behind the house in the open to dry. The fermentation dugout in question was of *omuzungute* tree, famous for yielding good beer, in addition to which it was a well-used one, usually quicker at getting results, and so it did not take a round before the juice began to ferment. In fact as soon as the press-men poured into it the thirteen pots of juice plus the one calabash and added fermentation flour to the juice, those present immediately saw the juice foam throughout the dugout and on seeing that Myombekere decided to pass the night in his friend's home, because he did not want to leave to Nkwesi alone the demanding work of drawing beer or to go to the trouble of traveling from his home back to Nkwesi's in the middle of the night to draw the beer before starting on yet another journey to go and inform his in-laws that he had already procured the required beer. And so he said to himself, "Let me sleep here so that, should the beer ferment during the night, we can draw it first and then I can go to my father-in-law knowing for sure I already have his beer."

Myombekere and his friend took dinner and then went to bed. When Nkwesi woke up from sleep for the first time the entire house was already smelling of nothing but banana beer! He felt he should wake up Myombekere and called him, "Myombekere! Myombekere! Myombekere!"

"Yes, Sir!"

"I think you should wake up so that we can take a look at this beer. What a beer smell! Could it be ready by any chance?"

The two men woke up, made a fire, and saw that the beer was foaming and had begun to overflow the dugout. Nkwesi poked a straw into the beer and tasted it and said, "We should sleep on a just little longer before we wake up again to draw the beer, because it is virtually ready." They went to bed again for a little while and at about cockcrow, just before the cock went, they woke up to find the entire house now smelling of nothing but really strong banana beer! They made a fire again and Nkwesi tasted the beer the second time, this time by drawing it in a tiny calabash and drinking it. When he took the calabash from his mouth, he told his friend, "*Aa!* my friend, today what you have here is beer to barter for a cow, really!" and passed Myombekere the calabash and he too drank some, after which he said, "You are right! Yes, it is brewed. Fully brewed."

Myombekere went out to call Nkwesi's sons from their bachelors' hut to come and give him and their father a hand. On his way back he went to fetch a pot from where he had kept the pots, from where he also brought filter grass for use in the funnel to remove fermentation flour and keep its residue from muddying beer in the pots. In the meanwhile Nkwesi's sons woke up and came into the house where the beer was brewing. Once in the house, the boys, still sleepy, went straight and huddled by the fire at the hearth, and on seeing them their father spoke to them sharply: "Look at these useless creatures! Did we call you here to came and warm yourselves at the fire? Go and fetch the beer pots for us quickly, so that we can draw this beer!" The boys went outside and brought the pots and came to attend to work and their father began drawing beer from the fermentation dugout. As soon as he filled a pot, one of his sons carried the pot and put it on a stand, one of the round holes which had been dug in the earthen floor of the hearth, and in that very instant another son of his brought him another pot. His third son was in charge of drawing excess beer from the pots being filled and putting it into one other pot so that beer wouldn't overflow and spill onto the ground as it frothed. Myombekere on his part was charged with holding the torch and lighting the hearth so that the others could see and do their work well and with giving the beer drawer fresh filter grass whenever the grass he was using became too thick with the residue of fermentation millet to filter well.

When the drawer filled ten pots, Myombekere woke up his friend's wives so that they could come and chew some *obukanza*,[16] and the women came and their husband put some banana beer in a bowl and put some more in a large calabash and gave it to them and they drank the beer. The drawer too served himself some, and likewise the owner, Myombekere, who said to the drawer, "Give me some too, and let me too witness what a great beer this *omuzungute* dugout has brewed, because a hunter who kills a prey is expected to have stains of the animal's blood on him." To which his sisters-in-law, the wives of his friend Nkwesi, responded: "Yes, indeed! For all we know, those to whom you are taking the beer may not even give you your wife, so that if you give them your beer without even tasting any of it you would be a double loser. He should give you some indeed!" Nkwesi too agreed with them: "What you say is right. What is more, those who will drink the beer tomorrow when it is ready for drinking will reward you with nothing but insults by saying: "*Aa! Hee!* The dog who pressed this banana fruit into beer knows how to brew real beer!" And Myombekere consented, "That's right!"

After that Nkwesi resumed drawing beer from the dugout and filling pots. He managed to fill only two more before he was done. When they counted all the pots, they found they had twelve pots of beer plus a big calabash, the thirteenth pot of banana juice having been lost in the millet residue. Seeing that Nkwesi told Myombekere, "This is the usual problem with banana beer! If you hadn't been here and we had drawn the beer in your absence you could have said, `They have swindled me of one pot,' since we had thirteen pots of banana juice in the dugout." Myombekere agreed with him and said, "It is just as you say. I can't deny it."

Before long all present heard the cockcrow, a single lead-cock bursting out, at which they said to the cock, "You found us awake, don't brag you woke us up!" Myombekere's sisters-in-law attacked him: "What do you say now! A short while ago we were telling you that it is already dawn and you were saying no. Do you hear that now?"

Myombekere replied, "I must admit you really can tell the night!" He then asked the women to give him a calabash in which to carry some *obukanza* for his niece and the boy at his home and they brought him one. He gave the calabash to Nkwesi and Nkwesi began filling it with the residue of the beer left in the dugout. Before the calabash was full, Myombekere's sisters-in-law were noisily remonstrating with him, "Tell him to stop. Don't take out all the liquid and leave us nothing but dry residue as if we were some monitor lizards. Don't forget we are the ones who helped you carry the bananas when that niece of yours was nowhere near here, so how can we count for less? Aren't we human beings like her? How can you then leave us nothing but dry residue?"

Myombekere told Nkwesi, "Please pour back into the dugout what you already have in the calabash and stir everything thoroughly so that the millet flour remains and the beer residue are well mixed before you draw again some for me with your wives seeing everything. As a matter of fact you should give way and let me give them the cup so that they themselves can do the drawing. To say the truth, we were both about to go wrong on that score, because matters of *obukanza* are usually women business." With that Nkwesi's favorite wife, who happened to be a woman overflowing with energy, quickly took the cup and her husband made way for her and she took the calabash they had brought for Myombekere and filled it full with *obukanza* and gave it to Myombekere.

Myombekere got up and said good-bye to everybody and added: "Let me go by my home and give my people there this *obukanza* before I take my message to the parents of my wife. If it were not for taking this *obukanza* home first and fetching my brother-in-law's basket in which I carried some hippopotamus meat he gave me, I wouldn't have passed that way; I would have gone to my in-laws directly from here."

Hearing that his sisters-in-laws told him, "*Aa!* You should pass by your home and find out how your people have passed the night, lest you leave them sick without knowing it," and added, "This can only mean that our brother-in-law is now hurting very badly from the pain of being without his wife, that's why he is in such a hurry."

That sixth night since the holing of the bananas ushered in the day of foaming beer,[17] the one day the beer is left frothing in the pots before it is fully ripe.

On arriving at the gate of his home on the morning of that day of the frothing of his beer, Myombekere called the people of his home and they awoke and Kagufwa came and opened the gate for him. Once in the house, he gave them the calabash of *obukanza* and then fetched his brother-in-law's basket and his herder's hat, in case it rained, and then gave Kagufwa instructions: "I would like you to go and see so-and-so and so-and-so on my behalf and tell them that I would like them to come here early in the afternoon, or thereabouts. And when they come, if I am not yet back, give them seats and tell them to wait for me, because I too intend to come back quickly. As soon as I get to where I am going, I will just inform my wife's parents that tomorrow I will bring them their beer and then come back. Even if they invite me to stay for lunch I won't accept; not at all. And so you will tell them to wait for me, do you understand?"

The child said, "Yes."

Myombekere took his spear and put it on his shoulder, put his *enkanga*[18] on his head, took his brother-in-law's basket and headed for the home of his parents-in-law. At the second cockcrow he was already in the area of the home where he went to take shelter on the day it rained on him while on that same journey and as the morning sun appeared in the sky he made it to the gate of the home of his wife's parents. The gate of the home was still closed and his wife Bugonoka was churning milk in her parents' house. When he got to the gate he called out, "People of this home!" The woman churning milk cocked her ears. He called again, "People of this home! Please let me in." Bugonoka recognized her husband's voice and quickly went to open the gate for him. He entered his in-laws' home and his wife relieved him of his weapon. Then, on looking at his head, she laughed and said, "How is it that today you have come wearing your herder's hat?" Myombekere answered, "Yes, I had to wear it because I was apprehensive of the cloudy sky, thinking that this time too it would pour on me like the other day." Bugonoka slowly escorted him home, took him inside her parents' house and gave him a seat.

Myombekere on looking around him saw a lot of women sleeping all over the floor, which was spread with grass as if in a wedding celebration. He was left wondering and saying to himself, "It appears people are celebrating a wedding here!" but he let that be. He first directed his voice towards the sleeping room and greeting his father-in-law, "Good-morning, father-in-law!" His father-in-law answered him back: "Good-morning, son." He sent over another greeting, to his mother-in-law: "Did you pass a good-night, mother-in-law?" and his mother-in-law greeted him back: "We slept well, son," and they all exchanged news of each other and finished.

After that Bugonoka too exchanged greetings with her husband and went on to ask him, "When did you leave your home to arrive here so early in the morning?"

"I left at cockcrow."

The other women sleeping in the house were also now uncovering their heads, some of them to see how Bugonoka's husband looked like, because there were among them those who had never seen him. Then Bugonoka told her husband, "Do you know that in the sleeping room there are, in addition to my parents, three other mothers of mine, aren't you going to greet them?"

Myombekere addressed greetings to each one of those in-laws of his, one after the other: "Did you pass a good-night, mother-in-law?" and the three of them too answered by turns his greeting: "We slept well, son. Are you all well in your home?" and he answered: "We are all well."

At that point his sister-in-law, the one whose name was Barongo, who happened to be a very cheerful person, jumped out of the sleeping room where she too was sleeping and said with a lot of laughter, "Do I hear in that outer room a person with a voice like that of my brother-in-law, Bugonoka's husband? *Uu!* I must be up, believe me, lest other women take my place under his chin before me!" The other women in the house laughed and said, "Barongo with her jokes! She is simply impossible!" Then the intractable Barongo came, with coquettish capers, and, without further ado, really sat under her brother-in-law's chin, right in between Myombekere's legs, raised to him her open hands with palms together and then greeted him: "Greetings, my brother-in-law! Greetings, my dear one! Greetings to you, the heart of my world!" and Myombekere answered her, "Greetings, my darling! Greetings to you the foundation of my household! Greetings you, the roof of my house!" And after that a whole line of Myombekere's sisters-in-law in the house streamed forward to come and exchange with him their greetings of endearments, that is all Bugonoka's female relatives in the house who called her "grandmother, aunt, child-of-my-mother and child-of-my father."[19]

When they were all done, Bugonoka told her husband, "Do you know that there are also five paternal aunts of mine in the house? Please, greet them."

Myombekere addressed to the women their male elders' greetings:[20] "Good-morning, my father-in-law", to each one of the five of them, and they too greeted him back one at a time: "Good-morning, son. How are you all in your home, son-in-law?" to which Myombekere answered, "We are well."

Only then did Myombekere finally say to his wife: "I must admit I am puzzled by what I see."

"Why?"

"Because of seeing so many people in the house. So I want to know, is someone sick or what?"

"Oh, I see! Your brother-in-law Lweganwa is already married. Today is the day for taking the bride to her parents' home for the bridal homecoming and tomorrow morning she will be taken there again for their newlyweds' breathing relief".[21]

"I see! So that's it! I should have known. *Aa! yee!* at last you have laid to rest my worries."

Myombekere then left the house to go and greet his brother-in-law in his house. He had hardly emerged from his father-in-law's house when he run into Lweganwa himself, who in turn had just left his house to come and bid good-morning his father. The two brothers-in-law went back together to Lweganwa's house,   greeted each other and exchanged news of their respective places courteously and properly. Lweganwa asked his brother-in-law, "Did you, by any chance, pass the night somewhere, midway on your journey? For, if you came from your home, how could you have covered all that distance and be here this early in the morning?"

"I didn't start off from mid-journey, I indeed started from my very home, only I left at first cockcrow, so that when I heard the second cockcrow I had already reached that place where I took shelter from rain the other day."

"That first cockcrow, the one at which you started your journey, was a false one, made by a cock deceived by this full moon into believing it was the approach of dawn."

"Yes, that may be. But whatever it was, that was the time when I got on my way, brother-in-law."

In the other house, as soon as Myombekere's many sisters-in-law finished greeting him, they got busy taking water pots and calabashes to go to the lake to draw water while Bugonoka remained behind and busied herself with cooking for the newlyweds and her husband.

Myombekere chatted on with Lweganwa, of this and that, waiting for the time when his father-in-law would leave his house and sit outside so that he could tell him of his errand.

While that was going on, back from the lake came the water-drawers carrying their water in pots freely balancing on their heads, in addition to which some of them carried under their armpits calabashes of all kinds and shapes[22] full of water, the skillful womenfolk at work!

On hearing that noisy chatter of the women returning from the lake Namwero left the house and came outside with a chair and sat in the sweet morning sun, and seeing that Myombekere too joined his father-in-law outside, sat down close by and kept quiet for a while, as befits a man seeking audience with his parents-in-law. Only after a while did he broach to his father-in-law the purpose of his trip: "My father-in-law, I am here to let you know that I have found what you sent me to procure for you. Today is the frothing day and tomorrow the ripening[23] day. And so I said to myself: `Let me go and inform him, so that he won't be taken by surprise on seeing loaded people invade his home without notice and say: Why didn't they inform me?'"

"If you have already found what we sent you to bring us, that's very good indeed. Bring it tomorrow morning, let's say not too early but before noon. We will be here. What is more, it will have come when there is no shortage of people to drink it. Don't you see how full of people this home is?"

"Yes, indeed! I can see you really have many visitors!"

In no time they heard Bugonoka calling Lweganwa and telling him to take his brother-in-law into his house to go and eat. In that same house Lweganwa's bride, her food-tasting maid[24] and her numerous sisters-in-law were served their own meal apart by the hearth of the house as Lweganwa and Myombekere ate theirs separately, which was *obwita*[25] with, as relish, *enembe*,[26] a potful of nothing but the really sweet *enembe* fish and only the big ones, plus a potful of the meat of the cow which had been slaughtered for the bride. While they were eating, Myombekere asked Lweganwa, "You really prepared yourself well for your wedding celebrations, my brother-in-law! Where did you get such fish, every single one of them so fat, within such a short time. Look at this! Where can one find this kind of *enembe*, each single one of them so overflowing with fat, as if the fisherman who caught them was picking only what he liked from the sea!"

"The succorer and last resort of the poor man is always the sea. When Mugasa[27] decides to smile on you, you get a catch enough to get you thorough your needs of the moment. As to this fish here, it was I who went to sea for about two days and Mugasa gave me and hence the catch. To say the truth it was the fish I caught which fought and won the battle of my wedding feast in this home."

After eating Lweganwa asked Myombekere, "Did you, by the way, bring my basket with you, brother-in-law?"

"Yes, I did. It was taken by your sister. She relieved me of it alongside my weapon when she opened the gate for me."

Shortly after that Myombekere got up and said, "I must be going back home." His hosts brought out his traveler's things, escorted him, and he went back to his home.

Back home Myombekere found the people he had sent the boy of his home to call already arrived, and already served lunch. They greeted each other and he told them why he had called them, that he wanted them to help him fetch banana beer from Nkwesi's home and to help him take the appeasement beer to the parents of his wife. All the men accepted and said, "We will gladly help you in this errand of restoring the foundation of your home, for you are doing the right thing. And when do we go?"

Myombekere said, "After we have fetched the beer we should all pass the night here together so that we can begin on the journey at cockcrow, because my father-in-law told me: `Bring it in the morning, even if it is kind of late in the morning, we will be waiting for you.'"

Myombekere's niece, that is the woman who had come to cook for him, was about to serve him food but he refused and said, "Today I don't seem to have my appetite with me; not at all. What's more, over there at my wife's parents' they cooked and I ate with my brother-in-law, and it was food of a really great feast, because he has just got married and they slaughtered for the bride a huge bull, and so there is some real feasting over there. Should your pleasure be fish, should you fancy meat, everything is there in plenty. Maybe that's why I am still full of up to now."

"Ever heard of food from one village crossing the borders of another village still in a person's stomach! *Aa!* Maybe you should just say: 'I simply don't feel like eating,'" those present told him.

Without further ado Myombekere, accompanied by his companions, seven of them, himself the eighth and Kagufwa the ninth, got on their way to Nkwesi's to fetch the pots of his banana beer, but not before he told his niece: "We are going, and may come back a bit late. Please look after the cattle. When the herder on duty for the neighborhood brings cattle from the pastures, go and meet our cows at the common pasture ground in time, lest they stray into people's crops and put us in trouble, because we are taking Kagufwa with us so that he too can help us carry whatever he is capable of."

And his niece replied: "Yes, Sir!"

While on their way, before they got to where Myombekere's banana beer was, since the mouths of many people together are never short of something to say, the men began saying things, as if siding with Myombekere in his plea to the parents of his wife for her return. They spoke of how parents marry off their daughters and take their son-in-laws' property as bride-price for nothing, with their daughters not staying any length of time in their husbands' homes, since you would, say today, hear people say such-and-such a man has married and before you know it, after just a few days, before even a year is out, you would hear people saying again: "The wife of such-and-such a man is not staying with her husband any longer, she went back to her parents' home," with that at times being the beginning of their divorce, with no clue as to what the man did wrong to cause the divorce. And then, should the husband go to his wife's parents in the hope of wooing back his wife, he would find that over there his father-in-law and mother-in-law were told by their daughter things which enraged them, when in truth they were mere fabrications of hers, a mere ruse for her to desert her husband. Never does it occur to her parents to say, for example, "This child of ours may be accusing her husband of things he never said, we can see that!" They accept without question and as the only truth whatever their daughter tells them. And even when their son-in-law goes to woo his wife back and states his case and it becomes obvious their daughter is the one to blame, they still will not take that into account. All they will do is to upbraid their son-in-law and say all sorts of bad things about him for having supposedly greatly wronged their child by insulting her. And should they decide to return his wife to him, they will not fail to discover some grievous fault he had committed, for which they will demand his appeasing them with banana beer or a goat or the like. Myombekere's companions went on to say that there are cases where only the father-in-law likes the son-in-law whereas to his mother-in-law and his brothers-in-law and sisters-in-law he is an enemy, which is what happens all too often in this country and that's why people's marriages are always so full of problems.

When they neared Nkwesi's home, they fell silent. The sun was just about to disappear behind the horizon as they entered the home. Myombekere called aloud Nkwesi, who answered and came out of the house in which he was. On coming out he in turn called out to his wives to bring seats for the visitors and his wives did so and the visitors sat down, and they all exchanged greetings and news of each other. That over, Myombekere got up, followed by Nkwesi, and the two friends disappeared into the house where the banana beer was and thereafter all their companions outside could hear was some murmuring in muted voices, without a single pot of beer being brought out. Finally those outside became impatient and called out: "Myombekere! Myombekere! Here the men are becoming impatient, they want to go home, night is falling!"

Myombekere answered them and said, "We too are about finished, give us just a moment," before adding, "Why don't you come and join us and give us your views?" The men outside got up and they too went into the house, where they were overwhelmed by a strong banana beer smell as soon as they reached the door. They found Myombekere and Nkwesi debating with each other the number of beer pots which were to remain in that home for distribution to those entitled to shares of the beer, namely, the men who pressed the beer, one pot, the village headman,[28] one pot, and one pot for Myombekere's friend Nkwesi and his wives and relatives to drink the following day. And so the men who pressed beer, who too were present, chose one large-size pot and strained and carried it to the bachelor hut of the young men of the home, came back and took away a second one, equally large, that one being for Nkwesi. Since all the pots were very large, they hesitated when it came to choosing the third pot, the one for the village headman's customary present, from among the remaining pots and Myombekere told Nkwesi, "My friend, if I bring that empty one we left outside, wouldn't that do for the village headman?" When the pot was brought, Nkwesi and the rest of the men agreed with Myombekere and said, "This is a fit present. Only an impossible headman wouldn't be satisfied with such a sizable pot of beer, especially when the present is from somebody who bought the bananas, a person who has no banana plantation of his own." And so the men took one of the huge pots and filled the smaller pot from it, with a lot of beer remaining at the bottom of the larger one. Myombekere then brought a bowl and poured into it that remaining beer for the men who had come to help him carry the beer to drink and managed to get from it two and a half bowlfuls for them. On drinking the beer the men discovered that it was no longer frothing, was already beer fit to drink, no longer the foamy liquid which causes people to belch through the nose but already tasting right like ripe beer.

Myombekere's companions had just finished drinking the beer when the village headman, accompanied by a royal prince,[29] arrived into Nkwesi's home: *bwaa!* [30] The visitors called, "People of this home! If the beer is ready give us some to drink."

Myombekere was reduced to scratching non-existing rashes in his head! He simply could not see how he could manage to take out of the remaining pots another pot, the fourth, to give the royal prince in the home, nor how he could contrive to pour beer from one of those large pots into a smaller one for him. That's why all he could do was to tell Nkwesi, "Could you please sit our visitors outside so that we could give them their entitlement to drink." In no time he saw people who were following in the wake of village headman and the royal prince flood the home of his friend! Once that crowd of people were properly seated outside, the village headman was presented with his share, the small pot which had been filled for him and then the prince was given his present, one of the large pots. Only then did Myombekere and his companions feel free to carry away their remaining eight pots of beer plus the one calabash and go away, leaving those in the home drinking the beer they had been forced to part with.

They arrived in Myombekere's home late in the evening, after the cows in his kraal had folded their knees and gone to rest. Myombekere went into his house and made in the earth of the house floor eight stands for the pots of beer they brought and came and told his companions to take the pots in the house by the hearth, where his niece held a torch for them to see as they did so, since it was already dark. The men finished their work and sat down to rest. A visiting elderly woman, old but still holding her own fairly well, came and greeted them one after the other until she had gone the entire round.[31] Myombekere exchanged news with her and inquired about her welfare at great length, because she was his grandmother, a sister of his father's mother, born of the same mother.

After dinner Myombekere spread on the floor beddings for the men

and they all passed the night in his home, ready for their early morning
journey.

Chapter VII

NOTES

1. Since Myombekere and his niece are seeing each other for the first time in the day, even though it late in the afternoon they greet each other by the morning greeting, and hence in the Kikerewe text the greeting she uses is the equivalent of "Good morning, Sir!" See note 11 of chapter I.

2. Mwibara or Mainland Ukerewe: The peninsula adjacent to Ukerewe island on the east and separated from it by a narrow canal called Lugezi (Ferry) was part of Ukerewe kingdom, the word *mwibara* being Kikerewe for "mainland." See Introduction on the parts of Ukerewe Kingdom.

3. *Embiso*: Ripening pit, a large round pit dug in the ground, usually inside a banana plantation, in which bananas are buried for ripening in preparation for pressing the ripe fruits for juice with which to make banana beer.

4. A friend of their husband is considered a brother of his.

5. *Olusabuzyo*: Here a wooden washbasin; and below a wooden container for drinking banana beer with. See note 12 of Chapter I.

6. *Ekizanda*: See note 20 of Chapter II.

7. *Ekilangi*: Solution of tobacco in water, which was taken for pleasure by adult Wakerewe, men and women alike, by the user pouring it up his or her nostrils and holding it in to take effect; also the name of the pipe-like calabash in which the solution was mixed and by which it was taken.

8. A rite for the bananas to ripen well and the ripe fruits to yield ample juice. The Wakerewe performed similar good luck rites for many of their important undertakings, especially those involving an element of risk or chance.

9. *Kufundurira*: "To uncover" the ripening hole enclosing the bananas for airing the fruits so that they would fully ripen.

10. *Kutemela*: To cut the *enfunzi* grass, a fine soft grass, or its equivalent, for use in pressing juice from ripe banana fruits in the press dugout. From the verb *kutemela* "to cut (grass) for".

11. *Embetezyo*: "Fermentation flour", usually the course flour of partially germinated *endwero* millet.

12. *Izungiro*: Dugout for pressing ripe bananas to get banana juice for brewing beer.

13. *Olutara*: Platform, in this particular case a rollable one made of very strong pieces of wood which is put over the press dugout and on which heaps of ripe bananas which have been mashed together with *enfunzi* grass are put for the press men to work on with their feet so that banana juice drips back into the dugout, from which more and more mash is taken until finally there is only banana juice left in the canoe-like container.

14. *Ensanki*: Mash of ripe banana and *enfunzi* grass saturated with banana juice.

15. *Embeterero*: "Fermentation vessel", which in the case of banana beer is another dugout like the *izungiro* above.

16. *Obukanza*: Fermentation flour saturated with sweetish banana beer good for chewing.

17. *Omubiro*: Banana beer on the foaming or frothing day, the day following the one on which banana juice is pressed and fermentation flour added to it or the day before the beer is ripe and ready for drinking, so that, as we see in the novel, "frothing beer" itself is already good (strong) enough for drinking.

18. *Enkanga*: Large conical hat made of strips of dry banana stem fiber worn mostly by herders as a protection against rain and the scorching sun.

19. See note 11 of Chapter I for the Kikerewe system of ranking people's relationships in general and within their extended families.

20. Among the Wakerewe the paternal aunt of man's wife is treated as if she were her brother, that is the man's father-in-law himself. See note 11 of Chapter 1.

21. "*Kwich'omwoyo*": "Breathing relief", one of the rituals of the wedding ceremony, in which, as we see in Chapter XXXIV, the newlyweds, with hardly any company, go to just chat and spend a day in the home of the parents of the bride.

22. *Emitaho, ebisusi*: See note 9 of Chapter 1 and note 20 of Chapter II.

23. *Ihira*: "The ripening day" of fermented beer, the day the beer was at its best for drinking and on which most of it was consumed (see *omubiro* above).

24. *Endumya*: The newlyweds' "food-tasting" maid, a woman, usually a young girl, chosen by the bride's parents from their very close relatives to be the officiant of the newlyweds' food-tasting rite of the wedding ceremonies, as we see in Chapter XXXIV.

25. *Obwita*: See note 14 of Chapter I.

26. *Enembe*: See note 32 of Chapter VI.

27. Mugasa: The deity of the waters.

28. *Omukungu*: See note 3 of Chapter III.

29. *Omuhinda*: A royal prince (or princess). In Kikerewe feudal society the brothers and sons of *omukama* (king) and his close paternal cousins were entitled to free treats from the public.

30. *Bwaa!*: See note 3 of Chapter IV.

31. The Wakerewe greeted one person at a time and it was considered very bad manners to greet people or exchange salutation news with them collectively. See note 11 of Chapter I.

Chapter VIII

MYOMBEKERE GOES TO APPEASE HIS WIFE'S PARENTS

At the first cockcrow, Myombekere and his companions woke up and immediately Myombekere went to the home of his neighbor Kanwaketa, who was among the men who helped him fetch his beer from Nkwesi's home, even though with him he had gone to sleep for the night in his own home next door. He had to go in person to Kanwaketa's home because he wanted his neighbor's daughter, an unmarried adult woman, together with Myombekere's own niece to accompany him on the appeasement trip so that he would have at least two women in his delegation. Kanwaketa's daughter joined the two friends and the three of them came back together to Myombekere's home. Myombekere then told his niece, "Bring that big calabash of beer outside; I want to put some of the beer in this *engunda*."[1] Myombekere's niece brought out of the house the big calabash of beer and Myombekere took the smaller beer calabash and filled it, leaving a good half of the larger one still full of beer. He then poured the remaining beer in a large calabash bowl which one day his wife Bugonoka made from her crop of gourds for use in her home as she said to herself, "Let me have this calabash bowl in the house, just in case I find some use for it. A poor person brings home nothing of value except whatever he or she chances to find, so even though the master of this home has no banana plantation one day he too may find somewhere a bit of banana beer and he could use the bowl to drink his beer. For, as our elders said, a cow-skin at home never lacks a sleeper in need of it." Then he called his carriers and they came outside and drank that beer together with his niece, Kanwaketa's unmarried daughter he had gone to fetch and the visiting elderly woman who arrived in his home the previous evening. Because that was the beer's ripening day, they all agreed it was really strong banana beer they were drinking.

After that the men carried out of the house seven pots of beer and the one *engunda*. The eighth pot, the largest of them all, Myombekere left at home, as the big one of the house for the demands of the owner's homestead. The six men, with Myombekere as the seventh, each placed a pot on his head. The two women were to help each other carry *engunda* of beer, the so-called *engunda* of fermentation flour residue.[2] In a presentation of beer to a person's parents-in-law in Ukerewe, there has to be *engunda* or some other small size container full of beer, called the mother-in-law's *obukanza*. When they all had their pots of beer on their heads, Myombekere took the lead and they started on their journey in that middle of the night.

At first they walked slowly and haltingly, because it was still dark, that night the first cockcrow, already gone by, having preceded the moon, which did not come out until they had walked for quite a while, and only then could they walk without difficulty. It was also then that the men began to feel the effect of the beer they had drank, for quite a lot of beer had remained in the big calabash after taking out *engunda*. Among them there was a certain man, whose name was Nakutuga, who walked with a limp, by tilts and jolts, because one of his legs was lame in the hip as a result of the polio disease he suffered in his early childhood. Before the moon came out, when he saw that his companions too were walking in bumps and jumps that way, he had said, "*He!* If today normal people have been reduced to walking the way you do, what will become of us the one-legged Nakatugas? Won't we leave behind broken pots before we reach our destination?" and that had made his companions, the other men as well as the two women, burst out laughing: *kwekwekwe!* And on his part the man had added, "You may not believe me, but we won't know all is well until we arrive at our destination, I am telling you!"

They had been walking for a fairly long time when they heard cocks from everywhere burst out crowing ceaselessly. Before long, it was the night sky of men's pre-dawn, and from there it turned into women's pre-dawn sky. After a while the *amabundazi* birds cried with their thick voices: *huu! huu!* and following that before long the travelers could see the white of their palms. In that very instant they heard the bird *kaseko* burst out whistling: *chalala! chalalalala!* leading the way for all the army of birds to join in and twitter, and *isenamunonza* of the sweet voice too sang, and so did the heavy and slow *engulye* sing its praises to Kalyoba[3] with *chumpuli! chumpuli chwe!*[4] From there on they began meeting other early risers, those on courtship errands, or some other trips of theirs, like going to sea for angling *enembe*, and the like. When they got in the vicinity of the village of Myombekere's in-laws, some of the men said, "We should take a rest here." Myombekere answered them, "No, try and hold on a little longer until we get to that river ahead of us, so that we can rest there while taking a bath in the river," and everybody agreed with his suggestion and said, "That's right; because taking a bath will refresh us a bit, so resting where we can also bathe is the right thing to do indeed."

They finally got to the river and put down their pots of beer and placed on top of pot covers their carrying pads.[5] Apparently some of the men had concealed inside those head cushions of theirs straws and now each one of them pierced the cover of his pot with a straw and fell on the beer. After a while Myombekere stopped them and said, "Stop, gentlemen, lest you reduce the pots to mere half-fulls and when we arrive at our in-laws our present is refused and we lose on every side, end up with nothing to show for all the trouble of making the beer. " The men took the straws out of the pots of beer and cast them away into the bush.

When they wanted to bathe, the men separated from the women, the men going to bathe at an upstream ford and the women at a down stream one. The men had just come out of the river and were still waiting for water on their bodies to dry a bit before putting on their clothes when they heard the two women cry out loudly from their side of the river: "*Wo!* Help us! Save us from a python!"

The men ran to them, holding their robes in their hands and putting them on only when they got near. They got to the women and asked them, "What has befallen you, to make you raise such an alarm?"

The women pointed with their fingers and said, "Don't you see that mountain of a python heaped in the water?"

The men looked and they too saw in the water a huge python, bigger than any anyone among them had ever see. Each and everyone of them exclaimed and said, "This can't be a python, may be it is a different kind of snake! Would it perhaps be the boa constrictor we hear about?"

Myombekere's niece, when she finally stopped trembling with fear, told the men what had happened: "As soon as we got here, we plunged into the water and bathed. And it was only at the end, when my companion had come out of the water and I was the only one left in the river, when all of a sudden I perceived those reeds over there shaking. On turning to look that way, I saw something gliding by, and when I took a better look I saw it was a python about to catch me with its coils! And that's when I cried out for help. What's more, I simply somehow found myself out of the water and it is my companion who gave me my clothes to put on while I was shaking all over with fear. I simply have no idea of how I got out of the river!"

Myombekere and his companions said: "This has to be expected! This river is too bushy. A place like this is bound to be a hiding place for all sorts of dangerous creatures!" They however realized that it was something they could not attack, since killing a python is such a strong taboo, and so everybody left the place and they all went back to their pots of beer.

It was now the sweet morning sun in which people enjoy to bask, the sun which feels really good on the body, the time of the day at which, if you are an elderly person blessed with children, you can't resist calling one of them and saying to the child: "Come, little dad!", if it is a boy, or "Come, little-grandma!", if it is a girl, "and scratch and open for me my itchy rashes." Those among the men who had never been to the home of the parents of Myombekere's wife then asked Myombekere, "Where exactly is the home where we are taking our present? Are we about to arrive?" "I can say we are getting close, but we still have some distance to cover. When we have gone past that hill, then we will be able to see and make out fairly clearly *amakukuru* [6] trees on the horizon; the cactus trees are in the very home of my parents-in-law."

With that the men took up their pots of beer again, this time placing them on their shoulders and not on their heads women-like as they had done so far, and the two women too took their *engunda* and Myombekere led the way and they resumed their journey. Nakutuga told them again, "What do you say now? Didn't I tell you, gentlemen, that we are like people at sea and can thank the heavens only when we have arrived back safely and you wouldn't listen! Is it not true now that Myombekere's niece here was about to lose her life on the journey? Had she been caught in the coils of a python as huge as that one and in the water at that, would she have survived?"

"Those are true words you are saying, good Nakutuga. What could have saved her in that water? It is simply terrible to imagine! That would have been sure death for her, that's all."

As they got very close to the home of Myombekere's in-laws, they were spotted by a child who could not restrain his tongue and so ran as fast as he could and reported to Namwero how he had seen people, men and women, carrying very many pots of beer. Before long, Myombekere's in-laws saw the visitors in question arrive. On seeing them the men who had gathered in the home, Nanwero's guests who had been invited to come and drink the banana beer, all got up to receive the visitors and relieve them of their weapons as well as of the pots of beer. The women in the home on their part busied themselves with finding chairs for the visitors, some of them having to run and get some from the nearby homes of the neighborhood, since it would not have been possible to get enough chairs from that home alone for all their visitors of that day, the invited ones and those who had trailed invited guests and many others who had just gate-crashed.

Myombekere and his companions were given seats and greeted their hosts, and then Myombekere told his companions, "Get up, please, let's go and greet my father-in-law." They got up and went to greet Nanwero, who they found seated in the shade of a grain store[7] with a group of men busy at *obusoro*[8] game they were playing. After exchanging greetings with him, Myombekere and his friends went to greet Myombekere's mother-in-law, who was inside her house in the company of their female guests. Then they came back in the shade of a tree where chairs had been placed for them and sat down.

Myombekere's companion soon began asking each other questions, in twos, in threes, all wanting to know the same thing, until in the end they put the question to Myombekere himself: "*Aa!* How is it that we are seated here in the midst of a mystery? Where is our wife Bugonoka?" To which Myombekere answered, "Maybe she slept at the home of his brother's parents-in-law, where yesterday she escorted her brother and his bride on their homecoming ceremony, and where today the newlyweds went back to breathe relief.[9] Maybe with her when she got there yesterday she never come back, she got married off to some other fellow over there, for all we know?" His companions could not help bursting out laughing. But immediately they felt they had to suppress their mirth and changed the subject and turned to asking each other for some *ekilangi*[10] tobacco and snuff, for those who used them, so as to avoid being frivolous and unduly hilarious in another person's home like children, who are forever up to one mischief or another and laughing for no reason at all sorts of foolishness.

Shortly after that they heard Namwero calling aloud his wife in the house and asking her, "Has Bugonoka not come back in that house?"

"No, she hasn't."

"What about Barongo?"

"She too isn't here; she accompanied Bugonoka where you sent her."

"What has taken them so long when where they went is so close? Get up, you Kasaka, and ran to call them. And, mark you, I am now spitting, and if this spittle is dry before you come back you are the one whom I will beat even more severely than those two!"

The young girl, who lived in the home, shot off, and since her legs were not yet encumbered with *enerere*,[11] those who saw her flash by could not believe their eyes! In no time she was back with the two women. When they came back, Namwero at once loudly reprimanded them: "What were you still doing there, to take so long?"

Bugonoka answered and told him, "The man you sent us to see was away from home when we got there; he had gone to the lake to fish his *olubigo*.[12] It was when he came back that we gave him your message and he fetched the roof-prop of his grain store and opened the store and took out for me what you sent me for. He was still wrapping it for us in banana fiber when Kasaka came and told us, `Grandfather is calling you, we must go back quickly. What's more, some visitors have also arrived at home.'  After wrapping for us the rock[13] salt,  he gave us this piece of *emamba*[14] and said, `Here, take him some fish and let someone put it on the fire for him,' and we left."

Her father thanked the man in his absence and said, "He has done well, the gentleman, to give me a bit of `*they-cook-grudgingly*'."[15] Everybody present laughed.

Bugonoka took the salt and the fish to her mother in the house and then came outside to greet her husband and the men who had helped him bring the appeasement beer. Then she went to her husband's niece and the unmarried woman she came with, carried their seats and took the two women inside the house.

Namwero got up and left *olusoro* game and called his wife and daughter and took them aside, somewhere behind the house, so that they could secretly confer with each other on how to treat the visitors who had helped their in-law to bring the appeasement beer. When they got to their chosen spot, they stopped and Namwero asked his wife, "By the way, how many pots of beer did they bring?"

"So you did not count the pots! How many had you told him to bring?"

"I told him to bring six pots."

"If I didn't count wrongly, I saw seven pots plus one *engunda*."

His daughter too joined in and said, "On my part I counted the people: they are six men, with my husband as the seventh, and two women, and no doubt it was the women who carried by turns *engunda* of beer my mother has mentioned."

"That is why I have called you here, so that we could agree on the relish with which we will serve food to our in-laws. If it weren't for them I would say we have enough relish in the home for any number of visitors, but, even if we could manage to serve them too with the relish we have, it still would not do for properly recognizing our son-in-law and his friends who have accompanied him here to appease us. In my view, it would be more appropriate if I made them a present of a goat, the big brown-and-white one. Wouldn't you say that would be a fitting present for visitors like these?"

"That would be a fitting present indeed."

"So get things going quickly, so that they can have something to eat. As for you Bugonoka, I want you to know you are going back to your home today. Your husband won't leave you here; you will go back together. Even if Lweganwa is late in coming back from his newlywed's breathing relief ceremony, you will not wait for him, you will just go, because he is already married, which is the important thing, all the rest is secondary. That's all. I have no more to say."

"On our part there is nothing which needs much preparation, since there is plenty of flour as well as cow meat, which is already cooked. Maybe you are the one who has to get things going quickly, have people slaughter quickly the goat you have given our visitors, that's all. As to flour Bugonoka needs to take with her to her home, we have plenty of that too."

After conferring thus with his wife and daughter, at once Namwero called out to the men who were at *olusoro* game: "Can three of you come here, or even four, that would be fine too." The men came and he told them to go and untether his big brown he-goat with white spots and long hair and take it and present it to his son-in-law before slaughtering it. In no time a certain man of muscular built who was among those who came had brought the goat, which he then took to where Myombekere and his companions were seated and said to them: "Welcome, sons-in-law; here is your relish with which your father-in-law would like to recognize you."

Myombekere and his companion answered the man back and said: "For us all that matters is our wife. We are, however, greatly honored by what our father-in-law has done for us. We thank him with great respect."

The man then took the goat away from Namwero's son-in-law and his companions. In that very instant the goat stopped crying: he had strangled it by the mouth, quickly twisted its neck backwards and given it a kick in the stomach, so that by the time he got it to the place of slaughter it was already dead and gone, with no sign of life left in it, and when his companions also got there nothing was left for them to do except to open the goat's skin at the abdomen and skin the carcass at once. The men skinned the goat and disemboweled it and took out the entrails. They were about to eat raw meat when Namwero got to them in time and said, "Gentlemen, don't finish the liver and the stomach eating raw meat, because this is relish we have presented to our son-in-law and his friends. I also hope with the skin too you cut it open nicely, the Kikerewe way of skinning a goat, because our son-in-law will take the skin with him to his home as a mark of our appreciation of his appeasement, so that he can proudly tell people, `When I went to appease the parents of my wife Bugonoka, my father-in-law presented me with a goat, whose skin is this one you see here.'"

The men who slaughtered the goat answered him back: "Here are the liver and the stomachs, we too haven't touched a thing by way of eating raw meat; nothing. As to the skin, here it is too; we cut it open nicely and skillfully." Namwero looked at the skin and found it was indeed nicely cut at the belly and even the decorative incisions they had put in it were very beautifully done and he thanked them. Only then did he allow them to slice off bits of the liver and the big stomach and they sliced off some, just sufficient for a taste of raw meat, since with the Wakerewe men it is said raw meat is worth a man dying for, and ate the raw meat after seasoning it with drops of the animal's bile.

Namwero then directed the men to roast one entire slab of ribs for his sons-in-law and at once the meat was rushed onto the fire in the cooking stones which had been erected outside. The man who was roasting meat called Bugonoka and asked her to bring him a plate on which to serve the visitors and salt to rub into the meat and Bugonoka did so. Namwero then told the men who had slaughtering the goat to cut into small pieces the rest of the meat and cook it all, with the sole exception of one leg, which he directed to be wrapped together with the animal's skin his son-in-law would be taking back home with him. So, apart from that, the meat of the whole goat, even the intestines, the stomachs, the pancreas, and the like, were to be washed and then each and everything put into one and the same pot and cooked.

The meat ready, the man in charge put the whole slab on a plate and took it to the visitors as it was, without even slicing it into smaller pieces, leaving it to the visitors themselves to cut up the meat and share it out, and put salt for the meat on the plate and went and placed the plate in front of the visitors and then went into the house to fetch a cup of water and, on his way back, picked up an washbasin,[16] brought it to them and they washed their hands. Then he left them eating and went back to attend to the cooking pot of meat. He had however not got back to the pot when the visiting sons-in-law called him and said, "Come back, please!" He went back and they cut off a piece of rib meat for him and he went away tearing at it with his teeth.

Myombekere and his companions ate roast goat meat and finished and put aside the plate and the knife they used to cut the meat and the things were taken away. As soon as   meat being cooked boiled and rock salt Bugonoka brought was put into the meat, before turning it over in the pot, the men cooking outside called aloud the women in the house and told them to put on the fire pots for preparing *obwita*.[17] The women put on the fire several cooking pots, others doing so inside Lweganwa's house as well, yet others going all the way to the neighborhood homes to cook from there.

Namwero sent Kasaka, who was a little granddaughter of his, on errand for the second time, to go and call the man who had given him a piece of *emamba*. The young girl, who was by nature swift-footed, shot off and got to the man and told him: "Grandfather has sent me to you, to tell you that we should go back together now, and that's all." The man in turn queried her: "Did the visitors you mentioned here the first time you came by any chance bring you presents of beer?" Kasaka laughed, her neck turned aside so that her eyes were on the wall of the house and not on the man, before saying, "Please let's go, lest they reprimand me and say, `Why have you taken so long?' Grandfather is the one who knows why he wants you; I don't." The man got up and the two of them came together to Namwero's home, where they found *obwita* cooks about to dish out the first round of cooking.

Shortly after that the women put on the fire pots for the second round of cooking *obwita* and in no time everything was ready and the food dished out, at the same time as the women who had gone to nearby homes to cook too had returned with food. Then some energetic men got busy and brought to the visiting in-laws water and food, so that those guests from afar could eat and start back before it got late.

The serving men lifted dishes of *obwita* and placed them in front of the in-laws, accompanying that with two pots of relish which had come from inside Namwero's house. Of the two relish pots one was the son-in-law's special relish and so it was placed in between Myombekere's legs. It was a pot of sweet *emamba* of the best type seasoned with butter. The second pot of relish was of minced dried beef. It was after that that the serving men strained and carried the big pot of goat meat and placed that too in the middle of the meal circle the visiting in-laws had formed, together with many large plates for serving meat. From among the men serving the guests food a designated person invited the in-laws to eat as required by Kikerewe etiquette: "Our sons-in-law, this is all we could afford!" and all the visiting in-laws responded to him at the same time and said: "For us all that matters is our wife, dear father-in-law."

The feast in front of the visitors was not of this world, it was beyond description! Those who saw it to this day are still talking about it and exclaiming in wonder!

Once left alone, the visiting in-laws selected Nakutuga to serve them, and he got up. First he placed into the hands of each one of his companions a large piece of goat meat and then served the relish from the two other relish pots, those which were cooked inside the house, by just putting everything on the serving plates for everyone to choose whatever he preferred.

In no time the men could eat no more and tried their best to force themselves on but to no avail! They left *obwita* almost untouched and didn't do much to the meat either. Maybe the only thing they ate and put away to some extent was the son-in-law's special relish, the one prepared in honor of Myombekere himself, but nothing else. In the end they had to admit to themselves their ineffectiveness and say: "How strange indeed! What a senseless thing the human stomach is! Before we ate we were so hungry we were saying to ourselves: `Today when we get something to eat we are going to eat until we burst,' and now in no time we are completely finished!  Think of that!  That's why our ancestors said: `The only great stomach is a woman's, which bears a child you can send on an errand.' That's indeed the only sensible one. Otherwise the stomach is an ingrate. You can fill it to bursting, as we have just done, and then after a mere short while it could even tempt you to steal something much bigger than it could possibly take! All the stomach knows is to cause people trouble, with never a word of thanks!"

When the visiting sons-in-law finished eating, Namwero got up and disappeared into his house, where he said to Bugonoka, "Take the seats of the two women who came with our son-in-law and let them join their companions outside."

Bugonoka did so and took the women to where her husband was seated. Once the two women were seated and settled, Namwero called some two men, who came and joined him in his house, where he showed them two pots of banana beer and told them, "You, please take this pot here to the seating of our in-laws over there and, you, take that other pot to our own seating over there and give it to the men to drink. As for you the women left in this house, take that *engunda* and drink the beer; that should be enough for you while we are still waiting for the newlyweds to return from breathing-relief at the home of the bride's parents. Even if they don't return until evening, we can wait, provided we have given people something to drink and released those who come from far to return to their homes. Wouldn't you say that's the right thing to do?"

His wife as well as the other women in the house agreed and said with one voice, "Yes, that's the right thing to do and released people from afar when it is still broad daylight like this."

The man who served beer to Myombekere and his companions was again Nakutuga, he was the one who was selected by his companions to draw beer from the pot and pass it around. That gentleman, even though he walked with a limp that way, was quick and good at whatever he did. After removing the cover from the pot of beer, Nakutuga first drew out of the pot a "poison-tasting share"[18] and gave it to Bugonoka to take to her mother. Bugonoka took the beer to her mother in the house and knelt down and gave it to her. Her mother told her, "Take a sip before giving me," and Bugonoka did so and then passed her the beer and said, "Here is your *poison* beer, it is being offered you by your sons-in-law." Her mother drank a bit of the beer before passing it to the other women, who drank it until it was finished and passed the empty bowl back to Bugonoka and she went back to join her companions at her husband's seating, because that's where her place too was.

Nakutuga received the bowl from Bugonoka and first poured into it beer for The-hand-that-feeds-me, that is the son-in-law Myombekere himself. He filled it full to the brim and got hold of it and handed it to him. Myombekere, before receiving the beer, folded tight his robe lest he stains it, should he spill any of the banana beer, you know how it is! and then took a really long draught, with eyes staring into the drink. He drank all the way to the middle of the bowl and then passed the remaining to his wife and Bugonoka received it. She too drank until she breathed out to catch breath and then passed the beer to the two visiting women, her companions with whom she was now sitting.

On seeing Myombekere pass his share of the beer to his wife that way his male companions said: "*Oo!* So that's it! A wife is simply someone too dear to a man! Imagine Myombekere sharing his beer with his wife, who is seated so far away from where he is, instead of sharing it with us seated here next to him! *Aa!* Yes indeed, Bugonoka, your husband really loves you! Very much so! You are the only one who wants to spoil your love for each other by remaining in your parents' home, when on his part it is obvious he loves you very much indeed!" All present burst out laughing.

Bugonoka on her part asked the men, "What about you the other men who are here, are you not married men? And don't you love your wives? If it is true that you and your wives don't love each other as you seem to say, why are you still married to them?"

The men responded: "*Aa!* What a thing to say! We are married men and we love our wives very much indeed, for they are the ones who cook for us something to eat, and the ones with whom we share whatever they cook for us. But when they desert us and go to live with their parents for ages the way you have done, then we no longer love them that much, because every man marries a wife to live with, so that she can take good care of his stomach. That is how it was ordained."

Bugonoka replied: "I see! So when your wives go to their parents' home, with a good reason for doing so, you stop loving them! Finally today you men have come out in the open and told us what you are all about!"

The men in turn retorted: "No, not when there is good reason. But what did our ancestors say? Didn't they say a distant dog never saves a hunter?"

Bugonoka agreed and said, "That's true, that's what they said. But what can a woman do if she has no other resort?"

The men answered, "Even if you don't know what to do, you still should stay with your husband; for, even if you go back to your parents, how does that help you find a better husband? Even if you have been struck by some mysterious disease you still should stay with your husband and let him be the one to take you to medicine men and women, so that if it is an affliction meant to spare your life you will get cured still living with your husband."

And with that they dropped the subject and that conversation ended and they all turned to enjoying their pot of banana beer. Nakutuga served beer to their entire round, giving a bowlful of beer to each one of them, the three women included. Passers-by who heard the noisy murmurs of so many people in that home also began dropping in unnoticed, until the home was full of quite a crowd. As a result the two lonely pots of beer were soon empty, so that some of the gate-crashers were reduced by their craving for beer to shamelessly snatching beer from the mouths of those they found still with some and most of those who came last did not even taste a single drop of the beer, having found nothing but empty pots.

As soon as beer for the in-laws was finished, Bugonoka went into her parents' house and got busy putting together what she needed for her journey back to her home. Her mother on seeing her said, "*Hee!* Everybody come and witness this! Bugonoka today is walking with some really resounding steps! Oh, no! This bit of banana beer must be getting to her head, because I have certainly never seen her walk with such a cheerful gait before! It appears this bit of beer our son-in-law has brought us knows how to get into a person!" The other women in the house said, "That's true. This is excellent banana beer, the kind to buy a cow with, in earnest!"

Bugonoka called her mother, who was sitting near the door with the other women, and her mother went to her in the inner-room where she was and asked her, "What do you want, dear?"

"I need flour to return to my home with, and a bit of meat. Aren't you going to give me a bit of meat? Where am I supposed to pick greens for cooking as soon as I get back to my home?"

Her mother called her husband and when he came she told him, "Give your daughter some meat so that she can go back to her home. It is time to start back, so that her husband's companions can get to their homes before night falls. What do you say?"

"Where did I put my sword-knife, I wonder! The truth is I haven't touched it at all since morning. Even with the people who slaughtered the goat for our son-in-law, we gave them some other knives but not the sword-knife. Has anyone seen it somewhere by any chance?"

"I saw you putting it on top of that *ekitwaro*[19] box, if I remember correctly. Let me look," his wife said. On looking she found it and brought it to her husband.

Namwero went to the platform where meat was being dried over fire and asked, "And where is Bugonoka herself?"

"*Uu!* Namwero, are you drunk!" his wife exclaimed.

"That's possible yes, since it wasn't water I was drinking but beer."

Mother and daughter laughed. The mother said to her husband, "I had to say that because you've just passed us, leaving me standing here with the child, you yourself seeing her with me, after which you asked for your sword-knife."

"Well, let her come this way with a tray then."

Bugonoka fetched a tray[20] and went to her father at the platform for drying meat and her father cut off for her a big chunk of meat from the beefy part of the leg of a cow and threw the piece on the tray: *pataa!* then took an entire slab of ribs and threw that too on the tray, and also got hold of the kidney and sliced off for her a good piece and put that too on the tray, before looking for the stomach and again cutting off a piece for her and throwing that meat too on the tray. And with that he finished and went back to sit outside.

Nkwanzi called Barongo and sent her to fetch her a green banana leaf from their banana plantation with which to wrap the top of a flour container, together with strips of banana fiber for wrapping the meat, and in no time Barongo was back and had put the green banana leaf over fire to singe it a bit so that it wouldn't tear easily before giving it to her mother Nkwanzi, her mother's sister. And since her mother was really good at packing tight flour in containers, she loaded into *ekitukuru*[21] basket flour which Bugonoka could not as much as lift from the ground unaided. As to the meat, they looked for some worn-out basked and tied the meat in it, after wrapping it in banana fiber.

That done and finished, Nkwanzi told Barongo to fetch her a few other things: "Bring here that calabash bowl and that butter pot, so that we can give her some butter for seasoning in her home the bit of meat she has been given by her father," and immediately Barongo brought the things her mother wanted, so quickly you would think she hadn't left to fetch them from anywhere. The calabash bowl which Barongo brought was so huge that after the pot of butter had been emptied into it there still remained room for more, and yet the pot had been full of butter to the brim. Nkwazi then reminded Bugonoka, "By the way, you should not forget your cow-skin and goat-skin robes; I perfumed them yesterday for you." Bugonoka fetched their *ekitwaro* and took out both her clothes. She then put aside the ordinary cow-skin robe she had on and put on her new very soft *enkanda*[22] her mother had perfumed for her and the entire house was at once invaded by the scent of *omugazu*.[23] Her mother then brought her daughter *enku*[24] and liquid butter and her daughter mixed the body perfume with oil and anointed herself. Bugonoka and her mother were still thus occupied when they heard Namwero call his wife aloud and say, "What is keeping you again in that house?"

"We too have finished, in fact. Bring out our sons-in-law's weapons, so that they can go home before night falls." In that very instant Bugonoka's mother was telling her daughter, "Take that large straw and sip some beer from this pot here."

"*Aa!* No, dear mother, I don't want to make a fool of myself on the way. That beer is for you here; you and my father will have something to drink with Lweganwa and his companions. I know when my brother comes back he will come thirsting for it. In fact, since your dear son loves his drink, I should say he'll arrive dying for it."

"Please don't remind me of that!"

People brought out the visiting in-laws' weapons. Before leaving to escort his visitors, Namwero sent away all that crowd of people who had flocked to his home, to the last one of them, those who had been drinking beer as well as those who found it all gone, to all of whom he said, "I want everybody out of my home. If you had come here for the banana beer, it is finished, there is none left, because it was some mere two little pots and one *engunda* which our son-in-law brought us for appeasement, and that was it. And so I am now leaving to escort my in-laws and the person I find here when I come back, unless he is the one who built this home for me, today he'll have to confront me in a battle of life and death!" With that people, who had all been noisily talking at the same time, fell dead silent and each one of them hastened to be the first person to leave until everybody was gone, right to the last person.

Namwero followed behind the departing crowd with Myombekere and his companions, whom he was escorting while carrying the skin of the goat he had slaughtered for them, in which he had wrapped the goat meat which had been put aside for his son-in-law. He escorted them until he came to a crossroads and then told his son-in-law, "Here are your weapons, son-in-law, I am now going back; I want to go to the lake and bathe a bit when it is still daylight. So here is your wife, I am giving her back to you. Go and live well with each other, without saying all sorts of bad things about each other again as you used to. Live in peace and harmony: childless women get married too; and even if your wife was not destined to have children, she is still your wife and you should continue to live with her in spite of that."

And so Myombekere said good-bye to his father-in-law: "Good-bye, Sir. Stay well, father-in-law," and his father-in-law replied: "Good-bye, son," after which Myombekere's companions followed suit and they too said good-bye to their companion's father-in-law and he likewise answered them back and they parted.

The departing men had to walk with restrained steps, so that Bugonoka and her companions, who were following behind at a snail-pace, could catch up with them. Bugonoka was still being counseled by her mother on the importance of being a good wife: "And now that you are going back to your home, my dear child, at once get hold of a hoe and cultivate your crop fields like a she-man. What is more, those sisters-in-law and brothers-in-law of yours who insulted you and called you barren, whenever they come to your home, if there is some relish in the house cook them *obwita* like your beloved visitors, because the Mkerewe elder once said: `You don't teach a bad dog a lesson by you yourself becoming a dog.'"

Before long Bugonoka's father got to where the women had reached and Bugonoka knelt down and said good-bye to him, "Good-bye, Sir, and may you pass a good night!" Her father answered, "Good-bye, my daughter. Have a safe journey." The two visiting women also knelt down and bid him good-bye and he too said good-bye to them. When the women got near to Myombekere and his companions, Nkwazi stopped and said good-bye to her daughter and her two companions. Then she heard the voice of her son-in-law saying good-bye to her from far: "Good-night, mother", with the voices of his companions likewise following suit. She answered them each: "Thank you, son. Have a safe journey."

Bugonoka's sisters, that is Barongo and the other family and clan sisters of theirs present, continued to escort their visitors for some more time, until they too finally said, "Good-bye! Here are your things, let us go back, we have escorted you far enough; we shouldn't delay you any further and make you arrive home in the dead of the night. Where the sun has already reached, it is all you can do to get to your place before sunset."

Myombekere said, "May be because we have women among us, the I-can't-walk-faster people, but otherwise, the sun still so high, if it were the journey of only us men we would have out-raced sunset. But since we have female fellow-travelers, for all we know, my sister-in-law, may be by the time we arrive it will already be the deep dark night in which you could kill a relative of yours without knowing it?

That said and done, Barongo, who was carrying *ekitukuru* of flour they had packed for her sister Bugonoka, approached Myombekere's niece and told her, "Here, take your things; you are on your own now!"

Myombekere's niece received *ekitukuru* of flour and her companions helped her put it on her head. She was still trying to properly position the head pad under the load on her head and her neck was still shaking this way and that way in search of balance when all of a sudden they saw that man they called Nakutuga sweep *ekitukuru* of flour from her head and place it on his before saying, "Could someone place a cushion on my head quickly, because this *ekitukuru* is grinding pebbles into my bold head, so that I can go home, in case you others are still enjoying your palaver."

On seeing that man, Nakutuga, shoot forth and snatched from that woman's head   the basket of flour that way, it was all Barongo and her female companions could do to keep from bursting out laughing. The man himself however took no notice of all that, did not stop or even look back, but forged right ahead at once and retraced the way which had brought them from home with *ekitukuru* of flour on his head, tilting and limping. He did not even bother to say good-bye to Myombekere's sisters-in-law!

When he got some distance away, Barongo and her companions asked, "Is the man naturally bad-tempered or is he a bit crazy, or has he perhaps been angered by something?"

Myombekere and his friends explained: "No, he is neither crazy nor a bad-tempered person, and neither has he been angered by anything, believe it or not. He is simply a jovial fellow who likes work and that was his way of telling us that we should be on our way at once and get back home when it is still daylight. That's all."

Barongo said good-bye to her sister Bugonoka: "Have a safe journey, dear sister, I too have only tomorrow night here, day-after-tomorrow I am off, to see how my husband is doing." Bugonoka answered her back: "Fine. And don't forget to greet my brother-in-law very lovingly for me when you get back home. And won't you be coming to visit me, and find out how I am doing, dear sister, and bring me some *kandoya*[25] sweet potatoes to eat? This year I am in danger of starving, you know, having been away from my crop fields for so long!"

Barongo replied, "I certainly will come, dear sister, if I can manage to find some time."   She then went to her brother-in-law Myombekere and put her hand on his shoulder and told him, "What do you have to say now, brother-in-law? The other day I told you: `Go and bring us the liquid of the banana plant quickly so that we can drink and forget our miseries,' after which I added, `Take it from me, the day you come with the yield of the banana fruit that is the very day you will leave with my sister!' So, what do you say? Haven't I won?"

Myombekere agreed, "You have indeed won our bet. You indeed foretold the truth. That's why our elders of yore gave us a riddle which says: `When a child day-dreams of a pumpkin at home people will have pumpkins for dinner!'"

Barongo kept on teasing her brother-in-law: "There she is, you are going with her today. Look how her skin is shining with lotion and how plump she is! Look how gracefully she moves in her soft robe of *enkanda* ! And then when you get home, since you men are such lunatics, you will begin beating my sister, with whatever you grab, including chairs, and shutting her inside the house! So you better take care! If I come to visit you and find you have been treating my sister like a dog, my brother-in-law, I will take her away from you and come away with her and let her marry some other man!"

"No, indeed, my sister-in-law, your doing so wouldn't be right. People staying together are bound to quarrel. You shouldn't take away from me my wife simply because I have quarreled with her, as if I were the only man in the world to do so, when quarreling is something we all do. Don't you and your husband, for example, ever quarrel?"

"Well, we quarrel. And that is precisely why I said the whole lot of you male creatures are lunatics. For, if you are not lunatics, how can you just get up and belabor with sticks a child of some of other people: *pupu! pupu!* as if she had done I don't know what to you!"

"Lack of sense in matters of men with women is never a one-sided thing, my sister-in-law: we are all insane. It is like real madness in the world. We are all mad people, except the vast majority of us are mad with our clothes on and only a few are raving mad and go about stark-naked."

"Well, have a safe journey, my brother-in-law."

Then all his other sisters-in-law said good-bye to Myombekere and gave Bugonoka her other clothes and the calabash of butter and the package of meat and they parted, the travelers to pursue their return journey and the others to go back home

After they parted with their escort, Myombekere's companions, among whom were some jocular young men, in addition to the fact that everyone had been drinking and they were all rather tipsy, began shouting cries of triumph, like people bringing home a bride from a wedding: "*Yahoo! hooyee!* We have come back with her; we didn't leave her behind, nooo!" And everybody would answer back in chorus: "*Hooyee! hooyee!* The bride's aglow with oil, *yee!*" And then they would concentrate on walking. Whenever they came to a place where there were homes in the neighborhood, the lead voice would start off that triumphant cry and his companions, the women included, would take up the chorus. Finally Myombekere too joined his friends in answering back that cry of joy, equally cheerfully, and they all continued accompanying their journey with ringing laughter.

As to Nakutuga, he never looked back since he put on his head *ekitukuru* of flour and was never to be caught up with. Whenever they saw someone in front and thought it was him, on getting near they found it was someone else. They walked until they had walked forever without ever catching a glimpse of him.

Shortly after that they met on the way Bugonoka's brother Lweganwa coming from the ceremony of breathing relief in the home of the parents of his bride, in the company of his new wife and their newlyweds' food-tasting maid.[26] They greeted each other, with Bugonoka playing with her sister-in-law a bit by lifting her bridal face-amulet and thereby uncovering her brow and enabling the men of Myombekere's party to have a clear look at her face, at which they all exclaimed, "Indeed, the man has married a real beauty!" Myombekere then asked Lweganwa, "Did you, by any chance, come across a friend of ours carrying *ekitukuru*?" "Yes, we left him taking a bath in that river yonder! Isn't he someone who walks as if he is limping a bit?" Myombekere and his friends answered, "He is the very man."

And so Myombekere and his companions hurried on, without slackening their pace again even once. When they reached the river, they found their man resting under the shade of *omugege* tree and told him, "What a way to treat your companions, Nakatuga, leaving us so far behind?"

"How have I treated you?"

"We thought maybe we had left you behind some place, having disappeared in the bushes to relieve yourself when we passed!" To which the man replied, "If you people are still deriving some pleasure in holding a palaver on the way, let me go ahead. Had you come with me, wouldn't we have got really far by now? I have been here waiting for you for a very long time. Look, I have taken a bath, done everything, and rested here until I was almost falling asleep. It was just now that I jumped out of my nap on hearing your cry of triumph and I was about to get up and resume walking when, on second thought, I said to myself, `No, wait for them, so that you can all travel together. Don't leave them behind.'"

His companions then asked him, "By the way, Nakutuga, aren't you afraid of that mountain of a python we saw in this river? How can you, this very same day, bathe in the same river, and all alone at that? You must indeed be a bold man, certainly not a man to play with!"

"Let's face it, has there really been no other people who have passed through this river since we forded it? In fact whenever we get scared we get scared for nothing, because the day the Almighty wills death for you whatever precautions you take you would only be deceiving yourself, they wouldn't bring you any extra moment of life," answered Nakutuga.

"Yes indeed! That's true; we can't say otherwise; no. What you say is how things are. However, our ancestors said: `The Creator protects you only when you too protect yourself.' If that is not the case, Nakutuga, why are you wearing this amulet?"

"I am wearing it to protect myself against the disease which made me walk limping the way I do. The medicine man who gave it to me, in case you are deaf and you want me to open your ears, gave it to me to ward off that disease, so that it would never attack me with the force with which it attacked me the first time."

"Well, there you are. Is that not protecting yourself? What greater self-protection can there be than that?" Everybody laughed.

After that the men told the three women to walk on ahead and they took off their clothes and plunged into the water of the river, as one of them said, "Yes, let's bathe a bit and wash off some of the heavy eating we had at Bugonoka parents', so that we can walk feeling a bit lighter." Another added, "Me, I even got stomachache as a result of that feasting. We were all happily shouting when on my part I was in really bad shape, but now look, plunging into this water has restored my well-being. When you eat because you have fallen on excellent food, the food goes into your stomach the wrong way and works havoc in you. As a matter of fact I am now feeling hungry again. If I were to get food now, I am ready to eat a good meal." Yet another man said, "Should I tell you why people never eat their fill of the good food they eat as visitors?"

"Please tell me, my friend."

"Unless I am the only one who feels that way, I would say it is because we eat while we are apprehensive of disgracing ourselves?"

"Disgracing ourselves how?"

"You want to tell me you don't know the disgrace I have in mind?"

"No, I don't."

"Come on, gentleman, don't be like a child. If, for example, you are a visitor somewhere and immediately after eating you say, `Gentlemen, I would like to go to the bushes to relieve myself', or if, before you know it, a little fart escapes you: *bwi* ! wouldn't that be disgracing yourself?"

His companions laughed and said, "That's it, indeed. That's what prevents most of us when we are guests from eating as much as we eat when in our own homes." And the man who had given that opinion said, "So you see now!"

After bathing in the river the men took their weapons and, as to their robes, since water hadn't dried off their bodies, they held them in their hands and took off running and put them on again only when they were about to catch up with their female companions. When they caught up with the women, some men relieved the women of *ekitukuru* of flour and the goat skin and meat and the men carried those presents they were given by Myombekere's parents-in-law and then their entire group tighten well and good the tendons of their feet and really walked.

It was at that very moment that Myombekere showed his wife the homes in which he took shelter the day it poured on him on his way to wooing her back. Bugonoka asked him, "Do you mean these homes very near here or which ones?"

Myombekere pointed them out by a finger "It is among those other homes, yonder, in the midst of those numerous *amakukuru* trees. Can you see that? Let your eyes follow my finger. Do you see now? That is the home of that great rain-maker."

Bugonoka finally saw the home and said, "I see! I see!"

Myombekere's companions asked him, "Who do you say lives in there, my dear man?" and Myombekere answered them back and said, "It is the home of a rain-maker. I am, to say the truth, the very person who was one day forced to go there to shelter myself from rain and, well, saw that which was not intended for my eyes. As a matter of fact it is a story which you can't retell without being called a liar. I, the person who chanced on where I shouldn't have been, am the one who will live all my days on earth with the memory of it all; never to forget it. But please let's leave this matter alone and talk of something else. Speed-up your walk, gentlemen, we are getting near. Since we are entering this thicket when the sun is still this high in the sky, we will get home when it is still daylight. Gentlemen, throw in clamors of triumph, let's hear you!" The lead voice started the chant of triumph which had been accompanying them on their journey and his companions took up the chorus.

When the sun was just about to disappear from the sky, at the time of the evening when the man who has brought home his cattle from the pastures is busy attending to his animals, and the women assisting the men milking cows are untethering calves of milk-cows and looking for soft tree leaves for wiping their milk containers with at the milk churn, our travelers stepped into Myombekere's home, still accompanied by their loud chant of victory.

Chapter VIII

NOTES

1.   *Engunda*:   See note 20 of Chapter II.

2.   *Obukanza*:   See note 16 of Chapter VII.

3.   Kalyoba or *Izoba*: The Sun, as a deity, also Providence. See note 21 of Chapter II.

4.   *Chumpuli chwe!*: Ideophones: *chumpuli* for "very early morning" and *chwe* for "clear daylight, the latter being partly based on the verb *kucha*, "to dawn". Here the expression is also onomatopoeic for the sound of the bird.

5.   *Engata*: See note 13 of Chapter I.

6.   *Amakukuru* (singular *ikukuru*): Cactus trees.

7.   *Ekitala*: See note 18 of Chapter I.

8.   *Obusoro*:   Board game on a holed playing-board (*olusoro*) with pebble for counters.

9.   *Kwich'omwoyo*: See note 21 of Chapter VII.

10.   *Ekilangi*: See note 7 of Chapter VII.

11.   *Enerere*:   See note 23 of Chapter VI.

12.   *Olubigo*: See note 3 of Chapter II .

13.   *Lunzebe*:   See note 17 of Chapter I.

14.   *Emamba*: See note 17 of Chapter II.

15.   *Namusyambakuma*: Men's nickname for *emamba* above, literally "they grind flour (for cooking a meal) grudgingly," because Wakerewe women who did the cooking did not eat the fish.

16.   *Olusabuzyo*: Here a wooden washbasin and below a wooden container for drinking banana beer with. See note 12 of Chapter I.

17.   *Obwita*: See note 14 of Chapter I.

18.   *Obulogo*: Poison; here the "poison-tasting" share of beer. See note 12 of Chapter III.

19.   *Ekitwaro:* Light cylindrical box made of the bark of a tree used, especially by women, for storing their articles of clothing, ornaments and other valuable possessions.

20.   *Olugali*:   See note 6 of Chapter I.

21.   *Ekitukuru*: See note 16 of Chapter V.

22.   *Enkanda:* See note 22 of Chapter VI.

23.   *Omugazu*: Incense from the barks of trees, one of which was *omugege*, used, among other things, by women to perfume their animal skin clothes.

24. *Enku:* Body perfume women wore by mixing with liquid or solid butter for anointing their bodies. In his note for his Swahili translation of his novel Kitereza writes: "*Enku* is made from buds in the roots of young papyruses, which are extracted and ground into powder. It is this powder which is mixed with solid or liquid butter to make the sweet-smelling ointment used by women".

25. *Kandoya:* Type of sweet potatoes.

26. *Endumya:* See note 24 of Chapter VII.

Chapter IX

BUGONOKA RETURNS TO HER HOME

In the homes of Myombekere's neighborhood children, women as well as men heard that great shout of joy coming into Myombekere's home and people poured out in all their numbers to witness Myombekere returning from his great adventure and found: *aa!* indeed, was that not Bugonoka? And so they asked, "Is what we are seeing Bugonoka or somebody else? For since when is Bugonoka so plump?"[1] And those who brought her from her parents' home said, "Indeed it is Bugonoka herself, in person. We should know, because we are the ones who wooed her back."

When Myombekere's neighbors had witnessed the scene to their satisfaction they went back to their homes, leaving in Myombekere's home only the people who had gone to fetch her.   Myombekere got busy and cut into pieces the meat they came with wrapped in the skin of the goat and gave it to the visiting old woman in his home to cook for them. The little boy Kagufwa shut the cows in the kraal, and when the gadflies disappeared with nightfall, he called the young woman of their home to bring him water so that he could milk cows and he milked the cows and finished. In the house the old woman boiled water in *obwita* [2] pot and then called Myombekere's niece and she came and made food and served the men. Since they were rather too many for the food, in no time they had already cleaned off everything and were licking their fingers. The young boy called the women in the house to come and take away the utensils and Bugonoka, who had declined to eat, brought the men water to wash their hands and took away the food utensils. All married women who had gone to their parents' homes never eat in their own homes the day they return, may be that's why they often come back in the evening, who knows?

After that the men settled down, while on his part Myombekere went to call Kanwaketa, the man who had given him his daughter to accompany his wooing delegation and to whom he had left the responsibility of keeping an eye on his banana beer in his house and on his home itself during his absence that day. He came back with both Kanwaketa and his wife, together with their two grown up sons, having left behind only Kanwaketa's mother, who was already too old to go places at night, and little children. Then he fetched logs of dry wood and piled them high on his courtyard fireplace[3] so that when they flamed they would turn dark night into moonlight. And when the fire was burning brightly to his satisfaction, he told two of the men present to follow him into his house, and into the house the men plunged. After a while, during which the expectant people outside heard nothing, out of the house the two men came, straining under the weight of a really huge pot of banana beer. On seeing that each and everyone of the men outside clapped his hands and uttered words of great thanks: "Your respects, Sir!" And immediately the mood became festive indeed, with all the laughter you can imagine, *aa! ee!* In no time a man had already jumped up and dug a round hole in the earth of the ground with the heel of his foot as he said, "Put it down here on this stand in the ground, gentlemen."

Myombekere called Kagufwa and gave him the duty of serving beer. The boy removed the cover from the pot and somebody handed him a beer drinking bowl Myombekere had brought from Kanwaketa's home and a small cup[4] for drawing beer with. Bugonoka told Myombekere's niece, "I think there is somewhere in the house a calabash bowl; please go and fetch it so that they can give us our `poison-testing' share." The young woman fetched it, rinsed it with water and handed it to the beer server and the boy poured in the bowl the women's "poison-testing" share and passed it to them. The women gave the beer first to the visiting old woman who had remained looking after the home that day and she sipped a bit of the banana beer and then passed it to the other women, who also sipped at it until everyone of them had a drink. Kagufwa continued serving beer until he completed the round of all the adult men present, giving to each his own bowl full to the brim. When he had served all the adult men, he dished out beer for his fellow young men present, one measure for every two of them, but this time without filling the bowl completely as he had been doing when serving adults, after which he was allowed to put in the bowl a rather small bit of beer for himself too. As the men paused a bit in their drinking, the women complained, "And so the `poison-testing' bit is all we'll get! Aren't we too going to have each our own measures?"

That jogged the memory of the men and they agreed with the women: "Indeed, what have we done? Please give each of them her own measure in their calabash bowl; let them too drink the beer, lest we forget the hand that feeds-us," and the boy served beer to each and every woman present, at the same time as Myombekere urged him to serve people generously: "Give people beer, child, and let them drink their fill. They should not drink their own saliva instead of beer as if they did not do a great job! Who would have helped me carry the beer to my parents-in-law had these kindly gentlemen refused? In fact, if I were a man of property, men like these deserve a real treat. As the Mkerewe ancestor said: `When you send another person's child into your millet store[5] expect him to chew a bit of your grain.' When you ask a person for help and that person helps you gladly, that is somebody you cannot thank enough."

The boy resumed serving the men, each one his measure, until he completed their round, and then served the women round again and again completed it.

At that moment, when everyone was still sober, people were nicely conversing with each other in an orderly manner, with only one person speaking at a time and the others listening, responding to what a person was saying only after he or she had finished whatever he or she was recounting, as they talked about the kingdom, the court of their sovereign *omukama,*[6] about their country as well as other countries, about rumors of what was going on in those other kingdoms, of men's adventures abroad, about the hunting of animals and how they are killed, about the killing of dangerous animals of the wild and safety measures to take, about marriages and love, about people's misfortunes, like famine and barrenness, about raising livestock and the other animals people keep, about gossip and people's behavior, and the like. Why go on? Who can tell all people talk about around a pot of banana beer? After that, and as the beer climbed to their heads, they became very noisy and disorderly, with two here carrying on a conversation of their own, three there another one, the young men over there with yet another conversation, the women too with one of their own.

When they reached that point and Myombekere realized that people were no longer talking sense, that others had begun going to urinate frequently as the night too was swiftly moving on and had already brought out of their lairs *ensimba*[7] and *amakara*[8] and all the creatures of the night, he said, addressing everybody, "Silence, please listen! Look here, ladies and gentlemen, this is beer, and all of us here are drinking and enjoying ourselves. However we are missing the boon companion of banana beer!"

"And who is this boon companion of banana beer?"

"*Enanga* music."[9]

"As a matter of fact we too were about to say the same thing, only, being visitors, we held back and said to ourselves, 'May be today Myombekere is not interested in that kind of thing!'"

"What could have happened to me that I wouldn't be interested in *enanga*? Has a relative of mine died? Even if I had lost a relative, today is a day of rejoicing, and, as you all know, beer makes the young as well as the old want to dance."

"Yes; somebody bring us the instrument quickly and let music remind us of all the good times we had forgotten."

Quickly Myombekere sent the sons of Kanwaketa to fetch the musical instrument from their home and in no time they were back with it, already tuned. Then Myombekere told his niece to bring a new cooking pot, one not yet stained with soot, in which to place *enanga* for resonance. The people who received the pot gave it to Myombekere, because he was very good at playing *enanga* tunes fit for adult company, was simply wonderful at the introductories and also had a really great singing voice and one which always blended well with whichever *enanga* tune he played: *dilira*! *dilira*! He began playing by singing an introductory about a childless woman who had lost her husband. He sang of how the childless widow mourned her departed husband, how she bewailed her lot at being left alone in the world by a husband with whom they loved each other so much, recounting how the women praised the beauty of her dead husband from the top of his head to the big toe on his foot.

His audience went dead silent, listening to the melody of the instrument and the pouring forth of his voice. And when his heart was really carried away with emotions, he zoomed to his instrument in a muted voice: *zuu*! *zuu*! as his fingers continued to make the strings of his instrument resound with music amidst complete silence from his audience as if there wasn't a single soul present! Then he lifted his voice a bit and began to sing of the misfortune which befell *Omukama* Lukonge and sang: "Misfortune is like destiny, Greatest-of-the-all-time-great,[10] I warned you you would be the cause of your own misfortune." On hearing that the women broke out in a peal of ululation:[11] "*Ililililili!*" And when Myombekere heard women's ululate he took up the song of the childless woman again and began to describe in earnest what befell her, how after her dead husband was buried the following day she cried aloud and wailed and wandered everywhere without knowing where she was going or what she was doing, how on the night before her dead husband was buried the woman was by his body the whole night, bewailing her lot alone, the poor woman, the childless woman, how for four days she mourned and wailed morning and evening wearing two mourning bands of the fiber of the black *entundu*[12] banana, one around her head and the second one around her waist, throwing herself this way and that way, all alone, with nobody to talk to as she used to talk to her husband, and how on the fifth day, the day of funeral bathing, instead of bathing she merely dipped her hands in the water of the lake searching for her husband in it and on not finding him there lifted the palms of her empty hands to the heavens in her misery, how the other female mourners told her, "Courage, dear sister, yours is the lot of us all: misfortunes befall human beings and not stones!"

When he came to where the childless widow cried, he was overwhelmed by compassion for the grieving widow and spoke on her behalf to the relatives of her late husband: "Come here, count and take back the property you paid for me as bride-price, for I am nothing but a barren woman, the useless female animal which the master slaughters for visitors while taking good care of the child-bearing cows! What kind of death will mine be, poor me? A person without a relative! A person better off dead and left without burial in the wilderness!" Then he raised his voice and called aloud his wife: "Bugonoka, where are you!" "Yes, Sir, my husband!" his wife answered and at once came forward and raised both her husband's hands in the air to congratulate him while ululating for him: "*Ililili!* Long live my husband!" To which Myombekere replied, "The same to you, my beloved, my fellow traveler, my inseparable life companion till death!"

That had been an introductory, and when Myombekere ended that piece he played the tune called *Amalende*, the tune about beautiful women, and sang the song of the tune and enumerated the beautiful women of this earth, all the women whose beauty is sung in *enanga* music, from the first to the last, and then made as if he wanted to put down his instrument and stop playing. On seeing that the men present insisted he played on and said, "Give him some more beer, so that he can keep on playing *enanga* for us; we want to dance. If he wants some snuff, that's fine too; because as long as this massive pot of banana beer is still upright in its stand in the ground, we have no intention of leaving and going anywhere else; not at all!"

The young boy of his home put in the drinking bowl some beer for him and he poured it down his throat and what remained in the container he passed to his wife Bugonoka and the daughter of his neighbor Kanwaketa and the visiting old woman of his home and the three women drank the beer and finished it.

Seeing that Kanwaketa's wife complained: "Poor me! Other women have husbands who share with them their measures of beer, but, dear sisters, what are the likes of me going to do?" She left to go and urinate and then came back. The other women laughed and seeing that she asked them, "You are laughing at me, have I shitted in my clothes?" and they answered her back and said, "*Aa*! we are just laughing at what you said before you left, that other women have husbands who share with them their bit of beer, we are not laughing at anything else. And why do you say that when your husband Kanwaketa is here? Can't he too share with you his measure like the husbands of those other women?" they asked her.

When that noisy dispute was dropped, the beer server gave a measure of beer to each and everyone present, but the first measure he drew out of the pot after serving Myombekere he gave to Kanwaketa, and when Kanwaketa too had drank until be breathed out like a watering cow he passed the beer remaining in the bowl to his wife as he told her: "Welcome, my darling, you the Foundation of my home, you the Roof of my house!" The women in the gathering laughed their fill.

Kanwaketa had every reason to call his wife the Foundation of his home, for he had two male children by that woman, his two sons who were drinking beer with him there, and he also had every reason for calling her the Roof of his house, because he also had with her female children, one of whom was drinking beer there with them, the one who had accompanied Myombekere to his wooing trip.

On receiving the beer Kanwaketa's wife thanked her husband and said, "Thank you very much, my husband. This makes me feel good!"

To which her fellow women added, "That's right! That Kanwaketa of yours wanted to eat like a lonely man and cheat you of your rights, as if you weren't here!"

That woman, the wife of Kanwketa, who happened to really like her banana beer, had given herself a name for her indulgence and she now told her female friends that her name was the name of some beer pots of this country and her friends asked her, "What are those names?" And she quipped, "Names of beer pots of this country." Her friends: "Very well, but their real names?" And she answered: "Those-who-never-pass-a-night-empty!"[13] And her friends laughed.

Then the beer server turned to the women round again, giving to each and every women her own measure of beer.

When people quieted down Myombekere asked: "Ladies and gentlemen, what song do you want me to play for you now, the one to which you would like to dance?" Some told him, "Any you choose for us. Play for us any you think is good to dance to and we'll dance," and yet others said, "Play Nakazenze[14] for us; that's the one we want." And so he was left to make his own decision and play whatever he liked. He had to retune his *enanga* first, because it was getting out of tune from being exposed to dew in the cold air of that late night. When he had it back in tune and keyed right for the song he had decided to play, he placed it back in the resonance pot, after warming the instrument over the bonfire he kept going to light up for their beer party. Then he told everybody: "Silence, please!" and everybody became quiet and he began with an introductory piece, which led him into the song he intended to play, a song called "Nakulinga." He began by humming and zooming to his instrument: "*zuu!*" and when the music got into him properly he raised his voice and sang and describe that man who was called Nakulinga: "Alas! Nakulinga, oh poor me! Alas! Nakulinga, oh poor me! The monster of Omururi[15] fellow, oh poor me! The monster of Omururi fellow! Brought here the awful white people, oh poor me! The awful white people from Europe, oh poor me! The awful white people who know no friendship, oh poor me! Whose friendship is the whip, on poor me!" The women broke out in prolonged ululation: *keye! keye! keye!.* The men could resist no longer and tightened their clothes and stepped into the arena to dance, two at a time, but not before telling their spectators: "Be good neighbors to our dance, clap for us, and we'll show you how papyruses dance in the flow of the river!" And people clapped for them all they wanted, in rhythm with the beats of the song which Myombekere was playing, and with that the sturdy fellows swayed and propelled their shoulders with real vigor, their guts pulled in until they were like *olukombwe*[16] weasel after it had vomited the ripe banana it had stolen. And the women's ululation rang on: *keye! keye!*

When the women saw the dancers became nothing but movement, when every part of their bodies was dancing to perfection, one after the other quietly dropped their hands to their haunches and took off some *enerere*[17] ornaments from their legs for giving to the dancers as prizes. The woman who wanted to give a prize to a dancer would get up from her place in the audience and make her way to the dance arena ululating and mimicking the dancers as if she too wanted to join in, all joy and laughter, and on reaching them she would break into an endless peel of ululation and sweep the ground with dance movements, moving around and in between the dancers any number of times she liked before breaking off her ululation and withdrawing.

The first couple of male dancers danced their fill and left the arena, and, on regaining their places in the gathering, immediately asked the beer server for a drink: "Young man, give us some beer, we need a drink, we danced so much that all we had drank is gone from our stomach." The boy gave them one bowl of beer full to the brim and told them, "Here it is, please share," and they received the beer and drank. Seeing that each and every person in the gathering too turned to the young man with only one thing to say to him, the same "give me some," and he obliged, took up his little cup and again served them all, including the women, and without forgetting Myombekere, their *enanga* player.

As soon as the first two male dancers left the dance arena, the women fell on the three young men present, the two sons of Kanwaketa and the boy in Myombekere's home, the one who was serving beer, and taunted them to dance by telling them: "You young men too get up and dance and show us what you're worth!" The young men got up and took position in the arena, feigning staggering as if they could not keep on their feet. On seeing that the adult males present could not help jeering at them: "*Wowoo!* Apparently beer has already rendered these poor weaklings incapable of even keeping their clothes on! They are gone past hope! Are they really still capable of dancing?" To which the little males replied, "All we want is for Myombekere to play Nakazenze for us. That's the song we would like to dance to." And so when people stopped making noise and everybody settled down Myombekere made his instrument sing Nakazenze.

That Nakazenze was a woman of legendary beauty and goodness and famed throughout Ukerewe for that, and that's why all *enanga* players sang

about her. And so when Myombekere had gone through the introductory
to the Nakazenze tune, had hummed and zoomed to his instrument in
muted sounds as if he was mourning, had picked up the introductory notes
again, he flourished his full voice and began relating the praises of that
woman called Nakazenze, how she looked, how she conducted herself
towards men, and sang:

Nakazenze my woman, *yee*! Nakazenze the good one.
When she walks people stop to admire, Nakazenze the noble one
She walks as if borne by the waves, *yee*! Nakazenze the perfect.

The daughter of Lwakarege, *yee*! Nakazenze the kind one.
When she walks people stop to admire, Nakazenze the noble one.

Nakazenze my woman, *yee*! Hospitable to visitors.

She's arriving by sea, *yee*! Nakazenze the noble one.

My wonderful visitor, *yee*! How will I requite her love!
She's arriving borne by the waves, *yee*! Nakazenze the good one.

For our bathing together,[18] *yee*! Nakazenze the perfect one.

When Myombekere finally leveled off his voice and limited his song to
snatches of: "*zenze, zenze, zenze, zenze, yeee!*" at once the three little males,
together as if of one body, moved and danced as if they did not have a single
borne in their bodies! Their audience rewarded them with the clapping of
their hands, the good neighbor of dancing, everyone clapping in rhythm:
"*Pwapwa, pwa, kabatu, pwa!*" The little men were dancing facing their
audience and when you looked at their bellies they had pulled in their guts
all the way and cut themselves into two like wasps, all of them dancing so
perfectly that it was not possible to say which one was better than the
other. When the women became really excited over the young men's
performance and the men too had nothing but praises for them, the
audience told the youths: "Now please turn your back to us, gentlemen!"
And at once the three male children turned to their audience that part of
their bodies on which women carry babies.[19] And when the audience had
again given the dancing youths all the clapping they wanted and
Myombekere had sang, sang well, really well, and the women had added
ululation to his music, the three youths began cutting short the movements
of their bodies until they concluded their dance.

Then they too left the arena and resumed their places in the audience
and somebody filled a bowl with beer and gave it to them, for the three of
them to share.

At that point Myombekere got so excited at seeing others dance that he too wanted to dance and stopped playing *enanga* and looked for Kanwaketa to relieve him so that he too could dance. Bugonoka realized that her husband was about to dance and at once dived into her house to take off *enkanda* [20] robe she was wearing, which she found too heavy and cumbersome to dance with. In an instant she was back, dressed in a skin of the bullock of a goat, and went straight into the dance arena to dance with her husband, who had already taken position in it and was waiting for Kanwaketa to play the song he wanted him to dance to. Kanwaketa too was not your run of the mill   musician, for he too was a consummate *enanga* player in his own right, skilled in all the age-old tunes. And so when he finished playing an introductory, he chose an elders' tune called *ekikuli*. [21] The lyrics of that tune narrated how the carefree unmarried women[22] used to sing without restraint to the music of their reed flutes whatever was in their hearts, as they roamed the ways and paths of the country having fun, especially during the dry season when people are free from work in the crop fields. When Kanwaketa played his *enanga* and hummed and zoomed to it in muted tones, his audience told him, "No, gentleman, flourish your voice quickly and sing and let people dance when they are still in the mood!" And as if that was what he had been waiting for, at once he raised his voice and sang:

A gluttonous male creature, oh woe is me!
has made me abandon my children![23]
A brutal male creature, oh woe is me!
kicked me with his feet!
Had I known what awaited me, oh woe is me!
never would I have married the creature!
I must leave my children, go back to my parents!
The stench of an odious old man, oh woe is me!
is like that of carrion!
The skin of odious an old man, oh woe is me!
is like that of a monitor lizard!
Sleeping with an odious old man, oh woe is me!
is like sleeping with a crocodile!
When an odious old man farts, oh woe is me!
you'd rather you were burnt alive!

And when Kanwaketa had narrated it all and come to the end of the song and gone back to the lyrics he had started with, the audience began clapping for Myombekere and Bugonoka to dance: *"Pwa! pwa! pwa!"*

Myombekere danced and pulled in his guts and cut himself into two like a wasp and moved and swayed as if moved by the wind! And when he really warmed up, he hoisted his shoulders and propelled them from up there in the air. The women ululated. Bugonoka on her part first danced bent close to the ground and with short and restrained shoulder strokes, and then suddenly she moved every part of her body with such intensity that a cloud of dust rose from her feet and enveloped Myombekere completely! Their spectators, men and women alike, taunted the couple and said: "Today is the day! Who will win this battle between husband and wife?" And one after another they poured into the arena to lift their arms in congratulations and to give them prizes while saying to them: "Long life! Long life!"

Each and every person present took part in that dance at Myombekere's home that night, with no exception, unless we want to count the old woman who was in the home visiting, who was the only person who didn't go into the arena and dance like the others, though she too from her place in the audience was clapping for the dancers and enjoying the action; and if you asked me who knows such things, I would say she too danced, because there was no way she could resist imitating the dancers and shaking her head and shoulders in rhythm with the movements of their bodies as I have often observed dance spectators do!

When all the people had danced and drank some more banana beer, Myombekere's companions told him: "Listen, gentleman, we are getting hungry. Tell Bugonoka to cook something for us, and if she can't cook at this late time of the night, let her give us the meat we brought and we'll roast it here on this fire."

Myombekere told his wife: "Did you hear what the men said?" and Bugonoka answered her husband: "Yes, I heard indeed!" Her husband added, "Go and bring us the meat, because all these men are to me real relatives of mine who deserve to be feted in this home. And so bring out all you want, my dear wife, it is I your husband who is allowing you. We will kill another cow tomorrow, if need be. What indeed is our cattle for, the poor childless couple we are?"

Bugonoka went into the house and brought out the entire slab of cow ribs plus a chunk of steak and gave the meat to the men and they put it on the embers in the fireplace. In no time they had taken it out of the fire, divided it out and eaten it all. After which they sincerely thanked Myombekere and said, "Only men like you should get married! Yes,

Myombekere! Look at how you have feted us the whole day long! For were we not feted first at the home of your wife's parents? That is in fact where we have just come from with our bellies full to bursting. And here we are, up to this moment still eating and drinking beer! How better could you possibly have treated us? Do you have to carry us on your back like we were babies? And so we want you to know that we thank you very much and very sincerely. The man or woman who does not thank the person who treats him or her well is an evil one, an accursed witch or witch doctor and nothing else."

Before Myombekere and his companions knew it they heard the first cockcrow go: "*Tata wee!*[24] and they responded to the crowing cock by telling it: "You found us awake, don't you ever brag you woke us up!" On hearing the cockcrow everyone among the men turned to the boy serving beer and said, "Give me some, please; I haven't drunk anything yet!" By that time those with bad stomachs as soon as they drank a bit more would get up as if they were going to urinate when in fact they went out there to vomit, before coming back to their places in the gathering singing:

"*Yebe!*[25] *yebeyebe*! We have drank our beer,
And given none to the unfortunate of this earth!
Our sovereign, *yee!* Our beloved bee, *yee!*
Of the palace of great conversation
The palace of hundreds of conversations, *yee!*
The palace of the rain-maker
Our sovereign, yee! Great bull, *yee!*
Who when he roars other bulls cower!
Our sovereign, *yee!* you of countless bananas
Before whose bananas other bananas are barren, *yee!*
Great one!"[26]

In the midst of that singing and merriment, people now perceived some of their companions already stretched like dead bodies on the ground. It appeared banana beer had got the better of them, especially since they had not slept a wink the whole night and were, in addition, taking snuff almost continuously. And so they had dropped off onto the ground without knowing it and sleep took over. Not long before that they saw the beer server, the young boy of Myombekere's home, pour the last bit of beer from the pot directly into the bowl. That done, the boy took the bowl of the last beer and placed it in front of the male adults. Then he lifted the empty pot and took it behind the house and from there went straight to his bed in the outer room of their house.

The men let the dregs of that bottom-of-the-pot beer settled in the drinking bowl, leaving clear beer above, and then drank and finished it off, after they had tried as hard as they could to wake up their friends who had fallen asleep so that they too could partake of the last drink of their pot but, *aa*! to no avail, their friends rewarding their efforts with nothing but groans as if they were breathing their last breath at that very moment!

Immediately after that Kanwaketa's wife told her husband, "Let's go home." Their two sons were among those who lay stretched on the ground and they woke them up. One of the two had vomited all over himself and instead of waking up he kept rolling in his puke with no strength to get to his feet until his parents finally gave up, with his father saying: "Leave him, a stray bull comes back home from the wilderness on its own," as he left for home with his wife and their other son, all three of them staggering all over the way as they walked, sometimes losing their way and going off into the bush or suddenly falling down: *bugutu!* on and on until they finally arrived. Except to this day Kanwaketa and his wife have yet to tell me whether indeed that night they managed to climb onto their bed and sleep in bed! As to the free woman of their home, their unmarried daughter, her parents had no idea of when she disappeared or where to!

That day Myombekere forgot to close the gate of his home, because he too left his courtyard bonfire staggering to the point of falling down, and so did Bugonoka. Once inside their house, the couple fell asleep stark-naked, unaware of it all. And since new day always comes, it finally dawned.

Early that morning the visiting old woman in Myombekere's house was the first to go out, to relieve herself, only to find first of all that the door of the house was wide open! Once outside, she had hardly gone behind the house when she was greeted by vomit and when she tried to go somewhere else there in turn she was greeted by mounds of the watery shit of banana beer drunks! She was shocked! At the courtyard fireplace the people who were left stretched on the ground at night were all gone. On looking towards the gate, she saw Myombekere's niece come sneaking into the home, accompanied by Kanwaketa's daughter, just the two of them, and she waited for them. She was about to bid them good-morning when they said to her, "You want to greet us as if we slept somewhere else when we all slept in the same house, only we left you still asleep to go to the bush to relieve ourselves!" The old woman responded: "I see!"[27] The three women went into the house together and woke up Bugonoka and she too got up and   then all the women in the house, including Kanwaketa's daughter, took empty calabashes and pots to go to the lake to draw water.

While the women were at the lake, Myombekere too woke up and went out of the house, where he too was immediately greeted by vomit and exclaimed, "*Uu!* What filth in this home today? Nothing but vomit and shit everywhere!"

So he went back into the house to get a hoe with which to bury the filth those drunks had left in his home. As he was coming out of the house with a hoe he ran into Bugonoka and her companions coming from the lake to draw water and Bugonoka, on seeing her husband with a hoe in his hands asked him, "In which field are you going to work this early in the morning? Don't you ever have a hangover?"

"I am going to bury the vomit and running shit drunks have spread all over this home. The whole home is nothing but the stench of carrion, unbearable to the extreme, you'd think you've run into a shitting bush in the season of heavy rains!"

"It is not surprising, given the complete lack of restraint with which they were attacking everything, the same people moving from beer to devouring roast meat that way! When you heap all that in one and the same stomach you are bound to put in something your stomach does not agree with. *Aa! hee!* What a way to eat! You'd think they were the fabled Mukingira of whom *enanga* players sing:

Mukingira, it's wrong to eat that way,
Child of Lake Lyamonde!
Mukingira, son of Lyegoba,[28]
Child of Lake Lyamonde!
For you the beer pot, for you the beer calabash,
For you *embete*, for you *embozu*,
For you the meat, for you *enfuru*!
Mukingira, it's wrong to eat that way!

When Bugonoka concluded her song, Myombekere and the two unmarried young women together with the visiting old woman all laughed their fill. And when the young women asked why such a song, the visiting old woman told them: "My children, may be you think that that's a mere song and a mere story, that no such a person ever lived?" The two young women answered: "*Nn!*" And the old woman told them, "We of our age today were born and grew up and became really big children before we ever heard of such a thing. But when we were nearing puberty, when our tiny breasts were taking shape on our chests, it was then that we began to hear that in the distant islands of Irungwa[29] there was a man named Mukingira, that he lived in the islet of Lyegoba. It was said that that man was incredibly greedy and an insatiable glutton, that however much he ate, he was never satisfied. When they cooked for him all the different types of relish you can imagine, every kind of fish, all in their separate pots, this pot here full of *embete*, the other one over there full of *embozu*, and yet that other pot full of meat to the brim, and even if they added to all that a huge pot of sweet *nabunyame*, the famed delicious sardines of those Irugwa waters, that one likewise packed to brim, and accompanied each and every pot of relish with its own dish of *obwita*, and put the entire lot between his legs, he emptied each and everything into his stomach, following that by drinking all the broth from all the relish pots and chewing and sucking dry all *ebisesya*[30] linings at the bottoms of the relish pots and emptying everything: *fufufu!*[31] And before long, in those very same days, we heard that man sung by *enanga* players, who had composed songs about him for their music. That's when the entire Ukerewe, even those like us who had never seen him, came to know of his misdeeds, now carried everywhere by songs like the one Bugonoka has just sung for us. And you want to take Mukingira's misdeeds for a mere song or a mere story! No, they are not, they are true happenings, because there did live such a Mukingira, who was a real human being. And that should not surprise you, because all the time we see that stories originate from the deeds of people and not from the deeds of stones or trees; never! It is only with the passing of time that those who did not witness those storied deeds come to think that may be they are mere stories, when in fact they really did happen."

Bugonoka said, "How is it that the information we receive from our elders sometimes differs? But I should not say it differs, because all I can say is that I too heard an explanation of this song at my parents' home, only a different one.

"A long time ago now, there arrived at my parents home a certain old man, really aged. It was before I got married here, but, I must admit, I was already a grown up girl, no longer what can be called a young child. That old man had been nicknamed One-who-speaks-his-mind,[32] which had become the name almost everybody knew him by. He was a man famed for his great knowledge of all sorts of things, and whatever he said was the truth and matter to take seriously. I heard my mother and others ask that man about this very matter of Mukingira and he told them: "It is true that

Mukingira was a real person, and that he lived in one of the Irugwa islands. But what we hear sung of him by *enanga* players, that 'Mukingira it's wrong to eat that way', is not merely about eating or drinking too much, even though, yes, that too was true of him. But his eating and drinking was sung only to avoid having to say to people the really unutterable deeds of that man Mukingira, which were that once he drank beer, and nothing but ordinary beer, he ran amok and chased every woman of whatever description he laid eyes on, wanting to perform the act of marriage with her no matter where. No wonder he performed the act of marriage with his own daughters, children of his very own blood, and his own sisters, born of the womb of his very own mother! And don't think that was all; no. When he went really berserk, he performed the marriage act with livestock, actually! That's how he became the subject of *enanga* songs throughout Ukerewe, his misdeeds thus becoming the talk of the length and breadth of this kingdom, forever."

Myombekere exclaimed really loud: "*Uu*! I see! So he was a real mad man! He was insisting on drinking beer when it was such a great enemy of his! A human being should die rather than do a thing like that! It is much better to smoke opium, if you must, and let people attach to your person the name The-opium-smoker, rather than insist on drinking beer when it disagrees with you in such an ugly way!"

That was how one thing led to another in Myombekere's home that day, how Myombekere's reaction to finding his home littered with the filth of drunks reminded Bugonoka of how people can abuse eating and drinking and end up wallowing in their own filth like Mukingira who ate and drank more than was good for his person and ended up shocking this entire kingdom.

When Myombekere finished burying all that filth, ridding the compound of his home of the stinking mess from one end to the other, he went back into the house and regained his sweet bed and rested and chatted with the people of his home while in bed, because that day he woke up dying from hunger, which is something anybody who has ever passed the entire night drinking banana beer will no doubt understand.

Bugonoka put a pot of meat on fire and left the visiting old woman and the little girl who lived in their home taking care of the relish pot so that she could go back to the lake with the other two women for more water. Then at once she turned to sweeping her entire house, from one end to the other, for she was a very clean woman and could never stand her house looking unkempt. And indeed how she found her house was not how she left it, for it had become messy beyond recognition! Every married woman knows how in need of cleaning her house always looks whenever she comes back home after being away for a number of days. Imagine therefore the state Bugonoka's house was in on her return, after being away for months!

Chapter IX

NOTES

1. Plumpness was a an important feature of feminine beauty among the Wakerewe.

2. *Obwita*: See note 14 of Chapter I.

3. *Ekikome*: See note 1 of Chapter II.

4. *Olusabuzyo*: Here a wooden container for drinking banana beer with. See note 12 of Chapter I.

5. *Ekitala*: See note 18 of Chapter I.

6. *Omukama*: See note 26 of Chapter II.

7. *Ensimba*: Wild cat with a skin like that of a leopard.

8. *Amakara* (singular *ikara*): General name for small wild animals of the cat family and, by extension, name for all "creatures of the night", wild animals which come out mostly at night. .

9. *Enanga* (pronounced *énaanga*, as different from *enánga*, the plural for *olunanga*, a "plate"): A zither, the Kikerewe most prestigious musical instrument and the instrument for the music of conversation and good company.

10. As related in the Introduction, Lukonge was the king of Ukerewe when the colonizing Europeans first arrived in that part of Africa and whom they exiled to Mwanza on the mainland for resisting their take over of his kingdom. This is the only place where Kitereza almost dates his story, which, as said in the Introduction, is otherwise situated in an undifferentiated pre-colonial past. *Lukwasilwandalira*: "Greatest-of-the-all-time-great", was one of the very many attributes and self-praises of King Lukonge.

11. *Akahira*: Sound of great jubilation made by ululating while vibrating the tongue and traditionally made exclusively by women.

12. *Entundu*: Banana plant with a shining deep-black stem. Bands of dry fiber of banana stems (and not only those of the rare black *entundu* banana) were tied around the heads and waists of the bereaved during the days of mourning. *Etundu* was also the term of praise for a woman with very soft and smooth deep-black skin, like that of Myombekere's wife Bugonoka herself in the novel, which the Wakerewe found extremely beautiful.

13. One of the ways of posing riddles in Kikerewe, in which the "unknown" name of the riddle, the one the initiator of the riddle gives at the end, solves the riddle and testifies to his or her wit.

14. *Nakazenze*: Name of a woman of legendary beauty, hence a song for which each musician had his own version. Myombekere's audience therefore wanted

to hear what he would improvise for them on that traditional song as testimony of his love for his returned wife Bugonoka.

15.   *Omururi (plural Abaruri)*: Member of the Waruri tribe from Bururi in Musoma on the mainland northeast of Ukerewe Island. It is in this song that we find the only mention of white people in the entire novel, where they are otherwise altogether absent in this African society of the past Kitereza has depicted for us.

16.   *Olukombwe*: Type of a weasel.

17.   *Enerere:* See note 23 of Chapter VI.

18.   A reference to the Kikerewe habit of a man and his wife bathing each other before retiring for the night. Myombekere evokes it here to allude to the romantic aspect of his love for his returned wife Bugonoka without offending people's sense of propriety, since among the Wakerewe sex was never discussed in public.

19.   *Oguheka*: Literally "child carrying part of the body", the back. As we see in the novel, Wakerewe women normally carried babies by strapping them on their backs with a piece of goat skin (before turning to the use of cotton cloth) called *engozi.*

20.   *Enkanda:* See note 22 of Chapter VI.

21..   *Ekikuli*: Reed flute.

22.   *Abasimbe*, plural for *omusimbe*: A free (unmarried) woman. See note 24 of Chapter II. Among the Wakerewe, unmarried adult women, whether divorcées or widows or spinsters, were in general free to do whatever they wanted and could therefore afford to criticize men. Kanwaketa's choice of this song for Myombekere and his wife to dance to seems to suggest that Myombekere, both as a man and as a husband, would win the approval of even the most critical women.

23.   In the patrilineal Kikerewe society, in case of divorce the children usually remained with the father.

24.   *Tata wee!*: "Hello dad!"

25.   *Yebe!*: "Hello darling!"

26.   In the song are some of the many attributes of *omukama* (the king) of Ukerewe.

27.   Kikerewe tradition was that one did not bid good-morning a person who slept in the same house with him or her, and hence the challenge of the two unmarried young women to the old woman, who, of course, knew they didn't sleep in the house.

28.   Lyegoba: One of the islets which constituted the Irugwa group of the minor

islands of Ukerewe Kingdom (see Introduction). Lake Lyamonde is the lake waters around yet another one of the islets, Lyamonde.

29. Irungwa : A group of small islands off the coast of Majita to the north-east of Ukerewe Island and the most distant of the minor islands of Ukerewe Kingdom. See Introduction on Ukerewe Kingdom.

30. *Ebisesya*: Linings, usually slices of papyrus stalks, placed at the bottom of a pot to prevent cooking fish from catching. Among the Wakerewe normally only women and children   sucked and chewed *ebisesya* once the fish in the pot was finished, and hence chewing them on the part of Mukingira is one more symbol of his greed and despicable habits.

31. *Fufufu!*: Ideophone for completely finishing off a dish of food.

32. *Namugambage*: "One-who-speaks-his-mind", here a person who tells the truth whatever the cost. Also see meaning of names at the end of this translation.

Chapter X

BUGONOKA SETTLES BACK IN HER HOME, HAPPY AND CONTENTED

Where he was, as he lay on his bed that morning, Myombekere thought of where to find a skilled artisan who would prepare for him the goat skin his father-in-law had honored him with. When he finally settled on the artisan of his choice, he called Kagufwa and sent him on an errand and told him, "Go and call Gwaleba for me. Tell him: 'Myombekere wants you; he has sent me here and told me: `If he is at home come back with him!'" The boy said, "Yes," and took off running, since he no longer felt the hangover from the banana beer, except that his eyes were still red like sparks of fire. He was in fact more than willing to go on that errand, since at that moment the one thing he desired most was a bath in the lake and Gwaleba's home was by the lakeshore.

He found Gwaleba at home and told him of Myombekere's message and he accepted, and the boy added, "Wait for me a bit, I am coming. I would like to take a quick plunge in the lake here, I won't be long. I will just jump into the water as soon as I get there and come back at once."

Gwaleba answered him, "Go and come back quickly then, and let's leave. By the time you come back, I too should have finished repairing this opening in the fence of my compound, torn down last night by some two unruly cows of mine while fighting with each other."

Back in Myombekere's home, when Bugonoka finished sweeping clean her house she gathered trash and took it outside to the household rubbish heap. As she returned into the house and was about to place a tray[1] in front of the grinding-stone and grind some flour, the visiting old woman in her house called her, "Child of my people, come and see! It looks to me as if this relish pot needs some water!"

Bugonoka lighted with a torch the inside of the pot and titled it to take a better look and said, "Dear me, you gave me such a scare for nothing! Only it's time we took it from the fire and put on water for *obwita*,[2] so that we can finish cooking breakfast and attend to other matters." Myombekere's niece was attending to the skimming of milk and was now filling *ebizanda* [3] with milk from the churn,[4] after scenting[5] the milk containers. It was at that time that Gwaleba arrived with Kagufwa, only to find Myombekere himself still on his sweet bed. The two men greeted each other and finished and then Gwaleba asked Myombekere, "By the way, are you not feeling well, my man? Why are you bedridden?"

"*Ha! ha!* I am fine. I am just resting in bed!"

"Were you, by any chance, at the home where last night women were clapping and ululating? [6] Where, by the way, was that *enanga* [7] dance?"

"It was here. That dancing was in this home. Yesterday, on coming back from appeasing my in-laws, when my companions and I arrived here with our wife, I thought and said to myself: `These people here are your real friends, whatever you say. They are the ones who helped you carry appeasement beer to your in-laws. What's more, they are aware of the one tiny pot of beer you left in this home, because they are the same people who brought here the banana beer from the home where you brewed it. Does it make any sense to deny them this one tiny pot of beer and, for all you know, end up drinking the beer all alone with your wife?' And my heart told me: `No! Give it to them to drink.' And that is what we drank here and it ended up being a real drinking party, since it was just us, with not a single gate-crasher."

"We heard, as I have said, the clapping and peels of ululation and said, `Wherever that is, they are enjoying their banana beer, the lucky ones, *a! e!*' And so it was here! And did you say you came back with Bugonoka?"

"Yes, she is among the women in the house. So you did not make out who was greeting you from back in the house? With others, that can be understood, but how could you fail to recognize Bugonoka's voice?"

"The one voice I made out was that of your niece, but none of the rest. I thought they must be visitors!"

"Anyway, I have called you here because I want you to prepare a goat skin for me. My father-in-law slaughtered a goat for us over there and presented me with the skin of the goat, with rather long hair. And that's why I have called you, my friend, after I said to myself that since you are such a skilled skin artisan you can make me an excellent robe out of it, instead of letting an amateur like myself handle the skin and end up with something which nobody can put on." That man Gwaleba was a skin artisan of really great skill, known throughout the country, since he was the one who prepared robes for the wives of the king[8] with the skins leopards and *emondo*[9] they wore. Preparing animal pelts and turning them into material for wear and making robes was his calling in life which had made him a famous man, and because of which whoever wanted a taste of rawhide meat his home was the place to go,   since there was always plenty of rawhide *ensyomoro* and *ebikoba*[10] for relish in his home, for, as the saying goes, "The child of a hide-thinner who does not eat *ensyomoro* and *ebikoba* when his or her father is still alive will never taste rawhide meat."

Myombekere and Gwaleba were still thus chatting when they saw Bugonoka bring them water for washing their hands and Kagufwa went and fetched a washbasin.[11] He was about to put the wooden washbasin down in front of the two men when Myombekere said, "No, not here!" and added, addressing Gwaleba, "Let's go outside; we shouldn't be like some greedy men who eat food hiding inside their houses."

They got up and went outside under the shade of a tree and Bugonoka brought them the food there. When she was about to return to the house, Gwaleba said to her: "Now I know! That's why Myombekere loves you so much: you wake up early in the morning to cook such a heavy breakfast for him! And how plump you have become since going back to your parents! What were they slaughtering for you all the time to make you so overflowing with health?"

Bugonoka smiled and said, "What could they slaughter for me, the poor people! I was eating nothing but *omusaga* greens.[12] May be my body has simply decided to be this way."

"Whom I you deceiving? Haven't you heard the saying of our elders of yore: `The bush thickens only when it rains?'"

"It's true that's what people say, but all the same you must admit if your body says otherwise you may eat all the good things you can name and all that will still be in vain."

The men were still eating when they heard a visitor calling: "People of this home!"

Myombekere answered, "Yes, Sir!"

The visitor added, "Are you at home?"

Myombekere responded, "Yes, we are."

The visitor entered Myombekere's home, but before he got where the other men were seated he squatted down, holding his bow in his hands. Myombekere called aloud the women in the house and said, "Would someone bring us a chair in that house!" and welcomed the visitor, "Please join us, gentleman; as you see, we are in the midst of combat." The man accepted the invitation, went to the meal circle and sat down and the woman who had brought him a chair relieved him of his weapons and took them inside the house. Because the man had found his hosts eating, he did not exchange greeting with them and he had to wait until they finished eating before greeting them. That's how the Wakerewe used to do in those days.

Inside the house the women, out of their usual unrestrained curiosity, began peeping outside and asking themselves questions: "May be it's someone coming to court you?"

The unmarried young woman of Myombekere's home said, "I have never seen him, not even once, before this day, that is if he is here to court."

Only when the men finished eating and washing their hands did they greet each other. Because the visitor was a total stranger to the other men, they exchanged greetings like acquaintances who hadn't seen each other for a long time, all of them greeting each other individually, including the boy Kagufwa, who greeted the visitor as his male senior, after Myombekere and Gwaleba had greeted the man as a peer. Myombekere asked the man, "What parts of the country should I ask you news of, gentleman?"

"Ask me news of the islands of Bweni."[13]

"Do you live on Bweni Island proper?"

"No, I live on another one of the islands, the one called Songe."

"And what's your name?"

"My name did you say?"

"*Nn* - -"

"My name is Mpazi."[14]

When the women heard that name they laughed and said: "It appears in those distant islands people have run out of names and have resorted to naming their children after ants."

Bugonoka answered back the woman who had said that, the little girl of her home, by asking her, "*Aa*! Come on, child! Have you really never heard in this country people called by names of ants like him, for example Mpigi, or Namuhani or Kachwera?"

"*Aa*! I must admit I hear them."

"And why are you surprised?"

After the visitor told his hosts the locality of his domicile and his name, the other men left it to him to tell them the purpose of his visit and he said, "Gentlemen, asking is seeking to see clear, and I am here to ask. I am on a courting mission, courting a woman whose parents live in our Bweni islands and have sent me to court in the home of a man who has moved into these parts of the country only recently, whose name is Nawanchuma. Could you tell me where he lives?"

"I see, that one. He stays uphill over there. Let's go, I will show you the way."

The visitor got up and Myombekere told the women in the house to bring his weapons and he escorted him. When he got him to the first crossroads, he gave him his weapons and said, "Go along this path, and when you get to that point over there you will come to a cattle-hurdle[15] across your way. Go over the hurdle. In fact as soon as you step over it you will see the houses of his home, they are clearly visible from there."

On returning home Myombekere told Kagufwa to bring the goat skin, as he on his part went to a platform where his niece had put thatching grass she had cut for thatching the roof of their grain store[16] and took some grass from there for spreading on the work ground so that the skin wouldn't get soiled while being pegged, and then fetched a bundle of pegs he had brought from Kanwaketa's home, enough to hold in place and stretch for drying any goat skin, even that of a big bullock. Gwaleba stretched the goat skin on the pegs he erected in the ground, using *empindu*[17] Myombekere had given him to pierce and thread the skin with, the way goat skins are pegged and stretched in the sun to dry, and finished his work.

That done, Myombekere told Kagufwa, "Go and call Kanwaketa and tell him to come at once with his ax." Kagufwa did so and Kanwaketa came with an ax. Then Myombekere told Kanwaketa and Gwaleba, "I need some relish in this home, the banana beer of yesterday consumed all what we had and left us in bad shape." On hearing that his two companions silently thanked their good fortunes: "What good luck! Thank the heavens!"

While that was going on outside, inside the house Bugonoka was at the door of their house taking strings of her waist beads out of *ekitwaro* [18] box and examining them to see how rusty they had become. And indeed she found they were already moldy and awful to look at and exuding a pungent smell from having been enclosed in the dampness of *ekitwaro* for so long without being aired even once. She used to wear six strings of beads around her waist before she felt she had a good waistful of beads, and she had altogether twelve of them, which she wore in two sets of six by turns, putting off one set as soon as it got infested with lice and the pests began biting her and replacing it with the other set, after rethreading the beads of that other set with fresh cotton. On the day her father and mother came to take her away, she had that very day replaced the set she had been wearing and put it away and so had gone to her parents home with the set of six she had just put on. She had beads of three colors, in equal strings of each, so that four strings of her beads were red, four green and four white, giving her altogether twelve waist-strings of beads, is that not right? *Aa*! that's correct! And so she was taking out of her *ekitwaro* the other six strings of beads she had left home so that she could clean them with cow urine she had collected for the purpose that morning and thread them afresh before putting them on to replace the set she had been wearing since she went to her parents' home. The other women in her house gave her a hand in removing seeds from cotton and in spinning some thread for the beads so that she could string them on new thread and shine them and make them look like new again.

That done, she descended to the lake to fetch water for her husband to bathe, and for cleaning their bed rawhide, after she had taken apart their bed for the purpose, because it had become infested with bedbugs. She made two trips to the lake. When she brought home water the first time, she found Kagufwa had already driven cattle out of the kraal and taken the cows to the neighborhood herder on duty and saw that one cow had been left behind, a young bull, black and white in color, which was at the moment lowing loudly. She put down her pot of water and before going back to the lake she asked her husband, pretending she did not know what was going on even though she knew everything: "Why is that cow lowing so loudly in the kraal? Is it not going to graze today like the other cows?"

Myombekere answered back his wife with the same pretense and jokingly, "Today we have placed an interdiction on that one and said: `Let that one stay there and cry its fill, because yesterday it ate Karungu's[19] grass too much'." Bugonoka too was determined to outwit her husband and answered him back: "If so, why is it that we humans are drinking Mutwenge's[20] water everyday and yet we have never seen an interdiction placed on us, even for one single day, and human beings being told, 'Today you humans are forbidden to drink Mutwenge's water because you drank too much of it yesterday'!"

"*Oo!* I see! So, my wife, you are still a child! So you have never seen, even on a single day, we humans placed under an interdiction and forbidden not to eat or drink!"

"No, never! I have never seen that and in fact you are just being unkind to this cow because it is an animal we keep, which cannot talk to you and make you understand how it feels, and that is why you can afford to punish it this way, but not otherwise."

"And to whom does this cow itself, lowing here, belong?"

"*Aa!* It is your very own property."

"Exactly. You are right on that score, my wife. And, therefore, let me ask you another question: 'And what about us human beings, whose undisputed property are we?'"

"We are the Creator's very own property."

"Exactly. That's it, my wife. That's the very truth of the matter. You have stated the real truth. And may I then give you the following explanation?"

"Please explain to me."

"You say you have never seen an interdiction placed on human beings, but won't you, the day I will stop breathing and die and my life become extinguished completely as we extinguish a fire, feel that the Creator, whose very own property I am, has interdicted me from eating and drinking, leaving you all alone on this earth?"

"I see! So that's what you are driving at! In that case I have seen that interdiction placed on humans. In fact I see it all the time."

With that Bugonoka was about to take up her pot of water again and place it on her head to go to the lake for more water when Myombekere told her, "Before you go, give us first some pot in which to collect for you cow blood for dying your *enduko*,[21] or don't you want it?"

"Thank you for reminding me. Of course I want it; how could I not! Won't I make bowls[22] any more?"

"That's why I too felt I should ask you, my dear wife, since I can't divine what is in your mind."

Bugonoka put down her water pot and went inside the house and brought out a big cooking pot and placed it by the door and told her husband, "Here it is, collect the blood in this one for me."

She was just crossing the gate of the household when she met Kagufwa, accompanied by a friend, a son of Kanwaketa, with whom they were coming back from taking their cattle to the neighborhood herder on duty. She went on to the lake to draw water and the two boys entered the courtyard, where they found Myombekere holding in his hands a pole on which was entwined a rope with a noose at the end, which he was about to put on the leg of the cow in the kraal. Gwaleba and Kanwaketa likewise were both already on their feet, standing guard by the gate of the kraal, just in case that bull should try to get out before it was roped. Once Myombekere roped the bull, he told the two men to open the gate of the kraal and to give way, so that the animal could come out. It was a strong young bull naturally bellicose, so that as soon as Myombekere put a rope on its leg it became raving mad. I shouldn't even go into details, because if you too have ever had to take a roped bull some place, you cannot but know fully well what happens to people on such an errand, how they can be made to run through thorns and briers against their will! And so, while still in the kraal, when that bull realized it had a rope on its leg, it gathered all its strength to drag the man who had roped it and when it said: "*Ku!* Myombekere, see me drag you!" within less than it takes to say it Myombekere was on the ground in the middle of wet cow-shit. He fell down without letting go the rope in his hands, so that had it not been for Kanwaketa, who jumped over tree logs in the fence of the kraal and quickly came to his aid and enabled him to get to his feet again, *aa!* that cow would have messed him up pretty badly by dragging him through that cow-shit mud and turned his hands into bleeding wounds with that rope or hurt him by throwing him against logs in the kraal fence! Was that cow simply mad or was that something else! When, even after it was held by two men, it pulled again with a: *ku!* the two men were lifted out of their stand and sent staggering about, and on and on they staggered as the bull pulled them along, still holding on to their rope. Near the gate of the kraal the bull spotted Gwaleba, who had climbed on some logs in the kraal fence waiting for it with an ax already raised in his two manly hands, to finish it off there and then, and the bull said: "You want me? Well, here I come!" and put down its head ready to lift the man into the air, just as Gwaleba on his part brought down his ax right in the middle of its damned skull: *po!* The cow fell down while crying out: *boo!* and the man broke out in self-praise: "I've got you, the strong short man; never ask who did it to you!" The women inside the house, who had been peeping by the open door laughed, and on seeing that the bull had fallen down with an ax sticking out of its head they said: "*Ee!* he has killed it. Look, it has fallen down with the ax planted in its head!" But apparently in axing it Gwaleba had struck it rather out fright, when he was carrying on and praising himself he was convinced: "I have axed it in the death spot, that's where my ax struck and thundered" when in fact he had just struck its right-side horn, from where the ax went on and split an ear, that was the blow which had made the animal bellow and fall down.

Throughout all that Gwaleba's two companions were still holding on to their rope, had not let go of it. Then all of a sudden the bull revived from the shock of the blow and got back to its feet and shook itself as if shaking off water from its body to dry and the ax in its head fell down quite some distance away. Gwaleba ran for the ax and grabbed it and, realizing that the animal was far from dead, the short strong man came back to do battle with the bull, which in the meanwhile had dragged Myombekere and Kanwaketa and sent them racing after it in every direction until they called on the two boys to come and give them a hand and ended by tethering the bull to a tree, where they now stood by helplessly looking on and panting. And so when they saw Gwaleba come, his ax aimed and raised high in his two hands and charging full speed at the bull they said, "Let's leave these two males settle their old scores alone!" Gwaleba on his part just kept on forging forward and making for the bull with the same resolve, never hesitating again for even one moment until he got to it. And when on its part the bull tried to rush him and stick him with its horns, our Gwaleba let fall his ax with full force: *pwaa*! and then stepped aside and the cow fell down: *ligiti*! Apparently his ax had this time caught the animal right in the very middle of the killing spot an it did not make any other single movement, so that when the men took the ax out of its head it was already completely dead. Only then did they pull its carcass to some grass-covered ground and slaughtered it.

Bugonoka too had witnessed the ordeal to which that cow subjected her husband and his companions as she was coming from the lake to draw water the second time, as a result of which she had not entered their home by the main gate but, so as to be as far as possible from that battle scene, had rounded the fence and made for the small hind gate and entered by that one.

The men skinned the animal and finished and then cut up the carcass, removing the limbs and slicing the meat into different cuts, after which

Myombekere gave his two companions their customary share of meat for slaughtering a cow for another person, and then took one cut, an arm, and told the men to cut it into smaller pieces and gave to each one of them a big chunk of meat from that part too, took a slab of ribs and sliced off some ribs for them as well. The meat that remained from those two cuts, the arm and the slab of ribs, he sent to his nearest neighbors, each and everyone of them. Then he asked his two companions to help him carry the rest of the meat into the house, and they put it in a place he had selected for the purpose. The other men wanted to go home, since they had completed their job, but Myombekere said, "No, please wait. Let's have some meat roasted for us and eat a bit of roasted meat before you go. What's the hurry for?" His companions responded, "We want to take this great food home, for our wives to cook before it is late so that at meal time we won't be pulling and struggling with hard meat as if we slaughtered the animal when it was already nighttime."

He managed to retain them and fetched his sword-like knife and cut some pieces of meat and put them on a wooden skewer and gave the meat to the boy of his home, after rubbing salt [23] in it. Before long the men were calling the boy: "You want to roast meat like a women! Bring it here; it is ready; it is meat for men. Have you ever seen men too roast meat until it is almost burnt like women? We men prefer our meat with a bit of animal-blood still in it. *Oho!* What are you trying to do to us, you child?" The boy put the meat on an a plate[24] and brought it to them..

Myombekere's neighbors finally bid good-bye to the women in the home: "Good-day and good-night, just in case we don't meet again today." The women answered, "Good-bye; and thanks. Greetings to your wives." Myombekere also bid the two men good-bye: "Have a good day. I am afraid I won't escort you; let me attend to this work." To which they answered, "Yes, indeed. Do so, because slaughtering a cow always means endless jobs. But, its madness notwithstanding, the bull was big only before being slaughtered, but now that we have slaughtered and skinned it, it does not amount to much anymore. And since it is such sweet meet, those you will give some to will have nothing but insults for us who butchered it, for not having slaughtered something bigger."

Myombekere answered: "True; it is just as you say."

He cut trees for building a barbecue platform, then cut into small pieces the meat he wanted to barbecue and finished, and left uncut some meat and said to himself, "Let me put aside this meat. Early in the morning

I will ran over and take it my friend Nkwesi who gave me the bananas for the beer with which I appeased my wife's parents."

And so in the morning Myombekere took some meat to his friend Nkwesi. Nkwesi saw him thus loaded and received the meat from him and asked him, "And did you come back with Bugonoka?"

"Yes, we did, and she is now in my home, back to stay."

On hearing that Myombekere's sisters-in-law, the wives of his friend Nkwesi, fell to teasing him: "So that's it! We should've known. So that's why on that day, the day your beer frothed, you were walking so fast in parts of the road you were leaving no trace of footprints behind!"

"I am sure you too have heard the saying: `Out of great expectations cunning hare dropped a precious load!'" And everybody laughed.

Myombekere stayed and chatted for a bit and then told Nkwesi, "Please give me my walking stick and the basket I came with so that I can return home; I left behind some work to do."

"Won't you stay for lunch?"

"No, I can't."

Nkwesi brought him his walking stick and the basket in which he brought him the present of meat and escorted him. After he had gone with him for some distance, he came back and Myombekere went on. When Myombekere arrived home Bugonoka asked him, "Are you back? Did you find them at home? Are they well?" "I am back, they were home and they are well, and they all sent you their greetings," he answered her.

A bit later Myombekere went to the barbecue platform and took from there some meat to send to the men who helped him carry banana beer to his wife's parents, put the meat in *ekitukuru* [25] basket and gave it to Kagufwa to take to them.

Kagufwa did so and came back and told Myombekere, "Where you sent me everybody to whom you sent me greets you and thanks you and told me: `Say thanks to him for us and tell him it was very kind of him indeed to give us this present of relish.'"

Chapter X

NOTES

1. *Olugali*: See note 6 of Chapter I.
2. *Obwita*: See note 14 of Chapter I.
3. *Ebizanda*, plural for *ekizanda*: See note 20 of Chapter II.
4. *Ekiyanzi*: See note 20 of Chapter II.
5. *Kuhagya*: To scent milk containers. The containers of milk, after they were washed, before being used were first scented with the smoke of nice-smelling *emisikizi* twigs, by being inverted over *omwotezyo* or "scented smoke" of *emisikizi* twigs burning in a small urn-like pot with a hole near the bottom called *empiki*. The milk churn, a large calabash with a long carved neck, was scented by introducing into its neck a burning twig of yet a different scent-tree called *omuchumulizyo*. Milk was poured into the containers with the scent-smoke still circulating in them so that enough of it could get into the milk and fill it with tiny foaming bubbles and give it a fragrance and flavor people found delicious. With the exceptions of babies, who were, as we see in chapter XIX of the novel, given fresh milk, skimmed milk treated that way was the only milk the Wakerewe drank.
6. *Akahira*: See note 11 of Chapter IX.
7. *Enanga*: See note 9 of Chapter IX.
8. *Omukama*: See note 26 of Chapter II.
9. *Emondo*: Leopard-like wild cat similar to *ensimba* in note 7 of Chapter IX. The skins of leopards and other beautiful animal skins were worn by royalty only.
10. The Wakerewe ate certain parts of cow-hide: in addition to *ensyomoro*, the meat obtained when thinning a hide during skin preparation, they also ate *emiguta*, fresh thick hide from the cow's feet and *ebikoba*, dry thick hide from the cow's head, after those hide parts had been singed and the hair removed and then stewed and seasoned with butter.
11. *Olusabuzyo*: See note 12 of Chapter I.
12. The Wakerewe considered it a sign of indigence to eat *obwita*, their staple dish, with greens as the main relish instead of fish or meat, and of all the greens *omusaga*, a wild spinach with a rather bitter taste, was considered the really needy person's last resort.
13. *Bweni*: One of the minor islands of Ukerewe. See Introduction.
14. *Empazi*: Big black ants with painful bites called by the English in East Africa "safari ants", because they often appear in interminable columns like those of safari caravans, on account of which they can be a real menace when they

invade people's houses or the kraals of their livestock.

15. Hurdle consisting of a tree log with two limbs erected in the middle of a fenced-in cowtrail, especially one leading to the homes of herdsmen, to control the movement of cows by forcing them to slow down, step over the hurdle by passing between its two limbs one at a time and thus fall into a single-file formation, so that, for example, they could be easily led into a kraal on their return home from grazing.

16. *Ekitala*: See note 18 of Chapter I.

17. *Empindu*: A long needle the size of a knitting needle with a flat harpooned sharp point used for weaving water-tight household utensils made of grass, like *engali* trays and *ebibo* bowls of notes 6 and 15 of Chapter I.

18. *Ekitwaro*: See note 19 of Chapter VIII.

19. Karungu or Lyangombe: The deity of the wilderness.

20. Mutwenge, women's substitute term for Mugasa: the deity of the sea. See note 27 of Chapter VII. Wakerewe women could not say words which were or sounded like the names of the parents or clan elders of their husbands and instead used substitute vocabulary. See note 23 of Chapter XVI.

21. *Enduko*: "Weaving-grass", fine strands of raffia-like grass used in weaving household utensils like *engali* and *ebibo* of note 17 above, by weaving the grass on fine ribs of papyrus.

22. *Ebibo*: See note 17 above.

23. *Lunzebe*: See note 17 of Chapter I.

24. *Olunanga:* See note 16 of Chapter I.

25. *Ekitukuru*: See note 16 of Chapter V.

Chapter XI

BUGONOKA PLANTS SWEET POTATOES AND MYOMBEKERE CULTIVATES BANANA

Bugonoka did not forget the counsel her mother gave her on the day she left her parents' home and returned to her own home with her husband after he appeased her parents. One day she was seated with her husband, threading her beads on strings while the two of them chatted about this and that when, all of a sudden, she told her husband, "Could you please put a new hoe on a handle for me. I want to cultivate a field of sweet potatoes, since the season for sowing millet is past. I don't want to waste my time and energy for nothing sowing millet which will end up as pasture for cattle, when I can easily get all the sweet potato seeding vines I need."

"I have both the hoe and the handle, so I can have a hoe ready for you at once, my dear wife. The only farm implement I think I lack is my billhook, whose handle was broken, but even with that I will make another handle and have the tool ready."

That very day Myombekere took down a hoe handle of *omusibi* wood which was hanging in the roof of his house over the kitchen fireplace seasoning with smoke, took a chisel from a large broken pot in which he kept his few handicraft tools and planed the handle with the chisel, worked on it to his satisfaction and replaced his tool in the broken pot. Then he sent Bugonoka to fetch some fire from the house and bring it to him a the courtyard fireplace[1] and to bring him two iron rods, one small the other one larger, for making a hole in the hoe handle, as well as one new big size

Wazinza hoe.[2] And Bugonoka did so and then returned to her job, the one we left her doing.

Myombekere then worked on the fire in the courtyard until it was fully going and the fireplace was full of live charcoal. Then he took his two iron rods and put them in the fire and kept on working on the fire using a rawhide shoe as bellows. When the iron rods were red-hot, he took them out of the fire and used them to pierce a hole in the head of the handle, which he held in place by stepping on it with one foot this way, working with the smaller rod first. When the smaller iron rod went through the head of the hoe handle, he put it aside and planted it into the ground to cool, sticking into soil the entire fired part of the rod and leaving above only its wooden handle. Then he began firing the spike of the iron hoe itself as at the same time he worked on enlarging the hole in the handle head with the bigger iron rod, fired red-hot in turn.

When he was satisfied with the size of the hole he had made, he stuck that iron rod too in the earth to cool, and concentrated on firing the hoe's spike. And when it got red-hot and was burning really bright, he took the hoe out of the fire and planted the red-hot spike into the hole of the hoe handle, quickly, before it cooled down and failed to burn well into the wood. As quickly he took hold of the hoe handle and struck the cutting-edge of the hoe against a log, immediately after which he got hold of a short heavy piece of wood and repeatedly knocked at the head of the hoe handle with it: *tutututu*! to drive the hoe spike farther into the wood. When the spike was no longer glowing, he said to himself, "Maybe I should now take the hoe out. I shouldn't force things and end up by breaking the handle head." The hoe spike had already peered through the head of the handle. And so he pulled out the hoe from the handle and fired the spike again and when it was red-hot once more he put it into the handle the second time, holding the hot iron hoe by a piece of rawhide, and repeated the process and again beat the spike into the head of the handle. Once more the hot iron spike showed no sign of holding and staying in place. It was on the third trial that on beating the hoe into the handle wood with the stick the spike went through all the way until the lobes of the hoe rested solidly against the handle head. He then tried the hoe by digging into the ground with it some three times with all the manly strength his creator gave him before telling Bugonoka, "Bring me some water and a washbasin[3] quickly!"

Bugonoka did so, knelt down and handed him water and a washbasin.

Myombekere poured water on the hoe in the handle with the water running into the washbasin and leaving behind the red hot iron hoe hissing from its contact with the water and making the water boil: *tokotoko*! and *fwofwofwo*! He then pulled the hoe out of the handle again, bent its spike a bit before planting it in the ground to cool and poured water on the head of the handle to cool the wood too. After that he took the hoe and drove it into the handle once more, and again tried it by digging with it and was satisfied he had fixed it right for farm work and told his wife, "I am done, dear wife, and the hoe is so well planted in its handle you would think it has always been there and it is not a newly fixed one! Why don't you come and see for yourself?"

Wife came and husband said, "Here it is, see for yourself. You should have no more excuse for telling people, `Myombekere refused to put a handle to a hoe for me, that's why I didn't plant sweet potatoes this year', since, alas, you women are always out to falsely accuse us men of all sorts of things."

"*Uu*! Myombekere, there you go again! I am sure even if women are inventors of stories as you say, they wouldn't go to the extent of saying that something is not there when it is! *A*! *hee*! *aa*! at least not that!"

"Why do you want to deny the truth? Don't we see everyday some worthless lazy women who are the very same people who go about spreading rumors everywhere that their husbands have failed to provide them with hoes and that's why they are seen daily roaming the streets and doing nothing while famine is ravaging their households like an evil-spirit, when the truth of the matter is simply that they are lazy creatures, that laziness is their only problem, but otherwise their husbands' homes are full of hoes ready for work?" Bugonoka was about to refute her husband's arguments when Myombekere gave her examples complete with names: "Take for example Nkarani's wife, the one called Nakuyenga, the daughter of Ababogo clan, does her husband not provide her with a hoe? What about Bandiho's wife, the one called Netoga, the daughter of Abahimba clan? And what about Mpongano, the wife of the late Kayobyo? Don't you see all these women behaving like lunatics, spreading all sorts of false accusations against their husbands similar to what we are saying: `My husband never gives me clothes to wear, my husband never provides me with a hoe, my husband is a bad man and does this and does that... that's why I can never plant my fields with crops.' Especially Mpongano, that one simply defies description!"

Bugonoka kept quiet and took the hoe in her hands and tried it by digging a bit with it and found it felt right for field work and said: "Yes, you have done good work! Only a lazy person complains against a hoe."

That same day Myombekere went and cut a tree for making a handle for his billhook, came and chiseled and fashioned the handle and finished it at a go. It was of a handle of *omukonyo* hard wood. Then he fixed the billhook in the handle after firing the spike of his iron tool to make sure the fixture would hold. That done, he sent his wife to bring him water for sharpening his work implement. He whetted it until it was so sharp it could cut through a fly which dared land on its cutting edge, and then went and hung it on a wall inside the house, already resolved the following day that tool would see some real action.

And so the following morning, when he judged dew had dried enough in the grass, he put his billhook on his shoulder and took his wooden rake and: *hoho*! off he went to clear his sweet potato lake-side fields.

The fields had become really bushy, overgrown with *amahule* and *amazuzume* mangroves and all sorts of trees, some of whose names even I don't know, which   were in turn overran and covered with thickets of vines and tree-climbers like *amasanzwa, ensikesike* and *amatungamamba*. And he got to work at once. Whenever his billhook became blunt, he whetted it on some rough stones around, never letting off to rest a bit in all that hot sun, dripping with sweat all over his body. He left his work only to go home for lunch at noon.

After lunch, the man sharpened his billhook properly again as he did the first time to get it ready for more work, and when he felt the sun was cooling off a bit, he took his work implements again and went back to his place of work and toiled. When he saw that the sun was about to disappear behind the horizon, he said to himself, "I should stop now, lest I work during the night and make people imagine strange things about me, say I till my fields at night because I use zombies to work for me. What's more, it's time to go home; I have worked enough."

He took his tools and left, passed by the cattle-watering strip of the beach where he took off his clothes and bathed in the lake, and went home to try and sleep off at night the pains and aches of his overworked body.

The following morning, at the twittering of the early morning birds, somebody called at the gate of the fence of his home, which was still closed: "People of this home!"

Bugonoka, who was already up skimming milk, was the first to hear the caller and told her husband, "It appears there is somebody calling at the gate."

Myombekere asked in a loud voice, "Is there someone calling?"

"I am the one calling, asking you to come and open the gate for me."

Myombekere went and removed the shutter from the gate of his home and the caller entered. As soon as he entered, Myombekere recognized him as the suitor of his niece and relieved him of his bow and they greeted each other while still standing, and then Myombekere told him, "Let's go inside the house." However the in-law-to-be, for fear of running into his mother-in-law Bugonoka,[4] declined the invitation and said, "No, father-in-law, this will do, out here." Myombekere called his niece and told her to bring the visitor a seat. The visitor sat down and settled and then asked Myombekere, "Is it true that my mother-in-law is back?"

"Yes, she has come back. She is in the house, decanting milk."

Once Myombekere confirmed his wife was in the house, the visitor got up and walked slowly and with meek demeanor until he got to the door of the house. There he stopped and raised a greeting voice to his mother-in-law inside: "Good-morning, mother-in-law?"

Bugonoka did not hear and the unmarried young woman being courted called her: "Woman of my people, you are being called!" Bugonoka responded and the unmarried young woman told her, "Your son-in-law, my suitor, is greeting you, he is by the door."

The suitor threw forth another greeting, "Good-morning, mother-in-law!" and Bugonoka answered the greeting: "Good-morning, son!" And they went on to exchange news of each other until they finished. Then man then went back to Myombekere and courted his permission to marry his niece, who had already given her suitor her consent and sent him to court the permission of her elders.[5] He had already come once before to court Myombekere's consent, only he did not find him at home, having come during those days when it was difficult to find Myombekere in one place because of what his life had become when his wife was taken away from him by her parents. He said to Myombekere: "Praise to you, Sir, father-in-law, help me found a household. I am a suitor, courting your niece, the one who has come to cook for you here. I came here the other day and missed you. When I asked your niece, she said, `He left early in the morning, but I don't know where he went!' The day before yesterday, when I went to her parents' home again to find out the state of my courtship, her parents told me, `Go again to court the permission of her uncle, since you did not find him at home the first time. If you see him this time, give him your message and also tell the woman you are courting to come here tomorrow morning, so that we can conclude the arrangements for her marriage and give you a wife, because, son of good people, we too feel you have done all we wanted of you and don't intend to drag on for a whole year the courtship of a divorced woman as if it were that of a young maiden; no.' That is my suit to you here, and so was it the first time I came, my father-in-law. Give me the foundation of a home. One person's generosity is another's salvation!"

"I too don't have anything to say, really. Maybe the only thing I am going to ask you is this: `Go and bring me two hoe handles, just two, and after that let my relatives give you the woman you are courting, so that you can have a wife.' The woman you are wooing too will do as you said, go back to her parents tomorrow, because we wouldn't be doing the right thing to retain here an unmarried young woman instead of letting her get married, for it was decreed since the beginning of time that a female child would leave her father and mother and go to found other people's homes, and that's how it has always been."

With that the suitor asked for his weapons, so that he could go back when it was still cool in the morning, for he was in a hurry to get back home for some work he had to do, and Myombekere called his niece and told her, "The visitor would like to go back, bring him his weapons." The unmarried young woman came out of the house with the visitor's bow, the visitor said good-bye to Myombekere and Bugonoka, the young woman stepped aside so that her suitor could lead the way and the two of them left Myombekere's home engaged in some intimate conversation of two lovers. After some time they stopped walking and talked on while standing still in one place until their legs got weak at the knees and they sat down, the female lover holding the bow, the male lover having already explained to her how her father and mother had sent him to fetch her, and the female lover too having agreed that the following day she would be going to her parents home early in the morning and would be staying there until the wedding day. Finally she gave her suitor his weapon and they said good-bye to each other and parted, her suitor going back to his home and she returning to her uncle's.

Back home her uncle had just finished sharpening his billhook and he and his wife had decided that Bugonoka would start that very day to cultivate the field which he began clearing the previous day. Myombekere left for the field first, and when he got there began raking together the grass and trees he had mowed down the previous day and piling them in one spot, so that when those coming to till the field arrived they could start working in the part already raked clear. He hadn't finished raking when he saw the tillers coming, three of them, that is the visiting old woman, his niece and Bugonoka, who was carrying on her head a load of sweet potato vines for planting. The women found Myombekere busy raking grass, seriously at work, no joke! On arriving Bugonoka put down her load of sweet potato vines and asked her husband, "Do we start cultivate this part or which one?"

Myombekere answered her: "Don't you see the side I have already cleared of grass? Where else do you want to start, when you see that I haven't even cut down the thicket on that other side? Just start with that side, if you are workers, people who have come here to cultivate the field!"

Bugonoka first gave the ground a trial cut, you know, with four strokes or so of her new hoe her husband put on a handle for her the previous day, as her companions looked on waiting for her findings, and then she exclaimed with a grunt: "*N!*"

Her husband heard her grunting and said, "What is that *n!* for, when what is needed is for you to hold your hoe like a she-man and scare this field and make it give way and disappear quickly so that you can begin tilling another one!" and everybody laughed.

With that Myombekere's niece as well as the visiting old woman too started digging as they told Bugonoka, "You should, we understand, scare the field this way: `*Ha!* I am cutting you!' if you want it to give way and disappear quickly as your husband told you." Bugonoka was the only one who had a new hoe while her two companions had used ones, though by no means worn out, used hoes still in good working condition and not remains of hoes of which people say hoeing with such hoes is digging with one's chest. Whenever passers-by ask people working with such hoes, "How is work?" they answer, "Work is fine, since we are here and hoeing, even though we are hoeing with our chests." And indeed when you take a look at the hoes in their hands you cannot but agree with them and say, "Yes, indeed you are right, you are farming the field with nothing but the muscles of your chests!"

The tillers, that is Bugonoka and her two companions, got to work, making rows of well-rounded mounds of soil on which to plant their sweet potato vines, slowly moving from one row to another, each one of them comparing her work with that of her companions to make sure she was

tilling and planting properly, at the same time as on his side of the field
Myombekere too was busy at his own work. He had finished raking grass
and was now back to attacking the bush with his billhook, so that all one
could hear was: *vutu! vutu!* stopping his mowing down of the brush only to
cut down a tree whenever he came across one, and cutting it his own
particular way. I am saying this because there are people who are left-
handed, even in digging the fields, while others, the majority, are right-
handed. All of a sudden the women heard Myombekere breathe a sigh of
relief: "*Yehuu!*" and on looking his way they saw that he had completed his
work. Bugonoka was the first to remark and tell him, "I see! You have
finished clearing the entire field!"

He answered, "It's true I have finished, only I hurt myself, my dear
wife."

All the three women asked him at the same time: "You are hurt
where?"

"My eye. I simply don't know what has got into it. I have tried to
agitate it with my hand, in the hope that whatever got into it might get out,
but in vain!"

The old woman said, "May be the poisonous tiny *akanalila*[6] dropped
into it?"

Her two companions retorted, "*Akanalila* in this broad daylight! I
thought the tiny insect flies about only in the evening, or does it do so in
daytime too?"

And the old woman answered, "And so you don't agree? How can this
water-side field fail to harbor the insect? And if they are around and it is
your bad luck to get it in your eye, what is surprising if it gets in? I now see
that you are not serious, you are yet to see what can happen to people in
this world!"

After that Myombekere returned home to fetch fire for burning the
grass he had mowed, brought the fire and put it on the grass and the fire
blazed, making grass which hadn't dried properly hiss and squeak: *zwii!*
from time to time exploding: *puu!* Then the field workers looked up in the
sky and found the sun was already directly over their heads and seeing that
Myombekere said, "We should be going home, ladies, for lunch; the
stomach is crying out for food. *Ahee!* You too want to finish your work in
a single day like me, when my work is the quick and fast one. As the saying
goes, `You can't cheat with a hoe, you can only cheat with a billhook.'"

"Let's finish planting these mounds we are on and then go home and come back later."

And so when they finished that they all left to go home, but not before looking at the work they had accomplished and saying, "Oh, yes! we have indeed put in a good start!"

After lunch the women went back to their lakeshore fields, to work on a bit more when they were still three, since Bugonoka's third companion, her husband's niece, had already told the other two women that on the following day she would be going back to her parents. Bugonoka could return to work in the field without worry, because there was enough flour at home and relish for dinner was already cooked. Myombekere was the only one who remained at home, lying on his bed, both because he had hurt his eye and because he had finished his man's job of clearing the field with a billhook, and since sweet potatoes was a women crop,7 what was there for him to do in the field even if he wanted to help! When he saw it was time to take a bath, he went down to the lake and bathed. From bathing he went to see the farmers at work and found the three women had already cultivated a whole large patch of the field! He was really impressed by what they had done! What with the fact that the soil of that lake-side field was still all wet as if it were the rain season, the cultivated stretch was simply something beautiful to behold! The women on their part, when they looked at his eye, now overflowing with tears and exuding rheum, exclaimed with anxiety: "*Ee*! There is danger of this eye causing you a lot of suffering!"

Myombekere answered: "There is always danger in all the work we do."

That day and at night Myombekere had a rough time. That eye would simply give him no rest from pain, the whole night long. The following morning Bugonoka took him to Kanwaketa's wife, who was skilled in removing splinters from eyes. When Kanwaketa's wife plied open Myombekere's eye she found he had indeed splinters in it. She removed the splinters and put into the eye some eye-drops. When the couple were about to leave, she gave them some more medicine and said, "When you get home put in the eye some more drops of the medicine, and before the morning sun has become hot you should see tears and rheum clear from the eye. Only as soon as you squeeze drops of the medicine into his eye he must lie on his bed with eyes closed for quite a while. And let's see how he'll do."

Myombekere got home and his wife treated his eye as their healer instructed them, and in no time, on taking a short nap and waking up, he perceived his wounded eye had already cleared. On seeing that, he got out of bed, completely restored, as if he had never hurt himself in that eye. His niece had already decided she couldn't return to her parents' home and leave his uncle with such an injury, and only when she saw that he was no longer hurting from the splinters in his eye did she tell him that she wanted to go back. Her uncle too gave her permission and told her, "In fact all this time I thought you had already gone, so you haven't?"

"*Aa!* Uncle, go without saying good-bye to you! In fact I had already decided I couldn't go and leave you so badly hurt and had said to myself, 'Let me wait and see how his injury will be and go when he has improved a bit,' for I certainly couldn't leave you in that condition, as if you were some mere stranger and no relative of mine."

To send her off, Bugonoka loaded her husband's niece with presents. She packed flour for her in a huge bowl,[8] full to the top, then filled their large calabash bowl with liquid butter and strapped it in a rope-hanger for easy carrying. Myombekere too put in his own send-off for his niece. He went to the platform on which he was smoke-drying the meat of the cow he had slaughtered and took some three big cuts of meat and put them in a medium size carrying basket, tied the meat in the basket nicely and gave it to her, just as the women too finished wrapping the flour ready for her journey. And so Myombekere's niece said good-bye to his uncle: "Good-bye, uncle, stay well in your home!"

Myombekere answered: "Many greetings to my brother-in-law and to your mother Mbonabibi and to your brothers," and she answered him back, "Yes, Sir."

Bugonoka took the flour and the calabash of liquid butter and the visiting old woman took the basket with meat and the two of them got up to escort her. When her escort got their departing companion to their neighborhood's common grazing ground, they put down her send off presents and then arranged them one on top of the other this way: the carrying basket with meat below and the bowl of flour on top of the meat inside the basket, where it fitted tight into the empty top, and lifted the combined load and put it on her head, and then put the calabash of liquid butter in her hands and she held it by the ropes of its hanger. Then the three women said good-bye to each other and Myombekere's niece went to her parent's home and her escort came back.

On getting home, Bugonoka and the old woman found Kagufwa ready for the morning round of milking cows. Bugonoka brought him water for washing his hands and he milked the cows and finished. Bugonoka then put in a pot[9] sweet potatoes for the little girl of her home to cook, put the pot on the cooking-stones and told her, "Here is a pot on the cooking-stones in which I have put for you food to cook and water to cook it with. And so, when it is time start the fire and cook food; we are now going to till. Yes! Do you understand?" "Yes." Then Bugonoka and the old woman put their hoes on their shoulders and went to till their lake-side field. Myombekere stayed behind at home, replacing logs in the fence of his cattle kraal where cows had broken through during the night.

At their field Bugonoka and the old woman first put down their hoes and went to cut sweet potato vines for planting from grown crops whose owners had allowed them to do so. They had been cutting sweet potato vines only for a short while when Bugonoka got hold of one she liked and pulled it before cutting, but the vine would not come out, apparently because it was entangled with other vines of the crop. Because it was her favorite sweet potatoes, she decided to trace it to its base where it appeared entangled. She was just bending down to disentangle it when on opening her eyes: *kigi*![10] a giant adder! She jumped and landed on the other side, far away, amidst cries of a frightened person: "*Yu!* Mother, I'm dying!"

The old woman asked from where she was, equally frightened by Bugonoka's cries, "What is it, dear?" and Bugonoka answered her, "I almost grabbed a giant adder, my dear!" The old woman hurried to her, clasping her seeding vines, some dropping down without her knowledge, and asked her, "Where is the terrible creature, dear?"

Bugonoka, still shaking with fright, took her to near where the snake was and said, "There it is, coiled over there!"

The old woman, whose vision was already cloudy, strained her eyes of an aged person and peeped and after quite a while she too saw the creature and found: *hii*! indeed it was some giant of a snake, grown almost too big to move! Overcome with fright, the two women hurried away from that field: *karukaru*! leaving behind some of the crop vines they had already cut, not daring to collect them all, since they now imagined that entire field of sweet potatoes to be swarming with adders. It was not until they were completely out of there and in the open that the old woman remembered to ask Bugonoka, "By the way, dear, what type of sweet potato was it whose vine brought all this on you?"

Bugonoka answered, "*Kandoya*, my dear."

The two women went straight back to till their field, because they had already cut enough sweet potato vines to plant the area they could possibly cultivate in a day. Shortly after they saw Myombekere coming with a fire smoking on a piece a broken pot held in the palm of his hand, on his right-hand shoulder a rake and a billhook. When he got near enough he said,

"How is work, farmers?"

"Work is fine, so to say, but we were about to die."

"*Yu!* What wanted to kill you?"

"We were cutting seeding sweet potato vines from the fields of the real farmers and had cut quite enough and were adding just a bit more when I came face to face with a giant adder, dusty beyond description, so big it could hardly move! That was what I was about to hold in my hand with a *kandoya* sweet potato vine I wanted to cut. Maybe today I woke up destined for death, for what else would I be now if not dead, had I been bitten by that huge snake?"

"*Aa!* By now you would be dead and gone, so don't ask what you would be. Indeed welcome back, my dear wife, from the monster's teeth, because by now I wouldn't know what to say. *Ahee!* What a day! May be even now the creature is still at the spot."

"Even if it is still there, what do you want if for?"

"To kill it."

"Are you crazy! You want to kill a snake! You, a grown up person, are speaking of killing a snake! Is it because you don't have children that you want to kill a snake?"

"And wouldn't it have killed you, had it bitten you?"

"It would have killed me, yes. And even if it had killed me, does that mean you would have killed it too? Wouldn't you have been afraid of the evil of your action catching up with you and harming you later on?"

The old woman said, "Indeed, child, whoever makes it his or her habit to kill the creatures that creep by the earth cannot escape evil falling on his or her head; not at all. If you keep on that way you will end up killing a python and then saying: `It's nothing!' However, my son, what we should do is to say no more of the matter. Anyway, who would take you to the creature and knowingly run the danger of doing a forbidden thing?"

"*Aa!* I too just said that as a kind of joke, otherwise I have no intention of doing the forbidden; no."

After calming their fears that way, Myombekere turned to the work which had brought him to the field, which was to rake together grass he was clearing when he hurt his eye the previous day. That done, he took the fire he had come with and torched the grass and it blazed and burnt everything down in no time. With that he told Bugonoka, "This is now work done, my wife, because I have now finished my man's work; only yours remains."

His wife answered him back: "Yes, this is now work done. Let's now see how Kalyoba[11] will decide matters. Should it grant us good health, we will cultivate the field to the end, should it withhold well-being from us, that's fine too, we'll go where everyone finally goes." On looking at the sun in the sky, they found it was already time for lunch and went home to eat. After lunch the two women came back and tilled their field until the evening sun had descended all the way down and completely disappeared behind the horizon.

From then on Bugonoka and the visiting old woman in her house fell into a daily routine of theirs of which they needed nobody to remind them. As soon as Bugonoka got out of bed, very early in the morning, at early dawn twittering of birds, when her husband was still asleep, she cleaned the bottom of her water pot and went to the lake to draw water. Since she was an energetic worker, sometimes she went to draw water that early in the morning after she was done and finished with grinding flour on her grinding-stone, and it was when she came from drawing water that she found her husband waking up and gave him water for washing his face. And on the days there was enough relish in the house, she never left home without first cooking breakfast for her husband. And when she had done all that, and skimmed milk and decanted it, she got hold of her hoe and in that very instant was off to till her field.

And so it did not take long before Bugonoka completed tilling her four sweet potato fields, of which she had started cultivating the most difficult one, the one which had become most bushy, the same one in which Myombekere hurt his eye. That too was the only one she tilled with the help of the visiting old woman, after which she went back to her relatives who were taking care of her in her old age. As to her remaining three fields, those she cultivated all alone, without a single helping hand.

When people who had planted *obubele*[12] millet that year threshed their harvest, Myombekere slaughtered a bull from his stock, a black bull incredibly big, the kind of bull owners of livestock reserve for slaughtering for mourners at their deaths, its hump so big that it had already cut itself into two. He had named it "The-entire-country".[13] That was the bull Myombekere slaughtered for millet and got from it enough millet to fill his grain store,[14] since in bartering the meat of the bull for millet for a really tiny piece of meat, almost smaller than that palm of your hand, he had put as a millet measure a men's meal bowl.[15] The one who filled that bowl with millet had thrown into his or her container a tiny piece of meat, and that was all he or she got and left with, and the one who did his or her best and filled the measure some two or three times got a corresponding number of the tiny pieces of meat. What with the fact that he had brought a real ruse of a retailer to work for him, a man called Mpuyangani,[16] a truly "unruly" man, true to his name, *aa!* It was something to behold! That man had a way of simply hoodwinking people who brought their millet to buy meat! No sooner had they filled his measure with millet than in that very instant he had emptied the millet into his big *ekitukuru*[17] basket and was already asking for more and telling people, "Bring the millet, quick, the meat for trading is almost all gone, since the owner of the cow slaughtered it intending to leave some for himself so that he too could eat some meat." What with the fact that in the days following the threshing of millet there is scarcity of fish, he had hardly finished saying that when the people were already scrambling to snatch from each other's hands the measuring bowl, with many of them spilling their millet in the scramble, which fell on the cow-hides he had taken care to spread on the barter ground! That was why Myombekere ended up with so much millet that he filled his grain store to the top. In fact that barter man of his did not all the time give people their due bits of meat for their measures of millet but, far from it, was grossly cheating others and giving them almost nothing for their millet! The truth is it did not take long before Mpuyangani had sold all the meat, because people poured in with so much millet that meat was finished even before many of them got there and a lot of disappointed men and women returned to their homes with their millet, especially since Myombekere's The-entire-country was a bull of legendary fatness in the area and the fame of its sweet meat could not have spread faster!

As for that Mpuyangani, when he finished his work Myombekere put something in the palm of his hand: one *ekitukuru* basket full of millet, one rather large cut of steak, plus an assortment of this and that from the entrails of the bull, and he took off with his meat strung on a rope, something with which to console himself in his home after his sweat and toil of a rather dubious kind that day in Myombekere's home.

When Bugonoka was tilling her sweet potato fields Myombekere on his part was preoccupied with some really important man's work in that home of his, the work of planting banana tubers in his backyard. What made him decide to plant bananas is this: First, he realized that the owner of a banana plantation or the man with banana beer was a person well known to the rulers of the country, from village headmen and princes all the way to the king himself. Second, he realized that a man with a banana plantation is a celebrity, true to the saying: "If you want to be famous grow a banana plantation." Third, as he himself had found out, the man with a banana plantation can end up possessing another man's property, such as a goat, like the one he himself took to a man with a banana plantation and bought twenty-five bunches of bananas from him, and many other valuables. Fourth, he had seen that the owner of a banana plantation can welcome in his home nobility even if he himself is the poorest of the poor, a childless man like himself. Fifth, he realized that with banana beer one can get people to help him do and finish very quickly many important jobs in people's lives, like preparations for wedding celebrations and other festivities, threshing millet, building houses, communal tilling of fields, dragging keels of boats from the forest to the sea, carrying planks for building boat frames, hauling canoes to the sea, carrying poles and thatching grass for houses, and many others. And sixth, he had found out that a banana plantation can often save a man from need and make him owner of whatever he wanted.

That work of cultivating a banana plantation made Myombekere go back and forward without end, asking for seed tubers, carrying them to his home all alone until he had finally planted in the backyard of his home two hundred banana plants. And because in this country people will never let alone a person, see him or her doing his or her work without wanting to know all about it, whoever met him on the way carrying banana tubers on his head would ask him, "What do you want these banana tubers for, Myombekere? Are you perhaps starting a banana plantation?" and on his part Myombekere would answer each and everyone who asked him such questions: "I want to have a few banana plants at home from which my wife can cut green banana leaves for covering her pot of sweet potatoes and cassava when cooking, because I have seen that too often her food is uncooked during the days of the easterly and the westerly and the northerly and the southerly wind!"

And people kept on querying him that way until finally some of them came all the way to where he was planting his bananas, after which their meddling knew no limits! Whoever came to him and found him in the field planting the bananas, or even if he wasn't there at all, he or she would begin tilling and planting for Myombekere with his or her mouth and finish the job in no time and then add: "Yes, here banana will flourish! Dig this way and that way, up to that place, inclusive of that bushy patch, if it too is part of your field. Especially in this area here where *engoro* grass is growing, that's where really flourishing banana will grow, banana trees which will bring down real bunches of bananas, bunches which require no less than two people to lift a single one of them from the ground!"

Whenever he heard such remarks Myombekere would be confounded and left wondering: "What is wrong with us people of this country of ours? *Aa!* I am simply lost, honestly! When you find another man quietly doing his own job you don't want to just greet him and exchange news with him and then keep quiet! Instead, first you don't honestly tell him what you really think of his work but you always praise him for it, and then should you in his absence come across another person and the two of you begin discussing his work you find fault with it and with all he has done, and anybody   who does not behave in that strange way is seen as somebody who   doesn't know how to talk! Does that make sense! I find the whole thing incredible, believe me! And why is it that these people keep on coming here like the fly in the saying: `I am the giant shit-fly inseparable from your stench?' Then on the road whoever meets you carrying banana tubers questions you without end, to know where you are taking them and what you want with them, as if you were the first person ever to cultivate a banana plantation in this country! And then here in my field I believe I am working all alone when apparently I am working with many people, I leave my home to come to this field all alone only to arrive here and get the impression that I am working with very many others! There is the co-worker of mine who comes here with a billhook in his mouth and as soon as you finish greeting each other at once he falls on clearing the bush: *pupupupu*! and finishes clearing the entire field and, when on my part I haven't dug even a single hole in which to plant a single banana tuber, he is already off planting. Then with my second co-worker my field is already a fully grown banana plantation, its plants already carrying very big bunches of bananas, he has, in fact, already arrived with a billhook and cut down the bunches, each bunch has taken two people to carry, it appears he has even drank *obutongora*[19] juice from the end-buds of the stalks of the bunches, a long long time ago! All that when I on my part haven't even got to digging the second planting hole, am still working on planting the first tuber, and already he is seeing a flourishing banana plantation from which he has already eaten ripe bananas, drank banana beer, got drunk on the beer and sung with intoxication, and since a long long time ago too at that!"

However he was prepared for them all and whoever came to him with such comments he would answer him or her: "What you see here is a banana plantation planted by the old ones of yore who first planted bananas and what I am doing is simply weeding it. Work not yet done needs doing. You can't take what is not there. You can't command your dog to catch what it hasn't spotted. To get somewhere you must journey. It's not yet time for drinking, ladies and gentlemen!" And with such words he parleyed with those who came to him as he was digging his field and let his real reasons for growing a banana plantation remain a secret of his heart and soul.

Chapter XI

NOTES

1. *Ekikome*: See note 1 of Chapter II.
2. Wazinza hoe: See note 18 of chapter V.
3. *Olusabuzyo*: See note 12 of Chapter I.
4. According to the Kikerewe extended family ranking of relatives, Myombekere's niece was a daughter to his wife Bugonoka, and hence Bugonoka was a would-be mother-in-law of the suitor of the young woman. See note 11 of Chapter I for the ranking of relations and note 7 of Chapter I for the custom which required a son-in-law and his mother-in-law to avoid each other.
5. Because Myombekere's niece was a free (unmarried) adult woman, *omusimbe*, and no longer a maiden, according to Kikerewe custom, as we see with the second marriage of Bulihwali in Chapter XXXVIII, she, and not her parents, was the one who chose her would-be husband. See note 24 of Chapter II and note 22 of Chapter IX and the second marriage of Bulihwali in Chapter XXXVIII.
6. *Akanalila*: Literally "that which urinates (into the eye)", a minuscule flying insect which causes very sharp though short-lasting pain when it gets into a person's eye.
7. Among the Wakerewe, sweet-potatoes and other vegetables and greens were considered women crops and therefore never cultivated or harvested by men. See note 14 of Chapter VI.
8. *Ekibo*: See note 15 of Chapter I.
9. *Omuzubo*: Drinking-water pot used as a cooking pot.
10. *Kigi*! : Ideophone for suddenly sighting something.
11. Kalyoba of Izoba: The Sun as a deity; also Providence. See note 21 of chapter II.
12. *Obubele*: See note 17 of Chapter V.
13: *Charokoba*: "The entire country", a colossus.
14. *Ekitala*: See note 18 of Chapter I.
15. For *ekibo* for serving food to men see note 16 of Chapter VI.
16. *Mpuyangani*: "Unruly one."
17. *Ekitukuru:* See note 16 of Chapter V.
18. *Obutongora*: Very sweet juice lodged in the leaves of the end-bud of the stalk of a bunch of bananas, which birds (and children) like to suck.

Chapter XII

MYOMBEKERE TAKES HIS WIFE TO HEALERS IN SEARCH OF FERTILITY

Myombekere and his wife Bugonoka both spent that day working in their crop fields and it was finally nighttime and the two were on their sweet bed when Myombekere first fidgeted in bed and then broke into a slight cough. When his cough ended he immediately yawned, without covering his mouth with the palm of his hand or *enkanda* [1] with which the couple were covering themselves as he would normally have done. "*Ahee!* What is happening today!" Bugonoka wondered. She almost burst out laughing but checked herself: "No, wait first for his yawn to end before you tell him what you want to say to him, since you are just the two of you here and it's not as if he will run away. No need to hurry." Then she heard her husband close his mouth with a whine, following that with chewing his mouth and swallowing saliva and again following that with what sounded like another slight cough. And that was when she finally said to him, "Whatever is afflicting you must be causing you a lot of pain, I am sure. You fidgeted and in that very instant you were yawning! Oh, dear me! *Yu!*

ahee! Poor me! At first I wanted to laugh and then I remembered and said to myself, `The world is full of all kinds of illnesses, maybe there is something wrong with your mate? *Hoo*! My goodness! Say nothing, you will ask him later on, that is if he is all right.'"

Your Myombekre on hearing that from his wife was ceased by endless laughter: *kakakaka*! infecting his wife with it and making her laugh until her sides ached. Whenever Myombekere laughed that way he slobbered excessively so that now on his side of the bed the cow-skin covering the bed became nothing but saliva and had his wife not wiped it off, *aa*! he would have passed the night on a dripping-wet cow-skin bed sheet! As to Bugonoka, that kind of heavy laughing made her sides ache and set tears streaming from her eyes endlessly, so that she too soaked her side of their cow-skin bed sheet, as you would expect!

It was when they finally stopped laughing that Myombekere told Bugonoka, "Tomorrow early in the morning I am going to the healer I told you about to tell him you are back, because I went to him twice while you were still at your parents' home and each time he told me, `Go home and come back when your wife is back.' So let me go and hear what he has to tell me and bring it back to you, for isn't it great to leave your own self on earth when you die?"

"Yes, it is a very great thing indeed, and that's why nobody likes to be without child, especially women. When you think about dying and leaving nothing behind you, nothing at all, disappearing altogether, with nobody at all to mourn you, dying like a dog whose dead body is eaten by the animals of prey in the wilderness, as if there are no healers in the world, *aa!* the pain inside you becomes unbearable! And since life is such a sweet thing, you cannot even kill yourself!"

"Why kill yourself, my dear wife, when barrenness can befall anybody? Don't you know of childless people who are also human beings living on this earth?"

"You can afford to say so because you are a man: if you marry another woman you can have children without any problem. But where will I get a child? It is true I see fellow childless people on this earth, but they never give up without first trying to drink the herbs of healers. Oh, dear me, how can we know anything by just sitting here like this!"

They dropped that subject and talked of some other matter, this and that, but even then mostly connected with their most important obligation, that of looking for fertility for Bugonoka. They would go everywhere, should that healer fail them they would go to another one, until they had been to all the medicine men and medicine women of Ukerewe kingdom, after which they would go abroad to other countries, wherever it is they will hear people say, "There is a healer in such and such a place." Finally they fell asleep.

And so the following morning Myombekere got on his way to the medicine man's home, to tell the healer that his wife had come back. He found the healer busy catering to his very many other clients, among whom were lepers, people suffering from epilepsy, from madness, people struck with muteness by witchcraft, people afflicted with spells of evil-spirits, people suffering from polio, from afflictions of breaking taboos, afflictions of curses, from all sorts of bewitchment, clients who had come to have their fingernail parings taken for making charms with, in addition to receiving drinking medicines and amulets for body fortification.

Finally he too was able to explain the mission of his visit to the medicine man, whose name was Kibuguma, and when he informed him that his wife had come back the medicine man told him, "Go and pass two days at your place and on the third day come with her here so that I can begin examining you."

Myombekere said, "All right," and bid the healer good-bye and left. He was already some distance away when Kibuguma sent someone after him: "Go and call for me the man who has just left this home, his name is Myombekere. Tell him to come back, because I forgot to give him all the instructions I intended to give him."

The messenger ran after Myombekere and caught up with him and told him, "I have been sent to call you back, Kibuguma wants you." Myombekere turned around and went back, got to Kibuguma and asked him, "I hear you are calling me?" Kibuguma responded, "Yes, I am calling you to tell you the following: When you come here with your wife, don't forget to bring firewood, all of which must be from one and the same tree, together with a brand-new cooking pot for cooking the medicine I will have prepared for you."

Myombekere said, "Fine," said good-bye to the medicine man the second time and went back home.

Back home Bugonoka first gave him a delicious little dish of sweet potatoes with *ekizanda* [2] of skimmed milk and he ate his fill, and then asked him about his journey: "Welcome back, did you find him at home, what did he tell you?"

"I am back, I found him at home, busy healing the sick. He sends you his greetings. And this is what he told me: `Go, pass two days, the day after tomorrow come with your wife. And when you come, come with firewood split from the same piece of wood together with a brand new cooking pot.'"

"He sends me greetings! Does he know me?"

"Are you telling me that people send greetings only to those they know? I thought that whenever you meet a person and exchange greetings with him or her, even a total stranger you have just met on the road, you can, if you so choose, ask him or her to send greetings to his or her spouse: greet your wife or your husband for me?"

"Well, you are right, I must admit."

At night Myombekere and his wife went to bed and slept and when it dawned they counted: one. That day too at night they went to bed and, since the new day always comes, it dawned and they counted: two. That second day Myombekere early in the morning went into the forest to look for a dry log of *omunazi* tree, found it and brought it home. Once back home, he took his breakfast and finished and was ready for work. He took his ax and split the log and got the required firewood of the same wood, fetched cords and tied together a faggot of the size a woman can carry comfortably. And at night that day they went to bed again, ready for their journey to the medicine man's home the following day.

The following day early in the morning, after Bugonoka had churned milk and poured her skimmed milk into *ebizanda*, she woke up the little girl of her home and told her, "There are sweet potatoes in this basket[4] here; when you see it is time wash and prepare them and cook, but make sure you peel the big ones, don't cook them with their skin on. Milk for drinking is in *ebizanda* up in the hangers; churn it around from time to time so that it doesn't curdle and spoil. And stay well. And do not leave the home to go anywhere before we return!" And with that husband and wife took their faggot of firewood and their brand new pot in which to cook their medicine and a hoe, used but still fit for weeding purposes, their fee for their healer, and left. The morning sun was beginning to warm up when they arrived at their destination.

That day Myombekere and his wife Bugonoka were the first clients to arrive in the healer's home, and so when Kibuguma exchanged greetings with them and finished and they took their seats and settled down, and when shortly after that he began catering to his clients of the day he started by attending to the couple. He told Bugonoka to follow him inside his house with her firewood and her new pot. Once inside, the healer brought medicine chipped with a chisel from a tree and put it in the pot the couple had come with and poured water in the pot until the medicine was completely covered. Then he told Bugonoka to place the pot on cooking-stones and cook the medicine. When the medicine boiled the first time, he told her to take it from the cooking-stones and bring it near the door of the house. Kibuguma then called Myombekere, who was still seated outside, and said, "Come into the house." Myombekere went into the house and he too took a seat by the door and the couple listened to Kibuguma talking to unseen powers in search of a cure which would heal them of the obstacle to their having children. The healer looked in that medicine which had been cooked with firewood from the same tree. He ordered the pot of medicine brought outside the door so that should a fly fall into the medicine and die he would know that the person seeking cure from him does not have long to live and if no fly fell into the medicine and died he would know that his patient still had very long to live on this earth. No fly fell into Bugonoka's medicine, so Kibuguma was really happy to begin healing the couple and said to Myombekere, "Your wife is a person of great destiny, because I find her omen very pleasing. I have also seen that what killed her children in the past was *ihuzi* 3 worms in her womb and nothing else. There is no other thing wrong with her at all, she is neither under a curse nor is she bewitched. And, Bugonoka, there is nothing wrong with your husband either. I have further seen that this woman has two eggs in her womb and that those eggs will give her children: one egg is an egg of a male child and the other one that of a female child. She will give birth to the male child first, after which she will give birth to the female child."

His clients on their part were agreeing with every word their healer was saying and prodding him on: "More of that truth!" or "See more clearly, healer!" And silently to themselves each one of them was saying: "What luck! Thanks to the heavens!" Especially Bugonoka, for whom everything was simply incredible! Thinking of what she was hearing she was saying to herself, "Can what this healer is saying really come to pass with me so that I will give birth to living beings, so that I too will hold on these two thighs of mine a child from my own womb! *Hee!* May be it is just healer's talk, he is adding raw trees to firewood just to swell the faggot! *Aa!* Anyway, since we are already here, let's listen to what he says and then wait and see what Providence decides."

When Kibuguma finished revealing their destiny to them, he called his wife, who was in the bedroom, and said, "Weroba, come and go and bathe your fellow woman!" Weroba came and Bugonoka took the pot of medicine and the two women left the healer's home with it until they came to a crossroads. Then Weroba told Bugonoka, "Take off your clothes so that I can bathe you." Bugonoka took off her clothes and then squatted right in the middle of the crossroads. Weroba then took the medicine from the pot and started bathing her with it, starting with her head and descending down to the big toe of each of her legs and bathing her entire body completely. After that Weroba told her to put on her clothes again, as she on her part got hold of the medicine pot and turned it upside down on the ground, pouring onto the ground all the medicine which had remained in the pot and leaving it there in the middle of the crossroads, and then took the pot and the two women returned home to Bugonoka's healer.

The healer told his wife Weroba, "Take that pot, because now it has become yours. To these two now it has become taboo, they cannot under any circumstances cook in it food or relish, even if it is nothing but mere greens, and eat that food. That is altogether a forbidden thing for them." Weroba took the pot and went to put it away with her other pots in the house, as at the same time Myombekere took the used hoe he had brought and gave it to Kibuguma as payment for the treatment he had given them. Kibuguma received the hoe and gave it to his wife and she put it away.

Myombekere then told Kibuguma: "As far as my wife and I are concerned, from this day we count ourselves your faithful disciples. And since you have initiated us, please adopt us fully, give us medication we can take while in our home."

Kibuguma agreed and sent his daughter, still a little girl, whose name was Bazaraki, to collect from the woods medicine for the couple. She was a child who already knew what she was doing, a young girl her breasts about to form and a very intelligent child who always did exactly as told whatever her father sent her to do. When her father called her and instructed her as to the medicines she was to collect, at once Bazaraki went into the house and took a chisel from its hanger, took a clean plate made of teak wood and disappeared into the wilderness to look for the medicines, got there and fell to procuring the medicines her father sent her for. At the first medicinal tree, she held her chisel in her right hand and her wooden plate in her left hand and began hacking chips of the tree into the plate she held underneath. When a chip she hacked off the tree fell on the plate face down, she took that one off the plate and threw it away, because those were her father's instructions to her, so that she kept only the chips which fell on the plate face up, because, according to her father's directions, that was the good medicine, the one to use to cure whatever disease the person seeking cure may be suffering from. And she chipped on until she had covered all the trees her father sent her to collect medicine from. That done, the little girl passed by their banana plantation, where she cut some strips of dry banana stem fiber as well as green banana leaves in which to wrap the medicine she had collected. She brought the medicine to her father and he examined it and found it was exactly what he had sent her for and told her to wrap it nicely in a green banana leaf first and then in strips of banana fiber.

Kibuguma gave the medicine to the couple and told Bugonoka, "Here is your medicine, but there are certain things you have to do. When you get home look for a calabash from the pervious year's harvest of gourds as the container in which to mix your medicine with water. Use only what you need and dry in the sun the remaining. You will be taking the medicine twice daily, in the morning before sunrise and in the evening immediately after the sun disappears from the sky. Only, both in the morning as well as in the evening, you will drink the medicine at the door of your house while facing east and with your legs stretched on the ground. Once the solution begins to weaken, you will pour that one out of the calabash and mix a new one, only the old medicine must be poured out nowhere else except into a shitting place in the bushes. You will come for more only when what I have given you is finished. If you yourself happen to be sick, your husband can always come to fetch it for you, it doesn't matter which one of you comes. What matters is for you to discipline yourself and make sure you don't misbehave with other men away from home and to observe the prescribed procedure for taking the medicine and for the two of you not to break any spousal sex prohibition at all while you are taking the medicine, that's all. As you know, no medicine can be effective and cure you of your disease when, in addition, you are afflicted with *amakire*4 disease for breaking a sex prohibition. And, by the way, the two of you should tell me if you are still kids, if you cannot discipline yourselves and keep away from the mischief of extra-marital sex, so that I don't waste on you my medicine for nothing. That is to say, if you are not ready to have children I shouldn't give you my medicine. Do we understand each other?"

"Is there any person in the world who doesn't want to have children? Having children is the one thing which every person on this earth longs for. And even with the like of us who don't have any, it is simply because we cannot do anything about it, but barrenness is something which all of us hate to see near us. Please just give us the medicine you have started giving us. We too know what you are talking about, otherwise why are we, two adults, here in front of you, if not to seek succor from our helplessness. Look at us, at our age, without the blessing of a single child alive, can we still be so easily tempted to misbehave out of our marriage, just like that, as if there is anything at all to be gained by that kind of thing?"

Having thus assured their healer, they were about to say good-bye to him when the healer, on seeing them preparing to leave, said another thing to Bugonoka: "By the way, I almost forgot. When you have mixed the medicine in a calabash of the previous year's gourd harvest, keep the calabash of medicine on the ground by the head bed-post of your side of your bed and always return it to that same place after drinking the medicine. It would be an excellent thing if you had in your house a female child who has not yet reached puberty, because it would be best if such a child were the one who held the medicine for you to drink."

"We have a female child in the house, one we are fostering, and she too hasn't reached puberty."

"Such a child is the one who should hold this medicine for you to drink. And tell the young child that before making you drink the medicine she should turn her back on you so that you are back to back. You will be sitting at the door of your house facing east and that child will be close to your back and holding in her hands the calabash of medicine for you to drink but facing west. That's how she should make you drink the medicine, her back against yours and, after giving you the medicine, she should be the one to take it back to its ground stand by the bed-post."

Then Myombekere and his wife took their medicine, said good-bye to Kibuguma and his wife Weroba and went back home.

Once back home Bugonoka looked for a gourd of the previous year's harvest, cut it nicely and cleaned it inside by scrapping and removing all its seeds and fluff. Then she unwrapped her medicine and put it in the calabash bowl and mixed it, went and fetched water which had been drawn fresh from the lake and poured the water into the medicine. When she finished she called the little girl, whose name was Nakiro,[5] and told her to take the gourd of medicine and the two went inside the house together and on to the bedroom. Then she told the little girl to dig a stand for the gourd in the earth of the floor next the head bed-post on her side of the couple's bed, and Nakiro did so and then stood the medicine calabash in it and the two came out of the house to attend to their other chores.

At sunset Bugonoka called the little girl and told her to bring the medicine gourd from the bed-post and then carefully instructed her as to how she was to make her drink it. And so when Bugonoka sat down by the door of her house and stretched out her legs, Nakiro sat close to her with her back against Bugonoka's back and the little girl held out the medicine to Bugonoka to drink. That done, the little girl took the medicine into the house to return it where she had taken it from, followed by Bugonoka, who too went into the house to start making dinner. It was already dark inside the house and Nakiro told Bugonoka, "Could you hold a torch this way so that I can see?" and Bugonoka lighted the house for the little girl with a flaming piece of wood. The child was about to cover the medicine with a lid when Bugonoka stopped her by reprimanding her: "Don't you dare cover the medicine, you little oversize-head creature! Are you the one who cast the spell of barrenness on me or what? Have you ever seen medicine covered?" Myombekere, who happened to be at the house door, told Bugonoka, "I tell you everyday that this useless creature of a child has no sense in her while you disagree, what do you say now? Is this child not of the same age as Kibuguma's daughter? And yet that other girl was carrying out perfectly well every work she was sent to do! *Aa*! This creature of ours here is empty headed, just like her mother!"

The following day in the morning too Bugonoka woke up Nakiro very early and the little girl held the medicine while Bugonoka drank it and it became their daily routine, as the healer directed, the woman and the young girl doing the same thing at dawn and again after sunset. And when the medicine was finished Bugonoka went for some more. She went with bowls[6] full of millet for the medicine man and this time all alone, her husband having been unable to accompany her because it was his round of duty of herding their neighborhood cattle.[7]

In Kibuguma's home his wife Weroba received from Bugonoka the present of millet she brought the healer and took it inside the house while Bugonoka remained standing outside. Then Weroba brought her a chair and she sat in the sweet morning sun together with the other clients of the medicine man she found already arrived. She greeted Kibuguma and finished and Kibuguma inquired for further news of her and asked her, "How is Myombekere?"

"He is fine, Sir; but I left him about to go grazing cattle, because it is his turn of duty in our neighborhood herding round."

"How many days does a home on duty herd in your area?"

"They herd for two days and on the third day they are free from duty."

"Oh, I see! They are just like us here. With us too that is how we herd."

On hearing that his male clients present told Kibuguma: "Herding rounds usually don't differ in neighborhoods where there are enough homes with cattle. Only neighborhoods in which there are few homes with cattle do you find turns of duty of some three of four days, otherwise throughout Ukerewe the turn of duty for most cattle owners is of two days for each home. In fact herding cattle in a four-day round of duty is almost like herding all alone, so that before you are through you have had more than enough of the smell of the wilderness and you are almost dying from exhaustion."

Bugonoka then told Kibuguma, "The medicine you gave us was finished yesterday, and so my husband woke me up early in the morning and said: `Go and bring medicine, because that is the most important thing. As for me, if when you return you find I have already left to graze cattle, just bring me something to eat in the pastures.' And so I would like to turn around and go back, lest I find the herder in bad shape, already dying of hunger. If the medicine is ready, please take care of me quickly."

Kibuguma went inside his house and brought Bugonoka another kind of medicine, different from the one he gave her the first time, and put it in her bowls and then told her: "This medicine is different from the one I gave you first and its job is to cure the disease of *ihuzi* which has been killing your children in your womb. With this one too you will mix the medicine in the gourd you used for the first medicine, putting a good fistful of the medicine in the calabash, enough for a strong mixture. This one you will take after cooking it mixed in the gruel of *endwero* [8] millet. The little girl of your home will decant the solution of the medicine into a small brand new pot and then use the solution to make the gruel, which should likewise be cooked for you by the little girl. Once you see that the gruel is ready, take the pot off the fire and drink the medicine gruel using *enkombyo* [9] spoon, morning and evening, as you did with the first medicine. But each time after decanting the medicine don't forget to tell the young girl to return the calabash of medicine to its stand by the bed-post, after adding in some water. The water for use in this second medicine has no restrictions, any will do, whether it is freshly drawn or it is water which has stayed in the pot overnight or even longer. And again when you see that the medicine has become too dilute go and pour the old mixture in a shitting place in the bushes. And then as soon as you see your period, even if the medicine is not yet finished, come and tell me, so that I can prepare for you at once yet another medicine."

With that Bugonoka said good-bye to her healer: "Have a good-day!" Kibuguma responded: "All right. Greet Myombekere for me, and tell him that Kibuguma on his part these days is dying for a taste of tobacco." To which Bugonoka responded: "I will, Sir."

Kibuguma's wife Weroba took Bugonoka's medicine for her and the two women left together, with Weroba escorting Bugonoka. Once they were outside the healer's home, Weroba said to Bugonoka, "Here is your medicine; I must go back and attend to the other visitors you left in our home. But, dear friend, should I reveal to you a secret?"

"What kind of secret, pray?"

"Drink this medicine in earnest and don't be afraid of it, because it rarely fails the women to whom my husband gives it. What is more, he has never given it to any other women so early in their treatment as he has done with you. May be that's why the other day we gossiped about you with him at night, on account of your omen being so propitious. And don't imagine he has given you the medicine with no good reason, for he is your seer. He would not have wasted his time giving you this medicine if he hadn't seen exactly how matters stand with you. I must admit I have rarely seen Kibuguma go wrong on women whose oracle he told by cooked medicine like yours; very rarely indeed. In fact I have seen him help even women who had never had a child at all and they too have born children, not to mention you, a woman who has brought forth life only you lost your children! It is only because you don't know the type of healer Kibuguma is that you may have doubts and say to yourself: `Maybe he heals people who are wholesome, but certainly not the likes of me.' Well, let me tell you, dear friend, go and drink this medicine in earnest and then let's talk about it again, one day, just the two of us, seated and settled somewhere, should it please the heavens to bless you. And so have a safe journey, and greetings to your husband."

"Thanks."

Once alone on her way Bugonoka went over Weroba's words: "drink this medicine in earnest", and thinking about those words of the healer's wife made her almost talk aloud to herself on the way like a mad person.

Back home she found Myombekere and Kagufwa already gone to graze cattle and on asking the little girl of their home about them the girl said, "They told me when food is ready don't look for them anywhere else except in the heath on the side of Ntamba's home, that's where you will find them. Then he called after me again after he had reached the common grazing ground over there and said I should tell you when you come and have cooked food not to forget to bring him his shoes, because over there the pasture is full of thorns, that whatever the case by the time of the scorching overhead noon sun you are bound to find them in that heath by Ntamba's home."

Bugonoka at once turned to cooking for the cattle herders. But first she quickly took off her special occasion robe she had worn to her healer's home and in no time had changed into a working dress. Then she came outside, swept together a handful of grass, then off to the courtyard fireplace[10] to look for fire, got some, turned around and was back into the house and at the cooking-stones and at once had thrown a hand inside the cooking-stones and swept aside towards the wall the ashes in it. She did that once and on throwing into the fireplace her hand the second time she cried out in pain: "*Yu!* "

The young girl asked: "What is it?"

And she replied: "I have burnt myself, my dear. I was thinking the fire had died out in here when in fact it is still live, and very much so."

She started a fire in the cooking-stones and when it was going properly, she took down a relish pot, inspected it carefully with her eyes, just in case there had dropped into it any unwanted matter, like flies or cockroaches or some tiny black ants and the like, and to ascertain there was still enough water for sufficient broth. Then she drew some water and added in just a few drops, her pot titled on one side, before giving it the fire it needed. When it was properly warmed, she whisked it off the fire and in an instant was boiling water for *obwita*.[11] The young girl had been grinding flour for the medicine and she too finished her work and gave the flour to Bugonoka and she put it away. When water in the pot boiled, Bugonoka put flour in the boiling water and then washed her hands. When cooking *obwita* all the time the cook needs to remove with her hands from her cooking spoon[12] excess food sticking to it and put it back into the pot so that it does not fall into the fireplace and a clean cook washes her hands before cooking *obwita* so that she wouldn't touch food with dirty hands. In less than it takes to say it, she had finished cooking, had dished out the food and nicely knead and shaped it in the men's meal bowl and had put their women's share of *obwita* in a women's bowl.[13] However Bugonoka and the little girl did not sit down to eat their lunch first before taking to the herders theirs, no, because a woman eating first and then serving her husband food later is not the Kikerewe way of doing things. That has never been heard of in this country, unless it is to start tomorrow or the day after tomorrow. Bugonoka called the little girl to come and help her carry food to the herders. She herself carried her husband's cow-hide shoes, the pot of relish, *obwita* dish and a cup[14] of drinking water and the little girl carried a big *ekizanda* of milk for Myombekere as well as Kagufwa's *ekizanda* of milk and they got on the way to the heath by Ntamba's home.

They found their two herders resting under the shade of a tree besides their herd of cattle lazily spread on the ground and served them food. And only after taking lunch did Myombekere ask Bugonoka, "So you are back? Did you find him at home, and did he give you medicine?"

"I am back. Yes, I found him at home and he did indeed give me medicine as well, medicine of a different kind. But leave that for now, I will tell you in the evening all about what Kibuguma's wife told me."

Bugonoka and the little girl took their food utensils and left for home. Before they had got any far, they met a certain man who greeted them and they greeted him back and he passed on, and shortly after that they heard him tell Myombekere, "How is your work of grazing cattle, friend?"

"Grazing cattle is still going on. And so I am watching the cows eat while I am dying of hunger!"

Bugonoka and the little girl laughed.

In the evening Myombekere drove the cattle from the pastures and his neighbors came to take away the herds of their homes and he and Kagufwa too drove their own cows home. And when Kagufwa finished milking the cows and Bugonoka prepared food and served dinner to the people of her home as usual and they all ate and Bugonoka took away her food utensils and went into the house and Myombekere and the boy Kagufwa too retired inside the house, dead tired after spending a whole day struggling with cows, their bodies full of aches and pains, Myombekere at once told his wife, "Dust our bed skins quickly for me, please, so that I can lie down and rest!"

"That is what I too was thinking."

Bugonoka dusted their bed sheets and then Myombekere stretched himself on the bed. His wife put away her kitchen utensils, replacing in its hanger each and every cooking pot of hers which was not in its proper place, putting back on the rack each and every drinking water cup of hers and putting away her each and every bowl where it should be until she was through and she too joined him on their bed. Myombekere was the first to speak by asking his wife, "Did you, by the way, tell me while we were herding cattle: `I will tell you in the evening all about what Kibuguma's wife told me'?"

"Yes."

"What did she tell you?"

"After Kibuguma gave me my medicine and explained to me clearly how I am to take it, having on my part already told him that you could not accompany me because of your neighborhood round of herding duty, I said good-bye to him. His wife Weroba then brought out of the house for me my bowl, in which her husband had already put my medicine, and escorted me. Once outside the home and on our way, when we came to that big anthill under *omulinzi* tree you may have noticed, I saw my companion stop and say, `Here is your medicine, dear friend, I must go back home now, to attend to the other visitors.  But I must reveal to you a secret, now that we are alone.'  To which I said: `What kind of secret, pray?' And she answered: `Drink this medicine in earnest, because it rarely fails those to whom my husband gives it, and because with the other women he has never given it to them so early in their treatment as he has done with you; never.' And for me it is her words of drinking the medicine in earnest which have left me wondering a lot. I thought the matter over and said to myself: `Does, by any chance, drinking the medicine in earnest mean drinking it all at a go or how am I to drink it?'  Because her husband had explained to me very clearly how I am to take the medicine and I understood him, and then his wife comes and tells me: `Drink it in earnest.' That's what has puzzled me. In fact I wanted to go back and ask him for an explanation, but, on second thought, I said to myself: `No; because if you go back to the man himself now, my friend, by the time he finishes treating all those other people you left there and becomes free for you to ask him for further explanation, you will arrive home to find your cattle herders already in very bad shape!' And so I just came home. That was what I was about to tell you when I said to myself, `It is better to tell him when he is home and rested rather than here in this wilderness when he is struggling with cattle this way, for he may fail to grasp the import of what you are telling him!'"

"I see! So that's it? In other words what you are wondering about is what Kibuguma's wife meant by her words: `drink it in earnest'?"

"Yes, because medicines in this country of ours do sometimes kill people. And even if the medicine does not kill you, it can still play havoc with you, for example blow out your stomach and disfigure you. So that's why I had to tell you about it, because two heads are better than one, as people say in this Ukerewe of ours, and add: `One can't hold a conversation, two can understand each other, three get at one another, and four shit fire.'"

"In my view, when Weroba told you `drink it in earnest' what she meant was that you should drink it every time of the day you are supposed to drink it and every day, as the healer instructed you to do, without ever skipping a round. And yet you are the one who went there! What would have happened then, if instead of you I were the one who had gone to see the healer alone? Wouldn't what I would have told you puzzled you even more? Indeed, given your worries, did you even drink the medicine you brought?"

"I did take the medicine."

"*Aa!* May be you did, may be you didn't. With so much going on in your mind, how could you feel comfortable drinking it?"

"I drank it, I tell you. Had Nakiro not already fallen asleep you could have asked her, because she is the one who cooked it in gruel for me".

Myombekere took his wife's assertion with a pinch of salt and said, "All right, let's see about that in the morning, if we are still alive." As soon as he stopped talking he fell asleep, exhausted from having spent the whole day running after cows in the pastures.

And so the following morning Myombekere asked the little girl, "I understand Bugonoka came with some medicine, who gave it to her to drink, I wonder?" and the little girl answered: "Yes, she came with medicine, it is in a bowl, and I am the one who put it in the gruel I made for her in the evening, when you came from herding cattle, and she drank it. I am also the one to whom she gave *endwero* millet and I ground the flour for the gruel during the day, before we brought you food in the cattle pastures."

Myombekere said, "I see. I thought that may be last night when she told me she drank the medicine she was pulling my leg".

Bugonoka herself said, "Let me bring the medicine itself and show you." She bought the medicine which had remained in the bowl and showed it to him. She also called the little girl and told her to show him the one already mixed in the calabash bowl and the child brought it.

Myombekere looked at it and said, "Now you have convinced me. Yes, you brought the medicine. Now I believe you, but I wouldn't had I not seen the medicine with my own eyes."

Then Bugonoka called the little girl to come and make the medicine gruel for her again. Quickly the little girl cooked the medicine gruel, gave it to Bugonoka and she drank it and Myombekere saw his wife drink the medicine with his own eyes, in broad daylight!

That done and finished, Bugonoka got busy preparing food for her cattle herders, after she had taken care of a number of other things she wanted done, since the neighborhood herders on duty usually drove their cattle from home rather late, at the time of the morning sun at which milk curdles, but not much later. A herder on duty who brought his cattle to the common herd too late risked being boycotted and left to herd his cattle alone, or, at best, he could find another person had already taken his round of duty and would thus have to wait another day to serve his turn.

Bugonoka served Myombekere and Kagufwa breakfast and the two herders drove their cattle from home and came to the collecting point and found people from the other neighborhood homes already waiting for them with their stocks. Then cattle of the entire neighborhood was handed over to Myombekere: "There they are, Myombekere! We gave you our herd of cows without a single one missing. Should you lose any, the blame is on you, should they be attacked by predators, again it's you we'll blame, because today you herd for us all."

"May God spare me of what you say, gentlemen. It is true misfortune strikes without warning, but all the same I say: `May God spare me of what you say!' children of worthy parents."

Myombekere then told his young companion: "Drive the cows, let's take them to the pastures when it is still a cool morning; and in the afternoon, when the westerly wind begins to blow, we'll drive them down to the lake and water them."

That day they went to graze their herd in another direction, away from the heath by Ntamba's home. But since what transpires in pastures where several men meet to graze cattle is like the gossip of women gathering firewood in the wilderness, we better not go into what they encountered while there lest we become snitches and get thrown into colonies of safari ants.[15] Let's go back to Bugonoka.

When Bugonoka finished cooking and serving breakfast to her herders and the herders left with their cattle to go and graze the animals, she took out a kitchen tray[16] and brought out millet for winnowing. The millet she got from trading meat had come from all sorts of farmers and was a mixture of almost everything: some of it was new, some old, some of it clean but also a lot of it soiled and some even with worms in it, the white and red millet worms as well as millet lice, and therefore full of worm-dust. Again some of the millet had been threshed on floors of rocks and was clean while some was threshed on earthen floors and therefore had a lot of sand in it. And there was all in all a lot of chaff in the millet. Every time before she ground the millet she had therefore first to clean it by scrubbing it with the leaves of *entobotobo*[17] eggplant before winnowing it and removing all the fluff and dust and sand form the millet. After cleaning her millet to her satisfaction, she put it away in her house for grinding later, because she rarely ground flour when it was already broad daylight. Grinding flour was work she normally did only very early in the morning, at cockcrow, so that by sunrise she would already be free to do other things. After putting away her millet, she sent the little girl Nakiro to Kanwaketa's wife by telling her: "Go to Kanwaketa's wife and tell her: `Give some dry cassava[18] to Bugonoka on loan, for mixing with her millet. She is taking her own cassava out of the molding heap tomorrow and once it is dry she will replace the measure you will give her. She does not want to grind her millet without a bit of cassava in it!"

The child went to Kanwaketa's and Bugonoka remained at home, seated under the porch of the door of her house weaving a grass tray. Quite a while passed before the girl reappeared, with dry cassava in some large bowl, full to the top. She put down the cassava near Bugonoka, knelt down and said, "This is what she gave me." Bugonoka put aside the tray she was working on and examined that cassava, feeling it with her fingers to see whether it was dry. When she saw that it was still feeling damp, she told Nakiro to bring from the house some kitchen trays for airing the cassava in the sun to dry. After sunning her cassava, Bugonoka asked the little girl, "Why did you take so long? Were the people not at home when you got there?"

"*Aa*! I found them at home. I delayed coming back because I found Kanwaketa's wife mending her *enkanda*. I understand a decoration in the skin had a tear in it and I found her mending the tear by sowing over it a new skin patch."

As the afternoon sun began to descend in the sky, Bugonoka put away next to the central pole of her house the tray she was making and hung her fine papyrus splits for use as ribs in her grass-weaving on the wall in the front of her house by the grinding-stone. She then took an empty water pot and little Nakiro took an empty calabash and the two went to the lake to bathe and to draw water. On coming back from the lake, Bugonoka took her cassava, already dry to her satisfaction, out of the sun and onto the grinding-stone to break it into fine particles for mixing with millet, and then brought her millet and mixed the two. That done she told Nakiro, "I have now served summons to this piece of work: the millet is mixed with cassava ready for grinding, and I count that work done. Tomorrow early in the morning it is simply a question of grinding the flour, after skimming milk, before going to take my own cassava out of the molding heap."

That done she sent Nakiro to untether the calves and to cut some soft tree leaves for wiping milk containers with. And when she judged Myombekere and Kagufwa were about to return, she put on the cooking-stones her pot of relish and warmed it, because she did not want her husband to stay hungry for long once home, coming from the ordeal of herding cattle as he would be. What's more, in Myombekere's home it was rare for people to eat their supper late at night; only once in a while did that happen, since everybody is bound to go visiting some place one day or another and return home late. But when everybody was home, that never happened. As a result some people began talking about him: "In the evening Myombekere never likes to eat in other people's homes! Where could he have eaten dinner already that early?   May be he fears being poisoned? In fact even when he is a guest drinking beer with others and people are invited for food he on his part will decline and say: `I didn't come hungering for more than one thing,' and he would just drink beer. May be he is a greedy person who doesn't want to eat in other people's homes for fear they too would eat in his home?" And indeed in those days many people were not eating in other people's homes for fear of being fed poisonous things, and also because they did not like to be considered tramps, or the like. In fact not eating too often in other people's homes was what was considered desirable behavior by everybody.

When Myombekere came from herding cattle that evening he brought home a log for splitting into firewood, because in those days the men were the real fetchers of firewood, daily. Bugonoka, on seeing her husband come home with such a heavy load, hurried to meet him and relieve him of his weapons. Myombekere sat down and asked for water to drink and Bugonoka brought him some, as at the same time she brought him and Kagufwa a plate of sweet potatoes with milk. They ate and then called her to come and fetch her utensils while saying, "We must leave some room for *obwita* at dinner, otherwise food will do us harm!"

Later on they took their dinner and went to bed and it dawned.

Early in the morning the following day Bugonoka was up as usual, since it was her custom to churn milk very early in the morning. While still churning her milk, she got up from the churn with her *empiki*[19] urn for scenting milk containers to fetch fire for putting in it from the courtyard fireplace. As she came out of the house and looked towards the kraal, she heard the cry of a mother-cow calling for its calf and went near and looked and found it was a cow which had just calved, the calf having just dropped down from its mother's womb.   At once she called her husband, "Myombekere, wake up, come and see your cow here, it has calved!"

"All right! Which one has calved?"

"The gray one."

"What calf is it, male of female?"

"How do I know! I looked from this far, how can I know the gender of the calf, or even how it looks like! All I had come to do, poor me, was to fetch fire from the fireplace here!"

Myombekere woke up and went outside, opened the gate of his cattle kraal and went in. He found the mother cow still cleaning womb jelly from the calf and the calf still lying prone on the ground, then he looked and saw it was a bull, black and white in color and told Bugonoka, "Just as I thought, my dear, the creature has calved a bull!"

"*Aa*! A bull is a cow too. Since that is what Lyangombe[20] has willed, what can you do?"

"As a matter of fact you are right, certainly. But, all the same, it is not the best thing that could have happened. I was hoping that, since it had a female calf as its first born followed by a male one, the one it has just weaned, it would continue to alternate the genders of its calves as other cows sometimes do, and so I was expecting it to bear a female calf. *Aaa*! Our hopes of counting on this cow for stock-raising are being shuttered! If your cows calve only bulls this way, when would you ever have a large stock!"

"Well, the fact is that what I see in this Ukerewe of ours, with the real Wakerewe like you, is that often you resort to a bull in your stock to achieve whatever you want done, like paying bride-price for us the women you marry, you know, or paying a debt to someone whose property you took, or getting yourselves out of need and want, or out of some other hardships human beings encounter, like famine, and others of that kind. Take us here, for example, did slaughtering your bull The-entire-country the way you did and trading its meat for millet that way not get us out of our need?"

"That must indeed be true, for what else can we say! What Providence wills to bless you with is what you should receive with both your hands."

Myombekere then lifted and held his cow's calf against his chest and carried it out of the kraal, its gray mother following him behind lowing for it. When he got into the compound of his home he laid it down on a patch of creeping grass and its mother resumed licking it clean, with its afterbirth hanging from behind. Then he told Bugonoka to give him water to wash off the cow birth jelly he had smeared himself with by carrying the tiny animal. Bugonoka brought him some water and poured it into a stone-trough in the compound of their home and he washed himself clean. She had some relish leftovers, and so after that she first cooked breakfast for her husband and when Myombekere and Kagufwa finished eating she took a hoe and went to the lakeshore to weed her sweet potato fields.

Back home Myombekere told the young boy of his home: "Would you please take a look and see if the after-birth sack of that cow has dropped so that you can go and throw it away in the bushes for the vultures or wild animals to devour and then come back and drive the cows to the herders on duty, lest you find the neighborhood herd already gone far and give yourself unnecessary trouble of looking for them." The boy looked for a stick and lifted the cow placenta from the ground where it had dropped by one end of the stick, but when he tried to put the stick on his shoulder and carry the afterbirth away it dropped down. Myombekere reprimanded him for that: "Look at that useless creature! See how he does things nonchalantly! He can't even lift the placenta of a cow by a stick! Give that stick to me, you oversize-head creature! This is how to do it. Can't you see! Will it fall off if you carry it this way, however far you want to take it? Here, don't waste our time, take it and throw it away; but come back quickly, you oversize-head, and take the cattle to the herders before it is too late, and then come back and fetch for me my billhook from Kanwaketa's."

The boy went and threw away the cow's afterbirth. He came back and found Myombekere scrapping soil from a hoe and took his herding stick and first went and opened the gate for the cows in the kraal before going to untether the milk cows from their pegs outside the kraal and driving the whole herd into the fenced-in trail leading from their home and took the cattle to their communal herder on duty. Myombekere on his part took a rope and went to tether in some grass the cow which had just calved, its tiny calf following along and butting its mother about while staggering unsteadily on its feet. That done, he took his hoe and went into his banana plantation to cover the bases of his young plants with soil and to weed the farm, which had become overgrown with weeds. The soil was fertile and so weeds simply took no time to grow during that season of heavy nightly rain storms. In those days this country of Ukerewe was a country of heavy rainfall, so that rivers were always full of water tumbling to the sea the whole year round, and that is why many people used to erect fish traps in the rivers and catch plenty of the tiny *ebigugu* [21] catfish and *enkorobondo*[22] sardines, fish women don't eat and the latter of which the Wakerewe have a riddle: "Enkorobondo-who-never-drink-river-water", even though rivers are their dwelling place and it is in rivers they are caught!

Hee! When Myombekere was busy in his young banana plants visitors came to his home and asked: "Where is Myombekere gone, child?"

"He is not at home, he has gone to till a field over there."

"Where is he tilling?"

"He is planting bananas."

"And the woman of the home?"

"I understand as for her she has gone to weed her sweet potato fields by the lakeshore."

And so the visitors followed Myombekere to his place of work. When they got to him, they first wished him good work the way people do to those working in a banana plantation: "Happy beer drinking, gentleman!"

"It's not yet the real thing but we are working on it, good people."

They greeted each other and exchanged news of each other respectfully, after which Myombekere asked them, "Which wind blows you this way?"

"The southerly and the easterly are what landed us here. And then we said, `No, we have to see what people are planting at this time of the year with the dry season almost here. What's more, the year is pushing on and it's time we looked for unwed women to marry!"

"Oh, I see! And over there where you come from, you didn't find any catch?"

"Well, with us fame reached us over there of a woman in these parts here, in that home next to yours, that's where people said she is to be found. But when we went there we found only an old woman at home. When we asked, she told us that the woman we want did not sleep in the home last night, she has gone to visit her uncle, who is said to be very sick. It is said that's where her father and mother too went early in the morning, together with a son of theirs. The other son, we were told, has gone to look for fish in their *olubigo* [23] fish trap."

"I see. So people have spoken to you about Kanwaketa's daughter. Yes, that one is there all right. She is divorced and even her bride-price has already been returned to her former husband. So it is all up to you, unless you don't have enough of what it takes, in which case you should get some help."

The men smiled. Then they complimented him on his work in the field and said, "Here you have hit banana in the wound, planted it where it was already growing! You think it's a joke? Especially in such fallow land, it is certainly not a joke! *Aa*! When the banana plant flourishes and begins to really dance in the wind here, you yourself will be amazed at what a great banana plantation you have. You will in fact be brewing banana beer without a break. You won't know what to do with banana beer in this home!" They then said good-bye to Myombekere: "And so, gentleman, keep on tilling the land. It appears we will have to make a point of coming to see you another time, when the woman who has brought us this way is back."

"Indeed, for our ancestors said: 'He who wants   men's big fish *enkuyu*[24] must first toil.'" And those visitors answered him back: "Exactly, brother", and left.

When his belly became too empty to bear, Myombekere went home to eat, only to find Bugonoka was about to send the little girl to call him for lunch. On seeing him coming, Bugonoka at once sent the little girl to meet him and relieve him of his hoe, as she on her part dished out of a pot boiled cassava for their lunch. The cassava slices were cooked together with *enkole*[25] beans so that the cassava looked as red as you could imagine, although at the bite of the tooth inside the slices were as white and as soft as flour, so that even a toothless person could eat them, in fact it felt as if you could even drink that boiled cassava with a straw!

After lunch Myombekere took his cow which had just calved to the lake to water it while he too soaked himself a bit in the lake. On his way back he met a certain woman, whose name was Kasigwa, who asked him: "It appears another cow of yours has calved, Myombekere?"

"It has, thank you, though it calved a bull. Yesterday while herding, I saw the ungrateful animal all restless but still thought it wasn't quite ready to calve yet, but apparently it was already in labor and that was why it was so jumpy. I must admit you women with children must have suffered beyond words!"

"Don't talk about that! Labor, real child labor I mean! *A!* Let me tell you, Myombekere: if it lasted say for as long as ten days or so, or even just longer by only a few more days than it does, we wouldn't bring children into this world alive, we would strangle dead all of them!"

"I see! It is that bad then!"

"Look here, let me tell you what a real ordeal child labor is: the egg of a female child has got its own kind of labor and that of a male child too has its particular kind. Then there is no saying that because I have already given birth to other children I have become accustomed to it and so this time it won't pain me much. *Aa!* Child labor is some incomprehensible thing the Creator just put out there! And when you men see women who are afraid of giving birth you think they are just being cowards, that it's no great deal!"

With that they parted, Kasigwa descending to the lake to draw water and Myombekere taking his cow home. On his way home Myombekere thought of what Kasigwa told him and said to himself: "What that woman said split wide open for you the truth of how little we men know about the tribulations of women!"

On getting back home with his cow Myombekere found Gwaleba seated in his home. They greeted each other in their own two elders' way: "Greetings, peer!" "Greeting, peer, my brother!" "Did you sleep well?" "Yes, we slept well." Then Myombekere asked Gwaleba: "We don't see much of you these days, where have you been?"

"I am in my home as usual, but I only sleep there: I am away from home the rest of the day, because I spend daytime at the palace of our sovereign *omukama.*[26] When I left this home on the day we slaughtered that cow which wanted to take us from this earth with it, I stayed in that home of mine for some two days only when on the third day I saw a courtier come for me very early in the morning and tell me, 'Come, let's go; the king has sent me to fetch you.'

"Where I was I farted in my seat and said to myself, 'You have been gobbling too many things at court for too long, you miniature excuse of a human being, today all you have ever eaten there will come out of you by the nose!' And so I got up and put on my raw-hide, for only the king has real skin clothes. When we got to him, I folded my miserable knee and raised these lame hands of mine to him and I paid him tribute and finished[27] and stepped aside, while inside me my apprehension knew no bounds.

"Much much later, I heard *omukama* call me: 'Gwaleba!' My heart went: *ku!*. I said, 'Yes, Great-giver,' and he said, 'I have called you because I have here some rather tiny job of mine.' I said, 'Hail to you, my lord!' 'Can you do it for me or may be you can't?' 'My lord, if it's something I know how to do, I will do it; should it prove something I am incapable of doing, Great-builder, you will surely find others of deserving skill to do it for you.'

"And at once I saw him beckon by a finger the chief courtier, the one they call Lwambicho, who went to where the king was reigning on his throne in the compound of his palace. He got close to him and knelt down and *omukama* whispered something in his ear and finished. Then, as we looked on, we saw Lwambicho stand up and cast his glance up and down the crowd of people who were gathered in front of *omukama*, as if looking for somebody he was told to look for, before I saw him too beckon by a finger another courtier, the one who came to fetch me from my home, whose name is Nsyana, and the two came and said to me: 'Come!'

"I became all tremor, since, as you too know, the king's Bukindo,[28] though the seat of bounty, can also be one's Life's-end. As we were about to enter the corridor of the *omukama*'s huge sleeping house *narunzwi*,[29] what should I see but *omukama* himself coming too! When I saw *omukama* coming, and realized I was with those two courtiers, Lwambicho and Nsyana, and remembered that those two were also the kings executioners, while I had no clue as to why *omukama* had called me, *ee*! I felt as good as dead and buried!

"I remained with the two courtiers in the corridor of *narunzwi* while *omukama* went inside the house. Much later, I heard the king call and say, 'Come!'   I too wanted to follow the courtiers into *narunzwi* when somebody standing in the door porch stopped me and said, 'No, you wait here; *omukama* called his courtiers only.'

"So I was left alone out there in that corridor, lost as to what to do, while from somewhere inside the house I heard noises of: *gunguru! gunguru!*

bogoto! bogoto! without even realizing that it was the noise of hides being moved about. And there I remained until my legs got weak at knees and pained, until I felt I could stand no longer and was about to squat on the ground when I heard somebody call me, 'You too, Gwaleba, you are being told to come inside.'

"I went in. I had just stepped inside the huge house and had not gone past its door posts when on glancing like this to my left to try and make out the person who had stopped me from entering the house at first whom do I see but the amazon Nabutuma, the mistress of the rites and ceremonies of *narunzwi*, from taking care of the king's horns of potent charms to tending the ever burning fire which was lit by the Abahembe clan people the day the reigning *omukama* was installed and is kept burning for him day and night until his death,[30] and the like, she who more than anybody else knows how to hail our *omukama* and pays him homage day and night, the speaker who knows what to say and how to say everything right and the one person on earth who knows how to properly do everything the king wants. That was the person seated there, near *omukama's* battle ax, placed there ready to finish off the sovereign's enemies, the traitors who may dare want to harm him inside his own house.[31] I had just seen her when she made a sign by her hand as if to throw me away in another direction and said, 'Go that way!' I then looked this way and that way and everywhere, not knowing where to go, dripping with sweat from my head to the big toes of my feet out of fear until I heard somebody say, 'We are this way!'

"Apparently there were other people in the house, all dead silent, whose work was to light the part of the house where Lwambicho and Nsyana had some work to do. But I can't say how many they were, because I was too overwhelmed with fear to know anything, that's why I don't even know on which side of the house the king's bed *engoro*[32] stands and to say I do would be to tell you lies. For me all I heard was Nsyana saying, `Come, we are this way!" and that's where I went and that's all I know.

" I had just got to the two courtiers when I heard *omukama* cough: '*Koho!*' In that very instant I heard by the door from where I had just come Nabutuma pay homage to our sovereign: 'Power to you, the Lion, power to you the Sun, power to you, Giver-of-habiliment, power to you, Generous-entertainer, power to you, son of Katobaha, power to you, son of Golita, power to you, son of Mihigo,[33] power to you, Punisher-of-offenders, power to you forever, son of a line of kings!' And what a voice that woman has!

Hii!   Where would you find even a man with a voice so powerful! Myombekere, that kind of thing you have to see with your own eyes to believe!

"When I got to where the courtiers were, I saw what is meant by a king's wealth! There in front of me were elephant tusks, hippopotamus teeth, rhinoceros horns, tails of giraffes and wildebeests, shinning bracelets, not to mention skins of lions, of leopards, of cheetahs, of the wild cat *emondo,*34 *ee*! Even if you wanted to look, what were you to look at and what leave out? And where could you find eyes to take in all that wealth? Then *omukama* spoke: 'Take out for him three lion skins, and let him start by working on those ones today. When he has finished that I will instruct you as to what he should work on next, until I tell him: Now go and rest in your home and come when I call you again.' Only when I heard *omukama* say that was my calm restored, but until then I had been dying with fear!

"And so that was the work I have been doing, and I did not finish it until yesterday. That's why you were not seeing me around. And today I am in desperate need of tobacco and that's what has brought me here in this home of yours, where I had just arrived as you came in. The whole night long and up to this moment these nostrils of mine have not touched *ekilangi*35 tobacco at all!"

Myombekere told Bugonoka to bring Gwaleba *ekilangi*. Gwaleba received the tobacco solution and poured it down one nostril, listened to it go to work in his head and poured the solution down his other nostril, ejected from his mouth a thick spittle and, his head thrown all the way back, spoke from his nose, his upper lip lifted and said, "Here is real tobacco, the kind of tobacco a person who wants to feel good and chase from his body every bit of cold needs!"

"Yes, it is indeed good tobacco. I put it into water for the first time only yesterday and when we finished eating and took it we couldn't hold its liquid up our noses long enough to let it take full effects, we had to blow it out quickly. And, in spite of that, it still made us groggy, made each one of us shake all over, and when we came out of it we drank an impossible quantity of water: I gulped a men's meal-time calabash full to the brim and emptied it and my wife likewise!"

Myombekere had just finished saying that when he saw his friend, that is Gwaleba, sweat until he was dripping with sweat and start trembling all over his body: *ligiligiligi!* before starting to fall limply all the way to the ground: *ligiti!* He at once called his wife, "Bugonoka, quick, bring some water to pour on Gwaleba, it appears he has been overpowered by *ekilangi*!" In less than it takes to say it Bugonoka had brought water and the couple had poured it on Gwaleba, on his legs, his arms and his head. It was not until after a really long while that he came to and said, "This tobacco is really manly strong, indeed! And since I went to it with all my craving, I did not even pay much heed to what you well telling me about it. All I heard, very vaguely, was you saying, `It was some insignificant bit of tobacco', but the rest I did not hear at all."

"Yes, it was some insignificant tiny bit of tobacco, not even enough to fill this palm of my hand, which was given me in some home I had wandered to."

"No, don't say that, my brother; if you have a bit of it remaining, give me some too and let me too go and make myself a brew at home."

Myombekere went inside his house and came out with the very package in which the plug of tobacco in question was wrapped and gave him some, enough for one brew of *ekilangi*, himself too remaining with just enough for brewing the solution only once. Then Gwaleba said good-bye to Myombekere and his wife and left.

After he left Bugonoka said to her husband, "I was really scared and said to myself, `Today we've had it. If this man dies here from this *ekilangi* his relatives will say we are the ones who killed him, poisoned him!"

"That's what passed through my mind too as I said to myself, `Poor us, why did we give him such strong *ekilangi*! If he dies in this home, won't that call for revenge on us from his people!"

"The owner of this tobacco has something of real value! He can buy plenty of property indeed with such good tobacco, that is if he cultivated a man-size field of it!"

"To come back to my friend who has just left, even if you have done work for the *omukama*, do you have to be so vain! *Ahee*! To shoot off and tell people things they didn't ask you to tell them, just like that, *aa!* It is the like of him who end up blabbing things for which one day they may find themselves being asked, 'Where did you get this information from?' And for such a question a person has no answer, and since it concerns matters of the great one he gets executed for nothing! Even if it was a way of asking for *ekilangi*, did he have to go off like that as if he were possessed by some evil power or   somebody had asked him to talk about such matter!"

"May be that's what he actually saw and he wanted to shared his secret with you, because you are his friend. Otherwise, can he really just talk to any person of such heavy matters!"

"Well, whatever the case, let's drop the subject and talk of other things, lest what we say should fall on the ears of strangers who were not even here."

And they talked no more about it.

When the medicine which Bugonoka was given by the healer the second time was finished, the following day Bugonoka and Myombekere, together, went to see their medicine man Kibuguma. They found other patients of his already gathered in his home and they all exchanged greetings with each other and Weroba gave the couple seats and they sat down.

Kibuguma attended to his other patients first before calling his initiate Bugonoka and telling her: "Come closer!" Bugonoka took her chair and went and sat near him. Then Kibuguma told her: "Could you give me your right hand?" Bugonoka stretched out her right hand to him, palm facing upwards. Kibuguma held her hand and looked into her palm. When he finished examining the palm of her right hand, he asked for the palm of her left hand: "Bring the other one!" Bugonoka became like a person to whom the barber says, "If you want a head-shave bring here that head of yours and sit still!" and she held out her left hand. Kibuguma held that hand too and examined its palm. As he was about to end his examination of that palm, he laughed alone and said, "Myombekere, come near me." Myombekere went closer. Then Kibuguma told him, "Your wife here last time came to this home alone to take the medicine you say got finished yesterday evening and on that day she told me in this home of mine here, `My husband has been unable to come with me because today he is on herding duty for our neighborhood,' and I too on that day told her clearly that her husband was not important on that day, but that with the medicine I gave her then, the one which had to be cooked with the gruel of *endwero* millet flour, she had to drink the medicine in earnest. I told her so because I had seen how your wife here is, and that's why I gave her that medicine of mine early and gave her clear instructions and told her: `Drink this medicine in earnest, but when you enter your monthly period, even if you haven't finished the medicine, come back to inform me, only that day come with your husband, because there will be something I will see in you.' And today the two of you have come and it is good you have done so. And since the two of you are here let me tell you what I want to tell you."

Myombekere said, "More of the truth, healer!"

Kibuguma continued with his conversation and said, "What I have seen in your wife today is a second thing, because the first time I told you that what was killing her children in her womb was *ihuzi* worms and nothing else. But today, after giving her that medicine, the one she has just taken, that medicine has enabled me to know the second thing, which is this: this *ihuzi* worm, since it is such a fierce one, needs four amulets, to be worn around her waist on a string of the sinew of a cow which was killed by a stroke of an ax on the head. She will wear two of the four amulets in front of her womb and the other two on her back as fortification against this *ihuzi* worm, which is simply ferocious. Starting today she will drink no other medicine. And should I tell you something else?

The couple said, "Do tell us all, our healer!"

"Starting today, when this monthly period she is in ends, relate to each other by the act of marriage; neither will her monthly period be followed by another one, not in the least, because her womb will conceive. And from that pregnancy of hers Bugonoka, unless something happens to her, will bear a male child. That's all I have to say and that's all I want to tell you. But when she will have passed four days after the end of her monthly period, on the fifth day both of you come back here, did you hear that?"

"We heard indeed."

When Kibuguma finished telling them that, he sent his wife Weroba to bring him a small stick for making the four amulets, together with the sinew of a cow which was killed by the blow of an ax on the head and *empindu* [36] needle and soot-blackened roof-grass. [37] Weroba did so and then fetched fire and came and made a fire at the door of their house, near the porch. Kibuguma on his part gave Bugonoka that cow sinew and told her to make for herself a string by which she was to wear the four amulets he wanted to give her. The healer finished shaping the four amulets as Bugonoka too finished making a cow muscle string the length of her waist and gave the string to the healer, who skillfully put on it the four amulets in such a way that two would be in front and two at the back of his patient's waist and gave them to Bugonoka, who put them on without getting up from her seat, by slipping the string over her head and shoulders and then dropping it to her stomach, at which point the men present turned and looked away from her and she quickly released the attachment of the cow-skin robe she was wearing and slipped the string of amulets around her waist.

That done, the couple got up, said good-bye to Kibuguma and his wife

Weroba and left for home.

On their way back home, the couple went over the events of the day. Myombekere said, "No doubt our healer, with these four amulets he has given us, has given us amulets for protection against the death of infants, since none of the two of us has a child living?"

Bugonoka responded, "It is true the healer himself did not tell us the amulets are a protection against infant death but, according to the ways of our people in this Ukerewe as we know them, yes, we both know that these amulets can't be for anything else except protection against infant death."

"Yes, because we all see all the time women whose children die in their infancy as well as those who lose pregnancies wearing amulets like these."

Once back home each one of them went about his and her business. Bugonoka, after she cooked food and they ate, took out a grass tray she was working on, sat in the porch of the door of their house and worked on her utensil. Myombekere on his part took a hoe and went to cultivate his banana plantation.

When it was time to stop working, Myombekere retired home, where he found Bugonoka on her part still working on her tray, but with darkness descending on everything around her she too went and put away her work in the corner of her house where she always kept it.

Making grass trays and bowls by patiently weaving strands of raffia tightly and solidly on ribs of papyrus splits is work which to the artisan is usually accompanied by pain in the back and at the bent of the neck together with a heavy chest and the risk of impairing one's eyesight, and for that reason Bugonoka usually worked on her handcraft only for some days at a stretch and then followed that by taking a break from the pain. Because she was not a lazy person, whenever she put aside one type of work she at once took up another. In fact that was why Bugonoka and her husband loved each other beyond words by a love equally reciprocated by both husband and wife. As a result whoever chanced to visit their home and stay with the couple, whether for two or three days or for one whole month, he or she left saying, "It appears these two are complete strangers to endless conflicts like those of the other couples I know or those between me and the people of my home!" I am sure they too had their domestic quarrels like everybody else, for, as people say: "Those who are side by side can't avoid rubbing against each other," but, by the look of things, their love for each other was real, because they showed it first and foremost by what they did for each other and by their ready forgiveness for each other and their quick reconciliations. That's why whoever visited their home had never seen either one of them show ill-feeling towards the other to the extent of sulking the whole day, like the moody couples I see in certain homes, who can't hide their ill-feelings for each other even to a stranger, to such an extent that a visitor in that home at once knows that the master or mistress is in a bad mood, only, alas, the visitor dare not ask why! Should he or she however have the courage to just touch upon the matter, at once he or she is bound to hear all about the couple's problems, either from the husband or the wife, since inside people's homes there are always some skeletons in the closet.

Hence the name   Myombekere,[38] for certainly that is what the lifestyle of a household is all about, because every man on earth has his particular way of managing his household. People's households you see everywhere are a very complicated matter. There is the household of a gluttonous man, who does not like at all to share whatever his favorite food is with his wife, the very woman who cooks that food for him, or with his visitors, whether they are from his wife's side or his very own side, and yet that same man may be living in harmony with his wife, the couple living together peacefully just like good people. There is the man whose home is founded on daily commotions and quarrels, who is always treating roughly the people of his home and forever quarreling with his wife or wives and his children. With that one too that's his particular *Myombekere* and his wives and his children may still be happy and contented. There may be yet another man who is head of a household and at the same time a notorious thief, who whenever he goes out comes back from his thieving with either lots of all kinds of food or some valuables, which he gives to his wife, who receives those stolen things with her two open hands of gratitude and, if it is something to cook, cooks it with great care and attention before they enjoy it together, and after they have eaten their fill husband and wife would break out in good-hearted laughter. For that man too, that is his *Myombekere*.

And what is true of husbands is also true of married women. Look, there is the woman who sits down to a meal and eats until she says, "I am satisfied," and then when she goes inside the house as if to put away the relish pot and the other food utensils and the leftovers, whatever that may be, leaving her husband outside at the courtyard fireplace, you will find her, no sooner than she is inside the house and still standing, cramming into her mouth whatever food was left over, including relish, as if she was chased from the meal still hungry! A man's wife is the cook of the household, yet there is the wife who when she is putting sweet potatoes in the cooking pot she is already chewing the raw food without a break so that you hear nothing but: *pokocho! pokocho! mugunu! mugunu!* and at the time of dishing out food from the pots again she is already busy stuffing herself by the handfuls without a break. Of that you say: I see! As to the leftovers of the previous night, that too she will gobble, in addition to cheating you, her husband, of your share of the food! When such a wife sees her husband going out, quickly she puts on the fire the quick-and-done-with pot and cooks herself her little dish of *obwita* and eats it with all the meat or fish relish remaining in the house and when the husband comes from wherever he had gone, if he has come back in the evening, he will at once hear his wife complain of having to pass the night without dinner and say: "Tonight we'll sleep on empty stomachs! Since you left by walking out casually, I thought that maybe you were going into the bushes to relieve yourself and so I came in the house and warmed the relish pot and took it from the fire and put it down. Then I said to myself, `No, let me try and see whether I can locate him in the nearby paths,' and when I couldn't find you I came back. I was just entering this house when I saw a wretched creature of a dog come out of the house licking its mouth and when I looked in the pot I found: *hii*! the creature had devoured the relish and finished everything and even overturned the pot, the monster!" saying all that to her husband when the truth of the matter is that she herself ate the food because of thinking only of herself and caring nothing for her spouse. Yet she and her husband may still be a married couple leading normal lives, that behavior of the wife being part of the particular lifestyle of their household. Whatever the case, there's no need to go into all the details of the matter, because the only man who does not know this is one who has never founded a home and likewise the only woman who doesn't understand what we are talking about is one who has never been married, though she too, should she live long and get married, sooner or later is bound to live the truth of this or heart about it and then say to herself: "Yes indeed, today I have seen for myself what I used to hear when I was still young," because an ancestor of this country once said: "What is spoken of comes to pass," and that's why what is seen and reported by a mere youth should be heeded even by elders.

However, let's return to people's households and their different lifestyles. The misdeeds of the husband or wife never come out in the open until the day the couple's marriage has ended and they have parted. Only then will you hear the husband reveal everything about his wife and say, "My wife Kasigwa, the one who went away, I loved her very very much, only she had one problem." On hearing that those present would respond and ask him, "Which one problem? Was she a witch or a thief?"

"I wouldn't have minded her being a witch, or a thief either, but that one problem of hers!"

"But which problem?"

"The one problem which made me no longer want her as my wife is this: she wets her bed like a small child, and she is so lazy that she cannot even scratch an itching rash on her own body. *Aa! hee!* gentlemen, can you marry such a woman? *Aa!* No! Even if you don't mind procuring for your wife new pelts for bed sheets you cannot all the same do so every day! How big would your herd of cattle be that would enable you to put on your bed a new cow-skin bed sheet daily without end! What's more, she simply had much more than her share of laziness: never willing to bestir herself, for ever sedentary: *lelelele!* like drinking-water cooling in a pot! Why should any man remain married to a woman who will end up killing the two of them with famine!"

At that point a woman in the audience would say to the man: "*Aa!* You loved her! Even though you tell us all this we know you loved her, and if she were to come back, say today, you would be the very first person to give her a fitting welcome back to your home."

"Did I deny the fact that I loved her! The truth of the matter is that I told you right from the beginning that I loved Kasigwa, that I loved her very much, so much that I have no words to describe my love for her. And then I added that she had only that one problem of wetting her bed and being lazy to the extent of not being able to scratch her itching rash. Is that not what I said?"

"Yes indeed, that's what you said."

And so it is with the woman who has left her husband with no intention of ever returning, she too never has any qualms about revealing the truth about her former husband's impossible temperament and whatever other character flaws he had. She keeps her husband's secrets only when they are still married, still in love with each other, but once they are divorced then everything about him becomes an open secret. Try, for example, to ask a woman who has had a nasty divorce from her husband the following: "Are you no longer at your home these days?" and, if you approached her right, you will indeed hear what she will tell you about her husband, what an awful man he is, starting with: "Where is my home?" That will be her first answer for you, and should you then retort by saying to her: "At your husband's," you are bound to hear, "At my husband's! Have I too ever had a husband?"

"Is so-and-so not your husband? I thought that, since he wedded you, he is your husband!"

"*Hee*! *yee*! *yu*! That one! Yes, it is true he is my husband, but he cast me away like a curse, and with me too I have no more feelings for him, because he called me a witch and made me a marked person among people. To say the truth, so-and-so is a man whose name I don't even want to hear, a man who for no reason decided to plant the stench of an incurable wound on me by labeling me a witch in broad daylight, branding me in my adult age with something unknown to either my father or my mother. And yet he is the one whose people's notorious witchcraft is known all the way to the king's palace. Even when he wanted to marry me people came to malign his people to my father and mother and said: `Do you really want to marry your daughter in that home of notorious witches and witch doctors!  Is your daughter for sale in exchange for potent magic or what?'  At which my father and mother asked those maligners: `I see! So they practice witchcraft?' To which those answered: `Don't even ask! Especially the mother of the man to whom you want to give your daughter, that woman never sleeps in her house but in other people's homes practicing her evil craft. That woman has witchcraft in her blood, having got it from her maternal grandmother, who was executed by *omukama* on account of her evil powers. It is said that that woman and her husband lived in Bukindo and she carried her witchcraft beyond limits and went and danced naked at night in the king's palace to bewitch *omukama's* wives and *omukama* saw her and aimed at her an arrow with a wooden head and: *bii*! the wooden arrow hit her right in the middle of her wretched belly and fell down beside her. You all know that our kings are the most powerful of the powerful ones in things of the supernatural, and you know too that it is said that to hurt a person of charmed life you have to hit that person with a wooden arrow, a real arrow or any other real weapon would simply not harm him or her. And after *omukama* struck her that way he swore at her in that middle of the night: Let that be your lesson, you dog, and make you stop coming here naked to dance your evil dance over my wives! The witch on her part took to her heels and returned to husband's home, at about the time of the first cockcrow, where she found her husband sleeping like a log, unaware she had ever left their bed! Shortly after that *omukama's* infant child died, and a few days after yet another infant child of the king was dead and buried! And when people were still mourning the death of the king's second child, it became the turn of a wife of *omukama* and she too was dead and buried. The king then dispatched his courtiers to seek the truth from seers and the culprit was found to be the grandmother of your intended son-in-law. And so the courtiers came back and gave the king the news they were dying to report, that the person who killed his two children and his wife was the mother of your son-in-law's mother. At once *omukama* ordered the courtiers to execute her and she was taken to the execution ground in the wilderness and executed, in front of the entire public. It was after that that *omukama* ordered the father of the mother of your son-in-law exiled from Bukindo and he went to live somewhere else. But at that time the mother of your intended son-in-law was already a grown up girl, already being courted by her present husband, the father of the young man who wants to marry your child. And neither is the father of the young man your ordinary human being: he on his part is famed for turning people into zombies. So if you are determined to give them your daughter go ahead and do so, but you shouldn't later on turn around and say: If we had known what a family of witches and witch doctors they were we wouldn't have given them our child to marry.' After that my father and mother wanted to say no to his marrying me, until some other people came to them and told them all sorts of different stories and said: 'The maligned suitor is often the best husband. All of us you see here are married men and women and yet there are people who still malign us all the time. Those people too are out to malign the young man's family for no reason and what they say about his people's witchcraft and evil powers may be mere fabrications of theirs. Those people may be nothing but the usual spoilers and jealous people of this country of ours, because in Ukerewe a man or woman cannot marry without being maligned first; that is something we have yet to see. If people will malign even married couples, how can you expect them to spare those still courting?' And my father heeded that and married me to him.

"So, there you are, he and his people are the ones who deserve that evil mark and yet now they are the ones who have made me a marked person.

"And when you come to the real truth about that so-called husband of mine, oh, poor me! Rape: he was forever trying to invade other people's wives, breaking into their houses when they were asleep at night and their husbands were away from home! Stealing: that's his favorite pastime, he will never see other people's property, however insignificant, left unattended and leave it alone. He even steals from the lake the catch of fish from other people's nets and fish traps in the middle of the night. That to him is what he calls work. And he does not spare other people's cows and goats either! What with the fact that he is a disgusting drunkard! Whenever he is drunk, *hahee!* he wants to do the act of marriage with his very mother and every female relative of his, provided they are female and pass in front of his eyes he will chase them so as to grab them and do the act of marriage with them! Where indeed can I start and where end when it comes to my husband's shameful deeds! Even with livestock, when he is drunk he will want to do the marriage act with animals as if they were human beings! As to beating his wives, for him, even when he is not drunk, that is his hobby. Finally I could take it no more, poor me, having had to put up daily with such a monster! I will, I am sure, find another man who is needy like me and who will want to marry me. Even though I have children there and he is the father of my children, it doesn't matter, I'll never return to that man, for don't we see everywhere children of the same mother with different fathers, children of divorced women who remarried?"

Anyway, we have arrived at all this due to the visitors of Myombekere's home who,   however long they stayed with the couple they never saw Myombekere and his wife Bugonoka embroiled in the ceaseless petty quarrels you find everywhere among people. No, not with them. And that was because of their love for each other. That's what side-tracked us until we finally came to the issues of the lifestyles of people's households, both on the part of husbands as well as that of the wives of men in this Ukerewe kingdom of ours.

Chapter XII

NOTES

1. *Enkanda*: See note 22 of Chapter VI.
2. *Ekizanda* (plural *ebizanda*): See note 20 of Chapter II.
3. *Ihuzi*: Kitereza in his note for his Swahili translation of his novel describes this disease as: "Worms which kill eggs in a woman's womb." See note 25 of Chapter II.
4. *Amakire*: Kitereza in his note for his Swahili translation of his novel says: "When a man's wife is pregnant, the couple must avoid extra-marital sex until the child is born, otherwise whoever of the two transgressed that sex prohibition can cause their newborn child to be afflicted with *amakire* disease, which calls for purification on the part of the spouses before it can be treated and cured". In fact *amakire*, as we see later on in the novel, can afflict anybody and not only children and can be caused by the breach of any sex prohibition, including the spousal one, which, as we see in the novel, married couples have to observe on numerous occasions as a condition for fulfilling rites.
5. Nakiro: In the original Kikerewe text the author has crossed out Bazaraki, the name he uses in his Swahili translation, and instead written in ink Nakiro everywhere, except in one or two places where he obviously overlooked making the intended correction. It is quite possible that Kitereza made the change in the original typescript, which was taken to Canada by his former employer the late Fr. Simard in 1952, where it still is, and a copy of which I have used for this translation(see Introduction), but never made the intended change in the carbon copy he remained with and on which he based his 1969 Swahili translation. It appears Kitereza had to make that name change because he uses names often for their meaning and he has used Bazaraki for the daughter of Bugonoka's healer Kibuguma, an intelligent and very responsible young girl of Nakiro age Myombekere and his wife Bugonoka evoke to reproach that little girl of their home, Nakiro, a niece of Myombekere, with irresponsibility and frivolity.
6. *Ekibo*: See note 15 of Chapter I.
7. Cattle-owning homes in a given neighborhood formed a "grazing community" in which homes took turns to graze the collective herd of the neighborhood. See note 4 of Chapter III.
8. *Endwero*: Type of millet.

9.   *Enkombyo*: Shells of lake crabs used as spoons.

10:   *Ekikome*: See note 1 of Chapter II.

11.   *Obwita*: See note 14 of Chapter I.

12.   *Omwiko*: See note 17 of Chapter VI.

13.   For men and women *ebibo*, see note 16 of Chapter VI.

14.   *Omutaho*: See note 9 of Chapter I.

15.   Male youths prone to telling lies and snitching on their friends to elders were sometimes punished by their peers tying them up and throwing them inside columns of *empazi*, the big black "safari ants" with painful bites. For *empazi* see note 14 of Chapter X.

16.   *Olugali*: See note 6 of Chapter I.

17.   *Entobotobo*: A wild eggplant.

18.   *Obutaga*: See note 4 of Chapter II.

19.   *Empiki*: Small urn-like pot in which twigs of a nice-smelling tree are burnt and their smoke used to scent milk containers. See note 5 of Chapter X.

20.   Lyangombe or Karungu: See note 19 of Chapter X.

21.   *Ebigugu:* Tiny catfish caught in rivers and ponds, especially during heavy rains.

22.   *Enkorobondo*: Tiny sardines caught in rivers, especially during heavy rains.

23.   *Olubigo*: See note 3 of Chapter II.

24.   *Enkuyu:* Name of a large fish with an abundance of scales, one of the kinds of fish Wakerewe women did not eat. See note 17 of Chapter II.

25.   *Enkole*: Type of very small beans.

26.   *Omukama*: See note 26 of Chapter II.

27.   The Wakerewe called the very humble way in which they greeted their king "*kulamucha*", to hail the sovereign. See also note 26 of Chapter II.

28.   Bukindo: The king's palace and the village in which it is situated. See note 8 of Chapter IV.

29.   *Narunzwi*: The king's sleeping house and largest house of his palace, so that any very large house is sometimes also referred to as *narunzwi* .

30.   On the day *omukama* was buried, fire in the entire kingdom was supposed to be put out completely and new fires started in people's homes only when, after the enthroning of a new *omukama*, a new fire for the new reign had been started at court by an elder from *Abahembe* ("Fire-makers") clan. The new king's fire was then kept burning in *narunzwi*, the king's sleeping house, day and night throughout the reign of that *omukama*.

31.   Kitereza grew up at the court of *Omukama* Mukaka, his paternal uncle who adopted him when his father died of smallpox when the author was only five

years old (see Introduction) and had therefore personal knowledge of the inside of the palace of the kings of Ukerewe. In fact we know from the annals of Ukerewe written down by *Omukama* Mukaka's son Alphonce Mkama II and quoted in the Introduction that it was indeed King Mukaka who, on becoming king in 1895, moved the residence of Ukerewe kings from Musozi where H.M. Stanley met King Lukonge in 1875 (see Introduction) to its present site and built in the palace that extraordinarily large house, *narunzwi*, and made the frightening amazon called Nabutuma its guardian.

32. *Engoro*: The king's bed, also name an itching grass. See note 4 of Chapter XXX.

33. *Katobaha, Mihigo, Golita:* Names of the kings of Ukerewe (see appendix II of Introduction). The king's titles here are some of the numerous attributes of the kings of Ukerewe.

34. *Emondo*: See note 9 of Chapter X.

35. *Ekilangi*: See note 7 of Chapter VII.

36. *Empindu*: See note 17 of Chapter X.

37.   *Enkazumbe*: Smoke-charred grass from the roof of a thatched kitchen.

38. "Myombekere" means "the lifestyle of a household", and also "Build (a house or household) for (her)", See note I of Chapter I.

Chapter XIII

A TALE: HOW MEN AND WOMEN CAME TO LIVE TOGETHER

Please, fellow men, now pay attention to me, because I want to tell you this sweet little story of our elders so that you too know how we met and came to live with women, and how after that we came to treat them differently from the way we treat ourselves. And you better listen carefully, for here goes my tale!

At the beginning all human beings, those you see now in this country and those living in other countries as well as all those who have ever lived since the beginning of time, lived like this: all the men, every male person ever created, of every race and color, lived in a country of their own, a single country inhabited by men only and ruled by a single sovereign, their *omukama*,[1] likewise a man. That's how they lived in their land of perfect happiness, doing their own cooking. And likewise on their part the women of the entire world too lived in a country of their own and they too were ruled by their female *omukama*.

The men on their side tilled the earth and grew food, and that was the only food they lived on and never tasted meat of any kind, neither did their *omukama*, who also lived solely on the food that grew in the earth. The women on their part did not know how to till land and did not eat the food that grew in the earth but lived on the meat of each and every wild animal of the entire animal race, and so did their female *omukama*, who likewise lived solely on meat and never ate any other kind of food. Their female *omukama* kept in her residence dogs, numbering one hundred in all, and it was those dogs which hunted for the women and killed every manner of animal everyday, on which the women fed.

One day the female *omukama* sent an official delegation of her female courtiers and female village heads [2] on an errand and told them: "Go, I am commanding you, to my fellow *omukama* in the land of men and tell him that I have sent you in his land to find out whether everything is fine with his people, and then come back and tell me whatever he will tell you." Her messengers left, carrying with them enough food for the journey to their destination and back, because it took fifteen night stops to go from their country to the country of men.

The delegation of women finally got to the country of men and went to the king of men and paid him homage. *Omukama* of men welcomed them warmly and prepared beds for them. But during meal time when he brought them food that grew in the soil they declined it and said: "In our country we never eat this food; it is taboo." On hearing which *omukama* of men and his subjects were all greatly surprised and *omukama* of men asked the women, "What do you live on in your country? What do you eat?"

"In our country the food we live on is the meat of each and every living wild animal."

"With us here too it is taboo to eat meat, and there is not among us a single person who eats meat. And how do you kill those animals whose meat you eat?"

"Power to you, *omukama* of men! Our *omukama* keeps one hundred dogs in her home; those dogs are the ones which kill the animals for us to eat."

On hearing that *omukama* of men became very interested in talking with the delegation of women, because his country was already ruined by wild animals which were destroying his people's crops all the time, and so he asked the female visitors, "By the way, since your *omukama* is my fellow sovereign, if I were to ask her to let her dogs come and kill for me the wild animals which are destroying our crops in this country of mine, would she give me some?"

"My Lord, she will, Great-giver, and gladly too."

"If she does so, how many do you think she would give me?"

"She could give you even the entire one hundred of them."

"In that case, when you go back you will be accompanied by some of my people."

So when it was time for the delegation of women to go back they said good-bye to *omukama* of men and he too sent warm greetings to his female peer: "My very warm greetings to my fellow *omukama*."

"Yes, my Lord," the women answered.

And so the women got on their way back, accompanied by the envoys of *omukama* of men, the women delegation still carrying enough food for their journey back, for they had carried enough meat to last them for more than thirty days. After traveling for fifteen days, on the sixteenth day the women stepped back into the residence of their *omukama* of women and the men from the country of men found that, yes, the residence of *omukama* of women was a really great palace! The visiting men paid the female *omukama* their homage and finished and stepped aside. Then her returning envoys stepped in front of her and told her how well her fellow *omukama* received them, gave them a house of their own to sleep in, and, in addition, tried to serve them food which grows in the soil. Those words "food which grows in soil" sent *omukama* of women together with all her people laughing uncontrollably: *kwekwekwekwe*! None among the women present could resist laughing. And when they stopped laughing they all asked, "And how does that food which grows in the soil look like?"

The returned envoys stood up and told their *omukama*, "Power to you, Great-giver! Some of it looks like the shit from our bowels, roundish that way, that's what they call sweet potatoes; then there is another kind, which looks like the hanging fruits of *amazungute*[3] trees, that's what they call cassava; then there are the grains of grass, which, when they ripen and dry, are harvested, threshed and winnowed to remove chaff, so that only clean grains are left. This grain they store in hut-like structures [4] in their homes, from which they get some as needed and grind into flour on a stone. This flour is what they put in a pot with boiling water, and, using a chiseled piece of wood they call cooking-spoon[5] cook and stir until it becomes something like a potter's clay, which is then dished out of the pot and put into bowls[6] for serving. That is what they call *obwita*.[7] We should perhaps show you some samples, my Lord, because the men we came with came with their journey food.

The returned messengers went with the men with whom they had come to where they had put the visitors' belongings and the men gave them some sweet potatoes and slices of cassava and leftovers of *obwita* and they brought the food and showed it to their *omukama* and her other people present. *Omukama* and the rest of her people exclaimed with great surprise and said, "Yes indeed, before you die don't say you have seen it all! All this time we call these people fellow human beings, because they look like us, and yet here they are, they feed on all sorts of filth from the ground and grains of grass as if they were pigs or some grass-eating wild animals!"

Omukama of women called the visiting men again and when they came in front of her she asked them, "Is it true that in your country you don't eat meat?" The men agreed with one voice, " Yes, our Lord, Great-giver,[8] it is true we don't eat meat, because to us meat is taboo. Secondly, may be our sovereign couldn't find someone to kill the animals for us, Great-giver." All the female people present as well as their sovereign were simply confounded!

After some time, the female *omukama* instructed her courtiers to sweep a house and get it ready as the sleeping quarters of the visiting men. It was then that the visiting men told *omukama* of women the behest of their *omukama* to her: "Great-builder, we have been sent to you by our *omukama* with this message: `Go to my fellow *omukama* and ask her on my behalf to give you one hundred of her dogs to come and kill for me the wild animals which are destroying the crops of my country. And, should she grant you the dogs, come back quickly.'"

On hearing that *omukama* of women responded, "Yes, indeed, there is every reason for you to go back quickly, since it also happens to be that our food, the food we eat here, as you have told me, is taboo to you. So go and sleep tonight and wait until tomorrow. Tomorrow morning I want my dogs here to go hunting wild animals for us first, so that I can give you the dogs your sovereign is asking for and you can take them to him and he can use them to put an end to the destruction wrought by those wild animals on your crops, lest famine strikes your kingdom and your people perish from hunger."

The men fell to singing the praises of the female *omukama*: "Power to you, the Sun, power to you, the Lion, Long live the Giver, power to you, the Generous one!"

At night they slept and it dawned.

At dawn the visiting men heard the female *omukama's* loud trumpets sound, followed by the shrill sounds of smaller hunting horns. And at once they heard an outbreak of dog howls, loud and haunting like the wailing of mourners for their beloved one who has just breathed his or her last breath: *uwoo! wooo! uwooo! wo! wo! wo!* In the palace itself crowds of people were gathering, every kind of woman imaginable, of every race and color. Then the female *omukama* gave the command and at once: *hoho!* the crowds of women took off with their dogs. The whole day they were gone, and gone they remained, and it was not until towards evening when the visiting men heard again the shrill and loud sounds of trumpets and hunting horns burst their ears. Not long after that they saw the dogs arrive, their mouths all red with blood, and shortly after that they saw countless women carrying on poles suspended from their shoulders countless whole animal carcasses and loads upon loads of meat, and they were left speechless with wonder!

In the evening the visiting men went to the audience of *omukama* of women and once in her presence two of them, both great speakers and people on whom *omukama* of men counted most and to whom he entrusted his important errands, Nkubitizi and another man, stood up and went in front of *omukama* of women and said to her: "Our Lord, Great-giver, we have come to ask for your permission to start on our journey back and to remind you of the request of our *omukama* to you, Great-builder."

Omukama of women pretended to have forgotten, as you all know sovereigns are wont to do, and said, "By the way, what was your request? I appear to have forgotten it. Please do tell me about it again, may be I'll then remember and see what it is all about," and the men told her everything anew and when they were done she agreed to their request and said, "Tomorrow go home, but make sure you leave very early in the morning, at cockcrow. As soon as the cock crows, I will send people to come and wake you up and tie leashes on all my one hundred dogs for you, so that they can escort you when it is still cool morning. They will also give you hunting trumpets and horns, both the big one as well as the shrill ones, for blowing for the dogs whenever you want to go hunting those wild animals destroying your crops and any other wild animals. However, there is one very important thing I must tell you, which is this: These dogs of mine must be commanded only once this way: `*Chi* catch!' They are not to be commanded two or three times like: '*Chi* catch! *Chi* catch!' or '*Chi chi chi* catch catch catch!' Never! If they are commanded two or three times they will go into the wilderness never to return and disappear for ever. That is the one thing which you have to explain to your *omukama* so that he can inform the people who will go hunting with the dogs. And so I hope your ears have caught what I said very well, because it is something you may not forget."

The two gentlemen assured *omukama* of women: "Our Lord, Great-giver, we swear in your very presence that we will not forget, Giver-of-habiliment."

After the men had thus sworn before her, the female sovereign told them, "You may go now. Say your good-byes now so that you can go to bed early, lest you start on your journey when you are still feeling sleepy."

The two men said: "Long live the Sun," and then the rest of the visiting men too went in front of the female *omukama* and bid her good-bye: "Power to you, the Upright-one. Have a pleasant rest, Great-builder, may you have power for ever, Praise-worthy-one!" and she responded to their good-byes: "*Mm*! Greet your *omukama* for me," and all the men responded to her together at once: "It will be done, Great-giver!" and left to go and sleep.

When the cock said: "*Tata wee!*[9]" the visiting men heard people come to wake them up, just as *omukama* of women had said. They woke up and quickly assembled their belongings, after which they were given dog journey food, that is meat, for the one hundred dogs. Although eating meat was taboo to the men, they were allowed to touch it, and so the men received the meat, got up and got on their way. And when their escort arrived at the place where they had been told they should stop, they gave the men the one hundred dogs, each and everyone of them with a leash around its neck, and the women and the men said good bye to each other and the women went back to their country of women and the men walked on with their dogs. In every place where they stopped for the night, the men first cooked their own food before cooking the journey food for their dogs, the meat they had been given for the dogs by *omukama* of women. And thus they traveled until they came to their last night stop, their fifteenth. The following day as the sun was setting, they arrived at the residence of their male *omukama*, together with their one hundred dogs.

Courtiers who had learnt of their approach had already informed their *omukama* that his delegation to *omukama* of women would be back that day, and so as they approached his palace *omukama* of men sent people to meet them and welcome them back, at the same time as other people were already preparing food for them. Before long the returning men arrived with their one hundred dogs. From where he sat in the interior of his palace *omukama* of men sent them word as to where they should keep the dogs and they did so. After that the king sent his returned delegation word again: "Go and tell them that after they have eaten and fed their dogs it's when they should come to see us."

So when the returning envoys finished eating and feeding their dogs, they went to pay homage to their *omukama*, leaving their dogs where they were instructed to keep them. Once in the presence of their *omukama*, each one of them humbly folded a knee and one after the other they filed before their king to give praises to him and then withdrew and joined the large audience already gathered in front of the sovereign. *Omukama* continued with the conversation he was having before the returned envoys came to him, told his audience how he was at a loss as to how to put an end to those wild beasts which were eating and wrecking so much destruction on their crops. Only much later did he call the name of one of the returned envoys: "Nkubitizi."

"Yes, Great-giver!"

"Come here."

Nkubitizi got up and went to sit directly in front of *omukama*. Once he sat down, *omukama* asked him how they went and how they arrived at the residence of *omukama* of women and Nkubitizi narrated to their *omukama* what happened: "Power to you, Great-giver! We journey to the place well and likewise came back well, Great-builder. We had no problem at all on the journey nor at any of our fifteen nightly rest-stops, both when going and when coming back. And things went well too when we arrived in that country of women, where we found your peer reigning, and she too wishes you a long reign, Great-giver."

"Is she well? And are her country and people well too?"

"She is well, and she reigns, Great-giver, and her country as well as its people are also well. She received us generously and gave us a house of our own in which to sleep, and we had just arrived when her people brought the food they eat in their country and when we looked at it we found it was nothing but meat."

All those in the audience of *omukama* of men exclaimed with great surprise and for those among them with weak stomachs it was all they could do to prevent themselves from vomiting and just frown with great disgust instead!

Nkubutizi continued: "And we have also come with what you sent us to request on your behalf, and their number is one hundred, Great-giver, just as the female visitors who came here to see you said. When we too got to their *omukama's* home one hundred dogs is what we asked for and that's what we were given, no more and no less, Great-giver. And once in their *omukama's* home, the morning of the day following our arrival, we first heard rolls of drums thundering in that very palace of their *omukama*. When the people stopped beating the drums, they sounded some strange musical instruments, one type of which they call trumpets and the other one, made of horns of wild animals, hunting horns. When they blow air by their mouths into these instruments they make piercing noises which can reach very far. As soon as those strange musical instruments were sounded, at once we heard their numerous dogs howling all at the same time: *Uwooo! woo! wo! wo!* while squatting on their haunches, their noses pointing up in the air. Each and every dog wore a leash around its neck. We simply had no words to express our amazement!

"Shortly after that we saw a huge crowd of people assemble, all of them women. And in no time those thousands of people were off, their one hundred dogs running close by behind them, to go and hunt in the wilderness and kill the wild animals for food the women would eat when they gave us their one hundred dogs to bring here. And so we passed the rest of that day in the palace, from time to time some of the palace people coming to keep us company and to query us about the food we of this country eat, which we showed them again and again and each and every time making them shake their heads in disbelief. As the day wore on, at the late afternoon sun, we heard again the trumpets and the hunting horns sound, just as I have already described them, and shortly after that we saw the one hundred dogs arrive, their mouths all red with blood, and immediately after we saw people pour into the palace carrying on shoulder poles loads and loads of meat, some whole carcasses of animals, all stiff dead, some chunks of the meat of the dead wild animals, carcasses too many to count, all of which they went and hung inside the residence of their female *omukama*.

"And so in the evening, after the sun had set, the female *omukama* called us and after we had been in her audience for a while we repeated to her the request you sent us to take to her, Great-builder, and she consented, explaining to us precisely how she was going to give us the dogs and how we were supposed to make them hunt for us: 'When you take these dogs to hunt, remember that you are to command them only once this way: *Chi* catch! Never are you to command them twice or three times. Did you understand or not?'

"The following morning, just before cockcrow, we woke up and assembled our belongings and we were given the one hundred dogs and got on our way back. We stopped for the night fifteen times on the way, Great-giver, and we have arrived here on the sixteenth day." Nkubitizi wanted to go on, to put in a string of additional information, when *omukama* stopped him: "Stop there!"

Hearing that the other courtiers laughed. Nkubitizi stepped away from the king, but not without a few words for his fellow courtiers who had laughed: "*Aa!* Yes, gentlemen, what are you laughing at! Isn't it only proper and fitting that when your *omukama* sends you on an errand and you come back you dutifully inform him, clearly and in details, all that you saw on your mission? So what is it you are laughing at? Do you then think that because my name is Nkubitizi[10] I am being truly the Garrulous-one, putting in things I didn't see, adding raw trees to firewood to swell the faggot?"

His fellow courtiers on their part answered him back: "We didn't laugh at your reporting to the king what you saw over there clearly and in details, we laughed because you kept on and on even after you had told all about your journey, so that we said to ourselves: `It appears to day Nkubitizi has decided to live the truth of his name! Look, *omukama* is telling him to stop and yet he is still going on and on, without paying heed,' that's why we laughed."

After sometime *omukama* told Nkubutizi: "Please bring us those strange instruments you say the women over there play when they take their dogs to hunt." Nkubitizi ran for the instruments quickly and came back and knelt before the king and began showing him and explaining the instruments to him, "This is what they call a trumpet, and this one here is the hunting horn."

"And what are these feathers for? And how do they play the instruments?"

"Power to you, Great-giver! These feathers are for cleaning the instruments of dust and cobwebs, this way. To play, they put the instruments on their mouths this way and blow in them."

"Please try to play for us a bit, so that we can hear what they sound like and satisfy our curiosity."

"No, I can't do that. Because if I play the instruments now when it is not yet time to hunt, the dogs will break out howling simply uncontrollably, and may even take off and scatter and run off in every direction and possibly get lost altogether. That, Great-giver, and all you great people of noble birth present here, is why I can't play the instruments. Because over there the female *omukama* gave us very strict instructions regarding such matters and said, "You should play these horns only when you are going to hunt, after you have put on leash all the dogs, and when you are coming back from hunting, after you have killed the wild animals, and never at any other time."

Omukama of men said a few words to thank his peer the female *omukama* for what she did for him: "My peer *omukama* of women has been very kind to me. I don't even know what to give her in return so as to fill her heart too with contentment and happiness as mine is at this moment. And to you all my courtiers present here, this is what I want to tell you: `Go and tell the nearby village headmen to summon the people of their villages to come here tomorrow early in the morning. I want each and every one of their subjects to come, because I want to take these dogs on a trial hunt at once in the area surrounding our palace, for we have already suffered enough from these wild beasts. You who have returned from this mission, go and sleep, because you are weary from travel, but remember to be here tomorrow morning to teach us how to make these dogs hunt for us."

The men of the returned delegation said to their king, "Power to you!" and the rest of the audience followed suit and everybody said good-bye to *omukama*: "Power to you, Great-giver, sleep well, Great-builder" and the king responded to them all: "*Mm!*"

And since the new day always dawns, it dawned. When it dawned, the king washed his face and then came out of his huge sleeping house and came to the palace courtyard, at about the time of the twittering of the pre-dawn birds, to see whether any of the people who had been on his mission abroad had arrived, and found that Nkubitizi and a number of his companions, some twenty and more, were already there squatting on the ground. The men came and paid homage to him and *omukama* asked them, "Are you the only ones who have arrived? The rest of your companions have not yet come!"

"Our Lord, it appears they have yet to arrive, Great-giver."

"Beat the drums."

The men put the drum-sticks on *emilango*[11] and the battery of palace drums spoke with their sounds of thunder and said: "*Gali kunu! gali kunu! gali kunu! Amageni! Amageni!*[12] and all the subjects who had been summoned by their village headmen poured into the palace, with not a single person remaining at home.

Then Nkubitizi took with him a number of his companion to go and help him leash the dogs and they left and then came back. The king had gone back inside his sleeping house and now was out again and shortly after that Nkubutizi and his companions left to go to the dogs again and in no time people heard them play the trumpets and the hunting horns from the land of women: *Hororrr! hororrr! hororr! Pyooo! pyooo! pyo! pyo!* and at once all the dogs sat on their haunches and looked up in the heavens and let loose their howls. *Ee! aa* ! What a scene in *omukama's* residence! What with the noise and commotion of that multitude of people and the thundering of the *emilango* to boot! It was something beyond description! The king too was overjoyed and became all cheerful. Nkubitizi was here and there and everywhere in that multitude of people, his trumpet on his mouth, skipping and jumping, turning the king's palace into his home and attracting the gaze of common people and village headmen alike.

When that chief courtier saw that those who had been summoned had all come, he ordered those who were beating the drums: "Stop!" *Emilango* stopped, at the same time as the players of the trumpets and the hunting horns too stopped playing their instruments. And at once   *omukama* ordered people to go hunting: "All you men assembled here, listen to me. I summoned you to come and hunt the wild animals which eat all our food. And so go now and hunt with these one hundred dogs which are here to help us kill those animals destroying our crops. They were given to me by my fellow *omukama*. But there is one thing which all of you must make sure to remember, which is this: These dogs are to be commanded only once like this: *'Chi!* catch!' That's all, until the end the hunt. You are not to command them twice or three times."

The men all agreed in chorus: "Power to you, Great-giver! We have heard you and woe to him who will dare to command the dogs twice or three times! We will be on the look out for him and you will know all about it on our return from the hunt, sovereign of the Reign-of-joy-and-peace."

And so off went the men, Nkubitizi and his companions leading the way, their dogs following behind. And when they got into the wilderness and began to beat the wild animals out of their hiding places, they released the dogs from their leashes and commanded them to hunt with: *'Chi!* catch!' and the dogs got into the wilderness and all over it and killed the wild animals, crop eaters and non-crop eaters alike, and killed them until they had killed countless numbers of them, until they killed them to the very last one, even though the place had been teeming with wild animals, those above the ground as well as those in holes under the ground, which the dogs had gone after and brought out already dead and cold. By the time the sun began to descend in the sky, there was not a single wild animal left alive in that area and the carcasses of dead animals lay scattered everywhere. The men then took with them some carcasses for feeding the dogs at home.

They arrived in the palace and told their *omukama* how their hunt in the vicinity of the palace had gone and how they had killed very many crop-eating animals as well as other wild animals, how they had left in the wilderness carcasses of dead wild animals piled high everywhere like stacks of ears of millet at harvest time. The king became really excited and told the village headmen and the multitude of people in his palace: "You all go home now. Those of you who live around here will, after you have eaten, take me to that place in the wilderness so that I too can satisfy my curiosity."

The village headmen and their subjects went back to their homes. Nkubitizi and the other courtiers remained in the palace and were served food and ate and then went to their *omukama* and took him into the wilderness. On getting where the dogs hunted the king too saw with his own eyes piles upon piles of carcasses of crop-eaters and other wild animals, mountains upon mountains of them, and he too exclaimed with great surprised and said, "Yes indeed, gentlemen, you have done good work! And these dogs too are really well trained and great hunting dogs, that's why *omukama* of women depends so much on them, and that's why too her people saw no need to till the land and they live on meat alone. *Aa! he!* This is simply incredible! And now let's go back home." And so the king and his people left the site of that day's hunt and returned to the palace.

They rested for two days and on the third day *omukama* told his courtiers to summon again the public, all his subjects from his entire kingdom, for a hunt. So *omukama*'s insignia was carried all around the kingdom and people were told: "Tomorrow everybody to the hunt! The meeting place: the ground of the tall *emihama*[13] palm trees." And on the following day all the men of the kingdom came for the hunt. In fact on that day the only men who remained at home were the very very old ones and the dead-sick, the bedridden ones and those who could no longer do anything at all except to eat and drink and bask in the sweet morning sun, and the men who were cooking for *omukama* and that's all. Otherwise the rest of the people of the kingdom, all the men of every race and color in the country of men, came for that public hunt. And when all the men had gathered at that ground of many *emihama* palms, as soon as they saw that dew had dried in the grass, since the ground they had gathered on was overgrown with grass and it was the season of clouded skies, Nkubitizi and his companions felt it was time to go to work and divided that multitude of people into many smaller groups for the hunt. That done, they sounded their instruments, the trumpets and the hunting horns went to the mouths of the players and sounded and resounded and the dogs joined in with their howling and there was such loud clamor in the wilderness that all those present witnessed what they had never seen before, and to this very day people have never forgotten the wonders of that day!

When the trumpets and the hunting horns stopped sounding, the men poured into the wilderness and commanded their dogs with: `*Chi*! catch!' and the dogs went after the crop-eaters and the other wild animals, those above the ground as well as those hiding in holes under the ground.

However what is destined to be is bound to happen. Also so many people had gathered for the hunt on that day and had been divided into so many groups that they simply could not all hear each other. As a result the order of not commanding the dogs more than once was simply not followed any more. So whoever saw a dog in hot pursuit of a wild animal urged on the dog by commanding it twice and even three times. When those dogs heard they were being commanded that way, *hoho!* they went on and scattered into the whole wide world and disappeared as if they had gone to heaven, for ever!

The men waited for the dogs to come back and waited and waited but the dogs never come back! And when they couldn't wait any longer, they left the hunting ground and went back home. Nkubitizi and his companions, who knew all about not commanding the dogs two or three times, returned with sorrowful hearts, so much that when they got in front of the king even the strength to tell him what had happened almost failed them completely, fully convinced he would execute them all. However when the monarch found out what had happened and realized it was inevitable, given the multitudes of people who had been out there, he did nothing to them and was only overwhelmed by sadness for being at a loss as to what to do.

Over there on the other side, when the female *omukama* in her country saw that the meat her dogs hunted for her people before they left was almost finished with no sign of the dogs being returned, she summoned her people and when they had all gathered in her Bukindo[14] she told them: "Listen to me very carefully, dear ladies. What we are witnessing shows that being too kind hearted at times can mean suicide, or so it seems. I was foolish enough to release my dogs to go to the aid on my fellow *omukama*, convinced they would be returned quickly. Apparently that was never his intention. For, look here, since I gave him the dogs to this very day we have heard nothing from him, not even a word to inform us whether the dogs arrived safely or not. And so, dear ladies, I have called you to tell you this: It is obvious to me that famine is already here, and in fact it is going to wipe us from the face of the earth entirely, kill us all, completely. And so I am giving you only today to stay here. Tomorrow I want you all to come with journey food, all of you, without a single one of you remaining behind, and we will go and bring back our dogs, because we can't just sit here and do nothing and neither can we send just a few people over there to go for the dogs, because they won't come to our aid in time, before the bit of meat we still have left has run out."

All the women answered back their female *omukama* and said: "Power to you, Great-giver! What you said is the only proper thing to do, that's how the matter appears to us too. We too agree that that is also the only right course of action to take, since by going over there the entire country of us we'll simply leave him no room for any more of his lies."

The following morning therefore *omukama* of women told her female courtiers to beat the palace drums and the courtiers put the drum-sticks to the drums and the battery of drums rumbled, but only those who lived near the palace could hear them. And realizing that she told her courtiers to beat the biggest drum, the one she had named Ears-of-the-country[15,] and Ears-of-the-country was sounded and the entire country heard and listened and came and assembled in her palace. No sooner were they all assembled than they saw their *omukama* emerge from her house. Those people of the country of women knew how to take good care of their *omukama*, who was beautiful beyond imagination, so that as soon as she came into the open her beauty completely eclipsed the sun! In addition to her amazing beauty, a good-charm amulet graced her neck and *obunerere*[16] covered her legs all the way to the calves. Her female courtiers played *ebikuli* [17] flutes in her homage, others ululated[18] and yet others chanted her praises to welcome her presence among her subjects: "Welcome, the Upright-one, welcome, Great-entertainer, welcome, Giver-of-courage, welcome, Giver-of-habiliment!" accompanying their praises with the clapping of their hands. She was a heavy woman, and what with her ornaments and the ponderous robe of *enkanda*[19] she wore, she was really hefty, but she never journeyed by walking, her people always carried her whenever she traveled. And so once she got outside her female courtiers brought her carrying chair, which was made of buffalo skin nicely sewn and attached to the frame, again by sinews from the legs of a buffalo, and placed her in the chair and carried her high, four carriers at a time, who carried the frame of her chair placed on their heads and never on their shoulders.

The carriers of the female *omukama* put their sovereign in her chair and on their heads and started on their way to the country of men, with other female courtiers leading the way and yet others following behind, while the female village heads with all their subjects walked at the rear, forming a procession of people incredibly long! While still on their way, after they had covered thirteen night-rests, the female *omukama* selected twenty of her most trusted courtiers and sent them as an advance party to inform *omukama* of men that *omukama* of women was on her way with all her people, lest they find him completely unprepared to receive them or on seeing all of a sudden so many people pour into his country without warning he should take them for enemies coming to attack him. The twenty women got to *omukama* of men and informed him they had been sent by their *omukama* to let him know she was on her way with all her people, that they had left her behind at the thirteenth night-stop and she might be arriving the following day or the day after that. *Omukama* of men prepared for the women a place to sleep and also sent his courtiers to his village headmen to tell them to inform their people that all of them were being summoned the following day to the royal village of Bukindo to assemble in the palace of their *omukama*, where the female *omukama* with her entire population of women was expected to arrive that day, the same female sovereign who was a very good friend of their *omukama* and who gave him the one hundred dogs to hunt crop-eating wild animals, who may be coming to find out from her peer how her dogs got lost.

The following day *omukama* of men told his courtiers to sound the palace drums the *emilango* were made to thunder in the residence of the sovereign and the people poured out in all their number to come and see why their *omukama* wanted them. When the people had assembled, *omukama* told his courtiers to call for silence and when everybody was quiet the king told his subjects, "I have called you here to come and welcome my friend, the female *omukama* who gave me the dogs which got lost during our hunt for the animals which were eating our crops. We have already with us here some of her courtiers, who arrived yesterday. They are the ones who informed me that their *omukama* will be arriving here today or tomorrow with all the people of her kingdom, but that, in spite of everything, she is not coming here with warring intentions. She is coming with nothing but peace in her mind. And that's why I have called you, to inform you of the nature of her visit and to tell all of you to be here to receive her and her people."

The day following that, as the sun began to descend past noon, people in the palace of *omukama* of men heard the shrill sound of the small drums of *omukama* of women and before long they say the vanguard of her procession begin to pour in. Seeing that *omukama* of men went into his huge sleeping house to change into his regalia and in no time he was out again and, as you would expect, ordered his courtiers to play the court drums and so his *emilango* thundered and the palace of *omukama* of men was filled with crowds of people and with such a commotion that it was indeed a scene to behold! And wasn't *omukama* of women carried high in her leather chair, and were *ebikuli* not at the mouths of her women courtiers, their sounds bursting open people's ears? And wasn't she eclipsing the sun by her shining beauty, and wasn't *omukama* of men of like beauty? And wasn't *omukama* of men the first to want to go and meet his peer?

When he was about to start off and go and meet her, his courtiers and village headmen told him, "No, Great-giver, stay where you are. We will go with your people to meet her." At once the people of *omukama* of men went off: *ku!* a whole crowd, to meet their visitors while still on their way.

The men got to the visiting women and relieved them of the things they were carrying, which included their clothing skins, pots, chairs, bowls, trays,[20] water cups,[21] their journey food, and the like. When they tried to relieve them of the chair on which they were carrying their female *omukama* the women said: "*No,*" and the women themselves continued carrying her, while now walking at snail pace, until they got to the palace gate and the female *omukama* herself told her carriers: "Put me down and let me walk into the palace, because we have now arrived at our destination," and her carriers put her down and she entered the palace of her fellow *omukama* walking.

As soon as she stepped out of her carrying chair all the men saw at once that she was an extremely beautiful woman, sparkling all over like crystal-clear spring water, pure from whatever side you draw it, for the entire of her was dazzling, from her person to the robe and ornaments she wore! And so from the entrance of the palace she walked, flanked by a crowd of her own people as well as the people of *omukama* of men, and when her procession got to where *omukama* of men was seated on his throne, the crowd of men and women flanking her halted and let the sovereign of women walk on alone until she came to *omukama* of men. Then she knelt down and greeted the sovereign of men: "Power to you, Sir! How are you, Great-giver?" and *omukama* of men responded to her: "Greetings!" She then got up and a chair of teak was placed for her on the right side of *omukama* of men and she sat down.

Much much later, *omukama* of men told his courtiers to stop playing drums, because he wanted to talk to *omukama* of women about her lost dogs. Everybody became silent and each and every person sat down, with the exception of the chief courtiers, who had the duty of keeping watch over that   crowd of humanity and making sure people did not start whispering and humming and zooming from underneath. In that very instant *omukama* of men sent out into the crowd a shrill whistle by his mouth like this: "*Chwiyo!*" Immediately the chief courtiers told people: "Silence, ladies and gentlemen, *omukama* wants to speak!"

When everybody became silent, *omukama* of men said to *omukama* of women: "We in this country wronged you. Your one hundred dogs which I asked from you to come and kill for me the wild animals which were eating the crops of the people of my kingdom arrived here safely. The following day I sent people to go and make them hunt in the vicinity of this palace and on that day they killed crop-eating wild animals without numbers, until they had completely wiped them out in that area. Then a few days after that I again sent out a royal message summoning people to convene for a public hunt, and since that second hunt was carried on by so many people they failed to observe well the instructions you gave to my envoys and told them never to forget, that is that those dogs were to be commanded once only, and instead, once in wilderness, they just did as they chose and commanded the dogs many times. When the dogs heard that, they took off and scattered to the whole wide world and disappeared as if they had gone to heaven. We waited for the dogs to come back and waited and waited but they never came back, to this very day. In the end we came to the conclusion that perhaps they had gone back on their own to where they came from. That is the wrong we people of this kingdom have committed against you. We do not deny it, because wrong doing appears to be the accursed lot of us men."

The female *omukama* on her part, when she saw that her peer had finished talking, responded to him as follows: "We too are here in your kingdom because of the same thing, to find out what happened to our dogs over here. Before those dogs came here to help you kill for you the crop-eating animals as you have said, Great-giver, I too had sent them to kill for us wild animals so that we would have enough meat to eat during the days the dogs would be here killing those crop-eating animals for you, and when we waited for so long without the dogs coming back, I finally said to myself: `No, I must do something.  Since we are meat eaters and the meat we have left is so little, I must call together people from my entire kingdom and ask them what they think we should do.  When my people  gathered, I asked them what they thought we should do and told them:  `Dear ladies, what are we to do, since our food is about finished? Should we send some people to my fellow *omukama* to go and bring back our dogs? Even if we could do that, by the time they come back we will be in very bad shape, famine will have already set in among us and caused us great suffering.' So I said that the thing to do was for us all, the entire country, to come over here and fetch our dogs. And everybody agreed with me and the following day we set out to come here. But now we too realize that what happened was not intentional wrongdoing on your part. All you too wanted was to save your country, because you had already suffered so much on account of those crop-eating animals. What is more, I too did not come here with the intentions of war, Great-giver; I came with nothing but peaceful intentions, just to find out what the matter was."

And when *omukama* of women finished saying what she wanted to say and said no more, *omukama* of men told his subjects to chant her praises and his people hailed her: "Power to you, Great-giver! power to you, Generous-one! power to you, Great-one!" In that very instant *omukama* of men whispered to *omukama* of the women visitors who had come to his country how they should abolish their food taboo regarding the eating of meat and of food which grows in the soil. He also asked her openly how she thought she could go back to her kingdom, what she thought they would eat, how they would survive, should she decide to go back to her kingdom with her people. And on her part *omukama* of women too, since she was by no means a fool, thought for a while and went over what *omukama* of men whispered to her and then bent her beautiful slender neck towards her peer in the manner of sharing with him a secret and said:

"Great-giver, I am of the opinion that I cannot go back to my kingdom, because I was being supported by my dogs, they were the ones which fetched for me and for my entire people the food on which we depended. And so, now that our dogs have disappeared, it would be impossible for us to go back to our kingdom. What we are to do next, that's what I don't know, and I am leaving it to you to decided for us, Great-giver."

On hearing that *omukama* of men raised his voice fully and rang out: "Listen, all you men gathered here as well as all you our women visitors, what my fellow *omukama* and I have just agreed upon here and now is this: This sovereign of women here together with all her people are not returning to their kingdom, because, as you all know, these women have come here to look for their dogs, on which they depended entirely for their existence, which procured for them all their food. And her majesty's dogs were with us and under our responsibility when they got lost. Therefore these visitors can never return to their country. They will stay here for ever. And so to all you men in my kingdom I hereby distribute to you one female visitor each, and I am doing so in keeping with the four divisions of people, which are the following: *omukama*, courtiers, village heads and common people. The female *omukama* will stay here in the residence of the male *omukama*, female courtiers too will each one of them be given to each and everyone of my courtiers, female village heads will go to all my village headmen to the last one of them and the female common people will likewise go to all my country's poor."

Nkubitizi and his fellow courtiers then fell to distributing the women to men and every male person got his female visitor, their *omukama* too getting his.

That over, *omukama* of men made the following proclamation: "From this day we have abolished the interdiction of eating food that grows in the soil as well as that of eating the meat of an animal of any kind. From now on we can eat anything we like, without fear, because any taboo since the beginning of time can be lifted by *omukama*. Should there be a person who cannot stand a given food, let that person not eat that food because it does not agree with him or her but not out of fear of breaking a taboo and saying to himself or herself, `Maybe if I eat meat my skin will all fall off or I will come to this or that harm.' No more; because whatever goes in the stomach never stays there. Our visitors likewise will from this day no longer be freakish about eating food which grows in the soil, of whatever kind. They too should begin eating earth food as they choose, without any fear of breaking a taboo by so doing, because starting today that taboo of theirs too no longer exists."

The entire mass of people chanted his praises: "Power to you, Great-giver! power to you, Generous-one! power to you, Giver-of-courage! May you pass a good-night, Great-builder!" and then his people got up and left to take their female visitors home.

And since that day in the home of each and every man there was to be heard the soft voice of a woman and in every house there lived together two people: a man and a woman. And I am sure you too in all your wanderings since morning till sunset you have never come across a third type of a person except these two: man and woman.

The dogs which got lost in the wilderness became what are today called wolves or wild-dogs, the descendants of those dogs of *omukama* of women which disappeared. And since nothing ever completely forgets its origin, after some time a few paltry dogs were seen trickling back to people's homes on their own in search of their mistress the female *omukama*. Those weaklings among the disappeared dogs are the dogs people keep in their homes today. The returned miserable species too still retained a bit of hunting skill when they came back, but real mastery of hunting went with the dogs which took off and disappeared into the wilderness forever, never to return.

And once people lived in twos that way in every house, a male and a female, and you all know what happens when grass comes too near fire, in no time people saw the female visitor in the king's home, the female *omukama*, with a big round belly. When people were still taking of that, all of a sudden they saw that the female visitors in the homes of courtiers and village headmen as well as those in the homes of the poor too had developed swollen bellies, in the entire country. And so procreation of the human race began and never stopped. Every woman who gave birth to a child brought into the world a female baby and every woman who gave birth again after that brought into the world a male baby and the entire kingdom was filled with the cry of babies: *nghalara! nghalara!* in every home and in every house.

On their way to *omukama* of men the women were so full of anger on account of he and his people failing to return their dogs that they carried that anger with them into their new homes and refused to eat the meat of all the animals of the wilderness where their dogs got lost. And from there on the women were never to eat the meat of the wild animals but only cooked it for their men,[22] after which they brought the heavy potfuls of the meat to their men, who piled heaps and heaps of it on plates for themselves with their women only holding torches and lighting the pots for them. And so the women now went along and ate *obwita* and all the other foods that grow in the soil, whereas regarding meat now even with the meat of livestock they chose to eat only the meat of a cow and refused to eat that of a goat and a sheep. And regarding wild beasts, they chose only to use animal horns, like the horns of *enkorongo*[23] and some other wild animals, in which they keep charms and medicines for keeping them alive and for healing their bodies. And of the food caught from the waters, they chose to eat only some and left it to men to eat hippopotamus meat and several kinds of fish, like *emamba*, *embete*, *enkuyu*[24] and some others.

Then we men realized that, because of their great meekness, women called their homes: "somebody's home," that when a woman accidentally caused her child to fall down, if other women of that home were present, you would hear those other women say: "You have dropped down another person's child!" that in fact even when the incident happened when the mother was all alone you would hear that mother of the child herself say: "*Yu!* Alas, poor me! Another person's child is hurt, what am I to do today?"

It was from that time that the good life the women used to have in their land of perfect happiness began to diminish and fade into memory and the women realized that their lives had changed, because when they were still in their country of perfect happiness, when men and women still lived separately, there was none of the ills of life you see today, like sickness,[25] death and all the problems which face mankind, and that's why witches and witch doctors were a thing unheard of and people lived for very long, since in that world of perfect happiness people lived until they were very very old and when they were so old that they could no longer even walk they molded and shed altogether the skin of their old age and in that very instant changed into new human beings with perfectly healthy bodies like those of adolescent youths.

And witness then all sorts of ills and sufferings invade human beings! Until in the end the men coined the saying: "Outsiders have killed our land." Witness malice enter the hearts of people and spread, witness envy take root and sickness and death enter the lives of people and dwell with them, as all of us can see happening daily! That's when "you have bewitched me" entered the language of human beings and the world of perfect happiness came to an end. That's when every person, of every race and color, became vigilant and looked for means of protecting his or her body against the doings of evil people and began wearing all sorts of awesome amulets all over his or her body to ward off death. And that's when everyone came to appreciate fully how sweet life is. That's when every person scrambled to tame creatures of the earth like crocodiles, snakes and the like he or she can set on those who have harmed him or her and avenge himself or herself at once.

And from thence consulting oracles and seers became the norm and overnight the entire kingdom of the human race teemed with healers, both male and female. That's when every woman of every race and color redoubled her efforts to procure for herself from healers medicines to cure every ill which befalls her body and to make herself liked in her foster home, now that she had become an outsider in her very own home. That's when there appeared in the world the barren woman who went to look for fertility medicine from healers. That's when there came into being a woman who felt her husband no longer loved her as much as he did when they got married and went to healers to look for love potions. And when women made a habit of looking for love medicines, some healers began giving them medicines with inordinate effects, capable of killing their husbands altogether or causing them some monstrous ills, like killing their manhood or swelling their stomachs. And since the women are the cooks of the food every man eats and the drawers of water every man drinks, now every time a man went to consult an oracle and the seer looked at his oracle this way and that the seer would often end by divining that the man's wife was the evil doer out to kill him. In the end men blamed all witchcraft on women, because women are always in search of all sorts of medicines and are forever talking about witchcraft, in their palavers, on the road and, above all, in their female-only gatherings by the lake or wells when they go to draw water and bathe.

Yes, that's true. That's how it is with human beings and their talking. For may be all of you too have heard the story of a certain man, who I think people say was a Mzinza by tribe, who, it is said, one day went for a walk in the wilderness and once there he saw the skull of a person who died a long long time ago, so long that the skull had become spotless white, with not a trace of hair remaining on it, nothing but white bones. Then that man, thinking he was above death, took a stick and, as if to belittle the skull, touched it with his stick and was about to flip it and send it rolling like a ball, and even went as far as addressing it aloud: "Little skull, what killed you?" Immediately the skull answered him back: "A tiny tongue like yours." On hearing that the man was simply confounded, did not know what to say and thought of what had happened and asked himself, "May be this is the skull of a person who could not hold his tongue, who was given to blabbering heavy matters of the kingdom and *omukama* had him or her executed! May be that's it!" Because that man thought he was above death like the people who used to live in the land of perfect happiness and it never occurred to him to remember and say to himself: "So this is it! This is what sooner or later I too will look like!"

And when badness among human beings grew until it festered, even the healers of the ills of witchcraft became suspect, with the patients they had cured accusing them of being the ones who had bewitched them and saying: "That's it; now we know! These very healers are also the wielders of evil power who bewitch people and make them sick so that they can go to them for treatment and pay them for that!"

And so after women settled forever with men badness grew and got out of bounds in the kingdom of what was once the land of perfect happiness, with men blaming everything on women. And that's why up to this day you always hear a man who is quarreling with his wife, before hitting her with a huge stick or smothering her with a   fist in the middle of her head or on another sensitive spot, angrily shout at her and say, "Let me beat you to death, you bitch, dog of dogs! Who's your relative here?" and then: *du*!

That is how we men met women and why we came to live with them, after which we considered them to be other beings than ourselves: dogs. And up to this very day when a woman is married she calls the home where she is married "another person's home" and the child she bears from her own womb "another person's child". She is so meek she grows up and becomes and adult and grows old and dies without ever possessing something she can call her own. And never will she rule again a kingdom as she once did in her land of perfect happiness, and whatever property she may possess will always belong to other people.

There you are! That's my elder's little tale for you! When the tiny red bird *enfuzi* is asked why it has red feathers it answers: "Where I come from we smear ourselves with red-earth." When the grain-eating *ensonsoni* bird of the long beak is asked why its mouth is so long it answers: "Where I come from we live on sucking juices."[26] So you too make of my tale whatever you will and don't ask me questions I can't answer, lest I too tell you lies.

Chapter XIII

NOTES

1. *Omukama*: See note 26 of Chapter II.
2. *Abakungu*, plural for *omukungu*: See note 3 of Chapter III.
3. *Amazungute*: Name of a tree which sprouts large fruits which look like hanging big cassava roots.
4. *Ebitala*, plural for *ekitala*: See note 18 of Chapter I.
5. *Omwiko*: See note 17 of Chapter VI.
6. *Ebibo* , plural for *ekibo*: See note 15 of Chapter I.
7. *Obwita*: See note 14 of Chapter I.
8. Used here and at other occasions in this chapter are some of the numerous attributes of the kings of Ukerewe. See also note 33 of Chapter XII.
9. *Tata wee!*: See note 24 of Chapter IX.
10. *Nkubitizi*: "Garrulous one", a disparaging name for a man who is too talkative.
11. *Emilango:* Battery of palace drums, the drums of the kings of Ukerewe, six in number and of varying sizes, from the smallest one of about three feet high and two feet across its surface to the biggest of about six feet high and four feet across the surface called *Matwigacharo*, "Ears of the country", which were played in the palace on all important occasions.
12. Kikerewe for: "They are here! they are here! they are here! The festivities! The festivities!"
13. *Emihama* , plural for *omuhama*: Very tall palm tree with a bulge in the middle.
14. Bukindo: See note 8 of Chapter IV.
15. *Matwigacharo*: "Ears-of-the-country", name of the biggest of the six royal drums of the kings of Ukerewe, *emilango* of note 11 above.
16. *Obunerere* or *enerere*: See note 23 of Chapter VI.
17. *Ebikuli*, plural for *ekikuli*: See note 21 of Chapter IX.
18. *Akahira*: See note 11 of Chapter IX.
19. *Enkanda*: See note 22 of Chapter VI.
20. *Engali*, plural for *olugali*: See note 6 of Chapter I.
21. *Emitaho*, plural for *omutaho*: See note 9 of Chapter I.
22. Wakerewe women did not eat the meat of wild game. See note 17 of Chapter II.
23. *Enkorongo*: See note 20 of Chapter I.
24. *Emamba, embete, enkuyu*: Some of the kinds of fish Wakerewe women did not eat. See note 17 of Chapter II.

25. Here Kitereza's tale forgets its beginning, where all the men gathered for the public hunt with the sole exception of the very old and the very sick and bedridden ones, unless we are to assume that the sick and bedridden were those awaiting rejuvenation.

26. Kitereza's ending of his tale is his way of saying: "That's me and that's my story", just as with the two birds in the riddles their truthful answers would be: "that's me and that's my color " and "that's me and that's my beak" respectively. Kitereza, of course, ends his tale by just giving the answers of the two birds and I have added on that last sentence only to bring out his understood meaning for the English reader.

Chapter XIV

BUGONOKA CONCEIVES A CHILD

But let us return to what we were talking about, the matter of Myombekere and his wife Bugonoka.

When the monthly period Bugonoka was in when they went to see her medicine man Kibuguma ended, the couple related to each other by the marriage act as they had been told to do by their healer, with Bugonoka still wearing the four little amulets around her waist, and four days after that the couple went to see their healer again, with Bugonoka taking with her for her healer a bowl[I] of millet, nicely covered by a piece of a green banana leaf. In Kibuguma's home they found the healer in the thick of his activities, in the process of talking with the unseen powers while a whole crowd of patients sat waiting. Weroba was the first to see the couple and said: "We have visitors!" and everyone turned to look, since we never trust the eyes of others, Kibuguma himself included. Weroba cheerfully received from Bugonoka the load of millet she was bringing as her present for her healer, took it inside her house and came out with two chairs and Myombekere and his wife sat down. The couple then exchanged greetings and news of their welfare with Kibuguma and Weroba and the other people present and finished and settled down.

Kibuguma administered to the patients Myombekere and his wife found in his home and finished and those patients left. He then went outside his home to relieve himself and when he returned to his healer's seat he asked the couple, "So you are back?"

"We are back."

"You Bugonoka, come here, I want to look at you."

Bugonoka got up, took her chair and went to sit near the healer and Kibuguma told her: "Let's see your hands." Bugonoka showed him both her two hands. Kibuguma touched her in the palm of her left hand and then examined the palm, and examined it again, and let go of that hand, then held her right hand and examined the palm of that hand too for just a bit and told her, "Come closer." When she was close enough, Kibuguma got hold of the nipple of her right-side breast and examined it, and examined it again, before taking up the nipple of her left-side breast and examining that one too, and examining it again, and then told her, "Take your chair and return to your husband over there."

Much much later, he called Myombekere: "Myombekere!"

The other man answered, "Yes, Sir!"

And then Kibuguma spoke openly and said: "I have seen that your wife has conceived a child, and I have also seen that her breasts are very badly contaminated. And so this is what needs to be done: let me bathe her here today with the medicine for *amatwera,*[2] because excessive *amatwera* can harm the child in the womb, and even after delivery *amatwera* remains a great danger to the life of the newborn child. And when you are ready to go, I will give her another medicine for bathing herself with at a crossroads. For two nights she will do so in the evening when it is already really dark and on the third day she will wash herself with the medicine at the same spot very very early in the morning, before the twittering of pre-dawn birds. If in your home there is no old woman who no longer sees her monthly periods to assist her in bathing with the medicine, then a young girl who hasn't reached puberty can also do, there is no problem."

He then called his wife Weroba and she came and he sent her to procure the medicine for *amatwera* and she went and brought it. Kibuguma then called Bugonoka and her husband and told them to follow him and they got up and he led them to the back of his house. Once there, the healer got busy and washed Bugonoka and rubbed her breasts, her head and her back with the medicine. And lo! Bugonoka's body exuded a strange red matter, and a lot of it! On seeing that Kibuguma said to Myombekere: "Didn't I tell you? Do you now see what your wife has inside her?"

"I see it."

"And you haven't see all. You just wait until I'm finished, please friend, and let's see whether you won't see wonders!"

"I'll see wonders indeed, since I am here."

At once Kibuguma took some more medicine in his hands and rubbed Bugonoka with it all over her head and neck, descending to her shoulders and armpits and her back, that way, and on to her chest and breasts, and finished. And then he asked Bugonoka: "What do you feel now in your body?"

"I feel my body itching very much, uncontrollably, making me want to scratch myself."

"That's it, but don't scratch yourself. The fact is that the medicine will itch only for a while and then stop."

And indeed after a while the medicine stopped itching. And after that lo and behold the medicine reveal the contamination which was inside the body of that woman! In that very instant Bugonoka's body turned completely white, with every bit of hair on her body turning completely gray, as Myombekere on his part just looked on without a word, not even a cough! And much later witness her look as if somebody had poured ashes all over her! And then, after another little while, all of a sudden her skin began peeling off, as it happens when a person who hasn't taken a bath for a long time takes a bath again for the first time.   Kibuguma asked Myombekere again: "How does she look to you now? Didn't I tell you you'll see wonders?"

"Please heal us, our medicine man! A wasted good deed is only the one done for animals which can't thank their benefactor."

Kibuguma called his wife Weroba and told her, "Come here!" And when Weroba came he whispered into her ear and said, "Bring me the urine of a spotless black cow!" Weroba disappeared into their house and after a while came out with the cow urine. Kibuguma spoke to his wife again, "Go back into the house." Weroba knew perfectly well what went with that cow urine, so she went back into the house and this time brought butter, also from the milk of a spotless black cow, together with a calabash3 full of water to the brim, enough water to bathe a person well. With that her husband told her, "Take your comrade and her chair into that enclosure and bathe her," and the two women took their things and went into the enclosed space to bathe, leaving Myombekere and the healer seated where the two women left them.

After a bit of time the women came back. Goodness! When Myombekere's eyes fell on his wife Bugonoka, what a shining-clean woman! Not a trace remained of all that strange matter which come out of her body or the pieces of her skin which peeled off! She was her wholesome self again, looking even better than before! Myombekere silently exclaimed with wonder but said nothing, kept it all to himself. And then Kibuguma told the couple, "Please come, let's go back and sit over there in the compound."

That done and finished, Kibuguma deliberately provoked his wife, knowing very well that she was a lazy woman when it came to kitchen work, by asking her, "Aren't you going to fetch from the fields at least a few sweet potatoes, however paltry, and rescue our rambling stomachs, since as you see we have visitors? Oh, I am sorry, *aa!* how can I forget. I should not hide behind you our visitors, I should just speak for us your hosts, since, as people say: `A visitor never leaves with your cows, and so can't finish your milk.' And so we can't count you our visitors as if you live here."

Weroba answered her husband, "You have already lost your case, because I have already invited our visitors to stay for lunch and my friend here has already answered and told me: 'We can't stay for lunch, that is if the treatment is over, because we have to hurry back home where we left the children all alone and one of the two is sick and we have cows to attend too as well.' I even tried to persuade her to stay by telling her, `Please stay here and wait for me while I go to the water-side fields to dig some sweet potatoes and come back so that I can chat a little with you,' with her still saying: 'Forget it!'"

Kibuguma retorted and said: "*Aa!* Do you hear that! Is that really true, Bugonoka?"

Bugonoka answered, "Yes indeed."

Kibuguma put in again, "I see! Well, I give up, poor me! All I was doing, anyway, was simply poking the tail of a snake to see where its head lies hidden, because, as you've heard, the truth is that Weroba herself hasn't even brought home from the fields the food to cook! My goodness! Is it indeed true that we no longer have households worth that name, that those died with our grandfathers! So late in the day and a man has yet to eat anything in his home as if he were a stranger in somebody else's home! *Yu! aa! hee!* Weroba, is this really the way to live! What a shame!"

Myombekere and his wife said: "That's how things are everywhere, as a matter of fact. Want has become everybody's lot. You simply stay on in your home because it is your home and you can't run away from your own household. Don't blame your wife for nothing, the poor woman, because she has simply been overwhelmed by having so many other things to attend to. It's we who have just wasted your time. As our people say: 'A lazy visitor is mere waste of time.' We are the ones to blame for having just wasted the time of both of you by keeping you from attending to your other work"

In response to which Kibuguma said, "Well, since she knows that in the mornings she has other things to do, why doesn't she prepare herself by digging up the food to cook and bringing it home the previous evening, so that the following day it would already be in the house? And so, my brother Myombekere, let me simply say no more on the matter, poor me! Because certainly things weren't this way when we were still young and growing up and seeing how our old men lived with our mothers. Then I never saw the master of a household speak to his wife about food and his wife dare to talk back to him by saying I don't know what. *Aa! hii!* That woman would have provoked real trouble! Believe me, no woman ever dared do that."

While Kibuguma was saying that to Myombekere, the two women had already separated themselves from their men and gone inside the healer's house, where they too were talking their own underground Kikerewe. Ask me: "Which underground Kikerewe?" and I will answer you: "Their women's secret talk," of which you could hear their two voices going on: *duduli! duduli!* and when Kibuguma stopped talking at once the two women too became completely silent: *di*!

Finally Kibuguma stood up and he too went into the house to get medicine for Bugonoka and came from the interior of the house holding it in his hands this way and gave it to Bugonoka at the door of the house where the two women were seated and told her, "Here is the medicine I told you to bathe at a crossroads for two days. The female child of your home who has not yet reached puberty you spoke of should bathe you in the evening after it has become quite dark, but make sure you are sitting down legs stretched in front of you and your back turned this way in the direction of the setting sun and your face looking in the direction of the rising sun. Do that today and tomorrow, and then the day after tomorrow do so very early in the morning, before the twittering of dawn birds, at the same crossroads, but this time sit with your outstretched legs and your face turned in the opposite direction, in the direction of the setting sun and the back of your head turned this way in the direction of the rising sun.

"And this is how you are to be bathed: The entire medicine will have been mixed with water in a calabash of a gourd of the previous year's harvest, with none of it remaining, and mixed using freshly drawn water and not with water which has spent a night or more in a pot, and the water which you will put in the medicine today will be the only water you will put in until the end of the treatment the day after tomorrow. Your outstretched legs will pass under the spread out legs of the young girl. She is to put the medicine container on the ground on her right-hand side and she is to take out of it the medicine three times only each bathing, so each time she must take care not to take out too much or too little so that the medicine can suffice for three days. At each bathing, the first time she will take out of the calabash a little bit of medicine, but not too little, and put it in each of her two hands. Then you will bend down, having taken off your robe, and she will start smearing your body with the medicine, starting at the bottom of your backbone and moving upward, while you remain bent down, working with both her hands. Let the medicine which will fall down fall down, but she should have most of the medicine in her hands as she works her way upward. When she comes to the middle of your head she will drop the medicine remaining in her hands in such a way that it falls on your thighs. Then she will take medicine out the container the second time as she did at first, again dividing it so that she has some in each hand, and this time you will straighten up, with your eyes closed, and she will start smearing you with the medicine from the middle of your head and work downward, tracing your body along your shoulders and your arms and when she comes to the palms of your hands, you quickly receive the medicine from each of her hands and at once throw it on the ground. Then she will take the medicine from the calabash the third time as already explained, while your eyes remain closed, and this time she will start out from your forehead and descend with your body to your chest and keep on descending all the way to the soles of your feet, before the little girl herself throws the medicine down.

"You will then get up and go home.

"The following day, the same thing. But on the third day, when the little girl has finished bathing you with the medicine and you get up, she will place the medicine calabash in the middle of the spot where you were seated on the ground and then you will lift your right foot and smash it with one stamp of the foot, accompanying that with the following words: "We have executed a witch," after which you will take your robe and put it on and the two of you will go home without turning to look back even once.

" And once you get home you will take a water pot in complete silence and go to the lake to bathe. Only after you have bathed can you speak again. And then you will draw water from the lake and go back to your home and you'll have finished your work. Did you hear me clearly, both of you?"

The couple answered him back, "We heard you indeed!"

And so Myombekere and his wife Bugonoka took their medicine and left.

While on their way, Bugonoka told her husband about their secret women's talk with Weroba in the healers house: "When you two were outside with your men's palaver we too had one of our own inside the house. Weroba was backbiting her husband and telling me: `This so-called husband of mine is being cynical about me in food matters when he himself never tills the land. Don't you look at him as he is there and think he too farms land like other men. I always work the fields alone with my miserable tiny children. He himself is lazy beyond belief! As soon as he strikes the ground with his hoe once you would hear him say: I am hungry, and there and then he puts his hoe on his shoulder and goes back home. For him, so it appears, because he has this healing skill of his nothing else matters, healing is all he knows, but talk to him of tilling the fields and he will sham sickness!

'Then when it comes to eating, even if you spend the whole night cooking and then cook the whole day you still will not satisfy his appetite. In the end I have come to think that he must have become such an insatiable eater only after he married me. And, come to think of it, that's quite possible, seeing all the time what men are capable of doing when we women let them get away with it. So, who knows? Just look at him there! During the planting season he depends on sending his patients like you here or your husband to help us with breaking the soil, with sowing, with weeding, harvesting, threshing, and sometimes even with carrying grain into our grain store,[4] to him that too is very hard work. In fact with me too I am still married to him simply because of these dear tiny miserable oversize-heads I call my children, but otherwise, oh, no! Tilling the fields single-handedly is unbearable, especially when, in addition to your own household, you daily have to feed so many other mouths too! *Aa! hee!* This is no life!'

"I finally felt I had to put on the appearance of agreeing with her and so I said: `It is true tilling the fields single-handedly is a problem, because that never brings home enough food; never. And, as you say, since you have those big-headed creatures of yours, you have to be really worried, since you cannot afford not to have something with which to allay a bit the hunger in their little stomachs, especially since children eat like locusts, without ever pausing. That could be a problem indeed! Also, my dear, let me seize this rare opportunity we have today of being alone this way and ask you this: By the way, dear, I have the impression that Kibuguma was your first husband, or was he not?'

"And Weroba answered me, 'You are right to ask. No, he was not. My first husband was another man, and I left in that man's home too children, a boy and a girl, and I left the man because that husband of mine couldn't pay my bride-price, and so my father came to take me away by force and I left still suckling my second child. It was not until I had been at my parents home for a month that the child was weaned and I took back to my husband and his relatives their child, and after some time my father took me back to my husband's home for divorce and I was divorced. It was after that this man courted and married me, when I was a maiden-divorcée.5 The boy I had with my first husband got married this year, and just recently, and the girl too is already being courted by a suitor, since children born one after the other usually also marry about the same time. And here in this home, dear friend, I have two dear little boys and three dear little girls, and I have no intention of hiding this fact from you, dear friend, because human beings living on earth can't be concealed.'

"That's what Kibuguma's wife told me. But after I thought over the matter I felt in my heart: `Well, even though this fellow woman has told me all those things about her husband, she too, like many of us, has a problem of her own: she is a lazy woman. For what else is she if not a lazy woman? Your husband simply asks you to cook some food for him and off you go backbiting him to strangers as if he had done something wrong to you or beaten you!'"

Myombekere said: "*Aa!* That's nothing but your usual women way of wanting to show yourselves in better light than your husbands. That's how all of you are, and the man who has never married is the only one who does not know it."

At home Bugonoka looked for the required gourd and mixed her medicine and then gave it to the little girl Nakiro and the girl took it into the house to the ground stand by the bed-post where she used to keep the other medicines. She carefully instructed the girl as to how she was to bathe her with the medicine that day in the evening and the following evening and early in the morning of the day after that. And so in the evening Bugonoka and the little girl of her home went to a crossroads and did as Kibuguma instructed, following all his directions, and on the third day very very early in the morning they concluded the treatment by an outright execution of the witch as the healer directed, and that job was finished and done with.

After that Bugonoka turned to the making of her grass trays[6] and bowls with perfect peace of mind and Myombekere too on his part everyday in the morning left to attend to the cultivation of his banana plantation. And since that year rain from time to time paid people surprise visits even during the dry season, working in his banana plantation became his daily occupation throughout the year.

And so Myombekere and Bugonoka waited for the outcome of the words of Kibuguma when he told Myombekere: `I have seen that your wife here has conceived a child.' Her first month to count was the month of September, the month of conception. Soon after that Bugonoka began to feel twitches in the lower part of her stomach. At first she doubted the whole thing and took it for the usual movement of her stomach worms. She simply could not be sure, because where she was she had already two miscarriages and she had never given birth to a child in the normal sense of the term, and then even that had been quite some time ago. What's more, she had already despaired and said to herself: "The witch or witch doctor who killed my two children inside my womb must have cut off my fertility and sealed my fate for ever and so I'll never conceive again." Those, however, were thoughts known to her alone. She had never shared them even with Myombekere. That to her was her secret of the saying: "Real secret lives inside a cow." And indeed it does, for have you ever seen your cow tell you what some other person had done to it? Even if somebody had hit it with the largest club you could think of when grazing, when it comes back home in the evening it still won't tell you, its master, that in your absence somebody gave it such a painful blow for nothing, when in fact it hadn't grazed anybody's crops.

When the new moon of the second month was about to appear, the time of the month when Bugonoka usually began her monthly periods, Myombekere waited for his wife to enter her period but *aa*! nothing happened. Her time passed and finally the month of October began and people played *enzamba* [7] to welcome the new month. That became her second month since she conceived. In the meanwhile those twitches in the lower part of her stomach continued without a break. The moon of the new month came and reddened and became a bright full moon without

Bugonoka entering her period, and it waned and was no longer beautiful and then moonless nights took over still with no period in sight. The jerks and starts in her stomach had now increased in frequency and intensity. Towards the end of that month, one day when Bugonoka was taking a bath she noticed that in her female parts the way to her womb had completely closed itself and remarked to herself, "I see! It appears what Kibuguma said has come to pass, I think!"

In the meanwhile she became plumper, all her body filled out and she became almost light colored in the face and really glowing, though she was normally of the smooth and beautiful deep black complexion of the black stem of *entundu* banana.

When the rains of the month of October, the month of *Ekimezo*, Germination, began pouring down from the heavens, Bugonoka, the woman who loved farm work she was, turned to tilling close to her home a field for planting greens like *omugobe, empwani* and *omususa* and the other vegetables which bear gourds for making household calabash utensils and water containers like cups, *ebisusi, ebizanda, enchuma* and *embilikira*, and for growing the different varieties of beans and peas like *enkuku, obutindego, obuzolika*, which people used to grow for use as relish in those days. But please don't ask me, "What about her trays and bowls , the kitchen utensils of woven grass she used to make, wasn't she ever completing any?" because I'll answer and tell you, "She was completing them and then trading them for millets of every kind, like *obubele, omugusa* and *endwero*. Sometimes fishermen too came to her wanting to buy the articles of her handicraft with their fish, like *embozu* catfish. Once she completed a tray she meant to sell, the buyer who wanted it would have to fill with millet to overflowing a really huge bowl she kept for the purpose in her house before he or she could take her tray. As to the fishermen with their *embozu*, for Bugonoka's tray they paid ten *embozu*. As for her bowls, the measure for barter millet was the new bowl itself, the buyer filled the bowl she had just made with millet to overflowing and paid for it that way."

And that's what a person's skill is all about: whoever has some skill can use it to feed himself or herself or to succor himself or herself from some other need.

Up to that time Myombekere still had his doubts as to whether his wife had conceived or not. With him it was still a matter of: "May be, may be not!" He was still waiting for the coming of the third month, the following new moon, because even regarding his wife not having had her periods he was still not certain as to what that meant and was saying to himself, "Maybe it is just jumping of periods, which sometimes happens to women!" As to why his wife was all shining and was putting on weight and sporting a slight fever at night, he didn't want to get into that at all and instead preferred to say to himself, "My wife is putting on weight because her kitchen is being good to her," because indeed that is how it is with all of us, men and women alike, we at times gain weight and at others lose it, just as it used to be the case with Myombekere himself. There were times he would put on so much weight that a person who met him on the way or found him sitting in his home wondered: "*Hii!* What exuberance of health in a man! Oh, no! A man shouldn't grow fat this way like a woman!" Some people would go to the extent of speaking openly to him and telling him, "No, Myombekere, you have become too fat! What is it that Bugonoka is feeding you these days? You have grown so fat your anus has bulged and a mass of flesh is hanging at the back of your head! But please do touch your ear for good luck, lest your healthy body should all go back to where it came from due to my mentioning it."

Meanwhile as Bugonoka continued to put on weight she began feeling aches and pains all over her body. During that second month inside the mother the thing in the womb is still a mere mass of blood, but one which is shining like the sun at the conception spot. If miscarriage takes place when that mass of blood is still alive, if you observed you would find it all agitation and shining like a real sun at that spot. The object has the same agitation inside the womb of the mother and that's the twitches we have talked about in Bugonoka's womb during those first two months. The eve of the third month came and the moon of November appeared and people played *enzamba* to welcome the new month and still Bugonoka did not enter her monthly period. At that point in her lower stomach the starts and jerks really intensified. During that period of third month the thing in the mother's womb is called "*ekina*", the smooth-bodied tiny lizard.[8]

A couple of days of that new month had gone by when one day at about noon on what had been since morning a bright cloudiness day Bugonoka and her husband were in their house, the husband stretched on their bed and the wife taking a nap on the floor of the front room by the milk churn while the little girl of their home, Nakiro, was playing with puppets of children made of millet stalks with her companions, the daughters of Kanwaketa, outside at the grain store in the courtyard. Where she was playing Nakiro sat facing the gate of their home and on looking up what does she see at the gate but a visitor, a woman, a loaded basket on her head, the sound of her *enkanda*[9] drumming against her legs with every step she took and the far-reaching *omugazu*[10] perfume she wafted along announcing her approach! The little girl went and woke up Bugonoka in the house and told her: "Wife of my elders dear, I see a visitor coming!" Bugonoka shot out of the house and made for the gate and on looking at the visitor who does she see but her sister, none other than the one called Barongo! And on looking again doesn't she see that she is carrying a baby on her back! At once she ululated,[11] I tell you! Myombekere too got up from his bed and on coming out doesn't he realize that the visitor in question is his sister-in-law! Witness how the couple jumped about with pleasure at the sight of their beloved visitor! They even forgot for quite a while all about greeting her! In the immediate they were simply all over her, Bugonoka whisking the *ekitukuru*[12] basket off her head and running to put it away in the house, Myombekere on his part, *hee*! that one wanted to make his sister-in-law sit down in the middle of the boiling-hot sun, on a chair which wasn't there, out of sheer happiness! It was not until Bugonoka had put down the basket in the front room of the house and rushed back outside and found her husband and their visitor still in the middle of that scorching overhead sun that she remembered to invite her inside the house and said, "Let's go inside!" and they finally made it into the house. Bugonoka gave her a high chair, since she was carrying a baby on her back, and she sat down and the couple and their beloved guest greeted each other with salutations of long-parted people, since they had not seen each other for many months, and duly exchanged news of their welfare until they finished. After that Barongo told her sister, "Give me some water to drink," and Bugonoka at once took a cup from a rack, knocked its mouth against the palm of her hand several times to rid it of any unwanted matter which might have fallen in it, passed it by her nose to detect if it had any unpleasant smell, in which case she would look for a better smelling one, and finding it smelling nicely drew water from the drinking-water pot and gave it to her sister and she drank some water and then breathed out a sigh of relief: "*Yehu!* now I am alive again, for I was really dying of thirsty! And the journey to this place is simply too long!" After that she took her child from her back and stood it on the ground to urinate, and then put it on her thighs while holding it in her arms and suckled it, as Myombekere and Bugonoka asked her how her husband was doing and how her birth of her male child had gone and congratulated her and said: "Bring into the world yet another one!" and she answered them the way mothers usually answer such congratulations: "There are none left."

Bugonoka got up to prepare food for her sister. And since women never sit back and relax even when they are supposed to be guests, when Barongo saw her sister busy cooking she herself got up and drew water from a pot for washing her baby. When Bugonoka saw her do that she said, "Why didn't you ask me to pass you the water, sister? You have just arrived from such a long journey, plus you traveled loaded so heavily, in addition to carrying a baby on your back! *Ahee!* That's enough to wear out anybody!"

"Well, even if I am tired I shouldn't find it too much work to do something right here inside the house as if it were going to work I don't know where!"

Within no time Bugonoka had finished preparing for her visitor *obwita*.[13] She came to the front of the house by the door where the visitor was sitting and took her chair into the inner room of the house and called the little girl Nakiro and said: "Come and eat with the visitor, because when you eat *obwita* alone when you are used to eating with other people you simply cannot enjoy food and eat your fill." When Barongo stopped eating Nakiro handed her *ekizanda*[14] of milk and she drank milk without a pause. She had just taken *ekizanda* from her mouth when Bugonoka told her, "Drink on, please, and finish it off. There wasn't in there the milk you can't finish; it was so little. Here milk is so plentiful we can't find enough people to drink it. We go to the extent of using milk as water for cooking relish and greens. As you can see, it has even become our water for cooking *obwita*, daily. The day enough visitors come to see us that's the day we are happiest, for we can say: 'Gentlemen and ladies, drink some of this milk for us.'"

That over, Bugonoka spread on the ground a cow-skin for Barongo in the outer room of her house by the churn so that her visitor could stretch down a bit. She could not take her visitor to their bed because it was teeming with bedbugs, so much so that they were out and attacking even during daytime. It was enough for a person to be on the bed for just a bit of time for the bedbugs to begin their assault on him or her. For the owners of that bed too, each night Bugonoka had first to spray the insects with water before the couple went to bed, otherwise they wouldn't sleep.

When Bugonoka judged it was the right time, she took an empty water pot and an empty calabash and woke up Barongo and told her, "The sun has cooled down now, wake up and let's go and plunge into the lake a bit when the sun is still warm, lest you begin to feel cold, because if you don't bathe you will simply be in terrible shape, with all the sweat you arrived soaked in."

Before they left Bugonoka brought to the door the basket Barongo came with and called her husband and they unwrapped their presents. She unpacked from that *ekitukuru* exactly twenty fresh *ensato*,[15] and under the fish there was quite a lot of millet, because it filled a tray and yet there was still left enough of it to fill two large cupped-palms. The couple thanked their visitor for the presents and told her, "This is very kind of you to remember us with relish. What's more, you are a mighty carrier, we must admit! Fresh fish is ever so heavy, and, on top of that, you had *obubele* millet, again known for being heavy to carry, all that on top of you, one person, with a child on your back to boot, not to mention the heavy *ekitukuru* basket itself!"

Barongo said: "*Aa!* You better thank my husband, the fisherman who killed the fish, if you must thank somebody, and not me, the spectator from the safety of sand on the beach. But these days their catch isn't so good. People say the coming new moon will be the month people will really catch fish in plenty. What is that month, by the way, brother-in-law?"

"It is December."

"That is the month. During that month an unexpected visitor is still very welcome, because there is always all the relish he or she can eat."

The two women then got on their way to the lake. Bugonoka took Barongo by her lake-side fields to show her the sweet potatoes she planted on coming back from her parents home. Barongo looked at the potatoes and exclaimed in wonder, "You really threw the whole of yourself into planting these sweet potatoes and said, `Let's see what will happen!'" Bugonoka bent down and dug at the roots of a *kandoya* sweet potato vine with a finger and found underneath a mature sweet potato and said: "I have in fact already started harvesting them. I have no reason to be unduly stingy with the crop, honestly. For whom would I be keeping the potatoes then? And I couldn't say your brother-in-law wouldn't allow me to start harvesting the crop even though it is ready until it is fully matured; no."

It was when they got to the lake and were bathing that Barongo asked her sister, "Whatever the case, you are pregnant, sister? I wanted to ask you while we were still at home but then I said to myself, `No, wait until you are alone and ask her then, since you are already here and for nothing else but to see her."

On returning home they found Myombekere erecting a platform outside near the courtyard fireplace[16] for smoke-drying some of the fish Barongo brought. Bugonoka took from the house a knife with a long handle and came outside with it. Her husband asked her, "Where are you going with a knife?"

"I am going to cut dry banana leaves for the visitor's bedding."

"I see! Go then, lest nightfall overtakes you before you are back."

"How can I come back at night as if I am going far, when I am going into Kanwaketa's banana plantation next door?"

In no time she was back with the dry banana leaves. There was in the home a spare bed-top for visitors, which was normally kept outside for fear pests would get into it. She fetched the bed-top, beat it with a stick to rid it of whatever dirt might have got into it and used it to make a bed for her visitor in the small third room[17] of the house and then told Barongo, "Come and rest here while we are cooking."

Barongo replied, "*Aa!* No, I don't want to fall sick from oversleeping! I slept so much during daytime, which was only a short while ago, and now you want me to sleep again. How will I be able to sleep at night?"

Bugonoka went over to the cooking-stones to prepare some nice relish for her visitor. You all know how it is in our Ukerewe: the people of Myombekere's home could eat the fish Barongo brought but Barongo herself couldn't, because a visitor who brings a present of relish or other provisions to a relative or a friend was never supposed to partake of his or her present when cooked in that home during his or her visit. A visitor would pass the night without eating at all rather than eat the relish he or she brought. That would be a great shame indeed to any real Mkerewe. If it were beer, yes. With beer people try to justify their unwarranted behavior by the proverb: "The bee loves the honey it makes," because the bee is the maker of honey, out of which it bears its children, but that doesn't prevent it from eating that very honey. And so the people of Myombekere home took supper with the tilapia fish Barongo brought them as relish while Barongo herself was given a different relish, *embozu* catfish.

After dinner they retired for the night. It was when everybody had retired to bed that Barongo asked Myombekere: "By the way, my brother-in-law, what do you think of your wife, when you look at her body and how she is?"

"The only thing I see is that she is my wife, with whom I live, that's all. But as to other things, I don't know a thing, my sister in-law."

"What I see is that your wife is not her usual self. And what I think, judging from what I have seen, is that this is her third month since getting the way she is. Am I to understand that you are unaware of this, my brother-in-law?"

"I was thinking that perhaps there's nothing with her that isn't usual with you women, since I hear people say that there are women who can skip several of their monthly periods and then resume seeing their periods again. And that's what I too, in my ignorance, imagine to be the case with your sister as well."

"And have you ever, since your marriage, seen her skip her periods for something like two or three months?"

"No, I shouldn't tell lies about her, poor woman, in her very presence, with her listening to what we are talking about. What do you say to that, Bugonoka?"

Since in those days Bugonoka once in bed took no time before falling asleep, it was as if she had been suddenly shaken out of deep sleep and her reaction was first to ask, "What are you waking me up for?" Myombekere repeated all her sister had asked him about her. Bugonoka, now completely awake from her nap, said, "What you are asking me about is something which has never happened to me ever since I got married here, not even once, unless it is something which has decided to start happening to me now in my advanced age. Otherwise it has never happened to me to skip even one month, leave alone two, of my monthly periods."

Barongo said: "That's what I am talking about with your husband. He too is saying that he has never seen that happen to you since the beginning of your marriage. Now then, brother-in-law, since your wife here has become a woman who toils for nothing every time she conceives, you shouldn't once again just sit down and do nothing about it: you must procure for her from healers medicine or amulets to protect her from the obstacle which has been behind her past miscarriages, whatever the obstacle is and whoever of you two is the cause of it in this home of yours. For indeed to add to yourself another life of your very own self is what all people on this earth most long for. Tell me, is there any other thing on earth as great as that? Do you, may brother-in-law, know of anything greater?"

"No, I don't, my sister-in-law. To bring into the world another life of your own is the greatest thing and the most desirable blessing on earth, because, as the saying goes: `The childless person has nothing but one's shin to send on an errand.' Among human beings the standing of the person with a child is greater than that of one who has only his or her own shin for a boy or girl to send on an errand, whatever else he or she may be. Even if you own countless cows, they would still be worthless to you. Look at you here, when this little child of yours cries, all of us in this house are cheered up. But when just the two of us, your sister and I, are in this house, there are times when the house feels like a bush or wilderness in which no human beings live. As to looking for medicines you talked about, we too since we saw you last on the day I appeased my parents-in-law on arriving back here did not stay for many days before going to look for a medicine man. The medicine man we found and who is still treating us is a man who lives out there called Kibuguma. He is the one who is trying to do what he can for us and who has given us medicines and the amulets your sister is wearing around her waist. Everything was given to us by that man, Kibuguma."

That matter was then dropped and sleep the relative of brain went to work and they all fell asleep.

Barongo stayed with the Myombekeres in that home of theirs for some ten days or so. Bugonoka even found time to take her to Kibuguma's home, because she said to her visitor: "I must take you to meet my healer and let you know him, so that should you come to see me and find me sick you will know where to go for my medicine if you are sent for it."

On the day she left, before leaving Barongo asked her sister, "Am I right in saying that the coming new moon will be the fourth month since you last had your periods?"

"Yes, unless things turn out differently, that's correct, it would be the fourth month indeed."

"I am asking you this because I intend to pass at our mother's, in your parents' home, informing her of your situation so that she too knows."

"If you are passing that way, please inform her and also tell her, `Bugonoka on her part says eat some while putting aside some for her, because when the coming new moon appears and becomes full moon she will come here to see Lweganwa's wife after the birth of her child.'"

"I will."

Bugonoka gave her sister sweet potatoes as a parting present, then called he husband to come and give her precise instructions as to what dry meat from the house they should give as present to Barongo's husband, his co-husband.[18] Myombekere directed her and said, "Take this piece, and this piece, and then give him also this one and that one," after which Bugonoka gave her sister additional presents: one bowl and one tray, both brand new, and a calabashful of butter. The couple then escorted their departing visitor and when they got to where they wanted to stop they said good-bye to each other and Barongo got on her way and the couple returned home.

When the new moon of the month of December appeared it became the fourth month since Bugonoka conceived. At that moment, when the thing in the mother's womb is four months old, it is called a "lizard".

On her part Bugonoka went on doing all her household chores as usual and performing every woman's job of hers, because laziness was something unknown to her. When she was about to go to her parents home to see his father and mother and his brother Lweganwa, she first sowed red millet on the ridges of a crop field she tilled in the month of November. There is nothing Myombekere's wife dreaded as much as famine in her house and she made sure she kept that plague very far from her home. And that too was the case with Myombekere himself. In fact in that home husband and wife had met each other's match, they were a couple of hot-blooded workers, two people who both loved work, because, as the Mkerewe of yore said: "If you want to unearth something you can't be afraid of dust." And keeping famine away from your home in this country means digging the earth every year, because if you stay home for a year and then a second one without cutting the ground with your hoe and then try to do something hurriedly the third year, you may find that you no longer have even seeds to plant, that you have to beg for seeds from other people, who will give them to you while reviling you in their hearts and saying: "Take the seeds, if you must, but are we the ones who prevented you from farming your lands? What were you doing when others were tilling their crop fields that you should put to test people's good will this way?" And may be that year on which you count to farm your lands the rains fail, and haven't you thus turned your home into the haunt of famine? Haven't you allowed famine to say to you: "You are my captive today, let me spread on the ground the ropes for tying you up really tight!" That's why Bugonoka tilled the land that way day after day, because her conviction deep inside her told her: "On the day I die if I die leaving behind me a well-fed home, that's fine. That's how it was meant to be, for all of us to die and leave our possessions behind for others to inherit. Because it is only when you die leaving behind you a well-fed home that you will have mourners, people who will come to bewail your loss and remember you by those things you will have left behind for them. But without anything left behind, who will be found to mourn you in a home where there is nothing to allay the pangs of a hungry stomach? Who wants any part of what people call a tobacco mourning, a funeral where the waking mourners have nothing to eat and all they can do is take tobacco! Who can stand such a mourning?" That's why Bugonoka, unless she was sick, never spared herself when it came to hoeing her fields and she had to be really sick to miss her farm work. Never was hers the habit of making a big thing out of every slight ailment and of shaming illness we see among the women of this country who are scared of farm work, who even when they go to their fields most of the time it is their hoes alone which are at their place of work while they themselves have wandered off to other women's fields in search of gossip, pretending they are looking for some snuff or *ekilangi*[19] tobacco· Such behavior was unknown to her.

When the moon of the month of December became full moon Bugonoka remembered what Barongo and herself had agreed upon, and when she was about to leave for her parents' home she put everything in order in her house first and gave precise instructions to the little girl she was bringing up in her home, her husband's helping hand from his relatives, as to what she would be cooking for Myombekere and Kagufwa. As to who would skim her milk, because the milk of her home was much more than the little girl could handle, she went to beg Kanwaketa's wife for help so that she would be coming to churn the milk for the people of her home during her absence and her female neighbor on her part agreed very willingly, because she knew Bugonoka was no idler likely to go and spend too many days at her parents' home, like some women we see in this Ukerewe of ours, who would say good-bye to their husbands and tell them: "I am going to see my parents, I won't be long gone, I will stay for two days only and be back on the third day," that being nothing but lies, the two days the female idler had spoken of to her husband often turning out to be two months, the woman not reappearing in her home until in the third month, so that by the time she comes back her husband has suffered a lot, and, if he has only one wife, she may even find him already thinking of marrying another one, because, as the saying goes: "Living alone proved too much even for the *enkorongo* [20] antelope of the wilderness," and, as some people also say: "A woman is like sun-dried tilapia fish which cooks sweetest with a layer of greens on top." So, if the husband of such a woman is a real man, a properly constituted male, we can say that in his home there will be no shortage of visits by divorced women and widows and spinsters during daytime as well as at nighttime to keep him bed-company. That's why such irresponsible women may come back only to find that their husbands no longer have any feelings for them, the worms of their manhood having become fond of other women, for the simple reason that men marry women as companions to live with, and so that they can take care of their husbands in matters of the stomach and the bed and cultivate food for them and, especially, so that they can bear children for them. And that's all. And there isn't a single man who marries a woman so that she can go and live with her parents; never. Even if a man has many wives, a man's wife overstaying at her parent's home is unacceptable behavior among the Wakerewe.

And so the following morning at the twittering of the pre-dawn birds Bugonoka loaded in *ekitukuru* basket her presents for her parents and put them on her head and got on the way. Myombekere too did not remain behind lying on his bed but escorted his wife, opened the gate of their home for her and accompanied her until they came to their neighborhood's communal grazing ground out there in the fields and they had to say good-bye to each other and he told his wife, "My very warm greetings to my father-in-law and mother-in-law and brother-in-law and his wife and their little baby!"

"All right. Stay well all of you at home."

"Fine. You too have a safe journey."

"Thanks."

Bugonoka got to her parents' home and the women in the home relieved her of her presents and put them away in her parents' house. Her father and brother were seated outside under the shade of a tree, making hoe handles with their chisels. Bugonoka went near them and knelt down and greeted them and they greeted her back and asked her news of her husband. Then she got up and went to her mother in her parents' house, where too she found her sister-in-law, Lweganwa's wife, who had just finished bathing her baby-boy and was now holding him on her thighs this way while suckling him. Bugonoka and her mother greeted each other and exchanged news of their well-being properly, and then Bugonoka looked at her sister-in-law and the two of them laughed, before greeting each other in their peers' familiar way and very warmly exchanging news of each other's welfare. Bugonoka asked her sister-in-law, "And so you have already given birth to your child, darling?"

"I have, thanks."

"And what kind of tiny creature did you give birth to, dear?"

"A tiny boy, my dear, who, I am told, has been named after your grandfather."

"Give us another one!"

"There are none left. But you had boycotted us, my dear, so many days have passed since you were here last and you had never come back to see us again, not even once!"

"I too felt bad about that, but being the only woman in my home, in addition to which I was looking for medicine from healers, I was simply caught up in so many things that I couldn't have come earlier. But please give me my grandfather, let me hold him a bit."

Her sister-in-law gave Bugonoka the child and she held it in her hands and then told her sister-in-law, "Give me some water, I badly need some."

Her sister-in-law said, "As a matter of fact you are some he-woman: you have just traveled what your brother is always telling me is a very long journey while carrying a load so heavy my mother-in-law almost fell down under its weight when she received it from you and yet, look, you have got here when it is still broad daylight, and that in spite of the condition you are in!"

She brought her drinking water and Bugonoka drank some and then breathed out a sigh of relief: "*Yehuu!*" before saying, "I was in fact lucky to have traveled under the cover of clouds; had I traveled in the hot sun I would still be on my way."

At once Lweganwa's wife turned to preparing food for their visitor, in her mother-in-law's house, since she had not yet started cooking in her own kitchen.[21]

It was not until evening, when the women were seated alone by their cooking-stones, that Bugonoka's mother queried her daughter about her condition: "By the way, Bugonoka, do you your self know how many months have passed since you have been this way?"

"The way I know it, this is the fourth month."

"And how do you feel in your womb, do you feel the thing moving about inside there or how is it like?"

"I feel jerks in my lower stomach all the time."

"We too were told of your condition by Barongo, who told us that our son-in-law took you to see medicine men and that you found a healer, and told us here even the name of your healer, only my memory has become so bad, oh, poor me! Otherwise she told us his name all right. By the way, daughter-in-law, what did Barongo say that man's name was?"

"I think I heard her say something like Kibuguma. Am I perhaps wrong, my dear?"

"No, that's it, you are right, that's what he is called."

Bugonoka's mother, Nkwanzi, continued: "And so it was Barongo who informed us that you took the medicines that Kibuguma gave you and that within a very short time you conceived. Does that mean that Kibuguma saw and divined well what it is that has been taking away your pregnancies, my dear?"

"As far as we are concerned, my husband and I, in our ignorance, think that, yes, he saw our problem clearly and even saw what had been causing my miscarriages and told us: `I've seen that what kills children in the womb of this woman is the *ihuzi* worm, that is what puts you in danger of ending up a childless couple.' Then that Kibuguma gave us the medicine for *ihuzi* worms and I came home and took it the way he had directed me. When that medicine became dilute, we went back and he gave me this *amulet* I am wearing around my waist, which is likewise meant to accompany the medicine for warding off *ihuzi* worms which keep on shooting out and killing my unborn children and causing me miscarriages."

"Yes, may be he saw what he said he saw, since he is the medicine man. How can we just dispute what he says when he is the seer. *Aa*! Let's just wait and see, because even the healers themselves say: `What heals is the Sun.'[22] Should the Sun grant us, we'll thank the heavens. Should it take away from us, *mh*! What is more, humans can only cure sickness, never death, against which there's no cure."

Bugonoka rejoined, "As our elders of yore said: `The boat sinks those in it still singing songs of hope,' and so should this medicine man fail and should we hear of another one, we will try that one too, because before we grow old we will not give up trying to have children; never!"

She spent five days at her parents home, during which time she helped her mother till ridges on which to sow red millet and then sowed the millet for her before leaving. The day she finished sowing the millet, at night her mother packed for her presents to take with her to her home and on the following day, the sixth day since she left her husband, she returned home, after being away for exactly the number of days they had agreed upon with her husband.

Once back in her home, the following day she went to see how things were with the red millet she sowed before going away and found: *aa!* yes indeed! It had fully sprouted as it should, with no empty patches anywhere! As she arrived home from the fields Kanwaketa's wife came in. The two women greeted each other and exchanged news of their welfare and Kanwaketa's wife inquired how everybody was doing at her parents' home, and then congratulated Myombekere by saying to him, "Happy wedding day, Myombekere!" to which Myombekere replied: "I am celebrating the day, thank you," and everybody present laughed. That said and done, Bugonoka made as if he was getting ready to do some work, and at once the wife of Kanwaketa realized that her friend wanted to skim milk and stopped her and said, "No, dear, let me churn my milk, you will churn yours tomorrow. You have just arrived from such a long journey, haven't had a moment of rest, and already you want to churn milk, as if I am not here! No, dear, don't do that. You could only do such a thing if you hadn't asked me to be churning your milk for you before you left. So please let me skim the milk. Even if I have neglected cleanliness and your churn is already smelling like an incurable wound, you can still pour away your butter and wash nicely your churn again and cleanse it of the stench I have given it, my dear." Bugonoka accepted her neighbor's offer. When Kanwaketa's wife finished skimming milk, Bugonoka took a sizable empty calabash bowl and filled it with butter and gave it to her, but, at first, her neighbor wouldn't take it and said: "*Aa!* Do you have to give me butter as if I cannot just churn your milk for you, dear?"

"Yes, I know you can churn milk for me for nothing, just out of your kindness, and that's why you should not think I am giving you this butter as payment for the work you have done for me. No, dear, I am just giving you some butter so that you can have something with which to season my husband's friend's relish, because I know you don't have butter these days, since all your calving cows stopped giving milk quite a while ago." Only then did Kanwaketa's wife receive the butter and her friend escorted her and she left.

As soon as she returned from escorting her neighbor, Bugonoka took an empty pot and went to the lake to draw water. She brought home water, put it down and went to fetch *omusunsu*[23] foaming herbs with which to wash her drinking water pot. She emptied the pot of water which was in it by pouring it into several other pots, like the *obwita* cooking pots, which too needed washing. After washing her pots, she boiled some water, fetched some gravel, pounded it with a stone into quite a bit of finer gravel, put the gravel into her calabash churn and poured hot water into the churn and   then put the churn into its straps and churned the hot water and gravel in it as if she were skimming milk until she was satisfied the churn was clean inside. She then took it out of its straps and brought it outside, somewhere by the fence of their home, emptied it of the water and gravel, rinsed it thoroughly with some more hot water until it was spick-and-span inside and then hang it on a stick in the fence of their compound and left it there to dry. In the evening, when she put on the fire her *obwita* pot and was waiting for the water to boil, she fetched her churn and scented it with *omuchumuliro*,[24] as part of her habit of doing every work of hers right.

That month of January became Bugonoka's fifth month of pregnancy. That's when Myombekere too became finally convinced it was real and his doubts were all gone, and that too was when even men and others who are usually ignorant of such things who saw her could all see that Bugonoka was indeed pregnant. During that fifth month the thing inside Bugonoka's womb became the fetus of a human being. Then the jerks inside her womb kind of stopped and she felt instead a different type of movement begin. Instead of jerks she now from time to time felt only something like blows: *gugu!* and then nothing again.

And thus she moved on with her fifth month until it became full moon and waned, and when it gave way to dark nights those blows became more frequent. At the same time that slight fever which accompanied her sleep at night persisted and increased. Myombekere whose hand kept on feeling her throughout the night is the only one who knew how boiling-hot she was at night! Regarding her sleeping, Bugonoka was now sleeping as if she had the sleep of three people, honestly! She rarely moved a muscle the entire night! To the extent that about cockcrow her husband would sometimes finally shake and wake her up while saying to her, "*Aa!* What type of sleeping is this today, Bugonoka? You haven't moved your body even once since you slept; not at all!" She on her part would wake up with a start and simply say, "Leave me alone, dear, let me sleep!"

But the fact that she had such a high fever throughout the night did not prevent Bugonoka from performing her normal jobs each morning by claiming she was this or that, no, lest I falsely accuse her of things she never did. As a matter of fact it was at the end of that month of January that she weeded her red millet crop. Also,   during that very month of January every morning she too went with the other people of her home for preparatory field work before the main planting season, to hoe the soil clean of grass and form the grass under-rows ready for the tilling of ridges on which to sow grain, and she always did so having already finished skimming her milk and cooking breakfast for her husband. And once in the crop fields she remained working until she retired with the others when the sun became too hot, since that grass-hoeing in preparation for the year's main field work of sowing *obubele*[25] millet was usually done only in the morning hours, except it was work from which a real hard worker retired always covered with dust from head to foot, so that even the beautiful ones were no longer much to look at, and as to the ugly ones, leave that alone!

All of a sudden a message of the death of a relative was brought to the Myombekeres, by a messenger who told them, "Bugonoka's aunt is dead, but not from sickness, for she was struck by lightning, which burnt her to death in a house." *Aa! hee!* Bugonoka and Myombekere found themselves in a real dilemma! The message was brought to them after sunset, and so Bugonoka could not leave immediately for the mourning, and neither could she show her grief by crying and bewailing her dead as people normally do on receiving such messages, even though her legs and arms were drained of all their force and she felt completely paralyzed by the pangs of her loss.

But you should not be too surprised and take Bugonoka for some insensitive creature. There was a reason why she did not cry and bewail the loss of her aunt there and then. Her husband was the first to remember that his wife was still under the treatment of a medicine man and was the one who stopped her by telling her: "My wife, don't cry and bewail your dead loudly, because the death of your aunt is already spilt water. Let's first find out what you can and can't do from Kibuguma, your healer, because, look, you are this way because of his divining and his herbs and even now you are wearing his amulets around your waist. I am the one who will go over there very early in the morning, at cockcrow, to ask him and let him tell us what to do, lest we break taboos we all know too well, alas, and get ourselves into trouble."

Bugonoka had no appetite for food that night and didn't touch her dinner, not even for a single bite. That night was a night of a deep sadness for the couple, both the mistress as well as the master of the house. Bugonoka held herself back from carrying out with the will of he-woman, although inside her she was dying with sorrow. To Myombekere, as you can imagine, that night was like one that will never end and as soon as the cock said: "*Tata wee!*"[25] he was on his way to see their medicine man and as the new day was about to dawn, before the twittering of the early morning birds, he was at the gate of the fence of Kibuguma's home, which was still closed with a shutter of thorn trees. He called out loud, about three times, "People of this home!" After quite a while he heard Weroba wake up Kibuguma: "Kibuguma, Kibuguma, wake up! I hear somebody calling at the gate, who he is, I can't tell." Kibuguma then asked aloud: "Hello! who is it calling outside there?"

"It's me."

"Who are you?"

"It's me your patient Myombekere."

Kibuguma jumped out of bed, grabbed his robe from a hanging rope on the way and held it in his hands, opened the door of his house and come out naked, his robe still just held in his hands, remembering to put it on and cover his nakedness only when he was already outside, where he walked agitating his eyes with his hands to clear them of rheum and see better. At the gate he took a good look and saw it was indeed Myombekere, all alone, spear in hand. He could not help asking him, "My dear man, are you a messenger of bad news, to travel in the middle of the night like this?" before opening the shutter of thorn trees at the gate, just wide enough for a person to pass through with his shoulders turned sideways like this. When the two men got into the house, Myombekere exchanged greetings with the people of the house and then said, "What has brought me here, my healer, is the following."

"Say it, and let's hear it!"

"Yesterday, rather late in the evening, we were brought a message that my wife's aunt has died and that she died from lightning, that lightning completely burnt down her house with her in it and burnt her to death. That aunt of my wife was living with a younger son of hers, who lives in a one man's household and who had built her a house in his home. That younger son of hers has three wives, the eldest of whom has two little male children, and three little girls, the youngest of whom is still sucking. As to the other wives, his second wife has one female child and a tiny baby boy, also still breast-feeding, and his third wife is pregnant and at such an advanced stage she could give birth any day. That's where our misfortune has befallen us, my dear friend. But what has brought me here is to ask you the following: `Can indeed my wife, the way she is now, still cry for and bewail aloud her dead relative and go to her mourning?"

Kibuguma answered him, "So I didn't tell you that she can't bewail aloud or attend mournings of her dead until after she has given birth? If that's the case, it was only an oversight on my part."

Myombekere returned home and explained to his wife that she could not bewail aloud or attend mournings of her dead, until after she had safely delivered her baby. Only then could she mourn and bewail her dead again.

The following day early in the morning Myombekere went to greet the people in the home where the death occurred. When he got there he found, yes, indeed lightning did strike a house and burn it down and really burn to death a human being in it. And, as a result, there was no mourning in that home either. And when he found that there was to be no mourning wake, he too returned to his home the same day. He explained to his wife how when he got there he found out there would be no mourning. Her relatives in that home would have to wait for a new moon and then make a ritual fire in the destroyed home, after which rain-makers would come and cleanse the people of that home of the ills of lightning and remove from the burnt down home lightning-residue left behind by the thunderbolt, following which her relatives would then move their home from that site and build a new one aside. And so Myombekere and Bugonoka could do nothing but stay back at home.

When the new moon appeared, Myombekere went back to the bereaved home for the delayed mourning and to help his wife's relatives build new houses at a new site, returning only when he finished helping them with those tasks of rebuilding their home.

February became Bugonoka's sixth month of pregnancy. Her stomach had now become really big. During that sixth month mothers speak of the thing inside the womb of a pregnant woman as a human being who is growing hair, because if miscarriage takes place then people would indeed find that the child who has come out of the mother's womb, even if still-born, has hair. But, even though her pregnancy had grown so big, Bugonoka still hoed her fields with it. Whoever met her at work in the fields would ask her, "How is work, Bugonoka?"

"Work is fine, thank you."

"This demanding farm work, especially given the way you are now, aren't you afraid you'll harm yourself?"

"Why should I harm myself when pregnancy is a robe the owner wears? Imagine you yourself throwing away the clothes you are wearing, what would people think of you?"

"*Aa! hii!* If people saw me throw away my clothes and walk naked they would no doubt call me a mad person, even the cynics bent on sneering would have to at least say I am a nitwit or complete idiot, because walking naked is not accepted behavior for normal people in this Ukerewe of ours."

And since people will always be incomprehensible, when they came across Myombekere during those days of working in the fields they found a few things to say to him too, and asked him, as if faulting him for something: "Are the people of your home well? How is Bugonoka? Has she, by the way, already delivered, or how are things? Wouldn't you say it is quite a while now since we heard she is pregnant?"

"We are all well. Bugonoka is well and in perfect health, she has not yet delivered, she is still carrying her delicate load."

"Myombekere, will shouldering this demanding farm work all alone, your wife being the way she is, not bring you to some harm this year?"

"Whatever we'll be able to do we'll make do with that. For what else is there to do? As the Mkerewe elder once said: 'There's no reason to wonder why so-and-so's harvest is abundant when his people and his in-laws were all well the whole year.'"

And so Bugonoka slowly moved on with that sixth month of her pregnancy, from time to time hearing those blows and kicks inside her womb, as in the meanwhile the couple worked on their *obubele* millet farm and tilled and sowed well to a finish, from one end of their crop field to the other, without a hitch. Because their field had been fallow, plus the fact that they always sowed their *obubele* crop with the aid of potent medicines, as usual in no time their millet sprouted from the ground into exuberant young plants. After a number of days passed, Myombekere and Bugonoka went back to the field and started weeding their millet before grass stifled it. But, although they began weeding the crop early, because so much rain was falling and grass was growing so fast, they felt they had to look for communal farmers to help them save their grain from weeds.

Chapter XIV

NOTES

1.   *Ekibo*: See note 15 of Chapter I.

2.   *Amatwera*: Kitereza in his Swahili translation of his novel writes: "Disease which afflicts a pregnant woman often resulting in miscarriage."

3.   *Omutaho*: See note 9 of Chapter I.

4.   *Ekitala*. See note 18 of Chapter I.

5.   *Omusimbe-zule*: A young woman with a single divorce was considered to be both *omuzule*, a "maiden-wed bride", and *omusimbe*, a free (divorced) woman. For *omusimbe* see note 24 of Chapter II .

6.   *Engali*, plural for *olugali*: See note 6 of Chapter I.

7.   *Enzamba*: Flutes, whistles and trumpets made of horns of animals, used in hunting with dogs and played to mark the beginning of a new lunar month.

8.   *Ekina*. Smooth-bodied small species of a lizard.

9.   *Enkanda*: See note 22 of Chapter VI.

10.   *Omugazu*:   See note 23 of Chapter VIII

11.   *Akahira*: See note 11 of Chapter IX.

12.   *Ekitukuru*: See note 16 of Chapter V.

13.   *Obwita*: See note 14 of Chapter I.

14.   *Ekizanda*: See note 20 of Chapter II.

15.   *Ensato*: See note 2 of Chapter VI.

16.   *Ekikome*: See note 1 of Chapter II.

17.   *Oluhongore*: A "cut-off bedroom". In addition to the two rooms of a typical Kikerewe house, the outer room, *omwalilo*, and the inner room, *omukugiro*, in a large house there could also be an additional inner bed room called *oluhongore*. See note 10 of Chapter I.

18.   *Omuswerani*: "Co-husband", a man married to a sister (or female family or clan relative with the rank of "sister" – see note 11 of Chapter I) of a man's wife.

19.   *Ekilangi*: See note 7 of Chapter VII.

20.   *Enkorongo*: See note 20 of Chapter I for the word and its derivatives.

21.   In situations where a young man married when still living with his parents, which was usually the case, his wife did not cook in her own house until she had harvested her own crops in her new home once or twice. Before that she shared a kitchen with her mother-in-law, learning how to be a good mistress of her own household while still establishing her own harvests.

22.   The Sun: See note 21 of Chapter II.
23.   *Omusunsu*: Herb with a clean scent which foams in water producing suds used as soap for washing household utensils and other things.
24.   *Omuchumuliro*: See note 5 of Chapter X.
25.   *Obubele*: See note 17 of Chapter V.
26.   *Tata wee*! See note 24 of Chapter IX.

Chapter XV

COMMUNAL FARMING

Myombekere saw how rain continued to pour down daily and relentlessly and discussed with Bugonoka about looking for helping hands so that they could weed their millet before they lost it all to weeds, and as a result he at once sent Kagufwa, the nephew of his who was staying with them, to call his mother. When that sister of Myombekere came, her brother told her why he had called her, hearing which his sister sympathized with the couple and told Myombekere, "Let me go and beg your brother-in-law to call together people he will find willing to accompany him here and help you save your millet crop in the face of such rains before you lose it to weeds."

Myombekere's sister went back and told her husband why Myombekere wanted to see her: "It is like this! And like that!" Her husband did not refuse either, but agreed with her and said, "That shouldn't be a problem, daughter of good people, because we see everyday people come to each other's help, even when they are just ordinary people to each other, not bound by any ties of kinship, so how can I fail to help the man whose sister is the foundation of my household? If I don't help him, that would be a great shame on my part, because when Myombekere gets a bumper crop I too greatly rejoice and thank the heavens and say: `That food is mine too, because Myombekere can never let me and my people, his sister and me and these dear little nieces and nephews of his, die of hunger.' And when we too get a good crop he too greatly rejoices for that, because what is ours is his too."

And so the following day, at about the afternoon sun, he went to summon his companions to accompany him to weed his brother-in-law's field the day after, and from young men and young women to every adult he found at home, with the exception of the sick, not a single person refused his call.

Back in Myombekere's home, no sooner had Myombekere's sister agreed to get them helping hands than Bugonoka took millet from their grain store[1] and winnowed it clean and the following day took it around the neighborhood homes to request her female neighbors for help in grinding flour. Her neighbors quickly ground the millet for her, because she too was always ready and willing to help whenever her fellow women took to her millet they wanted ground into flour for whatever occasions they had.

On the third day, early in the morning, Myombekere saw arrive in his home his sister with his brother-in-law and a big group of people, more than thirty of them, men and women, with their hoes, ready for work. As soon as they arrived they said, "We have no intention of sitting down. All we want is the work for which we are here. That's all."

Bugonoka's sister-in-law and her husband took the communal farming group to the field, as Bugonoka on her part went to request assistance from the neighborhood, to look for the women who would help her cook food for the communal farmers and bring them drinking water in the field. Myombekere on his side went to look for male help, men who would serve food to the workers and attend them during their feasting. And, what with the fact that instead of rain there was nothing but sunshine that day, as soon as the men and women got to the millet field they fell to weeding the crop without further ado, so that all you could hear was the sound of their hoes cutting the soil: *pupu! pupu!*

Before the workers in the field knew it, two of them, a young man and a young woman, had shot out of the pack and left everybody behind. The two youths were simply unmatchable in weeding millet and were in no time ridges upon ridges of weeded crop ahead of the group, making it impossible for anybody else to catch up with them.

Back in Myombekere's home Bugonoka and her female helpers got busy cooking. They first cooked sweet potatoes, but when they wanted to take the food to the field hoers Myombekere stopped them and said, "No, you can't serve my guests sweet potatoes without relish", and since he had slaughtered for them a bull, he had some men roast for them the two whole slabs of ribs of the cow, to which he added some more meat from other cuts good for roasting , after rubbing rock salt into the meat. The rest of the meat of the slaughtered bull was all cut into smaller pieces for cooking, the entire carcass, including the entrails.   If there was anything Myombekere left behind, then it was only one leg, plus the arm he meant to give to his sister before she went back to her home.

Those who took to the field workers sweet potatoes with roast meat found the two youths, the young man and the young woman, already through with their weeding, resting under the shade of a tree and drinking water. As to the others, the slow weeders, they still had waiting for them ridges upon ridges of unweeded crop, as the sun in the sky was getting to the high morning sun at which milk curdles. They put down the food under a shade of a tree and called Myombekere's sister and said, "We are to tell you that you should tell our in-laws to come and eat first before continuing with their hoeing." At once the farmers left their hoes in their allotted crop ridges, each one wherever he or she had got to, and came to eat.

The sweet potatoes were many and of the large kind, big enough to split into two, some even into as many as four slices each, but still they didn't get anywhere with those communal farmers, not at all, and neither did the meat. At the men meal circle, the server had just completed a round of giving one small piece of meat to each person and was now coming for some more meat from the plate [2] to serve a second round when he saw some incorrigible mischievous youths stretch their arms and scramble with each other and snatch from the plate the remaining meat, so that the server himself wouldn't have had even a tiny morsel of meat to go with his sweet potatoes had he not been fortunate enough to be still holding in his hands two small pieces he had already taken from the plate for serving to his companions, which then became his share. And when the other young men saw their friends scramble for meat they on their part pounced on the sweet potatoes. And even those who managed to snatch away some meat from the plate could still have it snatched away from their hands by their friends! On seeing that the women laughed at the men until they could laugh no more, so that some of them were almost literally dying of laughter! In fact the men did not get out of hand altogether only because Myombekere's sister finally had to reprimand them by telling them: "*Aa!* Look here, dear men, this isn't how to have fun, running after each other right into another person's millet when it has grown this high and trampling it on the ground!" With the women, who had formed their own meal circle apart from the men's, there was no fighting over meat. Their server, also a woman, managed to give to each one of them two small pieces of meat and they ate like well-behaved human beings. There was some attempt on the part of the girls to scramble for the sweet potatoes but an elderly woman present glared at them with her fiery eyes and they thought better of it and ate with proper manners throughout the meal.

After lunch they all went back to work, the young man and young woman who had completed weeding their allotment included, who went to help the others, with the boy helping Myombekere's brother-in-law and the girl helping Myombekere's sister.

The women who took lunch to the field then came back to cook food for the communal workers feast in Myombekere's home, where they arrived singing the praises of the farm workers and told those at home: "When we got there some of them had finished weeding their allotments and were already resting under the shade of a tree! At first we thought that perhaps they had fallen sick, since we human beings are always the `walking-dead', all of us. But in no time we realized that they had simply left the others behind and finished their work before the rest of their companions and were now just resting. Those who left the others behind are some two youths, mere children, a boy and a girl, and what ferocious hoers those two children are! Incredible! Indeed if such children were your own you could say, `Yes indeed, I brought into the world great human beings!' Because you cannot praise your child simply because he is alive and can eat. A person's child is praised for the work he or she does, especially farm work like that one. *Aa!* As a matter of fact, is a lazy person ever thought of well in this Ukerewe of ours? With youths   like those two we saw, if it came to courting for that boy a woman to marry, or that girl being courted by a suitor, *aa!* we are convinced nobody will find anything to say against their ability to farm the land; never! Something else to malign them with, that's always possible, but not on matters of cultivating the land."

After hearing that good report on the work going on in his crop field, Myombekere went to see how those who were cooking meat in the courtyard outside were doing, and on seeing that the meat was about ready he told Bugonoka to put *obwita* 3 pots on the fire at once, and at once women readied *obwita* pots, some scrapping them clean of crusts with *enkombyo4* spoons: *kwaru! kwaru!* at the same time as others took flour to go and cook food in the houses of nearby homes, at the Kanwaketa's and thereabouts. In no time they were back and dishes upon dishes of *obwita*, too many to count, had been assembled in Myombekere's home and taken into Bugonoka's house. When *obwita* was ready and people were about to go and call the farmers, they heard them returning on their own, noisily talking all at once. People in Myombekere's home laid on the ground under the shade of a tree logs of wood and movable door shutters for the men to sit on and, close by, spread grass on the ground for the women, where they would sit with their legs stretched out to one side, as women normally do at meal times.[5] The visiting farmers washed their hands and serving men brought dishes of *obwita* and placed them inside the men and women meal circles, and followed that by putting in front of the guests the huge water pots in which meat for so many people had been cooked and plates to serve meat on. Myombekere approached and invited them to eat with the word of welcome everybody uses in this Ukerewe of ours to invite his or her in-laws to partake of any meal, with the exception of sacrificial food: "Have something to eat, in-laws, that's all we could afford."

"For us all that matters is the wife you gave us, father-in-law," his visitors answered him.

Kanwaketa's son, whose name was Mugeniwalwo, was the man Myombekere told to go and dish the meat from the pots for the guests and eat with them while serving them. What with the fact that that young man, Mugeniwalwo, was a born joker, he would take from a plate one big piece of meat and as soon as he gave it to a host he would say: "I've given you the big one, dear man, lest once back in your place you revile Myombekere's brother-in-law by telling him, 'On the day you summoned us to go and weed your brother-in-law's millet the server saw fit to give me a bare bone with no meat on it to eat!'" And likewise with the women, he served all of them while saying: "I've given you the big one, dear lady, lest you should revile Myombekere's sister by telling her, 'The day you summoned us to go and weed your brother's millet, the server saw fit to make me eat a bare bone with no trace of meat on it and I ate *obwita* with hardly any relish, so that had so-and-so not helped me out with a share of her meat I wouldn't have eaten at all!'"   When the server came to the son-in-law's[6] pot of relish, the one Bugonoka had specially prepared in recognition of Myombekere's brother-in-law, he brought a really big plate and poured and piled in the middle of the plate the entire pot of relish and said, "Here is the pot of *emamba*[7], my dear men, serve yourselves as you please." And whoever took relish from that plate and put it into his mouth simply exclaimed in disbelief, because Bugonoka was a really great cook! Many of the men present returned on plates the meat Mugeniwalwo had already served them so as to eat that fish first and returned to eating meat only when it was all gone, because Bugonoka had seasoned it in a very special way, after the culinary skills of the Wakerewe women of yore.

After their meal, Myombekere honored his helpers with two pots of banana beer, one for the men and one for the women. As to the people who came to help him cook the feast and serve his working visitors, he honored those too with one pot of banana beer, for the men and women together to share. The visiting men and women drank their banana beer and finished it and likewise their hosts drank theirs and finished it in complete piece and tranquility, and if there was a single person who got drunk, then he or she must have shown his or her disorderly conduct after leaving, on his or her way home, wherever that was, but not while in Myombekere's home that day, lest I tell lies. Myombekere had bought that beer at Kanwaketa's, borrowed it in exchange for a she-goat he was to pay his neighbor, who still owed him three more pots of banana beer, according to the banana beer barter for a she-goat in those past times.

As Myombekere's sister and brother-in-law and their friends were about to leave, Myombekere went into the house and brought out the skin of the cow he had slaughtered for them, in which was wrapped the arm cut he set aside, and told his brother-in-law, "Here is a skin, my brother-in-law, go and make a bed sheet out of it for my sister, and here too is some relish for you all, to share when you get to your place."

His visitors thanked him and said, "This is very kind of you; we will, indeed, never stop thanking you!" With that their hosts brought out their hoes and escorted them and they left.

When Myombekere and the people of his neighborhood returned from escorting their guests, Myombekere told Kanwaketa's son, "Go and bring from the house the leg of a cow we kept aside, so that we can give some meat to the people who helped us with the work we accomplished in this home today!" He gave some meat to each and everyone of the people present, after which Bugonoka took into the house what was left. Then Myombekere told everybody still in his home, "Come, all of you, let's go to drink banana beer at Kanwaketa's," and each and everyone of them followed Myombekere, the only exception perhaps being Bugonoka, who remained at home busy cooking the meat which was left her and removing the hoof from the leg cut and washing the remaining entrails, otherwise the rest of the group took off in search of beer at Kanwaketa's. At Kanwaketa's Myombekere told his neighbor to give him his remaining three pots of beer and Myombekere and his companions drank the three pots of beer to the finish there and then. He returned home walking on unsteady feet but, alas! for him that day, since he was still sorrowing over his wife's loss of her aunt, he did not enter his home singing aloud the jolly drunk's song: "*The far off country where Balita[8] lives, where drunkards pass their nights instead of sleeping at home.*" No, he couldn't. He just walked on, staggering but all quiet.

But the following day he found it difficult to get out of bed, what with the fact that he didn't eat anything at night! Bugonoka went to wake him up after cooking breakfast, but try as hard as she could all her husband did was to keep on moaning, unable to bestir himself and get up from bed, and it was not until she brought water and poured some on his head and some on his feet that he come to and was able to get out of bed. She served him food and he ate, but rather half-heartedly, managing to eat with appetite only meat and broth but taking just a few pinches of *obwita* and leaving the food virtually untouched.

Then the couple resumed their normal life in their home, Myombekere busy with the cultivation of his banana plantation and Bugonoka on her part taking up again her favorite pastime of weaving with grass bowls[9] and trays.[10]

Chapter XV

NOTES

1   *Ekitala*: See note 18 of Chapter I.
2.   *Olunanga*: See note 16 of Chapter I.
3.   *Obwita*: See note 14 of Chapter I.
4.   *Enkombyo*: See note 9 of Chapter XII.
5.   Wakerewe women normally took their meals while seated on the ground facing the food sideways, their legs stretched out away from the dishes.
6.   Myombekere in this situation represents his sister's parents and hence in his home his brother-in-law is entitled to the very special treatment reserved for sons-in-law whenever they visit the parents of their wives.
7.   *Emamba*: See note 17 of Chapter II.
8.   *Balita*: Fictitious name of a place haunted by drunks meaning "where death awaits!" See list of names at the end of the translation.
9.   *Ebibo*, plural for *ekibo*: See note 15 of Chapter I.
10.   *Engali*, plural for *olugali*: See note 6 of Chapter I.

Chapter XVI

THE DISPUTE OF THREE MEN: MUGIMBA, MBALIRO AND NKARANI[1]

These three men, Mugimba, Mbaliro and Nkarani, came one day in the morning to that very home of Myombekere, just calling to see how he was doing, the way people call on each other all the time. Mugimba was the first to come and found Myombekere at the courtyard fireplace[2] of his home warming himself at the fire in the company of the boy living in his home. Bugonoka was in the cattle kraal collecting cow urine for washing her churn and all her other milk utensils and Mugimba and Myombekere and the boy were still at the fireplace when Mbaliro too came and joined them and they talked of whatever chanced to come up, of men, women and marriage, of parents and the upbringing of their children, of the raising of cattle, and many other things.

That's when Nkarani too came, and the men kept on with their conversations. Before long, they saw Bugonoka coming with warm water in a small cooking pot and on getting to the men she told them: "You better seat properly."

Mugimba asked her, "We better seat properly! Are we naked?" At which his companions all laughed. Mbaliro said: "This man here with his incurable jokes, *aa!* no! Come on now, is that what Bugonoka said: `You are naked, seat properly, fold your clothes well?' Don't you see her bringing water and pouring it in a washbasin?"[3]

Mugimba answered back Mbaliro in the same jocular vein and said, "Dear Sir, don't kill me, spare me, but all the same I heard such words from her, that's why I retorted as I did."

Nkarani asked Mugimba, "Since you retorted that way, how do your wives in your home invite you to eat?"

"It's me you are asking or someone else?"

"*Aa*! You, the one who has said so, who else?"

"Well, if it's me, then let me tell you."

"Tell me."

"The women of my home say it this way: `Form a circle with enough room!'"

"And is `form a circle with enough room' different from `seat properly'? And can you alone, with your two little boys, be told to `form a circle with enough room,' or do you perhaps now live with some visitors in that home of yours?"

"*Aa*! No, I am alone with my two little boys, but am I alone here, gentlemen, when in fact, as you see, we are three people, with the master of the home as the forth and this boy as the fifth! So why can't the woman inviting us to eat say `Widen your seating circle'?"

In no time Bugonoka brought them a dish of *obwita*4 and a pot of dried minced meat. Mbaliro said, "Indeed, so should it always be! You are a woman among women, a woman into whose home people come in the morning and go away with well-fed stomachs. Let's chase cold from our mouths!"

When they stopped eating, Myombekere took *ekizanda*5 of milk and churned it around and passed the milk to their elder, Nkarani, who was the oldest of all of them, followed by Mbaliro, who was in turn older than Mugimba, although Mugimba was aging fast and was big and towering and had hair all over his body and wore a very bushy beard, so that he too had become a graying old man like Myombekere's other two visitors. It was Myombekere himself alone who was still a young man of just the right age to be a master of a home, even though during those days he would normally have been judged too young to have a household of his own all alone, had his father not died early and their household fallen apart due to friction between brothers with different mothers. Whatever the case, compared to the other men we have talked about, he was a green horn.

Nkarani took hold of *ekizanda* of milk and put it to his mouth and poured the milk down his throat, his breath held in, until he finally took it from his mouth and breathed out noisily like a watering cow. Myombekere asked him, "Why didn't you drink the milk, doesn't it taste good?"

"I was afraid there would be none left for you the others. But as to tasting bad, *yu*! better talk of something else! Where can you find a woman who churns milk better than Bugonoka in our entire village? The woman who knows how to prepare skimmed milk full of tiny bubbles, milk which hisses like banana beer foaming in pots on the frothing day?" And with that he passed *ekizanda* of milk to Mbaliro, while adding words of thanks to the milk cow: "Can a man's life be complete in this country of ours without the precious *Buzimbe*?[6] It is true the Masai[7] stole all my cows, but I will always make sure I have at least one, come what come may!" By then Mbaliro too had finished downing the milk and retorted to that and said: "And if you don't have any like me, what do you do?"

"Why wouldn't I go begging for a cow to rear free of charge from the Wakerewe who possess cattle, who may feel compassion for me and grant me some of their cows to graze for them so that I can at least have milk to drink and console myself with that? For, as the Mkerewe woman of yore said: `If you have no fish or meat as relish for your food at least have a sip of milk.' Wouldn't you say that woman realized how important *Buzimbe* is?"

Mugimba put in and said: "By the way, what do you say of greens cooked with nothing but water and salt, do you find it appetizing relish?"

"*Aa*! I must admit, when it comes to that, nobody wants to eat that kind of green vegetables. Whoever eats that kind of relish does so only out of necessity, but that is not food fit for a human being."

"So you see now, my dear man! And yet you want to argue! Since when have greens tasted good when cooked with nothing but water and salt, without the milk-and-butter cow stepping in! As a matter of fact eating green vegetables cooked with water only is like chewing tobacco."

It was however after eating their fill of that good dish of *obwita* that the four men took up arguing in earnest: whenever they took up this subject and brought it to an end they jumped on yet another one. All the time their sweet *ekilangi*[8] waiting for them nearby: whoever wanted it poured it down his nostrils, listened to it going to work in his head and then blew it out, as they continued with their test of wits. After some time Mugimba suddenly came in with a kind of question and by said, "By the way, gentlemen, if I put to you a matter of mine which has always baffled me but which is something I observe all the time among people, can you give me an explanation for it?"

"Say it! If it is worthwhile explaining we will do so, and if we can't we'll leave it alone and you will find some knowledgeable people and they will explain it to you."

"Well, my question in this: `By the way, if your wife conceive a child, can you the husband know for sure she conceived in that or that month?'"

Then Mbaliro and Nkarani began throwing the challenge at each other. Mbaliro was the first to tell his friend, "There you are, Nkarani!"

"There you are, Mbaliro!"

"These are words to ponder indeed! Yes, indeed! Is that all, by the way? Have you finished, Mugimba?" Mbaliro asked.

"Yes, that's all. Because this matter to me has remained a puzzle, I have tried to look for an answer this way and that alone and failed completely. And today seeing this opportunity I said to myself: `No, today I must put this matter to my fellow elders, because the Wakerewe of old said: `A good cause gathers elders,' and we have become the few remaining elders, the ones people count on most."

Mbaliro then went on, "In that case let me blab my own views, gentlemen, because the Wakerewe put it this way: `There's no shame in losing a case at the king's[9] Bukindo.' In my view, to know that for sure, and know the very instant in which you made your wife pregnant, to know the very day on which she conceived, in my view, I think I will have to give up. However, since I am not afraid of being Mr. Split-opener of no matter what, let me all the same just go ahead and say what I know."

"Just go ahead and say it, man, what's there to fear?"

"Well, I am afraid, you see, of saying unbecoming words which could be heard by the mistress of this home inside that house who has just served us a delicious meal and who, since these are matters touching on sex, could give us a bad name by spreading it around that Mugimba and Mbaliro and Nkarani were saying ugly things about women and make us men to whom no woman would give even water to drink."

"Just say what you have to say, man, for who doesn't know how people are created? Every woman and every man knows it, for how else did he or she come into this world? Did he or she drop down from the sky?"

"In that case keep quite, if it is your pleasure that I be Mr. Split-opener."

"Speak and let's hear what you have to say."

"In this matter, from what I have always known, there are about three signs which will make you know a woman who is your wife has conceived before other people can possibly know. And here they are. The first one is not menstruating the way every woman does every month. But that alone isn't enough, because at times a woman may just skip her periods for may be one month and then resume seeing them. Count that as one sign. And then the second is the shining of her dear little face, because a woman who has conceived a child cannot but have a shining face, it is impossible for her not to. However ugly she may be she cannot but look a little bit beautiful in the face. Then the third symptom is the following: the body of a pregnant woman is hot throughout the night, runs a slight fever as if she is sick even though when she wakes up in the morning she goes about her daily business as usual. There are some women when they get pregnant their pregnancy induces them to sleep all the time, even during daytime all they want is to asleep. On my part those are the symptoms I usually see, but as to knowing the exact month and the exact day, before even noticing those signs, for me that appears an impossible thing indeed!"

When Mbaliro stopped speaking, Nkarani queried what he had said by asking him, "*Aa*! Mbaliro, do you really believe that the three things you have mentioned are the only clear signs that a woman has conceived?"

"Yes indeed, for what else can there be?"

"You have indeed named them correctly, except you have omitted the greatest of them all. So I've better name it openly. And here it is: When a woman realizes she didn't menstruate, she then begins to examine herself when bathing her female parts and when she notices that the inner way to her womb has shut itself off she becomes certain that she is indeed pregnant and it is not just a question of skipping periods. And during those times she begins to feel twitches inside her, confined to her lower stomach. But then I must tell you this, since you are the ones who have started all this talk: there is not a single one of us men capable of knowing for sure the day his wife conceived nor of being certain of even the month in which her pregnancy started. And if you don't agree with me, let me in turn ask you this question: `When you men divorce your wives when they are pregnant and they go and get married somewhere else and following that you sue them in court to claim your children, don't you more often than not lose your cases?'"

"*Aa*! Indeed we see often the women winning such cases against us men and taking away our children from us and our children becoming the children of those co-husbands of ours."

"And do you know why they defeat us?"

"Yes, that we do. The women often defeat us because of our inability to name correctly the months in which their pregnancies started."

Mugimba then asked Nkarani this: "By the way, for about how many months does the child stay in her mother's womb before being born?

"If it is a pregnancy without complications, if the pregnant woman isn't sickly all the time and as a result miscarries or her pregnancy runs to her back, a human being and a cow don't differ at all in their gestation. For, look here, if a woman were to conceive say today and the cow is also mounted this same day and it too becomes pregnant, then their pregnancies will keep pace with each other exactly: when the human female gives birth to a child the cow too calves. Therefore a woman's pregnancy with no complication is of nine months only and then the child is born and the tenth month finds the child already breathing air in the open, which is also the case with the pregnancy of a cow, as I have already said. On the other hand, a pregnancy with endless complications may miscarry with a whole lot of blood, but if, in spite of that, the pregnancy itself isn't lost, it is then said to have run to the back of the mother and that then becomes a pregnancy which is no longer spoken of in terms of months, no, but, instead, in terms of years. Often the women with that kind of pregnancy does not resume her menstruation. Even if the pregnancy had reached five months, when she miscarries that way it dissolves away and the swollen stomach of a pregnant woman disappears, because the pregnancy has run to her back, although the woman herself from time to time may still hear something moving or knocking about inside her. And to bring that pregnancy back to the front of the mother there is need to look for medicines, which are called the medicine for rescued pregnancy from drowning or the medicine for restoring pregnancy to the front of the mother. The woman carrying that type of pregnancy, once she takes medicines and drinks them in earnest and for a long time, whether it is for a year or even two years, people will all of a sudden see that pregnancy shoot out again fully grown, suddenly, like hernia, and within just a few days that woman gives birth to living human being and she too will suckle and bring up her child just like the woman who had a perfectly normal pregnancy. With the children whose pregnancies stay that long, when the child who is born is male he is named Butura and when it is a female child she is given the name of Katura,[10] because of having over-stayed in their mothers' wombs. Some of these children stay in their mothers' wombs two years and are born in the third year and yet others stay four years and are born in the fifth year."

On hearing that Mugimba strongly disputed what the other man had said, refused completely to have any of it and said, "I can't accept that! This matter of a pregnancy staying in the mother's womb three or five years, that simply can't be and I have to say no, poor Mugimba here! If so, Nkarani, where does the child keep all that time?"

"Why do you take me back to where I have already been, to the rear like I were a fart, you man? Didn't you then hear what I told you? You should realize that opium is no good for you, you should stop smoking it so early in the morning, it is harming you! How can you ask me: where will the child be? It will be in the womb of the mother. I was of the opinion that you are a Mkerewe, and how can you be a real Mkerewe and yet not understand such simple matter, as if you were still a child or you were from some far off country of some ignorant foreigners. For the truth of the matter is that the women who are wont to carry pregnancies for that long in their wombs that way are under the influence of some spell. Sometimes the spell is on the man who is married to that woman and at others it is on the pregnant woman herself. Oh, poor me, let me at least explain to those who are willing to learn and understand and leave alone the likes of you who will argue about anything including shit like a Muyambi.[11]   And to know the nature of that spell you have to consult an oracle and find out from seers whether you and your home and its people are wholesome or not. And that's how it is. When you find a healer he or she will reveal it all to you, including what is holding back that pregnancy. If what is needed is offering a sacrifice or wearing some particular dress the ancestor you are named after used to wear, the seer will divine all that and explain to you everything and when you come and do the required and your wife's pregnancy comes to the front again she safely delivers a living human being. So, did I in any way suggest that you'll take everything into your own hands when you know nothing, when the knowledge of what prevents the pregnancy from being born can only be obtained by consulting a healer and in no other way?"

Mugimba on his part responded to Nkarani by telling him, "Yes, I admit I am a confirmed opium smoker, but today I haven't smoked it since morning. And, yes, I am a real Mkerewe: you knew my father and his mother as well as my maternal grandmother, and you know they were all of them Wakerewe, and yet you have already found me to be somebody who argues about anything including shit as if I were a Muyambi! You speak of me being intoxicated with opium, excuse me, but it appears that with you too apparently *obwita* which Bugonoka has cooked for us this early in the morning in Myombekere's home here has made you drunk!"

Myombekere appealed to both of them by saying: "You mustn't quarrel, when both of you are elders! The enjoyable arguments we were having shouldn't lead to a quarrel." To which Mugimba retorted, "No, man, he is the one who said something unacceptable to me by telling me, `You dispute everything right up to shit.' Am I a Muyambi? And if he himself is not so argumentative, why was he named Nkarani!"

"Well, why were you given your name Mugimba, are you a rain-maker?"

"Yes, my namesake was a rain-maker indeed. Everybody knows that Mugimba was a great rain-maker, that he could converse with the heavens with amazing power and command it to rain. And it was to him that people whose property had been stolen went to consult oracles and be told who the thieves of their property were and have him strike down those culprits with lightening. Even the king knew of his powers. So you thought it was a name whose meaning was a secret, when it is common knowledge!"

Mbaliro said, "Whatever the case you must drop this matter. It is a great shame for two elders like you to carry on this way. Let what has been said go with the wind: it is a matter between men and that's how it should end, lest you harbor ill feelings against each other when you are people of one and the same neighborhood this way." And they all fell silent.

After that spell of silence, Mbaliro too had a few things he wanted discussed and started off by telling the other men: "*Aa!* What a pleasant palaver we had today, oh, dear! Everything we touched on turned into such interesting conversation, I can't believe it! Now let me too put to you something which has always puzzled me by asking you this: `By the way, gentlemen, how many months of the year do we have in Ukerewe?"

"There are twelve months in the whole year which comes and goes out of this sea."

Hearing that answer, Mbaliro then said, "I have, believe me, been on this earth a long time. I did not borrow this beard from the chin of a he-goat, it is a result of my aging after living for many years, and you can also see that on my head my hair has become the color of the gray-haired rabbit. But in all those years, I have never seen the Wakerewe stop arguing about the months in a year, year in and year out. When I go to Omulambo region I hear mentioned different months, when I come to Mumbuga I hear yet others, to Bwiro yet others, Ilangara again others, Mwibara likewise, not to mention the Islands,[12] where you reach the limit! During the planting season you could say, 'Oh yes! this is all right,' since at that time people are still arguing tolerably. But not during the dry season, when they have nothing to do except wander all over the country looking for banana beer. Then you will meet people in those drinking parties of theirs, the aged ones like me included, jaws all tensed, arguing until before they know it the planting season has gone by! All right then, even if the months of the year are twelve, what are their names? That's what I want to ask you and nothing else, and after that we will end our disputes, of which we've had enough for one day, for look how high the sun has got!"

Nkarani said, "Well, I think I still have my memory intact and so, if all you want are the names of those months, you will have them right now. So here are the names of Kikerewe months:[13] The first one is *Omuhangara*, and the following are the things seen during that month: rain accompanied by thunder and lighting falls during that month, often not without wounding of killing human beings and livestock, burning houses and splitting rocks. That too is the month in which big species of fish are caught in large numbers, in whole schools, especially *embozu, ensato* and *enkuyu*, which is also known as *enzegere*. Fish not caught in abundance during that month are the smaller kinds of fish, *eningu,* and *enembe* and the like. That is the month in which there is a lot of fog in the morning. In the olden days it was the time for grass-hoeing in preparation for planting *obubele*[14] millet. The second: *Omwiraguzu.* And what is seen during that month is the following: seaborne rain from pitch black clouds which originate from the Ukara Island side north of our island. And it is during that rain that really serious hoeing of crop fields takes place, when early planters sow every kind of grain, including the main food grain of *obubele*. The third: *Omwero gw'ilima*. Things seen during that month are the downpouring of rain and the continuing hoeing of the fields by each and every person, with the exception of the sick. The fourth: *Omuhingo*. What are seen in that month are the downpouring of rain, sometimes in intermittent very heavy downpours of foaming rain and at other times as light rain starting from cockcrow in the night and continuing to fall: *nzolinzoli!* that way until sunset, leaving cows mooing their fill in kraals or on tethering pegs, with the cattle owner who is moved by compassion for his lowing cattle and who is afraid his cows would die of hunger, knowing there would be no neighborhood herder on duty who will take the communal herd to the pastures that day, going to graze the cattle of his home alone in the rain, his *enkanga*[15] on his head. That's the month when, in the Mumbuga region of our island, tilapia fish of the best kind, *engonogono*, is caught in the *olubigo*[16] traps in countless numbers until the whole Mumbuga countryside is smelling of nothing but fish. That too is the time when in the evening *ebise*[17] crickets break out in their shrill cry with deafening intensity. The fifth: *Kaboza*. What is seen during that month is the daily falling of drizzling rain, of the type called 'girls-fun-rain', in which girls play while chanting: `Girls, it's raining, we are getting wet!' It is during that month also that the female Milky Way disappears from the sky and within a matter of days the male Milky Way appears. The sixth: *Omwiraguzu gw'echanda*.   What are seen during that month are the following: This is the month when the Milky-Way-Watchers of the Abakura clan are up on their watch-towers peering into the sky to see whether the galaxy can already be sighted, since sighting it is an important annual rite of theirs and they are the ones who tell people: `The Milky Way falls out of sight for fifteen days only before reappearing again.' That is the month when porcupines invade crops and take food into their holes in the ground where they live, storing people's crops for themselves before the farmers have yet to harvest! That too is the time when the cry of the white long-legged bird *entuletule* is most heard. The seventh month: *Omwero gw'echanda* or *Ikira lya Bukene*. What are seen during that month are the following: Water gets really cold, in the lake, wells and rivers and even in drinking-water pots, so that every time you drink water you feel as if your teeth want to fall out, because of water being so cold. That is the month in which harvesting and threshing of millet takes place and in which deep-sea fishermen catch *engere* fish in far off Mugabo.[18] Those too are the days of the stormy and fierce southerly *omulimbe* wind, which never lets down until it has capsized some seafarers. Were it not for the changing times of these recent years, you wouldn't fail to see all these things in that month. The eighth: *Bukene*. Because Kikerewe months sometimes run into each other, this month is often mistaken by many people for *Omutagato*, the warm month, when in fact it is Bukene, the cold month itself, and *Omutagato* is yet to come. And the things seen during that month are as follows: Sometimes there is to be seen a bit of fog and a rather overcast sky, from which sometimes rain may even fall, the rain people call `washer-of-the-threshing-stones.' That is the month the terrible easterly wind blows its worst. That too is the month the Abagere[19] fishermen bring their presents of pots of *engere* fish to *omukama* in Bukindo. It is also the month inveterate procrastinators finally thresh their millet harvests. The ninth:

Omutagato. What are seen in it are the following: People's bodies begin to feel warm, the cold of the month of Bukene leaves them. That month has, in addition, another name, which is the following: *Omuhunguru,*[20] the Shedding-of-tree-leaves, because it is during this month that many trees shed their leaves. It is also the month in which in our kingdom's mainland of Mwibara and in the forest zone of this island people set fire to grass and trees and during which the call for the hunting of wild animals is sounded. The tenth: *Ekimezo* or *Omumerezi,* the month of Germination. This is what is seen in it: The dry season rain begins to fall during that month, the rain which makes the burnt grass sprout and every kind of plant grow out of the earth and likewise the trees which had shed their leaves sprout new leaves. It is also during this month that an intelligent woman plants seeds of gourds for making calabash containers and sows seeds of other greens and plants whatever women crops she wants to plant without running the danger of black ants and other soil pests attacking her crops. The eleventh: *Kiswa,* Flying Termites month. What are seen in that month are the following: Rain of the start of the planting season falls. That's the start of cultivating ridges for sowing red millet. It is the time when men plant banana, and also the time the Wakara people from Ukara Island come to this Ukerewe looking for farm labor and till crop fields for the Wakerewe. *Kiswa* is also the time edible flying termites, *enswa,* from which the month gets its mane, and the other edible insect *amatondofwa,* fall. It is the time to start preparatory cultivation of fields for the main crops. The twelfth: *Olubingo*: What are seen are the following: Rain whose clouds gather in the east falls, but usually only in the afternoon, the rain people call `evening-guest'. It is rain usually accompanied by violent stormy winds of which the elder of yore said: `the evening-guest never blows twice', that is to say that the 'evening-guest' rain does not fall today and then fall again tomorrow. However, take it from me, that does sometimes happen, so don't count too much on that saying. It is during this month that some people sow early red millet, which then gets scorched by the sun of the *Omuhangara* month, for the sun of that month is a very hot sun: just make a point of being observant and you'll see what I mean! That rain of *Olubingo* is the rain whose lightning flashes in far off Buhekera country and the women of Ukerewe in the village of Musozi ran to bring into the safety of their homes their calves from the pastures where they were tethered, hence the saying you hear: `There it goes, that which flashed in Buhekera and in Musozi people struggled with their calves!' It is also during such rains that a

Mkerewe fisherman named Matulire of the Bayanza clan was in the far off land of Katoto fishing with his *amahumbi* [20] traps when his mother died and he received the message of her death: `Matulire, we have brought you news of bereavement, go and bury your mother, she has died,' and when he heard the heavens thunder forth: *drilili!* he answered the messenger and said: `Let her be, there are other men over there, they'll take good care of her!' And from that day on it became the saying of each and every Mkerewe, whenever he or she hears the sky of the `evening-guest' rain of the *Olubingo* month rumble around the sun: *drililili!* he or she speaks back to it and says: `There goes the rumble which prevented Matulire from burying his mother and made him say: there are other men over there, they will bury her!'

So there you have the Kikerewe months, my dear Mbaliro. Let's now get up and go home, oh, poor me! and leave alone the impossible disputes of these other men, if that's fine with you, Myombekere. And, in addition, in the whole year there are only four seasons, and so count groups of three months four times and you will get exactly twelve months in the entire year."

Mugimba said, "The months which Nkarani has narrated are just as he recounted them, because when my father was still alive he too used to narrate them to us that way as we sat at our courtyard fireplace."

With that Myombekere's visitors got ready to leave, but when Mbaliro tried to get up he exclaimed aloud: "*Aa!*"

The others asked him: "What is it?"

"Numbness has entered this leg of mine and so I feel as if I have *omulindi* cork tree log for a leg. What happened is when I tried to stand up I felt my leg dissolving beneath me and I simply couldn't lift it. Myombekere, come and give me some blows with your first on this foot; I can't stand firmly enough to beat it to life again on my own." Myombekere went and delivered him about three blows of his first on the foot and when he wanted to stop Mbaliro told him, "Go on, give it another three or four!" Myombekere dealt him another three strong blows on the foot and Mbaliro stopped his fourth blow before it landed and told him, "No, stop there, my dear friend, the numbness is gone, let me now try to stand up and see how it feels." He got up and walked limping as if he had stepped on a whole length of a thorn of the *omwongabutanga* thorn-tree and said, "Oh yes! my dear Myombekere, I can now see that numbness in the leg is a really manly enemy: if you get it when you have to run from a fierce wild animal you are as good as dead, indeed!"

"You are right, even without saying it."

Myombekere escorted the three men from his home. When he was about to return he said, "Let me go back, good friends; the dew has now dried in the grass and its time for me to go and plant my banana tubers I got yesterday evening from over there at Kanwaketa's, where we were drinking some banana beer."

"May be there's still some left?"

"May be, but I think it is most probably finished, he was so free-handed with it."

"Yes, I wouldn't be surprised if it was finished, because Kanwaketa is always over-generous with his banana beer, especially when he himself has taken a bit more than enough of it. Whatever the case his home is on our way, so let's pass-by and say hello to him and his people."

"Well, do so; who knows, you may , after all, even find he still has a bit of beer remaining, or again may be not. But you leave me a lonely man by breaking up such interesting conversation."

"Words are like saliva: they never dry up except the day you die."

"That's true though; yes, indeed!"

When Myombekere got back home, he first laughed alone in front of his wife Bugonoka before telling her, "Men with their incurable disputes, today two of the three men who were here, Mugimba and Nkarani, had broken into such an angry exchange of words it was bound to end up in a quarrel! It was by sheer luck that that didn't happen. In fact it was Mbaliro who saved the situation, who made them drop the subject and speak of something else by asking them a question about the months of the year, otherwise they were heading for a real quarrel, especially since Nkarani had already provoked Mugimba by throwing his stigma in his face by telling him: `You should realize that opium is doing you harm', and, as you too know, opium smokers never like to hear people revile them that way. *Aa*! And all that simply because the men would argue about anything, even the impossible! Didn't you, by the way, hear what they were arguing about?"

"*Aa*! Since I was hammering with *enkomanjo*[22] to reset the surface of my grinding-stone, I couldn't follow, I could only catch a word here and there, since I could not help hearing. It appeared to me that they first spoke of pregnancy. In fact pregnancy is the only thing I heard them talk about, poor me, lest I tell lies."

She was saying that only to poke the tail of the snake and discover where its head lay hidden and so, of course, her husband went into details and told her what their dispute was all about on the matter of pregnancy. When Bugonoka heard that, she uttered one loud exclamation: "*Yu!*" struck her thighs with her open hands and then said, "So that's it! Have these male creatures gone mad! If they are not mad, how dare they talk about such things, disgracing women in that shameful way! *Yu! aa!* Had I heard the creatures say what they said I would have insulted them there and then! You would think the monsters themselves are not married men, the way they carry on! *Aa!* I find them disgusting, I must admit."

"And what do you find disgusting in that? What is it that you don't know in all that?"

"Even if I know it, that doesn't mean I can talk about it in front of a gathering of people. *Aa! bee!* Myombekere! I should think that matters of a man and a woman are only meant for the two, and that's how it was meant to be, everything in its proper place. For that same reason I don't know matters of men, that is, even though I know them from being a married woman I cannot recount them to my fellow women that way; never! What would I possibly hope to gain by blabbing that way?"

"Well, you would be trying to inform them so that they too can know."

"Of such matter, oh poor me! Wouldn't that make me a shameless creature! Oh dear me, I better get up and peel my sweet potatoes and leave alone these incomprehensible males!"

"When a woman tells you the substitute name of her father-in-law[23] it is simply her way of telling you his real name; and since you are my wife let me be direct with you. Don't male healers treat your female bodies or deliver your babies when there is no midwife nearby? Or when a midwife fails, don't people ever fetch a male healer to deliver your babies, and that amidst a gathering of people, men and women?"

"Well, in such a situation, yes, because it is a matter of life and death, what else could they do?"

"That other matter too is similar, the two are in no way different."

They both fell silent.

Chapter XVI

NOTES

1.   The Names of the three men mean: Mugimba: Rain-maker; Mbaliro: Guessing; Nkarani: Noise-maker. See also list of names at the end of the translation.

2.   *Ekikome*: See note 1 of Chapter II.

3.   *Olusabuzyo*: See note 12 of Chapter I.

4.   *Obwita*: See note 14 of Chapter I.

5.   *Ekizanda*: See note 20 of Chapter II.

6.   *Buzimbe*: "Swelling", meaning "pregnancy", an allusion to a milk-cow.

7.   According to the Wakerewe's oral tradition, the Masai made two victorious cattle raids into Ukerewe Island and on the third raid the Wakerewe ambushed them, killed their leader and destroyed their force as they tried to retreat on foot through the then still shallow and fordable Lugezi (Ferry) canal, and put an end to their much feared raids for ever.

8.   *Ekilangi*: See note 7 of Chapter VII.

9.   *Omukama*: See note 26 of Chapter II. For the expression see note 8 of Chapter IV.

10.   From *kutura*: "To dwell (in the womb)".

11.   *Muyambi* (plural *Abayambi*): Member of people of foreign origin with the reputation of being too argumentative who lived for a long time in Ukerewe as guests of the ruling clan, the Abasilanga, until they attempted to pass for being members of the clan, so that when a Mkerewe was upbraided with being Omuyambi not only was he or she being accused of being too argumentative but also of being a Mkerewe of doubtful origin.

12.   The different regions of Ukerewe Kingdom. See Introduction.

13.   The names of the twelve lunar months of the year of the Wakerewe are: *Omuhangara*: January; *Omwiraguza:* February; *Omwero gw'ilima* ("Climax" of planting season): March; *Omuhingo*: April; *Kaboza* ("Interminable drizzle"): May; *Omwiraguzu gw'echanda* (*Omwiraguzu* of the dry season): June; *Omwero gw'echanda* ("Climax" of dry season) also called *Ikira lya Bukene* (Bukene's Tail): July; *Bukene*: ("The cold month"): August; *Omutagato* ("The warm month") or *Omuhunguru*: (Shedding-of-tree-leaves): September; *Ekimezo* also called *Omumerezi*: ("Germination" month): October; *Kiswa* ("Flying Termites" month): November; *Olubingo*: December.

14.   *Obubele*: See note 17 of Chapter V. Here Kitereza hints at his regret at seeing his people abandoning growing the more nutritious *obubele* millet in favor

of cassava.

15. *Enkanga*:   See note 18 of Chapter VII.

16. *Embigo,* plural for *olubigo*: See note 3 of Chapter II.

17. *Ebise* (singular *ekise*): Crickets.

18. Mugabo: An area in the middle of Lake Victoria on the west side of the lake far away form Ukerewe Island marked by stone pillars called *Oluti lwa Mugabo*, "Mugabo Pillar", which was the pass of schools of *engere* fish during the month of July, when for ages Wakerewe fishermen have annually sailed to place to catch *engere* in great quantities.

19. *Abagere*: Traditionally the fishermen who annually went out to distant Mugabo to catch the *engere* fish were exclusively the men of Ilangara, the part of Ukerewe Island facing the waters of Mugabo, who observed appropriate rites for the undertaking and who, like the other subjects of the king with specialized occupations, paid homage to their *omukama* by presenting him in his palace in Bukindo with loads of *engere* fish at the end of their one month fishing season.

20. *Omuhunguru*: "The moth in which trees shed leaves".

21. *Amahumbi*, another name for *emigono*, plural for *omugono*: See note 6 of Chapter II.

22. *Enkomanjo*: Very hard round stone used as a hammer for redenting the surface of a grinding-stone to reset its sharpness when it becomes too smooth to grind grain properly.

23. Wakerewe daughters-in-law were forbidden by custom to pronounce the names of the parents or elders of their husbands or use words which included or sounded like those names and instead used substitute vocabulary called *ensindo*, from *kusinda*, "to speak by substitutes", so that there is in Kikerewe a parallel vocabulary for a lot of words which is used only by women and only if required but which everybody knows. Breaking that name-calling prohibition was called *kutogola* and regarded very serious disrespect for the husband and his relatives on the part of the guilty woman, for which offense she would be expelled from her home until she brought from her people to her husband's home a basket of flour or its equivalent as appeasement. To discourage married women from taking the transgression lightly, the offending woman was punished together with all the other wives of her husband, if he had more than one, and all the women in the home and in the neighborhood married to her husband's extended family "brothers". See notes 20 of Chapter X and 33 of Chapter XXV for examples of *kusinda*.

Chapter XVII

CHARMING MILLET CROPS AGAINST BIRDS

It was raining daily at that time of the year, at times in foaming downpours and at others in never-ending drizzles, but that did not prevent those who were guarding their *obubele*[1] millet crop against birds from making their way through the rain to their crop fields, some wearing *enkanga*[2] on their heads and those who did not have *enkanga* protecting themselves from the rain as best as they could by old skins and hides, rags of former bed sheet skins already worn clean of their hair and torn and shredded beyond being of any other use. It was a year of unusually large swarms of grain-eating birds, from *ensole* to *enzeli*, and people had to really keep watch over their millet lest they lost it all to birds and harvested nothing. Since people never all sow at the same time, in some fields ears of millet were beginning to sprout a bit of grain while in others the crop was still even younger when a swarm of grain-eating birds descended on the crop from I don't know where! As you passed by each and every *obubele* millet field you scared off a whole army of birds of every kind, from *ensole* to *enzeli*, so huge a crowd that a person in a home nearby would hear them as they flew rumble through the air with a rolling din like pre-dawn rain and thunderstorm approaching from the sea.

People were finally overwhelmed by the task of guarding their crops against that army of birds and that in the midst of such rains, in which they stood shaking from cold the whole day long, and heads of households turned to the headman [3] of their village and said, "No, headman, save us, find us a bird charmer to cure our fields of birds lest we end up having tilled our lands for nothing, our entire crop lost to birds!"

As you would expect, the village headman could not but agree with his people, so that may be the only unexpected thing he can be said to have told them was: "Go and tell your children to tap the gum of *emibira* trees and use it to trap these grain-eating birds, like *ensole* or *enzeli*. Even if they catch only one of each kind that will do. Only you must remember this: don't bring dead ones. You have to tell your children to bring you live birds, because it is to those live birds the healer will give his medicine to drink. From our experience, that's how things are done. You can go now, to continue keeping watch over your millet and to look for the two charm items the healer who will come to cure our fields of this bird plague is bound to need. On my part, I too have no intention of waiting for tomorrow or I don't know which other day but will go to inform the medicine man on this very day, so that if he decides to come tomorrow or the day after tomorrow he'll let us know."

The men present thanked their village headman and said, "What you say is great, our village headman, and we too are in total agreement with you," and went back to their field watch-towers and to tell their children to trap the birds, some with gum and others with *ebitanda*4 bird-traps, as their headman got on his way to summon the bird healer.

In the evening, as the sun was about to disappear from the sky, a son of Kanwaketa caught *ensole* by his *ekitanda* bird-trap. Before the sun had completely disappeared from the sky, Kanwaketa and Myombekere took to the village headman that *ensole* bird which had been caught in a noose of the hair of a cow's tail on the boy's trap. They found the village headman already come back from summoning the bird healer, whose name was somebody, yes, Kahwerera. The village headman was surrounded by a lot of people, too many to count! However none of all those people had come with as much as single bird, and so when that *ensole* was brought and shown to him, he thanked Kanwaketa and Myombekere a lot and said: "Here are some men, real men who attack a job they have to do at once and do it and finish it that same day as men should do!"

Some of the other men present responded to the headman: "We too, headman, shouldn't be deemed unworthy. Our children too did set bird traps. Their only setback was that in these sunless rainy days their gum could not dry and set, but otherwise they did their job. It is not easy in the midst of such rains to make gum which is strong enough. If it shines and warms up they are capable of doing a bit better."

Another man took up the man who said that: "Why do you say: `they are capable of doing a bit better' when you should say: `they will make the right gum for trapping birds'! Don't we see them daily tap *emibira* sap when it is shinning and made real gum, gum you touch and say: `Here is gum on which a bird has just to land and it is trapped for sure?' and you want to tell us your stories as if we have never trapped birds with gum since we were born! Come on, man!"

And since a speaker is always unaware of whatever is amiss with what he or she says when others see it all too clearly, that first speaker, who thought he had said something really worthwhile before a gathering of fellow men, became the first person to go back on his words and say: "But that's what I too said, gentlemen!"

The others noisily fell on him, unsparingly, and told him, "You first said something different and all of us here heard you and now you want to bend things around, *aa! hee!* goodness!"

At once the village headman stopped them: "Please drop that, let it be carried away by the wind. Listen, and let me tell you how I went to see our bird healer, Kahwerera, the son of Mbali. Well, I went, and found him at home. We greeted each other and I stayed and chatted with him for a bit and then unloaded on him the heavy matter which had sent me there, which all of you men gathered here know, adding a bit of urgency in my request: `Please hurry to our rescue tomorrow!' And if you think I am telling lies, here is, what's his name again? Yes, Mafwere, with whom I went to the healer's home."

The said Mafwere joined in: "*Aa!* That's it, headman, that's what you told him."

The village headman took up again what he was saying: "When I told him about coming tomorrow he asked me, `By the way, those birds which are finishing your millet, what species of birds are they?' We answered him back quickly, my companion Mafwere and I saying together, `They are mostly *ensole* and *enzeli*.' At which he on his part said, `And you are telling me to come tomorrow, how can I do that when I have yet to collect my medicine! And, by the way, have you caught those birds, one *ensole* and one *enzeli*?' We said, `No,' and he rejoined: `You see, what did I tell you! Anyway, you can go back now. On my part tomorrow is when early in the morning I will go to procure bird medicine. When it gets to mid-morning, send somebody to come and fetch me. Otherwise, poor Kahwerera, why should I refuse to come to your aid when the medicine is not mine but belongs to my father Mbali and my grandfather Kazoka? For this medicine is not something stolen from somewhere, it is the heritage of my paternal family. Just as my grandfather and my father used to heal bird plagues, so will I come to heal your crops of birds. But I want to tell you this: When I come with my medicines, in the home you will take me to stay all the men in that homestead have to sleep with light arms, none of them is to play mischief with his wife at night.' That's what we have come back with, gentlemen. Did you hear it?"

"We have heard it, headman; if there is someone who didn't hear it then he's not here. Only we are still faced with one problem: how to catch *enzeli*."

The village headman said: "Indeed this *enzeli* has become a really big issue! God willing it should not rain tomorrow."

"May those be propitious words, son of kings,5 because your people our sovereigns are the makers of rain. Yes, it shouldn't rain so that we can make gum strong enough to trap *enzeli*."

In that very instant the headman picked the man who would go to fetch Kahwerera and said, "The person I have selected to go and fetch Kahwerera is Kanwaketa, and it is in his home too that the healer will be received when he comes to our village. Here in my home I will contribute one goat as relish for the healer and the people who will be accompanying him. And all of you the men of my village remember to tell your wives to take flour and sweet potatoes to Kanwaketa's home as food for our coming guests."

The men said good-bye to their village headman and got up to return to their homes and the village headman on his part went to put away the one medicine bird which had already been found.

So the following day people got busy trying to catch the *enzeli* bird. Before long the son of Mafwere too caught a bird, none other than the little bird *enzeli*, on his gum-trap and took it to village headman and the latter kept it. And indeed on that day no rain fell. And at the mid-morning sun, Kanwaketa, accompanied by Myombekere, passed by the headman's home before the two neighbors went to fetch Kahwerera.

The medicine man had already returned from collecting from the woods the medicines he needed to cure their millet crops of the bird plague when they arrived in his home and told him that their village headman had sent them to fetch him and that he would stay in Kanwaketa's home. The medicine man agreed and said, "Wait for me here for a while, I am coming.

I've got to fetch two companions of mine who live nearby here, my associates who accompany me whenever I go on such an errand."

He came back with his two associates and then went here and there in that home of his looking for a big piece of a broken pot on which to put his medicines, then he wrapped some other medicine in a green banana leaf and put it on top of the medicines he had put on the potsherd. That done, he quickly plunged into his house again, to look for his healer's dress, the skin rags healers wear across their shoulders when addressing their ancestors and the unseen powers or administering treatment to patients. His was of goat skin and he always kept it on a kitchen utensils rack. In no time he came out dressed for business: around his waist he had tied two goat skins, one in front and the second one behind over his buttocks. As to his healer's rag proper, he had it on already in its place across his shoulders, attached with a string over his right hand shoulder and worn with the head of the skin underneath the armpit of his left arm and meat-side to his body and hair-side out. When the men were ready to leave, Kahwerera's wife brought them food and they ate. Then Kahwerera went into his house once more and after a while came out with his walking stick in his hands and said, "Let's go, good people."

They all got up, the healer's two attendants carrying the medicines, one carrying the medicine on the piece of a broken pot and the other one the medicine wrapped in a green banana leaf, and got on their way. When they neared their village headman's home, Kanwaketa and Myombekere were about to take the healer to the headman's first when he said, "No, it is taboo for my medicines to be taken to any other home except the very home in which I am to be received and in which I will prepare my cure," and so Kanwaketa turned into another direction and into the way leading directly to his home.

On arriving in Kanwaketa's home, Kahwerera instructed his attendants to straightway place his medicines underneath a grain store.[6]

At once Kanwaketa took off to go and inform the village headman that he was back from where he had sent him and that he came with the medicine man, whom he left at that very moment resting in his home in the company of Myombekere. On hearing that the village headman told a son of his to bring from where his goats were grazing a goat as relish for the healer. His son run as if he were flying to bring the goat at the same time as the headman sent another son of his to summon people to take food for the medicine man to Kanwaketa's home. In no time the youth the village headman sent to bring a goat came back, carrying it on his shoulders, a rather big gray he-goat, and put it down. The village headman told Kanwaketa, "Take this relish, here it is. Slaughter it soon as you get home. The other things we will get together by and by. As to myself, I will come over there in the evening with the needed birds. Please give my greetings to the healer."

"I will."

Kanwaketa carried the goat and got on the way to his home. The goat, which he carried on his shoulder, was urinating on him throughout the way so that by the time he got home and put it down he was already all wet and messed up, in addition to exuding the stench of he-goat urine. He tethered it at *ilumba* tree in the compound of his home and left it there crying and at once went to Kahwerera and presented him with the goat by saying to the healer, "Welcome, here is you relish. It is being given to you by our headman, who, in addition, sends you his greetings. He too will be here in the evening, to greet you and to bring the accompaniments of your medicines."

Kahwerera answered him back, "Praises to him; this is very kind of him."

As soon as Kanwaketa said the goat was for slaughtering the medicine man's two attendants asked the medicine man for his sword-like knife: "Could you give us your mighty sword, master, so that we can lay this goat down over grass and slaughter it." The two men slaughtered the goat and skinned it and then called Kahwerera and told him, "We have finished, master," and he answered: "First remove this arm and this leg before going back to this arm, and then cut its stomach open, so that we can see how fat it is," and they did as their leader instructed them. On cutting open the goat's stomach they found its stomach membrane was as white as ash with fat and all present exclaimed their appreciation and said: "This goat is sweet beyond compare!" When the two men finished removing the entrails and the men present ate some raw meat seasoned with bile, the medicine man took one arm of the goat and gave it to Myombekere while adding, "Let me add to it a bit of entrails, lest you look like you are carrying the meat of a wild pig whose entrails people don't eat. And so, here is meat, friend, for your wife to put into hot water for you, please!"

Myombekere thanked him and said: "This is great, this is indeed rarely seen!" before taking leave of all present: "Stay in peace; we'll see each other later," and those he left behind answered, "All right." He got on his way to his home, the arm of goat meat he had been given dangling from his hands, he lifting it up time and time again   after walking from here to there, to take a good look at it, again and again until he finally got home and called his wife Bugonoka and said, "Come and receive these visitors."

Inside the house Bugonoka got up and maneuvered and moved her heavy body, only to come outside and find her husband all alone, not a single visitor in sight. She asked him, "Where did the visitor you told me to come and receive go?"

"Don't you see me, the way I am loaded?"

"I see! Yes indeed. And where did you get this reward for your venturing out?"

"In the homes of people. It appears our village headman has given relish to the healer of birds we had gone to fetch. I've just left him at Kanwaketa's, where the village headman has put him to stay, for how long, I don't know! And, by the way, I understand you should take food to him and his companions, that's what the headman said."

"That's right. In fact a son of his has been here to inform us and he told me, `Please take food to the healer of birds, he is at Kanwaketa's.'  I then asked him: `What kind of food are we supposed to send?' but he answered me when he was already walking away and since there was a wind blowing I didn't catch well what he said. He said I don't know what and what, I don't know!"

Bugonoka took some flour to Kanwaketa's home, where she found other women had already brought a lot of flour, and those who had brought sweet potatoes and bananas and cassavas too had brought heaps and heaps of food. On her part Bugonoka, since she had never seen the medicine man, asked Kanwaketa's wife, "And where is our healer himself, my friend?"

"It appears he went out for a while with his two companions and Kanwaketa; where too, I don't know! May be they have gone to Lumezya's home, where, so I understand, there is some banana beer."

"That could be, yes. May be that's where they went then, since men will even risk their lives for beer, and it's no joke! Let me start back and go to cook other people's meat lest it ends up half cooked and Myombekere eats while struggling to bite through and gives me a beating I could have avoided, poor me! But all the same I would have liked to see this medicine man who has come here, because I too would have liked to look at him with my own eyes, since people from all over and even from very far away have apparently seen him before me who lives next door to where he is putting up. Oh, what wretched luck I have!" And then as she tried to stand up his companions heard her cry out loud: "*Yu!* my leg!" And indeed she went back to the ground and sat down again. At that her fellow women laughed at her and asked her, "And where does that leg of yours pain you, dear?"

"It is a flashing pain which shot through my hip here, my dear, momentarily but really sharply and no joke!"

"And have you been feeling the pain for quite some time?"

"No, it has just started today, this very moment here in this house. When I tried to get up just now is when for the first time I felt it shoot through this hip like lightning: *myee!* and if I had been carrying something I would have fallen down."

Her women companions laughed. Kanwaketa's mother, Nanzala, asked them, "And so you find that to be laughing matter! Do you take her for a liar or may be you think she is putting on a show?"

"How can we take her for a liar? *Aa!* All we are saying is that may be it is a stomach worm which has outshot her in the leg, that's all. But we certainly didn't laugh at her thinking she is pretending, no. How can such an adult woman just pretend!"

Only then did Nanzala explain to the other women why Bugonoka had felt that way: "From what I can see Bugonoka has caught the disease of pregnant women people call *itango*, because that is how that disease shoots pain through the body causing a pregnant woman a lot of suffering. If it strikes when she is carrying a pot of water, she is bound to fall down before she knows it, leaving her pot or whatever else she might be carrying go smashing to smithereens on the other side. She simply wouldn't remember to save it, for *itango* is so painful."

They were still thus engaged with discussing Bugonoka's disease when they saw Kahwerera and his companions coming. On seeing him the women, from inside the house where they were seated, began beckoning each other and pointing him out in whispers and saying, "There goes Kahwerera, that is the medicine man! *Aa!* He is some real man, I must admit, as far as body build goes."

Nanzala said, "As far as bird plague is concerned, he does not simply cure it, he gives it a real thrashing. And no need to be surprised, my children, because it is his family's medicine, his heritage from his father and grandfather, and not medicine acquired from other people; no. As a matter of fact I saw a bit of his father, and knew him very well too, a very handsome man, with whom I danced quite a bit *someke* and *make* dance.7

I was a divorced maiden-wed woman[8] and he had just maiden-wed[9] the mother of this very man, but before he was born. And, as sure as you see me here, I could not but have my share of fun with him under the cover of bushes. Finally he courted me and I too accepted him and said to myself: `Yes, such a man should marry you!' The man's name was Mbali, and his father, whose name was Kazoka, was still living. And the father of this Kahwerera was a very handsome man, and big and tall, *aa*! When you saw him you said: `Oh yes! This is *Mbali*[10] indeed, male Cunning in person!'

Hearing that her daughter-in-law, Kanwaketa's wife, asked her: "And why didn't he marry you, mother-in-law?"

"At that time I too was still a real Nanzala, desired by many men and I too loving many men. When your father-in-law, Kanwaketa's father, saw me, in those same dances of ours, and talked to me his sweet words, which I accepted, we eloped and he took me to his maternal uncles. There we stayed as long as this number of months, two, quietly hiding out there together. Meanwhile on their part the relatives of my husband-to-be had gone to my parents' home some four times, and when they went there the fifth time my parents gave in and told them, 'You can go and brew for us twelve pots of banana beer, with one more pot, the thirteenth, as her mother's appeasement *obukanza*.[11] We won't be taking any bride-price from you, because our daughter has despised us. And you should tell that son-in-law of ours too to come here with his wife, in spite of everything, so that we too can know him, lest he should one day without knowing it beat us over some quarrel when he is our in-law.'

"It was then, as you would imagine, that we came out of hiding and my husband-to-be took me to my parents' home. In the meanwhile, without knowing it, I was already pregnant for a month, having conceived during that elopement of mine my first born child, the one who was caught and killed by *Kalazya*[12] the crocodile in the lake, where he had gone to water cows during his tour of herding duty for their neighborhood, already grown up and a married man.

"As it happened, at my parents' home things went smoothly for us: I wasn't as much as beaten. If anything, I only heard my father remark to his son-in-law-to-be and say, `What else can we do after the two of you have decided you are good for each other? All there is on our part is that we want to eat. And so go and bring us the banana beer we have mentioned and that's all. As to that wife of yours, if she listens to what we say and does not want to continue despising us, that one remains here until you bring that beer. Do you understand?'

" I saw my husband really cheer up and say: `Your honor, Sir, my father-in-law, and you too, my brothers-in-law, please give me the foundation of a home, be parents to me the way people become parents-in-law of fellow human beings.' And when he brought the requested beer I was wedded to him." And then old Nanzala added the following for the benefit of her listeners: "Now listen, you children! When you see a falcon after it has been rained on and is all wet and shriveled don't say: `There is no way that bird can prey on other birds!' and don't look at me now with all my teeth gone and say: `There is no way she can ever have chewed raw cassava since she was born!'" and those womenfolk let loose the loudest of laughter and with that concluded their palaver, each one of them getting up to go to her home and Bugonoka too braced herself to get up. Just as she got up, again a flash of pain went through her hip and again she cried out in pain: "*Yu!* my mother, this leg is killing me!" She finally stood up and limped on until she came outside, where she greeted all the men she had not come across that day and finished. Her husband's friend Kanwaketa poked a joke at her: "Today you seem to have overdone it in bending doubled with that hilarious laughter and ended up with paralysis, or is it just numbness?"

"Please don't say that, my dear Kanwaketa! What's more, may be it is you who has bewitched me, because it is while in your house that I caught this *itango*, which you now want to be paralysis and numbness. However, have a good night, and your visitors too."

"All right, you too go and sleep well."

"All right."

"Did you leave Myombekere at home, or did he just pass through and disappear again when he got back?"

"Listen to what that incorrigible joker is saying! *Aa!* Where would he be going to just pass through his home! I left him going to guard our millet against the birds as I came here, and may be at this time he too is about to come back home. Do you happen to want him?"

"Yes, I do. Tell him when he comes back to come and keep us company."

"All right. Do you perhaps have a bit of banana beer, Kanwaketa, in which case I should come back for a taste before I go?"

"You must be laughing at me! Poor me! From where can I get a bit of banana beer? Would my hair be so red and my mouth so dry if I had some banana beer!"

"From where can you get it? If that isn't a banana plantation, what is it then?"

"And what if there are no bananas in the plantation, can I press beer out of banana leaves or stems?"

"Let me leave you alone, poor me, you are impossible, lest I stay here until sunset, since with you the sun has just risen." And she left and limped on with her pain-stricken leg.

She got home as Myombekere too was arriving back and he told her, "What a swarm of birds today! These are not normal birds, they are something else! And they were not attacking millet the usual way either, today they ate the crop in a kind of frenzy! *Hee!* I found the children already dying from pain in their legs, for today it was simply impossible to sit down at all, they were up with slings in their arms all the time. There is especially *enzeli*, those birds are simply deaf to the noise of slings, nothing short of going over and actually shaking the ear of millet on which they are feeding will drive them away! Not even the explosions people make frighten them in the least!"

Then Bugonoka told him what had happened to her, how she had developed pain in the leg, which apparently was *itango* disease, and also informed him Kanwaketa wanted him over at his home for company.

Myombekere went to Kanwaketa's and found the medicine man seated in the company of his attendants while Kanwaketa was splitting firewood nearby. He had been there only for short a while when who should come into the home but the village headman, accompanied by a son of his and Mafwere, the latter carrying a pot of banana beer. When Kanwaketa saw them, he threw down his ax and took off quickly to meet them on the way and relieve them of what they were bringing. After people had exchanged greetings, the headman showed Kahwerera the birds they had caught. The medicine man examined the birds and examined them again and finally told the headman: "Now that we have obtained these requirements, our tasks are completed. And, truly, you should stop worrying and fearing that perhaps the birds will destroying your millet crop. Just forget that. Anyway, it will soon be the dawn of another day like this one and you will see for yourselves."

The village headman retorted: "Those are the words we want to hear, my dear Kahwerera. All we are asking for is for the Sun[13] to show you the way so that you can rid us of this plague, that's all."

"However, tomorrow your people will not hoe the fields, because hoeing the fields will break my charm on the birds. They will refrain from hoeing for only three days. Look here, let me count for you: their abstention is for tomorrow, the day after tomorrow and on the day after the day after tomorrow. Then on the day following that those who want to till the land can just go ahead and hoe, because there is no prohibition on that fourth day, which is the day on which I too will go back home. And, starting tomorrow, those on top bird watch platforms and watch-towers in the millet crops shouldn't shout and make noise to frighten away birds anymore, because that too would be breaking a prohibition. Frightening away birds too can break my spell on them. Did you, by the way, inform the people of all this, as I told you to do?"

"I did so since yesterday, and today too I have sent my foremen to every division of my village. Should there be any problem, that will be only because it is sometimes impossible to get everybody to listen, but, on my part, inform the people I did."

The village headman then told Kanwaketa to fetch the pot of banana beer he and his companions had brought and to put away in the house the two medicine birds, *ensole* and *enzeli*. The pot of beer was brought and the headman presented it to Kahwerera: "Please welcome, healer, here is some beer so that you and your companions can have something to drink. The woman without buttocks also undresses.[14] It is true it doesn't taste strong enough and it is barely drinkable, but it is banana beer you can feel in your body all right, and if you drink it like a man you can even get it to work a bit in you. Whatever the case, dear friend, that is the best I could do, and you can't know how bad or good food is unless you taste it."

"Praises to you, headman. What comes from a generous hand can only be good."

They drank the banana beer until they finished it. That day the village headman too stayed and dined in that home of Kanwaketa. Finally everybody left to go home. The headman left walking rather staggeringly, but still remembering everything Kahwerera said. That's why he had to pass by the home of a foreman of his and tell him that the following day early in the morning he should go and tell one of his fellow foremen to go with him in that early morning to the bird healer at Kanwaketa's, because they had an assignment to carry out, that of helping the medicine man take away hoes from people, should there be any found hoeing the fields. Secondly, they were needed to be with the medicine man all the time since the healer as well as his attendants who would be carrying his medicines wouldn't utter a single word while at their work, for a healer who is administering any cure whatsoever which involves what is called casting a spell never utters a word before completing his or her task. That's why our ancestors said: 'People are dead silent in the house as if they are casting a spell on hogs or birds!' And so the village headman had to send two foremen to assist the medicine man.

The following day early in the morning the medicine man was already busy attending to the task he had come to perform. The village headman's two foremen had both arrived well before sunrise. The healer's attendants too were up and about their task and in no time they had fetched embers and put them on the big piece of a broken pot they had come with the previous day. Then Kahwerera put medicine on the piece of broken pottery and spoke aloud to the elements while still in Kanwaketa's home and said: "To you the Sun, may this treatment of mine here today succeed and be good to me as it has always been whenever I performed it, giving a thrashing to the birds in all the parts of the land I have gone to heal! *Aa*! Let no other healer out of envy or malice dare step in the way of my success! And since this medicine belongs to my people, to my grandfather Kazoka, to my father Mbali, so let them lead the way for this son of theirs here, Kahwerera, so that this day he can rise up high with the falcon, Crusher-of-heads-of-birds, and win this war quickly."

When he finished addressing the elements thus, he took the two birds and made both of them drink some of his medicine. Then his two attendants took the healer's medicines and the three men, the healer himself included, fell completely silent and began communicating with each other only by beckoning and signaling with their hands and started out towards the crop fields.

In the meanwhile smoke was already coming out of the potsherd, now placed on the head of one of the two carriers of the healer's medicine, in thick clouds as if from an courtyard fireplace, incredible to behold! When they went past one millet crop field, the healer sprayed with his mouth the birds he had already drugged with some of that medicine he was holding in his mouth and then released them and they flew away. Then he sprayed all around him with his hands yet another medicine, the one for calling forth the Crushers-of-heads-of birds, the falcons.

When it was finally time, when the sun too had began shining clear and bright, that's when those who were on bird watch-towers in areas he had passed through saw a whole army of falcons, countless in number, relentlessly catch grain-eating birds in the air and the millet-eating birds die until they cried out and repented: "Why did we have to eat people's millet, the wretches we are! Where did what is befalling us come from?"

And so Kahwerera walked on, through the length and breath of the village, until he had finally covered it all, and during all that time the falcons carried on their job relentlessly. And since it is impossible to always have everybody in the community listen and obey, the headman's foremen that day confiscated hoes in numbers beyond belief! Even the wife of Mafwere was among the offenders, and yet it was her very own husband who accompanied the headman on the day they went to call on the healer for help. And, look at this, it was that very husband of hers who the previous night came to Kanwaketa's home with the village headman sweating under the weight of the pot of banana beer he was carrying, the beer they were bringing as a present for the bird healer Kahwerera! Can you believe it!

The medicine man finally completed going around the fields of the millet and came to a certain place and put down the ashes of his medicine and he and his companions started back home with their booty of a large number of hoes. It was not until they were completely out of the millet crop fields that he started speaking again and said, "Did you see or didn't you see?"

The headman's foremen answered: "You are simply beyond words! We have heard people speak of all sorts of medicine men but all those compared to you would simply have to surrender! What else can they do? Can they dare challenge the like of what we have witnessed! *Aa*! no!"

At Kanwaketa's the healer and his companions found the headman too had just arrived from taking a fish collection for their relish and they exchanged greetings. After that the two village foremen handed over to the headman the hoes they had confiscated from the offending people as the culprits themselves on their part began pouring into Kanwaketa's home to try and redeem their hoes. Those who had five hoes to redeem would come with a he-goat as ransom and some would bring a brand new Wanzinza[15] hoe as ransom for their other hoes. Many too had no ransom for their hoes but promise to find it, and some failed to do so and their hoes stayed for ever at Kanwaketa's waiting to be redeemed. But most of the confiscated hoes were neither ransomed nor did their owners promise to ransom them and were simply bundled together outright and given to the healer to take to his home.

The following day Kahwerera treated the fields the second time, and on the third day he did so again for the last time. That's when everybody recognized him for the real medicine man he was: because birds did not eat people's millet any more! Not at all. That's when each and everyone said: "Kahwerera the son of Mbali gave the birds a really good thrashing!"

After they harvested their bumper crop of millet, the village headman summoned all the people of his village and they all brought a collection of millet to his home, without a single person failing to do so. On his side Kahwerera, when he felt it was time, came to the headman's home to take his millet and found a whole grain store full of millet to the top waiting for him, out of which he took one large wicker basket of millet for the village headman and gave another basketful to the two foremen of the village headman for the two men to share.

Chapter XVII

NOTES

1.   *Obubele*: See note 17 of Chapter V.
2.   *Enkanga*: See note 18 of Chapter VII.
3.   *Omukungu*: See note 3 of Chapter III.
4.   *Ebitanda (ekitanda* singular): Bird traps consisting of nooses made of the hair of a cow's tail attached to a circular wooden frame.
5.   Many of the village headmen were princes. See Introduction and note 3 of Chapter III.
6.   *Ekitala*: See note 18 of Chapter I.
7.   In his Swahili translation Kitereza says of "*someke* and *make*" dance: "Dance of yore for adults, a wonderful dance indeed!"
8.   See note 5 of Chapter XIV.
9.   See note 2 of Chapter I.
10.   Mbali: Name (male) meaning "cunning".
11.   *Obukanza*: See note 16 of Chapter VII.
12.   *Kalazya*: "The extinguisher (of life)", fearful nickname for a crocodile. The Wakerewe feared that when people were caught by crocodiles it was often at the command of witches and witch doctors in   whose service those crocodiles were, and because of such fear they tended to allude to those creatures of their lake by   masked names, another one of which is "the monster apparition" we come across in Chapter XXX.
13.   *Izoba:* See note 21 of Chapter II.
14.   To the Wakerewe full and well-rounded buttocks are a highly appreciated feature of feminine beauty.
15   Wazinza hoe: See note 18 of Chapter V.

Chapter XVIII

BUGONOKA IN LABOR

The month of March became the seventh month since Bugonoka conceived. Now her stomach became a real balloon: the skin of a goat which formerly used to go around her body completely now could hardly cover the mere top of her stomach. All her flesh had deserted wherever else it should normally be and converged on her stomach, which looked round like a ball and swollen to bursting like that of the tiny toad *naturundubwi*,[1] and that fatness which people had been remarking in her had simply disappeared. And in that seventh month of her pregnancy the human being inside her began to play to such an extent that anybody near her could see it playing.

It was also in that month that she developed pain in her back, which caused her so much suffering that some people thought: "May be her time for delivery has almost arrived." Since, as you know, people will always concern themselves with other people's affairs like they were some business of theirs, to them she had been pregnant for long enough, even though she was actually only in her seventh month. But whenever her fellow women, those who are as ignorant of such matters as I am, asked her: "Dear, why don't you tell us the truth, if the time has come, so that we can call for you those who are no strangers to such matters?" she denied it. But still they would insist: "It is because she has never experienced normal child birth, that's why she can't keep good count of her days." And indeed had that pain she felt in her back at one particular time continued to torture her for let's say three more days, Myombekere would have invaded his mother-in-law's home looking for her to come to her daughter, because he had almost done so. Fortunately the pain lasted for two days only. What's more Bugonoka herself had been allaying her husband's fears by assuring him that her delivery time was still months ahead. But left alone, especially since he was Ndagabwene, Mr. I've-seen-it-before,[2] he had become so worried that he was thinking of calling their healer and his mother-in-law and nothing else. Finally that pain in her back stopped and Bugonoka became her normal self again. She could now feel the thing inside her playing so vigorously that when the couple were in bed and her husband put his hand on her stomach he too could feel it playing.

When the moon of the month of April appeared and people played *enzamba*[3] flutes for it, it became the eighth month of Bugonoka's pregnancy. The couple then had nothing left but to hope and say to themselves: "Now when this new moon which has appeared becomes full moon and disappears into darkness we will say: `This pregnancy has now seen eight months appear from the sea and go by since it was conceived. Let's now wait and see what the Sun[4] wills for us. Should it will Give-her, so will we get, and should our lot be Take-away-from-her, again that's what will befall us and then we'll say: The way we began is the way we'll end. We'll no more hope and say: May be in the days to come we too will get something, however little, so that we too can become human beings like other people who see their own selves come from inside their bodies. That hope for us will have died completely!'"

The wife of Myombekere in that eighth month of her pregnancy began to feel the thing play with redoubled vigor and without pause inside her stomach, which had so ballooned out that it had given her *ekiriga*[5] bent in her lower back, a feature she was not created with, and made her walk by shuffling along and looking as if she was about to break and fall backwards. During those days if a friend was sitting with Bugonoka chatting and Bugonoka was lying down reclined on one hand, that friend of hers could see from time to time something bulge on the upper side of her stomach and then disappear, a bit like what you sometimes feel happening inside your stomach when there are worms swimming in there and troubling you and they push tight against your stomach and then withdraw. And if you have never had stomachache caused by such swimming worms, ask somebody who has and he or she will explain to you what I mean. During the beginning of that eighth month of her pregnancy, before many days had passed since the new moon appeared, Bugonoka fell sick and Myombekere became really worried and said to himself, "What I am to do today, the miserable wretch I am? This sickness intends no good: if it does not kill the mother and the baby, still she will miscarry! What kind of sickness is this which doesn't give her a moment of rest?" Bugonoka too no longer knew what to think in the face of such ceaseless pain in her stomach. And finally one day she had to tell her husband, "You know, my dear Myombekere, there is something I don't understand!"

"What is it you don't understand?"

"I feel pain in the stomach all the time."

"Let me come; let me first go out and relieve myself and then come and listen carefully to what you are saying, because your words have troubled me."

And out her husband went and was gone for quite a while and then there he was, back accompanied by Kanwaketa's wife and Nanzala, Kanwaketa's mother, who was an old woman who knew herbs and a midwife who had helped many mothers, including those who came to her after their condition had become really bad, and delivered their babies safely. The old woman looked at her and then touched her on the stomach, as if feeling her, with her two hands, then felt her in her lower back, after which she asked the couple, "In your view, what kind of disease do you think this is?"

"We have no idea, and think that may be it is just a disease, which she has just caught. And we also think that may be her moment has come, since, as you know, dear Nanzala, that is something of which we have no personal experience. We are a lonesome couple, as you see!"

"I personally didn't see any disease here. It's true you have decided to call it a disease, but I have to be open with you and tell you what I have personally found: she is experiencing false labor and her delivery month is by no means due. No, it isn't! This is her eighth month, lest you are mistaken, my children." After Nanzala said that, she got up, and so did Kanwaketa's wife, and the two women said good-day to the couple and left. Then in the evening they came back, accompanied by Kanwaketa himself, whom Myombekere had not found at home when he went to call Nanzala, since people usually never stay put at home but are forever busy here and there and everywhere. When they arrived the old woman again examined Bugonoka and felt her as she did the first time and then asked her, "What do you actually feel inside you at this moment?"

"At this particular moment I feel the thing inside me playing about normally as it used to do."

"For now be calm and don't worry! Let's see how things will be tomorrow."

The following morning their neighbors came to see the couple again, and found Bugonoka already completely recovered, except perhaps for her body aches of a pregnant woman, for even though our elders of yore likened pregnancy to a robe and said: "Pregnancy is like a robe a woman wears," the truth is that when you compare a woman who is pregnant to one who isn't and observe the two of them you can in no way say they are equal; not at all: because the pregnant woman has no freedom of movement while the woman who is not pregnant is quick in all she does, since she has nothing in her that is weighing her down. Nanzala then told the couple, "What do you say now! Didn't I tell you that Bugonoka was experiencing false labor and nothing more, that she had no other sickness whatsoever? And, by the way, when we said good-bye to you and went away yesterday evening, what else happened after we left?"

Myombekere was the first to reply and said, "*Aa*! What else could possibly have happened? We just kept on bewailing our lot, likening our plight to that of a mourner who cries out: `You take away from the poor of the poorest.'"

Bugonoka put in: "To say the truth, he said a few other things too. When he heard me coughing in our bedroom there where I was from by the door here where he was, I heard him ask me with alarm, `Has the pain become unbearable again or what, my wife? Let me go and fetch my mother-in-law: this is a dangerous thing to do, for me to stay alone here with the dear child of other people in such a condition without informing her parents! ' And he was indeed about to start off when I stopped him and said, `But all I did was to cough, so why are you looking for your spear? Where do you want to go in this middle of the night?' May be he thought I didn't hear what he said."

The others laughed at Myombekere. When they stopped laughing, Nanzala added: "What you wanted to do was right indeed, my child, because we too grew up with our elders all the time telling us: `For a big fish call those with the right fishing gear!'"

Myombekere said: "Yes indeed, my dear mother, you have finally said what needs to said. People in this country are wont to deceive others, advising them to follow the so-called wisdom of the proverb: `Where the tilapia fish feeds is where it dies,' but when I looked at the situation here I found I was trapped in the middle and I said to myself: `You have to get up, you simply have to, even though it means leaving her here alone! You simply have to forget it's nighttime, because somebody else's child under your care is in a critical condition. This is the type of situation which, should the worse come to pass, can make her people very angry with you and ask you: Where were you for our child, in the condition in which she was, to suffer until she died without you coming to inform us? And what answer could you possibly have for them, when they see in front of them their child dead and cold? *Aa!* You will have nothing to say except to open your mouth and staring eyes and raise to them your empty hands begging for their mercy!'"

After some time Nanzala and her companions went back to their home, and then came back again to see the couple in the evening, to find out how they had passed the day and found nothing but peace and quiet with them. That's when Myombekere became himself again and made a resolution and said to himself: "I have to rest my heart on a stone so that it can stop being so jumpy and I too can behave normally like all the people I see daily in similar situations." And when he saw Bugonoka cheer up and regain her spirits and attend to her household chores again, he forgot all his worries.

Because Bugonoka was no longer in condition to walk all the way to the home of her healer Kibuguma, the couple discussed the matter when they were alone in the intimacy of their bed after dinner and Bugonoka told her husband, "I think you should make a point of going to Kibuguma's on my behalf to explain well to him my present condition."

"What you have said, my dear wife, has hit the baboon right in the middle of its bold head, as we say. And I won't be waiting for I don't know what other day; no. I am going there tomorrow and not a single day later."

Then they fell asleep.

Just before cockcrow Myombekere jumped from his sleep and when he found his body no longer feeling sleepy he got up from bed and took his robe from their clothes hanging rope and from there went to the wall of the house where he hang his weapons and began feeling the wall for his spear, searching for some three loops on the wall in which he normally slipped it. He then woke up Bugonoka and told her that he was on his way to Kibuguma's. His wife remarked to him, "Even so, you don't have to start off at this time of the night! You have got up in the middle of the night, mistaking it for pre-dawn!"

"Even if I have got up in the middle of the night, I still should start off, nothing will devour me on the way! As a matter of fact that way I will be able to come back when it is still cool in the morning."

"Is the sky not cloudy, by the way?"

"There are clouds in the sky, it is true, but most likely it will rain when the sun is already high up in the sky."

He had covered a considerable distance when he heard the sky heavy with rain rumble : *diririririri*! and he exclaimed to himself: "Will this day too for me be like the other day when I was going to woo back my wife, when it poured on me on the way until I could take no more!" but he reached his destination with no rain in sight. Kibuguma came to open for him the thorn-tree shutter of his home fence gate and the two men went together into the healer's house. When they finished greeting each other, Kibuguma asked Myombekere what had brought him there in that dead of the night and Myombekere told the healer how his wife had suffered from pain in the back and from another disease which women call false labor and added: "An old woman, Kanwaketa's mother, is the one who told us that. That woman herself is quite a reputable medicine woman in her own way: her healing includes making women stuck with the afterbirth expel it from their bodies and delivering babies who are wrongly positioned in their mothers' wombs. She is, in fact, the person people go to for help in our area in cases of mothers in need of repositioning right their unborn children. I hear some women say she can even smell a pregnant woman and tell from her smell whether her labor has peaked or not. And so I am here because my wife has been sick that way without a break, my healer."

"By the way, how many months have passed now since your wife conceived?"

This month is her eighth month."

"That's correct, and you should not think that may be you have counted wrongly; you haven't. However, since you are already here, let me give you medicine to prevent her from being stuck with the afterbirth and for shortening her labor."

"Do so, our healer."

Kibuguma got up and disappeared into the interior of his house and went to where he kept his medicines and was back in no time with the medicine, gave it to Myombekere and instructed him as to how it was to be taken. And so Myombekere got up and returned to his home.

Myombekere got home and explained to his wife how the medicine Kibuguma gave him was to be taken, and from there on everyday when Bugonoka went to the lake in the morning to draw water she went with the medicine her husband brought her and drank it over there while drawing water, because that's how the healer said it was to be taken.

When the new moon of the ninth month appeared, Bugonoka fell sick again. Myombekere went for Nanzala and the old woman came and examined her and said, "My son, it is true your wife is sick, but you shouldn't be alarmed, because her sickness is caused by the turning of the child: now the child inside her has turned so as to face directly the opening of the way out of its mother's womb. If you intend to call her mother, go and call her, so that she too can be by her child."

The following day Myombekere was on his way to call his mother-in-law. Once there, Nkwanzi on her part told him, "You can go back home, my son-in-law, I will come tomorrow." And the following day Bugonoka's mother came, loaded with presents. As soon as she arrived and exchanged greetings with her son-in-law, with no further ado she hurried on, directly to where her daughter was lying down in the house, and they greeted each other and then she asked her, "I hear you are sick, dear?"

"I am sick, but those who come to see me tell me that what is making me sick is the turning of the child. By the way, mother, is that how you too gave birth to us, with your pregnancies causing you so much trouble?"

"With me, poor Nkwanzi, I conceived my pregnancies in perfect health and with no complications, without ever experiencing pain anywhere in my body. What's more, in my case I never took any medicine on your account, I just gave birth to you feeling perfectly well. So matters of these kinds of sicknesses you are suffering from, my child, like pain in the back, false labor, a splitting head, *itango*[6], sickness of the turning of the child, I never experienced any of that. The only thing I experienced was labor and the after delivery pain. But, yes, I used to hear of other women experiencing your kind of suffering, but it is suffering more common with your type of pregnancies, with childbirth which is seeking to end barrenness in a woman, since there's no need to hide the truth we are still facing."

So, forced by the circumstances, Myombekere lived in the same house with his mother-in-law. They still kept their distance from each other, but they were not avoiding each other to the extent a son-in-law avoids proximity to his mother-in-law under normal circumstances, when people are all well and no sick person is involved.7 Bugonoka was the one who slept in the little third room of the house with her mother, Myombekere slept on the couple's bed in the inner room, the little girl on the floor of churning ground of the fore-room and the little boy on the sitting area of that outer room. Since Myombekere's house was spacious, the matter of finding a place to sleep for everybody while Myombekere's mother-in-law stayed with them in itself wasn't a problem, there was enough room in the house for everybody.

Nkwazi stayed with her daughter for two days and on the third day her husband Namwero too came to see their daughter. He found Bugonoka had woken up that morning feeling much better. Namwero on his part left the same day, after lunch. Nkwanzi escorted her husband and before returning to their son-in-law's home told him, "Let me see how she continues to do today and tomorrow and I'll come the day after tomorrow and may be stay for just a bit and then come back here, because this is her delivery month, it won't end before she delivers." And after those two days, since Bugonoka too had recovered, Nkwanzi went back to her home. And now that Bugonoka was well again she went back to doing whatever work of hers she felt she could still manage. And when her mother judged her time for delivery was nearing, the day before going back to Myombekere's home she woke up early to grind flour for taking to her daughter and the next day she said good-bye to her husband and took her load of presents and set off to see how her daughter was doing and arrived in Myombekere's home and stayed on.

Shortly after her mother's return, one day Bugonoka felt something like stomachache but somehow with the pain itself hurting her somewhere in her back, really intense pain, but which lasted only for a rather short time and then disappeared. On the following day Bugonoka felt the pain for the second time, only this time it lasted much longer and she had to bite her teeth and frown hard before it stopped and she was at peace again. And so she thought and said to herself, as if asking herself a question, "Oh dear, poor me! Why are these stomach worms causing me so much pain today? Don't I hear people say a pregnant woman   rarely suffers from stomachache? What then is this with me today?" But then the pain did not seize her again that day. Then the following morning, at the time when people can still be seen basking in the sweet morning sun, Bugonoka again felt the pain invade her stomach, with ferocious intensity. This time she finally asked her mother, "By the way, I feel inside me pain like stomachache and I first felt it the day before yesterday, and it is stomachache whose pain is gripping me in the center of my back. And today it has, it appears, decided to take matters really far! Oh, me! What kind of stomachache can this possibly be, mother?"

Her mother understood at once that it was labor, but since it is forbidden to mention childbirth pain by name as long as the pregnant woman is still in travail, she gave her an illusive answer and left her still engulfed in the darkness of her ignorance!

Chapter XVIII

NOTES

1. *Narutundubwi*: In his note for his Swahili translation of his novel Kitereza writes: "Tiny species of a toad so poisonous that if a cow happens to eat it the cow's stomach would swell and it would immediately die". The poisonous toad itself has a swollen round stomach which looks too big for its tiny body, a fitting image for the advanced pregnancy of a woman.

2. Ndagabwene: Fairly common male Kikerewe name meaning "I have already seen it (misfortune)".

3. *Enzamba*: See note 7 of Chapter XIV.

4. The Sun: See note 21 of Chapter II.

5. *Ekiriga*: Forward bend in a woman's lower back which accentuates her behind, a body feature the Wakerewe find attractive (sexy) in a woman. See note 14 of XVII.

6   *Itango:* Sudden leg muscle spasms in pregnant women which can cause her a lot of pain, as with Bugonoka in Chapter XVII.

7   For the custom of a son-in-law and his mother-in-law avoiding each other, see note 7 of Chapter I.

Part II

NTULANALWO AND BULIHWALI

Chapter XIX

THE BIRTH OF NTULANALWO

One day in the month of May, which was the ninth month of Bugonoka's pregnancy, Nkwanzi said to Myombekere, "Son, would you split for us some wood stumps for firewood, we need to keep a fire going in the house the whole night long. It appears your wife has developed stomach ache and we need some light in the house in case her stomach should trouble her at nighttime in these pitch-dark nights of the month. Should it happen that we have to stay awake all night attending to her, a light in the house makes things much easier." Myombekere went to a corner of his household fence where he had left lying some two sizable tree stumps of well-burning wood, split each stump into four pieces or so and called the young man who lived in his home to come and take the firewood to the women in the house.

At night, during dinner Bugonoka could not eat anything beyond the first two morsels she put in her mouth, literally two, before her stomachache gripped her again. You all know the particular way women eat, by cutting off with their right hand a large piece of *obwita*[1] from the bowl[2] of the dish and storing it in their left hand, from which they then take the morsels to eat. Well, she did not take from that piece in her hand another bite beyond the first two before she was gripped by those painful cramps in her stomach and had to give the food which was still in her hand to the girl who lived in her home. Dinner over, everybody went to bed, in the bright light of a flaming fire. And, as always, it finally dawned.

In the morning, at the hour of the sweet early morning sun, Bugonoka again felt the cramps in her stomach come on really strong. Her mother called Myombekere and her son-in-law came and squatted down outside in the porch of the house door and said: "You called me, mother-in-law, here I am!"

"I am calling you to ask you whether you could call Nanzala for us. We want to see her".

Myombekere was up at once and gone to fetch the old woman, and in less than it takes to say it he was already back with her. Nanzala exchanged greetings with the other women and learnt their reason for calling her and examined Bugonoka and examined her again before telling Nkwanzi, "I was assuming that, because you have born children of your own, you know all about our women ways but apparently you don't! Your child has reached this point and you have yet to seat her properly, to position her on the ground pad![3] It is obvious to me that her labor is almost climaxing, my dear".

So the two old women took Bugonoka into the inner room of her house and got busy to seat her on the so-called pad. They undressed her and put away her clothes and then made her sit on a block of wood with her legs apart, the way a Mkerewe woman who is getting ready to give birth to a child sits. You therefore now know that the pad I am speaking of is not a real pad, the cushion of which to carry or station things, that that's only a manner of speaking. Where Bugonoka now sat is called a pad for two reasons. The first one is that at that moment a woman is in a truly perilous situation, a situation of life and death. She could fatally topple from where she sat as easily as she sat there. The second reason is that a woman giving birth may not move an inch from the spot where Bugonoka was now seated until she has safely delivered her baby, hence at the moment a woman is delivering a baby she is trapped in a dangerous undertaking in which there is no escape, just as the pad on the head of a person carrying a load is trapped between the load and the head of the person with no way of escape. Take the example we see daily of a woman carrying a pot of water on a pad on her head and her pot of water weighing down on the cushion while her head is pressing up hard against the cushion on which she is bearing the pot. That cushion on the head of the water-carrier has no way of escape from its tight fix before she has reached her destination and put down her pot of water. Likewise a woman in that position is in a similar hard fix. That is the pad people speak of in the case of a woman giving birth to a child when they say: "So-and-so's wife has been on the pad for ever!" or "So-and-so's wife is still on the pad, she is still in peril!" and the like.

After Bugonoka was put on the pad and seated properly, her labor came on with redoubled pain and climaxed, and so the two old women with her focused all their attention to their job of delivering her baby. At once Nanzala held Bugonoka firmly and told her not to be afraid, to be bold like a man. In that very instant they saw something peeping out. On seeing that Nkwanzi told Nanzala, "Tell Bugonoka to push, because I see something peeping out."   On looking Nanzala too found that, indeed, something was peeping out but told Nkwanzi, "It is true there is something already visible but that is what we call the water-bag; the real object is yet to come."

Nanzala and Nkwanzi, bold like two he-women, then fell to instructing Bugonoka on how to give birth and told her, "Hold your breath and push for it to come out, because it is on its way." Bugonoka held her breath and pushed with all her might, as women do when giving birth. Before long they saw the water-bag come out, fully round, but only to burst open in that very moment and spill its water: *waya*! and at once the two old women saw the head of the child protrude just a little. Nanzala kept on repeating over and over the word "push" and telling Bugonoka: "Courage, dear child, courage!   Keep on pushing while holding your breath!" Immediately the child's head came out, but only the head, without the shoulders following suit, and apparently the ordeal of the shoulders is an altogether different affair, and a very tough one too! Now Bugonoka's pain became so intense she could no longer utter a sound, while the two midwives by her side kept on drumming into her ears the command to push harder. They we still urging her to keep pushing when all of a sudden they saw the shoulders of the child also come out. That's when Bugonoka too found she could hear again, because that ordeal of the shoulders had sealed her ears completely! And when the shoulders of the child came out, leaving inside the mother only the lower half of the child's body, Nanzala and Nkwanzi redoubled their command to Bugonoka to push relentlessly and Bugonoka did so and at once the child came out and dropped onto the ground.

At once Nanzala touched it with her hand and felt it to find out whether it was a boy or a girl and found it was a boy and told Nkwanzi in whispers that it was a male child. Bugonoka on her pad too heard the news. Then Nkwanzi in turn whispered to Nanzala, "So that's why he came out this way! He was ashamed to look at her mother because he is a male child, for that's how all male children usually came out of their mothers' wombs: face to the ground, because they are ashamed of looking at their mothers' nakedness, whereas every female child comes out face upward, facing her mother's nakedness."

As soon as the child came out, it at once put its fingers in its mouth, and that confirmed to the two old women that it was alive, since it was looking for a teat to suck. It came out with a very white object holding on to its stomach and stretching back to Bugonoka's inside, where it was joined to the placenta. When Nanzala saw that Bugonoka was not ejecting the placenta in time, that time was beginning to elapse and yet the placenta was still inside her womb, she said to Nkwanzi and Kanwaketa's wife, who was with them, "Why don't you take care of these two, the mother and her child, until I come back."

Nanzala found Myombekere seated outside while his ears and his heart were inside the house with his wife and she at once sent him to collect medicinal herbs from a nearby anthill: "Go and bring me the leaves of such-and-such a tree," as she too went to look for yet another medicine to go with that one. The two of them came back at the same time and Myombekere gave her the medicine she had sent him for. Quickly Nanzala pounded the two medicines together with a stone and went back into the house, where she found Bugonoka's afterbirth too beginning to protrude outside of her a bit. Right away she squeezed liquid from the medicine into Bugonoka's mouth and then rubbed the pounded herbs on her stomach, this way, before dropping some on the protruding afterbirth itself and at once the afterbirth dropped out of Bugonoka's womb completely and she was out of danger. That was when Bugonoka's midwives ululated4 to announce the great event. Kanwaketa's wife went to the door and told Myombeleke outside, "Aren't you going to congratulate us and ask us, `Is it a male or female child?' or `Did you have a safe delivery?'"

Hearing that Myombekere came back to life, as if from a swoon, and got up and went to the porch of the door of his house, where he was stopped in time by the women in the house who told him, "Don't you come this way! We are not yet finished with our business; you will see your visitor later!"

"I too had no intention of coming any farther than the threshold of this door here. Have you delivered into the world a baby boy or a baby girl?"

"A baby boy! A little fellow companion of yours."

"May she be blessed with yet another!"

Those inside the house laughed. Myombekere on his side was all smiles for having a male child for his first-born. Nanzala called out to him from inside the house and said, "My son, what do you intend to do for the stomach of this mother of your child, since that place from where this visitor has come now badly needs filling up?" Nanzala had hardly finished saying that when the child cried out and she called out to Myombekere again, "And do you hear how this one too wants you to do something for his stomach, since he too, now that he is here on this earth, wants to eat? Have you never heard people say: 'If you are starving hang around a sick person but never around a woman who has just given birth!'"
"I have indeed heard those words said and very often too."

Myombekere apparently took seriously Nanzala's words and set out, accompanied by Kagufwa, to look for fish from *embigo*[5] and *emigono*[6] fishermen. He came back with between twelve and fifteen *ensato*[7] and some three *embozu*.[8]

While Myombekere was gone to look for fish, back in his house Nanzala brought a rope made of papyrus cords and wound it around Bugonoka's stomach as was done to all women immediately after they gave birth to a child, so as to hold in her stomach and prevent it from extending out. Then she turned to separating the child from the placenta, because, as you have seen, the child comes out of the mother's womb attached to the placenta by a whitish rope-like object people call the umbilical cord. I am telling you all this because, since in this Ukerewe of ours delivering babies is normally exclusively female business, many men don't know well what goes on and need to be informed.

It was not until the afterbirth had come out that the women assisting Bugonoka could find a word to say; before that all of them had been speechless with apprehension, for Bugonoka's life was still in grave danger. And since Nanzala was a woman full of jokes, she got hold of the child's umbilical cord and sized well the length to cut, using the folded knee of the tiny baby as measure, for, as you may know, newborn babies never stretch out their legs at that stage, and then told the newborn baby: "Behave yourself now and let us give your body its life's knot."

Nkwanzi and the other women laughed and mumbled at the same time inside the house and asked Nanzala, "Tell us, dear, what can a life's knot on the body of a human being possibly be?"

"Do you really want to tell me that you don't know that all human beings, each and everyone of us, have body knots?"
"*Aa, aa!*"

"Well, in that case from now on you better learn that the life's knot of a human being's body, male or female, is his or her navel, because if when you are born your body is not given that knot you simply cannot live. Likewise, if we don't give this newly born baby his body knot at once we have nothing."

"Well! That's true, you know!"

Nanzala told Nkwanzi to pass her quickly a piece of papyrus string and the other woman tore a strand from a papyrus strip and gave it to her and she tied the umbilical cord of the child really tight with it, because if the umbilical cord is not tied tight enough once it is cut the baby may lose too much blood and die, just like that. She tightened the string on the umbilical cord at a point sufficiently removed from the body of the baby. Then Kanwaketa's wife passed Nanzala a splinter from a dry millet stalk for cutting and trimming the umbilical cord and Nanzala did so and finished that job.

Bugonoka had now left her pad and was engrossed in watching how the umbilical cord of her child was being trimmed, because she too was eager to learn that skill so that in case of need in the future she would know what to do. She did not want to have to ask other women what to do in a similar situation after she had had the opportunity to see with her own two eyes the job done in broad daylight. As usual, the cutting and trimming of the umbilical cord was done with the child still on the ground where it had dropped, next to its mother's placenta.

Nanzala finished trimming the baby's umbilical cord and took the child and held it in her two hands with its body inclined to one side, after which she joined together the toes of her feet, like this, and put the child on top of her feet, and then Mkwanzi poured water on the baby while Nanzala washed its entire body until she had washed it clean of the stains of the afterbirth. And what a red child! After washing it, Nanzala once more held the child inclined in her hands as water dried off its body.

Kanwaketa's wife went outside the house to uproot from the fields grass for making a bed spread on the house floor for the mother and her child and in no time was back with the grass and made the bed. Nkwanzi on her part went to cut three tender banana leaves from a shoot on top a banana plant in Myombekere's plantation and she too was back in no time with the banana leaves, on which the baby would sleep during the days of its confinement.

It was at that moment that Myombekere came back with fish he had gone to look for, and when the baby did not pee and shit in time Nanzala told her companions, "Go and call its father to come and give it a name. May be he is not peeing and shitting because he wants a name, for I have many a time seen that happen. Even with my own children, when I was still giving birth, that was something I witnessed often." The women called Myombekere and he came at once. As he entered the house, the other women told Bugonoka to put on her clothes and she put on something, just enough to cover her nakedness, not what can be called real dressing, because she was still in very bad shape, the way you all know women are after bearing a child. Myombekere was about to stop at the entrance of the house, since inside the house there was, in addition to his wife who had just given birth and was still being attended to, his mother-in-law,9 when Nanzala told him, "Come all the way to the bedroom. In this situation there is no room for avoiding the presence of your mother-in-law. There will be plenty of time for that later," and he went all the way to the bedroom. Because he was coming from sunlight outside, he couldn't see well and the old woman told him, "Squat down over there! Can you see better now or are your eyes yet to get used to the darkness in here?" "Now I am beginning to see clearly."

"Here is your child. Look at him and then name him, because he is causing us a problem: from the time he was born up to now he hasn't peed and neither has he shitted!"

Because it was first time matter for him, Myombekere did not know what people say to name a child, so he asked the women in the house how to go about it and they explained to him how to acknowledge a child and what to say. That's when he too knew what to do and remembered the name he wanted to give his child and spoke with a voice full of happiness, "Grow into an adult, your name is Ntulanalwo. If it was because you wanted a name that up to now you hadn't peed or shitted, urinate and relieve yourself as all human beings do." And all at once they indeed saw the child, still being held by its father, urinate and shit.

Nanzala said, "What do you say now! Didn't I tell you that I have seen this happen?"

And everybody agreed with her and said, "Yes, indeed! You saw what you say you saw. *Aa*! how can any of us dare contradict you after we too have witnessed this way the truth of what you say!"

With that the women told Myombekere to go back outside, and then laid the child on the green banana leaves, naked as it was born. Its body, still all folded up, was shaking as if it was feeling cold, as from now and then it put its fingers into its mouth. The women got busy and put Bugonoka's afterbirth on a short folding chair and carried it on the chair and went to bury it. The Wakerewe never bury a woman's afterbirth just anywhere, say in the wilderness or even in the courtyard. No. That's not their way of doing things: they bury the woman's afterbirth in the very house in which she gave birth to her child, and as soon as possible. However, there are two different ways of burying it. When it is the afterbirth of a male child, they bury it in the male side of the front room, that is the right-hand side of the room when you stand in the house facing outside, where they bury it in the earth of the house floor at the milk-churn. And when it is that of a female child, they bury it under the grinding-stone. The grinding-stone is removed and a hole big enough for the afterbirth is dug in the seat of the stone and after burying it and hardening the ground again, immediately seeds of a gourd of the previous year's harvest and some grains of *endwero*[10] millet are placed on top of the covered hole before putting back the grinding stone in its place. And so Nanzala and Nkwazi buried Ntulanalow's afterbirth by the milk-churn post, since it was that of a male child.

The day he was born Ntulanalwo did not suck the milk of his mother's breasts. No. The custom was that on the day a child is born, especially if it is born during daytime as Ntulanalwo was, the freshly milked milk of a cow whose calf had never died young is what the newly born baby would be given from a leaf of the end-bud of a stalk of a bunch of bananas, on which the milk is poured and then funneled into the mouth of the child bits by bits. And so the fresh milk of a cow whose calves had never died young was what Ntulanalwo took that day, during daytime as well as at night.

It was now time for Nkwazi to attend to boiling water in a large pot with which to cure Bugonoka's body of its aches and pains. When the water was really boiling and bubbling over, she told her daughter to get up so that she could go and massage her body with the hot water before the side-effects of child bearing overcame her and killed her, and at once Bugonoka got up and went behind her house. Nkwazi got hold of the pot of water and heaved it and took it behind the house, put down the water and then went back to the house to fetch a movable door shutter[11] on which to massage her daughter with the hot water. Once inside the house, she left instructions to the young girl who lived in Myombekere's home to look after the baby, because that was the time Nanzala and her daughter-in-law left to go back to their home, but not before Myombekere had taken from the fish he had brought two *ensato* and given them to Nanzala and given another *ensato* to Kanwaketa's wife.

Then Nkwanzi massaged her daughter with that boiling-hot water. Whenever Bugonoka tried to ward off her mother's hands as they brought that burning-hot water to her body, since her mother was handling the water with tree leaves she was kneading her daughter's body with and therefore was not touching the water directly and feeling how scorching hot it was, you would hear mother rebuking daughter: "You shameless creature! Where does this good-for-nothing creature come from, who fears water as if it were labor pain? Take away those hands of yours and let me give your body a proper hot-water massage. Do you really think if I massage you afraid of hurting you you will become wholesome again?"
"No, mother, the water is too hot, believe me!"

"Hot water is what mothers need after giving birth, and what do you want it to be? Have you ever seen cold water used to massage women after they give birth as a cure for the after-birth effects?

Bugonoka could do nothing but bear the pain she was writhing with as her mother kept on kneading her body with the hot water, on her head, on her back, with Bugonoka lying face downwards, and in her stomach, with Bugonoka now lying on her back, from now and then the daughter crying out really loud, "Mother, you will kill me, this water is too hot!" "Courage, I'm almost done", her mother would answer her. In the evening Bugonoka's mother gave her the hot-water massage again, until before her days of confinement were over she eventually got used to the scorching-hot water.

On that first day of the newborn child Nanzala and her daughter-in-law came back to bid good-evening to the mother and her new baby. They had just arrived when Kanwaketa too came. He found Myombekere raking together dry cow dung for burning in his courtyard fireplace[12] and at once asked him, "Has Bugonoka already given birth? Did she have a safe delivery?"

"Yes, she has already given birth, and safely."
"What child, man?
"A boy"
"May the daughter of good people be blessed with yet another one!"

And with that he was up again and said, "Let me too go and say hello! to her." On arriving at the door of the house, he called out, "Bugonoka!"

"Yes, Sir!"

"Good evening, my love! Good evening, my Sovereign!"[13]

"Good evening! And good evening again!"

"It is true that you have already given birth to a child?"

"Yes, I have indeed."

"What baby child did you bear?"

"A fellow companion of yours".

"That's goodness itself! May you be blessed with yet another one, daughter of Abazubwa[14] people."

Then they chatted on for a while before Kanwaketa said good-bye and left to go back to his home, accompanied by his wife and his mother.

The little girl in Bugonoka's house had brought Bugonoka some soft tree leaves for cleaning her baby with whenever it relieved itself, having collected the leaves when she went to cut some for wiping milk containers with during the skimming of milk. That same young girl, after the people of Kanwaketa's home left, asked Nkwanzi and the wife of her people, that is her uncle Myombekere's wife Bugonoka, "Why do women when they give birth have to be bathed with such hot water?"

Nkwanzi replied, "Is that what you find intriguing, daughter of worthy parents?"

"Yes," the girl agreed.

Nkwanzi was about to tell her the reason when she remembered that that was information meant only for women. The women of Myombekere's home were at that moment in the kitchen cooking and Bugonoka's mother at once sent the little girl outside, after telling her, "Go and peep first to make sure your uncle isn't somewhere near the door," and all that now said in whispers. The child went and peeped at the door and came back and said, "He is outside at the courtyard fireplace."

"What about the boy, your brother, where is he?"

"He too is at the fireplace with uncle."

"Well, if that's the case, listen well and let me tell you why women after delivering babies have to be bathed with such hot water."

"Please tell me, I too would like to know."

"That is done so as to cure mothers of new babies of the after-effects of bearing a child, because without treating them that way their bodies would continue feeling the ravages of child-bearing long after the child is born and that could kill them in no time. That's what hot water means to us women after giving birth to a child. Do you understand?"

"I have understood indeed, only, that being the case, I think with me there would be a problem: I will never bathe with it."

"And why not?"

"Because I'm simply too much of a coward to stand being burnt with such hot water?"

"Oh, I see! You are still too young, that's all. You don't know yet what is really important and what is not."

"I may be young all right, but I still find that ordeal too much to bear. Why is it that cows and goats give birth and yet they are never massaged with hot water?"

"So that's it! You are best left alone! So you have gone all the way to livestock and wild animals! I would like to think you do realize that those animals were created differently and that the human being too was created a different way! So how can you compare those different creatures to human beings! Child, have you lost your mind and become completely insane!" The young girl felt demolished, with nothing to say in her defense.

After dinner everybody went to bed. That day Bugonoka and her mother slept on different beds and did not share a bed as they had been doing. Her mother slept on the bed alone and Bugonoka on her part slept with her child as it lay on its fresh banana leaves, its body quivering as if from cold. As to the fire needed to light the house, it was flaming and lighting the house as never before, because Myombekere had fetched for firewood dry stumps of male trees and their hard wood was burning as bright as can be.

The following day at sunrise Nkwazi and the young girl Nakiro went to the lake to draw water for massaging Bugonoka, only to find that night the lake had been very rough, had been furiously raging the whole night and even now it was still rumbling and roaring, and, as a result, the water too was nothing but silt and the beach nothing but piles upon piles of lichens and seaweeds! Nkwanzi found herself asking Nakiro, "Where on earth are we going to draw water today, since it is nothing but silt?"

The young girl, who knew their lakeshore well, said, "We better go and draw some from over there, because that place is sheltered and the wind rarely hits it directly and the water over there too rarely gets as dirty as in this open shore." They took their pots and off they went and found that indeed on that side of the shore the water looked much better; so they quickly drew water and carried their pots and additional calabashes of water and returned home.

Once more Nkwanzi bathed Bugonoka with boiling-hot water as she had done the previous day. Nanzala and Kanwaketa's wife ran into Bugonoka as she was coming from behind her house after her hot bath and went into the house with her. It was when the visiting women sat down inside the house and saw the baby that they realized what they had done wrong and apologized aloud by asking: "What has made us so senseless today?"

"What did you do?"

"We must admit we have never seen the like of this! Imagine, we left home saying to ourselves, `Let's go and bid good morning the mother of the newborn,' and yet when we ran into her at the door and greeted her we completely forgot, altogether, to ask her news of her newborn! And yet it was we, and nobody else, who yesterday delivered her baby! How can anybody be this forgetful? Adults, in your proper minds, forgetting the very thing for which you set out from home! *Aa*! *hee*! what a shame! May be that's why our elders of yore said forgetting knows no child or adult. But, all the same, what did we take Bugonoka for today? Somebody else who resembles her or simply some sick person coming from taking a bath and looking this worn out!"

"I was thinking that I am the only one who behaves so weirdly, but apparently there are many of us around," Nkwanzi said. "Look at this! For example, in our neighborhood back at my home an elderly man and head of a household died, but there has remained in his home his grandson, the son of the old man's son, who too, it so happened, has followed his father in the land of the dead, like my relatives, who have all followed each other there. But that grandson of the dead man is already a whole mountain of a man, who too already has grandchildren of his own,   and yet since the head of that household died we up to this day have never stopped calling that home Kapapo's home.   Whenever we send children to fetch for us from there this or that we keep on forgetting and saying: `Go and fetch for me my bowl from Kapapo's home', never even adding something like `the late Kapapo's home,' not even that! Especially me! If he were a person from a large clan, with relatives everywhere like some people we see in this country of ours, his relatives would have cursed and hurled insults at me very many times, may be they would even have already accused me of witchcraft and said: `She is the one who killed him.'"

As Nkwanzi finished saying that, Bugonoka was heard silently hissing with pain while holding her stomach, like a person suffering from stomachache. The other women asked her, "Have you perhaps developed after-birth stomach pain, dear?"

"May be that's what it is, my dear. And it started troubling me during the night. I woke up from sleep to find an unbearable pain in this belly of mine. In the end my mother asked me what was going on: `Why are you fidgeting in bed endlessly like that?' And here I am again, I hear you carrying on your conversation all right but what I am actually listening to is my poor lot."

Nanzala said, "Your poor lot indeed, because after-birth stomach pain can indeed be excruciating during the mother's days of confinement. You need herbs to treat the pain or you will soon be unable to eat and so continue to weaken. And feeling weak and sick when you are still surrounded by the sickly smell of the healing wound of your child's navel makes things even worse."

"Why can't you get us some such herbs, dear, if you know them?"

"Do you think they are something to fetch from far? Myombekere has in fact found some in his banana plantation. Myombekere, please come here!" Myombekere came and Nanzala told him, "Bugonoka has developed after-birth stomach pain. Go and fetch her some *eminankonge*[15] sweet canes to chew and that will cure her of it."

Myombekere in no time brought *eminankonge* canes and gave them to the women in the house, who gave them to the little girl Nakiro to peel. The girl peeled and cut and put on a tray[16] pieces of wild sugarcane until Nanzala said, "That's enough! It is never quantity which cures. You the others eat the remaining," and the old woman put the tray in front of Bugonoka and she chewed some.

Before she finished what was on the tray, she began to feel fine and told those present, "Please keep these for me somewhere; I'll eat some more later." Her mother removed the tray of *eminankonge* and put it away.

Chapter XIX

NOTES

1. *Obwita*: See note 14 of Chapter I.
2. *Ekibo*: See note 15 of Chapter I.
3. *Engata*:   See note 13 of Chapter I.
4. *Akahira*: See note 11 of Chapter IX.
5. *Embigo*, plural for *olubigo*: See note 3 of Chapter II.
6. *Emigono* plural for *omugono*:   See note 6 of Chapter II.
7. *Ensato*: See note 2 of Chapter VI.
8. *Embozu*: Type of catfish.
9. For mothers-in-law and sons-in-law being required to avoid each other see note 7 of Chapter I.
10. *Endwero*: See note 8 of Chapter XII.
11. *Ihara*: See note 6 of Chapter III.
12. *Ekikome*: See note 1 Chapter II.
13. Myombekere and Kanwaketa are neighbors and friends and hence consider each other brothers, and because of that they have with each other's wife a joking relationship of peers-in-law. See note 11 of Chapter I.
14. *Abazubwa*: One of the clans of Wakerewe. Addressing a person by evoking his or her clan was both a mark of intimacy and a way of paying tribute to a persons ancestors.
15. *Eminankonge*, plural for *omunankonge*: Wild sugarcane.
16. *Olugali*: See note 6 of Chapter I.

Chapter XX

CONFINEMENT OF THE NEWBORN BABY

The day after Ntulanalwo was born, in the morning, after Bugonoka had had her hot-water massage and chewed some *eminakonge* wild sugarcane to calm her after-birth stomach pain, which when it gripped her made her writhe and wince and wring her stomach so much, medication was applied on the wound of the child's umbilical cord cut for the first time. It was also starting that day that the newborn baby was bathed endlessly and water became its perpetual companion in its first period of growing up, during which it would be bathed time and time again throughout the day, as the custom was. Only at nighttime were newborn babies bathed may be only once, because their mothers were sleeping. But even then, when the mother woke up, even if it was in the dead of the night, there were mothers who would bathe their babies at that time too, since their is no interdiction or taboo against bathing babies at night, should the mother's sense of cleanliness desire it.

That morning, after bathing Ntulanalwo, Bugonoka and Nkwanzi again fed him with freshly milked milk of a cow which had never lost a calf by infant death by giving him the milk from the leaf of a bud of the stalk-end of a bunch of bananas, after which the women brought the medication for treating the baby's navel wound: the sap of red *kasaka*[1] leaves (others use *entobotobo*[2]). They applied the medicine on the baby's wound cautiously, dropping on the wound the sap of red *kasaka* skillfully so as to apply it just on the wound of the cut umbilical cord while making sure none of it touched any other part of the child's body. The treatment was then repeated in the evening at twilight, before dark set in.   After that Bugonoka was told she could suckle her child.

She took the child in her hands and put the teat of her breast into its month: the child sucked really greatly! Everybody present was filled with joy on seeing that and said, "You see! The poor fellow was already starving, except he couldn't tell us because he cannot speak! Poor fellow!.."

Nkwanzi then went to fetch some more fresh tender banana leaves, since the old ones had wilted. Kanakweta too had dropped in to bid the mother and her baby good evening, accompanied by his wife. After some time Myombekeres' neighbors got up to return to their home and on seeing them about to leave Bugonoka told Kanwaketa, "Kanwaketa, aren't you staying for dinner?"

"No, I can't. I must hurry back to milk cows. Dinner will have to wait for another time."

"I can't blame you if you won't stay. How do I know you haven't lost your appetite from nausea at the thought of eating with the mother of a newborn baby?"

Immediately Kanwaketa's wife jumped in and said, "As to that, you don't need to say it, Bugonoka! Mothers of new babies nauseate Kanwaketa beyond measures. You look here, during those day when I was still bringing them into this world I would tell him, `What about joining me,[3] dear, so that we can eat together for company and good cheer?' And his answer would always be, `Is that food or what, which I must eat with the mother of a newborn baby!"

"And what can you say to that, dear friend? Doesn't that prove me right?"

"You are indeed right, I can't deny it, but, in spite of that, I would advise you to take the words of this woman with a pinch of salt. Still I must hurry and milk the cows, the sun is deserting the sky."

"Why can't the young men of your home milk the cows, so that you can wait for dinner and eat with me?"

"I must leave you alone, you are incorrigible! You are like a parrot, once you start talking you never stop. Let me go and attend to that blind milk-cow of mine, the troubles of which you too know. And so have a good night, and may the new born suck well."

"Good night, dear. You too sleep well."

The morning of the second day after the child was born, Nkwanzi boiled the water for massaging Bugonoka and when it was ready she hurried out to collect tree leaves with which to massage her daughter, since the young girl, Nakiro, was attending to milk, and was back with the leaves in no time and on coming back she told Bugonoka, "My dear, I have just been given a real scare by a monitor lizard! I had just broken off a branch from *umukora* tree and was picking from it the leaves I needed when I heard something noisily running through the undergrowth and charging right towards me. When my eyes fell on it, it was already almost on me, hardly any distance away! I was convinced it was a snake and jumped away yelling: `*Yu*! mother, I'm dying, a snake is biting me!' And with that I fell down: *gangara*! on the other side. On looking again, I realized that it was some huge monitor lizard, and: *chorwe*! it disappeared into a hole in an anthill. I exclaimed: '*Aa*! My father![4] If I were a man and had a big stick with me today I would have pursued and killed this monster of a lizard!' Do you mean to say that you here didn't hear me yelling! I was afraid that even my son-in-law heard me!"

"We here heard nothing at all. There is indeed in that area a huge monitor lizard. It has, in fact, almost wiped out our chickens. I have been nagging your son-in-law to plug the holes of that anthill but to no avail. You didn't hurt yourself, I hope?"

"No, child, I only trembled all over with fright. When I woke up from where I had fallen and then remembered that monitor lizards are known to bite people and that their bites are said to be really dangerous, I was overcome with fright. Even on my way back here in the cow-trail I was passing through I kept on turning and looking back, thinking that may be the creature was still pursuing me!"

"You have every reason to be afraid, since, as our ancestors said: `To a person who has been attacked by bees there is no safe bee,' and also: `The person who has been bitten by a snake runs away from the harmless *ekina*[5] lizard,' and again they said that whatever opens a mouth bites. As to giant lizards biting people, yes, I too have heard here men talk about it and say, `To battle the monitor lizard you have to take precaution and remember to wrap a rag around your private parts the way the Wakara[6] people dress, because the creature is wont to go for a man's private parts looking for his nakedness to deprive him of his ability to found a home.' Imagine the monster of a creature doing that to a man! *Hee*! Won't that man become a living-dead like legendary Bubwi,[7] the man who was living and yet completely dead, like a new cow-skin rendered useless by over-scraping and thinning so that it is nothing but holes and tears!"

"My child, don't tell me about Bubwi! That one was a real living-dead. Listen and let me tell you about him, that is if my son-in-law is not within hearing. Nakiro, do please check on him for us." Once Nkwanzi was assured that her son-in-law was at a safe distance, she went back to what she was saying: "We too grew up being told how badly handicapped that man Bubwi was. How that Bubwi was a man blind in one eye, seeing only with one eye. Start counting and say: one! How he was lame in one arm, which was all shriveled and he could not cultivate his crop fields. Say: two! How on one of his legs two of his toes were missing, the big-toe and the following one, so that he walked in jerks and starts. Say: three! How he was dead beneath his underwear rag and could not marry. Say: four! How that man Bubwi was circumcised and his skinless penis taboo[8] to all Wakerewe woman, so that even if he could marry he would not have found a woman to marry in this country, because he was a forbidden thing. Say: five! And that completes the list of the handicaps of that man called Bubwi you hear of in stories."

"My goodness! All that on a single human being! No wonder people likened him to a new but over-thinned cow-skin which nobody can wear because it is nothing but gaping holes and tears! Of what use could he possibly have been on this earth? Good for just eating and sleeping! Indeed that one had really been cursed by the Sun![9] *Aa*! *bee*! mother, I think I'd better get up and go to bathe and leave Bubwi alone with his handicaps!"

"Take the toilet leaves with you as you go out; I've put them in a basket by the grinding-stone," her mother told her.

While bathing Bugonoka told her mother, "You simply cannot imagine the hunger I am feeling today in this stomach of mine! In fact I began feeling very hungry this way at cockcrow, so that even now I was seemingly quietly lying down on that bed of mine while the truth is that hunger was killing me."

"To say the truth, things would have been much worse were it not for the fact that you were suffering from after-birth stomach pain, because there is nothing to compare to the way a mother eats after giving birth when her baby child is still in confinement. I would say that if that were the normal way all women ate, grain in   grain stores[10] of people's homes would never make it to the following harvest. Never!"

On returning inside the house the two women bathed the child while the child itself rang out crying with a manly voice, kind of heavy. It was

Nkwanzi who was bathing it and who responded to its crying by telling the child, "No more crying, little dad. What! A man afraid of water! No more crying, please, I won't beat you any more. *Aa*! *hee*! Quit crying, little grandfather. What a child! If God wills and he grows up he will have a great singing voice."

"What of his father's singing voice, shouldn't he inherit a bit of it? Don't people say a shit-heap resembles its shitter?"

When the child was dry enough Nkwanzi gave it to its mother and Bugonoka suckled it, and after that Nkwanzi brought a branch of red *kasaka*, broke a small leaf from it and sap came out and she put the sap onto the child's navel wound and treated it.

That morning after breakfast Myombekere went to Kibuguma's home to get instructions regarding the shaving of the child's birth-hair once its period of confinement was over. He came back and told the people of his home how Kibuguma was sending them his greetings and how he was greeting the little child and each and every person in his home, and how if he omitted anything at all in their home in his greetings then that must be the chickens, since it was only chicken that he Myombekere did not hear their healer mention! He wanted to tell them everything Kibuguma had told him but Bugonoka stopped him and said, "No, you should always wait until there are fewer eyes and ears around before talking about such matters. There are still too many people abroad. Wait, you will tell us later, after dinner." So that day when they finished eating their evening meal Myombekere told his wife and her mother, "Once I got to Kibuguma's, I waited until he finished his other engagements and then I approached him and said, `What has brought me here, my healer, is this: I want to ask you how we are to bring the newly born child outside for the first time. And, also, can we shave off the child's inside-the-womb hair?' And he answered me back and said, `Just bring the child from confinement to the outside normally, as is done with all children. You yourselves will also shave off the hair he was born with. Except when the time comes to shave off his hair after he cuts his first tooth, that's when you will bring him here and I will shave him. Do you hear me?' And I said, `Yes, I hear you'. Then I got up and they gave me my walking stick and I came back."

Bugonoka said, "I see! So that's what he said. It's fine then. And thanks to him, our healer!"

On the third day, after Bugonoka had been given her hot-water massage and Ntulanalwo had been bathed and his navel wound treated, some two men called at Myombekere's home on their way from *omukama's*[11] palace. The two men told Myombekere, "Ask us news of Bukindo,[12] that's where we are coming from. We went there on the day before yesterday to pay our homage to our king and we have come back from there this very day. Except we left our master not feeling well. In fact if that illness of his persists it will turn into serious sickness, judging from what we were able to observe. But this is a secret we are just sharing with you and don't tell it to other people and put in danger of being sent to their execution some two miserable and poor creatures we are!" All this was said in whispers to Myombekere, with just the three men present. After that the two visitors took their leave. Myombekere invited them to stay a bit and wait for food but they declined and said, "No, thank you. We must be on our way before it gets too hot, for it appears today will be a cloudless day." Myombekere escorted them and came back and informed the women in his house that the two men were coming from Bukindo where they claimed to have left the *omukama* not feeling well, that the men shook their heads when they told him that and added, "Should the illness he has persist it is going to be sad news for the country." Then he added to his listeners, "But all I want is to share with you this information and, since you women tend to blab whatever you know, please don't let this out to anybody. Even if some other people speak to you of it, pretend to be surprised, as if you have never heard a thing about it. And under no circumstances are you to be the first to speak of it."

"We too find this kind of news too big for us, because it is heavy matter. We too would be afraid of blabbing in such a situation, my son," his mother-in-law said.

They had not quite finished with that when they heard a person calling at the gate of their home: "People of this home!" On glancing that way, Myombekere saw that it was his brother-in-law Lweganwa, Bugonoka's brother of the same father and same mother, accompanied by a brother of his from his father's side, carrying on a pole on their shoulders fresh fish, many *ensato*[13] together with two big pieces of *emamba*,[14] and he said to the women in the house, "I win: I have seen our visitors first!" The women retorted, "Who are they?" and he, "My brothers-in-law." And at once he had shot off to meet the visitors, got to them, bubbling over with happiness, and told them, even before greeting them, "Look at the type of visitors one should always receive in his home! What a lucky day for us!" He gave his visitors seats and then heaved the heavy load of the welcome present of provisions and took it into the house, where his mother-in-law got out of his way and he carried it in one stretch all the way to the inner room, where Nakiro laid a movable door shutter[15] on the ground for him and he deposited the fish on it before immediately going back outside to exchange greetings with his brothers-in-law. He greeted Lweganwa first, since he was the older of the two, a bit older then his companion. Lifting to him his open hands joined together he said, " Greetings to you, my brother-in-law. How are you? And is your wife well? And your little child?"

"Greetings, my Sovereign,[16] my brother-in-law. We are all well, except the day before yesterday our little child had a fever, but now it is doing better and beginning to cheer up again."

Then Myombekere went on and asked Lweganwa, "How is my father-in-law?"

"He is fine, except the day he came back from visiting you here he arrived in the evening after dark and said, `I have hurt myself. I fell into a porcupine hole on the way and sprained my leg.' And in the morning he sent me to fetch for him some herbs, *obwanda* and *amakugwe*,[17] with which to massage with hot-water his injured leg. We massaged his leg that way morning and evening for some four days before we saw him begin to walk a bit better, limping, supporting himself on an old hoe-handle and making it all the way to the lake. He is now back to walking normally, but during the first few days we had feared he would become lame, especially given his advanced age."

"Now I see! That's why our ancestors said it is never too late for misfortune to strike. Imagine, my father-in-law left this home in perfect health, only to be met with injury on the way! *Hee*! And we back here with no way of knowing, all this time convinced that you were all fine when the truth was another matter!"

Then Lweganwa and his brother, whose name was Kamuhanda, went into the house to greet the women. After which Nkwanzi asked his son, "Do you still catch fish in plenty or how is it?"

"We are still doing well, but the catch is no longer that big, and yet our *olubigo*[18] trap is in deeper waters, so you can imagine how poorly those whose traps are nearer the shore are doing. Yesterday early in the morning I went into our *olubigo* and I came back with one hundred *ensato* and some five odd ones, and then I went back there late in the afternoon and again I caught another one hundred *ensato* and some other five odd ones plus one *emamba*. When my father saw that he told me: `You've better take this bit of fish to your sister, because somebody from those parts told me here that she has already given birth." And so I decided to go and tell my brother Kamuhanda you see here to come to our home at cockcrow so that he could help me carry the fish and accompany me to come and see how the mother of the new baby is doing, because a helping hand makes work easier."

Myombekere thanked him and said, "This is indeed very kind of you, my brother-in-law, because with me here I have indeed had a hard time trying to get fish. It is true that with us too our *emigonzo*[19] fishermen still go to sea and they too do catch enough fish, only they simply ask too much for it. And even if you tell them that your wife has just given birth to a baby, you would very likely hear them at once answer you with the most disheartening of words: `If it is true that your wife has born you a child, why didn't you slaughter a cow for her?' And so you get nowhere. All you can do is to keep what you have in your heart to yourself, because it wouldn't help you to retort by asking them, `How often do you see men slaughtering cows for their wives whenever they bear children?' With the like of them that would simply be wasting your time, for the truth is, if you were to visit the homes of those very people who speak so glibly of slaughtering cows, you wouldn't find as much as cow footprint nor a trace of cow-dung in their compounds. And so you let all your thoughts stay and die inside you and put out pleading hands to them so that they could sell you some fish, since you have nowhere else to go. You are a person in need and they the ones who have what you need. And if you tell them, `I have a sick person at home, please sell me some fish for my sick one,' their answer for you is bound to be: `If we hadn't gone to sea, what would you have done? Since there are plenty of fishermen everywhere in this country, go and buy fish from other fishermen, those you know will sell you fish without delay. With us here we are not yet ready to sell, we are still repairing our *emigonzo* and we won't put them aside when they are still in such a state of disrepair as if we are being chased by something.' So you give up completely, like a person in a fight who has been beaten and overcome and has no other recourse except to plead for mercy. And should you tell them: `I have a death in my home, sell me some fish to take to my people so that they can prepare food for the mourners who waked the whole night by the body of their dead with hunger in their stomachs,' don't imagine they will say: `This is a person struck by misfortune, let's sell him fish at once.' No. What they will do instead is, as it were, to butt you hard in the lower part of your stomach by telling you: `Hadn't we gone fishing, wouldn't people have come to mourn your dead? Go and kill a cow, since a funeral is the proper occasion for slaughtering cows,' and embarrass you and put you to shame by ridiculing you that way in front of a crowd of people. And being subjected to such shocking language has become our daily lot in our dealings with our fishermen here, and still we have nowhere else to go. We have become what our people of old had in mind when thy said: `A starving person has no ears.' And when they finally sell you that fish of theirs, there again you run into further trouble. When you say, `Sell me this one here,' there too, *hee*! you see them behave as if you are forcing them. Instead of selling you the fish they first press it with their fingers, feeling and examining it fastidiously, wasting your precious time. And when you think of the need you left behind in your home and realize that you came to buy fish and you have found it and you have what is needed to buy it and yet you are not buying any, my brother-in-law, you are simply left without knowing what to do! For, as you know, our elders said: `You can't break a person's arm for what is his or hers."

Lweganwa said: "*Aa*! Just as you say, my brother-in-law, for what else can you do? You can't fight a person over his own property. That would make you everybody's laughing stock and a person who has lost his senses. It is obvious that you people over here are really an unlucky lot when it comes to matters of fish, and we can't but pity you. Compared to us, things are really terrible with you here. In our part of the country we are indeed much better off. For example, in our neighborhood, in just the homes of my father's relatives, in the month just gone by, April, each and every one of those homes was full of *ensato*, and of the best type, *engonogono*,[20] and yet we traded nicely with buyers who poured into our homes daily with their millet, always taking care to throw in a bonus fish for them. For, however much fish a person has caught, why should that make him rude to customers? *Aa*! *hee*! What a wretched way to treat people! Can Omusese[21] treat a fellow Omusese that way? May be, my brother-in-law, those people you are speaking of are people of another tribe!

"*Aa*! They are the indigenous and pure Abasese of this country themselves, not some Abakwaya[22] or Abaruri[23] as you might imagine; not at all."

"There must be something wrong with them."

Sometime later that day Myombekere told his visiting brothers-in-law, "Let's go to Kanwaketa's home, we may get there some banana beer to drink."

And indeed there was banana beer at Kanwaketa's. Kanwaketa gave Myombekere and his brothers-in-law a whole pot of beer and they drank it in Kanwaketa's very home, in the company of some other three men. Some other people who too had heard there was beer in that home and had come to look for some were already drinking their pot of beer in the courtyard, while yet others were drinking their beer inside Kanwaketa's banana plantation.

So people drank banana beer and kept on drinking and before they knew it a drunkard marred their company, bent above all on provoking a fight with Myombekere's brothers-in-law. Myombekere tried all his best to restrain him, to make him leave alone his visitors, to no avail. And then the drunkard turned on Myombekere. With that Myombekere too lost his temper, completely, and the two confronted each other and in no time were locked in a wrestling match: *gingiri gingiri*! and down went the drunkard. People around cheered the two men on, joined in by those who had been drinking in the banana plantation, that is those among them who could still stand up, and the rest of the crowd which had been gathering in the home in search of beer, as Myombekere on his part now was squeezing the drunkard by the throat. Then he let go of his adversary's throat and got up from him. And that's when the drunkard became really mad. Whoever he saw near him he hit and shoved and pushed, until finally he broke the pot from which Myombekere and his companions were drinking their beer. And when Kanwaketa saw the drunkard break his beer pot, a pot he treasured so much that he had given it a name: Beehive, he too became raving mad with anger and was about to fight with the drunkard when young men present stopped him and said, "Leave him alone, allow us to give him the thrashing he deserves, because he has already spoiled our company too much and, as if that were not enough, he has even broken a whole pot of beer and poured the drink on the ground! What he has done is like smashing to pieces *omukama's* drum!!"[24] And with that those young men got hold of sticks and rained blows on the drunk, so much and by so many of them that nobody knew who inflicted a wound on his head. Even Lweganwa and Kamuhanda belabored him, to pay him back for having insulted them and for having fought with their brother-in-law Myombekere. When the young men judged the drunken fellow had taken enough beating, they took him from Kanwaketa's home and escorted him to his own home.

When calm was restored, Kanwaketa called Myombekere and went with him in his house and told him, "I am rather short of beer today, my friend. You too know that there was not as much as I usually have when I brew beer. And so let me see if I have anything left for you. There is this one sizable *engunda*[25] here, so go and drink this in your home with your visitors and our mother-in-law, or may be she never partakes?"

"A real Mkerewe woman like her not to drink banana beer! What problem could she possibly be having? Even with those of our women for whom beer doesn't mean much, they too will always at least take a sip."

And so Kanwaketa took the small calabash of beer and told his friend, "Let me see you out and then come back to wait for this awful drunkard. For you know what a habitual trouble maker the creature is and how quick he is to go for his weapons whenever he fights with people. Should he come back, he will find us waiting for him and if he comes armed we too have weapons." Myombekere came out of the house and went to take his brothers-in-law and the three of them left. Kanwaketa had already gone ahead and was waiting for them at the gate of his home with *engunda* of beer, which he carried concealed under a goat-skin he was wearing. As soon as he escorted his visitors out of the gate, he gave the beer to Myombekere and they said their good-byes and parted.

At Myombekere's home Bugonoka had just been given her hot-water massage and Nkwazi was now treating the child's navel with herbs for the evening round. "Glad to see you back alive! What on earth was that commotion about, which could be heard all the way to this place: Beat him, beat him!" Bugonoka asked.

"We were the ones fighting with that awful creature Bandiho, because he pestered us beyond measures. He began by hurling insults at my brothers-in-law here, simply unbearable! Then he turned on me and we confronted each other and in no time he had caught me around the chest. When he tighten his hold on me I said to myself: `Let me teach you how to behave, you awful creature, if since you were born you have never seen how people fight.' And so we struggled with each other and before he knew it he was on the ground where we plant crops. People cheered us on and I held him by the throat and squeezed. Then I said to myself, `Leave the creature alone; that should teach him a lesson,' and got up from him. And that's when the fellow went raving mad, attacking everybody until he ended up breaking Kanwaketa's beer pot. There was still some beer in the pot and all of it spilled to the ground and became a pool. *Aa! hee!* When

Kanwaketa saw that he went after the drunkard raging with the anger of two people and said: "Why did he break my most valuable beer pot Beehive and pour all my beer to the ground! You'll pay for this or kill me first, you dog without shame!" People present stopped him and said, `You better leave the matter alone and allow us to teach him a lesson for you.' And indeed Bandiho was taught a lesson, though unfortunately the creature never learns. Whatever the case, the men did their work, gave the poor creature a real beating, goodness!

After that Myombekere presented to his mother-in-law the beer Kanwaketa gave him: "Welcome, mother-in-law. Here is a bit of beer for you from Kanwaketa. To say the truth, in spite of the fight which broke out, there wasn't much. He didn't have what he usually has when he brews beer."

"Tell our son-in-law I thank him. Maybe you should put it away until we have finished preparing food and are free to attend properly to that work, because our people of old said: `The sheep protested to the butcher: slaughter me gently, one job deserves another and your other jobs can wait,' and again they said: `The hare protested: you can't do two jobs at the same time.'"

Myombekere then spread on the floor near the entrance of his house, on the milk-churn ground, the hide of a cow to make a bed where his brothers-in-law would sleep. Lweganwa and Kamuhanda could not wait to stretch out a bit and fell on the cow-hide like tree logs, for you too know what happens when a person who has been sipping beer for quite a while lies down to take a rest. But in no time Lweganwa was up swaying on his feet and saying, "Brother-in-law, I am all sweat and I feel as if I want to throw up. May be I should go out." He had hardly finished saying that when he was already outside behind the house and was vomiting really big! In an instant Myombekere too had followed him there, with a calabashful of water. When Lweganwa stopped vomiting Myombekere poured water on his head and Lweganwa washed his head with the his right hand while propping himself against the ground with his other hand. Then he coughed and cleared his throat and told Myombekere, "That's enough, my brother-in-law. I am all right again now that I have vomited a bit. Somehow that's how I am. Whenever I take a lot of beer, I have difficult breathing until I vomit and once I have vomited the beer this way I feel fine and if there is still some it is then that I can drink without vomiting again. I simply don't know what's wrong with my stomach!"

"That's because every human being is created differently, my brother-in-law."

After dinner at the courtyard fireplace[26] Myombekere's brothers-in-law went back in the house to their bed by the house door and drank the beer Kanwaketa gave them from there. Slowly they found themselves giving up, having taken enough, and fell asleep until the new day dawned. Early in the morning the women got busy preparing food for them and their hosts escorted them and they left. As they were leaving Lweganwa's mother told her son, "Greet your father for me, and tell him: `As for her, she wants to see Bugonoka regain her strength a bit before coming,' and also tell him that, if the mother and her child wake up in good health, tomorrow we are outing the child."

And with that the two brothers, Lweganwa and Kamuhanda, went back to their homes, bringing with them the news they had heard at their beer drinking of the previous day, news of the illness of their country's king.

Chapter XX

NOTES

1. *Kasaka*: Name of a herb, of which there are two varieties, one whitish and the other reddish in color.

2. *Entobotobo:* See note 17 of Chapter XII.

3. Except in the rare cases where a married couple lived all alone, Wakerewe men usually took their meals separately from the women of their homes, so that a husband eating with his sick wife or his wife who had just given birth to keep her company was supposed to be an expression of affection for her.

4. *Tata*!: See note 5 of Chapter V.

5. *Ekina*: See note 8 of Chapter XIV.

6. Wakara: The people of Ukara Island (see Introduction). The Wakara used to dress by draping the barest cover over their private parts and were therefore seen by their much better dressed Wakerewe neighbors as people who went about naked.

7. *Bubwi*!: Possibly a combination of *bu*! and *bwi*! onomatopoeias for a big and small fart, respectively.

8. It was taboo for the Wakerewe, male or female, to be circumcised, and so the marriage of a Mkerewe woman to a circumcised man would be condemned.

9. *Izoba*: The "Sun". See note 21 of Chapter II.

10. *Ebitala,* plural for *ekitala*: See note 18 of Chapter I.

11. *Omukama*: See note 26 of Chapter II.

12. Bukindo: See note 8 of Chapter IV.

13. *Ensato*: See note 2 of Chapter VI.

14. *Emamba*: See note 17 of Chapter II.

15. *Ihara*: See note 6 of Chapter III.

16. For greetings according to relationship ranking see note 11 of Chapter I, and for joking relationship between brothers-in-law and sisters-in-law see note 29 of Chapter VI.

17. *Obwanda, amakugwe*: Names of medicinal herbs for treating sprains and dislocations..

18. *Olubigo*: See note 3 of Chapter II.

19. *Emigonzo,* plural for *omugonzo*: See 4 of Chapter VI.

20. *Engonogono*: See note 2 of Chapter VI.

21. *Omusese* (plural *Abasese*): Indigenous Mkerewe, as opposed to people from other tribes who lived in Ukerewe (and non-Wakerewe who wanted to pass

for Wakerewe). However, when used by Wajita and the other people the Wakerewe wanted to exclude by that insiders' name, it is the non-Wakerewe's pejorative name for Wakerewe.

22.   Abakwaya: See note 5 Chapter I.

23.   Abaruri: See note 15 of Chapter IX.

24.   *Engoma*:   Drum(s). The drum was also the emblem of the kings of Ukerewe (and other related Bahinda kings of the lake region -- see Introduction) and so the word also meant "kingdom" and "sovereignty".

25.   *Engunda*:   See note 20 of Chapter II.

26.   *Ekikome*:   See note 1 of Chapter II.

Chapter XXI

BABY NTULANALWO'S FIRST OUTING

On the fourth day from the day Bugonoka gave birth to her child, the piece of umbilical cord at the child's navel fell off. The mother looked for it and easily found it and went to keep it on tray,[1] because she knew it had a function to perform the following morning, the day of her child's first outing.

When Nkwanzi was informed by her daughter of the matter, she told her son-in-law, "Son-in-law, with us here in the house the child's umbilical cord has dropped. And so, if you have a little brother of yours, it doesn't matter whether he is of the same father and same mother with you or not, please know that today in the evening there is the cutting of *ebisisi*[2] sticks. It is that little brother of yours you will send to cut *ebisisi* sticks you will bring back with you, and then tomorrow morning we will out the child. The sticks have to be two sticks from *omulama*[3] tree."

As the sun was descending towards the horizon, Myombekere went and told a brother of his from among his father's relatives to cut *ebisisi* for him as directed by his mother-in-law and so in the evening he brought home *ebisisi* sticks and took them straight into the house. Bugonoka told him, "Put them on that tray over there, because that is where we have already placed the child's umbilical cord as well as the seeds of food he will come out with," and Myombekere did as he was told.

When it was dark enough in the evening, Myombekere called Bugonoka so that they could go to perform the rite of relating to each other in the horn, that is both of them were going to urinate in the same horn of a bull as sacrifice for *ebisisi* so that the spirits of the two of them would become inseparably one. Without that, they would live in danger of harming their child with *amakire*[4] disease. They went to the ancestral shrines of their homestead[5] and Myombekere took from a peg in a shrine hut a horn of the bull of a cow and urinated in it until he felt that was enough and cut short his urine so as to leave space for his wife's urine and passed the horn to Bugonoka, who received it, squatted down and she too urinated in it. *He!* with her she released a real flood and filled the horn to the brim and on to overflowing! Myombekere laughed, with a muffled voice, and so did Bugonoka herself. Then she gave him back the horn of urine and he received it by his left hand and proceeded to pour the urine behind the ancestral shrine, very close to it, right at the poles of the wall of the shrine hut. That done, he returned the horn to its peg in the shrine and Bugonoka went back in the house to her baby and he went to sit at his home's courtyard fireplace.

Suddenly in the house a small snake reddish in color dropped from the roof and smacked to the ground and remain immobilized for some time on the spot where it fell. Bugonoka was the first to cry out loud: "*Yu!* mother save us!" In that very instant she had jumped and snatched her child from where he lay and was at once on the other side of the floor clasping her baby in her hands. Myombekere too, who had heard his wife's cry, had in that very instant jumped from the courtyard fireplace into the house to find out what the danger was. On arriving inside the house he found the snake still lying where it had hit the ground, not far from where the bed of Bugonoka and her child was, and since he had come from outside with a stick with which to save from danger those who had sounded the alarm, he raised the stick ready to hit the snake.

At once his mother-in-law stopped him: "Don't! Don't kill it, son; that's taboo! Do you know what has brought it? For this is not a snake like the snakes we see everyday: it is a snake of the shrines. Let your wife give you some water, then sprinkle it with water from your mouth."

Bugonoka brought him water, while still clasping her child in her hands, and Myombekere took some water and held it in his cheeks and at once sprayed the snake with it. *Aa!* In that very instant there was nothing to be seen! The snake had disappeared, altogether! They searched and looked everywhere with torches and even undid the beddings on the ground where Bugonoka and her child were sleeping, but all in vain! Then Nkwanzi told Myembekere, "It is obvious that it is of your shrines. Your departed relatives had only come to see how the child is doing and had not come with bad intentions at all. You should dispel all your fears, because there is no longer any reason for you to be afraid."

Bugonoka rejoined, "Now I see! So that's why people say: `You see it only once like a snake of the shrines'. For look, as soon as it was sprinkled with mouth water we did not even see how it disappeared."

"You are indeed still little children!" Nkwanzi said. "Apparitions from the shrines are seen only when they make their presence known, that's the only time you can see them. How can you then know how they disappear! Nobody can know that. It is some kind of mystery. It is a happening which paralyzes a person's senses as a stone-blow on the shin paralyzes the leg."

After dinner they went to bed and it dawned.

When it dawned and began to brighten up and people everywhere were waking up, Nkwanzi told Myombekere: "Son-in-law, aren't you going to fetch some feathers for the amulet of *enkona*,[6] and *olusombwa, olubingo* and *olusinga*,[7] and *omulindi*[8] for making a shield for the child.

Myombekere went to Kanwaketa's and invited Kanwaketa to come to his home that day to eat the meat of his child's *engozi*[9] goat, before going to his neighbor's mother Nanzala to ask her for the feathers to put in *enkona* amulet, and she gave him some. Before leaving, Myombekere told old Nanzala: `Please come as soon as you can'".

"That's right, go ahead, we too are on our way."

On his way back home Myombekere went into the fields to look for *olusinga, olusombwa* and *olubingo* and brought the plants home, where he was instructed to put those ritual items too on the tray where already the piece of the child's umbilical cord was, alongside the ritual food seeds, namely the grains of *endwero* millet, some *enkole*[10] beans and pumpkin seeds of the previous year's harvest. Myombekere did so, and also put on that tray sinews of a cow which was killed by a blow of an ax on the head. Then he went out again, carrying with him a billhook to go and cut *omulindi* cork wood at the lake shore and in no time he was back.

He returned home to find Nanzala and her daughter-in-law already arrived, making *enkona* amulet while the other women in the house were making straps for the child's *engozi*, and sent Kagufwa to call Kanwaketa and also to fetch his neighbor's *kanabuhotora* [11] ritual spear for offering sacrifice to the ancestors as well as some green banana leaves on which to slaughter *engozi* goat, and in no time Kagufwa and Kanwaketa arrived bringing with them some green banana leaves as well as the miniature healer's spear. Quite a number of men, mostly Myombekere's relatives he had invited to come and eat the meat of the goat of his child's *engozi*, had already gathered in his home. The Wakerewe may bring a child out into the open for the first time at any time during daytime, morning or evening, whatever the parents of the child prefer, the only exception being noontime, for outing the child at noon is not a Kikerewe custom.

The women in the house made *enkona* amulet with the sinews of a cow which was killed by a blow of an ax on the head, enclosing in the amulet the feathers of a real eagle together with the feathers of the small bird *kamunyamunya*, which is also known as *entangamarwa*,[12] to counteract the striking power of the eagle, made a string by some more of the cow sinews for the child to wear the amulet with and made straps for the child's *engozi* with suitable cords and finished, and then started their women side of the rite of taking the newborn child into the open for the first time. The newborn child, Ntulanalwo, was put on the back of the young girl of the home, where he was strapped by *omwigereko*,[13] the goat skin the child's mother used to wear as a top cover for her *enkanda* [14] robe. The child was already wearing his *enkona* amulet, in such a way that it was in his hair at the crown of his head,   all this while still inside the house. Then the women poured water into a washbasin[15] of average size, into which was to be dipped an aspergillum of *olusombwa* held together with the leaves *olubingo*, and gave the washbasin and the aspergillum to Nkwanzi and Nkwanzi held the washbasin in her left hand and the aspergillum in her right hand. The young girl who was carrying the newborn baby was then made to hold a Wazinza hoe[16] by the handle. Bugonoka on her part held the tray containing the piece of her child's umbilical cord and the grains of *endwero* millet, some *enkole* and some seeds of the previous year's pumpkin harvest.

Those preparations ready, the women's party came out of the house, with Bugonoka leading the way, the young girl who was carrying Ntulanalwo following her, Nkwanzi following the girl and Nanzala and her daughter-in-law at the rear. Once outside, the women told the young girl: "Dig here: behold your field for crops!" The young girl struck the ground with the hoe, three times or so. Immediately Nanzala told Nkwanzi, "Make rain for them, the ground of their crop field is too hard!" and Nkwanzi dipped the aspergillum of *olusombwa* and *olubingo* leaves in the washbasin and sprayed with water the young girl and baby Ntulanalwo while uttering loud and clear the words: "It is raining, it is raining, friends!

You must run, dear girls, lest we get soaked so far away from home!" The girl ran, followed by the rest of the women, all laughing, as if it were a joke, when in fact they we concluding their part of the rite.

At the porch of the house door, the women unstrapped the child from the young girl's back and gave it to Bugonoka and Bugonoka took her child and sat right in the middle of the of the door of her house and placed her child on her lap. The women then shaved off from the child's head the hair he was born with, using the water in the washbasin to wet the hair. That finished, they turned to their daily household chores, like grinding flour for cooking food for the people who had come to eat the meat of the newborn's *engozi* goat.

Then it became the turn of the men to perform their part of the ceremony, for which a diviner had already arrived to look into the entrails of Ntulanalwo's *engozi* goat. A brother of Myombekere, the oldest of his relatives on his fathers side, spoke to Myombekere: " Aren't you going to offer to the ancestors the goat, so that it can be slaughtered?   Hold *kanabuhotora* spear in your left hand and the goat in your right and take the animal near the middle of the door of your house, over there near the child, and call upon the ancestors quickly, so that people can go ahead and slaughter the goat."

Myombekere got up and took *kanabuhotora* spear and with no more loss of time he had got to the he-goat, untethered it and brought it to the door of his house, there where Bugonoka was still seated holding her child on her lap. On getting there, he squatted down and uttered the sacrificial words by telling his son: "May you accept your goat: here it is, the one we have given you to be sacrificed for your *engozi*. May it bring you nothing but good health!" Then he prayed to his ancestors, naming all his departed forebears he knew by name: "*Bananka, banyonyo, babusunga, babugoteka,*"[17] and adding, "And all you our ancestors, from the first one to the last one, come and join us and accept the goat of this child of yours, which we want this day to sacrifice for his *engozi* so that he may be blessed will good health and well-being." With that his clan elder told him, "No more, that's enough."

The diviner who had come gave his sword-like knife to some young men present and then he himself quickly got up and went to strangle the goat[18] with the help of Myombekere. When the two men killed the goat, the diviner told those to whom be had given his long double-edged knife to give it back to him so that he could slice open the goat's skin at the belly and let them skin the animal. In no time he had slit open the skin of the goat along the middle of its stomach and at once the young men went to skin the goat at the door of Myombekere's house, at the same time as Bugonoka and her child were told they could now go back inside the house, because their part of the ceremony was over, since the child had remained outside only to wait for the offering of his goat to the ancestors.

The young men finished skinned the goat and the diviner disemboweled it and removed the parts of the entrails he needed for his divination, namely the food stomach, the spleen, the heart, the lungs, the liver and the intestines. He began seeing things and saw that *engozi* of that goat was propitious for the child, and also saw that there would be a war in Ukerewe, a terrible one, in the years ahead, together with a locust plague where locust would descend on the land and completely destroy food crops, and that there would also be other pestilences like an epidemic of boils, and that there would be a season of too much rain and a season of drought. Then he took the intestines of the goat in his hands and saw good signs in it and that in that home of Myombekere there was health and prosperity. He turned over and searched the goats intestines again and again, all the while, as had been the case from the start, a person constantly pouring water on the goat's interior parts he was examining. The diviner saw that Bugonoka would have another child.

Inside the house the women were ululating[19] without break in jubilation for the happy news they were hearing. The diviner then put down the intestines and took the heart of the goat. He shook his head and put that part of the entrails down and took the goat's lungs and blew air into them and inflated them and turned them upside down to look at the throne of the kingdom, the health of the king. *Hi*! what a sight! As soon as he sighted the throne, those present saw him shake his head with great sadness.   His audience was reduced to watching him without comprehending a thing. Until eventually they asked him, "Why have you been reduced to shaking your head that way? Share with us the news, whatever it is, because all of us here are people of the same clan, and there is no outsider here you can fear to trust with a secret. The only outsider here besides yourself is Kanwaketa, a respectable elder who would simply not blab as if he has never been witness to what can be revealed through a sacrificial animal and who, besides, is our friend".

"Is that your wish, that I should be Mr. Split-opener of no matter what?"

"It is."

"If that is your wish, so be it. What I saw then is a throne which is toppling and not resting upright in its stand. And since that is your wish, let me spill out everything and not leave things I see unsaid as if my divination is of outside origin and not a gift of our own home passed onto me by my father and grandfather. And so I have seen that our king's illness is no ordinary illness from which he will recover, and only a few days and nights remain before you hear that he has followed his father in the land of the dead. Then Abasilanga will fall on each other fighting over the succession of their reign. Look how the populace is up in arms, bows and arrows in hand! It is true there will be no loss of life, but strife will reign in the palace of the rain-makers, until another king is seated in the throne. *Aa!* May what you have heard not be blamed on me! I have just repeated what I have been told by the goat of *engozi* of Ntulanalwo the son of Myombekere. Let no one come to ask me how I learnt all this, poor me!

"Yes, it is as you say. You have learnt all these things from the sacrificial goat, because you were blessed with the eye that can see such things. You had been here for quiet a while before that but you hadn't said any of those things until you saw them in the goat's entrails. So without it you wouldn't have known them. *Aa!* All we can do is to wait and see how it will all come to pass. As our people say: `We the subjects are monkeys and catch another branch the instant the one we are on breaks.'"

Myombekere's elder brother said, "I see that all of you here are still little children. The truth is, *omukama*[20] is not mourned the way we ordinary people are mourned. Only the drum[21] mourns him. And so, should what has been said come to pass, the one among us who will still be alive will see what he or she will see. So to us ordinary people the passing of the king should not concern us much. It is true we will feel sad, because it is the death of our sovereign, our ruler, but our attitude, we poor souls, should be this: `Whoever marries my mother becomes my father.'  It is for us that the Mkerewe of old coined the saying: `In this Ukerewe of ours a mourning which doesn't concern you is for you a wedding.' That's all; I have no more to say to you. You have better attend to the business for which we are gathered here."

Since the seer too had finished his divination, he gave them permission to cut up the meat so that all the sacrificial animal could be cooked and eaten and consumed to the last bit there and then. The cutting of the sacrificial animal completed, Myombekere's clan elder told him,

"You must cut from each of the different parts of the meat a tiny piece of sacrificial meat and serve food to the ancestors."

At once Myombekere did as he was told and cut off from each and every part of the goat's meat a piece of meat, tiny like this, and put the pieces on strips of green banana leaves and took the sacrificial meat to the gate of his household, which stood facing east this way. Once at the gate, still upright on his feet, he began giving food to the ancestors while loudly invoking them and saying: "*Bananka , banyonyo, babusunga, babugoteka*, may you accept this food and eat some meat, which I am now giving you, so that your child may be blessed with good health and well-being." He then placed the pieces of meat on every part of the entrance of the gate of his home, everywhere. That done he left the gate, still carrying some pieces of meat on two strips of fresh banana leaves, and went to his home's ancestral shrine huts and there too repeated his loud invocation of his ancestors and said: "To all our ancestors, from the first one to the last one, may you partake of this food, may you accept with kind disposition your dish of meat I am serving you here so that your child will know of no illness when carried in the skin of this goat which we have sacrificed for him today, so that he will always be blessed with good health, so that his footsteps would be acknowledged by the cries of frightened termites whenever he treads the earth!"

With that Myombekere finished giving food to his ancestors and the meat of the sacrificial goat was cooked by men on cooking-stones which had been erected outside in the compound of his home, as custom dictated such meat to be cooked. Refuse from the stomach of the goat had been emptied at the door of the house where the goat was slaughtered and left there until after eating, when everything, right up to the banana leaves on which the animal was butchered, would be hauled away and taken and thrown at a crossroads. The meat of the sacrificial goat was eaten this way: As the men outside cooked the meat of the goat, the women in the house cooked sacrificial *obwita*[22] with *endwero* millet flour, and when the food was ready once again Myombekere served food to his ancestors the way he had done the first time, again invoking them loudly, but this time feeding them cooked meat with *obwita*.

On seeing that, the boys present burst out with stifled laughs and the adults at once rebuked them: "You dogs! Shameless creatures! What are you laughing at! Is this a game to you! Stop, you are too big for that, lest it becomes a habit," and the kids were silenced. Then the women in the house quickly brought to the men outside some five dishes of *obwita* of *obubele* millet flour and a sixth one of *obwita* of the red *omugusa* millet flour, in addition to the sacrificial one, a tiny one like this, the one of *endwero* flour, making all together seven dishes of *obwita*. The men then all sat down in a meal circle at the door of Myombekere's house, the place where the goat had been slaughtered, around the green banana leaves on which the goat was slaughtered and on which were the refuse from the animal's stomach. The large water pot in which the goat meat was cooked was placed inside the meal circle and meat dished out of the pot onto some three big plates[23] from which the men ate meat. The men started off their meal by eating the sacrificial *obwita*, the tiny dish of *endwero obwita*, before turning to the rest of the food as each one of them pleased, those who preferred *obubele* millet eating *obwita* of *obubele* and those who preferred *omugusa* millet likewise eating *omugusa*, as the man who was eating with his little boy beside him urged on his child to eat, forcing into the little boy's hand some more meat when the tiny hand was still full and telling the child, "Eat, little dad, you need it to grow!" The seer was served the head of the goat and told: "Here is your dreams' head, because you are our diviner and the head belongs to you and to nobody else." The tongue of the goat was given to Myombekere's elder brother, the head of their clan. The others ate the other cuts of the meat, each one of them taking this or that piece until they finished all the meat to the last bit, discarding the bones onto the goat's stomach refuse while all the time sending away crying with blows any dog which tried to get near those bones, until they finished their meal and moved away from the place.

The diviner then instructed the men on how to prepare the skin of the goat for use as *engozi*. They were not to prepare it like the skins for wearing as clothes, nor like the sacrificial robes of men or of women, nor like the healer's rags, nor the cow-skin robe men wear to sacrifice a cow in prayer for prosperity, nor like the woman's *amwegereko* top-cover, nor like the rain-maker's rag, nor like the usual ritual skins men wear whenever they offer sacrifice for good health and well-being, nor like the skin men wear when making sacrifice to ward off diseases and epidemics and misfortunes of every kind, nor like any other ritual wear.[24] The goat skin for use as *engozi* was prepared in a unique way, because the day the goat is skinned is the very same day the skin must dry, be made into *engozi* and be used to carry the newborn child. None of that may be postponed until the following day. To make sure the skin dried quickly, it was scraped with stones and gravel again and again all the time until it dried on that very day and straps were attached to it, because leaving any of that work unfinished is taboo. That too is how Ntulanalwo's *engozi* was treated and it dried and straps were attached on it and it was made into *engozi* that same day. And since that day happened to be a day of bright sunlight, it took no time at all to dry and Nkwanzi put straps on it and made it into *engozi* and gave it to Bugonoka and Bugonoka used it to strap her child on her back.

Then Myombekere turned to making his child a miniature bow and supplied it with its arrow, both bow and arrow made of a stem of *olusinga*. His child was a male person and so he had to grow up knowing how to use a bow and arrow, weapons with which to defeat his enemies should he ever be attacked in his lifetime. Myombekere had also to make a shield for his son, and so he divide into his house at once and come out with a chisel for working on the *omulindi* cork wood and in no time the shield was ready, complete with a hand grip. He was then instructed to take all those items into his house and stick them into the roof of his house in such a way that they were directly over the door of the house, alongside all the other objects of the outing ceremony, the grass aspergillum of *olusombwa* and *olubingo* leaves together with the two *ebisisi* sticks, taking care to place one of *ebisisi* sticks on the male side of the door, that is on the right-hand side when inside the house facing outside, and the other stick on the female safe of the door, the left hand side of the door when inside facing outside. As to the piece of the child's umbilical cord, that one was thrown underneath its parents' bed.

That done and finished, he wrapped together in the green banana leaves the refuse of the goat's interior and the bones of the meat and the morsels of *obwita* which had escaped from the hands of the men and dropped down as they were eating and hauled off everything to a crossroads, got there and threw down everything in the middle of the meeting place of two footpaths and returned home. The sun had already begun to descend in the sky.

As soon as he got back home, his relatives and the diviner said it was time for them to leave. Before they left, the seer told Myombekere: "Let's say you have some two important functions yet to perform in this home of yours today. You must first achieve the rite of *ebisisi* and follow that by achieving *engozi* rite. So in the evening you will call your wife for the two of your to go and relate in the horn and thereby achieve the two rites at the same time, because the two have been performed on the same day.

With that on your part, you the husband, both the sex prohibitions of *ebisisi* and that of *engozi* will be lifted, and   from then on those sex prohibitions for the protection of the child will bear on the baby's mother alone. You would be free to go with other women outside your wedlock as much as you like, with no fear of harming your child with *amakire* disease.   For fortunately we are not like Abakwaya[25] people, of whom we hear that with them the husband lifts this sex prohibition with the mother of the child as the intermediary, body to body, when the women has just delivered a child! *Ahee*! What strange human beings these people must be! We are certainly much better with our intermediary of the horn, with the husband and wife just urinating in a horn, which gives the   man's wife time to become wholesome again."

Myombekere too joined in and said," It is true, our way of doing things is certainly much better, because that other thing! *Aa!* no!"

With that Myombekere's visitors said good-bye to their hosts and left.

In the evening Myombekere and his wife did as he was told by the diviner and matters were concluded and everything was well and settled for the couple.

Four days passed and on the fifth the new moon appeared and people played *enzamba*[26] flutes for it. Bugonoka and Nkwanzi heard people playing horn flutes and whistles to welcome a new moon and   brought Ntulanalwo out into the open to show him his month, the first one to appear since he was born. Once outside, holding the child in their arms, they lifted him up towards the moon and said, "Ntulanalwo, there is your first month, look at it!" Then they took the child inside the house again. Nkwazi stayed with her daughter until she regained her strength and then went back home to her husband. Sometime before that a cow, fully grown, had one day come back home from grazing with the other cows in excellent health only to fall down and die on reaching home, without any sign of being sick, and so there was some smoked beef in Myombekere's house and Bugonoka's mother went back to her home with a basketful of dried meat as her send-off present.

Chapter XXI

NOTES

1. *Olugali:* See note 6 of Chapter I.
2. *Ebisisi:* Two ritual sticks used in the ceremony of outing a newborn baby, that is taking the child out of the house in which it was confined since its birth and bringing it outside into the open for the first time.
3. *Omulama:* Name of a tree literally meaning "long-lasting-one".
4. *Amakire:* See note 4 of Chapter XII.
5. *Amazu g'abakekuru:* See note 6 of Chapter VI.
6. *Enkona*: An eagle. The eagle was deemed to be the cause of polio in children, and hence a child who suffered from polio was said to have been "struck" by an eagle and the amulet to protect children from polio was called the *enkona* (eagle) amulet.
7. *Olusombwa, olubingo, olusinga. Olusombwa*: grass-like shrub; *olubingo* or *ibingo* (plural *amabingo*): slender sugarcane-like cane; *olusinga*: small woody plant with a slender straight and branchless stem. *Olusombwa* and the leaves of *olubingo* were held together and used as an aspergillum, and the stem of *olusinga* was used to make a bow and an arrow, the weapons with which to out a male baby child.
8. *Omulindi:* Cork tree which grows among lake mangroves.
9. *Engozi*: Piece of goat-skin (later on cloth) with which to strap a baby onto the back of its mother or baby-sitter, the way Wakerewe women normally carried babies.
10. *Enkole:* See note 25 of Chapter XII.
11. *Kanabuhotora:* Miniature one-piece all iron ritual spear about three feet long a person held in his or her hand when offering sacrifice to ancestors.
12. *Kamunyamunya* or *entangamarwa:* Names of a bird which literary mean "tiny great shitter" and "beer brewer", respectively.
13. *Mwigereko:* Kitereza's note for his Swahili translation of his novel is: "The skin of a goat which a woman wore on top of her robe of very soft cow skin. Women would wear *omwigereko* to cover their breasts so that their sons-in-law would not see them, because a son-in-law seeing the   breasts of his mother-in-law would be a very shameful thing indeed!"
14. *Enkanda*: See note 22 of Chapter VI.
15. *Olusabazyo*: See note 12 of Chapter I.
16. Wazinza hoe: See note 18 of Chapter V.

17. *Bananka, banyonyo, babusunga, babugoteka*: Conversational formula for saying "so-and-so and so-and-so" many times, from *nanka* or *kananka* (plural *bananka* or *bakananka*), "so-and-so".

18. Traditionally the Wakerewe killed a goat by strangling it, as they do on a number of occasions in the novel.

19. *Akahira*: See note 11 of Chapter IX.

20. *Omukama*: See note 26 of Chapter II.

21. For the drum as the emblem of the kings of Ukerewe see note 24 of Chapter XX. Palace drums, *emilango*, were played at all important palace occasions, the sad ones included. For *Emilango* see note 11 of Chapter XIII.

22. *Obwita*: See note 14 of Chapter I.

23. *Enanga*, plural for *olunanga*: See note 16 of Chapter I.

24. It would appear Kitereza here simply wants to tell his reader that animal skins as clothing material were prepared differently depending on their intended use.

25. Abakwaya: See note 5 Chapter I.

26. Enzamba: See note 7 of Chapter XIV.

Chapter XXII

THE KING DIES AND A NEW ONE IS ENTHRONED

Shortly after the seers prediction, in that very mouth, the moon of the month still a bright moon, Myombekere and Bugonoka heard people say: "*Omukama*[1] has passed away." The couple exclaimed sadly and said, "*Ahee!* Goodness gracious! Our beloved and kind king has really passed away!" And for a long while the whole country was no longer the same, sadness reigned everywhere and the land became quiet as if the entire population had deserted it. People began circulating in whispers all sorts of rumors, claiming to have heard all sorts of bad things. This person here would tell another person there: "Do you know?" and his or her companion would retort, "*Nn!*" and with that he or she would tell that other person who had bewitched *omukama* and killed him and who was about to be installed on the throne, claiming that Abagwe[2] had already made their choice: "Don't you know *omukama* was killed by his brother so and so. Apparently the throne is so sweet that he killed his own brother so that he would become king!" To which his or her companion would rejoin: "So he is the assassin! *Hee!* The throne must be luring indeed if a man can kill even his own brother for it!" Hearing which his or her companion would in turn rejoin, "I have, in fact, met a person who learnt it from Abagwe themselves, that person is also the one who revealed to me the secret that Abagwe have selected such-and-such a prince to become our new king."

But all those rumors were said in muffled mumblings, only in: *hihi*! *hihi*! Two people in this place would mumble theirs and yet another two in another place would have theirs, in all of which there was a majority side with a common version of things and yet you still found a minority's different point of view as well. And should a member of the Abagwe king-makers clan happen to pass by, a crowd of people would rush towards him, just in case he would say something for them to hear, and seeing that he would make a sign by the hand to say no, to keep that crowd of people away from him, because for Abagwe the time following the death of the king was one of pressing and grave matters, like settling the inheritance of the dead king's personal belongings, making preparations for his burial, in addition to selecting from among the princes another good man fit to rule the country.   During those days a drum in *omukama's* palace was heard endlessly sounding by repeated strokes of a single drum-stick mourning the king.

Myombekere and people like him who had never seen the burial of *omukama* found themselves in the palace of the dead king milling aimlessly at the edge of the huge crowd of people which gathered daily in Bukindo.[3] Whatever the case, there was nothing else for them to do, since the burial of *omukama* was a matter for Abagwe only. One day Myombekere was in that endless mass of people when he came across a person who let him in the secret that the body of the dead king would be buried that day in the evening, and so Myombekere decided to return home first and when he got home he shared that bit of information with Bugonoka, to keep her informed of what was going on. At home he stayed only long enough to eat a bit of sweet potatoes and then in the evening was back again in Bukindo, hoping to see how it would all happen, only to be met by the news that the body of the king had already been taken out of the palace on the quiet and onto the lake and put in a boat and carried to the foot of *Kitale*[4] Mountain, the burial ground of the kings of Ukerewe. Myombekere was confounded and said to himself, "I who wanted to see it all has ended up seeing nothing!" And so he ended the day by returning home to tell Bugonoka nothing except that he didn't see a single thing of *omukama's* burial!.

The following day Myombekere, as he had been doing on the previous days, passed by Kanwaketa's home and the two neighbors went together back to Bukindo, to find out which prince would assume the kingdom drum[5] as well as to learn the name of the person who buried *omukama*, that is the one who cut the first hoe on the ground to dig the dead *omukama's* grave. As soon as they got there, what would they see but a lot of people armed to the tooth, with spears, bows and arrows and carrying on their shoulders quivers of all sizes and shapes! The two neighbors held each other's hand as each said to himself, "What brought us here in the midst of such a raging war?" But each kept that to himself and aloud they both simply said, "Let's wait and see what happens next!" So that was it! Those armed people were the party of the prince who had been selected by Abagwe to become the new *omukama*! Myombekere and Kanwaketa had arrived at the moment when the members of Abagwe clan and maternal relatives of the appointed prince were escorting the prince into the palace to be attired in the king's regalia, and after a short while the two neighbors saw that armed crowd come out of the palace again. Seeing that Myombekere asked one Omusese,[6] rather advanced in years, "And where are they going again now?"

"I thought you were a Mkerewe?"
"Yes, it's true I am a Mkerewe, but this is my first time to see the installing of *omukama* on the throne and that's why I am asking."

"As I see it, now they are taking the prince who is to become king to Igalagala[7] rock to test him and see whether he can become *omukama* by making him climb the rock before they can install him on the throne to rule".

"Well, well! Now I see what this is all about!"
The prince and the procession of his followers were gone and stayed gone for quite a while. Finally Myombekere and his companions saw that huge crowd of people returning to the palace singing a victory song, which was joined in by the crowd which had remained behind in the palace sending out a cry of great jubilation in which multitudes of women rang out peels of ululation:[8] *keyekeye! keyekeye!* in the midst of *emilango*[9] drums, which at once thundered and rumbled beyond belief! Myombekere and Kanwaketa found themselves bodily swept forward by the crowd and caught in its mood of joy and celebrations, their sadness at the loss of their dead king altogether forgotten. It was then that they learnt the name of the prince who had become their new *omukama* as well as that of the person who had buried their dead king, at the same time as they witnessed cows without number being slaughtered to celebrate the enthroning of the new *omukama*.

In the days which followed the installing of the new king on the throne, all the dance groups in Ukerewe with their lead singers were summoned to Bukindo to dance for the new king their dances of the day. So into Bukindo people poured in countless numbers from each and every village of the entire Ukerewe Kingdom like eggs of a pregnant jigger burst-open. *Aa! hee! we!* What can I say! What was one to see and what leave out! There was simply too much of everything: the dancers, the spectators, those who had come to simply pay homage to their new king as well as those who had come to do so by bringing him presents of banana beer, of cows and goats, as the new master of the land himself reigned on his throne in the middle of the compound of his palace!

Finally Myombekere and Kanwaketa also made to Bukindo their citizens' visit and paid homage to their new *omukama*. Kanwaketa made the visit with six pots of banana beer. As for Myombekere, his banana plantation was not yet mature enough, had just began to bear fruit and could not as yet produce enough bananas for making beer. He hadn't even drunk from it the farm tasting beer people speak of. What he presented himself with before his king was a young bull of fair size whose mother had already calved twice after it. And what a palace reception for the two neighbors and friends! They were received by *omukama* himself as his beloved visitors! Call it my lies if you like, but I am convinced that those who accompanied them on that visit have yet to forget the day! Yes, I know, the one who did not witness their reception is even this very moment calling me a liar. But, believe it or not, that was a real royal treat for the two neighbors. As the saying goes: "A man with no provisions cannot tell fellow seafarers: `Let's land over there and cook something to eat,'" and *omukama* has it all.

Before returning home they said their good-byes to *omukama*: "Long live our King; have a good night our Sovereign", to which he answered "*Mn!*" Since the king had a cow slaughtered in their honor, when they left the palace and passed through the home of the courtier in which their presents had been received, they were given back their walking sticks together with some meat of a cow to carry back to their homes with them. Back in their homes, they shared with their wives all they had seen in Bukindo in the midst of dancers and courtiers, and when they got to describing the treat *omukama* gave them they simply did not know where to stop! Their wives too were overjoyed. What with their husbands bringing home some meat from the palace! *Aa*! What happiness! Just listen to how all excited Bugonoka became on hearing what her husband told her: The following morning, after cooking breakfast for her husband, she went to the lake to take a bath and came back home, took out liquid butter and shined her body, fetched her *enku*[10] and perfumed herself and told her little child Ntulanalwo she had laid down on his *engozi* stretched on the ground, "Come, let met put you on my back so that we can go to dance for our king," and off she went!. Nakiro and Kagufwa on their part had already left for *omukama's* palace long before! And when Bugonoka got to the dances and the other celebrations in Bukindo that day she completely forgot everything else, to the point of almost forgetting to feed her child! She did not even realize that it was getting dark and that she had milking of cows to attend to and as a result that evening all the calves of her home sucked their fill of their mothers' milk and not a single cow was milked! That was the day Myombekere wanted to teach her the lesson of her life! In fact what held him back was the fact that their child was still so tiny, but if let's say Ntulanalwo was already a bit bigger, he surely would have beaten her, because he was boiling with anger.

That incident passed and the couple put it behind them and went back to the two of them having one wish and one word.

Chapter XXII

NOTES

1. *Omukama*: See note 26 of Chapter II.
2. Abagwe or Abasita: The clan or king-makers. Though the king's heir was normally his oldest son, in Ukerewe succession to the throne was not strictly by primogeniture and elders of that clan could select any other son of the dead king or any other Muhinda (plural Bahinda), "Prince", to become king.
3. Bukindo: See note 8 of Chapter IV.
4. The kings of Ukerewe were buried at the foot of Kitale Mountain by the lakeside some two miles northwest of present day Bukindo Palace and four miles northwest of the Old Bukindo at Musozi. See note 31 of Chapter XII.
5. *Engoma*: The drum as the emblem of the kings of Ukerewe and their kingdom. See note 24 of Chapter XX.
6. Omusese: See note 21 of Chapter XX.
7. Igalagala: A huge steeply sloping granite rock near Kitale Mountain burial grounds of the kings of Ukerewe of note 4 above. The final rite in the enthroning of the new king by Abagwe (or Abasita) king-makers was to make the king-to-be climb up and down the huge rock without touching the rock while wearing leopard skin slippers on his feet, a trial the main significance of which was to confirm that the king-to-be was perfect physically and not lame in anyway, since no man in any manner lame or in any way missing any part of his body, including his foreskin from circumcision, could become king of the Wakerewe.
8. *Akahira*: See note 11 of Chapter IX.
9. *Emilango*: See note 11 of Chapter XIII.
10. *Enku*:   See note 24 of Chapter VIII.

Chapter XXIII

NTULANALWO IS BESET BY DISEASES

And now witness Bugonoka put on weight and become really plump, her strength fully restored, once again attending adeptly to all her daily work as she used to before she gave birth to her child. When she was going some place, she strapped Ntulanalwo on her back with his *engozi*.[1] On the day she was tilling her crop fields or grinding millet on her grinding-stone, again on her back is where Ntulanalwo would normally be. In fact that's where he was most of the time whenever she was doing whatever she was doing, be it cooking *obwita*[2] or digging up sweet potatoes. But since Bugonoka was bringing up a young girl in her home, at times she strapped Ntulanalwo on the back of the little girl and then she herself attended to whatever she wanted to do.

And bit by bit Ntulanalwo was a month old. With the passing of time the child became all round, his body nothing but folds and lumps of flesh, so that on washing him Bugonoka had to open those folds before she could reach the hidden parts underneath, and a lump of flesh covered his entire neck. Whoever passed by at those times when the child was not carried in his *engozi* and hidden from view and saw the child could not help exclaiming with amazement at how chubby it was!

Shortly after that Ntulanalwo's parents brought him a baby-sitting amulet, which he wore hanging across one shoulder, and filled his arms and legs with ornaments which made the child look even bigger. Whoever found the child out of his *engozi* and saw his face and his fingers and toes could also not refrain from saying, "This child takes after his father completely! He looks like Myombekere in every way as if it were Myombekere himself who went into Bugonoka's womb and came out! Even his fingers right to their fingernails are nothing but Myombekere! He is indeed Myombekere in everything, the only exception being his hair, which resembles Bugonoka's!" Bugonoka's hair was remarkable because she had *kaheke kalagalika*[3] hair most admired by the Wakerewe, the short bristle naps which look like scattered grains of cereal on the head, and not the unwanted slimy hair[4] of Abakangara,[5] which people sometimes called the hair of a larva.

It was in that very month that Ntulanalwo went down with a stomach disease, the stomach pain common in babies which makes the child's excrement stop being the watery stuff newborns in good health empty from their bowels. All the child was doing now instead of emptying its bowels was twisting and writhing and bringing out nothing but foam. Bugonoka and Myombekere became miserable indeed, until finally they confided in other people, since, as the Wakerewe of old said: "To hide a disease is to want it revealed by mourners," a saying the Bakwaya[6] people too have in their language. The people they consulted told them that their child was experiencing stomach pains caused by *ilezi*[7] disease, and that it was *ilezi* which prevented him from emptying his bowels normally like children do when still sucking and instead made him bring out nothing but foam. They told them that what they needed were medicine for the stomach pain and another medicine for *ilezi* disease itself. And indeed when the child was given those medicines he became well again and resumed noisily releasing liquid waste from his bowels as all newborns in good health do, and Bugonoka too went back to keeping by her all the time some soft toilet leaves for cleaning her child.

Before long, in that same month, one day the child went down with serious fever. That night Myombekere and Bugonoka did not sleep a wink. The following morning Myombekere filled a calabash[8] with millet and then with his finger scooped some saliva from the child's month and put it in the millet and took his child's *ekisano*[9] and went to look for a seer to find out the cause of his disease. The seer he went to told him that his child was sick because he wanted the articles of wear his namesake[10] used to wear when he was alive, which were an iron bracelet and a small wrist bell. "And so go and get them for him at once," the seer said. Once back home Myombekere went to look for the needed objects. And indeed when he obtained them and put them on the child in no time the fever left his child.

A few days after that the child stopped sucking normally his mother's milk and sucked in jerks while crying all the time, nighttime and daytime alike. Again the couple consulted people to find out why their child had stopped sucking well. Old Nanzala came to see the child and examined it in the mouth and found it had *amahanga*[11] baby teeth. "I see! This child has *amahanga* and needs to have them extracted. That's why he is not sucking well and he is crying so much. Up, quickly, let's take the child to Mfwanabwo; she is the one around here who knows how to extract *amahanga*."

The women went to see Mfwanabwo and told her, "Please cure us".

"Who is sick?"

"This child."

"Give it to me, let me take a look at it!"

She took the child in her hands and felt the back of its head. At once Mfwanabwo went into her house to look for the instruments she needed and brought them, sat on a chair and told Bugonoka, "Hold your child in your hands in a slanting position like this," and then she proceeded to extract *amahanga* from the child's mouth until she had removed them all, placing them on a leaf of a tree one after the other. The child cried until it could cry no more. There was a lot of bleeding in the child's mouth throughout the operation, to the extent that Bugonoka was trembling all over with pity for her child. After removing the child's *amahanga* Mfwanabwo went to fetch medicine with which to treat the wounds in its mouth, brought it, fetched a piece of a broken pot and took it to the courtyard fireplace,[12] where fire of the previous night was still smoldering, so that it did not take long for the potsherd to get hot. She then put the hot piece of pottery near the child and placed on it the medicine, which she had separated into two balls, placing on the potsherd one ball at a time. In no time the medicine was warm enough and she took the tiny ball of medicine and kneaded it on the child's *amahanga* wounds. Whenever the medicine she was using cooled, she put it back on the warm piece of pottery and at once took the now warm other tiny ball of medicine and kept on kneading with medicine the child's mouth wounds repeatedly with rapid hand movements. The child cried until the ears of those present were ringing with its cry! Only when she judged she had treated the wounds sufficiently did she stop: apparently those who treat children are completely devoid of pity! She then told Bugonoka and Nanzala, "Let me bring you medicine with which to continue treating the child's wounds."

She went somewhere behind her house and came back with the medicine, already made into a ball, and wrapped it in a piece of a green banana leaf and told Bugonoka, "Here is the medicine to go with. Divide it into two small balls the way you saw me do here and when it gets to the overhead noon sun knead his wounds with the medicine again and repeat the treatment in the evening and that will do it. Both times, put a potsherd over fire in your kitchen and when you judge it is warm enough take it the middle of the door of your house before it cools and treat the child from there. And take these *amahanga* with you, and when you come to a crossroads throw them there and walk on straight to your home without ever turning to look back. Did you hear me?

"I have heard you"

Bugonoka took her child's *amahanga* and the two women left with their sick child and when they came to a crossroads Bugonoka did as Mfwanabwo told her and the two of them continued walking nonstop and without ever looking back and returned home. At noon Bugonoka kneaded her child's wounds with the warm medicine and did so again in the evening. At night, at about cockcrow, the fever left the child and Ntulanalwo sucked normally.

Ntulanalwo's second month moon appeared and during that month his parents saw their child develop something like a small boil on one of his jaws! Finally Myombekere and Bugonoka called people to come and see what their child had. Everyone they asked told them the same thing: "I don't want to hide things from you, I want to tell you openly that your child here has caught *obuto*[13] disease. And so you have to see healers and procure him medicine at once before this disease overwhelms him and harms him, especially since it is on such a bad spot." So they asked everyone who came to took at the child for medicine for *obuto* disease and all sorts of healers gave them all sorts of medicines: some gave them amulets for the child to wear around his neck, or on his arms, so as to bring the small boil to a head quickly, others amulets for making the boil die out instead of coming to a head, and others yet, in their desperate search for a cure for their child, made them herbs pounded still green and mixed with butter from the milk of a black cow, which they rubbed on their child's boil, again so as to bring it to a head quickly. *Aa!* what didn't they try! But all in vain. Finally a certain man spoke to them of a medicine man he knew: "As far as I am concerned, Bihemo is the person who knows the cure for this disease, because something like this is what happened to a child of mine when it was still in its after-birth confinement until its mother and I had lost all hope. We had tried remedies from all sorts of healers, this sure healer and that other reliable one, all in vain! Until finally somebody told us of this man and I went to fetch him and he came and examined our child. After that I saw him take from his bag a small piece of wood this size together with a razor of white metal, like the ones healers with potent medicines use to make incisions in their patients' bodies for counteracting witchcraft when they treat patients struck with muteness by magic spells, and used it to cut the stick into two small amulets. I brought him some thatch grass blackened with kitchen fire soot from my house and some fire and *empindu*[14] needle and placed those things in the middle of the door of my house for him. Then with the red-hot point of the *empindu* he burnt through the amulets holes through which to thread a string of the sinew of what animal I don't know. After that he took a length of animal sinew from his healer's bag and trimmed it with his razor to the right size and then slipped on it the two small amulets he had made and tied then around the left arm of the child, since *obuto* was on its jaw of that side. And within very few days our child was cured. So, if you want my views, that is the real healer, the one I can personally vouch for, because he cured my child when I had lost all hope."

Myombekere fetched that medicine man and the healer examined his child and made the two amulets for him and put them on him and within a matter of very few days Ntulanalwo was cured of his *obuto* disease.

During all those days when Ntulanalwo suffered from one disease and then another, his parents protected his well-being by observing the sex prohibition incumbent on parents nursing a sick child. With that treatment Ntulanalwo was healed and Bihemo became for Myombekere and Bugonoka, for the rest of their lives, the healer who finally cured their child of *obuto* when they had lost all hope, a disease whose scar continued to mark Ntulanlwo's jaw until he was an adult and until he died and went to his grave with it.

In that second month after Ntulanalwo's birth Bugonoka's sister Barongo came to visit her the second time, to see her sister after the birth of her child. She found her sister's child already laughing to its baby-sitters, having recovered from all the illnesses which beset him following his after-birth confinement, a baby in perfect health. She stayed with her sister for about a whole month before her great pleasure of looking at her sister and her baby cooled down sufficiently and she went back to her home.

It was during that second month since his birth that Ntulanalwo began seeing. Everyone who came to Myombekere's home and found him carried in the hands of his baby-sitters would approach him, click his fingers at him and then pass his or her hand before his eyes and say: "*Yee!* Can you see! Look at my fingers!" and Ntulanalwo would turn his neck following the movement of the hand of the person who had clicked his or her fingers at him and everybody then realized the child had began to see. In the third month, Ntulanalwo's language became crying, as it usually is with all babies. When he suffered from his different diseases again his talking had been crying. For that we say: "Noted." When he was hungry he cried, and even when he ate his fill again he cried. When he felt hot and sweating he cried and when he was being washed to cool him down again he rang out crying you would think someone was beating him. And so we say that his language at that time was crying. During daytime, Bugonoka would often spread Ntulanalwo's *engozi* on the floor by the milk-churn near the door of their house and he would fall asleep there, but not with closed eyes the way people normally sleep, and those who came by and found the child sleeping that way would tell Bugonoka, "It appears your child sleeps like the fish *ensato!*"[15]

"And what is to sleep like *ensato?*"

"It is to sleep with eyes open and not with the closed eyes of a sleeping person".

"Is that supposed to be a disease too?"

"No, it's not a disease, but a child sleeping that way is often caused by the mother of the child having been too fond of eating the sweet heads of *ensato* while she was pregnant. That's what we too were told by out elders when we were growing up."

"May be it is true, because when I was pregnant I used to stuff myself so much with the heads of *ensato!* May be that's why my child is sleeping that way!"

"It is, for you can't imagine our ancestors saying something they hadn't seen."

A number of days passed and then Ntulanalwo began sucking his mother's milk only to throw it up immediately, with his eyes turned upward. Bugonoka and Myombekere were at a loss as to what was happening! And since our people of old said "to ask is to know," the couple inquired for enlightenment from other people until finally one person told them that their child was suffering from *oluzoka*[16] and also told them where to find a healer to cure him of the disease, and Myombekere went to fetch the healer and brought him to his home to see his child. The healer examined the child and then told its mother, "Please give him a breast to suck and let's see how he reacts. What disease can this be?" Bugonoka suckled her child. Ntulanalwo had gulped down no more than some four mouthfuls when he stopped sucking and remained immobilized on his mother's breast and in that very instant threw up the milk he had sucked. When the medicine man saw that, he knew at once what the disease was and said aloud: "I think the child is suffering from a stomach diseases. He has *oluzoka*, that's what makes him suck milk while throwing up this way. He also has another stomach disease, the one called *empingizi*.[17] Let me therefore give you powdered medicine which his mother will smear on her breasts for the child to suck with her milk every time he sucks. If his disease is what I think it is, the child will be cured of having to throw up every time he sucks. And now bring me a small hoe." He was given a small weeding hoe and left for the wilderness to procure his medicine. When he brought it, he went and sat down in the porch of the door of Myombekere's house and then took a sword-like knife form its sheath and carefully worked on a root of a tree he had brought from the wilderness with the knife, flattened it out, cut it into two bits and measured them against each other and made them of equal length. Then he told Myombekere to bring him some fire, *empindu* needle and some grass blackened with soot from a kitchen fire and Myombekere brought him what he asked for. The medicine man made fire with the grass right in the middle of the house door and then put the point of *impindu* in the fire and when it was red hot used it to pierce a hole through one of the two pieces of wood by burning holes in it from opposite sides until they joined and put that one aside and did the same with the second piece. He then took a strip of the skin of a monitor lizard which was killed by a blow of a stick and slit from the skin a cord which could go through the holes in the two pieces of wood, after making sure it was long enough to go around the child's chest.

He then told Ntulanalwo's parents, "Let me put around his chest this *empingizi* amulet, because it is *empingizi* which causes the child to have such labored breathing, and if the worm of that disease is the ordinary one we know, it will leave the child's chest and he will be cured." And at once he put on the child the two amulets, in such a way that one hung right in the middle of his tiny chest and the other one at his back in line with his backbone, and with that the healer concluded his treatment of the child.

He chatted on a little longer before telling Bugonoka, "When you are bathing your child, don't take off this *empingizi* amulet. Even at night let the child sleep with it, even when carrying him strapped on your back or on the back of whoever is carrying him he should always be wearing it. And with the powdered medicine for the child to suck with your milk, when you see that it is about to get finished, come for some more before it is actually finished." That said, the medicine man left, with Myombekere escorting him for a while before returning home.

So when Ntulanalwo wanted to suck, Bugonoka first spit several times on the teat of the breast she wanted to give him, put on it the powdered medicine and then held the child in her hands, his head and mouth on the side of that breast and the child sucked. As soon as the child put her mother's teat in his mouth and sucked and swallow a bit and the milk got into his stomach, his parents heard a worm in the stomach of the child announce itself aloud: *chororororo!* Apparently the medicine had got to it. Shortly after that they saw Ntulanalwo rapidly kick about with his tiny legs and then begin to suck by mouthfuls, really greedily, and gulping the milk. With that Bugonoka felt her child was on his way to sucking well and scooped with her finger, like this, the saliva of the child from its mouth and smeared it on the teat of her other breast and then quickly put on it the powdered medicine and transferred the child to that other breast and the child sucked that one too. There and then the couple heard from the child's stomach the sound of yet another worm: *chororororo*! and at once they saw the child stop sucking at the same time as the labored breathing in his chest stopped too and he began to breath quite normally. Following that Ntulanalwo got busy playfully pedaling his legs on her mother's lap. Myombekere and Bugonoka saw their child was indeed cured and said, "Here's a healer indeed! You'd think he was some witch or witch doctor who had cast the disease on the child and then lifted it!"

None of the amulets the many and different healers gave Ntulanalwo was removed from him once he was cured. He continued wearing them all and remained loaded with a whole collection of amulets even when he was in perfect heath, so that they would continue protecting his body and prevent a recurrence of his old diseases, because when a disease strikes again often times it comes to kill.

Because Ntulanalwo had been so beset with diseases, it was not until the end of his third month that people told his mother: "Sit down the child before it is too late, lest he develops an ungainly gait."

"How do I sit him down."

"You dig a stand in the earth and place him in it, and after you have done that for a number of days you sit him on your lap. Do that every time after suckling him. Did you think children are the ones who decide on their own when it's time to start sitting up?"

"I must admit, in my ignorance, that is indeed what I thought".

"That's not surprising. With something of which you have no experience, you can't just imagine and know how everything is done, when you don't even have a clue of what to do. But now that you have born a child, should God bless you and let this one remain with us here on earth and grant you yet another one, then you will know what to do and how to nurse and bring up children."

As the fourth mouth went by, slowly Ntulanalwo finally could sit still in the stands his baby-sitters were digging for him in the earth and remain steady without swaying in every direction and threatening to topple over. Finally it was no longer necessary to dig a stand in the ground for him and he could sit steadily anywhere on the ground or on a person's lap. He then became a greater pleasure to baby-sit than hitherto. Now Myombekere too from time to time would place him on his lap, and when the child showed signs of being tired of sitting there he would place him on the ground and keep him occupied by making him play with leaves of trees or of a cassava plant, and the like, calling its mother or its baby-sitter Nakiro only when the child finally appeared determined to burst out crying.

And so days went by. Whenever Ntulanalwo had a fever for two or three days, Myombekere went to see a seer with *ekisano* of millet or of the roots of a tree stamp or a cock to find out the cause of his child's sickness, whether it was the evil doings of witches and witch doctors or some ritual matter or whatever it was, and thus know the nature of his illness and quickly do whatever was required for his child to be cured. One day Ntulanalwo got really sick and was boiling with fever and Myombekere collected from the child's mouth a bit of saliva and put it into a tiny calabash, put some millet in it and then threw some of the millet to the roof of his house and yet some more of it into the kitchen fire, where it exploded as the grains popped open. And because it was night, he put *ekisano* of millet by the bed-post of their bed for the night and early in the morning, at the hour the early morning birds all sing at once, got on his way, his *ekisano* in hand, to look for a seer who would enlighten him. When he arrived in the home of one seer and finished exchanging greeting with the medicine man, the seer asked him, "My dear man, what brings you this way?"

"I've come this way to know what I can't see".

"I see!"

The seer then called his wife who was in the house and said, "Bring here a tray[18] for us," and his wife brought it. The seer then received Myombekere's *ekisano* and poured the millet on the tray and examined it, shook the tray of millet and turned the tray into another direction and again examined the millet. And when he had seen everything clearly, he pronounced his divination for Myombekere to hear and said, "I see that the sick person is a child."

"May you see more, healer!"

"I see that this child of yours was struck by the spell of an evil spirit whose path his mother crossed on her way back home from your lake-side crop fields while carrying the child. You have to look for herbs to cure him of the evil spell and give him a medicine vapor infusion before what he got into overwhelms him."

Myombekere was really sad, for he knew that whenever the spell of an evil spirit strikes a grown-up the result is usually chronic illness, if not death. "If it can do that to an adult, what will it do to a tiny infant whose body is still devoid of any resistance to disease! All the same, let me go and try to look for some herbs for the child, as the seer told me. Only this time we are up against something really formidable!"

He got home and shared what he learnt with Bugonoka, told her that the diviner had told him "this and this and that," and went on to say to her, "But as the seer was nearing the end of his divination for me, he concluded what he was telling me in a disheartening voice and said: `Go and look for the herbs with which to cure him and give him a vapor infusion before what he got into overwhelms him.' Those words of his are what made me understand that our child's sickness is a grave one indeed and that's why he decided to simply leave me in the dark that way."

Bugonoka had to agree with her husband. And when she looked at her child seated on her lap and looked at him again, over and over, she found tears streaming down her cheeks before she knew it, on account of the great pity she felt for her child.

At that very moment, before Myombekere had left his home to go anywhere, as luck had it, there was Nanzala, accompanied by another old woman, a visitor of hers. The two old women had come to wish Bugonoka good day and see how her sick child was doing. After they exchanged greetings with Myombekere, whom they found seated outside, Nanzala said, "What misery for a young child to be sick day in and day out this way, afflicted with all sorts of unknown diseases! *Aa!* He should get well so that we the adult too may feel good!"

The other old woman rejoined, "Indeed, the child should get well, for not only is illness never good for anybody, it also kills all joy in the patient's people. It is true our ancestors said: `Whoever walks in the sun gets hot,' but illness which never leaves a person has to be dreaded, for it brings only misery. For, my son, water which leaks into a boat drowns its passengers." Myombekere agreed, "It is indeed as you say, my mother."

The two old women then went inside the house to see Bugonoka and the child and once in the house put a hand on the child to feel the fever and found him boiling hot and exclaimed, "What a fever!" Shortly after that, they saw the child break into a sweat until he was dripping wet from his head to the soles of his feet. Old Nanzala on seeing the child sweat so much while having such a high fever said, "This child may be sick or suffering from whatever other disease he has, but it appears he has been struck by the spell of an evil spirit. Otherwise, what we see wouldn't happen. And, Myombekere, if I may ask, how are you nursing your child, my son?"

"Just as you see me. For how else can I nurse him, when I am all ignorant of everything".

"What I want to know is: `Have you tried to seek the knowledge of a seer, or are you just nursing your sick child like a foolish person?'"

"Even without your saying it, it is true I am nursing him like a foolish person, but all the same when you arrived here you found me just returning from having his *ekisano* looked into, and what the seer told me is exactly what you have just said, my dear mother, that the child is under an evil spell and nothing else. And even now I was about to come and see Nanzala and ask her whether she could find me some herbs for treating sickness caused by spells of bad spirits. And now here you are, the two of you, and you have seen clearly the nature of my child's illness, so please help me, my mothers. Only a person can help another person. Fetch me some herbs to at least try and help my child, because our people of old said: `The boat sinks those in it still singing songs of hope.'"

Nanzala told Bogonoka to put back the child in bed and not to continue carrying him in her hands when he had such a high fever. Shortly after that Nanzala and her companion left to go and look for medicine with which to treat Myombekere's child. The little girl Nakiro wanted to follow them but they sent her back. In no time the two old women were back with medicine. They first asked Bugonoka for a pot in which to cook it and Bugonoka gave them a pot and they put the medicine in it and poured into it a lot of water, gave the pot to Bugonoka and she took it to the cooking-stones. They told her to cook it until it boiled up only once and then to take it from the fire. When it was ready, Bugonoka, seated on a chair with parted legs, put her child on her lap and then placed the pot of the boiling medicine under her thighs, after which Nanzala completely covered the mother and her child with *enkanda*[19] cow skin and mother and child were immersed in the hot vapor of the pot of medicine. From time to time Nanzala would stir the medicine in the pot, sending off a lot of fresh steaming vapor towards the pair engulfed over the pot inside *enkanda*. When she saw both of them sweat to dripping with sweat, she uncovered them, satisfied the child had responded well to the medicine, since he was sweating profusely. She then told Bugonoka: "In the evening do the same thing, because the preparation is the same as you have just seen. If he is sick because he was struck by the spell of an evil spirit, after that he should improve." Nanzala and her companion then left.

As the sun was about to set, though still fairly bright outside, Bugonoka did as she was told by the old woman. When she and her child had been over the steaming pot for some time and were drenched in sweat, she beckoned her husband with her hand to come and uncover them. She had to call him by beckoning him that way because it is taboo for one covered over the pot of that medicine to utter a word while under treatment. Myombekere did so and found the two of them, mother and son alike, dripping with sweat. Bugonoka then took the child to the door of the house to dry and when he was sufficiently dry she suckled him and noticed that the child was sucking a bit better.

The following morning Myombekere and Bugonoka woke up to find their child had no more fever and they were overcome with joy. They then called the herbs they had treated him with "medicine", because when medicine doesn't cure you it becomes "stuff". When Nanzala came she told them, "Today too, at noon, immerse the child in the vapor of his medicine and conclude the treatment by doing so again in the evening. Then, when darkness sets in, Myombekere will take the pot of medicine and go and pour it at the middle of a crossroads and take the pot and come home with it."

Myombekere and Bugonoka said, "All right," and did as they were directed at noon and in the evening. Then they went to bed and slept and it dawned. Ntulanalwo was now playing all the time. But, all the same, it is clear that the spell of an evil spirit is a formidable enemy. Had medicine not been found for Ntulanalwo at once, given the condition he was already in, he would not have survived to grow up. No, he would have certainly died.

Once Ntulanalwo could sit up properly alone he began to gather soil by the palms of his little hands and eat it whenever he was seated on the ground. One day Bugonoka was busy doing her household chores while her son too was busy eating sand when all of a sudden she heard him retch as if he wanted to vomit and then cry. Bugonoka went and examined her child and discovered what had happened: Ntulanalwo had choked on a piece of grass he had tried to swallow! His mother then struggled to force-open his mouth and put a finger in his throat until the piece of grass finally came out, a really long one. From that day on Bugonoka took real care that that wouldn't happen again. Before putting her child on the ground now she first swept the ground to clear it of all bits and ends of grass. Except she had no way of putting an end to his eating soil and finally asked some people about it: "By the way, what am I supposed to do so that this child will stop eating soil?"

"What can you do when that is how all babies are, always grasping this and that and putting it in their mouths and eating soil along with grass and choking themselves with it daily. Eating soil is the hobby of all children, from the first to the last, and, do whatever you will, you will never succeed in stopping a child from eating soil when it is on the ground. For babies at this age are what people call `snake-catchers', because they don't as yet know what from what or what to fear and what not to fear. Also during this period a child keeps on eating soil like that on account of its gums itching, because it is about to teethe and it wants something with which to rub that itch. Is this child of yours here too, by the way, about to cut his teeth?"

"This one! Not now; he is not anywhere near there yet!"

"Well, call us liars if you want, but you will soon see for yourself that we are right, for he is about to grow teeth."

A few days after that, in that same fifth month, one lone small tooth indeed did appear in the mouth of Bugonoka's child, in the gums of the lower jaw. That was good, because when a child cuts his or her first tooth in the upper jaw gums he or she is considered a freak. Myombekere and his wife agreed they needed to know what to do regarding protecting the health of their child by observing their parental sex prohibition attendant on their child's teething and the lifting of the prohibition.   And so Myombekere went to their healer Kibuguma to ask him how they would perform the rites of their child's teething. Kibuguma told him: "From today you are no longer to play about with outside women. Even if the woman is a long time girlfriend of yours, you shouldn't go with her again, because doing so is transgressing and you risk harming your child with *amakire*[20] disease. And if you achieve with your wife the rite of your child's teething after committing such a transgression your child can come to grievous harm, or even die. I don't want to hide the truth from you, I have to be very open with you, because you are a dear client of mine. And since you are still a young man, you have to really discipline yourself until you have consummated the rite of the child's teeth with your wife by your relating to each other body to body. Only then will you be free to go with outside women as you like. However, when you have related to each other with your wife and consummated the rite, the following morning bring here your child for me to shave off his hair."

On arriving back home Myombekere recounted to Bugonoka what Kibuguma had told him and said, "From today we have to protect the teeth of our child, because if we transgress against the teeth sex prohibition great harm can come to him and he can even die. And in the morning on the day following the night during which we will relate to each other to consummate our child's teething rite, we will take the child to our healer, together with our last dues of hoes to him, so that he can shave the child's hair."

Myombekere and his wife did as their healer bid them and the day which followed that they woke up early to take the child to the healer for the shaving of the child's hair. Bugonoka strapped Ntulanalwo on her back, put millet in large bowl[21] and wrapped a cover on top of it and Myombekere on his part took with him two iron hoes and off they went.

They arrived at Kibuguma's place and presented him with their gifts and Kibuguma properly accepted them. After that the healer told his wife Weroba to shave Ntulanalwo's head and Weroba shaved clean the child head. Then the healer and his wife escorted their visitors and Myombekere and Bugonoka with their child came back to their home. The prohibition thus lifted, Myombekere resumed going with outside women as he pleased. And so the couple continued with their lives, and Ntulanalwo's teeth grew.

Within a few months after that they saw their child begin to crawl. He began by dragging himself forward on his bottom. Slowly he stopped crawling on his bottom and moved on to what is called crawling "cow-like", that is bottom up in the air, one knee of his tiny leg folded and the sole of his other tiny leg working the ground in movement. All that time still pursuing his hobby of eating soil, sometimes going about it by peeing on the ground and wetting the soil first and then with his tiny fingers scooping that soil and dirt, all wet with urine, and putting it into his mouth and eating it. Whoever went near him, Ntulanalwo rewarded him or her with a smile, displaying to him or her his row of tiny teeth, his little chest and tiny lips dripping with a mixture of his saliva and the dirty muddy soil he was eating.

The first word which his mouth fancied during those days of crawling was: *tata tata*! Slowly he began to prattle what only he could hear and understand: *dalidali*! *dadadada*! over and over. As months continued to roll by he finally began to utter words, one at a time, which people could hear and make out, though not so easily. As days stretched on, since Ntulanalwo already saw clearly with his own eyes, during lunch he would be attentively watching his mother as she held *ekizanda*[22] of milk in her hands and put the milk to her mouth to wash down the sweet potatoes in her mouth and again he would follow with his watchful eyes the movement of her hand as it went to the sweet potatoes on the tray. From there he began asking her mother something in incomprehensible words like "*nn*!" And so that was it! That was his way of asking for food! That's what Bugonoka soon realized and began to give him some skimmed milk mixed with water, and eventually to hand-feed him a bit of sweet potatoes, mashed with her fingers. The child was tasting and soon he began to eat, just as in the saying of our people of yore: "Tasting is eating." And from there Bugonoka began to give him sweet potatoes to hold in his hand and eat on his own, and also *obwita*. She had in her house a very small plate[23] and it was on the tiny plate that Bugonoka would put for his son tiny bits of *obwita* and mix them with broth for relish and the day Ntulanalwo was really hungry he would attack those tiny pieces of food until his tiny stomach was round to bursting like that of a she-goat expecting twins. And when Ntulanalwo began eating food like that, his flowing excrement of a child feeding on milk slowly gave way to real cooked-food shit of human beings.

Now from time to time our Ntulanalwo would fancy things and act his fancy, like the person who wets his or her bed. He would suddenly fancy words comprehensible to people, sometimes by just bursting out as if asking for something and saying, "*Yumbu*!"[24] The adults then would understand that he was asking for sweet potatoes. Sometimes it would be, "*Ita*!" and they would know he was asking for *obwita* , or, "*Anya*"[25] and they would know that he wanted to shit, or, "*Manya*!"[26] and they would understand he was asking for meat. And bit by bit he began calling his mother: "*Yaya*!" in response to which Bugonoka would say, "Yes!" and Ntulanalwo would then may be tell her whatever he wanted.

From crawling cow-like Ntulanalwo started to stand up on his own. But at first he seemed kind of shy about it, never doing it except in front of people he was used to, like his baby-sitters, and when he stood up in front of them they in turn would encourage him on by clapping and singing for him: "Steady! steady! Big one! Big one!"

And when he entered his second year he began walking by holding onto the wall of their house until bit by bit he made steps without holding onto anything and eventually walked standing on his own feet. He did not delay walking like the children we sometimes see being dragged about inside a trellised basket[27] before they can walk. Not Ntulanalwo.

Chapter XXIII

NOTES

1.　*Engozi*:　See note 9 of Chapter XXI.

2.　*Obwita*:　See note 14 of Chapter I.

3.　*Kaheke*: Short bristle African hair, considered by the Wakerewe to be the most beautiful hair, the best of which was *kaheke kalagalika*, "loose-grain" *kaheke*.

4.　*Omuterere:* Literally "slimy (hair)", long and soft African hair, which the Wakerewe considered uncomely.

5.　Abakangara:　A tribe of cattle herders, foreigners in Ukerewe, a light-complexioned peopled with the long and smooth *omuterere* hair above the Wakerewe found uncomely.

6.　Bakwaya: See note 5 of Chapter I.

7.　*Ilezi*: Kitereza in his notes for his Swahili translation of the novel describes the disease as: "Stomach disease which prevents a child from emptying its bowels, which afflicts mostly children still sucking and makes the child trying to relieve itself keep on twisting and stretching its body with nothing but foam-like excrement yellowish in color coming out of its stomach."

8.　*Ekisusi*:　See note 20 of Chapter II.

9.　*Ekisano*: An oracle or its medium, that is the object a seer or healer uses to divine a person's oracle, which among the Wakerewe could be millet, a hen, the entrails of a cow or goat or the roots of a herb, usually those of a common herb called *ilambwanzoka* , literally "that which a snake licks", which the person in search of divination uprooted after "harming" it by scratching its stem and removing some of its soft bark by a single downward stroke of a thumbnail.

10.　For the procedure and importance of naming children, see note 1 of Chapter I.

11.　*Amahanga*: False teeth. Kitereza's note for his Swahili translation of his novel says: "Teeth which grow in the mouth of a baby giving the child a very high fever and making it cry all the time, for which the parents have to take the child to a healer who knows how to cure *amahanga* to have them extracted."

12.　*Ekikome*:　See note 1 Chapter II.

13.　*Obuto*:　Kitereza in his note for his Swahili translation of his novel writes: "Disease of boils in infants, in which boils erupt in the head or neck or throat of a child. Often the boils don't heal quickly or their scars continue to fester even after the boils appear to have healed". *Obuto* literally means "childhood (disease)". When the same kind of boils erupt in an adult the disease is called *obubi*,   the disease of "badness (or ugliness)", no doubt because it could be such a terrible affliction.

14.   *Empindu* : See note 17 of Chapter X.

15.   *Ensato*: See note 2 of Chapter VI.

16.   *Oluzoka*: Kitereza's note for his Swahili translation of his novel is: "Stomach disease which causes infants to vomit whenever they suck milk and which, if not treated in time, could eventually develop into epilepsy."

17.   *Empingizi*:   Kitereza's note for his Swahili translation of his novel is: "Stomach disease in infants which causes them to breathe with difficult, panting and laboring for breath."

18.   *Olugali*: See note 6 of Chapter I.

19.   *Enkanda*:   See note 22 of Chapter VI.

20.   *Amakire*:   See note 4 Chapter XII.

21.   *Ekibo*:   See note 15 of Chapter I.

22.   *Ekizanda*: See note 20 of Chapter II.

23.   *Olunanga*: See note 16 of Chapter I.

24.   *Yumbu* for *enumbu*: Sweet potatoes.

25.   *Anya:* Version of a child learning how to speak of *kunya*, "to shit."

26.   *Manya:* Version of a child learning how to speak of *enyama*, "meat."

27.   *Olugega*:   See note 19 Chapter V.

Chapter XXIV

THE WEANING OF NTULANALWO

Ntulanalwo sucked the milk of his mother's breasts for two complete years. One day, when he was still sucking, after he had grown his incisors, his mother touched the breast on which he was sucking and since he was greedy and selfish and did not want anybody to touch his mother's breasts, Bugonoka all of a sudden felt her child biting hard the teat of her breast: *kekeche!* His mother took a tiny twig from a broom and gave him a few measured strokes with it while saying, "Never bite me, you tiny freak! Suck nicely, the way human beings suck!" The child cried and cried as if he would cry for ever! Myombekere was in his banana plantation pruning banana plants of dry and wilted leaves and came home out of breath from running, his heart racing and his ears blocked, and at once asked Bugonoka why the child way crying like that, and it was not until he knew the cause of it all that he calmed down and became himself again. Since that day Ntulanalwo never bit his mother again. From then on Ntulanalwo just sucked nicely his mother's milk day in and day out. From that day too, whenever Ntulanalwo cried for no reason and kept on crying for too long, Bugonoka would get hold of a tiny whip and threaten him with it: "Quiet! Stop crying lest I beat you!" and immediately he would stop crying completely as if he hadn't been crying, with only the streaks of tears remaining to show he had cried at all. Bugonoka on seeing her child respond that way when still as young as he was, hardly capable of understanding anything, could not help saying to herself. "I see! Now I understand why our ancestors said: `Straighten a tree while still young, for an old one can't bend.'"

When Ntulanalwo's legs became strong and really steady and he was no longer wobbling but now walked normally, Myombekere and Bugonoka discussed the question of weaning their child, and deliberated about who would stay with him and bring him up[1] after he was weaned. If Myombekere's mother was still alive, may be she would have been the one to bring up Ntulanalwo. But Myombekere was already an orphaned child, without a mother and all alone like the lonely little red bird *efunzi*.[2] And so the person fit to bring up their child for them was Nkwanzi, Bugonoka's mother. It was true that Myombekere had sisters and they two could be considered, but those relatives of his were not the couple's favorites. Myombekere and his wife Bugonoka were first of all afraid of their domineering behavior, and then they still remembered what those sisters of theirs said when they were pressuring Myombekere to divorce his wife and marry another one and have children so that he wouldn't die childless. It is true their intentions were good, for they wanted him to have children, because in this country of ours a childless person is treated worse than a dog.[3] And not only that, he or she is never given proper respect by people, because childless men and women throughout their lives are treated like juveniles and are often considered by people with children to be no better than useless spinsters and confirmed bachelors, adult men and women without spouses. That's why people insultingly allude to a childless man or woman as " a milk cow which haunts the company of calves." When people with children discussing matters of parenting see a childless person approaching they beckon each other and say, " No more: here comes a milk cow which haunts the company of calves," at which one of them would ask, "Who is coming?" and should the childless person coming happen to be already gray-haired, at once you would hear the person who was asked that question answer, "We are talking of the gray-haired one from our neighborhood. Here he comes! Say no more lest he hears and takes everything to juveniles." But, in spite of their good intentions, the words Myombekere's sisters said were nevertheless bitter ones, over which anger still lingered in the hearts of both Myombekere and Bugonoka. That's why Myombekere said, "It is true with me I no longer have anything to say against my sisters, because our past misunderstanding has been cleared. However, having tasted what they are like I can't swallow poisoned food knowingly. I am afraid if I give them my child to bring up for us, especially since my sisters indeed know how to say really ugly words, should at anytime anything happen to our child, they are capable of creating real trouble between me and my father-in-law and mother-in-law and make them take away my wife from me again, and this time for good, when, as you see, she is the only wife I have a bed for in this home of mine! It is much better to have the child brought up by my mother-in-law and father-in law. Should their home prove propitious for him, if God grants him life he will stay with them until he is grown up. I too know what the Wakerewe of old said: `A child is never born of a single parent.' The child's maternal grandparents are its parents as much as its paternal ones."

And so Myombekere was now left with only one thing to do, which was to inform his mother-in-law that it was to her that Ntulanalwo would go after he was weaned and that he would be hers to keep and bring up. And when he went to see her, the only thing his mother-in-law on her part said was to agree. If she said anything else besides that to her son-in-law then it must be the following: "By the way, when are you weaning the child?"

"With us, if it were not for the difficult of getting fish for the weaning occasion, if say we get the fish tomorrow, the day after tomorrow we are ready to take him off his mother's breasts."

"That's fine then. Go and look for fish tomorrow and we too will look for some on this side, and likewise with me count on seeing me in your home on the day after tomorrow. And, concerning matters of how to wean the child, it would be a good thing for you to consult that mother of your friend. Oh, me! Is her name Nanzala, or what is it?"

"You mean the one with whom you delivered your daughter's child?"

"Exactly".

"You are right, her name is Nanzala".

"That's the one I mean".

Myombekere came back and recounted to Bugonoka about his mission to her parents' and how on the day after the following day her mother would be coming to their home for the purpose of taking back with her her grandchild.

The following day Myombekere went out early in the morning to look for fish with which to wean his child, or rather fish for him and the people of his home to eat, for, as usual, the child was only a cover, since the stomachs of the adults too needed to be fed. Has anybody ever seen the fabled person called "Never-eat-parent?" That is a mere invention of parents for teasing their children, just as our parents too teased us with the joke when we were children, as a trick to find out whether we had become intelligent human beings capable of distinguishing right from wrong. One day when our mothers brought to our fathers' lunch gathering plates[4] of peeled[5] potatoes accompanied by *ebizanda*[6] of skimmed milk our parents told us: "As for you, boys and girls, there is no food for you before you bring here Never-eat-parent, whom we left on the common grazing plain over there. Whoever comes here before finding Never-eat-parent and bringing him here will simply not eat." And off we went, running, fighting over which footpaths to take, climbing over each other to cross hurdles in cow-trails, some of us falling down, others pushing on, shouting our heads off to call the person we were looking for: "Never-eat-parent, *woowe*! Come with us to our home, you are wanted," and all that for nothing! And our parents would laugh and laugh until they choked with milk. You, on the other hand, went on calling until some of you become hoarse. And when the adults called you back and said, "Come back, here he is, already with us!" there too you began another race, challenging each other as to who would get back first and see Never-eat-parent before the others? And when you got back home you found nothing and turned to asking the adults, "And where is he?" to which they would answer, "He was here all right, but when he heard you coming shouting like that he was frightened and thought that people who were coming while shouting that way may be wanted to kill him! And so he said to himself, `I've better get out of their way; they don't want to share their food with me!'" And so you weighed the matter in your childish minds and said: "Wait, tomorrow when they send us to fetch him on coming back will come back quietly and catch him eating with our parents." And then the following day you went for him again and again you found nothing, until you finally realized that the adults were simply playing tricks on you. As to Never-eat-parent, that is somebody who has never been found anywhere and never will!

At about noon Myombekere was back home, under the weight of a shoulder pole loaded with fish front and back. From where she was, on peeping who should Bugonoka see but her husband carrying the whole length of *emamba*,[7] as long as can be! And on a looking again, well! well! so the back of the pole too was loaded, with three *embozu*[8] catfish and four *ensato!*[9] She ran for a movable door shutter[10] and put it on the ground under the shade of a tree and Myombekere deposited on it his abundant provisions.

He scaled, cut and cleaned the fish he brought, and then went to

Kanwaketa's home to consult Nanzala on the weaning of their child. Nanzala explained to him everything: "With us the Wakerewe, the rite of weaning a child is similar to all our other rites for lifting the sex prohibitions for couples, like the one attendant on moving into a new home or using a new roof of a house or a new grain store[11] or a new roof of the grain store for the first time. And so this is what you will do. You will sleep with empty arms and then the following day you take the child off her mother's breasts. The child's mother then will smear both her breasts with cow dung and whenever the child tries to suck, his mother will stop him by telling him, rather sharply, `Don't , there is shit! Don't you see! It stinks!' But there has to be available for the child every food he may want to eat: fish, *obwita*,[12] sweet potatoes and skimmed milk, with which his baby-sitter will try to keep his belly contented throughout daytime. And at night his babysitter will come to sleep with the child let's say here, for fear the child might suck his mother's milk at night. And once you take the child from his mother's milk the mother will pass three days without bathing and on the fourth day she will go to bathe and wash away the milk of her breasts. Then at night that day you will relate to each other with your wife in bed. That is what achieving the rite of a mother's milk is."

Myombekere and Bugonoka did as directed. The following day Bugonoka's mother came in, loaded with presents. On seeing her arrive, Bugonoka at once took off running to relieve her mother of the big basket[13] of presents on her head. Myombekere got up and went out of his mother-in-law's way as custom demanded. Not long after that Nkwanzi saw her grandson pass by her and called him: "Come and greet me, my husband! *Yuu*! so you already can walk!" Ntulanalwo came near and Nkwanzi lifted him and put him on her lap. In no time he no longer wanted to stay on her grandmother's lap and got off and made his way to his mother at the kitchen in the inner room of the house. When she found her mother cooking *obwita* he told her "*Yaya, ita*!" His mother said, "You want *obwita*, son? Wait until it is cooked and I'll give you some, my little one." When the food was ready she dished out relish and told her son, "Come this way and eat *obwita* with the visitor." Nkwanzi put small pieces of *obwita* for the child on his plate and was about to put on rather much when Bugonoka stopped her and said, "Don't put on much, dear mother, this child today has already eaten too much, he will fall sick from overeating!"

"That's how children are, and you think this one has eaten much when he hasn't eaten anything yet! You wait when he weans. That's when you will see him eat until you are simply amazed. Don't you see children who have just been weaned always sporting stomachs round to bursting! And what do you think is the cause of that if not eating much this way?"

"I do indeed see them, I must admit, only I thought that may be it is a disease, or that may be that's how children are supposed to be after they are weaned".

"No, for many of them it is eating and not a disease".

In no time Nkwanzi had stopped eating and so Bugonoka asked her mother, "Why didn't you eat, mother?"

"*Aa*! I ate my fill. What with *embozu* for relish, this was quite a meal!

In the evening Nanzala and her daughter-in-law came to visit and when they lingered outside with Myombekere Bugonoka told them, "My dear women, aren't you coming into the house?"

Kanwaketa's wife answered, "We are coming, only the sun is kind of living us behind, night is about to envelop the birds with darkness, as the Wakerewe say. And, as you know, for us women when the sun sets it ushers in our difficult task of cook for our masters: should you serve him badly cooked food, you would be rewarded with blows, and even when you do everything right, you only breathe relief and say, `*Yehuu*! today was my lucky day; I have escaped through some narrow and hidden path like a rat! What will my lot be tomorrow, poor me?'"

Myombekere responded to Kanwaketa's wife and said, "I see! So, my sister in law, you find your chores a real burden?"

"I must indeed admit, brother-in-law, that we lazy women do find cooking for you our husbands a real burden. In fact, my brother-in-law, it is a wonder we still managed to grow fat. It must be by special blessing of the heavens! Even you wouldn't put on weight if your were forever worried like us! But just listen, my brother-in-law, and let me conclude by telling you this."

"I am all ears, give me the words!"

"Don't you yourself see how the carefree women, the unmarried ones,[14] the women who have no home to run and no husband to keep them for ever worried, are always so round?"

"It is because you married womenfolk are simply overworked, my sister-in-law. The woman, all alone, tills the sweet-potato and cassava fields and harvests those crops, again alone, and peels that food and washes and puts it in the pots and cooks it, after looking for firewood to cook it with.

And when she has finally cooked the food she still has to dish it out of the pots and serve it. Of all this we say: `Noted!' Then yours alone too are: grinding of flour, picking of greens, cooking of *obwita*, weeding of men's crops, taking away utensils on which you have served us men food, before concluding your chores of the day by making ready the bed so that your husbands can go to sleep. I should not, by the way, forget: should you be a mother, that is even worse, since for you alone too is the duty of bringing up children from infancy almost all the way to adulthood, for a growing-up child is almost inseparable from his or her mother. And so the truth is, my sister-in-law, that you women are simply overburdened with work."

"I see! So you too realize that! I thought you would deny it".

"No, I did not mean to deny it. I agree with you entirely, because I see how you women toil ceaselessly all the time."

That day at night Nkwanzi and Nakiro went to sleep at Kanwaketa's home with Ntulanalwo. On that day Bugonoka had pulled apart their bed to fight the bedbugs with which it was infested and at night she put is back again and properly spread the bed for the night and she and her husband went to bed, but with their backs turned on each other.

And since it always dawns, it dawned.

Early that morning Bugonoka made *obunzingwa*[15] and gave it to Kagufwa, together with *ekizanda* of milk and six cooked fish, *ensato*, to take to Kanwaketa's as food for Ntulanalwo as well as the other people in that home. And during the three days the people of her home stayed at Kanwaketa's Bugonoka spoiled them with whatever food they wanted to eat, but during all those days Bugonoka and her little son Ntulanalwo did not see each other. On the fourth day Bugonoka went to the lake to bathe and in the evening Nkwanzi and Nakiro brought Ntulanalwo to his father and mother. As soon as they arrived Bugonoka took her child and the other two women went back to Kanwaketa's home. Myombekere had only one house in his home and they too knew that was the day Myombekere and Bugonoka had to achieve all the rites of weaning the child so that the couple could free themselves from the sex prohibition attendant on separating a child from its mother's milk. The Mkerewe of yore said: "The host puts away in his house a visitor's walking-stick without the visitor seeing but, because everybody knows where to put a visitor's walking stick, he knows where his too is kept."

Myombekere and Bugonoka and their child went to bed. Then sometime during the night Myombekere remembered the words of a

Mkerewe of old overcome with curiosity: "No, this is too much! To be sure your concealed treasure isn't rotting you have to uncover it and peek!" Anyway, we won't recount all that in details as if we were possessed and in need of a healer to chase evil from our minds. If you have ears, you have ears, if you don't, leave things alone, lest people call us mad even though our legs have never known the touch of the madman's iron fetters.

The following morning, when it was still dark, Nkwanzi and Nakiro returned to Myombekere's home. They found Bugonoka cooking *obunzingwa* as journey food for Ntulanalwo. After that she put the food in Ntulanalwo's small bowl,[16] dished out of a pot some relish for the child and put it in whatever container it was she put it in, and immediately fetched her mother's basket, in which she had already put for her some *obubele* millet, through not too much, since she would be carrying Ntulanalwo on her back as well. She added in the basket some dry *embozu* catfish, and, finally, put in her son's journey food. Nkwanzi in a hurry to leave said, "Will you please hurry up, my dear; I would like my son-in-law to accompany me for some distance early so that I can arrive before it gets too hot."

Bugonoka responded, "I too am now done," and with that she wrapped a cover over the top of the basket and placed on top of it a hand of ripe bananas and went to take Ntulanalwo from their bed and fetched his *engozi*[17] and strapped him on Nkwanzi's back while the child himself slept through it all. Myombekere took his spear and came out of the house first, ready to escort his mother-in-law and his son, and mother and daughter said their good-byes and the travelers left.

Because it was still dark, Myombekere did not walk far ahead of his mother-in-law as custom demanded, since it was still dangerous nighttime, and remained near enough to warn her of porcupine holes in the way. When there is sufficient reason, a son-in-law does not have to keep at a distance from his mother-in-law.[18] That was sanctioned by our ancestor who in times of sickness said: "An outsider cannot look after your mother-in-law for you," and in times of death: "I always row other people for nothing, why can't I ferry my mother-in-law to mourn her dead?" And, as you know, in a boat the mother-in-law sits in front while the son-in-law sits behind her, naked.[19] So I am asking all of you this question: "In our tiny canoes we call *empanza*,[20] is there anywhere to hide in daytime?" And your answer is: "No, because there is no hiding place for an adult in that one rower dugout." With Myombekere too he now escorted his mother-in-law that way, walking ahead but close by, warning her of holes in the way, and it was when they could see in the palms of their hands and they had arrived where they began to come across other travelers that Myombekere increased his distance a bit between him and his mother-in-law. When finally the sun came out of the horizon and they were now passing by people's homes, he put down his mother-in-law's basket and then went and took cover behind a small near-by bush and said good-bye to her from there and returned to his home as his mother-in-law and his son Ntulanalwo went to theirs.

Chapter XXIV

NOTES

1. It was customary for Kikerewe couples soon after they weaned their children to take them to their parents or close relatives for bringing up so that the children could experience being part of their extended families from very early in life. In the case of young couples their children's grandparents or other elderly relatives also wanted to help and free the young parents to have more children.

2. *Enfuzi:* Name of a tiny red bird with lonely habits, the totem of the Abasilanga clan of the rulers of Ukerewe; also name of a soft common grass used in the pressing of juice from ripe bananas for making banana beer, also used for making temporary bed-spreads on house floors.

3. Kitereza here may be partly speaking from his personal experience of being a childless man. See Introduction.

4. *Enanga*, plural for *olunanga*: See note 16 of Chapter I.

5. Wakerewe women peeled only sweet potatoes intended for the men of their homes and cook their own share of the potatoes with the skin on.

6. *Ebizanda* , plural for *ekizanda*: See note 20 of Chapter II.

7. *Emamba*: See note 17 of Chapter II.

8. *Embozu:* See note 8 of Chapter XIX.

9. *Ensato:* See note 2 of Chapter VI.

10. *Ihara*: See note 6 of Chapter III.

11. *Ekitala*: See note 18 of Chapter I.

12. *Obwita*: See note 14 of Chapter I.

13. *Ekitukuru:* See note 16 of Chapter V.

14. *Abasimbe* plural for *omusimbe:* See note 24 of Chapter II.

15. *Obunzingwa:* *Obwita* cooked with milk and butter instead of water, considered a treat for children or food for a sick person with no appetite for ordinary food.

16. *Ekibo*: See note 15 of Chapter I.

17. *Engozi:* See note 9 of Chapter XXI.

18. For the custom which required mothers-in-law and their sons-in-law to avoid each other see note 7 of Chapter I.

19. In his Swahili translation Kitereza has added to the text the explanation: "In olden times males never wore clothes while at sea: that would have been transgressing against Mugasa, the deity of the waters."

20. *Empanza*: Dugout or canoe for a single rower.

Chapter XXV

NTULANALWO IN THE CARE OF HIS GRANDPARENTS

After many days, about three moths, Bugonoka loaded in a wicker basket[1] presents with which to visit her son Ntulanalwo. And loaded she was indeed that day! Hear this: the basketful of flour, a package of meat and smoke-dried *embozu*[2] catfish, a new tray[3] for her mother, a new tiny bowl[4] she had made specially for her son, a new calabash[5] for her mother to draw water with, a new *engunda*[6] for her father's banana beer parties, *enduko*[7] raffia for her mothers to make trays and bowls with together with *empindu*[8] needle for her to work with, ripe bananas for her son to receive when he came to meet her, so that he would not merely feed his eyes on the loads on her head he couldn't eat, and a calabash bowl full of butter for her son to put on his skin after bathing before going to bed.

At her parents' Barango's daughter, who was in the home, was the first to tell Bugonoka's mother, "I've seen our visitor first!" From inside her house Nkwanzi on peeping outside and looking that way saw her daughter coming and really loaded and hurried forth to help her with her loads of presents, and on seeing his grandmother going to meet a visitor little Ntulanalwo too followed behind, on the double. As soon as she was relieved of her loads, Bugonoka carried her son in her arms and told him, "Greet me, Ntulanalwo!"

"Greet me!"

"You have grown up?"

"Mm!"

"Say, your stomach is so full, what could you have eaten already?"

"Sweet potatoes with milk."

Bugonoka exchanging greetings with her father and her brother and then joined her mother inside the house.   Nkwazi said to her daughter, "To tell the truth, dear, we here had said you people don't seem to miss your child much, for it has been quite a while since I left your place! Isn't this the third month since I left, before you finally decided to come and see us?"

"It is and you are completely right, it has been a long while. But we miss him all right and we too are always talking about you here and wondering how you are doing. The fact is we did not come to see you sooner because your son-in-law fell sick. First he was down with serious fever and stayed in bed with it for some six days, which made us really worried. Then when the fever left him, he was overrun with an outbreak of rashes. Seeing that, those who claim to know everything in this world began to say: "Myombekere is covered with rashes from head to foot, he must have stolen something from hippopotamus hunters'[9] charmed safety keep, that is what happens to such thieves!" And he suffered from that disease for a whole month and a half before his rashes were finally cured and his skin became normal again. And then before long he erupted boils, one on the buttocks here and the other one on a thigh here, and that too became a serious disease from which he suffered for half a month before the boils came to a head and a healer put a razor on them and cut them open and drained them of pus. Only then could he have some sleep and sit on a chair and was able to walk again. That's what befell us at our place. Oh yes! our ancestors must have had my husband and me in mind when they said: `Before a war counts casualties it hasn't begun!'"

"I see! So things were that bad with you and that's why you delayed coming! Imagine, we here completely unaware of all that!"

Bugonoka stayed with her parents for about ten days, taking advantage of her stay to pay mourning visits to her parents' relatives in the area in whose homes people had died since she was there last, and then returned to her home.

So Ntulanalwo stayed under the foster care of his grandfather and grandmother, who babied him day in and day out as all parents do with their children when they are still young. At night when her grandmother cooked *obwita,*[10] she scooped off a piece and put it aside, together with some relish to accompany it, as leftovers for him to eat next morning, and every morning Ntulanalwo's daily song became: "Grandma, I want *obwita*" and Nkwanzi would give him last night's food she had kept aside for him. And, his eyes full of rheum, streaks of snivel all over his mouth, snot hanging from his nose, the palms of his little hands all filthy and black as if he had been foraging in soot's anus, as the Wakerewe say, your Ntulanalwo would eat his food, quietly putting away in his little stomach morsel after morsel. And when he couldn't finish the food, he gave it back to his grandmother to keep for him to eat again later, for you are all aware of the insatiable greed of little children which makes them eat all the time from morning to sunset. And again during daytime when Nkwanzi cooked sweet potatoes for lunch she kept some aside for Ntulanalwo, for him to eat all the time and as often as he wanted.

Before long, Ntalanalwo was infected with the eye disease *emboga*,[11] which stayed with him for quit some time, during which time his grandparents treated him by eye-drops from herb medicine until finally he was cured. And about four months after he was cured of *emboga*, he was afflicted with a stomach disease which made him throw up bile vomit. As soon as he ate his last-night's leftovers in the morning, his stomach became upset and he threw up bile vomit. At first his grandfather and grandmother said, "May be it is chilly morning wind which doesn't agree with him." When days went by while that stomach disease of his continued, they realized that it was cold overnight leftovers which did not agree with the child's stomach, and from that time on his grandmother began cooking for him his tiny dish of *obwita* early in the morning or slicing off something for him from his grandfather's breakfast. When that was tried Ntulanalwo's stomach calmed down and the vomiting stopped.

One day Ntulanalwo did not eat his supper in the evening and after people had gone to bed, sometime during the dead of the night, he shitted in his bed. Nkwanzi, with whom he shared a bed, woke up and found the child boiling with fever. She woke up Namwero, who asked her, "What's the matter?"

"I am calling you for you too to witness what has happen to our children's child".

When Nanwero woke up and felt the child with his hand and found the child had such a high fever he said, "This is a serious disease! The child has just fallen sick today and already he is in this condition! *Aa*! We can't handle this alone!"

"It is indeed a serious disease, since before today we have never know him to suffer from anything like this. No, we can't handle this alone. May be you should wake up Lweganwa and tell him to go and inform our son-in-law and Bugonoka to come and see their child. We cannot stay with him without letting them know as if there is nothing wrong with the child in the face of such a serious disease. As our elders once said, `The big fish in *omugonzo*[12] trap is for the owner of the trap.'"

"Yes, what you say is right. We are adults and have seen people get sick, but not this way. What's more, this child is yet to have his blood let and that, more than anything else, is what frightens me."

Nanwero woke up Lweganwa and Lweganwa came, accompanied by his wife, and found the child just moaning and groaning and really boiling with fever! Lweganwa went to call his brother Kamuhanda, and since it was a bright night, with a full moon shining in the sky, the two brothers didn't even wait for cockcrow but took their spears and set off in that very dead of the night.

When the pre-dawn birds twittered, Nanwero got up and filled a small calabash with millet, scooped a bit of the child's saliva with his finger from the child's mouth and put the saliva in the calabash of millet and set off to have his grandchild's sickness told. When the got to a seer, he gave him his *ekisano*[13] of millet and the seer divined and told him: "Your child is very sick and he has a very high fever."

"May you see clearly, seer!"

"However, he has been struck by the spell of a bad spirit!"

"May you see it all!"

"If you don't give this child herbs needed for treating the spell of an ill-spirit without delay, he may come to serious harm. And please don't take things lightly, lest the worst befalls your child."

Nanwero was an adult and knew the medicine needed for those afflicted with the spell of an ill-spirit and did not say anything more or waste any more time. As soon as he got back home, he took a bowl and left for the wilderness to collect medicine for fumigating Ntulanalwo with, brought it and Nkwanzi fumigated him as required. When the vapor of the boiling pot dried sufficiently on Ntulanalwo, his grandparents plied wide open his eyes and examined them, because the eye tells people nursing a sick person a lot about the patient. If your patient's eye is fallen, even if he or she is deceiving you with the word of his or her mouth, you have reason to be down-spirited, because his or her eye is not looking right. When Nkwanzi wanted to carry Ntulanalwo back to bed the child told her,

"Grandma, I want to go and relieve myself" and Nkwanzi carried him behind the house. The child purged and purged until finally he brought out a bright-red worm. Nkwanzi called her husband, "Nanwero, come!" He went and Nkwanzi showed the worm to him and said: "Look at what came out of this child's stomach!"

"I see it now, the child is really sick and the cause of his disease which gives him so much fever is in his stomach!"

"I think that's why when I asked him to eat something he refused; he must be feeling really bad inside his stomach."

Nkwanzi took the child back to bed and covered him with the skin of a goat, but only up to the neck, this way. Nanwero then went to the lake to look for fish in his *olubigo*.[14] In no time he was back, the front and back of his shoulder pole loaded with as many as thirty *ensato*[15] and four *emamba*.[16] He put the fish in the ancestral shrines first.[17]

Before long Lweganwa and Kamuhanda were back accompanied by Myombekere and Bugonoka, all dripping with sweat. They all went straight into the house to see how Ntulanalwo was doing and found the child still boiling with fever. His parents, father and mother alike, were rendered speechless, before finally asking when and how their child's sickness began. Nkwanzi was the one who went first: "It was like this and like that." Nkwanzi was still relating that when they heard Ntulanalwo ask for water to drink. His grandmother drew water from a pot, made him sit up on the bed and helped him drink some, which he did with his teeth chattering as if he wanted to chew the water container. Nanwero told Nkwanzi, "Don't give him much. Since he has began to want water when he is purging this way you have better grind a bit of *endwero*[18] flour quickly and mix it with the medicine I once treated Lweganwa with when he purging this way and make some gruel for him." A sister of Barongo, whose name was Kabunazya, who was that day also in the home, quickly ground some *endwero* and since *endwero* millet is soft and easy to grind in no time she had finished and Nanwero brought the powdered medicine, white as flour, and told Kabunazya to make the medicine gruel quickly. The girl made the gruel, from time to time putting drops of it on the palm of her hand with the wooden cooking spoon and tasting it to see whether it was ready. Then she took it from the fire and cooled it. When the gruel cooled sufficiently Nkwanzi brought *enkombyo*[19] spoon and washed it clean and dried it and then made Ntulanalwo sit up and asked him, "Do you want some water, dear?" Ntulanalwo agreed: "*Mn*." Nkwanzi took *enkombyo* and used it to taste the gruel herself first and found that the medicine was not bitter but only slightly sour and was also cool enough and yet still warm before drawing from the pot of gruel *enkombyo* full of medicine and making the child drink it. Ntulanalwo took about three spoonfuls of the medicine and on taking the fourth, before drinking it all, those present heard inside the child a worm noisily leave his chest and make its way to his stomach: *chururrr*! Nanwero said, "Did you hear that? There goes the worm which is aggravating his disease. The medicine got to it and now it has left the position from where it was afflicting him and it is descending to his stomach."

"Yes, we too heard it."

"Don't be afraid, keep giving him the medicine until it has got to all over his body and then let's see how he will feel tomorrow." After a while Ntulanalwo refused to take any more of the medicine. His grandfather said, "Don't give him any more. Keep it and warm it up for him when he asks again for water to drink".

Since it was still early in the day, Myombekere, on seeing how seriously sick his child was, found he could no longer bear just looking on at what filled him with so much pain and finally told Nanwero, "I can't just stay here. Please tell me where I can find a seer who takes plant roots for *ekisano* so that I too can seek enlightenment and pass the night knowing what makes my child sick," and his father-in-law told him. When he got to the open fields he uprooted a stump of a shrub and got on his way to where he had been directed.

Bugonoka too where her husband left her had a lot of thoughts of her own gnawing inside her. The pain and suffering of her sick child was killing her inside and reminding her of her passed days of barrenness and her two abortions,[20] and on remembering that she told her mother aloud, suffocating with anger and hardly knowing what she was saying, "I now see that with me my female sex organ feeds on shit!" What she wanted to say was: "If I were not a woman but a man like my husband and could personally go to look for seers and healers wherever I could my child, who may be is about to die, would be cured."

Hearing her daughter say that to her, Nkwanzi realized how much she was hurting inside and tried her best to console her: "No, my child, that's not how to nurse your sick one. To nurse well you have to be strong, to have hope inside you, and not to give up so easily. Do you think you never got sick? You did, but I had to nurse you with hope, by propping my heart on a stone and not trembling with fear that way. In your child's case, your father has already consulted a seer, because, yes, I agree with you, in this Ukerewe a human being is never nursed with bare eyes, without taking his or her *ekisano* to seers to find out the cause of his or her illness as well as looking for medicine for its cure. And that is exactly what your father did this morning and as you see there is medicine in that pot even now. And my son-in-law likewise, after he arrived here, did not sit back and just watch like an idiot. No, he too this very moment is out doing the right thing. And so, my dear child, you need to be courageous, man-like, to rest your heart on a stone for support, because whoever walks under the sun is bound to get warm and also because whoever despises medicinal herbs despises life, because they do cure."

In that very instant Ntulanalwo asked for water to drink and so Nkwanzi warmed the gruel mixed with medicine and made him drink some. When the child drank about four spoonfuls those present heard the worm inside him make noise again, leaving the child's chest and sliding down to his stomach: *chururr*! and they exclaimed and said: "Oh, it must be those worms in his stomachs which are giving this child such a terrible time!"

Finally it was time to fumigate the child with medicine vapor for the evening round. Ntulanalwo and his grandmother had not left their steaming pot when the child coughed: *koho*! and cleared his throat of the cough and was about to swallow it when he was told by those present, "Spit in the pot." Ntulanalwo did so. Snot was hanging from his nose and those present cleaned him and dropped that too in the steaming pot. They were still thus occupied when Myombekere came back from having his sons oracle told. He rested a bit and his mother-in-law and his wife asked him, "What news did you bring?"

"The diviner told my oracle and said, 'The child has been struck by the spell of a bad spirit, that is what is making him so sick. I didn't see any witch or witch doctor who is after him. All the same, go and make him wear around his neck the amulet for cooling fever and send him to bed tonight wearing it. And because you have yet to let his blood, tomorrow morning when the sun has quite warmed up take your child outside and let someone make incisions in his temple, two on each side of his head. And, since he also has *amagogore*,[21] if that's all he has, the two of you, you and your wife, will protect him by observing the attendant sex prohibition. If you do that you child will be cured.' That is what I have come with. But when he told me about the amulet for cooling fever I asked him, 'If I may ask, what is an amulet for cooling fever?' and he gladly explained to me everything clearly: 'You will shape a small granite stone of reasonable size, tiny like this, and then you will take a strip of dry banana stem fiber and tightly wrap and tie the piece of stone in the middle of the strip and, using the rest of the strip, make strings of sufficient length on each side of the stone and have the child sleep wearing the amulet around his neck.'"

And so as soon as he was done telling them that and making sure they too understood everything well, he went to prepare that amulet for cooling fever as he had been directed and came and put it around his child's neck as the child lay in bed.

After dinner everybody went to bed. A bed had been prepared for Myombekere on the ground of the milk-churn in the front of his father-in-law's house, Bugonoka with her mother and the sick child slept in the inner room, where a bed big enough for the three of them had been made and the sick child in the middle had enough space so that he wouldn't be squeezed in by the two adults and lack sufficient air while he had such a high fever.

When the night was really advanced and the creatures of the night had come out of their lairs to roam the wilderness, Ntulanalwo asked for a drink of water to wet his parched throat. His bedmates woke up and Bugonoka warmed the pot of medicine gruel and gave the child the medicine and then put him back to bed. As soon as he fell asleep again, some *enemba*[22] cried: *tetetetete*! The adults nursing the child all exclaimed: "This disease is becoming complicated, otherwise witches would not bring their *enemba* to cry in our home in the middle of the night." That passed and in the house those who fell asleep fell asleep, since when people are looking after a sick person there are bound to be some who can't sleep and those who can. And when it was really late at night, what with cold heavy dew in the air, now those asleep went into real heavy slumber. Nanwero, who was still awake, heard as if people were throwing something at his house: *tiri tiri*! Shortly after that he heard people knocking together *enkomanjo*[23] stones: *poo poo po*! Finally he exclaimed in a heavy voice to himself, "*Yu!*" As it happened his son-in-law on his side of the house too heard what his father-in-law heard and when he moved about in bed and pretend to cough Namwero called him, "Son-in-law!"

"Yes, Sir!"

"Did you hear what happened outside?"

"I heard, father-in-law".

Then just before cockcrow the two men heard some owls cry from on top the cactus trees of the household fence: *wuwu! wu!* This time Nanwero got up from his bed in the interior of the house quietly and passed by the cooking-stones and took out a piece of firewood live with fire on one end. He had just got to the hearth when Nkwanzi tried to stop him: "You man, don't go outside, unless you never listen! Who are you to confront witches and witch doctors? It is true it is our people's way to scare away owls with firebrands, but I am afraid for you and I don't want you to go out. Our ancestors cautioned against such behavior when they said: `Water which leaks into a boat is after drowning those in it!'" Still Nanwero did not pay any heed to what his wife was telling him. Then the owls were heard crying from the top of their very house. Nkwanzi said, "Now hear that! Don't go there if you have ears, or have the evil ones bewitched you already?" But her husband was still adamant and silently forged on, his firebrand in hand, and was joined by his son-in-law as he passed by his bed. He opened the door of his house and the two men got out. The owls were still on the roof of the house and Nanwero sent flying the firebrand after them, all that done in complete silence. On hurling the piece of burning wood at them the birds flew off and scattered and the two men went in different directions of the compound, one going to urinate this way and the other that way, and then returned to the house. Before they dropped off to sleep they heard the cock crow.

And indeed Nkwanzi's fear for her husband was founded. The two men too had been dying with fear even as they were going out, because they too knew it often happens that people who go out at night to hurl burning firewood at owls crying in the compounds of their homes or at the roofs of their houses many times come to harm. There are those whose arms, after hurling firebrands at night birds, remain stiff in that stretch-out position, enable to fold again. There are others who on their way back to the house can't find the door of their houses, when it is in fact wide open. And many of them, even when they managed to return to the house with no difficult, once inside often the hair on their heads would feel as if it were leaving their heads and they would tremble uncontrollably and then lose their power of speech for ever, having been struck mute by the spell cast on them by witches and witch doctors, the owner of those owls.

Finally sleep carried off Nanwero and Myombekere too and they woke up only at the twittering of the early morning birds. Nanwero and his wife were the first to go out of the house and when they opened the door and came out on looking into the compound of their home their eyes were met by four *enkomanjo*, black in color! The couple exclaimed and said, "No wonder! It appears this night witches and witch doctors were dancing in our home the whole night long and that's why our bodies are all aches and pains!" Nanwero added, "What's more this is something new here. We have never seen the like of this!" Lweganwa and his wife too came out and they too saw that, yes indeed, witches and witch doctors danced in their home during the night.

When Myombekere's mother-in-law went back inside the house to the child, Bugonoka and her husband too came out to witness what had befallen them at night and when they too saw what was outside they were left speechless! Myombekere on his part listened to thoughts forming inside him and said to himself, "I see, this is that kind of place!" And then another voice spoke to him differently and said, "This kind of place is everywhere. It is just as people say of the cock which crowed bragging of its country to a new cock in the area: `My beautiful country!' and its companion answered  back: `It is wherever you are!'" And on hearing that other voice inside him he calmed down and thought again and said to himself: "This kind of place is everywhere indeed, for where are my parents who gave me life? And didn't my wife lose her pregnancies twice,[24] didn't those children die when they were still in their mother's womb and in the place where I live, never having been to this place which I want to malign by calling it a bad part of the country? Let's just wait and see what the Sun[25] will allot us." Bugonoka too on her side did not know what to say. She became a most unhappy person, one who could only look and see but could do nothing, like the frog of which people say: "The staring eyes of a frog never prevent a cow from watering."

Nanwero sent Lweganwa to call for him *amagogore* healer, a man called Mukweru, who happened to be a relative of theirs. He did not live very far from their home and so it did not take very long before he came, accompanied by his wife Kazolika. Nanwero told him how witches and witch doctors danced in his home the whole night with their *enemba* and owls crying, and how they were knocking together black *enkomanjo* in the home and showed him the black stones: "There they are even now, in the middle of our compound."

Mukweru and Kazolika were both nonplussed and said: "*Yu!* We are in big trouble! We have never seen anything like this in our neighborhood here!"

Nanwero rejoined, "I too have just told my son-in-law here that this is something new, not a familiar sight." The others present agreed and said, "Yes indeed, this is something new here. It is true people die here too, but all the same this has never happened in our neighborhood. Until now the like of this was something we heard of happening in some other neighborhoods. And if we have among us women of such evil mischief who bring out their night chickens[26] with their malefic songs to come and hold their wicked dances in other people's homes, they must end their evil habit. They must never repeat this! Never! Let them drop their wicked habit as completely as they stopped sucking their mothers' breasts when they weaned. We did not name names, say so and so, no, we have told the whole lot of you together. He or she who inherited that evil dance from his or her father and mother and does not want to put an end to it has better leave this place, because he or she is endangering the tranquillity of our neighborhood. Otherwise, should this happen again, we will take the matter to seers and find out who is behind it and the culprit will have to deal with us all. Be he a man so fierce that other men would rather run through a herd of rhinoceros than face him or a woman who bears twins every time she gives birth, he or she will have it from us all!"

That over Ntulanalwo was brought outside to have his blood let and his *amagogore* treated. Somebody brought a razor and some water in a washbasin[27] and some in a cup[28] as well. Mukweru called Myombekere and Bugonoka and told them, "The child has plenty of *amagogore* in him, I can feel it in the heavy throbbing of his blood-vessels when I hold the back of his head in my hand. It would be better if you let his blood first before I save him from *amagogore* in time, before the disease overwhelms him." Bugonoka was skilled in shaving heads and making blood incisions, and she took the razor and made a gesture of whetting it by lightly stroking her shin with first one side of the blade and then the other in a few rapid strokes and then whistled at it for it to excel in sharpness, this way: *chwiyo!* and followed that with the words: "May you cut the hair and spare the brain?" and at once she dipped the palm of her left hand in the washbasin and wetted the child's temples and shaved clean a patch on each side of his head, finished and made two incisions in each patch, four altogether, more symbolic than anything else, as the child's father rested his hand of the child's shoulder. That done, Mukweru disgorged from the child's throat an abundance of *amagogore*, some coming out through his nose and some through his mouth. Ntulanalwo cried and cried until his voice was ringing like a bell! When Mukweru was satisfied he had cleaned out of the child's throat all the mess of the disease, he let him be and said, "I'm done. Bring him a solution of ash-salt[29] and give him some to drink. He should be all right now."

Bugonoka quickly fetched a hoe from the house and came and buried her child's *amagogore*, and then told Namiti[30] to boil some water with which to wash from him stains of *amagogore* blood mess. Ntulanalwo finally calmed down, and then asked for gruel. After that he was left sitting outside, in the shade of the roof of a grain store[31] surrounded by everybody in the home, instead of being taken back into the house. Bugonoka went in the house to make for him very light gruel of *obubele*[32] millet cooked with some milk and gave it to his son and the sick child noisily drank some four mouthfuls of the gruel and then wanted to pause a bit but those present urged him to drink on and said, "Keep on, drink on, son! Let it scorch your throat and warm your chest so that you can get well again. Yes, that way!" He was given a second serving but only sipped at it a bit and refused to drink any more, shook his head to say no. But he had already drank enough to make his healthy companions happy and so they displayed their white teeth to the sun and jokingly taunted him: "Mwizanalwo,[33] you didn't as much as take a sip of the gruel, when it was you yourself who asked for it!"

"I am satisfied."

"And what do you feel like eating now?"

"Fish."

Lweganwa's wife brought some *emamba* but somebody among those present told her not to give that fish to the child: "Not that one: *emamba* tends to upset the stomach. Better give him *emumi*[34] catfish, which has soft fillet and is more suitable for a sick person." Nkwanzi retorted and said, "You don't even need to remind us of that, because his being able to eat something is what makes us all here happy. Ever since he fell sick he simply wasn't eating anything and had us so worried we don't even want to be reminded of it! And so, unless it is something we don't have, he deserves to be given whatever he desires to eat."

After their patient drank gruel and gulping some fish,[35] visitors from the neighborhood left and he was taken back into the house, put to bed and covered with a goat skin. At a bit past noon, his parents and grandparents woke him up and put a hand on him. He was covered with sweat and the fever had left him. They then bathed him, since he hadn't taken a bath since he fell sick. It is true the usual advice is: "Put water on a sick person," but with Ntulanalwo those nursing him were afraid to bathe him while he had such a high fever, because they were not sure they would be doing the right thing, since some of the diseases in this country don't want water anywhere near them, like yellow fever, for example, of which they also say: "Yellow fever and blood don't go together," meaning the letting of blood, whether by incisions or by horn-suction. After some time Ntulanalwo asked for something to eat and was given *obunzigwa*,[36] which he ate with a bit of fish. He had just eaten and those nursing him hadn't even washed his mouth, so that it was still all oily with the butter of *obunzingwa*, when Myombekere's two sisters arrived. After they exchanged greetings with those present they asked, "How are you all and how is the patient?"

Bugonoka said, "Here he is, today he is feeling better. It is today too that his fever seems to be leaving him, after he was disgorged of *amagogore*. But the child has been seriously sick, and, especially since he hasn't been eating, he is not himself anymore, all his body is gone and only the head is left, as you would see for yourself were it not for the fact that, coming from outside, your eyes are not yet accustomed to the dark in here for you to see clearly."

Myombekere's sisters rejoined, "As for us, dear woman, we knew nothing of this sickness when suddenly, yesterday sometime in the evening, a person brought us the frightening news: 'I have come to inform you that people came to fetch urgently Myombekere and his wife to go and see their child who is sick, and it is said he is very sick and they may or may not find him still alive.'"

The older of the two sisters, the one whose two children, the young boy Kagufwa and his little sister Nakiro, were being brought up in Myombekere's home went on, "With me where I was something inside me died and I felt dizzy. I told my husband, `There is no human being alive any more over there!' No sleep came anywhere near me the whole night and all the while this heart in me kept on racing.  Finally I said to myself, `You better tell this man to escort you this very moment and go and take your sister with you, since she lives on the way, so that you too can know whatever there is to know, so that even if the worst has already happened at least you will know.' So I woke up my husband. It happened to be about cockcrow and before we got to the home of my sister here we heard the night crier split the sky with its sound, and so the two of us at once set off. But we were traveling with cocked ears, afraid to hear the cries of mourners. When we approached your neighborhood we came across a man and asked him whether he had any news of this home and fortunately he said he did and gave us the news, the good man, for he was all good to us, unless we want to invent things against him. He is the one who calmed us down by informing us that the sick child today is feeling better."

Bugonoka's younger sister-in-law on her part apparently had a different impression of the man and said, "You should have seen my sister confront that man to get the news! With me, I must admit, I am afraid of men who look so frightening on the roads, poor me! I always fear that if you ask such a man a question the way he doesn't like if he is carrying a spear he may decide to plant it in you."

Those present all laughed but one of them said, "Oh yes, you are certainly right! You have to be careful, because there are some terrible male creatures who don't want to be asked questions by women. Yes, such men do exist and you are not imagining things."

In the evening Myombekere's sisters said, "There is indeed some distance between this place and where we live! Look how our legs are now paining!" They had, in fact, bruises in their thighs from walking so hurriedly over such a long distance. After dinner Bugonoka boiled some water for them and they bathed and washed their bruised thighs and felt much better.

That night Ntulanalwo slept without fever. The following morning, when the sun was bright and warm enough those nursing him brought him outside and made some gruel for him and he drank it. At noon he took lunch with his grandfather and his uncle and his father. Seeing that everybody became all joy and was left with only one thing to say about their child's sickness: "It comes suddenly but leaves slowly." Myombekere's sisters on seeing that the child was well again decided to leave the following day and the next morning they left. It was decided Bugonoka would stay on for a little longer and see how the child's convalesced but that Myombekere would leave at once and go to attend to other matters of his home.

During her child's convalescence, before Bugonoka prepared anything for him he asked him first what he wanted to eat, because by custom the Wakerewe always ask a sick person what he or she wants to eat before cooking food for him or her. It is asking a person in good health what he or she wants to eat that people find disgusting. Such behavior is condemned and the person who asks is considered a senseless person and a greedy and inhospitable individual. And should the person asked be of the mind to let you know how angry and insulted he or she feels by your asking him or her such a question, be not surprise if he or she responds to you ironically by telling you, "No, I have just eaten my fill, don't waste your time," when in fact he or she hasn't eaten anything that day, and if he or she is a relative of yours and not some gate-crasher he or she could openly tell you: "Why do you ask me what I want to eat as if I am sick?"

Bugonoka watched her patient convalesce for some five days and on the sixth day, when she saw that Ntulanalwo was now well enough, that he was strong again and no longer walked dancing on his legs, she too went back to her home.

It was not until a whole month had passed that Myombekere and Bugonoka went back to see how Ntulanalwo was doing. They found the child once more chubby and as healthy as can be, and on seeing their son in perfect heath they decided to return to their home the same day. Nanwero and Nkwanzi tried their best to make them stay for the night and told them, "You should rest for the night and then go back in the morning!" but they refused and said, "We must go, it doesn't matter how late at night it will be before we get back home, since it happens to be full moon and there's nothing to be afraid of, since, as our people of old said: `One who goes home can't get lost.'"

Ntulanalwo stayed under the foster care of his grandfather for many year. He became six years old then in his seventh year he lost the incisors of his childhood teeth, before it would become the turn of his other teeth too to go. He then became a herder, to be found racing after livestock in the pastures of the wilderness, looking after his grandfather's cattle with his uncle Lweganwa. Among children games, his first favorite and the one which preoccupied him most was hunting with bow and arrow, with his little bow his grandfather made for him and furnished with four arrows made of the stalks of *olukenke*[37] grass. The quarries he hunted were the ordinary lizards and the smaller smooth-bodied ones, *ebina*,[38] those were his wild animals he killed daily, on their house, in the grass and on rocks in hills and mountains. The day he killed the big lizard, the one fond of nodding its head repeatedly, that day he would say, "I've killed an elephant" or a buffalo or a rhinoceros, and the day he killed *ekina* he would say, "I've killed a hare" or some other small wild animal.

And so Ntulanalwo played with his bow and arrow and days came and went, until one day he took aim at the right eye of a boy in his grandfather's neighborhood, a boy of his own age, and shot him dead right in the eye with the arrow of *olukenke* grass and blinded him in that eye. The parents of the child came charging red hot into Nanwero's home to pursue the masters of that home, in a real battle of life and death! It was only because old Nanwero himself too was still a real man and firm and not someone to be easily tramped on by another man and because there was, in addition, his son Lweganwa to reckon with in their home that the fury of the man whose child his grandson had wounded didn't bring Namwero to harm, otherwise that man would certainly have left behind a dead body in Nanwero's home, since he came armed. When the aggressor realized he had gone to look for honey in the hive of killer-bees, he turned around and went to the village headman's home to lodge a complaint against Nanwero, that   his grandchild had hurt his son and completely blinded him in the eye.

As soon as that man left his home, Nanwero got hold of Ntulanalwo and gave him a real beating with a slender twig of a tree while admonishing him: "Never again your mischief, you tiny freak! Never again your mischief of shooting your friends in the eyes, never again, never again, never again, you tiny freak! Never again your mischief of being wild!" Ntulanalwo cried until he was hoarse, while at the same time telling his grandfather, "I'll never do it again, grandfather! I'll never do it again!" On hearing the child cry and resound like a bell that way Nkwanzi came out of the house to try and placate her husband's anger and said, "Stop beating that other people's child, he has cried enough!"

Nanwero turned to his wife and glared at her with an angry eye and said, "What is this one here saying now? Should I leave him and beat you instead? Is what he did, according to you, something good? *Aa*! Hear her say: '*Nyoko nyoko*!40 other people's child!' Is a child from Bugonoka's bottom not my child? What type of nonsense is this one talking?"

Nkwanzi on seeing her husband get so mad with anger at her took cover in the house and Nanwero was left alone talking to himself outside and saying: "I can now see that you women are real dogs, without any shame! The only thing you miss is a tail, otherwise you would have been real dogs! When his parents gave me the child to bring up did they say:

`Whenever he causes an accident, baby him, don't beat him and try to correct him!' In which kingdom were you brought up not to know that a tree is straightened when still young? A pampered child grows up to be a person with no discipline in life, because he or she was spoiled in his or her childhood, and the child who is reprimanded a bit by his or her parents grows up knowing how to behave. And you want to tell me I don't know what and what!"

His wife answered him back from inside the house and said: "Please, I was just saying that may be you could inadvertently strike the child on a sensitive spot, the haunt of his soul, and kill him, since, my dear Nanwero, with a human being there isn't a single one you can say this one can't die easily, my dear. It is true the child has done something wrong and it would be cynical of me to pretend he did not do something bad, that he acted well. That is not what I had in mind, dear."

The two of them said no more.

All that could be heard from Ntulanalwo now was endless hiccups accompanied with sniffling and coughing.

The following day Nanwero was summoned to the village headman's home. When each of the two men, the accuser and the accused, stated their cases, the headman judged them as follows: "Both of you have simply to drop the matter and forget it, because this is a bad accident which happened when two children were playing together. There is no other way of judging this case, because this accident is not an act of an adult who knew what he was doing. And, with children, if you let these two alone this very day they can very easily go back to playing together as usual."

Nanwero and that other man left, and the man went home and nursed his child's eye until it was well again. Ntulanalwo and his companion went back to playing together as usual and only the adults concerned continued to look at each other with a bad eye. As time went by they too resumed their normal relations, though the residue of bad feelings remained.

Ntulanalwo was still at his grandfather's home and he was now eight years old when one day, as he and his uncle were taking their cattle to the herder on duty in their neighborhood herding round, he killed   *entamba*[41] by hurling a stick at the bird, after which he asked Lweganwa, "What is this bird called?"

"It is *entamba*."

"Do people eat it?"

"They do, only in a rather complicated way".

"Complicated how?"

"You have to eat it while running; you can't eat it while seated as you eat other birds."

"And why must you eat it while running?"

"It is said that if one were to eat it while seated or standing still that person would loose his mind, become a real madman walking naked in public and never be normal again."

"Well, if that's how to eat it, let me take it home, where I will eat it the way you say I should. By the way, if I ask grandfather, will he tell me the same thing?"

"Well, let's go, and when we get home you just ask him and you will hear what he will tell you."

Ntulanalwo took his *entamba* and they returned home and once home he went to his grandfather and told him, "Grandfather, I have killed a bird."

"You have? Let's see."

"I'm told it is *entamba*."

"How did you manage to kill *entamba*, such a clever bird?"

"I killed it with a short stick. I hurled the stick in a whole bunch of the birds in flight and killed this one."

"Now I see that you have become a grown-up, since you can kill even *entamba*."

"Grandfather, is it true that the bird is eaten?"

"It is eaten, only you have to eat it while running. As you are here now with me, if you want to eat it, after you have barbecued it, you would have to start from the home gate over there and run all the way to the common grazing plain yonder and return back home here still running and having finished eating the bird. That's how to eat *entamba*."

"And what will happen to you if you just eat it normally, without running, grandfather?

"If you eat it sitting down of standing still you will loose your mind, become altogether insane, never to be a normal person again."

So Ntulanalwo understood that what he was being told was not a "so-I-hear" thing but the truth. He therefore went to the household trash-heap and plucked his bird completely clean of its feathers, except for the head, because that is how he used to see Lweganwa pluck the birds he killed. Then he went back to his grandfather and asked him, "What is the reason for plucking birds while leaving feathers on their heads?"

"The reason is that if you plucked the feathers of the birds' head as well you too would loose the hair on your head completely and become all bold, for ever, never to grow hair again on your head and be forever laughed at by people as a hairless person."

And so Ntulanalwo was enlightened, for, as our ancestors said: `To ask is to be enlightened.' He at once collected some dry twigs of trees as firewood for barbecuing his bird at the courtyard fireplace,[42] for he knew that if he went to the kitchen inside the house the women were bound to chase him away and tell him, "A bird is never barbecued indoors, it is taboo to do so! Go and do that at the fireplace outside. What might your country of origin be, I wonder? It certainly can't be Ukerewe!" And so Ntulanalwo put his bird over the fire he made at courtyard fireplace. When it was half done, he opened its belly and removed the bile and the entrails, then got hold of its head and squeezed the brains out with his hands, because Wakerewe never eat brain, not even that of a goat or cow. He then put his bird over fire again until it was really well-done. Then he quickly took it from the fire and deposited it on a leaf of *omulumba*[43] tree, and when the bird cooled enough he went with it to the gate of their household and started eating it by biting off its head, and then munched   while running and went for another bite as he swallowed the one in the mouth, chewing everything, its tiny bones included, on and on, running while eating until he finished and returned home already done with even savoring the stray bits of bird meat in his mouth, after which he went back to his grandfather and told him, "I've finished eating my *entamba.*"

"And from this day you too will outrun all your competitors in foot races, because you have eaten the swift-flying *entamba* the way it should be eaten."

Another day Ntulanalwo was grazing goats near a small hill on which there was *ikunu*[44] tree with a large hole up its trunk when he saw a woman of advanced age approach him and greet him: "How did you sleep, my little one?

"I slept well!"

"How is your grazing?"

"I'm at it."

"Do you know whether *entamba* ever nest up this tree?"

"Sure they do, since even now you can see their nests in the tree."

"If you know how to climb trees, could you climb up and bring down for me one nest of *entamba*, my child, for you are just like one of my very own."

Ntulanalwo climbed up the tree and dislodged for her from the tree a nest of *entamba* and climbed down carefully with it and placed it in her hand and the old woman left. When Ntulanalwo returned home, as soon as he finished tethering his goats to their pegs he went to ask his grandfather about the incident: "By the way, grandfather, when I was grazing the goats today I saw a woman looking for a nest of *entamba*. What did she want if for? Does it too have some use?"

"The nest of *entamba* heals, and may be that's why she was looking for it."

"And what does it heal?"

"It heals many things, my child, but then the people likely to know all the different diseases it heals and how it is used in each cure are the medicine men and women themselves, people with those healing skills. The little I know in the matter is the following: the nest of *entamba* is medicine for the cure of the disease of *amazilane* and *oluti*,[45] which are diseases which give people afflicted with them irregular heartbeats all the time. And as to how it is used as medicine, it is used in combination with three other ingredients. The first ingredient is prepared by hacking chips from a teak tree, pounding those chips of teak wood on a stone and then drying them. Then iron refuse from a smithy is pounded together with the teak wood ingredient. After that some rock salt[46] is added to those two ingredients, and then the nest of *entamba* is mixed with those three things and the mixture is ground into powder. What results then become a thing of one name, medicine for the disease of *amazilane* or the disease of *oluti*, or of something else, depending on the disease the healers want to treat. But to be able to know all the diseases   *entamba* nest cures and in combination with what ingredients, from the beginning to end, you would have to be a healer yourself, otherwise that is not possible.

"So that's how it is! Now I know."

When Ntulanalwo became a big boy he finally knew that Myombekere and Bugonoka were his parents, since they kept on coming to see how he was doing, and knew why Nanwero was his grandfather and Nkwanzi his grandmother. But still his parents did not concern him much and he did not feel attached to them as he was to his grandfather and grandmother who were bringing him up. In fact he knew they were his parents only because, as the Wakerewe say, `blood relationship has a scent of its own', otherwise were it not for that overpowering scent of blood relationship people speak of Ntulanalwo would never have realized that

Myombekere was his father and Bugonoka his mother. Whenever the couple came to see him at that moment he wanted very much to be with them, but when they left and returned to their home Ntulanalwo never missed them the way we sometimes see happening with children in foster homes.

When Ntulanalwo was still in that foster home of his, Myombekere's brother, the elder of their entire clan, died. Because the man had children, he was buried in his own home and not in Myombekere's home, as would otherwise have been the case. Still, the first to cut open the ground for the dead man's grave, the man who buried him, was Myombekere, with the son of the deceased only seconding Myombekere. The death of that brother of his, a member of his very own family, meant that Myombekere had to send for his son so that he could be present when he and his wife performed their death rites, because if Myombekere and his wife were to achieve their death rites when he was away, when the deceased was such a close clan relative of theirs, their child would live in danger of *amakire*47 disease, should either of them break a sex prohibition and then have anything to do with their child before performing a purification rite. Nanwero and Nkwanzi therefore went with Ntulanalwo to that mourning and people mourned the dead man and finished and the mourners scattered and Myombekere and Bugonoka in their home performed their death rites and finished.

Ntulanalwo however stayed on with his father and mother in their home. His grandparents left earlier, as soon as the mourners went to bathe their grieving after the four days of mourning, and left him behind and said to themselves: "Leave him, his parents will bring him back after they have completed their death rites." But even during the days he stayed with his father and mother in their home, he did not like his parents' home, neither did he like the people of the area, nor their way of doing things, nor the food he ate at his parents' home. What with the fact that his parents put a lot of restrictions on him, by forbidding him to go to far off places, like wandering off to the hills, and to play in certain homes, like the homes to which they themselves didn't want to go, even though they tried to lure him by treating him to all sorts of good food, none of all that counted with Ntulanalwo! He was dying with nostalgia for his grandparents' home and saying to himself: "What an awful place this is! I wish I could go back to grandfather and grandmother. It is wonderful over there and, what's more, there are a lot of other boys to go places with and chat with, whereas here the people are no good and at home they are all the time rebuking me and even forcing me to go and look for firewood and are always sending me on errands without end! It is true that here there is plenty of bananas and banana juice, but, all the same, I am fed up with being rebuked all the time." When Myombekere and Bugonoka realized that, although they were giving their child all sorts of good things in their attempt to make him get used to their home and thus cure him of his nostalgia for his grandparents' place, they were not getting anywhere with him, Bugonoka returned him to his foster home.

After some days since his return to his foster home, Ntulanalwo suffered from *emboga* eye disease as well as boils, which kept on erupting on his buttocks time and time again. Nkwanzi and Nanwero looked for *emboga* medicine for him and put eye-drops into his eyes. Then they realized that his eye disease had its origin in the blood-vessels in his head and looked for someone with the skill of puncturing blood-vessels and the blood in those vessels was let and his eyes cured. Ntulanalwo was then told that he should swallow often *obusahwa*[48] fruits to prevent a recurrence of his eye disease. As to his boils, they cured those with a razor, cutting them open as soon as they came to a head. He would be held down firmly, lying face-downward on the ground, and the person skilled in cutting open boils would, with a very sharp razor, cut deep into a boil with repeated short strokes and then squeeze the boil with his or her fingers, draining out a lot of pus, with sometimes the hard core of the boil coming out too, leaving the cut boil oozing with watery body fluid streaked with blood. The wound left behind would then be treated by applying butter to it. Bit by bit he was finally cured of boils too. With his boils too his elders had something to say to Ntulanalwo and   told him, "Most of the time boils are a result of eating *amafwitanda*[49] fruits." When Ntulanalwo heard that and then remembered how sweet those fruits were, how delightful to the palate, and also how his friends with whom he played went into the woods to look for and found and ate the fruits daily without suffering from boils as often as he did, he found the idea of giving up eating the fruits on his own a really difficult thing to do! Fortunately for him, after a while the boils also completely stopped afflicting him. Before long he erupted large rashes which festered and sored and gave out watery puss. Nanwero and Nkwanzi treated him as best as they could with *omwitankole*[50] and *hakili*,[51] the reputed medicines for curing people of rashes, but in the case of Ntulanalwo the son of Myombekere to no avail! So his grandfather kept on inquiring everywhere for a cure until finally he came across a person who had suffered from that type of rashes and he told him of the medicine man who had treated him with the powder of burnt tree leaves mixed with butter. Nanwero went to the medicine man and he cut the leaves for him and burnt them and gave him the medicine. When Nanwero applied the medicine on Ntulanalwo's rashes, the child was cured within a matter of days.

In the days which followed, Ntulanalwo's favorite pastime became playing in the lake with his friends, since his grandparents' home was near the lakeshore. He played in the lake and learned how to swim and dive, how to somersault in water, how to angle and catch *enfuru*[52] sardines from the top of rocks in the lake, and how to do other things of that kind in the lake with his playmates.

One day the children were angling *enfuru* and when they felt that the fish wasn't taking their bait well any more, they turned to their game of swimming way out in the lake, swimming and diving until their eyes were red like eyes of people who hadn't slept a wink the whole night! One of their games was diving and remaining under water in pairs, side by side, the small fingers of the paired boys' adjacent hands linked, to see who would win by holding his breath and remaining under water longer than his companion. Ntulanalwo was linked to a companion of his under the water in that way when all of a sudden his companion pulled him with a lot of force: *ku*! and he found himself violently jerked out of position and really roughed up, as if in a fight, so much that the surrounding water too stirred and churned. Seeing that, unaware of what was happening, Ntulanalwo said to himself, "Maybe my friend wants to pick a quarrel; I must leave lest his throttles me under the water," and so he came to the surface, his head already covered with sand and mud. It was when he surfaced that he heard the others, but this time adults, shout to him really loudly: "Ntulanalwo, save your self! You are going to die!" he turned and looked back and saw torrents of water rising to the surface, the water itself all mud and silt and on hearing that alarm: "Save yourself! You are going to die!" he was overwhelmed with fear. He realized that he was the only one still in the water, that all his friends were already on the shore. When he had looked back he had seen no trace of his playmate with whom they were chained together by the small fingers of their hands. So our Ntulanalwo became a frog and swam in bounds and leaps and in less than it takes to say it he was already on dry land. As soon as he stepped on the shore on looking back at the lake he and the others saw a crocodile surface and show them the body of a human being, that of Ntulanalwo's playmate with whom they were linked under water by the small fingers of their hands. With that his fear redoubled and he trembled all over and all of a sudden those present saw him just drop down to the ground: *ligiti*! at the same time as adults present sent out a cry of alarm: "*Wu*! *luluu*! a crocodile has killed a person!"

People in all the homes around came pouring to the scene of the accident, from men to women, even the women nursing newborn babies. The women on finding out it was a child of one of them who had been killed at once wept and wailed, for you know how readily women cry. The men brought harpoons and jumped into boats and canoes and began the search for the person who had been caught by the crocodile. They were still searching in the part of the lake where he had been caught when they saw at a distance the crocodile exhibit the human body again and then toss him up this way and catch him before disappear with him under the water again, this time completely and for good as water disappears in the flour of a dish of *obwita*. The men continued their search until sunset and when dark set in and they hadn't found the body they went to their homes to sleep for the night. The following day they resumed the search and again that day too they came out of the sea empty handed. The search went on throughout the four days of mourning, each and every day the men coming back empty handed. On the fifth day, the day the mourners of the person killed by the crocodile were to bathe his death, the mourners went to bathe at the lakeshore where the accident had occurred only to find, lo! the body of the dead child lying on sand on the beach, at the exact spot from where the children had gone into the lake! On examining the body, they found it did not have a single mark to show it had been caught in the teeth of a crocodile nor a scratch from the crocodile's clutches! The only thing visible was blood which was flowing form the mouth and the nose of the dead body, and nothing else! Nanwero and the other people exclaimed and said: "So people are right when they say, `The body of the victim of a crocodile and of a person who drowns are often not found until the day of the bathing of their deaths!' Look! With this child too it is on this day of the bathing of his death that we have found his body brought ashore by the crocodile. So the crocodile didn't kill him so as to eat him; this was wanton killing!" Others said, "*Aa*! The owners of the crocodile had not sent it to catch and eat him or even intended him to be the victim. He was killed by mistake, the intended victim was another person, and that's why the crocodile has returned him without a tooth mark or scratch."

Following that accident Ntulanalwo was strictly forbidden by his grandparents fostering him to play again in the lake as he had been doing. They broke to pieces his fishing line with which he used to angle *enfuru* and then told him: "From today, if you are a human being, never play that way in the sea again. And if you persist in not doing as you are told we will take you back to your parents' home, to your father and mother to give you a good beating and teach you how to behave." And in those days Ntulanalwo indeed became scared of the waters of the lake, and if he went into the lake again at all then it was only when he accompanied his grandfather or his uncle to catch fish from their *olubigo* trap, and even on such occasions, though already in the lake, he did not bathe by swimming about but dipped himself in and out of the water like a kingfisher. *Ahee*! Who wouldn't fear the monster with such terrible teeth! And, let's face it, who loves to die!

When enough time passed, however, Ntulanalwo, like everybody else, forgot the past and had no more memory of what nearly happened to him, and with that he was no longer afraid of anything and went back to bathing in the lake like other people and he too resumed swimming again and angling *enfuru* like everybody else.

His grandfather and grandmother saw the boy was becoming incorrigible and sent for his father to come for him, lest their child should end up badly hurt or cause some serious injury to some other people's children. For Ntulanalwo had indeed become an incorrigible child, the child the Mkerewe calls "the impossible one whose father and mother have given up." His grandparents were afraid they would be blamed by Myombekere's paternal relatives, who would say: "Those who brought up this child spoiled him beyond salvation by bringing him up with petting and babying and never disciplining him, that's why he is so unruly."

Chapter XXV

NOTES

1. *Ekitukuru*:   See note 16 of Chapter V.
2. *Embozu*: See note 8 of Chapter XIX.
3. *Olugali*: See note 6 of Chapter I.
4. *Ekibo*: See note 15 of Chapter I.
5. *Ekisusi*: See note 20 of Chapter II.
6. *Engunda*:   See note 20 Chapter II.
7. *Enduko*: See note 21 of Chapter X.
8. *Empindu*: See note 17 of Chapter X.
9. *Abanyaga*: See note 9 of Chapter II.
10. *Obwita*: See note 14 of Chapter I.
11. *Emboga*: Kitereza in his note for his Swahili translation of his novel has three meanings for the word: "1. Eye disease which makes the eyes overflow with rheum all the time (the one used here). 2. Purification medicine people wash their hands with after a burial (the one we encounter later on in the story at the death of Myombekere in Chapter XXXVI). 3. Very soft greens, liable to cause a running stomach if not eaten with moderation."
12. *Omugonzo*: Se note 4 of Chapter VI.
13. *Ekisano*: See note 9 of Chapter XXIII.
14. *Olubigo*: See note 3 of Chapter II.
15. *Ensato*: See note 2 of Chapter VI.
16. *Emamba*: See note 17 of Chapter II.
17. *Amazu g'abakeluiru*: See note 6 of Chapter VI.
18. *Endwero*: See note 8 of Chapter XII.
19. *Enkombyo*: See note 9 of Chapter XII.
20 In the beginning of the novel Bugonoka's pregnancy which aborted was one, followed by the pre-mature birth of a child who lived one day only.
21. *Amagogore*: Tonsillitis. Kitereza's note in his Swahili translation is: "Disease in which the patient has a high fever and loss of appetite, whose treatment consists in the healer introducing a finger in the mouth of the patient and disgorging from his or her throat a lot of black and red blood."
22 *Enemba*: In his notes for his Swahili translation of his novel Kitereza writes: "Bird deemed to be the harbinger of misfortune."
23. *Enkomanjo*: Very hard round stone used as a hammer to redent and resharpen the surface of a grinding-stone. See note 22 of Chapter XVI. The stone is

usually the color of granite, so that a black *enkomanjo* is a rare object in Ukerewe.

24. See note 20 above.

25.   Providence. See note 21 of Chapter II.

26. Owls and *enemba* above.

27. *Olusabuzyo*:   See note 12 of Chapter I.

28. *Omutaho*:   See note 9 of Chapter I.

29. As different from rock salt. See note 17 of Chapter I.

30. Namiti: The girl, whose name is a very common female Kikerewe name meaning "born of medicinal herbs", appears only here in the entire novel and without any introduction and we can therefore only assume she is one of the inmates of Namwero's home, possibly Barongo's daughter we encounter at the beginning of the chapter.

31. *Ekitala*:   See note 18 of Chapter I.

32. *Obubele*:   See note 17 of Chapter V.

33. Mwizanalwo: Name meaning "born with death", a women's substitute vocabulary, called *ensindo*, a word Kitereza has put in brackets after the name, for Ntulanalwo, a common male Kikerewe name meaning "Death is my eternal companion". In the same sentence Kitereza instead of using *enkumba*, the ordinary word for gruel or porridge, he has used *enzagami*, again with *ensindo* in brackets, in his attempt to reflect real women speech in Kikerewe. For the custom of women using substitute vocabulary see note 23 of Chapter XVI.

34. *Emumi*: Type of catfish.

35. *Kumila*: Literally to "gobble" fish or meat or any other relish, meaning to eat relish without the food it is supposed to accompany. See note 20 of Chapter VI.

36. *Obunzingwa*: See note 15 of Chapter XXIV.

37. *Olukenke*: Very tall grass with a smooth jointless stalk.

38. *Ebina*, plural for *ekina*: See note 8 of Chapter XIV.

39. *Omukungu*:   See note 3 of Chapter III.

40. *Nyoko*: Your mother"! as an insult. See note 2 of Chapter III.

41. *Entamba*: A martin. See also meaning of names at the end of the translation.

42. Ekikome: See note 1 Chapter II.

43. *Omulumba*: See note 16 of Chapter II.

44. *Ikunu*: Name of a tree with a very large trunk when fully grown.

45. *Amazilane* or *oluti*: Hookworm disease. In the Kikerewe text Kitereza speaks of them as if they were two diseases but in his Swahili translation they

are said to be two names of the same disease. Literally *amazilane* means "a marriage taboo" which forbids men and women from a given clan to marry in another clan, like the one we encounter in Chapter II between Myombekere and the woman he comes across on the road and begins to court, and *oluti* here means "the spine" (the word also means a small wooden cooking spoon).

46. *Lunzebe*: See note 17 of Chapter I.

47   *Amakire*: See note 4 of Chapter XII.

48   *Obusahwa*: Name of very tiny and abundant fruits of a tree called *isahwa*, which are usually not eaten although edible.

49. *Amafwitanda (plural for ifwitanda)*: Very sweet and fleshy wild fruits and the tree bearing them.

50. *Omwitankole*: Kitereza's note for his Swahili translation of his novel says: "Medicinal herb which is a very good cure for rashes when mixed with butter and applied on the patient's skin."

51. *Hakili*: Another medicinal herb for the cure of rashes.

52. *Enfuru*: Sardines.

Chapter XXVI

NTULANALWO LEAVES HIS GRANDPARENTS AND RETURNS TO HIS PARENTS' HOME

When Myombekere received the message from Ntulanalwo's grandparents calling for him, he went to take back his child. He said to himself: "Well, just as they want. They have tired of having a helping hand in their home and a herdsman for their livestock. As I say, with me that's fine, just as they want. Let me bring him up myself, for to whom can I bundle him off, who will tolerate him as if he were the child of his own blood? You all know the saying of this country our ancestors left us: `Ugly to other mothers beautiful to its mother!'"

And so Myombekere came back from the home of his wife's parents with his son Ntulanalwo, Myombekere in front with his bow and arrows and Ntulanalwo following behind and he too carrying his own small-size bow suited to his own age as well as two small wooden-headed arrows, *emisonga,*[1] their shafts decorated with cock feathers, ordinary chicken feathers you see around the neck of any cock. From time to time Myombekere would tell Ntulanalwo, "Walk on as fast as you can, my dear man, lest it gets dark before we get anywhere," because they left his wife's parents' home when it was already noon. It was not until they walked past the thickest jungle on their way without encountering killers people speak of, who ambush travelers and strangle them, without encountering predators like lions and leopards or other fierce animals of the wild like elephants, rhinoceros, buffaloes and *embulabwoya,*[2] without encountering anything remarkable and began to see homes of people alongside the road that Myombekere's anxiety left him and father and son walked relaxed, stopped walking with hurried steps.

After walking on for some distance farther they heard a commotion of many people, who sounded as if they were chasing after something or surrounding and cornering something. Myombekere kept on hearing that commotion, which sounded as if it was getting nearer and nearer, and said to himself: "Remember you are a man, get ready and die like a man. May be people are making that loud noise because of some fierce animal, which may run into you as it tries to escape its pursuers!" He therefore took from his shoulder his quiver and dislodged from it three arrows, a barbed arrow, a spear-shaped one and a poison-arrow. He put the poison-arrow on the string of his bow and held the other two arrows in his right hand and again hung his quiver across his shoulder and kept manly ready for battle that way, ears cocked, one ahead one behind like the hare of the wilderness, eyes all alert, his heart hard like iron, his legs steady and his steps sure. Father and son walked on. Because Ntulanalwo was like what our ancestors had in mind when they said: "The child of *enkuyu*[3] fish of abundant scales is born with a lot of scales," he asked his father, "Should something come our way threatening our lives, can I too shoot it?"

"Yes, if it is a dangerous animal you just shoot it, because you are not a women, who dies crying for help, her hands held out pleading for mercy. With a thing like that just shoot it, that's not forbidden, my son, because a man dies like a man."

As they walked on, the noise increased and became really loud, and when they got nearer the source of the noise Myombekere heard people saying, "Come this way, you are in its way of escape, and especially since it is yet to be struck by a weapon, it is still too dangerous," and he understood that whatever it was had not yet been struck by those hunting it. What he did not yet know was what it was that so many people were hunting. When he came near the bush people had surrounded, he too told his son, "Come this way, next to me here," and the child moved closer to his father. And isn't his son too now on the ready, his small *omusonga* arrow strung on his bow? *Hee*! The wonders of this world! Was this what the old man of yore meant when he said, "To underrate another person is to betray your own insignificance?" There was a man named Ngwebe in the throng who sent flying in the bush where the hunted thing was a lump of soil, which apparently landed where it was lodged, on that very side of the bush where Myombekere had positioned himself with his son. No sooner did Ngwebe throw into the bush the lump of clay than people saw emerge from there a real giant of a snake, *ensota,*4 its body already the color of a dry tree trunk and, *hi*! immense and pervasive like the dawn of a new day, its crest waving at its head, eyes red like sparks of fire, and come tearing by the tops of trees in the bush and making straight to where Myombekere was. Before it got to Myombekere his son, without uttering a sound, pulled tight his little bow and let go his *omusonga* arrow right into the belly of the giant reptile: *puu*! and the boy's wooden arrow went right in and remained planted in the giant snake! When the reptile tried to strike the child, Myombekere, who hadn't moved an inch from the stand of his feet, at once let fly his arrow into its neck: *puu*! and his poison-arrow went in and took root. The reptile turned around its head to go somewhere else, only Ngwebe too was already at the scene and at once he too brought down his spear with all his strength into the damned belly of the creature: *chipiki*! The giant *ensota* became a plaything on the ground.

On seeing that, the whole crowd rushed that way to see for themselves that giant of the fierce snake, which had become a real threat to the lives of travelers, turned into real danger hiding and waiting to ambush everyone who took that footpath. They also came to see the man who had saved them by killing the dangerous monster and found that its killer, the one whose weapon hit it first,5 was a small child! Everybody was really surprised and people remarked to each other: "Yes, indeed, now we see it! To underrate another person is to betray your own insignificance! This little boy is the one who has brought tumbling to the ground this giant of a terrible creature which had proved an invincible enemy to all of us adults, with all our years behind us! No, it can't be! May be this is not an ordinary child, he has something else working for him!" When the people looked at the mountain of *ensota* lying dead down there on the ground and then looked at the child who had killed it, the men were simply reduced to exclaiming with wonder, shaking their heads in disbelief and saying, "If you have a son like this child, you can really count on him! When this child grows up he will be somebody really remarkable!" They then lifted Ntulanalwo's arms up in the air in congratulations and asked Myombekere, "I this bold child the son of your own blood or in what way is he your child?"

"Yes, he is the child of my own blood."

"What is his name."

"He is Ntulanalwo."[6]

"*Hii*! He has a manly name as well!"

The women of the area began to arrive on the scene in all their numbers and asked who the killer of the monster was. They found their men crowded around Ntulanalwo and hiding him from view and asked them to give way so that they too could see him and on seeing Ntulanalwo the women fell to taking from their waists strings of beads, to holding his arms and raising them in the air in congratulation, accompanying that with peels of ululation[7] and presenting him with their waist-strings of beads until the beads around his neck were too heavy for the child to bear and Myombekere had to relieve his little son of his hero's trophies.

That done and finished Myombekere and his son pulled their weapons from the reptile and Ngwebe too retrieved his spear and then Myombekere asked how they had spotted the giant snake and the people told him, "Bunoge was grazing cattle on his turn of the duty for our neighborhood when he saw this *ensota* in *omukoko* [8] tree over there, where it struck his cow killing it on the spot and where the cow's carcass is still lying in a heap. Come, so that you too can see it."

The men went to the tree, where they found Bunoge's dead cow had already swollen like a mountain where it lay, its stomach round like a ball about to burst open due to the venom of *ensota* in its body. It was a deep brown cow and when one touched it, however slightly, the hair of its skin fell off, and seeing that all those present who had never see such a thing said, "Yes indeed! *ensota* is a snake of very deadly poison! The meat of this cow in now unfit for people to eat because that poison is everywhere in its body, otherwise it wouldn't be shedding its hair this way at all. Its skin too is now useless, since its hair will all fall off!"

With that Myombekere and his son left to continue with their journey, leaving behind the men at the scene disputing whether or not they should slaughter Bunoge's cow. When they got home and told Bugonoka what had befallen them, she ululated with joy and then went and raised up high the arms of both her husband and her son in congratulation. Ntulanalwo's parents put away for him the strings of beads and the bracelets which he had received as presents for his great feat.

The following day Myombekere sent for Kanwaketa and told him: "Dear brother, look at what happened: my child and I were on the brink of death. I therefore want to congratulate my child and myself and I am offering my white bull over there for butchering, for us to eat and celebrate, for, had we died, it would have been enjoyed not by us but by our mourners."

"What you say about congratulating yourselves is the right thing to do, my brother, because, had you died, instead of this happiness we would be in real grief." And at once the two neighbors and friends went into the kraal, put a rope on the bull and herded it into Myombekere's banana plantation, where they butchered it and finished the job.   And in Myombekere's home people ate cow meat to celebrate with great joy the heroic feat of Ntulanalwo killing *ensota* as well as his return to his parents' home. Namwero and Nkwanzi heard of it and they too came to congratulate their grandson and their son-in-law and take part in the celebrations.

Myombekere's sisters however heard of the occasion differently. You all know how good our people are at connecting words and adding things onto them and elongating them as if they were making ropes of them, how a person will hear something from a friend and how from there he or she would twist what he or she heard and make it something else. Myombekeres sisters too were told something else. The person who told them the news about their brother got it twisted this way: "Your brother was coming from the home of his wife's parents when on the way he was struck by *ensota* and killed on the spot. It is said that it was his neighbor Kanwaketa who carried his body back home and he was buried and that was days ago, so that the day of his mourners bathing his death is possibly tomorrow." It was some time in the evening when the news reached one of the sisters and she went off crying and wailing to fetch her sister and the two bereaved women, accompanied by their husbands, got on the way to Myombekere's home. When they got to Myombekere's village, still some distance from Myombekere's proper neighborhood, their husbands went to get some more information from the home of an acquaintance of theirs who lived in the area and on inquiring the man told them, "Myombekere is alive, and isn't even sick. Who ever told you what you heard lied." Then he recounted to them what actually happened. On learning the truth of the matter Myombekere's brothers-in-law were overcome with joy and returned to their wives running and told them: "Myombekere is alive and all his people in his home too are all alive and well. The only thing there is that they are feasting to congratulate themselves for their narrow escape from that terrible monster of a snake, and that's all." Their wives stopped crying and went to their brother's home quietly and found people in the home in the middle of their happy celebrations, with not a thing to complain of! And when things turned out that way, the sisters too joined in the celebrations and for a good two days and it wasn't until the third day that they went back to their homes with their husbands.

And so Ntulanalwo came back and stayed in his parents home, obeying his father in all he wanted of him, doing everything he was asked to do, because he simply changed and became a different person. His old behavior simply went away and disappeared as a bird disappears from sight in the air. He became a good boy to both his parents and their relatives and a very beloved companion to all his playmates, a boy who regarded as his father every adult man he saw and as his mother every adult woman.

Chapter XXVI

NOTES

1. *Emisonga*, plural for *omusonga*:   Wooden arrow, derived from the verb "*kusonga*", which means to finish off killing a prey already hit.

2. *Embulabwoya*: Animal whose name means "Hairless", so that today the word has become a euphemism for a human being in a homicide. Kitereza in the note for his Swahili translation writes: "Hairless animal which used to abound in the forests of old Ukerewe, the last of which was killed by the famous hunter Nkona (name meaning "Eagle") who lived in Nanonge, the village of the residence of the queen mother the mother of Omukama Lukonge son of Machunda, an event witnessed by many old people I knew."

3. *Enkuyu*:   See note 24 of Chapter XII.

4. *Ensota*:   Kitereza in his note for his Swahili translation of his novel says: "Very large and long snake with deadly poison. In the olden days in Ukerewe there were two kinds of *ensota*, one with a crest on its head and the other without a crest, both of which were equally deadly poisonous. *Ensota* with a crest when alarmed moved with its head up in the air, moving by its tail-end only while making a whistling sound which could be heard from a great distance. If *ensota* bit a person or an animal, even a buffalo, the animal would die on that very spot from its poison, even though the snake itself, whose two types were equally huge and frightening to look at, did not feed on human flesh or the flesh of animals."

5. In a hunt, the man who was counted "the killer" of the prey was the one who struck it with his weapon first.

6. Literally Ntulanalwo means: "I walk (or live) with death". See note I of Chapter I.

7. *Akahira*: See note 11 of Chapter IX.

8. *Omukoko*: Name of a very large evergreen tree with a lot of branches and foliage.

9. *Narutundubwi*: See note 1 of Chapter XVIII.

Chapter XXVII

THE BIRTH OF BULIHWALI, NTULANALWO SETTLES BACK IN HIS PARENTS' HOME

When Ntulanalwo was still living at his grandfather's home, his parents had a second child, his baby sister. Bugonoka had started off her married life with a period of barrenness and when she sucked and weaned her son Ntulanalwo she again lived for three years without conceiving another child, so that she was almost losing faith in what her healer Kibuguma divined and spoke before her and her husband: "She will give birth to a male child first and then give birth to a baby girl."

The couple were in their fourth year after the birth of their only child when they went back to their healer for help and their healer gave them medicine again and again Bugonoka drank the medicine until she had taken sufficient of it and she conceived the pregnancy of her child Bulihwali and gave his son Ntulanalwo a little sister. The gap between Ntulanalwo and his little sister was larger than usual, because a woman plagued with barrenness conceives with difficulty, unlike normal woman with no such complications who give birth to one child after another, who usually suckle their child for one year and wean it in the second year when the mother is already pregnant again. With such women, after quite a number of years have passed one day the woman looks around her and suddenly realizes she already has quite a gathering of human beings in her home, all born by her! It is true nobody can have enough children, but all the same her eyes cannot but be pleased with what she has done, for which she would congratulate herself: "I can see I have born some children!" Everywhere she turns she hears the voices of her children. Before she has had a moment of rest, she hears form this side a child of hers calling her, "Mother, I want leftovers," or, "Mother, I want sweet potato," and yet another one, "Mother, I want a bath," and another one yet, "Father, I want to sleep," and the like. And the joy of life in many children like that fills the parent too with great happiness. The childless man or woman on the other hand sits all alone in his or her house or in the compound of his or her home until finally he or she can no longer stand the unsettling thoughts in his or her mind and says to himself or herself: "No, I shouldn't stay here alone this way; let me may be look for some company at so-and-so's, rather than stay here all alone like this, as a result of which the sun seems to stand still and it takes forever before night comes!"[1] So because Bugonoka's child-bearing was that of a barren woman who has to drink the medicines of healers for a long time before she conceives, she did not bear another child after Ntulanalwo was born until in the fourth year after he weaned. That pregnancy went well with Bugonoka and she carried it without any complication for the entire nine months and then brought into the world her baby girl. And Myombekere gave that baby girl a name reminiscent of their suffering over their barrenness and said: "May you grow into an adult, you are Bulihwali."[2]

Bulihwali too, like her brother Ntulanalwo, was taken to the home of her maternal grandparents to be brought up by Namwero and Nkwanzi[3] as soon as she was weaned.

For now however let us put aside matters of Bulihwali the daughter of Myombekere and Bugonoka and take them up again later when we recount her life and how she fared until her death.

The year Ntulanalwo came back to his parents home from living with his grandparents was also the year Myombekere's nephew, that is Kagufwa, who was living in that home of Myombekere, went back to his parents. His father came to fetch him so that he could go and get married, since the courtship of his wife-to-be was about to be concluded. Myombekere gave him a present of a bull for slaughtering for the bride in his wedding celebrations and Myombekere's brother-in-law, Kagufwa's father, thanked him sincerely and said, "Thank you very much for this much needed present, brother-in-law, you have indeed been very generous to your nephew."

"If I don't give Kagufwa something for his wedding I would be a person devoid of all sense, because he was my savior when I badly needed help in looking after my livestock, not to mention the fact that he almost lost his life for me, for Ntamba would have killed him and he wouldn't be here with us now, had his swift foot not saved him. In fact, brother-in-law, even if you hadn't paid bride-price for my sister, the mother of this boy, I would still give him something to help him get a wife, because he toiled so much for this cattle. I wouldn't have heeded those of our people who say: 'A man goes to look for something to help him meet his marriage expenses from his mother's people only if his father paid bride-price for his mother, otherwise to do so would be shameful, since his maternal relatives never received a thing from his father.' Even if that were the case and you hadn't paid his mother's bride-price as you did, with Kagufwa I would still give him something of value for his wedding, for our ancestors said: `One who dies working dies eating.'"

A year passed after Ntulanalwo returned to his parents' home from his grandparents, during which time he helped his father graze their livestock. Since in those days looking for firewood was men's work,[4] Ntulanalwo too every time and without fail would, like his father, return home from grazing livestock carrying a faggot of firewood for his mother to cook with. The day he wasn't herding cattle he went to angle *enfuru*[5] and when he brought the fish home his father would congratulate him and say to him, "How was your work in the sea, fisherman?" To which he would answer, "Work in the sea was fine." On his way home from angling when people he came across asked him for some fish: "Aid us with a bit of fish, Ntulanalwo?" he would answer those he didn't want to give his fish to, "All a handout does is to whet the appetite," which would make those people burst out laughing, and when he gave fish to some those on their part would thank him by raising their two hands to him in gratitude and telling him, "Thank you, son of Myombekere, there has never been born a man as generous as you! Thank you for saving me from want this way, son, may the person who speaks ill of you precede you into the ground as *ebisesya*[6] linings precede fish at the bottom of the pot," meaning that whoever wished Ntulanalwo ill should die before him. When Wakerewe women want to cook fish, they first line the bottom of the pot with *ebisesya* before putting in fish so that fish doesn't catch at the bottom of the pot and burn, and that's why a Mkerewe wished his or her fellow human being good health and long life with that saying.

Finally Ntulanalwo mastered milking cows and saved his father from having to squat in the middle of the mud of cow dung during heavy rains. Myombekere congratulated himself: "I now see that bearing children is indeed a great blessing! No wonder people long for children so much and are so frightened of barrenness! Now I realize that barrenness is a deformity. Yes indeed! May this child grow up quickly so that I may give him a wife with whom to have children of his own and perpetuate himself and spread our clan!"

Myombekere too now had a banana plantation, from which he had already bought things of value from people, like goats, and iron hoes and, yes, cows. He bought goats first and when he had acquired six goats he bartered them for a bull, and again when he had bought as many as twelve goats and saw a person with the young female of a cow who wanted goats he added a calf-bearing cow to his herd, since twelve goats was the indisputable exchange value of a female cow, and hence the saying of our ancestors: "We are quit like the buyer and seller of a heifer!" And since Myombekere too had become a reputable banana beer brewer, a man in whose home multitudes of people thronged in search of a drink, one day he had brewed beer in his home and the beer was still not quite ready, still foaming, and yet the morning sun had hardly began to climb in the sky when dignitaries upon dignitaries as well as the ordinary nobodies were already pouring into his home to drink free banana beer. Apparently the person who said: "Where there's a carcass is where the vultures gather" wasn't wrong, he was dead right. Myombekere placed pots of his beer in front of people and the people drank the beer and the beer got to their heads and they started talking in twos here and in threes there.

When he saw people talk in such groups everywhere, he too began to seek out and whisper his secret to one dignitary after the other, important people who he happened to know had daughters he could court for his son Ntulanalwo. He whispered his secret to as many as five people that day, of whom not a single one refused or had any strong objections to the idea, unless I want to lie and put words into their mouths, the good people, with the exception of perhaps only one of them, who felt he had a few man to man words to say to Myombekere and told him: "There is a taboo between my people and yours and our clan and yours cannot marry, neither can we partake of each other's sacrificial meal, no, because of that taboo between us bequeathed us by my ancestors and yours." Myombekere too had to consent that, yes, a great prohibition stood in between them, for who, except an insane person, would knowingly eat food that is taboo to him or her?

The beer drinkers all gone, Myombekere and Bugonoka went over the issue of looking for a wife for Ntulanalwo. They wanted him to marry young, before staying for too long as an unmarried young man, since he was their lonely male child. They also wanted him to marry the daughter of a really great man, to have wife who, even if not the daughter of the king or of a prince, would at least be a daughter of a prominent man and not of some miserable poor nobody. They also wanted their son to marry a woman who was, in addition, a beauty and a woman of excellent character and who was also good at hoeing the land, because they were really afraid, since we are all mortals, of leaving their Ntulanalwo after they were dead living in misery because of a lazy wife.

Their child Ntulanalwo himself, however, had not yet been completely cured of his inclination for mischief. One day he went with some other boys to catch birds, *ebikuhwe*[7] and *enzuli*,[8] in *obubele*[9] millet fields after harvest. When they caught what they caught they called it a day and left for home. On their way back home when they came to a crossroads where there was some sandy ground, Ntulanalwo said to his two companions he was with: "What do you say, men, if we hold a wrestling match? If you throw me down, take my four *enzuli* birds, here they are, plus this one *ekihuhwe*, make that five!" On hearing that his friends, who had caught many more birds of each of the two kinds than he and were therefore not particularly worried about losing a few, even if they lost the match, readily agreed. One of his companion was called Kikunami[10] and the other was named Kahwagizi.[11] Kikunami was the first to come forward and give Kahwagizi his *enzuli* and *ebikuhwe* to hold for him and Ntulanalwo too gave his birds to Kahwagizi to hold for him. In less time than it takes to say it, Kikunami and Ntulanalwo were in each others grip and struggling with each other and rushing each other this way and that way all over the sandy patch. At that very moment a certain man, an adult, whose name was Busengezuzo, was passing by and on seeing the two boys in a wrestling match he too stopped on the spot to watch the match and urged them on, as if they were two fighting bulls, and told them: "Today is the day, men, he who goes to the ground won't eat food at home, *brurr*! That was my game! *Ah*! son of my father! struggle, male ones, so that we can tell the strong man from the weakling!" Kikunami wound a leg catch around Ntulanalwo's leg and brought the two of them down in a female fall, a draw,[12] with both of them falling to the ground sideways, with that man Busengezuzo still taunting them hard, *we*! The boys got to their feet again, wiping sand from their heads. But that fellow Busengezuzo was not giving up, was still bent on setting them on each other, and so he said: "*Brurrr*! You shit out of a fight, my men!" When Ntulanalwo heard that word shitting out, he told his friend: "Let's have a repeat, Kikunami." His friend agreed and they gripped each other's torsos again: *gingiri gingiri*! Ntulanalwo wound a leg catch around the right leg of Kikunami and before he knew it Kikunami was on the ground, the back of his head in the dust of the sand. Both Busengezuzo and Kahwagizi jeered at the defeated boy: "*Woo*!" Kikunami dusted himself and then took from Kahwagizi four *enzuli* and one *ekikuhwe* from his catch of birds and gave then to Ntulanalwo.

Seeing that Kahwagizi threw out a challenge at Ntulanalwo with a cry of self-praise and said: "*Aa! ee!* My name is Kahwagizi! I feed on thorny cactus and rinse my mouth with the bitter milk of *olukoni*[13] euphorbia! Come, give me a turn! We shouldn't feel so scared to come near you as if you have thorns on your body, dear friend, and let you go away bragging and saying: `I scared them!'"

"What you say is true indeed, Kahwagizi. What with the fact that his is making off with your catch of birds, he is indeed bound to brag, and why not? *Hee! aa*! I too will go away saying: `The son of Myombekere beat them and took away their *enzuli*.'"

So Ntulanalwo and Kahwagizi gripped each other by the chest: *gingiri gingiri*! that way and this way! Before he knew it, Kahwagizi found Ntulanalwo's leg twined around one of his legs and whenever he tried to lift Ntulanalwo and free his leg, he found his opponent simply immovable, glued upright to the ground as if by a spell impossible to break! And as Kahwagizi struggled to figure out some counter move, he was already on the ground and his leg: *cheke*! broken! Ntulanalwo cried out in self-praise and said: "I'm done with you, so remember this name: I am the son of Myombekere!" And immediately he leaped to where their birds were kept and took from Kahwaguzi's catch four *enzuli* and one *ekikuhwe*, which made it five birds, the prize promised the winner of their wresting match, which gave him, counting with his own catch, twelve *enzuli* and three *ebikuhwe*, and then took off running and returned to his parent's home with his loadful of birds, leaving Kahwagizi still on the ground, groaning with the pain of a broken leg, so that Busengezuzo had to lift him up and then slowly escort him back to his parents' home while supporting him.

The man got the wounded boy to his father and mother and the parents of the boy asked him what had caused their son's injury and Busengezuzo recounted what he witnessed. Kahwagizi's parents then, without a word said, turned to massaging their child's foot, for what else could they do when their son's injury was the result of children play. To say the truth, the way I see it, Kahwagizi was a bit older than Ntulanalwo, except that Ntulanalwo had a fattish body with round sturdy legs, the never-break legs, but, apart from that, Ntulanalwo was certainly the younger of the two boys.

When Busengezuzo left the home of Kahwagizi's parents, he passed by Ntulanalwo's parents', to make sure Kahwagizi's father wouldn't arrive there before him when he went to complain to them about their child breaking his son's leg, because Busengezuzo couldn't wait to tell Myombekere what a real man his son was. I am sure you too know of individuals whose mouths have things to tell all the time like liars. Busengezuzo too was a man of that kind. When he arrived in the home of Ntulanalwo's parents he found only Myombekere and Bugonoka at home, Ntulanalwo himself having already left with some other friends of his to look for firewood in the woods. And when he arrived, no sooner had he finished greeting Ntulanalwo's parents than he uninvitedly began hedging, the way you daily see people do when they are determined to blab to others something, and with a forced laugh he pretended to ask a question: " Isn't Ntulanalwo at home?"

"He was here with some friends of his, spinning cow-tail hair for making bird traps to catch birds with in the harvested millet fields; may be they have gone out for a walk."

"Yes, my dear Myombekere, you brought into the world a lion of a man!"

"Why?"

"I found him yonder at that sandy ground out there wresting with his companions, two of them, with himself the third, on their way from catching birds, *enzuli* and *ebikuhwe*, *aa*! I found him wrestling with Kikunami, the son of Malyalya. I had been standing there for just a little while when I saw the two of them fall to the ground in an inconclusive female fall. In no time I saw them grip each other's torsos again and in less than it takes to say it your son had put a leg grip on the leg of his opponent and in an instant I saw Kikunami[14] topple over all the way into the heap of sand on the ground. Apparently they had wagered *enzuli*, for immediately I saw Ntulanalwo take from Kikunami's string of bird-catch four *enzuli* and a fifth bird, *ekikuhwe*, and add the birds to his own catch. Then when the son of Lusalira saw Ntulanalwo throw down Kikunami and then take his birds he bragged and swore his self-praise like you've never heard! It was indeed a spectacle to behold! And so he went in for your son, kind of angrily. Before I knew it, they were in each other's grip, rushing each other this way and that way all over the sandy patch: 'Here, down you go!' but Ntulanalwo said: `No!' In that instant I saw that your son had a few tricks waiting: before he knew it, his opponent's right leg was trapped in the grip of your son's left leg. Kahwagizi tried all he could to spin around Ntulanalwo and throw him down: here you go! but *aa*! your little man was glued upright to the ground as if by a spell impossible to break! When Kahwagizi resorted to violent shakes and moves in search of a counter trick, I saw your Ntulanalwo lift him only once and send him tumbling down on the other side: *tini!* while Ntulanalwo himself remained standing upright like a dry tree. Then I saw your son leap up and in one stride snatch the wager of birds he had won from his opponent's catch and run straight this way. However, without Ntulanalwo realizing it, Kahwagizi's leg had been broken and that's why he remained lying in the sand that way. When I saw Kahwagizi behave like a baby about to cry I went and lifted him from the ground and found that his leg was broken at the knee, his kneecap dislocated so that it now stood behind the leg in the bend of his knee. So I persuaded him not to cry by telling him, "Don't cry, because you are the ones who wanted to wrestle, it was a game for all of you; so you can't cry now, like a woman. Bear it silently, I will support you and walk with you slowly and take you to your parents' home. What is more, of the two of you, you and Ntulanalwo, you are the older, so that it was Ntulanalwo who in wrestling you was risking taking on more than his match. Such a mere kid shouldn't make a grown-up young man like you cry as if you are a good-for-nothing fellow." I think when he heard that he was ashamed and so he didn't cry and I walked him slowly until I got him to his parents' home. But I left Lusalira going to look for *obwanda* and *amakugwe*[15] with which to massage his son's leg with hot water and did not hear of anything else out there. That's why I passed this way, thinking that perhaps Lusalira has already been here to vent his anger on you."

"*Aa*! We are yet to see Lusalira here. May be he has let the matter be, since it is a matter of children play."

"Possibly, yes. That's what I too told him, how the children had been just playing and nothing else, that they hadn't been fighting."

"In fact, with us here, our son himself hasn't told us about it; hadn't you come to tell us we would still be completely unaware of it, unless perhaps he spoke about it to his mother. Bugonoka!"

"Yes, Sir."

"Are you, by any chance, aware that Ntulanalwo has caused an accident?"

"What accident?"

"He has injured the leg of Lusalira's son."

"I know nothing about that. He just plucked his birds, singed them over fire and then gave them to me. In fact that is what I am cooking this very moment. But he didn't speak to me of anything else."

Busengezuzo finished hawking the words of his mouth and went away, leaving Myombekere and Bugonoka waiting to see whether or not Lusalira would come to charge them with their son's felony. Sometime in the evening Ntulanalwo came back home, and during dinner his father asked him, "Is it true that you have injured Kahwagizi the son of Lusalira?" Ntulanalwo told him how he wrestled with his friends and defeated them, how it was Busengezuzo who was urging them on and added, "But I personally wasn't aware that Kahwagizi was injured, because he was still on the ground when I left. And I left quickly like that because I thought that when he got up from the ground he might get up looking for a fight. But it was Busengezuzo who taunted us to wrestle on."

Myombekere said: "I see! Busengezuzo was urging you to wrestle as if you are his fighting bulls! What a rotten adult! Imagine, you had hardly left with your friends when he was already here, and what he told us is something else, not like what you say. But all the same, my son, if you listen to what I tell you, you should never again engage in such mischief with other people's children. I don't want accidents like that in my home. If that is how you used to behave when you were at your grandfather's home, know that with me here you are never again to indulge in such mischief and go about challenging people older than you. If Kahwagizi weren't older than you, you can be sure Lusalira would have already been here to charge us with the injury you have caused his son. The son of a human being should be praised for his goodness and for his obedience to his elders, and you want to be known for ugly charges people bring against your parents on account of your doing things of no use to anybody at all! It would be better if people came here with some defendable charge against you, like your eloping with a young girl. That is some understandable felony, for which even if asked to pay things of value as compensation a person gladly does so while saying: `My son wants a wife!'"

When Myombekere waited for days without Lusalira coming to his home to complain against Ntulanalwo and without hearing a word whispered on the issue, he told Bugonoka, "May be the injury of the son of Lusalira turned out to be not so serious."

"So it appears, for had it been as serious as Busengezuzo told us here it was, the injured person being the son of the Lusalira[16] I know, let's face it, he would have been here to complain a long time ago, and really belligerently, or would have already taken us to the village court at the headman's.[17]

"*Aa*! He would indeed have already come. It doesn't matter though, since today or tomorrow I intend to go in those areas, to the home of Matogo *emigonzo*[18] fisherman to look for fish, and I will call at the Lusalira's on my way, to greet them and find out how serious Kahwaguzi's injury was."

"You man, please don't go calling at Lusalira's and find yourself courting revenge! It was your child who injured their son and now you want to simply walk into their home! How do you know what they may do to you? Maybe even as we speak it is you they are discussing, the way people are these days! What if they kill you?"

"Still I will pass through, because my son having injured his son in a children game can't be reason enough for him to shoot me with an arrow or spear me as if my son had committed some heinous crime against him. I now see that with you women this fear of yours will never leave you! Am I never again to take a walk and go and look for fish for the people of my home because of this so called Lusalira, as if all the men in the world would rather run into a herd of rhinoceros than face him!"

So the following day in a sweet morning sun Myombekere took his quiver and removed from it six arrows and took his bow and left to look for *emigonzo* fish in Matogo's home. Since the cow-trail he was taking passed by Lusalira's home, when he came to the man's home he got out of the trail and took the footpath which led right into the home, got to the gate of the homestead and called, "People of this home!"

Lusalira answered form inside a house, "We are here!" and came out at once and found there in front of him no other person but Myombekere! When Lusalira wanted to relieve him of his weapons, he said no, because he felt he had to take precautions and was saying to himself, "In case something really bad has happened to that child who was injured by my son and they want war with me we'll shoot it out!" And so he refused to part with his weapons and told Lusalira, "No, leave them, let met keep them, because I am still proceeding yonder to the Matogos' to look for *emigonzo* fish. People told me that he is going out to sea and catching a lot of fish these days. And is it true or did those who told me simply feed me a pack of lies?"

"Those who told you are right, they did not lie to you. Our fishermen are catching so much fish these days! Over there on the peninsula almost every man is out fishing with *emigonzo*, but the man who is really catching a lot of fish is the one you mentioned. In fact when you get there you won't know what to choose and what to leave: should you want *ensonzi*,[19] that's up to you, should you want *embozu*,[20] again that's up to you and should you want *emamba*,[21] there again that's up to you, should want *embete*,[22] there too that's up to you, and if your Bugonoka too eats *emumi*,[23] that's what is especially abundant at Matogo's. In fact coming at this time you have come at the right moment indeed, when the fishermen land their heaviest catch of the day and are still on the seashore."

"You mentioned Bugonoka eating or not eating *emumi*, *aa*! we in that home of mine eat everything, I must admit; may be the only thing we don't eat is a dog!

"You want tell me that Bugonoka eats *emamba, embete*, goat meat and mutton?"[24]

"*Aa*! At least not those! Please don't say that! Those are things of which their ancestor told our women: `Don't eat these!' I am only speaking of ordinary relish which the women who want can eat, but certainly not the forbidden foods! *Ahee*! To say the truth, for us who are not fishermen, if a friend should happen to give you a section of *emamba* on a day there is no other relish at home and you return home with that *emamba* piece and nothing else to show for your search, that day you will see the mistress of your home grinding millet while dragging her hands over the grinding-stone and with no flour dropping from the stone! No, I wouldn't dare mention what I know is out of the question for her to eat."

They were still standing and hadn't greeted each other and when they finished their chat they greeted each other and then Lusalira called his son Kahwagizi and said, "Bring a chair here for the father of your friend" and Kahwagizi brought Myombekere a chair. He was still limping and the injured leg was still tied in a cast of stick ribs. When Myombekere saw the child come limping that way with that cast of sticks on his leg, he pretended to know nothing about it and asked with feigned surprise, "What happened to the child?"

Lusalira hadn't said a single word in answer when Myombekere heard Kahwagizi's mother say, "Your son wanted to kill my child, and it was by sheer luck he didn't. Now, as you can see, he comes out of the house a bit, but the day he was injured as well as the following day we had become very angry indeed, and I don't want to hide it from you, for we were on the verge of coming to your home to demand retribution. In fact things are as they are because we were fortunate enough to find excellent medicine for treating his leg, medicine on which the healer who gave it to us must count very much, judging by what he wants from us for it.

"I am completely unaware of all this."

"Didn't your son tell you that they wrestled on their way from catching birds in harvested millet fields?"

"May be he was afraid of what would happen to him when we found out, since he had done something wrong."

"It is possibly that."

"By the way, what fee does the healer who gave you the medicine for the boy's injury want?"

"When the injured person is male, he wants a he-goat, and in the case of a female patient, he charges a young female goat."

"*Yu*! What exorbitant fees! *Ahee*! I have never heard a healer charge so much for this kind of treatment. I now see that healers have no pity; all they care for is to acquire property!"

"*Ha*! Healers being considerate! Haven't you ever heard the saying `Clan go, for here comes healing' or `The healer spares the property of neither father nor mother?'"

"No wonder healers have no feelings!"

"But we are saying all this simply because we don't have that precious goat itself, otherwise we would simply pay and say nothing about that, since he has cured a human being for us. For can a goat turn into a relative of yours?

"Indeed, we are saying all this gratuitously, for how can anything be of greater value than a human being? If you don't have the goat, when the healer comes to demand his payment come and get one from my home, where I have this one young he-goat, already seconded by another calf by its mother. I am sure that healer too, if he were to see it, wouldn't be dissatisfied with it, since it is fat and not lanky, a he-goat of good value. Please come and take it, because I am giving you the goat just because I would like to help and I am not saying, `Let me pay on their behalf because it is my child who is responsible for this terrible thing.' No, I don't have that in mind."

Lusalira answered him back, rather coldly, and said, "Yes, let's talk a bit more about that when the healer comes to demand his fee." That lukewarm answer was the result of the wife of Lusalira having cast an oblique look at her husband before he answered. After that Myombekere left and Lusalira escorted him. When he came back from escorting Myombekere, his other wives, for he had many wives, discussed what Myombekere had said with Kahwagizi's mother and then asked their husband, "What do you think of the words of Myombekere, who, without being asked by anybody, wants to help by giving you a goat? What do you think of that?"

"What I think of it is this, and if I am mistaken please correct me, but all the same I will tell you."

"Speak, we are listening."

"It appears to me there are two possible meanings in what he said. The first meaning is that for him of his own initiative to want to pay me compensation for a wrong done by his son to my son is like laying a trap for me. He wants to see whether I am a wise person or a stupid man who will accept retribution decided on by just the two of us, when I did not even lodged a complaint against him at the village headman's, so that one of these days I could find myself having to pay him much more, because I too have children and my children too are for ever pouncing on other people's children. It is true I don't have a goat, but all the same I will desperately look for it somewhere else rather than accept Myombekere's. Because, when I look at myself, I have to admit I am a madman and I know that Myombekere too is a madman like me and two madmen cannot afford to have a vendetta between them. And the second meaning is this: I see Myombekere as a person who wants to wave his wealth before my eyes. And now I see what this is all about: he has put himself forward and said, `Whenever my son commits a crime I will be silencing complainants by paying them with my property so that they won't lodge suits against me at the courts of village headmen or even at *omukama*'s[25] court.' Yes, that's it. And so he has hardened my heart and my spirit completely against him. Even if when the healer comes to demand his fee he comes choking with impatience as if it were impending vomit, I will go to look for his payment goat somewhere else rather than at Myombekere's. Let him have all his cattle, it is his wealth, and let us live on our lives in our poverty. And, when you look at it, this man flaunts his wealth and yet all he has is a lone male child and that single female of his for a wife! But, we'll see! Short of his finding some way of curing mischief in that so-called son of his, *aa!* we are here and we'll see what we'll see! My dear wives, that is what my heart has told me; if I have erred, please correct me."

The mother of Kahwagizi took up the matter and said, "In all you have said, you haven't erred; no. Because, if you go and take from his home that so-called goat of his, what would you then do if tomorrow or some other day in the future one of your own sons here should accidentally injure that lonely son of his? All children are restless creatures, for ever picking at each other like chickens, and we can't pretend we don't know what we all know too well. We therefore have every reason to fear making fellow parents pay us retribution for every accident their children cause ours. So if you are a person who can listen to good advice, you shouldn't go to fetch his goat. Let him live with his abundance of wealth and you with your poverty. What's more, the whole thing is over, since your child is healing. But that son of his, *aa!* will end badly! He is bound to commit a serious crime and plunge his father and mother into real trouble, believe me! Here I am, if I am still alive you will talk to me about it!"

All the man's other wives said, "We too are for your not going to fetch that goat, that's all."

"I am glad that's how you feel, because I was afraid you would be of a different opinion," Lusalira agreed with his wives and added, "If it is a question of his so-called wealth, let him keep it to himself: he does not feed me, so why should his wealth concern me as if my life depends on him."

On returning from buying fish from *emigonzo* fishermen Myombekere decided to take a different way and did not pass by Lusalira's again. He had bought plenty of fish and when Bugonoka saw him coming she went to receive him, relieved him of the load of fish and welcomed him home: "Welcome! And how was the fish-hunt?"

"I'm back. In fact it took me this long because of spending some time at Lusalira's; otherwise I would have been back long before this."

"And how is the wounded doing?"

"He is there all right, but now he is almost healed. I found him still wearing a cast of sticks on his injured leg, but then he is the one who his father sent to bring me a chair outside by telling him, "Bring a chair for your friend's father to sit on," so I watched him walk as he came. It is true he is still limping slightly but he should be well again in a matter of days. As to the medicine man who treated their child, Lusalira told me that, since the patient was male, once their child is healed they will pay the healer a he-goat. However, Lusalira doesn't have the goat and so I told him he can come to take one from here, where I have one big enough for the fee, already seconded with a calf by its mother. And so, should he came here to fetch the goat while I am away, just give it to him. That's all I found in Lusalira's home and nothing else. There was nothing like wanting to pick a quarrel with me on the part of anyone in their home, no, and to say there was would be to tell a lie about them, honestly. Now I see that this Busengezuzo fellow is somebody to be wary of indeed. He wants to create enmity between me and Lusalira for nothing!"

"I see! He must be a senseless fellow. That idiot! I too will from now be wary of whatever he says. I find him disgusting!"

Myombekere turned to cleaning and cutting as needed the fish he bought, as Bugonoka washed her cooking pot so that that day the people of Myombekere's home would forget the hardship of having no relish to eat *obwita*[26] with. He then sang the praises of *emigonzo* fishermen to Bugonoka, how they were catching so much fish, especially Matogo, who was catching so much more than all the others, adding, "May be he has a fish-attraction medicine, otherwise he wouldn't be catching such an abundance of fish!"

"What does he barter his fish for, that Matogo?" Bugonoka asked him.

"He trades it for millet, cassava[27] and arrows. And what a multitude of buyers he has, like the crowd of spectators at a dance! And apparently scarcity of fish is killing us everywhere in the country, for among them you find nobility of all ranks pleading their cases, this one saying, 'For want of relish I have passed three nights without food!' the other one saying, 'Four!' and so on."

"Well, there can be no nobility when it comes to taking care of one's stomach. Haven't you ever heard people call the stomach `the eternal creditor'? If you want to be shy about it you may find yourself starving. It is true people have plenty of grain in their homes, but it is not food yet, because it can't be eaten alone. You need fish and meat as relish before you can eat *obwita*, and even though we have greens, unless you have cows and can season your vegetables with milk and butter, eating *obwita* with greens cooked in water with nothing in it is forcing matters, eating the food only because you can't do otherwise, and try all you can the tasteless greens in your mouth keep on going one way and *obwita* the other way, when there is only one throat for the food in your mouth!"

Myombekere and Bugonoka waited for days and days for Lusalira to come and fetch the goat Myombekere had offered him with no sign of him or word of his ever intending to come. And since as people say: "A cow-skin in the house never lacks a needy sleeper,"   one day when the Myombekeres saw a man come to them looking for a black goat like the one they had offered Lusalira, a rain-maker who wanted a goat of that color for his rain sacrifice, they gave him the he-goat and in exchange he gave them a female goat to bear many more other goats for them.

It was now two years since Ntulanalwo came from living with his grandfather and grandmother and back to his parents' home and almost thirteen years had passed since he was born.

Chapter XXVII

NOTES

1.   Kitereza and his wife Anna were such a lonely childless couple. See Introduction.
2.   Bulihwali: Name (female) meaning "When will suffering ever end!". See note 1 of Chapter I.
3.   Children being fostered for some time by members of their extended family was customary. See note 1 of Chapter XXIV.
4.   By the time the author was writing, in Ukerewe looking for firewood had already become a women's job, hence Kitereza is here possibly admonishing his fellow Wakerewe men by reminding them that this is their job, according to old Kikerewe custom. See note 14 of Chapter VI on the division of labor between men and women in Kikerewe society.
5.   *Enfuru*: Sardines.
6.   *Ebisesya*: See note 30 of Chapter IX.
7.   *Ebikuhwe*, plural for *ekikuhwe*: Name of a bird.
8.   *Enzuli*: Name of a bird.
9.   *Ebubele*: See note 17 of Chapter V.
10.   Kikunami: "The one who bends over," from the verb *kukunama*, "to bend over." In the Kikerewe text Kitereza puns on *kukunama* and *kukunamuka*, "to bend over " and "to topple down", respectively. See also meaning of names at the end of the translation.
11.   Kahwagizi: Literally "the rash one". See also meaning of names at the end of the translation.
12   In Kikerewe wrestling, the two contestants grip each other's chest to start a match, and winning is throwing the opponent down in such a way that the back of his head touches the ground. When both the contestants fall down sideways the fall is called a "female" fall and counted a draw.
13.   *Olukoni*: Euphorbia shrub, whose plentiful white sap looks like milk but is certainly not palatable.
14.   See the pun on *kukunama* and *kukunamuka* in 10 above.
15.   *Obwanda, amakugwe*: Herbs for treating sprains and dislocations. See note 17 of Chapter XX.
16.   Lusalira: Literally "bitter taste." See also meaning of names at the end of the translation..
17.   *Omukungu*: See note 3 of Chapter III.

18.   *Emigonzo*, plural for *omugonzo*: See note 4 of Chapter VI.

19.   *Ensonzi*:   A rare catfish of *emumi* type (below) whose flesh is full of fat and which   is considered a   delicacy, though it must   be eaten with great moderation because it tends to cause purging and nauseates easily. See note 62 of Chapter XXXVIII.

20.   *Embozu*: See note 8 of Chapter XIX.

21.   *Emamba*:   See also note 17 of Chapter II.

22.   *Embete*: See note 17 of Chapter II.

23.   *Emumi*: See note 34 of Chapter XXV. Many Wakerewe women did not eat this fish too, although it was not one of the kinds of fish taboo to them, because they found eating it repulsive due to the fact that the fish, which is prone to swimming upstream and into the ponds and pools of the marshes in large numbers during the season of heavy rains, eats everything it finds, including excrement and worms and other filthy-looking fish nutrients, some of which fairly often can be found still intact in the flesh of the cooked fish during a meal!

24.   These were among the kinds of meat and fishes which were taboo to Wakerewe women. See note 17 of Chapter II.

25.   *Omukama*:   See note 26 of Chapter II.

26.   *Obwita*: See note 14 of Chapter I.

27.   *Obutaga*: See note 4 of Chapter II.

Chapter XXVIII

MYOMBEKERE COURTS A MAID
FOR HIS SON TO MARRY

When Myombekere saw how much his son had grown, he started early to court a maid for him to marry, because he did not want him to become a mature young man without a wife, for Wakerewe of means in those days found wives for their sons and married off their daughters when they were still innocent youths, that is before they reached puberty. The maid Myombekere went to court was a girl he had spotted in Kalibata's home, Kalibata's own daughter, whose name was Netoga. And when you saw that child Netoga herself you said to yourself, "This is indeed Netoga!"[1] and added, "Indeed Kalibata begot a daughter!"

On his first visit to Kalibata's home to court his daughter, Myombekere took one barbed arrow and, instead of a second one, the stem of a reed, the sign that the traveler was a man of peace and not of war, a man looking for nothing else but women to marry. He set out on his journey very early in the morning, long before dawn, because that was how courtship was supposed to be carried out in those days: the suitor always woke up to go courting when people were still asleep in their homes, and as a result he could even conclude the long courtship process without people finding out that he was courting so-and-so's daughter. Things were done that way as a measure of precaution against maligners, even though people of bad will always still managed to find out and tried to taint other people's courtships. When he got to Kalibata's and the door of the gate of that man's home was opened and he got into the home and entered

Kalibata's house and was relieved of his bow and the bow was put away in the inner room of the house and he was given a seat and he sat down and exchanged greetings with the inmates of the house and finished, he broached his mission by saying: "Taking a rest is for the legs but never for the mouth. Deign, Sir, to help me build a home! I have come to seek from you, my dear brother, a home. Be a parent to me, dear peer of mine, as you are a parent to this daughter of yours I am asking from you."

Kalibata pretended to be hearing this for the first time, as if he had never discussed the matter with Myombekere, and yet on the day they were drinking banana beer together in Myombekere's home that was precisely what their tête-a-tête over which they laughed in merriment was about. This day, however, Kalibata became a different person and his reply to Myombekere was: "Are you courting for yourself or are you courting for somebody else?"

"Yes, in a sense I am courting for myself, though actually I am courting for my son."

"I see! Unfortunately I have no daughter fit to court in this home of mine."

"You have and I have seen her, otherwise I wouldn't be here falling at your feet with begging hands."

"I have no single female child. May be the one who told you of the girl meant to direct you to a different home or may be he or she had seen here girls from homes of the neighborhood who had come to chat."

That day Myombekere went back with nothing, with no way of knowing what to expect from Kalibata. Then he went back courting the second time and said, "Deign, Sir, to light for me the path which has brought me here, allow me to raise hands of a supplicant to you asking you to become a parent to me as people become parents-in-law to others. For our ancestors left us a saying: 'He who be gets a daughter begets a son and he who begets a son begets a daughter.' But Kalibata still stuck to what he told him the first time: "I have no daughter."

He courted Kalibata's daughter for almost a year before he heard from him a second answer: "Keep walking."[2] And from then every time he went to woo his daughter the man's only answer to him was always: "Keep walking!"

Finally he spotted another maid to court for his son and from that time on the day he did not go to court in Kalibabata's home he went to court in that other home. There too he got a similar answer: "I have no daughter. Keep walking."

Shortly after that he got a third answer from Kalibata's: "Keep coming to see us for a chat and let's see what the new year brings us."

For the rest of that year, he kept on courting in both homes. However before long that second courtship escaped him, for we cannot say the courtship died, my dear friends, as if it were the loss of life! He now concentrated on his first suit, there at Kalibata's home, and continued courting right into the second year, during which time all he got during his visits was chatting with Kalibata of all sorts of things, of rain pouring down so heavily that food crops like cassava and sweet potatoes were rotting in the ground, of drought, of how the wells of those who lived upcountry were drying up from the drought, of how cows had no grass to eat that year and of how what and what were people's only hope of surviving the drought, or how everyone would flock to Ukara Island in search of survival food,[3] of how *omukama*[4] could be dethroned by popular demand because he had refused to make rain for his people, because when that happened and a new king was put on the throne people would indeed see it rain cats and dogs until the industrious farmers tilled the soil and rocks alike.

As days went by one day Myombekere heard Kalibata say to him words which gave him some hope: "Now you should court here with breaks, because when you come the next time I intend to send you to court in the homes of our relatives as well. What's more, you have courted enough and two gentlemen like us shouldn't be so hard on one another."

In the meanwhile Ntulanalwo himself was reaching puberty, his voice had thickened, his face was covered with pimples and he exuded a male smell like that of a he-goat. Now his favorite pastime became night dances, because he found them occasions for merry-making with his dance companions and places where he could get girls with whom to play privacy games in the bushes and in bachelors' huts, games in which he sometimes included adult women, those who were free[5] and even married ones. When his parents learnt of those games of their son with women they were overwhelmed with joy, for that meant that their son was a proper male. Myombekere had star ted courting a future wife for him when he was still too young, before he had reached puberty, and had therefore no way of knowing for sure that their son was all right as a man, so that one day he found himself telling Bugonoka, "It is true we have started courting a girl for our son to marry, but, my dear wife, should the Wakerewe whose daughter we are courting grace us with the goodness of their hearts and give us a wife and the great day comes and the bride is brought in this home and then our Ntulanalwo doesn't prove himself a man, wouldn't that disgrace us completely in the eyes of people? With us men the best thing is to court a maid for your son when you know for sure that he plays privacy games with girls in dancing places and in his bachelor's hut or when you learn from his fellow young men that your son yesterday or the day before yesterday fought with so-and-so on account of an unmarried woman who lives in so-and-so's home. That is when you too can go courting feeling good and saying to yourself: `Oh yes! I begot a sharp razor of a man!' What do you say, my wife, isn't that a good feeling?"

"I must admit there are times when   your questions catch me unprepared for them and as a result I fail to find a quick word to say in answer. But, all the same, let me too instead of answering you ask you a question: 'What do people value most in this world?'"

"What people value most in this country of ours are long-life, marriage, begetting children and food to eat."

"You see! So you know that. And that is my answer too. How, for example, would you have married me if you were not a proper male? Or how would you have begot that Ntulanalwo of yours himself without being a proper male? Or would you have expected the woman you would have married to bring to you other men's children from the wilderness? And how would that wife of yours have loved you if you couldn't relate with her the way a married couple relate with each other?

"No, if you are that kind of a male you can't marry a woman, because you are a dead body and the dead never beget children."

"And so my answer to your question is that courting a maid for your son while knowing he is not a dead body is a very good feeling indeed and can never be a bad thing. Because the day that son of yours brings his bride in a home like this one and their wedding is properly achieved that is when you the parents can go out in front of people full of pride. But if the newlyweds marriage is not achieved you simply would not know how to face people, because your male child has proved a dead body and that is nothing but disgrace! If you want to know how it is, listen and let me tell you the rest. You hear all the time mothers ask their sons the morning after the night of their wedding day: `Are we to bathe or no?' Why do they ask the bridegroom that question? They ask because what saves them from shame and disgrace is finding out that the marriage of their children was consummated and so they can go and take a bath and perfume the house as befits the occasion. And when everybody who comes to greet the newlyweds finds the scent of *omugazu*[6] pervading the house and wedges shaved[7] into the forehead of the bridegroom's mother as if she too were a bride, won't the visitors understand that a marriage has been consummated in that home?"

"Why not when the people in the home are merry and the signs of people celebrating a wedding can be seen."

"Let me tell it all to you, dear husband of mine. Yes, it is true that parents courting a woman for their son without knowing whether he is disposed like a man or not does at times bring nothing but disgrace to the parents, because there are times when parents find brides for their sons who are dead and useless and their sons themselves know it and yet have not told their parents about it and on the night of the wedding day of such a son all the useless fellow does is to awkwardly fumble about and do all sorts of things except what he is supposed to do! And in the morning when the useless being is asked whether he will bathe or not he has no answer for those who ask him. And at that moment the parents of such a son can only bewail their lot and say, `*Aa*! Father of our fathers! With us the prospect of a new household is dead and gone! Had I known I had a dead home-founder I wouldn't have wasted my time wading through early morning dew to wake up gentlemen asleep in their homes, not to mention wasting my bride-price property this way! I was counting myself a parent among parents when the truth is that instead of a son I begot a living dead!' Such sons are the ones of whom we sometimes hear people say: `They have bewitched him, that's why he is not a man like other men.' And when the situation remains unsolved you see the parents of such a son restlessly turn to taking out their oracles to have them told by the seers so as to know whether there is some bad knot to undo on the being of their child. If it is a mere question of worms weighing him down in his lower stomach, they will look for medicines for him to drink before it is too late. And among them there are those who do all that in vain, without succeeding to find a cure for their son and their son's wife returns to her parents' home; and, yes, she is right in going back to her parents, because she cannot remain married to another woman like herself. And there are also those blessed with their good luck who in going here and there among the healers and seers finally strike upon a good healer who treats their child and cures him. But, as for you, keep on relentlessly courting a maid for your son Ntulanalwo, because he is a proper man. I haven't been without inquiring all the time among the girls who go to dances with him and those for whom he builds mock kitchens in their children open-air plays of house-keeping. Among them I have enemies, I am sure, but there are also those who like me and who have told me that your Ntulanalwo has already got girl friends among young girls of his age. And to say the truth, come to think of it, I too find that so-and-so's daughter is much more respectful to me these days than she used to be in the past. And that is what I had to say to you and now you have heard it all."

Myombekere paused in going to court in Kalibata's home and took a rest of some days in his own home as he had been told to do by Kalibata himself. But then he remembered the saying of our ancestors: "A sentinel never sleeps!" So the following day very early in the morning he was up and on his way to Kalibata's home, got there and said, "Kalibata, deign to give me a home. I am back for the same reason for which I have been journeying here so often, because our ancestors said: `The person who feels cold is the one who approaches the fire.' What's more, you must admit a lot of time has passed, gentleman, since I began journeying to this home. I may be exaggerating, but I think may be this is the third year since I began coming here. It has been such a long time! No, Kalibata, you shouldn't butcher me and leave my carcass lying in dust on the ground like I were porcupine which people don't eat. Please give me a word of substance, a word which can get to me, which I can feel in my heart so that it can give me the strength I need to keep on journeying here. In fact I too have a word of my own inside me, only I fear to say it to you."

"Say it; if it is for me, I'll hear it."

"Yes, I think I will have to say it aloud, because you are you and I am me and you won't know what I have in me unless I tell you. What is more, our ancestors said: `Wherever you see *omukama* is where you hail the throne,' and you too here are my king and I am now raising to you my empty hands of a supplicant that you may give me the greatest present on earth to a man: a wife. And so, why should I not tell you openly what is in me? And even if I keep quiet that word I have for you in me will give me no rest for not letting it out, so I have better utter it. And so, my dear Kalibata, I am afraid of being called by the names of the people of this country.

"What are they called?" "People-of-this-country."

"And their growing-up name?"[8] "Those-who-journey-for-nothing."

The mother of the girl being courted and the rest of the female inmates of that house burst out in uncontrollable laughter. It appeared to them an apt description of Myombekere, a man who had had it with going to so much trouble daily, wading through dew-soaked grass so early in the morning, tree stumps and stones in footpaths knocking out toenails on his feet, without ever being rewarded with some meaningful answer, an answer to encourage him in his courting! My guess is that even the young girl being courted laughed from her bed in the interior of the house, even though of course I can't know for sure what I didn't actually see. But what I know is that all those in the interior of that house laughed until they forgot all restraint. Just imagine, they laughed until the master of that home, Kalibata, reprimanded them sharply and said, "What is this now? Have you never heard people speak of `to-journey-for-nothing' or has it turned into something new to you? Whatever the case, keep quiet so that we can continue with our conversation!" Quiet thus restored Kalibata told Myombekere, "Can you really consider these few days you have been courting here such a long time as to call it three years?"

"Yes, three years or even two years are to me a long time. Every farmer farms his lands so as to harvest and have some food in store, but with me I have been just farming for ever. And as to time, isn't what I said the time which has passed since I began coming here?

"No, because I keep count of time by making monthly knots on a rope and so I know. This year in which we are is the second year and we are still in its sixth month. It is the year after this one which will be the third year."

"Still to me that is already a long time; I certainly can't call it short."

"Since I have also been a suitor like you, I must admit that's how things appear to all suitors in a courtship. And so it would appear that with you, if we were to give you our daughter, you are ready to marry her to your son this very day?

"*Yu!* Not only I am ready, but I would say: `Heaven be praised!'"

"So you think I am like these other people's name?"

"What are they called?"

"They are called these-other-people."

"And their growing-up name?"

"Never-let-go."

"As to that I will have to say yes."

"Well, since you have nicknamed yourself Those-who-journey-for-nothing, I've better call myself by the name of the people of this country.

"What are they called?"

"They are Wakerewe."

"And their growing-up names?"

"Yes-to-everything."

"Yes, that would be a good nickname indeed, because if that became real I would rejoice and say: 'Yes indeed, anything worthwhile can only be given you by a fellow human being!'"

"Since I am the one who told you that next time you come I will send you to court in the homes of our relatives, so go and do so." Kalibata then told Myombekere the names of his relatives and the villages in which they lived and finished and then added, "When you have finished presenting your suit to all those to whom I am sending you come back and tell me what my relatives said to you and then we'll know what to do next."

"Praise to you! There simply is no need for me to say anything more. Let me just go and do what you have directed me to do and let's see what the Sun[9] has in store for us. Can you spare a bit of *ekilangi*[10] for me? In my home we had none at all last night. I thought I still had a bit of tobacco in the house, but, what with the darkness, we looked and looked for that second-rate tobacco somebody in the homes of our neighbors had given me but couldn't find it, in spite of searching with torches. In the end we were forced to resort to used tobacco emptied from past brews. *Aa!* You can't call that *ekilangi*, it was an act of sheer desperation. You can't feel anything with those tobacco rejects. In fact in our part of the country this year we don't know where we'll get tobacco; it is rare to see anybody hawking any, and so all we do nowadays is to wander about daily bothering people begging for some."

"We in these parts are no better. It is by sheer luck that the men on the peninsula over there are in position to save us. They are the ones who planted some this year and, yes, they still have it, because I see them around exchanging it with people who hawk goats."

"How many balls of tobacco would they give you for a young she-goat?"

"Unless the scarcity of tobacco has changed their price, normally if say you bring a young she-goat already seconded with another calf by its mother and it is of good size, not lanky, you should get not less than twelve balls of tobacco, and in the case of a he-goat you would get six balls, in both cases plus an additional flat piece for sealing the bargain."

Then Kalibata told his wife, "Bring us that *ekilangi* for this man here to take some, unsatisfactory as it is, because it appears he hasn't tasted any for a long time." Kalibara's wife brought *ekilangi* and gave it to her husband while kneeling down and he received it and said to Myombekere, "Let me take off the poison for you."

"I would say this so-called poison[II] we speak of all it does is to impute bad intentions to people. Otherwise, how can anybody poison something which he or she too is going to take and then that poison kills others while he or she remains unharmed?"

"You should not dispute that, because it is a custom bequeathed us by our ancestors. They must have seen it happen to say so and it is not just a manner of speaking; no."

"Yes, that could be true. But those ancestors of ours, are they never wrong?"

"There are times when they are wrong, but most of what they say is the truth."

Kalibata held *ekilangi* in his right hand and tilted it so that he could better see whether there was enough for the two of them; if not, he himself would then take just a little bit and leave the rest for his visitor, for a visitor always comes first to his or her host or hostess. And when he saw that there was enough liquid to satisfy up to even four people, he lifted *ekilangi* with the arm in which he was holding it and threw back his head and poured the tobacco liquid in his left side nostril before quickly switching and pouring it in his other nostril and he was done. The liquid saturated with tobacco went deep into his nostrils, filling his mouth with saliva and at once Myombekere saw his companion, his nose still pointing up in the air, send out of his mouth a neat jet of saliva: *chilililili*! before passing the tobacco solution to him, and he too threw back his head and poured it into his nostrils. Then the two men stayed that way, their noses pointing into the air to let the tobacco liquid take effect in their heads, whenever one of them wanted to speak speaking through the nose as if suffering from a chronic cold. After sometime they both blew it out of their noses and at once Kalibata told his wife, "May be give me some water, it appears this *ekilangi* has intoxicated me." Kalitaba drank water his breath held in and breathed out only when he finished drinking. He was about to give back to his wife the remaining water when Myombekere said, "Give me some too; I too need water to drink. *Hii*! What a strong tobacco! It burns your inside like fire! No wonder it makes one thirsty! If you take too much of it it is liable to overwhelm you completely and if you didn't know where to stop it could even throw you to the ground. Is this the tobacco you told me the peninsula men have and that they barter it for goats?"

"This is it. Where else could we find tobacco? They are the only ones who planted some by irrigating it with lake water."

"Those people this year will really purchase a lot of property with such tobacco! Let me go back now, but when I come again I will come with the goat I have told you about, accompanied by a friend to help me bargain for a good price. If you have a little bit to spare, my dear Kalibata, could you give me some? There is no point in my being too shy to ask when I am so desperately in need and risk dying with craving for tobacco back home, poor me! I shouldn't be like the person in the saying: `One who doesn't call for help dies in an animal trap.' Let me call for help instead of keeping quite, because it isn't right to say you don't eat something when you do."

Kalibata went into the inner room of his house and after a while came back with a sizable slice from a tobacco ball. Then he fetched soot blackened kitchen-roof grass and wrapped the plug of tobacco in it to prevent it from losing flavor and weakening, brought a strip of banana fiber and wrapped everything in it, tied it into a beautiful package and gave it to Myombekere and with that Myombekere said, "Please see me out, friend, we have been chatting for a long while. Let me return to my home and see how the cattle of the Wakerewe[12] I keep there has been faring. Thank you for everything. But, all the same, please don't cling to what you have. Please, mother, help me, for you too know that you women were created to build other people's homes."

Kalibata's wife answered him, "I do know indeed, but haven't you ever heard people say: `A woman dances without jumping from the ground'"[13]

"I have heard that, it is true, but don't you too in your women way ever let yourself really go until your spectators say: `So-and-so's wife doesn't jump only because she doesn't want to, because women are not supposed to dance while jumping, otherwise she could very easily jump as well as any man!'"

"I can see I better leave you to your fellow man, your match in your battle of wits!"

Everybody laughed and Myombekere left.

Myombekere got home and told Bugonoka the good news he brought back from Kalibata's home and her heart was likewise filled with joy and she told her husband, "Let us wait until you finish taking your suit to those you have been told to see and report to Kalibata whatever they tell you. Then I will count one day and the second day I will go and pass the night somewhere nearby so that I can make it to his home very early in the morning of the following day and court my turn. Because it looks like we may have some good news coming and we can't afford to be nonchalant about it. And what about this tobacco they have given you, is it any good, Myombekere?"

"Don't ask, it is real fire! I was given a taste of its *ekilangi* this morning and it was only because I took it with moderation that I managed to stand it, but had I really let myself go at it it would have knocked me to the ground. Even then both Kalibata himself and I had to drink a lot of water after taking its *ekilangi*.   Kalibata also told me that it is still available somewhere in their area and that its owners want goats for it. When I go back to report to him the progress of our courtship I should may be go with Kanwaketa to help me bargain for some of that tobacco in exchange for my goat."

"I see! Then it is excellent tobacco and must be taken cautiously and in moderation."

Chapter XXVIII

NOTES

1. Netoga: "The heart's desire", from *kutoga,* "to long for something." See also meaning of names at the end of the translation.

2. There is punning here in the Kikerewe on the name Kalibata, which means "Eternal traveler" and Kalibata's answer for Myombekere: *libata*, "keep walking" (traveling)."

3. The people of Ukara Island, Ukerewe's neighbors, though living on a much smaller island than Ukerewe and more overcrowded, had a long history of manuring their fields and managing their lands and food reserves better and in the times of crop failure and other causes of famine they used to succor the Wakerewe with their stores of grain.

4. *Omukama:* See note 26 of Chapter II. The king was deemed the supreme rain-maker of the kingdom, and a king who failed to end a long draught by making it rain could be dethroned, as it happened in 1867 with Omukama Ibanda, the brother and predecessor of Omukama Lukonge of the Introduction.

5. *Abasimbe*, plural for *omusimbe*: See note 24 of Chapter II.

6. *Omugazu:* See also note 23 of Chapter VIII.

7. *Kutemelela*: "To trim the face", by shaving two wedge-shaped marks, *ebyeyela*, one on each side of the face to elongate the hairline and broaden the forehead. In general the Wakerewe never shaved their faces except in that particular way and only the newlyweds and some of their female wedding attendants.

8. A conversational device in which the speaker's "riddle name" reveals his or her wit. See note 13 of Chapter IX.

9. *Izoba*: The Sun, Providence. See note 21 of Chapter II.

10. *Ekilangi*: See note 7 of Chapter VII.

11. The custom of the host or hostess first "poison tasting" what he or she offered people was reserved for beer and did not apply to food. See note 12 of Chapter III.

12. Myombekere avoids saying "my cattle" so as not to sound bragging about his wealth to his son's prospective in-laws.

13. Only Wakerewe men danced while lifting one of their legs and striking the ground with their foot in rhythm with the beats of the dance.

Chapter XXIX

MYOMBEKERE COURTS THE CONSENT OF THE RELATIVES OF HIS SON'S BETROTHED[1]

That day Kanwaketa set out very early in the morning to go...Where could he have been going? Anyway, let's leave that alone for the moment. And so he went by Myombekere's to bid the people of his neighbor's home good morning before leaving.[2] Myombekere woke up and came out of the house and exclaimed, "What! It is already a bright new day! Thank you for coming, for if you hadn't woke us up today we would most likely have kept on sleeping past sunrise! It would have been one of those days when a person feels lousy the whole day on account of oversleeping. Surprising as it may seem, both Bugonoka and I were awake until the first cockcrow. Then we drifted off into sleep for a little while before waking up again and then: *whee*! we slept once more until now! When you called I was hearing you as if in a dream, in which we were running from Masai[3] enemy warriors. The Masai were chasing us, hard by, ready to kill us with their long-bladed swords. We were a multitude of people all running away, mixed, with women among us. We ran until we were ready to drop dead, with some of us being stabbed and wounded and others killed. The women, who as you know were created with an abundance of tears, cried to the point of drying up the fountain of tears in their heads. I am afraid what I dreamt of was too vivid to be an ordinary dream. My dear Kanwaketa, you'll see! This year or the one after this the terrible thing may come to pass, because the dreams of my head tend to prove true. Here we are, if both of us are still alive, you'll come to tell me here how right I was."

"Yes, I agree with you. In dreaming there are times when a person foretells the truth and I can't disagree with you there. You may remember just a few days ago when you and I were here together and Kahwamama told us he had dreamt he found his wife Nabutwema committing adultery and two days later indeed he caught her red-handed committing adultery with Byekwasyo."

"Yes, indeed! Sometimes the human head sees it in advance all exactly as it will happen."

"And that's why just now I gave you the most convincing evidence of what dreams can tell us so that you would release me from your tales sooner, otherwise I won't make it to where I am going."

"And where are you going this early in the morning, my friend?"

"I am going to visit sick people in yonder villages."

"I see! In that case wait for me. We'll go together, for I too want to leave early to go courting the consent of the relatives of my in-laws-to-be to the marriage of my son to their daughter."

"Hurry up then."

Myombekere took a bit of time to take his bow and arrows and his delay in the house made Kanwaketa The-impatient-one and he said, "You man, what is keeping you in the house! Did Bugonoka cast a spell on you when you married her and is that why you are never in a hurry to leave her house? You need a second wife to make you a man who is master of his actions, because you are becoming hopeless, my dear friend. *Yu*! Bugonoka, would you please release him so that we can go. *Ahee*!"

"*Aa*! One moment! Here I'm, please."

Myombekere came out of the house and the two men set out. After traveling together for some time, they parted and each went his separate way. Myombekere finally got to the village in which the first man whose consent Kalibata sent him to court lived and began asking people where the man's home was. He would therefore walk into a home and ask: "Ladies and gentlemen, I am a suitor asking for directions. Where does so-and-so live in this location of yours?"

"Of what clan is that so-and-so, and what is his father's name?"

"His clan is Muhunga and his father's name is so-and-so."

"I see, that is the one you want. You have, in fact, already left his home behind."

"I see. This then is what people mean when they say: `Never-ask passed a night next door to his destination.' And am I to go back by the footpath I came with or do I take another way?"

"Let us direct you properly. We too are travelers and don't want you to refuse giving us directions should we stray into your neighborhood."

"As you say, traveling is for us all; and how can anyone let the Creator's own human being sleep in the wilderness like a beast by refusing to give him or her directions?"

"What's more, that isn't correct behavior among our people, even if perhaps that is how people behave in some foreign countries we don't know of. So, to get there take this way and stay on it and walk straight ahead until you come to a rather big cattle trail fenced in with *olukoni*[4] euphorbia, and when you leave that cattle trail behind a bit you will see on your right another fenced cattle trail with a cattle hurdle[5] of *omuzangate* tree at its entrance. Step over the hurdle and then look up ahead of you like this and when you see a lot of tall *amakukuru*[6] cactuses go there; that's the home, those cactus trees are the fence of the home of the man you want."

"Thank you very much. You have indeed helped me greatly."

"Have a safe journey; and when you get back greet the people of your home for us."

"Thank you. Have a good day, in case we don't meet again."

"Thank you."

Myombekere did as directed and got to that man's home, where he found the master of the home present and took a seat and said, "Deign, Sir, to help me build a home! I am a suitor, sent to court your consent."

"Who sent you?"

"I was sent by Kalibata."

"Which one of his daughters are you courting?"

"I am courting the one called Netoga."

"Are you courting for yourself or for somebody else?"

"I am courting for myself, yes, but in actual fact I am courting for my son."

"And what did you say your name was?"

"My name is Myombekere."

"I see! You must have been courting for a long time then?"

"Yes indeed, it has been a long time, because this is the second year."

"On my part, I had thought that perhaps the courtship had been discontinued! It appears that brother of mine doesn't let go easily when it comes to giving away his daughters in marriage.!"

"May be it is as our ancestors said: `Things which matter are decided by the Almighty.' He too wanted to see how the Almighty would direct the course of events."

"On my part, I have no objection. Let him go ahead and give your son a woman to marry, because a man cannot find another man ugly, only women have their preferences among us."

"Praises to you, gentleman. Become a parent to me as you are a parent to the girl I am courting, because what I want from you is a family relation. I want you and me to be people of one family, who visit each other, love each other. I want us to share a meal around a courtyard fireplace,[7] for I am asking you for someone who will look after this stomach of mine, which, with each and everyone of us, will never let us be until it is satisfied, because of which it was given the fitting name of `The-eternal-creditor'. And so please see me out, because I am still traveling to many other homes on this same mission of mine."

"Won't you wait to see the woman of this home make fall with smoke to the ground of her kitchen the little[8] lizards?"[9]

"Thank you very much, but no. We'll eat another day, since eating never ends: As you can see, even now it is eating I am seeking from you."

"Don't forget that our old ones of yore gave us this saying: `To eat is to eat today, because we don't know what we'll eat tomorrow and we don't remember what we ate yesterday!'"

"I have to agree with you on that: to eat is to eat today indeed!"

The master of that home escorted Myombekere and then, as he was giving back to him his bow ready to turn back, Myombekere said to him, "Look at me, I was almost forgetting!"

"Forgetting what?"

"Kalibata told me: `Ask the man whose consent you will court first to show you the home of another man you have to see; they are close neighbors.'" And Myombekere told the man the name of that other man he had to see.

"Come, let me show you his home. It is that home over there, the one in which can be seen five houses and that tall *omulumba*[10] tree," accompanying his directions by pointing things out with a finger of his hand.

After walking for a while, Myombekere arrived in that other home. The master of the home was present, occupied with sacrificing a goat for his wife and surrounded by a gathering of people who had come for the sacrifice. After Myombekere courted the man's consent the master of the home told him: "Let them go ahead and give you a woman to marry. That's all from me," and then asked the other men gathered there, "Is that not how it is supposed to be, gentlemen?" The men all agreed: "That is exactly how it should be, for how can a man find another man ugly?" And one of them added, "Courting the consent of the relatives of the betrothed is exactly like informing people of the death of a relative of theirs, because it is informing them that their female relative is leaving the home of her father and mother and going away to found a home for other people, just as announcing the death of a person to his or her relatives is informing them that their beloved one has left them."

People made some noisy remarks on that and then Myombekere thanked the man for his generous answer, asked for his bow and then returned home, to go and continue courting the consent of some more people in the other places he was sent to by the father of his son's betrothed.

Back home he told his wife how that day he hadn't put a morsel of food in his mouth and his wife was moved with pity and said, "My poor husband, today you must have traveled on the bad road of which people say: `A bad road never reveals what it has in store for you.'"

"I've never seen such a journey! I haven't put into my mouth even one tiny piece of sweet potato. You would think I was traveling through an uninhabited wilderness when in fact I was visiting people's homes the whole day!" Immediately after dinner he went to bed and fell asleep, worn out by the day's journey.

The following morning, before he left again for his consent courting, Myombekere went first to bid good morning his son Ntulanalwo and told him, "Today, when you take cattle to the herder on the neighborhood tour of duty come back home quickly, don't disappear and go to your pleasure walks. I want you to weed the banana plantation, the part around *isuguti*[11] tree, where the weeds are already choking banana plants. Make sure you dig up really deep *esorwa*[12] weed, shake all soil from its roots and then pile it aside and once it is dry we'll burn it. And if on coming back I find you haven't done the weeding, we'll see! For, as a male child, when your parents begin courting a girl for you to marry you should realize you are no longer a little boy and say to yourself: `Now I am a grown-up.' But you, instead, want your daily occupation to be promenading and eating while lying down like the spoiled goat we hear in tales which used to eat while lying down. I am going, but if I come back and find that part of the banana plantation still as it is you'll see me!"

"You just go, I'll weed."

Apparently his father did not hear well what Ntulanalwo said, may be due to the fact that he had turned his back on him and was already some distance away, from here to there, and so Myombekere turned around and asked his son, angrily, "What are you saying by mumbling to me things that I don't hear? You accursed creature! Do you want me to come and give you a beating? Can you really insult me and talk back to me mumbling through your teeth things I can't hear, me, your own father?"

Ntulanalwo on seeing his father react angrily that way to the point of wanting to beat him, realized he did not hear what he said and cautioned himself: "If I don't repeat without delay what I said he can come and really rough me up inside this little hut of mine," and so told his father: "Father, what's the matter! I told you I will come back to weed once I take the cattle to the herder on duty. *Ahee*! Maybe you didn't hear what I said, but that's what I told you!" And when Myombekere heard his son answer him back humbly that way he walked on to his consent courting mission without further ado.

Sometime that morning, when Bugonoka finished skimming milk, she asked her son, "Why were you insulting your father at night before sunrise, you child?"

"*Aa*! You think I insulted him? I agreed to come and weed the banana plantation, except it appears he didn't catch what I said and thought he heard something else. But the truth is, I didn't in anyway insult him, mother. If I had, since we are just the two of us here, I would tell you."

"You know, you have to behave well, you child! Don't you want to get married?"

"*Aa*! I do."

"And how can your father go ahead and court a girl for you and wed you to her if you don't behave well? You will have only yourself to blame if he changes his mind. Everyone will say: `That son of his is simply an impossible child, his father and mother have simply given up trying to correct him. That child is a real mad man. What's worse, he is some roadside beauty, good to look at but completely useless: he is lazy to the extreme, a hoe to him is taboo!' Tell me, is that all right? Is that good behavior in a person's child?"

"No, it is not good."

"If you know it is not good behavior, why do you these days spend the entire daytime in the wilderness, looking for *amavune*[13] wild fruits in pasture lands. Can you live on those wild fruits?"

"I think I am wrong in that, mother."

"And so today make a point of returning home quickly from taking cattle out to pasture and come to weed where he directed you to. There is no point in making your father angry that way. Which country do you come from not to know that when parents curse their children they die unmarried?"

Ntulanalwo drove cattle to that day's neighborhood herdsman and came back, took a hoe and son and mother weeded and finished that part of the banana plantation, because Bugonoka had understood the situation this way: "My husband was not directing his anger at his son alone but at me too. His son was just a scapegoat but the real target of his anger was me. Now that his time is all taken up with courting a wife for Ntulanalwo, he is afraid his banana plantation will be ruined by weeds, and so I too must now take serious care of it, lest this man gets disheartened and stops courting a wife for my son, poor me! Then People will say of the courtship: `They capsized when they had almost landed,' as is sometimes said of sea voyagers. For, as everybody knows, when adults are gathered for a palaver and one of them breaks wind, since adults can't afford to disgrace or shame one another, children will be falsely accused of having fouled the air, if there happens to be children nearby, and if there is no single child nearby then a dog is falsely accused of the fart. And my man too wanted to reprimand his son as well as me."

When Myombekere came back from his courting and had something to eat, he went to his banana plantation to see whether Ntulanalwo did the weeding he told him to do and found that the entire area he wanted weeded was clean and the soil all shaken out of the roots of the *esorwa* grass and the weeded grass in turn nicely piled aside in one heap. On looking again in the weeded area he saw Bugonoka's footprints! He was really pleased to see that, so much so that he went back home humming as if singing some song to himself and on getting home he asked Bugonoka, "Did you do the weeding all alone, Bugonoka?"

Bugonoka answered, "Ntulanalwo is the one who, as soon as he came back from taking cattle to the herdsman on duty, took a hoe and went to weed first and when I finished grinding flour I too followed him there and when it was time I came to prepare lunch and left him cultivating the field alone. Then later on he too came home and ate lunch here with a number of his friends. After lunch he made *empiru*[14] for his friends, who had brought him their wood, and after that they all left together saying they were going to the lakeshore to look for reeds to make shafts for their *empiru*, after which they would go to bathe in the lake. But today he did some hoeing all right. In fact, had his friends not come here and tempted him, today he had no intention of leaving home at all."

"That is good, indeed. I have also seen the weeding you did and I am really pleased. We have indeed to keep on barking at him, that way maybe he will end up a human being like others. But if we let him alone he will end up a lazy and useless creature, this son of ours!"

"It is possible, indeed. As our people of old once said: "Straighten a tree while still young, for a grown tree won't bend.""

"Actually, I am trying to restrain his wanderings this way because it is said: `A man for whom they are courting a bride is prone to drowning.'"

"That is in fact true, and that's why with some parents when their son's courtship is close to conclusion like ours they would never allow him to go to sea at all."

After that Myombekere went to Kanwaketa's to ask Kanwaketa to accompany him the following day to go and buy tobacco with a he-goat. He found he wasn't at home. On asking his wife his whereabouts she told him that the village headman's[15] messenger had just come to fetch him and the two of them had left together in the direction of Ntamba's neighborhood. He was still seated chatting in Kanwaketa's home when he indistinctly heard people talking with low voices in the narrow footpath leading to the home by a side gate. The voices were getting closer and closer, as if coming into the home, and, on looking up, there, already by him, was Walyoba carrying a pot of beer, doing his best to walk steadily under the heavy load on his left shoulder. At once Myombekere jumped up from his seat and cheerfully said: "Should we relieve the visitor of his load, Walyoba?"

Walyoba answered by telling him: "You deceived me, up on you, you don't deceived me, you don't' drinked it!" That's how Walyoba answered him in his foreigner's Kikerewe all wrinkled up like that.[16] What he wanted to say was : "If you want to relieve me of the pot relieve me of it, only if you don't you won't drink the beer."

Myombekere helped Walyoba put down the pot of beer. The wife of Kanwaketa brought seats outside and everybody sat down. After Myombekere finished exchanging greetings with those who had just arrived, the headman asked him where he had been and Myombekere told him that those days he was busy courting and so he was rarely at home during daytime. The headman told him that he had come to fetch him, together with Kanwaketa, to go and confiscate beer from Ntamba's home, because Ntamba had already brewed beer once without giving him his headman's homage-beer, and so this time too when he waited for him to bring him the beer to pay him his due respects with Ntamba nowhere to be seen he told his son Galubondo and the village crier Walyoba the Jaluo to follow him, adding, "Believe me , dear Myombekere, today I was really mad with anger at Ntamba, especially when I remembered that case of yours when he beat your nephew to the point of death! I said to myself, 'This time if he dares refuse us my village headman's share of beer I will deport him from my village and be done with him forever.' You too know that our two kings, the late son of kings as well as the reigning one, both gave me the right to eat from you my subjects when they installed me your village headman, and who is he to deny me my share of our *omukama's*[17] food in my village. Today indeed he was going to suffer the consequences of my worst wrath. And where in this country then would he have gone to live where *omukama* is not sovereign and where when people brew beer they don't pay respects to their village headman by giving him his customary present of banana beer? Indeed he would have been in real trouble had he refused to give us the beer. What's more, I would have beaten him thoroughly and maybe even demolished his houses so that he would realize the wrong he had done and repent: `I see! I did something really wrong in not giving my village headman   beer due him!'"

Myombekere took up where the village headman left off and said, "This reminds me of the proverb: `What concerns this *bulera* concerns that *hungwe*[18] too.' As you know *bulera* and *hungwe* are different names of the crow, just as Ntamba and Myombekere are different names of brewers of banana beer. And this goes for Kanwaketa too, for he too is a brewer. Only Walyoba and your son Galubondo among us here have no banana plantations and can say they are not concerned with such a problem, but me and Kanwaketa here cannot afford to laugh at this mad man, Ntamba, and neither do we intend to backbite him or to ingratiate ourselves into your favor, but all the same we would like to state the obvious. And it is obvious to me that this colleague of ours has transgressed. What does Ntamba mean by brewing beer twice and on both occasions more or less refusing to pay you homage by offering you your headman's customary share of the beer? You were given the right to eat the food of the land over which you are head by our king and banana beer is that food of the land for our sovereign and his village headmen. And so how can he refuse to give you your customary present of beer when you are his village head? Has he found another headman besides you whom he feeds with your rightful share of beer? *Aa*! What a mess! Kanwaketa, if I am mistaken please correct me, and since our village headman himself is here let me hear how the two of you see this matter."

"Myombekere, do you hear me? Do you want me to tell you something?"

"Tell me."

"What you have just said is exactly how I feel. Ntamba has grievously transgressed the rule of the land by refusing his headman his customary present of beer when the headman is the ruler of his village. He has acted as if he wants to rule himself and that especially is what disturbs me most about him. Ntamba himself daily sees people brew beer in secrecy but even in such cases never failing to equally secretly beckon their village head to partake of the brew. *Ahee*! gentlemen! Why brew beer which is so little that it doesn't enable you to observe what in this country is a binding obligation? It is true, as Myombekere says, that we too have banana plantations but let what befalls us befall us: committing felonies is the accursed destiny of all men. That however shouldn't prevent us from saying loud and clearly that in this case Ntamba has erred."

The headman joined in and said, "Anyway, let's drop the matter, since it is now behind us. It appears this Ntamba has decided to keep us guessing what he will do next, so let me too leave him guessing what the future may have in store for him. Today was the second time, but let him continue to be a man and me a woman. Should he bring me his nonsense again the third time however, that would be his third and last. Even if he gives me his beer, like he did today after I went begging for it, I won't accept it. Take it from me, unless I am not the son of that great woman my mother or unless I die today. But if I live long enough, may my son Galubondo here and all of you present taunt me with empty brags if I don't put an end to Ntamba's affront. Even today what served him was the fact that he realized he was in trouble and so hastened to give me this huge potful of beer, bigger that any he has ever offered me in paying me his respects. Still, the bad eye which Galubondo and Walyoba cast on him unsettled him greatly."

Galubondo took up what his father was saying and added, "Ask me who was looking at him when Walyoba told him: `You have refused us our beer for too long, today you will give us all your beer and then add a he-goat to it!' I never saw a man so frightened! His whole body began quaking so that his lips trembled. That man was really frightened! By the time we went to fetch this beer he could hardly utter a word. That's how Walyoba managed to deprive him of this huge pot without him saying a single word. And then, it appears, he still thought we would drink the beer in his home as we usually do, but instead Walyoba put the pot on his shoulder and walked away while talking fast to himself in his people's incomprehensible language! That is when we saw even the beer beggars who were around decide to drop back, otherwise they would have followed us all the way to this home.

The village headman then said: "Kanwaketa, my man."

"Your respects, Sir, my headman."

"You better do what needs to be done otherwise this pot of beer would be waiting for the multitudes to arrive."

Kanwaketa sent a son of his to bring a beer drinking bowl[19] and a tiny cup[20] for drawing beer with and the young man began serving the beer. The headman told Myombekere to go and bring his wife Bugonoka to drink some beer. Bugonoka came accompanied by her son Ntulanalwo, who had *enanga*[21] with him. Seeing that village head said, `Now, young man, I have heard for a long time now people praise you and say that you are an excellent *enanga* player like your father; today you will play for me some of your songs, because your fellow young men are really full of your praises." Galubondo said, "Father, do you think those who praise him are exaggerating? The son of Myombekere plays very beautiful tunes and has a great singing voice; all of us who have heard him play can testify to that." In no time other people were flocking into Kanwaketa's home to keep village head company and drink his beer. Even without the village headman's presence that's how beer is: it attracts and gathers together people more than anything else.

When people had taken enough beer, especially since some of them were simply adding finishing touches and were already tipsy, they began talking of all the topics on earth (how could they talk of those of heaven as if they had ever been there, poor people!) and ended up talking of the After-life: how the After-life eats up all people indifferently, how After-life fears no *omukama*, does not respect nobility of whatever rank, does not respect parents, and as to childless people, don't bother to even speak of that! You know what our people of yore said: "A pot of beer is the boon companion of conversation," and they wanted to go even further when the village head stopped them and said, "Quiet now, so that we can listen a bit to sweet *enanga*. Let this child play some and awaken forgotten feelings in us all."

All present agreed with their village head: "Yes! We now know why *omukama* chose you and made you our ruler: you know the right things to say at the right moments!" People quieted down and the noise died out and Ntulanalwo asked their headman, under whose chin he was seated, "Which song do you want me to play?"

"Don't you play any songs of your personal composition?"

"Well, I would like to know your preference."

"With us whichever song you play we are ready to enjoy."

Ntulanalwo was given a pot in which to place his *enanga* for resonance and he began to tune his instrument. When it was ready, he put it in the pot and played first an introductory tune, singing to it, at first all low and soft, the way his father used to do, and after a while, when the music got to his head, he raised his voice. On hearing that his mother together with Kanwaketa's wife and all the girls present who were a bit grown-up ululated.[22] He finished playing the introductory tune and played some adult songs and adults hummed along and warmed up and got excited. Then he played dancing tunes and everybody danced, the young and the old ones alike. When the village headman took his turn to dance he really moved his body and propelled his shoulders, no joking! The women gave him a peel of ululation, at the same time as the men accompanied his dance movements by clapping for him, all in step with the rhythm of the music! The village head danced until he was dripping with sweat and people raised his hands up in the air in congratulations! Finally the pot of beer was drunk and finished and people scattered and only then did the village head too return to his home. That's when Myombekere told Kanwaketa that the following day he was going to report to his in-law Kalibata the response he got from the people whose consent to his son's marriage to Kalibata's daughter he was sent to court and that, in addition, he wanted Kanwaketa to accompany him, since he wanted to go and buy tobacco of which Kalibata had spoken to him. Kanwaketa asked him, "When do you want us to start off?"

"I would prefer we started off at about second cockcrow, because we'll be walking while dragging along with us a goat."

"In that case, don't bother to come here to wake me up. Since your home is on our way, I'll pass by your place for you."

"Fine."

That day Myombekere and Bugonoka and Ntulanalwo ate no dinner, their only dinner that night having been the beer they drank at Kanwaketa's home and nothing else.

And so at second cockcrow Kanwaketa woke up and when he got to Myombekere's gate he called, "People of this home?"

"Yes! So you've arrived! I was beginning to say that perhaps Ntamba's beer has played havoc with my friend, since you are one of those who went to confiscate it and we don't know what that Ntamba fellow is capable of."

"Don't remind me of that! On my part, you see me here, yes, but the truth is my stomach is in very bad shape, I walk feeling so light, especially since last night we in my home went to bed without eating anything. I am feeling really terrible!"

"My man, that was the case with us here too. We too had no dinner. Perhaps this Ntamba fellow put something in his beer! *Aa*! Honestly, what a strong banana beer! Whoever had a sip of it got dead drunk as if something had gone wrong with him or her! Maybe the young men like my son Ntulanalwo fared better, but with us old bones the beer did give us a real beating, even without saying it!"

"Especially in my home, we were really finished! No, we can't go in this condition. If Bugonoka has something in her kitchen she'd better do something for our stomachs first. Otherwise, Myombekere, we'll get there already a sorry sight."

Bugonoka heeded that plea and quickly woke up and prepared some food. After eating that early morning dinner of theirs, Kanwaketa told Bugonoka, more in jest than anything else, in a brother-in-law to sister-in-law spirit: "You know, my Bugonoka, you are the only woman who can really cook, other women simply mess up! May you live in this house in good health forever, for you have indeed breathed new life in us. Without you we would have fainted before getting where we are going or arrived only to fall down from dizziness in our in-laws' home. Today those people would have wondered and said, `They are epileptics!' Imagine that! That would have been the one great blemish on our persons for which our son would have been denied the wife we are courting for him. *Aa*! And so have a good day in this home of yours, we are off to look for whatever we'll get."

"Go ahead, and may everything go well with your mission."

Myombekere brought a rope of papyrus cord and put it around the goat's neck and the two men started on their way. The goat cried until it stopped crying and walked until it refused to walk anymore and did exactly as in the saying: "The goat says no by lying down." When the two men saw the trouble it was causing them, when its turns of lying down became frequent and when they tired of its crying out that way in that early dawn, in addition to the fact that it was delaying them on their journey, Myombekere lifted it and placed it on the bend of his neck, the way people carry a goat on their shoulders: the head of the goat facing his right shoulder, the front legs, what people call the arms of a goat as if a goat too has hands which can catch things, outshooting that bend of his neck and hanging over his right-hand side breast, that is if you are carrying the goat left-handedly, and its belly pressing right against the bend of his neck and its hind legs hanging over his left-hand side breast and its small tail whisking away at flies, as if it too has an animal tail to speak of when all it has is a stump! When he had carried it for a while, his companion told him, "Give it to me and let that sweat on you dry up a bit." Myombekere passed the goat to him and he too loaded it on the bend of his neck. After a distance of from here to there, he told Myombekere, "This young goat is really healthy, my dear man."

"Why?"

"I know a healthy goat by its weight and, look, this little goat too is really weighty."

"I see! So that is how goats are. That's something I didn't know. It hadn't occurred to me that a healthy goat would be more weighty. I though all goats are heavy the same way, whether lanky or not."

"A goat like this little thing, if we were not taking it where we are going to buy with it something we want but were instead to put it to the knife, I tell you that day we would eat so much that we would camp out in the bushes emptying our bowels, on account of its sweet meat. It would, I think, be necessary to drink a bit of banana beer first, if we wanted to really enjoy it and eat by swallowing its fatty meat without chewing, because chewing such sweet meat could prove nauseating."

Then they walked on for just a little longer and arrived in Kalibata's home. The gate of his home was still closed with its shutter of *entalama*[23] thorns. Once in the home, they tethered their goat to a peg in the compound of the home and went to Kalibata inside the house. Myombekere reported to him the replies he got from the homes to which he sent him and finished and then made another courting plea: "But, my dear Kalibata, do please quicken up things a bit for me. You don't have to be like the people of this country."

"Who are they?"

"People of this country."

"And their growing-up name?"

"Never-let-go."

"Well, I am the name of a village of this country."

"What is it?"

"Village of this country."

"Its growing up name?"

"Impatience. Because, as far as I am concerned, now you are the only one I am waiting for. If you hurry up, so will I. And so today I m sending you to court the consent of the relatives of the mother of the girl you are courting, some of them are in that village over there and for the others you will have to cross the sea and go to Ukerewe mainland, and also to the Islands,[24] to Irugwa, where there is a single home, and that is all. And when you come back to see me, come with a house screen[25] for partitioning my house and you will have done everything I want you to do. And now tell me, Kanwaketa, is that not how people should talk?"

"*Aa*! You have spoken like a man indeed. There's no denying that. Myombekere can only blame himself now, in case he dislikes traveling to places."

"What about you helping me out, man?"

"If you send me to help you, I will. Why should I refuse to help you, if you ask me to help you bring home the great prize?"

Myombekere then asked Kalibata to take him to where he could buy tobacco. As soon as Kanwaketa untethered the goat from the peg on which it was tied, the goat gave one strong jerk on the papyrus rope in his hands and the rope snapped and it was gone. And since it was a rather wild goat, like the goats of the minor islands of our kingdom which are left to roam the island hills at will, in an instant it was already by the gate of Kalibata's home and out into the bushes, running as fast as it could. Kanwaketa and Myombekere were left confounded and immobilized by not knowing what to do, stunned like people who had just killed another human being, especially Kanwaketa, who looked as if he had actually passed out. It was in fact Kalibata who brought them back to life when on coming out of his house he at once asked them, "And where did the goat you came with go?" At once Kanwaketa took off running to look for the goat, which had by now got really far in the bushes, with Myombekere following suit, at the same time as Kalibata called a son of his to come and help the visitors catch their goat.

The youth flew to their help and found the two adult men already at the limit of their strength in their struggle to catch the goat and told them, "Please take a rest and don't bother, old men, leave this to me. Racing after goats is my favorite hobby." And indeed that goat did not make the rounds of two bushes before the youth had it in his hands and gave it to the two adult visitors. Only then did they become themselves again and recover their voices and call out to Kalibata: "Please come with our weapons and another papyrus rope for tethering this naughty creature!"

Kalibata came and led the way to take the two men to the adjacent peninsula where the tobacco they wanted to buy was. They got to Namusya's home, the home of the owner of tobacco, and Kalibata told the man, "Here are visitors, come to challenge your boasts about the quality of your tobacco. They want tobacco and they have a goat. So here they are!" After exchanging greetings with his visitors, Namusya sent his wife to call some neighbors of theirs for him to come and witnesses their barter of tobacco for a goat, and in no time the neighbors had come, a whole troop of three of men. Namusya told them, "Gentlemen, I have called you because I have here a barter of tobacco for a goat. Here is the goat, take a look at it and tell me whether it is a healthy goat fit to buy and if so determine what you think is its right barter value in tobacco, because the value of a barter item is best judged by the eyes of many. What's more, seller and buyer concluding a bargain the two of them alone isn't the thing to do."

"Maybe our people of old found barter concluded between just two people, between buyer and seller alone, undesirable because, should later on one the two parties raise a problem about the bargain, then people would say: 'This is an impossible case to judge, because there is no single other person who witnessed the trading,'" Namusya's neighbors said. "But here we are, your witnesses, and we find this goat satisfactory. It is small, but then it is also young, after some more grass in it this is a very big goat. And although it is a he-goat and not a female, people need he-goats too in their herds to breed more goats. And the price we have determined for it is this: Give these men twelve balls of tobacco plus two flat pieces for the witnesses to the bargain and that's it, because that is the price we usually see in the trading of a he-goat for tobacco[26] and we were not born yesterday, we are all adults who have seen quite a bit of things."

It was as if those men had made any further bargaining unnecessary and the deal was concluded. At once Namusya went to untie the roof of his grain store,[27] which was full of balls upon balls of tobacco, and took out the twelve balls and two flat pieces for the buyers.   Myombekere and Kanwaketa too were satisfied with the sizes of the balls of tobacco. Myombekere took from his purchase one ball of tobacco and gave it to Kalibata and took another one and gave it to the three men who witnessed their deal. Namusya too acted like a man and went back into his store and brought five flat pieces of the commodity and   first gave one flat piece to each of his three neighbors and then gave another to Kalibata and yet another one to Kanwaketa. The buyers wrapped their tobacco in some old kitchen roof grass blackened with smoke to preserve its flavor then put it inside some worn-out carrying basket[28] they were given and left. When Myombekere and Kanwaketa came to where they had to part ways with Kalibata, Myombekere told Kalibata, "Let me go and court where you have sent me. In the meanwhile, expect to see my wife in your home not tomorrow but certainly the day after tomorrow. She too wants to present her plea to you."

"I see! That's a nice thing to do on her part. Please tell her to come, we'll be home."

The following day Bugonoka went to pass the night in the home of relatives of hers she had spoken of who lived in Kalibata's neighborhood and the morning after that she woke up early and went to Kalibata's home. She found the master and mistress of the home both present and exchanged greetings with them, after which Kalibata asked her, "Where do you come from, lady, in case I have relatives in that part of the country and you can give me news of them?"

"Me? I see! I am the wife of Myombekere."

"What is wrong with me today? I must have lost my senses!"

"Why so?"

"What else can I be but an insane person? Imagine going to a person's home, finding her there, drinking her beer, being in fact the beneficiary of her present of a whole pot of beer, and then when you meet her again you don't recognize her, as if when you went to her home you were already drunk! My mother of mothers! It was just yesterday and here I am with no memory at all of you! I see, so it's you, Bugonoka herself! *Ahehee*! what a great pleasure to see you!"

"It's me."

"Myombekere must have escorted you this way in the night for you to be here this early in the morning?"

"Oh, dear me, don't tempt me to lie to you! I passed the night in this area of yours, in the home of this woman with me here."

"And how are you related to Tilumanywa's wife?"

"My maternal grandmother is from her family. The father of this woman here and the father of my maternal grandmother are children of the same father with different mothers."

"She is a close relative of yours indeed."

On hearing that the wife of Tilumanywa asked Kalibata, "So all this time you have been seeing me you were taking me for some dead-end person, with no relatives?"

"*Aa*! Never; not that! Poor me, I simply didn't know that you two were related. Otherwise how could I call you a dead-end person when I happen to know that there isn't a single year which passes without your going away from that home of yours to mourn a relative? Look, even at this very moment you bear signs of a person in mourning. How then could I dare suggest you have no relatives like the miserable poor lonely me!"

Bugonoka then pleaded for her son's courtship and finished. Kalibata told her, "On my part I have no more reason for dilly-dallying, what remains now is entirely in your hands. So it is up to you to speed up things, daughter of Namwero. The day your husband comes to report to me what he was told in the homes to where I sent him to court, let him come with the house screen I asked from him and it is on that very day that I'll send him to fetch the bride's escort[29] and bring this matter to a conclusion. I too would like to see the end of it as soon as possible so that I can be free to attend to my other concerns."

"Praises to both you and your wife. Let your giving hands be kind to us and succor us the way the nobility of the land succors poor people, you children of worthy parents!"

As Bugonoka and her relative got up to leave, Tibwenigirwa, Kalibata's wife, told them, "Please wait for food, dear women. Human beings walk with their stomachs and not their backs in front and to journey with your stomachs flat like your backs is like walking backwards."

Bugonoka replied and said, "No, thank you, dear woman. Let me go, because I'm all alone at home over there. It is true that even now I am here because I am looking for food, for your daughter's food in my home, but there will be another time for me to eat here. What's more, I am still passing through the home of this woman here and I don't want to start on my way back late and arrive in another person's home at nighttime and be beaten by my master while he is telling me, `Maybe you hadn't gone over there to court but to have a nice time with your grandmother's relative!'"

"Come on, dear, does Myombekere too ever beat you? Whenever I see him here so cheerful I say to myself: `Surely this man never loses his temper in his home and never reprimands his wife.'"

"You surely don't mean it? Dear woman, where have you ever seen a man who never beats his wife, who never gets angry with a woman he calls his wife, in this country of ours? The way I see it, with all of us women our husbands treat us as if we were some creatures they own!"

As Bugonoka and her relative entered the latter's home they ran into Tilumanywa returning from fishing in his *olubigo*[30] and the man said, "So you two are just coming back! How was your bride-hunting adventure?"

Bugonoka answered him, "The bride-hunting adventure was fine, my brother-in-law, but our people say: `Don't grind flour for food before the quarry of the relish is in your hands.' So I've better ask you: `How was the fishing adventure?'"

"The fishing adventure was good and I have the quarry here with me, as you can see. I came back half walking and half running, afraid you'd by now have been back long before and I'd find you, my sister-in-law, already angry with me for keeping you waiting."

"We too have just got back this very moment."

"But you must have done quite a bit of courting, because you left quite a while ago."

"Yes indeed, we did quite a bit of courting. And how could it be otherwise when that was what sent us there, my brother-in-law."

"*Aa*! You should always state the reason for your visit to your host at once, lest you be like the man who went to borrow a seeding bull, of whom people say: `He arrived and said nothing. After a while the owner of the bull was served food and his visitor joined him and they ate together, again the visitor saying nothing. Before long another man came in the home and found the men still eating, but with that other visitor when the master of the home invited him to eat he declined and chose to state the reason for his visit first: Thank you for the invitation but let me first tell you why I am here. I have come to borrow this bull of yours. I want it to seed my cow. That's why I am here. Hearing that the first visitor said with great surprise:

Hear that! Your bull is what I too came to borrow, and now look, this man comes later and asks for it before me! What am I to do now?   And those present laughed and said: Well, your mouth has let you down, so contend yourself with *obwita*[31] you are eating and let the man who stated his need on arrival take the bull, and the owner of the bull too agreed with them.' But tell me, my sister-in-law, to spend there so much time you must have received some good news, grounds for good expectations which people say kept the hyena standing outside a house the whole night long?"

"We shouldn't sing our own praises, since we are yet to get what we want. But, all the same, yes, there appears to be good news for us over there. Only it is still the milk of a heifer of which people say: `don't count on it before you drink it.' All the same, in our ignorance, we believe there is indeed good news over there for us."

Bugonoka was given something to eat and then her female relative loaded a container with presents for her and she left and went back to her home. At home she found Myombekere weeding his banana plantation and told him what Kalibata told her, how everything now was in their hands, they the suitors, and how the house screen remained the only really needed thing. Husband and wife left the banana plantation and came home, and Bugonoka took out of the container the presents her relative had given her husband. I see! So in that *ekitukuru*[32] basket there was fish, twelve *ensato*[33] and thirteen *emumi*[34] underneath *ensato*. On seeing the present of so much fish Myombekere asked his wife: "Does my co-husband[35] catch fish in abundance these days, I wonder?"

"He does indeed. For example, on the day I arrived I found people in his home busy smoke-drying fish, and when my relative served me sweet potatoes my relish was a whole *ensato*. When she came to take away utensils after I had eaten, she found I had left on the plate the whole upper half of the fish starting from the middle of the stomach, having only eaten the tail half with the sweet potatoes before I was full, and on seeing that she told me, `Don't do that to me , dear.  If you can eat no more sweet potatoes at least eat the rest of the fish.  This remaining little piece can't be put back into a pot.'  And so I got to gobbling fish after saying to myself, `This is my lucky day!' and put it all down my throat to the very last bit. She was the one who offered it to me, so I couldn't be reproached with greed, because she had given me the relish without my asking for it. Another voice in me told me, `You risk being sung with songs like: She eats too much, the greedy female, gobbling[36] all alone an entire *ensato*  each meal!' That voice in me in fact took me all the way to the puzzle about Abasilanga,[37] of whom people say: `The Abisilanga people are like *omugono*[38] fish trap, they swallowed a fish whole.' But then yet another voice in me said, `Here you are not a gate-crasher, a stranger among people who don't know you. The mistress of the house is a close relative of yours who will never say anything like that about you. Better eat, you woman, lest you be a fool for letting go a prize-quarry after it had fallen down between your legs!' Once that other voice told me so I got down to really eating the fish to the finish, sucking its bones clean before throwing them down. There was quite a bit of broth remaining on the plate and that too I poured down my throat and left the plate dry. And at night the same thing: every person was served a whole *ensato,* and likewise at the meal I ate today before coming I was given a whole big fish. And you are asking me whether he is catching an abundance of fish! Let's say it was just my bad luck that today your co-husband did not catch *emamba,*[39] or else you can be sure he would have given you that men's food in addition to what I brought. Yes, he is catching a lot of fish and a visitor in that home can eat his or her fill of fish."

"Did you say that Abasilanga are like *omugono* because they swallowed a fish whole?"

"Yes, that's what I always hear people say, even though I don't think I know for sure the meaning of the puzzle."

"That reminds me of another thing said about Abasilanga. People also say of them: `Abasilanga are like the udder of a she-goat which never suckles another mother's child.' And do you know the meaning of the two puzzles or not?"

"*Aa!* This latter one is obvious, its meaning not as hidden as that of the other."

"If so, what is the meaning of the second puzzle? Say it, go ahead!"

"The meaning is that Abisilanga don't take care of each other like people of other clans do. And if you want a good example of that, here is one: Whenever the king dies the Abisilnga princes are up in arms against each other over the succession to the throne. And as soon as Abagwe[40] have selected one of them and put him on the throne as the new king that one proceeds to send in exile almost all his brothers and remains alone, enjoying his sovereignty with the Ukerewe populace. What do you say, is that not the meaning?"

"With that puzzle if it were archery people would say: `you have hit the baboon in the center of its bald head.' As to the other puzzle, I too hear daily people speak of the Abasilanga being *omugono* and swallowing fish whole. And there are those who may give you an obscene explanation, that this or that Musilanga had sex with his daughter or with his sister and made her pregnant with a child and that that is the meaning of the puzzle. And if you ask another person that one too may come out with yet another explanation, that a certain Musilanga actually swallowed whole *ensato*, because he was so greedy and such a glutton! And so on your part on leaving that second person you realize that the two explanations of the puzzle are themselves equally puzzling. Let me tell you, my Bugonoka, a big clan is bound to have skeletons in the closet. Whatever the case, let's drop that subject, we are done with it. Let's talk of something else."

Chapter XXIX

NOTES

1. When the parents of the young girl being courted send to their relatives the parents of the would-be husband of their daughter to woo their relatives' consent to the marriage, the courtship becomes official and all the other suitors of the girl, who may have been several, are informed by the girl's parents that their daughter is already betrothed to a suitor. Usually before that stage is reached, the parents of the girl would have already made sure their close relatives have no objection to the marriage.

2. Among the Wakerewe a person greets all the inmates of his or her home on waking up, first thing in the morning, however early it might be. Likewise the head of a family would not leave his home to go on a journey without first finding out how people passed the night in the home of a close neighbor and friend like Myombekere is to Kanwaketa.

3. *Abakwabi*: Kikerewe for the Masai, the warrior people of today's Kenya and Tanzania from the mainland to the north-east of Ukerewe. See note 7 of Chapter XVI.

4. *Olukoni*: See note 13 of Chapter XXVII.

5. *Ekitambuko*: See note 15 of Chapter X.

6. *Amakukuru:* See note 6 of Chapter VIII.

7. *Ekikome*: See note 1 Chapter II.

8. *Ebina*, plural for *ekina*: : See note 8 of Chapter XIV.

9. A humorous way of saying "please wait for food."

10. *Omulumba*: See note 16 of Chapter II.

11. *Isuguti*: Name of a very large and tall tree.

12. *Esorwa*: Name of a creeping grass, a weed very difficult to uproot from crop fields because its roots grow very deep and sprout into new shoots very easily.

13. *Amavune*: Name of a wild fruit found mostly in grasslands.

14. *Empiru*: Arrow with a round wooden arrowhead, used by boys for shooting birds and in archery games.

15. *Omukungu*: See note 3 of Chapter III.

16. Walyoba was Omugaya, Kikerewe for the Jaluo people of Mara region of Tanzania and neighboring Kisumu area of Kenya, far away from Kitereza's Ukerewe. Kitereza in his original Kikerewe text does capture to perfection the atrocious accent and grammar and usage aberrations in the Kikerewe of the non-Bantu Jaluo man from those distant lands, which I can only indicate in my English translation.

17. *Omukama*: See note 26 of Chapter II.

18. *Bulera* and *hungwe* are different names of a crow.

19. *Olusabuzyo:* Here a wooden container for drinking banana beer with. See note 12 of Chapter I.

20. *Omutaho:* See note 9 of Chapter I.

21. *Enanga:* See note 9 Chapter IX.

22. *Akahira:* See note 11 of Chapter IX.

23. *Entalama:* Name of a thorn tree.

24. For "the Islands", the collective name the Wakerewe gave to the minor islands of Ukerewe Kingdom, see Introduction.

25. *Olusika:* Screen, usually made of papyrus stalks, used as a bulkhead for partitioning rooms in a house, and, by extension, any wall inside a house or building.

26. In the previous chapter, when the exchange price is mentioned first, it is only the female goat which is said to be worth twelve balls of tobacco whereas a he-goat is said to be worth six rounds only, so we have to conclude that Kalibata, Myombekere's first informant, did not know the correct exchange price, or that this is one of the few instances where Kitereza forgets a detail in his long story.

27. *Ekitala:* See note 18 of Chapter I.

28. *Olugega:* See note 19 of Chapter V.

29. *Ensendekeleza:* Bride's escort, the woman, usually a paternal aunt of the bride, the bride's parents designate to accompany the bride throughout the several days of wedding celebrations at the home of her parents and in her new home at the bridegroom's.

30. *Olubigo:* See note 3 of Chapter II.

31. *Obwita:* See note 14 of Chapter I.

32. *Ekitukuru:* See note 16 of Chapter V.

33. *Ensato:* See note 2 of Chapter VI.

34. *Emumi:* See note 34 of Chapter XXV.

35. *Muswelani:* See note 18 of Chapter XIV.

36. For the Wakerewe fish is relish meant to accompany a main dish and eating fish (or meat or any other relish) alone was considered being gluttonous. See note 20 of Chapter VI.

37. *Abasilanga* or *Basilanga*: The clan of the *omukama* (king) of Ukerewe. See Introduction.

38. *Omugono:* See note 6 of Chapter II.

39. *Emamba:* See note 17 of Chapter II.

40. Abagwe, also called Abasita: Clan of the king-makers of Ukerewe. See note 14 of Chapter V.

Chapter XXX

MYOMBEKERE MAKES A HOUSE SCREEN[1] FOR THE PARENTS OF HIS SON'S BETROTHED

Myombekere debated with his wife what of the two errands, courting the consent of the relatives of their son's betrothed and making a house screen, should receive priority. Bugonoka told him, "The way I see it, you should make the screen first and finish it and free yourself to concentrate on courting and court without interruption the consent of the people you have been sent to, so that as soon as you complete courting the blessing of those relatives of our in-laws you can take to Kalibata his screen on the same day you go to report to him the responses you got from your courting trips."

"Indeed two heads are better than one! Yes, I think that's what I should do, because, if I hurry off courting before making the house screen, it means that I will not be able to report at once to our in-laws the response I get from their relatives but will have to wait until the screen is ready, and to delay making my report after I have accomplished my mission isn't the best thing to do. Yes, I will finish one task first, make the screen first, so as to free myself to concentrate on courting. So let's see what tomorrow brings us, and if we wake up in good health Ntulanalwo and I will go into the lake swamps to cut papyrus stalks for the screen. As to Kanwaketa, leave him for now; I will call him to help in the slicking of papyrus cords[2] for plaiting the screen with."

The following morning Myombekere and Ntulanalwo took their billhooks and went into papyrus swamps at the lakeshore. Myombekere told his son, "Lead the way and let's go! You'll learn what a terrible itch papyrus dust can give your skin, if this is your first time to go into a papyrus swamp." And son led the way and father followed.

On their way to the swamp Ntulanalwo asked his father, "Father, can you tell me this: Where does itch dust you mentioned come from in a papyrus swamp when papyruses have no grains and itch-dust usually comes from grain?"

"So you think itch-dust is found only in grains?"

"From what I see, yes."

"What about leaves of *amabingo*[3] canes or *engoro*[4] grass? Don't you see they make your skin itch and yet they are not grains?"

"I do, but in that case I think it is because they both have hair like that of a larva, which also causes the skin to itch. But what can cause the skin to itch on a papyrus, which is all smooth?"

"What an argumentative child! You just walk on, let's go, so that we can come back home before it gets too hot. As for itching, that's where we are going and so you'll see, especially when the sun begins to boil. So there's no need for you to ask: `Where is it?' and : `Where does it come from?' Do I look like some ignorant fellow to you? If you ask such questions in front of adults they'll all laugh at you and say: 'Where does he come from not to know that papyruses cause skin itch?' Before you ask such questions, don't you see that a papyrus carries an ear at its end?"

"I know that, and some people use those papyrus stem-end ears as a substitute for *enfunzi*[5] grass in the pressing of banana juice for beer."

"Well, the cause of the itch is in that stem-end ear. If you examine that papyrus crest you will notice textures jagged like teeth, like the edge of a mat or the jagged edge of the large bone at the back of *engere*[6] and *enembe*[7] fish."

"Then I know why they cause itching, father, because with *engere* fish too, if you catch it on your line and you are not careful in taking it from the hook and its back bone pierces your skin, it leaves behind a scorching pain."

"And what do you think I am trying to tell you? That's it."

They got to the papyrus swamp and folded tight their clothes ready for business and father and son, each a billhook in hand, went into the swamp, this time with the father leading the way to clear a trail into the swamp. When he had cleared a path sufficiently far into the swamp he told his son, "This is enough, come in. But be careful, look where you step all the time, because this swamp has many dangers in ambush."

Ntulanalwo asked, "Which dangers in ambush?"

Myombekere, who loved his son beyond compare, explained to him: "Of the many dangers in ambush here there is the python and the black water cobra. The latter snake, if it bites you , you must never leave the water; you have to remain in the water where the accident happened until you have been given medicine to counteract its venom. You hear that, my dear child? If you leave the water, immediately you are out the venom of the snake will overwhelm you and you will die. Then there are the many other different kinds of snakes too, and there is also the monster apparition."

"And what is the monster apparition, father?"

"You don't know the monster lizard, what women call the extinguisher?"

"No!"

"From today know it: it is the crocodile."

"I see! I have never heard that name for a crocodile."

"There are also the hidden gaping holes, which will swallow you completely to the hair on your head if you slip off the floor of papyrus suckers and bases where we are standing, for you shouldn't imagine that we are on dry land: we are right out in the deep waters of the sea. And, my dear child, in here however good a swimmer you are that won't help you, because you will be trapped in the mesh of papyrus suckers and roots. And aren't those ambushes and aren't they many?"

"They are many indeed. I now see that in here you must keep your eyes open and be alert, expecting anything all the time."

"Exactly."

Then Myombekere cut one papyrus stem and tossed it to his son and said, "There is your sample: cut only the stems of that kind; that is the kind which will give you a really beautiful house screen, the kind we want. What is more, that is how a Mkerewe does whatever he does: whatever you make should be beautiful so that others can appreciate your workmanship. If it is a household object like the house screen we want to make, whoever comes to your home and sees it should exclaim in admiration and say, `Whoever made this screen is a real craftsman!'" And with that father and son took up positions away from each other, one here and the other one over there, and began cutting papyruses, with Ntulanalwo using the sample given him by his father as a guide. And so they worked and cut down papyruses without a pause: *pu pu pu*! you would think they wanted to level the whole swamp! And when the sun warmed up, Ntulanalwo began working while scratching himself all the time like a person afflicted with rashes and yet without a single rash on his skin, that being the work of papyrus itch-dust his father was talking about on their way to the swamp, which he was now experiencing first hand and which hadn't spared his father over there in his own corner either.

When Ntulanalwo saw that where he was there was no more papyruses fit for cutting, he moved to another spot in search of good ones. His father hadn't as yet told him to stop and so taking a rest was out of the question. You know how it is, friends! *Aa*! How could he just stop working when he wasn't his own master? As our ancestors said: "Measuring the depth of a ford is not for the short person." Ntulanalwo had just moved from here to there when lo! he saw something, most of its body completely under water and the rest partly concealed by papyruses which had fallen down and now lay overrun by creeping *amatungamamba* [8] vines, its head resting on top of papyrus suckers this way. You know, the curiosity of children! And so when Ntulanalwo had observed it well and had seen that it had horns but not like those of a goat, he at once retraced his steps, walking backwards, moving cautiously as his father had instructed him, stealthily that way until he got to where his father was and told him in whispers, "Father, come and see! I have seen some creature over there, its body under water while its head was above water resting on the suckers of papyruses like this. I also saw that it has on its heads horns much longer that those of a goat."

"*Aa*! You child, don't be making up things now?"

"No, I am not making up things; not at all. If you think I am lying, come I show you where I left it, you will see it."

Myombekere lifted his billhook and felt its edge with the thumb of his right hand and found its sharpness still intact, still razor-sharp and more. It was his trusted tool he used to cut *emihongora*[9] hard wood trees in the forests for use as house poles. Father told son, "Let's go, let what will happen happen! Dangers are for men to overcome. Don't be afraid and don't tremble."

"All right."

"Do you still remember where you saw it?

"Yes, I do."

After walking stealthily for just a bit, Ntulanalwo told his father,

"There it is, father," pointing at it by a finger of his hand.

"*Aa*! My son, thank you for setting a hunting dog at a prey already in sight. Follow me, but make no noise." Myombekere moved a bit faster, still stalking the animal, and Ntulanalwo likewise, with not a sound made, got close and then stood firm, turned and looked back to make sure his son was far enough so that he wouldn't hit him with the back of his billhook on lifting it. Ntulanalwo saw his father lift his billhook with both hands, his legs apart and firmly planted down and at once ducked by bending really low, still without making a single noise, at the same time as he heard the sound of the blow of his father's billhook: *puu*! at which he too jumped up quickly and landed his billhook right there on the creature's damned nasal: *pwaa*! Father and son heard the creature whine with a goat-like cry: *mee*! They had killed the animal there and then. Myombekere was already holding the head of the animal ready to drag it out of the swamp and Ntulanalwo gripped a front limb of the dead animal as his father told him, "Careful not to drop your billhook in the lake and lose it; hold it firmly. We have killed here meat for relish, my son, Karungu[10] and Kalyoba[11] have willed it to us. This is the *enzobe*[12] antelope you hear about."

"So this is it? And what was it doing here in the middle of a papyrus swamp?"

"That's where *enzobe* live, coming out to eat only at night and sleeping during daytime. This one too was asleep, that's why we were able to kill it. Had it been awake, we simply wouldn't have had a chance."

"And what do they eat?"

"*Enzobe* eat grass, and are particularly fond of sweet potato vines, that is their favorite dish."

They dragged the animal out of the papyruses and saw it was a huge she-game. It had no horns, what had looked like horns to Ntulanalwo from a distance were its ears, for only a male *enzobe* has horns. On examining it well, they saw that it was pregnant and at a very advanced stage. Myombekere was carrying his double-edged sword-like knife and he took it out of its sheath and told Ntulanalwo, "Hold the animal for me this way, I want to skin it. The papyruses we have already cut are enough; we'll leave them there to wilt and loose a bit of their sap and we'll come back for them tomorrow, if we wake up in good health. We cannot wait any longer to attend to this heaven's bounty, we simply can't; no! Whatever the case, the sheep in the proverb told its butcher to slaughter it carefully because `one task deserves another.' Ntulanalwo held the animal as he was told and his father skinned it.

Father and son had just finished skinning the animal when a certain man, whose name was Kurobone, arrived at the scene unnoticed. He too was coming from the papyrus swamp, where he was uprooting young papyruses for making cords. Without anything said, on getting where father and son were he threw down his bundle of cord   papyruses and, without even greeting them,   immediately said, "I second you in killing this animal, gentleman! *U!* Did you just find this *enzobe* here or did you kill it, and with what?" Myombekere recounted to him how they killed the animal. Looking at it without its skin that way Kurobone exclaimed in wonder at how full of fat it was and said, "This *enzobe* must be pregnant, for this is not ordinary fat!" And he too, the clever fellow, took out his sword-like knife and began helping Myombekere to disembowel the animal. As our people say, "The clever man eats a share which isn't his." At once the two men removed the animals entrails and placed them aside and Myombekere told his son, "Go and wash the entrails in the water over there, stabbing the animal food stomach over and over so as to rid it of its dung quickly, then bring the meat back here and let water drip out of it so that it won't be dripping on us and messing us all over when we carry it home. It is true people say: `When you kill game you carry its blood stains,' but all the same we should rid its entrails of as much animal dung as possible. Isn't that so, Kurobone?"

"That's true, dear Myombekere, carrying a lighter load is preferable to carrying a heavier one."

It was indeed true that that *enzobe* was so full of fat because it was pregnant. After disemboweling it, on opening up its stomach they got out of it a female baby child which was on the verge of being born, just a few days before its birth was due. When Kurobone removed the liver, he at once cut off a piece and became the first of the three men to taste the animal's raw meat,[13] after which his companions followed suit, seasoning raw meat with bile juice and eating until they consumed the whole liver to the very last bit. Then they cut off pieces of the animal's food stomach and ate raw that part too, likewise after spicing it first with bile drips, and thus our men savored a bit of their meat before it was cooked, the way things were supposed to be!

When each of the three men had been apportioned his customary share fof meat for butchering an animal, they proceeded to sharing out meat cuts ready to carry them home, each one of them placing his load of meat on a shoulder carrying pole. The two adults divided equally between them most of the meat of the adult *enzobe*, so that Ntulanalwo was given to carry only the unborn animal's carcass and the entrails of the adult *enzobe*. Like the adults, Ntulanalwo too carried half of his load hanging in front and the other half behind his shoulder pole, and thus loaded the three men left for Myombekere's home. Kurobone was thus forced to leave behind his bundle of cord papyruses at the spot. It was safe, though, because in those days the fact that it was a well tied bundle showed it belonged to somebody and so nobody would dare take it. On their way back home whoever came across them and saw them loaded with meat that way would congratulate them for their good hunt and say, "Good hunting men! Aid me out with a bite please!" and they would answer back, "Ask my shoulder for that!" and if the one who asked was Myombekere's acquaintance Myombekere would then give him a bit of meat. And so it was throughout their way until they finally got home.

In Myombekere's home Bugonoka found herself ululating[14] out of sheer happiness! Myombekere told Ntulanalwo, "Gather together some firewood and make fire at the courtyard fireplace[15] for roasting some meat, because the day you slaughter a cow in your home you eat roast meat." He then took out an entire slab of ribs, Bugonoka brought the men a plate[16] for the meat with some rock salt[17] and Myombekere rubbed salt into the meat, and when the fire was burning well Ntulanalwo roasted meat using a raw stick of *imeya*[18] tree as a skewer. As his son roasted the meat, Myombekere could see that it was so sweet its melting fat was threatening to extinguish the fire! When he judged the meat had roasted long enough he told his son, ""Isn't that enough, man? You want to roast men's meat until it is burnt as if it were for women! Look at how the entire home is full of the smell of burning meat! What with the wind blowing that way, even those in Kanwaketa's home will in no time smell it." He had hardly finished saying the man's name when he heard Kanwaketa himself speak to him, already at the gate of his home, "You men, I am coming to visit you and you are backbiting me!"

Myombekere answered by telling him, "Your omen is a propitious one, and you will also live a long life."

""And when could you have butchered an animal, since I have been here and Bugonoka told me that you left early in the morning to go to the papyrus swamps?"

"Is there no animals for slaughter in papyrus swamps?"

"And what animal did you find?"

"Say kill, please, and not find."

"Did you go out there with bows and arrows? If not, with what did you kill it?"

Myombekere recounted to him how they killed the animal, after which he told him, "Come and join us, we are about to eat."

After that Myombekere told his son, "Ntulanalwo, go and bring us a bundle of pegs for stretching and fixing these two hides," and the men pegged and stretched taut the two animal skins, after which Myombekere shared out the meat and Kurobone was given a forelimb for having seconded the killing of the animal, even though you can't second the killing of a prey which is already dead, so that the person who really seconded the killer was Ntulanalwo. Myombekere and his son, however, being people of one and the same home as they were, had found it difficult to point that out to Kurobone and embarrass him and had let him get away with his claim. After that Kurobone left, but not before Myombekere had added to the man's share of meat a bit of entrails. As he was leaving, he told Myombekere and Ntulanalwo that the following morning he would pass by so that they could all three go back together to collect their papyruses they had left behind. Myombekere remained in his home cutting up the rest of the meat, after he had given Kanwaketa a whole hind limb and his neighbor too had left to take the meat to his home. Ntulanalwo then made a barbecue fire over which to smoke-dry meat his father was cutting up.

As you know, people's homes are never without visitors and that day too, in the evening, as Myombekere and Ntulanalwo were smoke-drying their meat, they saw Lweganwa with a companion of his arrive in their home: *bwaa*![19] Ntulanalwo quickly jumped away from the barbecue to meet his uncle and relieved him of his weapons and took them into the house. Myombekere called his wife, "Bugonoka, hurry and bring out seats for our visitors!"

The visitors exchanged greetings and news of their welfare with their hosts and then Lwegannwa said, "I am here to accompany this friend of mine, who has been sent to court the consent of the relatives of his betrothed in these parts of the country." Bugonoka went back into the house to attend to her cooking and outside Myombekere recounted to his brother-in-law how they killed that *enzobe*. On hearing that Lweganwa told his nephew, "I can see it! Child of my sister, you are greatly endowed with the blessings of Karungu of the grass and the wilderness, and, should the Creator will you long life, you will be a great hunter." Shortly after that Bugonoka brought outside food for the men and Myombekere told his visitors, "Brothers-in-law, get out of that barbecue smoke and go over there. It appears your sister wants us to confront some invader!" When Lweganwa and his friend were about to carry their own chairs, Myombekere protested, "Oh, no! Please allow me to carry the seats for you, lest you lower me in the esteem of your friend here, who would go away saying: `That brother-in-law of Lweganwa is some mean fellow, really cold towards his visitors!'" Everybody laughed.

At cockcrow Myombekere' visitors were already up. Myombekere wrapped for them a bundle of *enzobe* meat of the size he decided to give them and then escorted them out of his home. Since at night people don't usually escort visitors, as soon as they entered his cattle trail Myombekere gave them their weapons and returned home and his visitors went their way.

That morning, as the sun began to warm up, Kurobone came to Myombekere's home and Myombekere and his son left with him to go back to their work of the previous day. As they got to the papyrus swamp, before going in, Ntulanalwo spotted a bird in the process of swallowing whole a snake and he exclaimed in wonder. His companions asked him, "Why are you exclaiming?"

"I am amazed at that bird! What kind of bird is that struggling to swallow whole a snake which is wriggling about that way? Can't the snake bite it?"

"That is *namukokoro*,[20] a bird which feeds on snakes, scorpions and lizards, big and small, all of which it swallows whole that way, never chewing. It appears that is how it was created. The bird itself is poisonous too and if it bites a human being he or she can die. The bird called *isemututu*[21] is also like this one, it too attacks snakes. It is quite a spectacle if you find those two birds in combat with a snake. Whenever the snake swells its head and then shoots forth its length to strike *namukokoro* or *isemututu*, at once you see the bird put out a wing to receive the bite, thus rendering the venom of the snake useless, since it gets no further than the feathers of the bird. And when the snake turns this way to withdraw its head, the bird strikes the snake on the head with its beak. And on and on until the snake is finally exhausted and immobilized and *namukokoro* then swallows it and keeps on putting it away down its throat while the only thing the snake can do is to wriggle its tail. That is how *namukokoro* swallows a snake, always head first, the way *ensozu*[22] and the kingfisher swallow *enfuru*[23] sardines whole. Head first too is how the bird called *kimbara*[24] swallows the big tilapia fish whole. Its throat swells and its long neck contracts to a stump and in no time *ensato* is put away in the stomach of *kimbara*, the bird reputed to shut the door of its home by its back.[25] The only fish which even *ensozu* can't swallow is the eel, because when *ensozu* catches an eel and takes it to a rock above the surface of the water and swallows it, the eel slips through the bird's bottom onto the rock and when *ensozu* turns around it finds the eel wriggling on the rock and making its way back to the water. Seeing that, the *ensozu* swallows the fish the second time and once more at once and as easily the eel would slip through the bird's bottom onto the rock. Finally *ensozu* gives up: should it keep on pursuing the impossible and stay without food the whole day? There and then the eel returns into the sea and *ensozu* goes back to chasing after tiny sardines, its daily food."

Myombekere and his companions found Kurobone's bundle of young papyruses intact at the place where they had slaughtered their *enzobe* and likewise Myombekere's papyruses were untouched where they had cut and left them. Kurobone told Myombekere, "Let me help you carry your papyruses out of the swamp before I take my bundle of cord papyruses home. Where, by the way, do you want them deposited first as we carry them out of here?"

"If you ask me, I would prefer your helping me to carry them all the way to Mbulamugani's home, because that's getting them very near my home, from where I can make three trips, or four if necessary, and carry everything home."

"I'll help you; let's go at once and come back for more."

The two adults carried a real man-size bundle of papyruses each. From where they were to Mbulamugani's wasn't what you'd call a distance you walk until you begin to tire, for the man's home was in the vicinity of the swamp of papyruses, and after the men had walked for just a while they arrived and put down their bundles of papyruses and placed them leaning against the stem of *omulunba*[26] tree in the compound of Mbulamugani's home, before going back for more and carrying away everything. They then untied the bundles and spread the papyrus stems on the ground and sunned them.

In the evening Myombekere, the married man he was, had a pot of water heaved for him behind his house by his wife Bugonoka for him to bathe at home. Behind the house there was a washbasin,[27] kept there permanently for bathing purposes. Bugonoka poured some of the water in the washbasin and then called her husband to come and take a bath, as she waited for him with oiled toilet leaves with which to rub his body so that his skin wouldn't become scratchy but wood look well cared for and smooth the Kikerewe way, because bathing with water alone among the Wakerewe was only for the very poor, the ones people called "*enkombyo*[28] spoon body-scratchers." While Myombekere was taking a bath, the couple saw a person walking outside along the fence of their home, already behind their house, almost opposite where they were. At first the couple only heard something and thought that it was noise made by a calf which had broken its tether or perhaps by a dog attracted by the smell of smoked meat. On looking, however, they saw it was a man. You are telling me! My dear friend, the way Myombekere yelled at that fellow! "What wretched dog is this, which dares skirt my home instead of using the gate? What are your likes after, who prefer to pass behind people's homes instead of taking ways people normally use? Who are you, you wretched creature? For your impertinence, today it is your life or mine!" When the fellow heard Myombekere thundering that way, he took to his heels with: `let youth in me prevail!' and with: `my swift-limb, don't deny me life!' Myombekere and Bugonoka almost dropped senseless to the ground with laughter on seeing the fellow run without looking back like that, the goat skin he was wearing trailing him noisily: *kabatu*! *kabatu*! Myombekere was angry because passing behind another person's house is unacceptable behavior and rightly so. For if a man or woman is your visitor, why wouldn't he or she enter your home by the gate instead of trying to sneak through your fence that way? That behavior is like the following other habits which almost everybody in this Ukerewe of ours abhors, and here they are. When we were young and growing up, we avoided passing too close to other people's homes, be it nighttime or daytime. Also if we chanced to pass by the gate of another man's home, it was forbidden us to cough or blow our noses, because there is no way for you to know whether at that very moment the masters of that home are eating or not, and if they are they would be justified in hurling insults at you, or even beating you, because your coughing would have enraged them, you would have fouled their appetites during their meal, which is behavior no one can defend, so that even if they had beaten you and you had tried to sue them at *omukama's*[29] court you'd have been chased away with insults.

The following morning Myombekere sent Ntulanalwo to call Kanwaketa to accompany them to the papyrus swamp and give them a hand in uprooting cord papyruses, and once in the swamp the three of them fell to uprooting the young papyruses for making cords, each one of them working in a spot of his own away from the others. Ntulanalwo had been working for just a while when he heard the noise of something moving in the papyruses in what sounded like starts and halts. The sound kept on increasing as if coming towards him, but he still couldn't see what was causing it. He thought to himself: "If I cry out in alarm before I see what it is, my father will be here ready for the worst, thinking that perhaps I am wounded, and when he finds I am not wounded and fails to see what has made me cry out he will beat me really badly, may be even kill me! So I've better tell Kanwaketa first." He went and told the latter in whispers and Kanwaketa asked him, "Ntulanalwo, was it still moving in the papyrus thickets when you left?"

"Yes, even now it was making dry papyrus stalks and leaves rattle as if it were trying to climb over them."

"Let's go and see, but walk without making noise." "All right."

So they walked stealthily and when they got close Kanwaketa too, who was in front, heard the noise of something moving about and made a few steps back and beckoned Ntulanalwo to signify to him that he too had heard it. Then they saw a huge monitor lizard run from underneath foliage. Both Kanwaketa and Ntulanalwo laughed. Myombekere asked them, "Why are you laughing?"

"We are laughing because over here your son heard something moving in the foliage towards him and he came to call me to go and find out with him what it was, and when I came I found it was a huge monitor lizard, a really ancient one, everything about it already turned into one mass of scales. That's what you hear us laughing about. I was telling him, `Because yesterday you killed *enzobe* you assumed *enzobe* are lined up in here and today too this was yet another one!'" Myombekere joined them in laughing.

They uprooted cord papyruses they wanted and carried them home. After lunch the three men turned to slicing stems of young papyruses along their lengths, three slices each stem. Then they sunned the strands by placing them standing against a prop, until they would wilt and be ready for use as cords. Myombekere kept watch all the time to make sure the papyrus splits wilted quickly by turning them around and moving them to a new sunning area whenever where they were was no longer in the sun as the sun moved on in the sky. All the way to sunset. The following morning, early, he took some of the wilted slices of papyruses to the homes of his neighbors so that they would give him a hand in making cords, before coming back home to begin himself too making some more cords, work in which Kanwaketa came to help him accompanied by a number of elderly people who had come to his home for a palaver with him, who also joined in and helped and the group of men attacked that work and completed it.

That day at night Myombekere told Bugonoka she would need to grind flour for food for many people, because he wanted to invite expert craftsmen to come and help him make the house screen the day after the following. The following morning, therefore, Bugonoka took grain form their grain store,[30] winnowed it clean of dirt and grain dust with its pungent smell, removed sand from it, which was quite a lot, because Myombekere's home had no threshing rock and their millet had been threshed on their earthen threshing ground next to a nearby anthill, and picked her grain clean of all foreign matter until it was ready for grinding. Then she put it on her head to take to the homes of her neighbors for the women of their neighborhood to help her in grinding the millet. Myombekere on his part left early in the morning to buy fish from *emigonzo*[31] fishermen for the craftsmen who would be working in his home. Bugonoka returned from taking millet to the women of their neighborhood to find her husband too already returned and asked him, "Already back?"

"Yes, and here is what I have managed to get."

Bugonoka cast down her eyes and looked and saw a whole really long *emamba*[32] and four large *embozu*,[33] of the size people call "welcome-everybody", and was really impressed and exclaimed, "Oh, yes! Today you have indeed put together a treat for your craftsmen!"

"Well, you know the saying: `When you send another person's child into your grain store expect him or her to chew  some of your grain,' and yet another one which says: `He who dies working dies eating.'

"You are right, indeed."

In the afternoon Myombekere went to solicit the help of three renowned craftsmen, so that he would be the fourth and Kanwaketa the fifth, to work on the screen. All the three men agreed and said, "We'll be in your home first thing in the morning." The next morning, as the sun began to warm up, the craftsmen arrived, some of them with their children trailing behind, having left home very well aware that over there where their fathers were going to do some work there would be some real feasting, eating as much as they liked. The five men all assembled, Myombekere told his wife to bring water in which to soak the papyrus cords so that people could begin the work they came to do and sent Ntulanalwo   to bring some cords and a washbasin in which to put water for soaking the cords. He then made five wooden splinters with which to plait the house partitioning screen and cut pegs for stretching above the ground ropes on which to plait it and the men stretched taut ropes on the pegs and began making their house screen as their children present passed them knives and cords and papyrus stalks.

In the house Bugonoka put on the fire two huge pots of fish, one full of *emamba* and the other one of *embozu*. And so the men got to work and worked on and on until when it got to about noon they raised from the ground a brand new house screen, a real beauty to behold, and really large: three fully stretched arms and a half measure of from the tip of an arm to the middle of the chest!

When the three craftsmen who had come to help Myombekere finished eating, they left. Myombekere then told his friend Kanwaketa, "Let me assign you the homes which are nearby, where you will go courting on my behalf, because, my dear friend, people have to come to each other's aid in times of need. As for me, tomorrow I want to cross over to the mainland, court in the homes I was assigned there and then proceed directly to the islands of Irugwa.[34] When I come back, I would be grateful if I found you have already saved me from having to journey to the homes you will have gone to, my dearest of friends.

"You just name for me the homes in which you want me to help you court. I'm all agreeable, because you are my friend, we have always been on excellent terms with each other and I can't, all of a sudden, today refuse you assistance you need. *Ahee*! Myombekere, imagine that! How then can we call ourselves neighbors if we are on such bad terms that we can't help each other when in need? My dear brother, have we been enemies all these days? For, if we are not enemies, how can we live in discord like *amazwengya*[35] birds, the roommates who never share a word, as people say! Helping each other has always been our people's way of life, so that when in need even a person who is not related to you deserves your assistance. And so, for that assignment, my dear Myombekere, you don't have to worry, because I too want to see Ntulanalwo get a life companion. So if you want to cross the sea tomorrow, you just go ahead with no anxiety in your heart, knowing for sure I will court as you will direct me."

Myombekere then recounted for him the homes in which he wanted him to court on his behalf. Kanwaketa got up to return to his home and Myombekere escorted him out of his ancestors' dwelling place[36] and before leaving him told him,"My man, goo-bye, and maybe I won't be seeing you for sometime. For if I wake up in good health I intend to leave home really early. I want to cross over early in the morning so that I can finish courting in the mainland in time to pass the night in the island of Bweni, as a step to Songe Island, where the people of Songe will ferry me to Majita, from where I will set sail for Irugwa Islands.[37] And as for you, my dear brother, keep an eye on my home for me, because when the master is away his home is in disarray."

"All right. Remember to bring us *Nabunyame*,[38] the sweet sardines of Irugwa."

"Who will give me Nabunyame in Irugwa, where I have no relative or friend?" They both laughed and parted.

Chapter XXX

NOTES

1.   *Olusika*: See note 25 of Chapter XXIX.
2.   *Emihotora*: Papyrus cords, also young papyruses which are uprooted for making the cords.
3.   *Amabingo* , plural for *ibingo* or *olubingo*: See note 7 of Chapter XXI.
4.   *Engoro*: Here the name of a grass. See note 32 of Chapter XII.
5.   *Enfunzi*: Here the name of a grass; also name of a tiny red bird, the totem of the Basilanga clan of the kings of Ukerewe. See note 2 of Chapter XXIV.
6.   *Engere*: See note 18 and 19 of Chapter XVI.
7.   *Enembe*: See note 32 of Chapter VI.
8.   *Amatungamamba*, plural for *itungamamba*: Creeping vine which grows on the lake shore and on the surface of shallow waters.
9.   *Emihongora* plural for *omuhongora*: Name of a hard wood tree.
10.   Karungu or Lyangombe: See note 19 of Chapter X.
11.   Kalyoba or Izoba: The Sun, Providence.   See note 21 of Chapter II.
12.   *Enzobe*: Type of waterbuck found in lake swamps.
13.   For Wakerewe men eating of raw meat see note 11 chapter IV.
14.   *Akahira*: See note 11 of Chapter IX.
15.   *Ekikome*: See note 1 Chapter II.
16.   *Olunanga*: See note 16 of Chapter I.
17.   *Lunzebe*: See note 17 of Chapter I.
18.   *Imeya*: Name of a tree.
19.   *Bwaa!*: See note 3 of Chapter IV.
20.   *Namukokoro*: Name of a snake-eating bird.
21.   *Isemututu*: Name of a snake-eating bird. Kitereza's note in his Swahili translation of the novel says: "A type of bird which eats snakes and rats and chicks and which is deemed to be the night companion of witches and witch doctors, in other words to be the chicken of those witchcraft practitioners."
22.   *Ensozu*: Large bird which lives on fish.
23.   *Enfuru*: See note 5 of Chapter XXVII.
24.   *Kimbara*: Fish-eating bird which catches large fish.
25.   Possibly a reference to the actual habit of the bird *kimbara* once inside its nest.
26.   *Omulumba*: See note 16 of Chapter II.
27.   *Olusabuzyo:*   See note 12 of Chapter I.
28.   *Enkombyo*: See note 9 of Chapter XII.

29. *Omukama*: See note 26 of Chapter II.

30. *Ekitala:* See note 18 of Chapter I.

31. *Emigonzo* plural for *omugonzo*: Fishing device comprising of a row of large hooks attached to a rope. See note 4 of Chapter VI.

32. *Emamba*: See note 17 of Chapter II.

33. *Embozu:* See note 8 of Chapter XIX.

34. For the mainland and the minor islands of Ukerewe see Introduction.

35. *Amazwengya*: Name of a bird. Kitereza in his Swahili translation note says: "White-feathered birds with thick voices which move in groups and   retire for the night in a selected tree, from where they cry noisily all night long." The saying is used for spouses who share a home and a bed but never seem to agree on anything.

36. A man's home is the dwelling place of his ancestors.

37. Irugwa Islands are a group of the minor islands of Ukerewe, the most distant from Ukerewe Island, located off the coast of Majita, the homeland of the Wajita, the "Abakwaya" mentioned several times in the story. For Wajita in Ukerewe see Introduction.

38. *Nabunyame*: Very tasty sardines (*enfuru*) with soft bones and a lot of fat, found only in the lake waters of Irugwa Islands.

Chapter XXXI

MYOMBEKERE GOES TO IRUGWA ISLANDS ON HIS SON'S COURTSHIP ERRAND

The following day before leaving, Myombekere instructed Bugonoka and his son Ntulanalwo to cultivate around his banana plants and weed the plantation during his absence so that on coming back he would find it free of undergrowth and all he would need to do would be pruning the plants. He then took his weapons, for, although he was on a courting trip and was therefore not supposed to travel armed, he was going to the mainland,[1] the dwelling place of dangerous animals. They exchanged their good-byes with Bugonoka, he told Ntulanalwo to take good care of their livestock and he was gone.

He crossed over to Mwibara[1] at the Lugezi ferry and went to court in some homes in Kisoria Peninsula. When he finished, he went to Bweni Island and passed the night on the island. The following morning Bweni people took him in a tiny canoe[2] and dropped him on Songe Island. There too he slept one night and the following morning the people of Songe Island ferried him in a boat to Majita. In Majita he traveled by land and went to pass the night in the home of a friend of his in a village called Ebugunda. There too he slept one night and the following day that friend of his ferried him first thing in the morning to Irugwa Islands. They got to the island they wanted and pulled their boat onto a good landing shore and then took their weapons, leaving in the boat their oars and the bail,[3] as every seaman did in those days, sure that nobody would steal such things. Myombekere and his friend asked the first people of that island they saw for the home of the man they were going to see and the two friends ascended from the shore to the man's home. The women of the home receive Myombekere and his friend and relieve them of their weapons and took them into a house with the master of the home nowhere to be seen. Myombekere asked, "Is the master of this home not at home?"

"He is in but in bed; he has been ill for a long time."

"In which house is he? We would like to greet him."

One of the man's wives, in whose house the sick man was, got up and led the way and Myombekere and his companion followed her. Once inside the house, she gave them seats and then went to the bedroom to her husband, where she sounded as if she was waking him up. The man coughed and cleared his voice and his wife said to him, "There are visitors in the front room come to greet you."

"Are they male or female visitors?"

"They are men and have just landed ashore."

"Give me my robe, I will get up and go to greet them."

His wife gave him a robe and an old hoe-handle for a crutch to support himself with and he got up and joined the visitors seated by the house door. They exchanged greetings like long parted people and exchanged news of their respective homes and then Myombekere asked the master of the home, "What are you suffering from?"

"Our diseases on earth are innumerable, my brother, and I am told I suffer from *enzusi*[4] rheumatism. I have been twice branded with re-hot iron to no avail, the treatment bringing me no relief at all. And so I have been reduced to keeping my bed, day and night, listening to pain killing me, my dear brothers. There are days I can't even eat. *Aa*! And what a flood of thoughts invade my mind on that bed of mine as I lie there suffering! And no sleep either, even if I close my eyes for as long as I can hoping that maybe sleep would finally come, *aa*! I simply can't sleep! And so I spend the entire night listening to the pain with my wide-open eyes. Could you please tell me of some medicine or of some healer you have seen treat people suffering from this disease of mine? If indeed I were to find a healer to treat me and cure me of this disease, I would be forever indebted to him or her! I don't have a goat, but that day I would look for one from those with livestock and slaughter it to congratulate myself. I am a poor man, with no animal skin with which to make a drum in this home of mine, but on that day I would stretch a piece of sailcloth over the mouth of a bowl[5] or some other container and make myself a drum and go and play it from the waters of the sea, which never discriminates the rich from the poor."

"You have indeed suffered greatly, my brother, because *enzusi* is a terrible disease indeed. How can anybody afflicted with that disease walk? Look at how you have wasted, been reduced to bare bones! How can a sick person have appetite for food? No, you simply can't eat properly."

"Gentlemen, I can't indeed."

"I must admit I too don't know of a healer of the disease, but, all the same, I hear that those who can cure *enzusi* by branding the patient with hot iron do exist. The earth is large, such healers are bound to exist somewhere. So keep on asking, for that's the only way to learn about anything. That's why our ancestors said, `Never-ask passed a night in a stranger's home next to his sister's.' Please accept my plea! I am a suitor sent to you to court your consent!"

"Who sent you?"

"I was sent by Kalibata."

"Are you courting for yourself or for somebody else?"

"I am courting for my son, the child of my own blood."

'Which daughter of his are you courting?"

"His daughter called Netoga, the oldest child of his wife Tibwenigirwa."

"I see! So that's the one you are courting. Tibwenigirwa calls me her grandfather, her mother comes from our family. Go and tell Kalibata to give your son a wife without further ado. I haven't anything else to say, because a man cannot find another man ugly. Apart from that, the only thing which really matters to me is to ask you in turn to tell my son-in-law Kalibata to look for a healer for my disease. That's all." Then the man called on his wives to cook food for the visitors.

Myombekere and his friend passed a night on that Irugwa island too and left the following day, early in the morning. Once in the middle of the lake they were suddenly caught in a strong easterly, simply ferocious and before they knew it all of them were thrown into the sea. They were now four of them, since on leaving Irugwa the two friends had given a lift to two other men, and they all went over while their boat itself remained floating. The men fought for their lives and swam like frogs, and that Mukwaya[6] mainlander too was as good a swimmer as his insular companions. At the same time they raised an alarm and some *emigonzo*[7] fishermen who happened to be in that area of the lake fishing came and rescued them, caught their boat and bailed water from it for them and the four men climbed back into their vessel, you'd think they'd never capsized! The wind too died down and the waters became calm again and they took up their oars and resumed rowing until they landed in Ebugunda in Majita, pulled their boat ashore and left for their destinations, Myombekere and his friend going to the latter man's home and their two passengers each one going his separate way.

Myombekere's friend recounted to his wives how they capsized and were rescued from the lake and then told his sons to strangle dead a goat so that he and his friend Myombekere could congratulate themselves for their narrow escape from death, for it was only fitting that as survivors they should congratulate themselves for having escaped form the jaws of death. Within no time the young men had finished skinning the goat and had stretched the skin on pegs and the goat's meat was being cooked. Since the Abakwaya women are not finicky in matters of food like our Wakerewe women and eat goat meat, there was real feasting for the whole household, to such an extent that Myombekere and his friend forgot all about their almost fatal accident in the lake.

The following day early in the morning Myombekere and his friend went to the lakeshore to see whether there was any boat leaving for Ukerewe. They found there a big boat of eight passenger seat-rows. On asking a man they found by the boat, he told them that he and his companions had landed the previous evening from Irugwa and that the boat belonged to the people of Irugwa who were escorting *omukama's*[8] resident envoy on the islands, *omusiba*[9] of Irugwa, to pay his homage to their king. On hearing that Myombekere told his friend, "This is the vessel for me, my friend, for I cannot be afraid of the long sea journey when I am bound to travel by water, since not matter which way I take I must cross water to get back home. And even if I travel through Mwibara dry land, that too is traveling through danger, through dangerous beasts capable of killing me. And, if it comes to that, I'd rather die in water with company, so that whoever cries and mourns one of those other dead ones mourns my death too, rather than die a lonely death on dry land."

The two friends returned home and Myombekere was given something to eat, and after that his friend told his wives to give their visitor some new cooking pots, a send-off presents he felt was appropriate for his departing friend, something to put into Bugonoka's hands when she welcomed him back home. The man's two wives took from their stock of pots one cooking pot each and Myombekere was given two new cooking pots. His friend then took a carrying pole and tied the two pots on one end of the pole and on the other end he tied the skin of the goat which had been slaughtered for them, in which he had wrapped a whole hind leg of goat meat. Myombekere then told his friend, "Please escort me to the lakeshore. It is much better to wait beside the boat at the lake, lest the king's deputy takes off with me sitting here and I am left behind, because now the wind is about to die down and his people can take to sea any time." At the lakeshore they found *omukama's* deputy already arrived and the boat ready to row off. Myombekere greeted *omusiba,* by paying him homage like he were the king himself, and then asked him for a place on his boat as a passenger. He told *omusiba* that he was a Mkerewe from the main island and the king's deputy agreed to take him and said, "Go ahead and put on board your belongings, because I too am going to Ukerewe Island, to pay homage to *omukama.* Only I'll land at Kitale."

"Praises to you, my lord! That doesn't matter, because it would still be in the same land, son of the king." As soon as the boat was ready to row off, Myombekere's friend went back home to his wives.

When the men in the boat had all put on board their belongings, they carried high *omusiba* and seated him in the boat, after which they noisily worked on turning the boat around, vigorously prodding the bottom of the lake with their oars to point the prow of the boat to the sea and the stern to the land, all of them already out of their clothes and naked as they were born. That done, at once they all climbed into the boat and sat down, and when each man had taken his place on a row, Myombekere too was given an oar and became part of the team of rowers, since he appeared to the other men to be some real piece of a man: heavy-set, his body rigged with muscles like the trunk of *omusense*[10] tree with a fully seasoned core. And at once the singer of the team of rowers started a seafaring song. The boat pilot told the rowers in the front of the boat, "You ahead, give us the oar beats quickly so that we can begin rowing. What's wrong with you, gentlemen? Do you want us to pass the night in the sea? We others want to arrive before dark in Omulambo,[11] the dwelling place of great things, so that we can go and drink our fill of banana beer at the palace of the Giver-of-habiliments."[12] On hearing that the men of Irugwa islands at the front of the boat set the pace by rowing in rhythm as a team of rowers does and the rest of the men began rowing properly and answering the song of the boat singer. Finally, the singer stopped singing and people took a rest and poured their *ekilangi*[13] up their noses and let it take effect and blew it out and rested until they were rested enough and ready to row on again. When it was time for another sea-song, everybody wanted somebody else to sing, and so it became: "So-and-so, a song please!" "Give us a song, you so-and-so!" Myombekere then said something to them all in a form of a question: "What do such men fear who when asked to sing in front of their fellow men become all pretenses and excuses?"

"What indeed, dear man!"

"As for us, we'll croak out our share as best as we can. Let he who wants to laugh laugh."

"That's it, dear man. Sing for us something so that we can row this boat."

Myombekere then began to sing in a low voice and without much force:

"Ndelembi,[14] *ee*! Ndelembi" and the chorus answered him by humming like a mother cow calling its calf: "*Mm*! yes dear, *hii*!" Hearing that, Myombekere said to himself, "Now wait and see how I'll sing for you until your heads are afire with my song, for none of you has ever heard me sing!" "Ndelembi, *yeee*! Ndelembi!" and the chorus kept on answering him with their humming, their elbows out, the oars in their hands digging the waters of the sea: "*Mm*! yes dear, *hii*!" When Myombekere took up the song again this time he fully let himself go and rang out with the beautiful voice he was created with:

"Ndelembi, my brother,
Let your daughter go,
Let her get married!"

His chorus too answered him back with full and ringing voices and sang:

"*Ee!hee!ee!hee*!
Ndelembi, my brother,
Let the child get married!"

And in turn Myombekere took up the song again with yet a more refined voice, ringing out beautifully, the type of singing which sets afire people's heads in a boat, rowers and passengers alike, his voice rising and then descending as if he was coming to the end of his song, the chorus already aware that at that seeming end of his song they would take him up and answer him and harmonize with him as his song wanted, blending well their voices to his, as he too joined their refrain and added to it his beautiful voice and embellished the chorus. And when he sang on until the end of his song, witness your Myombekere hear a peel of ululation[15] of congratulations ring out from the wife of the king's deputy, who was in the boat with her husband, and fill the whole boat: "*Keye! keye! keye!* Long life to you, son of worthy parents!" On hearing that ululation his head caught fire and he sang on to the limit of his skill, so that if his singing were madness his audience would have said: "Now he has become raving mad!" The man sang a song and cried and mourned for himself even though he was still alive and sang as nobody has ever sung! And during all that time the rowers their elbows all out, their armpits relentlessly opening and closing, the oars in their hands digging the waters! Then a certain fellow among them, oh, dear me! I shouldn't say he was being provocative when he too was rowing, poured oil on fire with: "*Haha! haha!* Good health to you all, my mother's husbands! Water never breaks the rower's bones! Nyacheyo[16] (the name of their boat), carry your children, take them to the Rain-makers seat, the seat of the Stinging-bee, the seat of hundreds of conversations, the seat of the sovereign of countless thousands, where perfume and incense dwell, where skin robes abound, in the palace of great language, the home of Those-of-sparkling-teeth. *Haha! haha!* Men, today you've had it!" When the king's deputy heard his sovereign thus hailed, all his memories of good times were aroused in his head: he awarded Myombekere a *Wazinza*[17] hoe and to the other rowers he promised as their reward his bullock of a goat, which was already so big it could be bartered for three goats, to which add a small one as bonus and count four goats. He told his men: "When we return home from Bukindo[18] the goat is yours to slaughter on arrival."

His men as well as Myombekere sang the praises of *omukama*'s deputy: "Long life to you, son of kings!"

Then there was another song break and rowers took a rest, those who wanted to chat chatted, those who wanted to bathe in the middle of the sea told the wife of *omusiba* to close her eyes: "We here want to bathe, deny us your eyes," and Waburuza, the wife of *omusiba* of the king, denied them her eyes and the men jumped into the water and bathed, and those who wanted to drink water drew water from the lake with the bail and drank some water while others did so using their cupped hands. It was not until *ekilangi* users had poured liquid tobacco up their nostrils and had let it go to work in their heads and then blown it out and the bathers had climbed back into Nyacheyo and settled in that the wife of the king's deputy reopened her eyes again. At that very moment, before rowing had resumed, one man wanted to urinate and asked for the urinary horn *emborogero*[19] and it was passed to him and he urinated in it and then poured the urine into the lake and the boat's urinal was placed back in its place. After that the front rowers started rowing and set the pace. Their singer, Myombekere, then said, "Let me try again," and sang another seafarers' song in what appeared to be a foreign language, possibly a Kikwaya song: "Young girl, *yeee*! Young girl!" And the chorus answered him with loud humming and he continued: "Young girl Nyabuunde, pass me *ekalangita*,"[20] and the rest of the men answered him by humming in chorus. And if you want to really know the meaning of that song here it is: it is more or less a man calling and pleading with a young girl and asking her to pass him whatever he wants, something like:

"Young girl, *yeee*! Young girl!

Young girl bedecked with beads,

Pass me some *ekilangi*."

And as for their singer Myombekere himself, as they journeyed on and neared the islands of Busyengere and Kweru-kwa-mune, his head got so fired up with singing and rowing that before they knew it his oar broke into two and our man swore an oath: "I'm done with you, oar! Never ask my name, for now you know me!" And everybody in the boat laughed, *omusiba* and his wife included. They were still thus distracted when all of a sudden Myombekere snatched form the hands of another man an oar and said, "Give me this heavy and proper oar and become a passenger, or bail out water, if that is your pleasure, and let us row the boat." "That's right, our man, let him give you the oar so that you can row; we'll give him another, this tiny one over here!" And Myombekere resumed singing for them while rowing.

They passed by the islands of Kweru and Busyengere nonstop, without landing on any of them, and pushed on, but once out in the middle of the waters of Busyengere, the dwelling place of *enkungurutale*,[21] the sea all of a sudden looked as if it wanted to roughen on them without any wind blowing and the men fell to praying for the mercy of the deity of the waters, and after praying to Mugasa[22] that way they saw the sea calm down again and *enkungurutale* itself make its way down to the bottom of the sea, but otherwise that monster of the sea had already emerged on them. Once *enkungurutale* sank down to the depths of the sea the men cheered up again and rowed in a single stretch all the way to Kitale and their vessel safely ran onto the sand of the lakeshore: *chekwee*! and they jumped out and hauled it ashore. *Omusiba* and his wife were carried high and placed on dry land beyond the reach of the lake water and the boat was left alone safe and secure in the landing place and the travelers set out for Bukindo. Myombekere put his belongings on his shoulder and accompanied the people bound for Bukindo, who told him, "Dear friend, do come to Bukindo to join us for a chat."

"Indeed if I get some time I'll come, since you say you intend to stay for some time here. You have been so kind to me, I would be a senseless person not to want to see you again before you leave."

They walked together for some time and then parted ways, Myombekere going to his home and his fellow travelers going to Bukindo.

It is impossible to describe Bugonoka's happiness that day! She saw her Myombekere come back, safe and sound, as healthy as ever! She too knew what the Wakerewe say about the place he had been to, Mwibara: "Mwibara counts the lives of people,"[23] meaning it kills them, for it is teaming with dangerous wild beasts. Her husband too could have died there, since all of us are Ntulanalwos,[24] death's fellow travelers, and there is no point in anyone of us pretending he or she doesn't know it. She also knew the Kikerewe saying: "The sea is nobody's playground," and, indeed, there isn't a single tree in the sea on which to climb and save yourself when in danger of drowning, none at all, I am telling you! And that was why Bugonoka was so happy to see her husband come back safe and sound and as healthy as ever. And since she was kind-hearted and loved her husband like honey, until she saw him come back she was all the time worried about him and saying to herself: "Poor me! I wonder what will happen to him!" And so, before his return, everyday when she finished doing her house chores on remembering her husband she would take her chair and place it in the porch of the door of her house and sit there, in that home of hers, directly facing the gate of their household, pretending to be busy doing this or that but actually on the lookout for his coming back, ready to go and meet him and cheerfully welcome him back home. And then at night she had been dreaming about him all the time. There was a day she dreamt of him having arrived back home, engaged in a nice conversation with her, in which he was telling her news of where he had been, only to wake up and find she was in their bed all alone. Another night she dreamt he was being chased by two rhinoceros, which forced him to climb a very very tall rock, at the bottom of which the two beasts then laid siege and waited for him till sunset and did not leave until nighttime and Myombekere was forced to pass the night up there on the top of the rock. And it was especially that type of dreams which had filled Bugonoka's heart with so much pain, had made her all the time worry about her husband so much and imagine: "Poor me! Maybe he is no longer alive!" So seeing him again after what seemed an eternity restored her to herself.

She prepared food for her returned husband with the choice relish she had made sure would be there on the day he returned and served him radiating happiness: looking at her she appeared to be smiling without actually smiling! Immediately after eating Myombekere went into his banana plantation, to see what had become of it, accompanied by his wife, and found it was completely clean of all weeds and said to his wife, "I must admit you accomplished what I told you to do. What remains now is only my work, pruning."

It was not until after dinner and late at night that Myombekere recounted his journey and what befell him on his return from Irugwa Islands and how he capsized. Bugonoka was filled with pity for him: "*Yuu!* Mother of my mothers and father of my fathers! And here we were, eating and filling our stomachs as if nothing had happened! *Aa! ee!* And so that was why I had those terrible dreams daily! You were at death's door! Father of my fathers! Poor me! *Yee!* With such a death you would have been what the Wakerewe call `the dead with no mourners except birds!' *Yu!* That would have been an unspeakable thing! And we wouldn't have known about it either, until much later."

"You are right. From that end of the world across the waters, you wouldn't indeed have known until much later, because it is far off, all the way to where a Mkerewe calls 'in the ear of an owl,' where nobody ever goes."

"Indeed that's obvious, no need to say it. Even if the sons of your friend were to inform us, that would only be a long time after, when you had already become a thing of the past, completely gone and forgotten!"

"Well, these cooking pots are your present from the wives of my friend Mbarwa, and that hoe is a gift given me by *omukama's* deputy of Irugwa Islands. He and his people were on their way to Bukindo to pay homage to the king and they gave me a lift in their boat. I think he gave me the gift because I have become the names of the people of this country."

"Who are they?"

"They are Wakerewe?"

"What about their growing-up name?"

"Voice-traders."

At once Bugonoka understood that Myombekere had sung for them sea songs and laughed all the way to ululating. And then the couple went to bed.

The following morning Kanwaketa came to greet Myombekere and Myombekere told his friend about his journey, how he capsized, how he was given a lift by the king's *omusiba* of Irugwa Islands, how he sang, how he saw *enkungurutale* near Busyengere Island. Hearing that Kanwaketa asked him, "What saved you?"

"Prayers. You know how it is, every boat has its own medicine man. An endowed person made an incision on the small finger of his left hand and then put his bleeding finger in the water of the sea and with that we saw *enkungurutale* sink back to the bottom of the sea. That's what saved us and we resumed our singing while rowing until we landed at Kitale. That's all I can tell you about my journey, dear brother, a journey in which I became an unwilling witness to miracles. At this very moment I would have already been food for fish, *ensoga*[25] and *ensalali*,[26] as in the saying: `Whoever dies in Mugasa's waters is food for *ensoga* and *ensalali* and whoever dies in Karungu's[27] wilderness is food for worms and maggots."

Kanwaketa in turn told Myombekere the answers he got from the homes where he had sent him to court on his behalf before he left. And then Myombekere said, "Today I'll rest at home, but tomorrow I'll be at Kalibata's door to see what he says."

Chapter XXXI

NOTES

1. Mwibara: Mainland Ukerewe. See Introduction on parts of Ukerewe Kingdom.
2. *Empanza*: See note 20 of Chapter XXIV.
3. *Olusabuzyo*: See note 12 of Chapter I.
4. *Enzusi*: Kitereza in his note in his Swahili translation says: " Disease of the nerves which can cripple the patient, called *baridi ya bisi* in Swahili and *rheumatism* in English," the disease Kitereza himself was later to be afflicted with, from about 1957 to his death in 1981.
5. *Ekibo*: See note 15 of Chapter I.
6. Mukwaya, singular for Abakwaya: See note 5 of Chapter I.
7. *Emigonzo*, plural for *omugonzo*: See note 4 of Chapter VI.
8. *Omukama*:   See note 26 of Chapter II.
9. *Omusiba*: The king's resident representative in the minor islands of Ukerewe Kingdom.
10. *Omusense*: Name of a big tree with a rugged trunk.
11. *Omulambo*: One of the four regions of the island of Ukerewe and the one in which *omukama's* palace, Bukindo, is situated, the remaining three regions being Ilangala, Mukituntu and Ngoma.
12. For many other attributes of *omukama* see notes 33 of chapter XII and 29 of Chapter XXXII.
13. *Ekilangi*: See note 7 Chapter VII.
14. *Ndelembi*: Traditional Kikerewe wedding song, still current.
15. *Akahira*: . See note 11 of Chapter IX.
16. Nyacheyo: "The floating-one."
17. Wazinza hoe: See note 18 of Chapter V.
18. Bukindo: See note 8 of Chapter IV.
19. *Emborogero*: Literally "where the cow moos", horn of a cow used as a urinal.
20. *Ekilangita*: Term of endearment for *ekilangi* above.
21. *Enkungurutale*: Kitereza in the note for his Swahili translation of his novel says: "Colossus shark which dwells at the bottom of the lake, which capsizes and drowns people when it surfaces and runs into a sea vessel. It has a big crest on its back with which it can pierce a boat and sink it. Usually as soon as the sea-travelers see many small fish jump into their boat they at once know *enkungurutale* is around and tell the pilot of the boat to sacrifice to

Mugasa, the god of the lake, at once. The pilot then immediately takes a knife and makes an incision in the little finger of his hand and puts his bleeding finger in the water of the lake while saying this prayer: 'We are asking you, our Mugasa, to save us, your human beings, from this danger we are now facing!' And after that prayer from the pilot the boat would move forward again: *enkungurutale* would disappear and the travelers would be safe again". However, *enkurungurutale* appears to be a legendary creature of the lake whose description tends to differ according to whoever claims to have witnessed one of its elusive sightings, the most prevalent description being that of a colossus snake-monster which dwells at the bottom of the sea.

22.　Mugasa: See note 27 of Chapter VII.

23.　In the Kikerewe text there is a pun here on *mwibara*, "the mainland", and *kubara*, "to count", so that *"Ibaralibara"* , in addition to rhyming, also means "Mainland Ukerewe counts (human lives)": traversing it is putting one's life in grave danger from   every kind of fierce wild beasts with which, until very recently, it was teeming.

24.　Ntulanalwo: Name signifying "death is my eternal companion." See note 1 chapter I.

25.　*Ensoga:* Name of a savory big sardine with silvery scales.

26.　*Ensalali*: Anchovies.

27.　Karungu or Lyang'ombe: See note 19 of Chapter X.

Chapter XXXII

MYOMBEKERE REPORTS TO THE PARENTS OF HIS SON'S BETROTHED THE RESPONSE OF THEIR RELATIVES TO THE COURTSHIP AND PRESENTS THEM WITH A HOUSE SCREEN[1] AND SENDS THEM BANANA BEER FOR SEALING THE COURTSHIP

On returning home from escorting Kanwaketa, the first thing Myombekere did was to take down the house screen which he made before leaving for Irugwa, bring it outside, give it a dusting to rid it of cockroaches and cobwebs and scrutinize it to make sure mice hadn't damaged any cords[2] in the structure. When he was satisfied it was still all right, he beamed with happiness, gave the screen another thorough dusting and spread it on the ground and left it sunned there as he told Bugonoka, "A courtship article should be presented when it is still in good condition like this, so that those for whom it is intended are pleased with it. That way you too don't feel ashamed of what you have brought and can find the right words you need to converse with your hosts and speak without any worry as if you were in your own home."

In response Bugonoka said, "A courtship article is like a borrowed robe, with which the borrower cannot be too careful. For when you borrow another person's robe to wear on such and such an occasion, however careful you may be it is very difficult to return it to the owner without having damaged it in one way or another or having done to it something over which the owner could be displeased, like wrinkling it when putting it away instead of folding it nicely the way perhaps the owner usually does, so that when you return it to him or her and he or she receives it without saying a word most probably he or she has done so only to spare your feelings, otherwise, were he or she to tell you the truth and point out how you had spoilt his or her robe in this or that way you would certainly be overwhelmed with shame, if you are a sensible person, and say to yourself: `Yes, I have indeed disgraced myself!' A courtship article too has no room for even the slightest of blemishes, because, as people say, in courtship no blemish can be a small matter. And with you too, since courtship is your present business with Kalibata, yes, you should take to him something good, something he can receive with sincere thanks."

The following day when it dawned your Myombekere, early, at about the second cockcrow, took his bow and collected his house screen and opened his household gate and was gone. He arrived at Kalibata's and was received and taken into the house and, as you would expect, fell to reporting how he courted in the homes to which he was sent the last time, the homes of the maternal relatives of the maid he was courting for his son. He started with those in this island of Ukerewe and finished and went on to those of Mwibara[3] and finished those too, detailing what he was told by each person he was sent to, leaving out nothing. Then he recounted his journey to Irugwa, the route he took and the night stops he had, how he found the person whose consent he was sent to court suffering from *enzusi*[4] rheumatism and how that person sent him to tell his son-in-law Kalibata to find him a healer, everything from the beginning to the end. And then Myombekere told his hosts about his return journey, how the boat he was in capsized and how he would have drowned had he not been rescued by *emigonzo*[5] fishermen, and how he returned only the day before the previous day and said to himself, "I must go at once to report what I was told and bring my in-laws the house screen they asked me to make for them and find out a bit more clearly how my courtship stands." And with that he concluded his report and held his peace.

Tibwenigirwa, the mother of the girl who was being courted, said to a child nearby, "Go and bring home for me my water pot from the courtyard gate where I left it as I was on my way to draw water from the lake, lest passing cows kick it and break it. I must put off going to the lake and listen to this conversation."

Kalibata first weighed what he had heard silently in his own heart and then said aloud: "My dear Myombekere!"

"Yes, Sir!"

"Long live each one of us, my friend!"

"That should be mankind's eternal blessing!"

"In my view, life is dear to each and every human being and not to me alone or to such-and-such person alone. All of us, without exception, want to live. And here we are, you capsizing that way when everybody and all your relatives know you are courting in this home. Had you died, wouldn't they have all said: `It is that courtship which killed him?' Correct me if I am wrong."

"No, you are not wrong. What you say is the truth."

"It is true we ordained for ourselves that before a man can marry he must be sent to court the consent of the betrothed's relatives wherever they are, even in the Islands,[6] but that custom of ours has never made sense to me at all. And so with me the question of refusing your son a wife can no longer arise, not in the least. It is true words of more or less maligning you have reached us here, but let's say nothing about that, since the whole thing is more or less silly. It would, in fact, appear that the person who said those things about you here simply had nothing else to malign you with. And so perhaps I might as well reveal it all to you, so that you won't leave this home with a troubled mind because of not knowing what it is all about. This is how it happened. A certain person came here, some man called Ntamba, and said in this home the following: `Are you people of this home the ones who want to wed your daughter to Myombekere's son?' We here, my wife and I, said, `Yes. By the way, what sort of a person is that Myombekere himself? Do please tell us, for we too want to know, to make sure we are not about to throw our daughter into a patch of thorns.' And when we said that he told us: `Myombekere's wife is a woman of terrible temper, who is forever fighting with other women on the lakeshore where they draw water and breaking their water pots. She provokes even men, daily. In addition, she practices witchcraft, much as her appearance might fool you! What is more, the people of Myombekere's home cultivate their fields at night, never returning from the fields until the dead of the night.'[7]

"When he told us that, since he was still present, we pretended to agree with what he was saying and added to it and said, `Thank you very much for revealing this to us. You have indeed saved us, dear brother, since this is what our ancestors had in mind when they said: When you have no relative in a conspiracy you die before you know it. '

"And that Ntamba fellow then took up our rejoinder and said, `In fact if you wed your daughter to Myombekere's son the entire Ukerewe kingdom will exclaim in wonder and say: Kalibata must be a madman, and if he is not mad then he has bartered his daughter for some magical powers or potent witchcraft! Otherwise a man like Kalibata would not marry his daughter into Myombekere's home. Myombekere's wife was barren, completely, and in her desperate search for fertility she revealed her witchcraft in broad daylight by killing a relative of Myombekere as the price she had to pay for the magic which gave her children, and only then did she conceive that child of hers they call Ntulanalwo, for whom they are courting your daughter. And so, if you are determined to give her son your daughter in marriage, that's up to you, but the truth is that that woman Bugonoka is real malediction, a real witch.'

"Then after a time he went away and as soon as he left my wife Tibwenigiriwa and I went over the matter between the two of us and said, 'What a turn of events! We had approved this Myombekere the way people approve fellow human beings and then here comes this man to pour filth into our relationship! *Hee*! Maybe that's why people say that no man ever marries without someone trying to malign him! And so, whether the accusations are true or not let that be as it may, but we won't go back on our word and kill a person's courtship after it has reached near conclusion this way. What's more, we have already put the poor man through so much trouble. Whatever the truth might be, for us Myombekere has become our in-law and nobody else will marry our daughter except his son. We will have nothing to do with this Ntamba's accusations?' By the way, what is your relationship with that man? Is he some relative of yours or what?"

"I am not related to Ntamba in anyway, neither is my wife, neither are we related to his wife. I think this is sheer malice on his part, for he bears me a grudge. And let me tell you the origin of his grudge against me, since you are the ones who have brought up this subject. This is how it happened. On a day I had gone to woo back my wife from her parents' home, two of my cows, literally two, grazed in his millet crop, not even to the extent of destroying even one single ridge of the millet, and at once Ntamba came, raging mad, and immediately fell on beating a boy living in my home, a nephew of mine, who was looking after the cows, and beat him to the point of death. In fact the child was saved only by his swift foot, otherwise Ntamba would have killed him on the spot. And then the same Ntamba was off running to lodge a complaint against me in the village court at the village headman's.[8] And so the following day we went to the headman's home and court was held to hear our case and I threw him in the dust of the earth in our legal contest and he and not me was ordered to pay judgement fee to the village head together with an additional fine of one goat for his brutal beating of my nephew[9] and there the matter ended. And lo and behold from thence ensue enmity between us! *Aa!* We became enemies like smoke and the remaining eye of the one-eyed person, as our people say! We stopped greeting each other: whenever he came across me you would think he had encountered some predator, and likewise his wife and those of his relatives who knew of the incident. As a matter of fact we did not resume greeting each other until very recently, after my wife had conceived, born and weaned her son for whom I am looking for a home-building companion from you. And so it appears that his grudge against me did not die out in him but simmered on like the injury of the blow of a stick, which can still prove deadly long after the deed like the transgression of a taboo, as can be seen by how he has shitted incredible stench all over me in this home! Let me assure you, here and now, my dear Kalibata, that if that man had some potent potion with which to harm us and the opportunity to do so he would have killed me and the rest of my family to the last person a long time ago. But that is the truth of the matter and there is no other ground for enmity between Ntamba and me."

"I see! We now can see that it is nothing but a grudge which is making him lose his bearings that way! Whatever the case, with us you don't have to worry: we will give your son a wife."

"Praises to you! Please receive me with willing hands and deign to grant me that which I seek from you."

"We are pleased with the house screen you have brought us; it is satisfactory. But regarding what I told you, that the day you bring me a house screen would be the day I would send you to bring the bride's escort,[10] I must confess here in front of you that I simply lost control of my tongue and ended up saying what I said when in fact there is still one other important function which should precede fetching the bride's escort."

"Whatever you say, as long as you don't change your mind. And, dear friends, what can that other important function be which precedes fetching the bride's escort?"

"Rather than keep on beating around the bush, I'd better come out with it openly for you. The remaining function which I want you to perform for me is this: `Go and bring me four pots of banana beer for sealing the courtship and you will have done it all."

"In that case let me go and try my best to look for the beer; should I be fortunate enough to find some, I'll bring it." And with that Myombekere left to return to his home, with Kalibata escorting him.

When he got home Bugonoka asked him, "What news did you bring back with you this time?"

"My dear wife, this time I am bringing you something altogether new!"

"And what might that be?"

Myombekere recounted to her how Ntamba went to malign them in their in-laws' home and how the father of their intended daughter-in-law had asked him to send their in-laws four pots of banana beer for concluding the courtship. Bugonoka was really shocked on hearing how Ntamba maligned them. Then, after a moment of silence, she told her husband: "It would take you forever before you can press bananas and brew the beer! Maybe you should go to your friend Kanwaketa and plead with him for help so that he can give you the beer and you will give it back to him when you next brew your own." Myombekere agreed with what his wife proposed, and as soon as he finished eating he left to see Kanwaketa, whom he found chatting with his wife. They exchanged greetings and the couple inquired about Myombekere's courtship: "How is household-founding?"

"A quarry in the wilderness is not yet relish."

They all laughed. After that Kanwaketa's wife told Myombekere, "What you say is true though, because you cannot celebrate a wish before you possess your heart's desire."

Myombekere took up that and said, "How can you? For example, with me today the father of my daughter-in-law-to-be has asked me to bring him four pots of banana beer for concluding the courtship and told me: `If you don't bring me the beer there will be no wedding.' And it is those words which have brought me hurrying here to see your husband, thinking that, since he already has bananas ripening in the holing pit,[II] I can plead for his mercy so that when he brews his beer and it comes out well he will give me the required number of pots, as a loan to be paid back when I brew my own next."

Kanwaketa responded: "Why call that a loan coming from me? Isn't this what people mean when they say: `Friend save me from drowning in my deep waters so that I can live to save you from your shallow ones?' I don't see this simple matter as something to worry you at all. You can therefore calm down, dear brother, and count fully on me. Let's just wait and see whether that holing pit will be propitious for us and give us good beer, because we don't have long to wait before fulfilling that obligation. Today we have cut the grass for pressing the ripe bananas with and tomorrow, should we rise from our beds in good health, we will press the fruits. And so the day after tomorrow would be the foaming day. Let me see! That is the day you will take from the brew the four pots your in-laws want and also the day you will go to inform them that the following day you would bring them the beer they asked from you."

Myombekere sincerely thanked his friend and said, "Dear brother, you have really saved me. You have indeed helped me greatly, because I had began to really worry and say to myself, `This is going to put off my son's wedding for many more days: all the time it will take to cut the bunches of banana, to hole them, to air the holing pit, to cut the press grass, to press the ripe bananas, what an eternity'![12] And so, since on my part I feel I have already waited too long for my son to marry, I will indeed gladly accept and take to my in-law the beer you are offering me, because your brew is almost here."

The following day Ntulanalwo together with the sons of Kanwaketa and some companions of theirs from nearby homes pressed Kanwaketa's ripe bananas and obtained thirteen pots of banana juice plus a near full fourteenth one. That day Myombekere and Kanwaketa stayed only to see to it that the bananas were properly pressed before descending to the kings palace in Bukindo to pay their homage to their *omukama*[13] and his *omusiba*[14] of Irugwa who had given Myombekere a lift in his boat on his return from courting in the islands. On arriving in Bukindo they found *omukama* had just lifted session from the palace courtyard and retired to the interior of the palace, where he was resting in his rest house.[15] On coming across a courtier they asked him, "Would you happen to know the home in which *omusiba* of Irugwa is staying?"

"He is staying at Kazoba's over there. He too was here keeping *omukama* company and just left when the sovereign withdrew to rest."

Myombekere and Kanwaketa went straight to that home of Kazoba, paid their homage to the king's deputy and exchanged greetings with the people of Irugwa who landed with him. They had just been there for a short while when six courtiers arrived, each one of them carrying a pot of beer. Myombekere and Kanwaketa beckoned each other and exchanged confidences in whispers: "It appears we journeyed with propitious feet today! So let's now wait and see whether we will be lucky participants or not." *Omusiba* told Kazoba, "That pot of beer is for you to drink with Myombekere and his companion." Myombekere and his companion sang *omusiba's* praises. Of the remaining five pots of beer, the king's deputy took two and gave them to his people and the remaining three were taken into the house. Kazoba and Myombekere and his friend fell to drinking their pot of beer as on the other side the people of Irugwa too attacked theirs. Soon after that Myombekere and Kanwaketa had to say good-bye to *omusiba* of Irugwa and his people and leave, since there was important work awaiting them back home.

As to Kanwaketa's beer, the following day became its foaming day and it was drawn and Myombekere took out four pots plus one calabashful, the beer Kanwaketa promised him, and carried it to his home.   Then, immediately, he took his weapons and set out to go and inform his in-laws that he had already obtained the beer for concluding the courtship. He arrived and told Kalibata, "My journey to your home today is to let you know that I have managed to obtain the beer, which is today frothing and will fully mature tomorrow. And so I said to myself: `Let me go and inform him, lest we gate-crash into his home with unexpected presents and possibly find him absent and be forced to retrace our steps with our presents.'"

"What you say is true, because with us poor folks we never stay put in our places of domicile like kings."[16] They both laughed.

Myombekere told Kalibata, "Please see me out, because today I simply can't stay; what with my having to look for people who will help me carry here our things tomorrow. For, as we have been saying, my dear friend, nowadays everything has become really impossible! We have all become perpetual wanderers. What's more, these days people no longer volunteer to help others as readily as they used to. It would appear malice and envy have increased beyond measures in our people, unless of course people here are not as bad as those in our part of the land."

"Please, say nothing about that! For if I were to tell you about people's behavior here in this part of our land you would feel disgusted to the point of vomiting! You would definitely say your area's people are still much better. *Aa*! *ee*! My dear man, maybe we should say nothing at all about that and talk of other things."

With that Myombekere said good-bye to the mistress of the house: "Have a good day," to which Tibewenigirwa answered, "No, you must at least allow us to escort you out of the haunts of the ancestors of this home." And so Myombekere went back to his home.

Back home, as soon as he finished eating the welcome bit of sweet potatoes his wife served him, he was off to look for people who would help him carry his pots of beer the following day and found the four he needed for his four pots.

At night when Myombekere and his wife went to bed and slept, no sooner had the cock crowed than the four men arrived and told Myombekere, "We came walking ourselves out of breath, convinced that maybe we are already late, since you told us that as soon as the cock crows we would start on our journey, and even now we were afraid that perhaps you have found other helping hands and are already gone, and here you are, still sleeping! We now understand why our ancestors said: `Upcountry travelers kill themselves hurrying to catch a boat only to find fellow travelers by the sea still comfortably seated in their homes.' And so, man, please bestir yourself and let us start on the journey and come back in time to solicit a drink of banana beer from Kanwaketa."

"My dear men, I couldn't agree with you more; I was just waiting for you. And so come inside the house, so that each of you can select what he wants to carry." The men went inside the house, kind of racing, to see who will get there first and carry the lightest load and who will get there last and carry the heaviest, true to what people mean when they say: `The first cow drinks clear water and the last one silt." The men brought the pots of beer out and Myombekere led the way carrying the calabash of beer and they followed after him. They arrived at Kalibata's and somebody in the home open the household gate for them. Since it was an expected visit, it did not take long for Kalibata, the master of the home, to get out of bed and come to meet the visitors, and as soon as he came out of his house he saw that, yes, they were indeed welcome visitors, like the visitor in our ancestors' saying: "The beloved visitor of the beautiful nappy hair loaded with presents of simsim and cassava,"[17] for already the aroma of banana beer was pervading the entire compound of his household as never before! The visitors were relieved of their presents and the presents taken inside a house. Food was prepared and they were served a meal and ate. If among them there was a man who had never eaten that early in the morning, well, that day he too had an early morning breakfast, for fortunately, as our elders said: "There's no cold or dew in the stomach for it to need the day to warm up first before it can eat."

After the visitors ate, Kalibata told a son of his, "Lift and take this pot of beer to the visitors for them to drink," and added, addressing Myombekere, "My fellow parent-in-law, it is your fault if this bit is all I have to give you and your companions. So please accept from me this tiny pot of beer and let each of you drink whatever little he will be fortunate enough to get."

Myombekere answered him: "To us the important thing is that you give us a wife, my dear co-parent-in-law. As to eating, my brother, let that wait for another day, whenever we will find something to eat together." Myombekere's companions also joining him in answering Kalibata and said, "With us the important thing is that you give us a wife. As to eating, that never ends. What's more, even a lot of food gets finished just like little of it, for there is nothing in the world which people eat which never gets finished."

Kalibata's son began serving beer, by first drawing out of the pot his mother's poison share,[18] which was passed to her in the inner room of her house where she was seated. Then the boy put another share of beer in a bowl[19] and gave it to Myombekere. Myombekere received the beer and then drank just a bit and passed it to his son's mother-in-law-to-be, Tibwenigirwa, and said, "My co-parent-in-law, please accept this share of food from my mouth, lest you censure me for greed and for not thinking of you," to which she replied, "That is very kind of you indeed, my fellow parent-in-law." The women in the house received the beer, and, as they had done with Tibwenigirwa's poison share, poured it in their women's calabash bowl and returned the drinking bowl to the men. As the boy serving beer poured another share in the wooden bowl, Myombekere told him, "Put in some more, until the bowl is full to the brim," and the boy filled the container to the brim. Then Myombekere told him, "Take it and give it to your father." The boy stood up, took the share of beer and handed it to his father. Kalibata said, "Take a sip first before giving it to me, dear child." No sooner had the boy sipped at the beer than he took it from his mouth, kind of frowningly, shook his head and followed that by a slight cough, and seeing that Kalibata said to him, "What do you say now! Aren't you the one I hear daily boasting of I don't know what and what? You don't seem to have much to say today!"

His son responded, "No, father, this beer is too strong! Really!" Kalibata took the bowl of beer and emptied it in one breath, to the last drop. The men present were struck with wonder at Kalibata's drinking stamina and exclaimed, "Dear friends, what a stamina the man has! With the like of us, if you tried to empty into your stomach such a huge bowl of beer in a single breath there is no way you would leave the spot where you are alive! No way!"

To which Kalibata himself responded, "As a matter of fact nowadays my drinking stamina has slackened due to age. Otherwise in my former days, when I too still counted myself a man with his own strength, I wouldn't call emptying such a tiny container of beer drinking beer. I used to empty three such tiny things, pouring them all down my throat each in a single breath, all alone, before I had taken enough beer to make me feel a bit tipsy."

And the other men exclaimed really big: "*Yu!* You must have been an incredible person. In fact there aren't many of your kind in this world; not at all!"

Before the visiting men had completely emptied their pot of beer, Kalibata told his in-law, "Now this is something concluded. Go and pass two days in your home and on the third day go and fetch the bride's escort (he told him her name and the village in which she lived), then on the fourth day give your legs some rest by staying at home and on the fifth day, whether it will be you yourself or somebody else you will chose to send on your behalf, come here in the morning to find out when the wedding will take place. That's all I want to tell you, my dear in-law, because once people drink banana beer on account of a female child there should be no more delay in giving her away in marriage."

Myombekere and his companions joined in and said all together: "Exactly! Yes indeed!"

And so Kalibata brought out his visitors' things and the visitors went back to their homes. Once they got to Myombekere's home and were served food, they all set off to go to Kanwaketa's to solicit a drink of banana beer.

On seeing Myombekere, Kanwaketa told him, "This time, my dear fellow, it was as if there were something wrong with my brew! The sun had hardly warmed up when I began to see people arrive here in twos and threes at a time. And in no time I saw our village headman too arrive, with not less than ten people, maybe more. I therefore took out his village headman's pot and gave it to him and it became all his. Then the people who pressed the bananas also said, `Give us our share and let's drink it and be done with it.' On my part I tried to plead with them in whispers and told them, "Can't you hold on for a little bit, so that we can wait for Myombekere to come back, my dear men?' And when they insisted I gave in and gave them their pot. Before those had finished drinking theirs, I saw arrive here the crown-prince so-and-so, he too in the company of an entire crowd of people, as if they were coming to confiscate everything in this home. I felt my heart jump in its seat and I gave them seats and they sat down, while inside me I was saying to myself, `It doesn't matter, I'll wait and hear what they have to charge me with, since committing felonies is the accursed lot of all men, and mine today won't be the first.' And when they had sat down and rested for just a bit I heard the crown-prince call me, `Kanwaketa!' I answered, `Yes, Sir, son of *omukama*!' And he told me, `Give me beer to drink.' I answered him and said, `It is beer you want, son of the king? Let me bring you some, so that you can eat what belongs to your family's reign. It is true that I don't have much, but let me deprive my mouth of as much as I can, son of *omukama*, so that you can eat what is yours by right for being your people's.' So I personally stood up and went to fetch a pot of beer and placed it between his legs. He refused it and said: "Look at how this man wants to play with me as if I were his joking-mate![20] This paltry container is what you are bringing me while you have inside the house huge pots all full of beer! Do you want me to lose my temper and send my people inside the house to bring here all the beer in there?'

At once, before I had even answered him with a single word of pleading for mercy, I heard the people he came with plead my case for me and say, `Have mercy! Have mercy, son of *omukama*! A little food is also something to eat. Maybe that is all he has.'

The crown-prince answered them, `Why did he brew the beer if he knew it would be so little? In that case let him take back into his house his tiny pot, it is too paltry for my eyes.' At once I stood up, lifted the pot and took it back into the house and then took out the big one I had hidden away and brought him that one. When I brought him that big pot, I saw my lord and master cheer up and everyone with him express his satisfaction, but before that the royal prince had begun to rage with anger. And so his people uncovered the pot and served the beer.

"And I was still encumbered with those when what do I see but three courtiers arrive: *bwaa*![21] A voice inside me said, `Today you've had it! You are running away from a dog you can't outrun, as people say! Here I am still saddled with this master and still trying to placate his anger and then here comes yet some other masters! It appears that what I have brewed today is no ordinary beer but beer destined to spell disaster for me!' This time with those masters as soon as I gave them seats and they sat down, without saying as much as a single word I went straight into the house and brought out for them the pot of beer the crown-prince had declined and gave it to them there and then. Fortunately those other masters of the land on their part did not find that potful an unfit present for them, the good people, and I shouldn't accuse them of untrue things. Those have just finally left this home this very moment, after people told them of some other banana beer somewhere up hill, where too a brew matured today.

"In the meanwhile I was all the time concerned about you and saying to myself, `Look at how bad things can be! Today Myombekere and his companions will die of hunger in their own home, for now that this beer has been exposed this way, will they find any of it still remaining?' When those people had finally all left me and I still had a bit of beer left, only then did I cheer up and say to myself, `Let me put aside for Myombekere and his companions what has been spared me by the mouths of the masters of the land, so that they too will at least be able to slake their thirsty, be it only a little,' for with me here today I was like the fabled Ketandala."22

Among the men who had helped Myombekere carry beer to his in-laws there was one biggish adolescent and the strapping youth asked Kanwaketa, "And what happened to that Ketandala?"

Kanwaketa at once explained to him that that Ketandala was a man accustomed to hunting in the wilderness and killing daily all sorts of wild game as food for himself and the people of his large household when one day, while hunting as usual, in the company of other men, he killed the animal of prey we call a leopard, and Kanwaketa continued: "When the famous hunter saw the sizable carcass of the leopard with its thickset neck, he was overwhelmed with joy and said to himself, 'There is some real food here!' And on perceiving how beautiful and colorful the skin of the animal he had killed was he further said to himself, 'Today I have obtained for my wife a really beautiful robe, of the kind she has never worn!' At that point his companions told him, 'Please, let us help you skin your animal so that we can finish quickly and go home, because it is getting late.' The men skinned the animal and finished, having cut its fingers from the carcass as they skinned it so that the animal's fingers remained on the skin and the animal's carcass was left fingerless.

"The famous hunter himself had never killed a leopard nor seen a dead leopard being skinned, neither did he know that the Wakerewe never eat the meat of a leopard, and so he was puzzled a lot by what he saw and finally asked, 'Men, why are you today skinning this animal in such a strange way?' His companions asked him, 'Why do you say so?' and he answered them, 'I always see animals being skinned without their fingers being cut off from their carcasses but remaining on them, and here you are today skinning this animal and cutting off its fingers and taking them off with its skin?" The men laughed at him for his display of ignorance and told him, 'Usually the animals which are skinned that way, leaving their fingers on the carcasses, are the animals people eat, even though there are some few others which are skinned that way and yet people don't eat their meat. Whatever the case, this is an animal which preys on human beings and so the Wakerewe never eat its meat. And the way it was skinned is how the lion, the cheetah, and the *ensimba* and *emondo*[23] wild cats too are skinned. What's more, its carcass must be left behind here in the wilderness.'

"Immediately he regretted   and said to himself, 'Why then did I kill the creature if people can't eat it?' but in that same instant another voice inside him said: 'Even if its meat can't be eaten, let that be so, provided you have obtained for your wife a beautiful skin to wear!'

Kanwaketa continued, "The men then tied the leopard skin on a carrying pole and carried it on their shoulders and set off to go to Ketandala's home while singing *ekibegi*.[24]

"Then early the following morning his hunting companions came to tell him, `Get up, let's go and present this skin to *omukama*, because this skin is never worn by common folks.' That news too became a great puzzle to the famous hunter, but again he kept his thoughts to himself. And so he got up and went, but only because he had to, otherwise he wouldn't have gone. And so he and his companions set out for Bukindo, playing their *ekibegete* music from his home all the way to the compound of *omukama's* palace. As soon as the king's courtiers heard *ekibegete* music, they went to inform the king and said, `Long live our sovereign! We have come to inform you that we hear in the distance the music of people who have killed a dangerous wild animal,' to which the *omukama* answered, `If that's the case, bring out the drums and sound the palace *emilango*,'[25] since all those who killed fierce wild beasts and went to present the king with the skins of a lion or leopard or the short and long horns of a rhinoceros or elephant tusks were received by *emilango* thundering and rumbling in the king's palace and bringing out crowds of people in all their numbers to come and see how those killers of the brutes paraded their show before *omukama* as he reigned on his throne in the middle of the compound of his palace, the hunters dancing to the music of *emilango*, moving this way and that way and enacting their hunt in well marshaled ranks. Once in the palace compound Ketandala and his companions, therefore, dropped their *ekibegi* and danced to *emilango* music, moving their bodies as if they had no bones. The women congratulated them with presents of rounds of beads from their waists and *enerere*[26] from their arms and legs. Oh, what a show! Before long, *omukama* came from his house to the palace compound. The hunters went to pay their homage to the king and recounted to him how they hunted the animal and how they killed it. *Omukama* then asked them who the killer was, that is the one people call the first-hitter, as well as who it was who seconded him and who in turn followed the second-hitter, and then *omukama* gave order to the courtier in charge of preparing skins of such fierce beasts whenever they were killed in the country to go and peg and stretch for drying the leopard skin. During all that time *emilango* sounded without a break at the skillful hands of their drummers, calling to life forgotten joys from the hearts of those who had killed a fierce animal as well as those who hadn't in the ranks of the untiring dancers to whom women relentlessly sent peels of ululation:[27] *keye! keye! keye!*

"When the leopard killers finished making their presentation to *omukama*, they took up their *ekibegete* dance again, which was now joined in by women so that the men now danced with female partners[28] and the dance really warmed up as never before! *Omukama* watched them dance for a while then left and returned inside his palace. When the sun go to the time of the day when *omukama* takes his daytime meal, a slave of his came to tell them to stop dancing because the king was about to take his meal. And so the hunters left the compound of the palace and their whole group went to the home of the courtier where the headman of their village was received whenever he came to pay his village's homage to the king. There they were given sweet potatoes for lunch. After lunch, they saw two men come to that home carrying pots of banana beer. So that was it! The two pots of banana beer was a present from *omukama*, who was bringing the leopard killers something to drink. But they were too many for the beer and they had to content themselves with a sip each, not one of them slaking his thirsty enough. In fact some of them did not taste even a single drop of the beer, so that all they knew of it was the number of pots they saw and counted, but never found out how the beer itself tasted. No, they simply couldn't.

"Sometime in the afternoon a man came and said to them, `The king was taking a nap but he is now up and has even finished taking his bath and he has sent me to you and said: Go and tell them to dance.' On hearing that the humorous ones among the men who were dying to resume their dance hailed their king in his absence and said, 'Power to the son of kings, hail to the Sun, power to the Giver-of-habiliments!'[29] and they all got up to resume playing their *ekibegete* and their entire jubilant group flocked back to the palace compound, where *imilango* were again made to rumble and thunder, bringing to the dance women of every age and color in countless numbers like the eggs of a pregnant jigger burst open, from the woman with her child strapped on her back or trotting beside her to the one without child, until the crowd of people at the dance became countless like a farm of ants. Dear son, can you imagine a crowd of people so packed that if you threw a stick into it it would simply have no chance of ever dropping to the ground?"

The strapping youth answered back Kanwaketa: "*Aa*! Of course I can very well imagine that, just keep recounting"

And Kanwaketa continued: "As the afternoon advanced, at the time when the sun begins its descent to the horizon, *omukama* came out to the palace compound again to watch dancers. On seeing that, the sea of people fell on each other to come and bid good-evening to their sovereign. Then *ekibegete* crowd went back to their heroes' dance and the other part of the crowd trooped back to *emilango* dance. After a while *omukama* sent a courtier to tell all the leopard killers to come to him so that he could give them presents he wanted to give them and to tell *emilango* dancers to halt their dance. Once in front of the king, the hunters got down each on one knee and, with eyes lowered to the ground, hailed their king and said, `Power to you, the Upright-one!'

After a little while *omukama* called the real killer of the leopard, the one whose weapon struck the animal first, by his actual name. The man replied, `Yes, Sir! Great-giver!' When he appeared to be taking his time to get up from where he was, at once courtiers told him, `Up, quickly, go to the front!' The man went to the front and sat on one of his legs with the other leg folded and *omukama* told him, `I am giving you a heifer as your reward, because you are a real man.' Ketandala hailed his sovereign and said, `Power to you, the Sun! Power to you, Giver-of-habiliments!'[30] He then embraced the feet of the king as if kissing them and withdrew and went and sat down some distance away. *Omukama* then called the second and the third hunter to hit the leopard and they too did as Ketandala had done and were rewarded with a she-goat each.

"That done the headman of the hunters' village, who had accompanied them to the king's palace, said good-bye to *omukama* first and the hunters followed suit, after which they were given their cow and two goats and they drove their animals and returned home with their palace rewards.

"In Ketandala's home the men found a home completely empty of relish, and yet when a group of hunters kill a fierce animal they must be feted and feasted by the killer, their companion whose weapon struck the animal first! And so his companions, with raillery, reminded Ketandala of his obligation to them and told him to barter the heifer *omukama* awarded him and he bartered the female calf of a cow with herdsmen for two bulls. The man who seconded him in the killing of the leopard as well as the one who came third to him were also made to barter their two female goats for a he-goat each.

"The hunters made camp in that Ketandala's home for some four days, dancing their *ekibegete* day and night, feasting on what our ancestors called `free-bounty', where no obligation is owed in return. By the time the four days were over, they had emptied the poor fellow's grain store[31] of its millet and cleaned his sweet-potato field of its entire crop. As to the two bulls of his barter, they had slaughtered both and ate the meat to the very last bit. When they left Ketandala's home, they moved to the home of the man who seconded his killing of the leopard, where they stayed for one day, during which time they ate the he-goat of the man's barter, and on the following day they moved to the home of the man who came third in hitting the leopard before concluding their dance in celebration of killing a dangerous animal and that man too slaughtered his he-goat for them. Only then did they undergo the rite of fortification[32] and put behind them their great feat. And that's why our ancestors called the leopard hunter: `the hunter of meat for the wilderness and skins for the kings.' And so, young man, don't you now see well and clear what happened to Ketandala and how he toiled for nothing: how the meat of his leopard was left in the wilderness, its skin sent to the kings, his prize cow fed to the butcher's knife while his store of millet and his sweet potato crop completely disappeared overnight. And he wasn't even allowed to keep the skins of his two bulls they had slaughtered: he had to give away again one of the two skins to the medicine man who fortified him against the effects of killing that predator, since he had nothing to give him as fee for his fortification medicine."

The young man responded and said, "This is really great! Now I understand perfectly well! I am rendered speechless, because I see that Kikerewe is a language of great depth. I must also admit you our elders really know how to speak and don't talk anyhow like we young people!

Myombekere then told Kanwaketa, "My dear man, today we have come to ask you for some beer to drink determined to be like the fabled person named You-must-give-me, because we too are certainly not leaving this home before you give us some beer."

Kanwaketa responded, "I must admit you are right. I shouldn't feed you on all words and no food. It was this young man who delayed me giving you something by asking me for that explanation. As you know, the Mkerewe of old said: `A good word is like a medicinal herb: you learn it from others.' And so how could I deny this son of good people medicine as if he were an enemy of mine?"

Myombekere and his companions said, "You are indeed right; except we happen to be really thirsty and we would very much appreciate your giving us a taste of whatever little your royal visitors left you. Anything at all will do. We are however not demanding it of you like those other visitors of yours. We are people who are just appealing to your kindness with no claim to anything of yours. So please treat us as you see fit."

Kanwaketa called a son of his and told him, "Go and bring these men that miserable slender-necked pot I have been left with so that they too will have eaten something in this home." His son brought the pot of beer and Kanwaketa presented it to the men and said, "Please welcome, dear brothers, to this bit of beer. In fact it is only thanks to the fact that the men who were here heard there was another brew yonder up hill that you found me still having even this bit."

Myombekere said, "Praises to you! To give a little is better than to give nothing. Those who were here before us ate their destined share, so let us too eat ours."

And so the men drank beer and word led to word.

They hadn't finished the beer when there arrived in the home a group of more than eight people. Kanwaketa was convinced it was the crown-prince who had come back with his followers. However, it turned out these were other people altogether. They didn't even bother to take seats. As soon as they saw Kanwaketa, they called him aside, to whisper something to him out of other people's hearing and told him, "Brother, don't think we have come to maybe beg for something from you . We have something of value of our own with which we want to buy beer from you, if you have some left. We were playing *olusoro*[33] board game with this man here and when he lost to me to the tune of six waist-strings of large green beads, I told these other companions of ours, `Tell me where we can go and get some beer, I'll buy some for you to drink.' That's when they told me, `Come on, let's go to Kanwaketa's. Today is the drinking day of his banana beer, that is if you are not kidding us.' And that's what brings us here, my dear brother. And when we saw you over there with company, we said to ourselves, `It is much better to take him aside and ask him when he is all alone than asking him before such a gathering of people, since it may very well be he doesn't want it known to some of them that he has any more beer left.'"

Kanwaketa told them, "Go and take a seat out of the sun under that shade of a tree first. In the meanwhile, give me what you have so that I can first go and ask the mistress of this home, since she is the would-be wearer. Maybe she doesn't like this type of beads."

The men gave him the strings of beads, the whole six of them, and he took them to his wife. As soon as his wife's eyes fell on the beads she jumped about with joy and asked her husband, "Where did you get such beautiful beads?"

Kanwaketa answered her, "The men over there are the ones who have just brought them, and they say they want to buy beer with them."

His wife asked him, "And how many pots of beer do they want for them?" and Kanwaketa answered, "They want just one pot of beer for the whole lot of six waist-strings."

His wife said, "It's a pity we don't have the beer, otherwise I would say give them. In fact this would have been greatly overpricing on our part," and her husband rejoined, "If you like them, let me buy them. As you know, we now have remaining three pots of beer. Let me give them one out of the three, rather than give the beer to people to drink free, when something of value like this has come our way. Then we will be left with our own spare pot plus the pot for my fellow banana plantation owners to drink."

And so he called the men and gave them their one pot of beer and gave the strings of beads to his wife, who went to deposit them in her *ekitwaro*[34] box. The men carried their pot of beer into Kanwaketa's banana plantation and drank it until they emptied it and went back to their homes.

Chapter XXXII

NOTES

1. *Olusika*: See note 25 of Chapter XXIX.
2. *Emihotora*: See note 2 chapter XXX.
3. Mwibara: Ukerewe mainland. See Introduction.
4. *Enzusi*: See note 4 Chapter XXXI.
5. *Emigonzo*: See note 4 of Chapter VI.
6. The Islands: For the minor islands of Ukerewe see Introduction.
7. The Wakerewe believed that witches and witch doctors use zombies to cultivate their crop fields at nighttime.
8. *Omukungu*: See note 3 of Chapter III.
9. Here again Kitereza forgets a detail of his long story: when this incident happens in Chapter IV of the novel, Ntamba's is made to pay just the one goat of *endamuro*, judgement fee.
10. *Ensendekelezya*: See note 29 of Chapter XXIX.
11. *Embiso*: See note 3 Chapter VII.
12. For the process of brewing banana beer see chapter VII.
13. *Omukama*: See note 26 of Chapter II.
14. *Omusiba*: See note 9 of Chapter XXXI.
15. *Enengo*: In the note for his Swahili translation of his novel Kitereza writes: "The *omukama*'s house in which he rested during daytime, chatting with his wives and select company while drinking beer," and, by extension, a rest house in a homestead or one used as such on an occasion.
16. *Abakama*: Plural for *omukama* in 13 above.
17. *Obutaga*: See note 4 of Chapter II.
18. For the significance of the "poison tasting " share of a drink see note 12 chapter III.
19. *Olusabuzyo*: Here a wooden container for drinking banana beer with. See note 12 of Chapter I.
20. *Omugurwe*: See note 30 of Chapter II.
21. *Bwaa*! See note 3 Chapter IV.
22. Ketandala: "Leopard-killer."
23 *Ensimba, emondo*: Wild animal of the cat family whose colorful skins were reserved articles of wear for the wives of the king. See note 7 of Chapter IX and note 9 of Chapter X.
24. *Ekibegi* or *ekibegete*: Name of a warriors' dance performed to celebrate the killing of a leopard or a lion.

25. *Emilango*: See note 11 of Chapter XIII.

26. *Enerere*: See note 23 Chapter VI.

27. *Akahira*: See note 11 of Chapter IX.

28. *Kusinja*: A man dancing with a female partner.

29. For many other attributes of *omukama* see notes 33 of chapter XII and 12 of Chapter XXXI.

30. See note 29 above.

31. *Ekitala*: See note 18 of Chapter I.

32. *Kutimbika*: To fortify a person with potent medicine against the potential harm of spilling human blood or killing a beast which spills human blood. It was believed that without such fortification the person concerned would lose his or her mind.

33. *Olusoro*: See note 8 of Chapter VIII.

34. *Ekitwaro*: See note 19 of Chapter VIII.

Chapter XXXIII

NTULANALWO GOES TO KALIBATA'S HOME TO MARRY HIS DAUGHTER: PAYING BRIDE-PRICE, BRINGING THE BRIDE HOME, BULIHWALI AS THE NEWLYWEDS' FOOD-TASTING MAID[1]

Myombekere remembered that his daughter Bulihwali, Ntulanalwo's sister, who was being brought up at her grandfather Nanwero's home, had to be fetched, because he and his wife felt she should be the newlywed's maid for the food tasting rite of her brother's wedding. He reminded his wife of that and the issue was settled and Bugonoka prepared herself for the journey and the following day she duly set off, carrying with her a bunch of ripe plantains, of the type called *kasankara*, which she would cook at her parents' home for her daughter to eat on their journey back. She arrived at her parents' home and they all exchanged greetings and news of their welfare with each other and finished, and then she told her parents, "I have come to inform you that Ntulanalwo's wedding is approaching, and also to fetch Bulihwali."

"And why do you want to take the child with you?"

"Don't you think she should be the newlyweds' food-tasting maid at her brother's wedding?"

"Yes, that's right. You are doing the right thing. And when is the wedding?"

"Myombekere yesterday was told by our in-laws to stay away today and tomorrow and on the day after tomorrow to go and fetch the bride's escort[2] and the day following that to give his legs a bit of rest and on the next day to send somebody to find out when the wedding is to take place."

Nanwero told his wife, "Nkwanzi, you'd better get ready. Send for Barongo tomorrow to come and accompany you to the wedding celebrations." To which Bugonoka said, "Yes indeed, Lweganwa should go and call her first thing in the morning and tell her to come with her daughter."

The following morning Bugonoka woke up early to cook ripe plantains she had brought as Bulihwali's journey food. Then Nkwanzi put a present of millet in an *ekitukuru*[3] basket for her daughter, just enough for her to carry on the long journey, where she would also have to carry her daughter who was still too young to walk all the way for such a long distance. Nanwero on his part came out with two Wazinza[4] hoes, the bride-price articles of those days, and stuck them in the basket of millet.

Myombekere was simply overjoyed to see his daughter who he hadn't seen for a long time. As soon as Bugonoka unstrapped the child from her back, he took her in his hands and then placed her on his lap, overwhelmed with happiness at seeing his daughter grown a bit bigger than she was in the days following her weaning, and only when he had seen his fill of her did he let the child go to her mother in the house. Shortly after that Kanwaketa's wife happened to come by and she too carried the child in her hands as soon as she saw her and exclaimed, "*Yu!* How chubby the child has become and how fast she is growing! You would think something is stretching her out!"

Bugonoka rejoined and said, "You say what I would say, for I too have a feeling that may be when you live with a child in the same home you never notice how fast he or she is growing. With her, when I saw her last when she fell sick shortly after we weaned her and I visited her, she wasn't anything like this, and so this time on seeing her I was simply amazed!"

The following day Myombekere was off early in the morning to fetch the bride's escort. He found the woman at home and told the escort of his son's bride, whose name was Munegera, "What has brought me to see you is this: the day before yesterday Kalibata told me to come and see you. He said: `Go and tell my sister Munegera to come and be my daughter's bridal escort.' And so if you are going today, that's your wish, but tomorrow is when you would be needed, since it is on the day after tomorrow that I will go to find out when the wedding is to take place."

Munegera answered, "Today I will have women in the neighborhood help me grind flour to take with me and then go over there tomorrow. You have done your job, and so don't go back worrying that perhaps I won't go. There's no need for you to worry because I am certainly going, for who have you ever heard refuse an invitation to eat?"

And with that Myombekere went back to his home. I believe you all know the Kikerewe saying: "The bridegroom's home celebrates a wedding long before the bride's people." And so in Myombekere's home everybody became consumed with the wedding celebrations fever, which could be seen in everything there, I am telling you! Ntulanalwo too was here and there and everywhere, fetching his aunts, that is Myombekere's sisters, and the many and sundry of their relatives his father and mother sent him to. Millet was taken out of their grain store,5 winnowed and cleaned of all sand and dust and sent for grinding to the women of neighboring homes as is always done, ready for the celebrations of Ntulanalwo's wedding, and every female relative of his who was invited assembled in Myombekere's home, and since some of the women came with their unweaned children, the home became one really big and noisy gathering of people. Among the assembled women, those God created with beautiful voices were already trying out their voices, singing low, testing their voices to find out how they would sing for their Ntulanalwo's wedding, with their listeners taking them up and answering the choruses of their songs. And as their singing really got into them, the singers would raise their voices, and likewise their choruses, in answer to which women drumming on folded rawhides would really heat up, as people gathered from everywhere to watch their performance. Many in that crowd answered well to the parable of this country which says: "Love them all and let music choose one for you!" We are not calling them marauders, oh no! Thank God! We are only saying that not every man in that crowd of people at the women dance came there to merely listen to the beautiful voices of the singers: the young men came to look for women to flirt with. We don't want to hide the truth from you like the son-in-law who won't mention his mother-in-law's name even though everybody knows he knows it!6 No, we don't, for the truth of the matter is that dance does not only warm up the spirit but the heart as well.

On the day he was to learn of when the wedding would take place, early in the morning Myombekere sent a person to Kalibata's home and when his envoy arrived there he told Kalibata, "Praises to you , Sir! I am an envoy sent here by Myombekere who told me: `Go and find out whether the wedding is today, then come back quickly to inform us early so that we too will know what to do.'"

Kalibata answered him, "Go and tell them that the bride's escort came yesterday, and so, if all is well with them, the wedding is today. Let them come in the evening, after their womenfolk have arrived, since the women always come to weddings first and their men follow suit. "

The envoy said, "Yes indeed, that's how we see things done in our Ukerewe, and we too won't depart from our people's way of doing things. And so I must be off. Escort me so that I can report back quickly what you have told me and those over there too can have time to prepare themselves." Kalibata escorted him and he left.

And so in Myombekere's home that became a really busy day. On the side of Bugonoka and her fellow women, others fell to grinding millet, others turned to making the wedding amulet for Ntulanalwo to wear after getting married, others to uprooting grass for making on the floor of the house the bed-spread on which the newlyweds would sit, others to drawing water from the lake and attending to all the other chores of womenfolk on such occasions, like washing cups[7] for the newlyweds and their companions to drink water with and so on. At the same time Myombekere with his fellow men on their side too were attending to their preoccupations. Myombekere dispatched his nephews to go and collect firewood or fetch firewood logs from the woods or split the logs already in the home into firewood with which to cook the wedding feast and sent yet others to the lakeshore to buy fish, because, as our elders said: "Before you invite vultures fill your tray[8] with rats." Myombekere's other important task of the day was to get together the articles of bride-price the bridegrooms wedding party would take with them to their in-laws. Ntulanalwo himself, with the help of a number of his companions, was off to look for people who would escort him to his father-in-law's home for the wedding. In the homes he went he invited whoever he found home, whether she was an unmarried woman[9] or a married one, a young bachelor or a married man, to them all he said, "Ladies and gentlemen, come and accompany me to my wedding. Save me from drowning in my deep waters and let me live to save you from drowning in your shallow ones." The wedding escort he thus managed to put together comprised of fifteen men, with Ntulanalwo himself the sixteenth, and twenty-one girls and women, that is altogether a total of thirty-seven people.

When it got to the time of the day when a bridegroom and his companions usually go into a man's home to marry his daughter,

Myombekere sent ahead the women party with some five iron hoes. Then after sometime the men followed, with three goats, with Myombekere reminding the men as they were leaving: "As to the bride-price, you'll present that tomorrow and not today, to Kalibata, in the presence of the people who will have gathered around him."

With that Ntulanalwo got hold of his bow and, escorted by his companions, went to marry.

They had been on their journey for quite a while when a certain elderly man, whose name was Katetwanfune, the man Myombekere had chosen to lead the wedding procession, joked with Ntulanalwo and said, "Today Ntulanalwo will curse the night and say: `Will it never dawn!' and then tomorrow he will curse the sun and say: `Will it never set and let me be what I want to be with my wife?'"

"My goodness! Hear this man's incorrigible ranting! *Aa*! How did you discover all that in my heart?" Ntulanalwo retorted.

"I imagine it has to be so, because if that wasn't what you are thinking you wouldn't be going to marry." In that very moment the man's eyes fell on Ntulanalwo's cow skin robe he was wearing and he saw that he was wearing it upside down: the hair of the skin to his body and the meat-side of the skin on the outside and he said, "Well, my dear man, what do you say! You don't want to admit what I say about you and yet here you are, so overwhelmed with happiness you are wearing your robe inside out. Is that really how people normally dress, the hair of their skin-wear to the body and the meat-side of the animal skin outside?"

"I must have just got it wrong. I thought it was all right and was completely unaware of this."

The rest of his companions burst out laughing and added, "Today we would indeed have become the laughing stock of the whole world, if on arriving the people over there had found their son-in-law dressed in this strange way! For on such occasions the bridegroom is always the center of attraction, the one person everybody is looking at, over whom people are beckoning each other and pointing him out to those who haven't seen him. Today we would have indeed disgraced ourselves in broad daylight! And all of us, without exception, since people would have said, `His wedding companions escorting him are also nothing but a bunch of hoodlums, without a single sensible person among them!'"

A man called Buzebe among them asked, "Are you all telling me that the only thing you see amiss with Myombekere's son is the way he is wearing his robe?" to which his companions answered, "What else is amiss?" and Buzebe told them, "If you observe, you will see that he is also holding his bow upside down, the end point entwined with cord pointing to the ground and the end which normally touches the ground pointing upwards."

Ntulanalwo said, "What's wrong with me today, gentlemen?"

And Katetwanfune answered him, "What else can it be but the excitement of getting married, which is making you do all those strange things?"

Ntulanalwo agreed, "Maybe that's true, because I don't remember my mind ever being so distraught!"

To which the other man answered, "And why shouldn't you be distraught when today all that matters to you is your bride, whether they will actually give her to you?"

In Kalibata's home the men found their female companions already arrived, seated in a separate group of their own in the home. People in the home came to relieve them of their weapons and took the goats they came with and tethered them on poles of grain store stands. The guests then got seated and exchanged greetings with the people in that home, and after that fell completely silent: *di*! When Ntulanalwo and his companions talked at all, it was only in whispers, otherwise only the inmates of that home talked. Kalibata's unchallenged voice could be heard from one corner of his home to another, repeatedly calling out aloud to the women: "Get food ready quickly, so that our in-laws can eat and people can begin to dance." The women redoubled their effort to get ready the first serving of food, which would be for the people of the home, and in no time food was ready and the people of Kalibata's home together with those who had come to celebrate with them the giving away of their daughter were served first.

Before the bride ate, the bridegroom was called inside the house to join his wife-to-be for the ceremony of tasting ritual food[10] at the cooking stones of his mother-in-law's kitchen. Once in the house, Ntulanalwo was told to kneel with his bride on a block of *omulindi*[11] cork wood. The two of them then bent down and put out their tongues and licked crop seeds and other foods the bride and bridegroom taste in the ceremony of *kurumya*: a bottom-of-the-pot crust of *obwita*,[12] some raw *enkole*[13] beans, some grains of *endwero*[14] millet and a piece of cooked fillet of *embozu*[15] catfish.

The ceremony over, the girl returned to her place on her bridal-spread in the inner-room of the house and sat down and was given food to eat with her entourage, among whom was her paternal aunt who was her official bride's escort, and Ntulanalwo went back to his place in the gathering of his companions outside.

After Kalibata and his male companions were served food and women in the house too finished eating, the women turned to cooking for the bridegroom and his wedding companions, and pots of *obwita* were cooked in each of the many houses of that home. When food was ready, Kalibata told his sons, "Tell our in-laws to form a meal round and serve them food." His sons did as they were bid and their in-laws seated themselves properly in two meal rounds, the visiting men forming theirs first and then their female companions forming their separate round close by.[16] A whole pot of water with several cups for drinking water was brought at the in-laws eating place and water was poured in two rather big washbasin[17] and one was given to the men and the other one placed in front of the women, and the in-laws washed their hands and finished and the washbasins were dragged away and put aside. At once Kalibata's oldest son went inside the men's meal circle and some people passed him dishes of *obwita* and pots of fish and he placed them in front of the men and then did the same for the women round. Then people passed him plates[18] on which to serve fish and, finally, they passed him the son-in-law's special pot of relish and after that he invited their in-laws to eat: "Please welcome, sons-in-law, this is all we could manage,"   to which the bridegroom and all his companions answered, "Father-in-law, the only important thing to us is your giving us a wife." Kalibata's son then, from inside the meal round where he still was, served their guests relish by putting fish on the plates and the visitors ate their meal. That was the day when even the women ate *emamba*[19] mistaking it for smoke-cured *embozu* catfish, for that *emamba* was so well prepared and so well seasoned, what can I tell you! The milk-woman who made the butter with which that fish was seasoned and likewise the woman who cooked the fish will never have their like again in this world! Oh yes, the good old Kikerewe cuisine is gone forever!

The bridegroom's party were still eating when a child among the bride's company made a sound as if stifling a laugh. Kalibata left his place at the courtyard fireplace[20] of his home where he was seated, for it was already dark in the evening, and went to the door of the house from which the stifled laugh of the girl was heard, really raging mad! I'm telling you!

When he got there he thundered angrily: "*Aa*! Which bitch dares to giggle while our sons-in-law are eating! Is that the manners your mother taught you, you worthless creature? Do that again, you empty-headed thing, and you'll see me! What impertinence!" Complete silence fell over all the inmates of that house: *di*!

When the bridegroom and his companions finished eating and the food utensils were taken away, a woman among them confided to another woman in whispers, "My dear woman, I must admit that I was puzzled by that fish which was seasoned with butter, because when I ate it, and ate some more of it and some more again, I encountered what felt like the skin of *emamba*. Yes, dear, here it is, I still have it."

Her companion felt in her hand and touched it and exclaimed with a big: "*Yu*! Why don't you throw it away?"

Unfortunately a man in the male side of their bridegroom's party heard that last remark and said, "You shouldn't throw away whatever it is you speak of throwing away! It simply isn't done. What outrageous mischief in women!" He thought that they were speaking of maybe some sizable piece of fish, which he thought, rather than throwing it away simply because they had eaten their fill, they could give it to him and he would gladly guzzle it. The woman who held it, rather in jest, handed him the fish skin, convinced that he would throw it away once he realized that it was bare fish skin with no flesh on it. As it happened that man was rather funny and not altogether right in the head, and no sooner was the fish skin in his hands than he showed it to the rest of the men and the other men said, "It looks like the skin of *emamba*!"

The women adamantly disputed the men's claim until the men said, "Since you are bent on disputing the fact, why don't you drop the matter and let us give the skin to Katetwanfune to keep, so that tomorrow when it is daylight we can examine it well. Whatever it turns out to be, that's fine with us," and the women agreed: "All right!"

As soon as the in-laws finished eating, since those who had come to dance for the wedding celebrations were already assembled, the bride's female companions at once set on foot the *lwakalera*[21] dance. Those with beautiful voices rang out and the rolls of rawhides resounded as never before and *lwakalera* dancers moved their bodies as if they had no bones in them as the maracas players rattled their instruments and the women spectators rewarded the performers with ululation[22] from every side: *keye! keye! keye!* As soon as *lwakalera* dancers concluded their turn dancers of other kinds of dances started dancing their current dances of those years.

After a while, Ntulanalwo's sisters-in-law came to fetch him and took him to the bed they had prepared for him and he retired for the night. As for the rest of his companions, they were given a hard time throughout the night by the bride's party: where they were, all night long they were sprayed with water, cow-urine, urine, sand! And so for them they passed a night of no sleep and no rest, so that even the good meal they had eaten became to them a bane rather than a blessing, especially to those with weak stomachs, who found themselves belching like people who had overeaten! And as the night advanced, at the dead of the night when wild creatures roam the wilderness, the boys and girls as well as married women and married men kept on disappearing as if going to relieve themselves in the fields but apparently not for that! They had other matters of their own to take care of! Shortly after that people heard loud noises coming from those fields followed by the sound of the blow of a stick: *tu*! Well, well! A certain man who had come to the dance with his wife had caught his wife with another man!

Everybody flocked to the fields, to see and hear out the couple. But when people questioned the husband, "Tell us, since you beat your wife this way, who is the man you say you found your wife with; can you identify him?" the husband answered, "When I looked for my wife at the dance and could not find her anywhere, I said to myself, `Let me look for her over there in the fields,' and when I walked out of the home and came across boys and girls, paired off and standing here and there or squatting in some dark nooks in the cow-trail fence, when I saw and realized who they were, I left them alone. From there I kept on walking further afield, for a little while, and when I got to that place over there I heard people whispering. On walking on a bit further I heard movements of people in the grass and I said to myself, `Listen well, you!' Then I heard the pair speak in clear voices. That was when I heard this wife of mine here telling her man, `You are the one who delayed coming, we don't have any more time now. We must return to the dance at once, lest my husband begins looking for me and discovers I am absent. And he is bound to do that any time now, because the dance will soon end, it's time for us to go home.' And when I heard that I shot out and went straight for them. As it happened, apparently the man had heard me coughing and he was apparently already up and on his feet and so I had just got to them when I saw the fellow sprint and run away. That is when I raised the alarm and caught this woman by the hand, so that she too wouldn't run away from me like that creature of a fellow. See for yourselves, here is the bedding they were lying on. And I have tried as hard as I could to make her tell me who is the man she was with here with her telling me nothing but some made up story: `I had come to relieve myself and was just about to squat here when you arrived and said: I have caught you committing adultery, when the truth is that there was no man whatsoever with me here.' That's why I am beating her this way."

On hearing that the people who had rushed to the scene judged his case this way: "Listen to reason, both of you. You man, stop beating your wife, because you are beating her without cause: you cannot say she committed adultery when you don't even know the man you are accusing her of committing adultery with. And since you don't know the man, adultery would be impossible to prove by simply showing some bedding, in a case where there is no collaborating eye-witness." And with that people returned to their dance, some saying as they went back, "This is a man who is jealous of his wife beyond measures!" Some others even kind of ridiculed the man and said, "If I were as jealous of my wife as that man is of his, I wouldn't take her to a dance with me. No, I would leave her at home for fear if I went with her I would disgrace myself in public the way this fellow has disgraced himself today."[23]

As soon as the signs of dawn appeared on the horizon, the women of the bride's party called the bridegroom's female companions and said, "You must wake up and sing. You cannot remain here in silence as if you did not come for a wedding," and the bridegroom's female companions got up and assembled at the door of the house in which the bride was and sang the song of welcoming the break of a new day:

> *Lead singer*: When the new day is about to dawn
> *Chorus*: It cuts asunder eyelashes.
> *L. S.*: From the sky, when it's about to dawn
> *C.*: It cuts asunder eyelashes.
> *L. S.*: From the deep dark night, when its about to dawn
> *C.*: It cuts asunder eyelashes.
> *L. S.*: When the day of many words is about to dawn
> *C.*: It cuts asunder eyelashes.
> *L. S.*: When the day of many jokes is about to dawn
> *C.*: It cuts asunder eyelashes.

And so on and on until it was finally sunrise and a bright new day.

Then the singers took a short break and those who wanted to relieve themselves went to do so. As to the women of the bride's party, some took pots and calabashes to go and draw water while others went to collect cow-urine for bathing the bride and cleaning the soles of her feet and for washing *enerere*[24] she would wear on her feet and on her arms.

After that the women of the bridegroom's party joined their male companions, and that was when Katetwanfune told them, "Come here, so that we can settle our last night's dispute." He then showed them the fish skin they had given him the previous night and said, "Here is your fish skin over which you were arguing with us last night." The women looked at it and found it was indeed the skin of *emamba* and became really ashamed of themselves and felt disgraced and exposed, with nothing to say in their defense. The men told them, "What do you say now? Come on, let's see you vomit! Don't we always tell you that you women do eat men's relish surreptitiously like thieves with you claiming you never? Here you are now! Today your secret is all out!"[25]

Ntulanalwo too woke up and his sisters-in-law brought him water and he washed his face and then he joined his companions and sat down.

Finally Katetwanfune saw Kalibata come to seat outside and the men in his home gather around him and he and his companions took the articles they had come with as bride-price and placed them in front of their in-laws and he told Kalibata, "Father-in-law, what we have is what you see in front of you. Please accept our presents and give us a wife. We are, above all, people who believe in what our ancestors said: `Bride-price never gives you a wife, what gives you a wife is a kind word.' And so, father-in-law, the woman with no buttocks also undresses,[26] and because of that we don't actually have much to say, except that our only hope lies in your kind word and the kind word of these noble people gathered here."

Kalibata told the men who had gathered in his home to witness the bride-price he was being given for his daughter: "There you are, gentlemen. What is already in the open cannot be discussed in secrecy. The man has finished what he had to say and it is now up to you to say whether you find the bride-price adequate or not, so that whatever you will not be satisfied with can be given back to the owners."

An old man among Kalibata's people said, "What can I say, since my eyes no longer see clearly!" His companion laughed, and he rejoined, "Well, I must say so because at my age the torch of my eyes no longer lights things as clearly as that of the eyes of you newly-mint people," and the others agreed, "Indeed, we cannot dispute that." Then the old man went on: "If I am not mistaken, I see some three goats." The others said, "Yes, there are three goats: one is a she-goat that hasn't calved and two are he-goats." And the old man went on, "And so this young she-goat, which is already pregnant with a calf, is for Kalibata, for rearing, and then one he-goat is a paternal parenthood present for Kalibata's father, and the other he-goat is a maternal parenthood present for the father of Tibwenigirwa, the bride's mother. As for the bride's escort, she will receive her present on the other side on the day she will leave the bridegroom's home, that's when she will be given her goat. And the five hoes I see correspond well with the number of the entitled. Maybe what needs to be done is for you to examine them for defects: the one in which you will detect weak spots in the metal, put that one aside, let it go back to the owners, to be replaced by another one at some later day. That's all."

Some among the men present asked the old man, "And who are the entitled for the five hoes? Please explain to us, old one?"

And the old man said, "To explain I would say the distribution of those five hoes is as follows: One hoe is a present for the baby-carrying *engozi*[27] straps of Tibwenigirwa, the mother of the bride Netoga. The second hoe is bride-price for this home, what we in our old people's way call the hoe for the voice of the homestead. The third hoe is for the bride's womanhood, the hoe for cutting under the bride's steps. The fourth is for the bride's ointment maid. And the fifth hoe goes to the bride's ululation lady. Those are the main entitled recipients of the bride-price articles you will normally see at a wedding.[28] The only required item remaining are arrows, which you should be given at the time the bride is about to come out of the house, and then the job is done. The milk-sucker's[29] present you hear of, that one is given to its entitled recipient over there at the bridegroom's home, after the bride has lived in the home for some months, or even a whole year. And that relative of the bride too receives the present of a young she-goat, even though a he-goat is also acceptable. Do you know understand or do you still have questions?"

"We understand, old one," his listeners answered.

That over, some of the men present put out their hands to examine the hoes for metal defects. A man would get hold of a hoe by its spike, shake it to feel how weighty it was, inspect its metal looking for weak spots with the eye of an expert and, finding none, he would then place the hoe on top of his head, still holding it by its spike, and then shoot it with the middle finger of his right had this way: *ta*! and at once he would hear it ring out: *dee*! and the others present on hearing the hoe ring out that way would say, "That one is forged right indeed! Omurongo[30] of Matale of Uzinza did a real master's job!" The men went through all the five hoes with each and every one of them ringing out: *dee*! that way and without detecting in them any weak spot or any other metal defect which would make them when struck give out a dull sound: *duu*! and sang the praises of the hoes and said, "These would indeed be welcome allies with which to pay crop fields a visit!"

Katetwanfune and his male companion finished presenting their bride-price and withdrew and rejoined their gathering, where they had left Ntulanalwo seated.

When the sun warmed up fairly brightly, Kalibata called out to the women in the house and said, "Get ready whatever you have decided to do, for you women never seem to be in a hurry. These people here passed a sleepless night and now you want to keep them here the whole day long for no reason! Do you intend to prepare them a meal before they leave?"

Inside the house the women gathered around the bride exclaimed with a big: "*Yu*!" which Kalibata heard and said, "Did I do something wrong by telling you what I said? Or did I perhaps speak in some foreign language you don't understand?"

Hearing her husband say that, Tibwenigirwa told Munegera, "Dear woman, you have better plead with your brother for us before he loses his temper and let him know that we too are about ready and that we are a bit behind only because we had been waiting for those who had gone to draw water."

Munegera quickly got up and went to the door porch and told Kalibata, "No, my dear brother, you didn't do anything wrong. You are right in telling us what you said, for how can your concern for our visitors be something wrong, my dear brother? Only we were still waiting for those who had gone to draw water for bathing your daughter, but now we too are almost ready."

Kalibata on his side in answer to his sister said, "And so you are the courageous one sent to confront me! Are you taking me for a fool who doesn't know anything? Well, let me disappoint you and speak out, because I never like being contradicted by a woman, and that's the truth. Look at how what you are saying is betraying you! I saw you collecting cow-urine a long time ago, shouldn't you by now have finished your so-called bathing?

And so don't you imagine that inside that house is today out of bounds to me. You just wait, let me escort this visitor of mine and then I'll be back and you'll see me. *Hee!* So you better hurry up or you'll have to deal with me!" The women became completely silent and when they spoke again spoke only with their voices lowered all the way down to the ground, as if in whispers, as in the meanwhile Kalibata himself left to escort that visitor of his he had spoken of.

Where Ntulanalwo was he could see and feel that his father-in-law was a real man in his own home, a red-hot brand of a man and not one of those pushover males who are afraid of their wives on their daughters' wedding day and daren't raise their voices in favor of the bridegroom and his party, who as a result could leave the man's home with their bride only after night has already fallen, the type of men who would go along with the confusion the bride's mother causes when, on hearing her daughter shed crocodile tears over her impending marriage, on seeing her sniffling over and over with her endlessly runny nose, she encourages her to let her tears pour down by whining along: "My only baby is going for ever, oh dear friends! I hear her crying right inside my womb, oh dear friends! I tremble and I feel dizzy, because my child is leaving me and going to other people's home!"

As Kalibata left to escort his visitor the women of his home began on their ritual of preparing the bride, which included bathing her with water and cow-urine and rubbing clean the soles of her feet with a toilet stone; paring her fingernails and toenails and shaving wedge-marks[31] into her forehead; shaving off her under the clothes (pubic) hair, smearing her entire body with cow butter, from her head to the sole of her foot, and making her wear on her legs and on her arms her bride's *enerere* and beads around her waist and across her chest and her bride's band-and-veil[32] of intricate patterns of multicolored tiny beads over her face; putting on her her bride's neck amulet, likewise decorated with patterns of multicolored tiny beads; perfuming her with *omugazu,*[33] after chasing form the house all unmarried girls and boys lest bridal perfume should give them bad luck and kill their chances of getting married in time.

As soon as the women were through with their preparations, the men in the bride's party began to pester Ntulanalwo asking him to give them presents of arrows until they had deprived him of all his arrows, leaving him with his bow and its cord and nothing else, after which they turned on Katetwanfune and the bridegroom's other male companions, depriving them of their arrows in a really serious scuffle, to the extent that some of the bridegroom's companions who tried to resist surrendering their arrows were seriously injured, their hands bruised as if they had been burnt with hot water, their palms full of wounds and cuts and scratches from arrowheads! And yet they couldn't even lose their temper! Even in the case of the bridegroom's men who had come to the wedding with borrowed arrows, their noisy protesting and arguing didn't help them, because the men of the bride's party were answering them back by telling them: "What are you taking us for? Some idiots who have never been to a wedding as the bridegroom's companions? If the arrows aren't yours, we are taking them all the same. Let the bridegroom come and redeem them from us later on if he chooses to, and if not he will know how to pay the owners on your behalf." What's more, many of those people who confiscated arrows from the bridegroom and his male companions weren't even Kalibata's relatives, who could at least claim to be entitled to the presents; not at all. It appears many of them were just people from his neighborhood. But that didn't prevent them from saying, "If you came here with the idea that Kalibata was some unfortunate poor fellow with no relatives of his, that's too bad for you! You will go back to your homes with nothing but your bows."

When that commotion over arrows went too far, Kalibata, who was now back home, called out with a thundering voice and said, "You who are demanding arrows from our in-laws have to stop now, because you have carried matters beyond bounds. Look, you have wounded some people in their palms and all over their hands. Arrows are things of value, and where have you ever seen things of value growing wild on trees for people to just pick? Whatever the case, I want you to stop. I don't want this kind of behavior in my home."[34]

After that, inside the house one of the bride-price hoes was put on a handle and then the bride's mother, Tibwenigirwa, took the hoe and cut the earthen house floor with it once and the bride stepped over that mark of the hoe on the ground, and mother and daughter repeated that three times. Then the women in the house called Kalibata and said, "Tell little Mahendeka to come, we want him here; but tell our sons-in-law to give him an arrow."

As soon as Mahendeka went into the house, the bridegroom's companions all go to their feet, ready to receive their bride without delay. Unfortunately for them that time hadn't yet come, and the bridegroom and his companions were kept on their feet until their legs began to pain, until the sun had burned and scorched them thoroughly! Even Ntulanalwo, who was left standing in the shade of a grain store, sweated until he was all wet. And yet there was no sign of Mahendeka coming out of that house. What happened was that as soon as the little boy entered the house he was given *obwita* on which his sister Netoga had pinched a few times and then left the food alone.

Outside the house the women of the bridegroom's party were now singing a *lwakalera* song, as some of them danced moving their bodies as if they had no bones in them. They were singing a lullaby for the bride, babying her and telling her not to cry, the way a small baby-girl is babied in the house of her father and mother:

Lead singer: *Yee*! Our only child.

Chorus: She longs for what she wants, *yeye*!

L. S.: Maybe she wants some cassava.

C.: She longs for what she wants, *yeye*!

L. S.: Maybe she wants some bananas.

C.: She longs for what she wants, *yeye*!

L. S.: Maybe she wants some sweet potatoes.

C.: She longs for what she wants, *yeye*!

Then in the house the ointment maid and the ululation lady asked for their fees and they were each given a new Wazinza hoe and were out of themselves with joy and demonstrated their happiness by jumping about and running here and there inside the house, with the bride's ululation lady ringing out peels of ululation! In that very moment Mahendeka, the bride's little brother who was to raise up the bride, linked the little finger of his right hand to the little finger of the right hand of his sister Netoga while holding in his left hand a barbed arrow he had been given by the bridegroom's men as his fee for raising the bride, and then told his sister: "Stand up and go and get married!" and led her from the inner-room and brought her to the door of the house. As to Netoga herself, tears poured down her eyes in torrents, mixing with the oil ointment on her chest to look like dripping sweat.

The men of the bridegroom's party too now stood crowded at the door with their female companions, but only out of sheer excitement, with no official function there, and when Katetwanfune, their designated leader, also came to the door he pushed all of them out of his way and without further ado swept the bride from the ground and placed her on his shoulder and ran as fast as he could. Netoga struggled on his carrier's shoulder as if protesting and wanting to be left alone so that she could return to her parents' home, but Katetwanfune paid no heed to her and, holding the bride fast and steady on his shoulder, he run on. *We!* Netoga then burst out crying loud, wailing like a mourner, with the bridegroom's other companions on their part running after her, accompanying her with endless shouts of jubilation! As for Ntulanalwo, he was following behind, walking at a snail pace in the company of the bride's escort, his female father-in-law,35 who too was dripping with oil like the bride herself.

The carriers of the bride pushed on until they got to a considerable distance and then put her down and waited for her escort and Ntulanalwo. When those two arrived, the bride's escort told the carrier of her niece, "You must carry my child carefully, lest you injure her with your shoulder bone in her stomach, since you are carrying her like a bundle of dead weight. It would be better you carried her seated on your shoulders," meaning with one leg on top her carrier's left shoulder and the other leg on top his right shoulder, his head in between her legs. The bride's escort added further instructions to her niece's carriers: "When you get to a river, don't carry her across; put her down and wait for us to arrive first."

And so when the bridegroom's wedding party got to a river they put down their bride again and waited. When Netoga's aunt caught up with her, she sat down right on the ground and placed her niece on her lap and held her like a baby. And so the bridegroom's companions noisily pestered her and told her, "Give us our bride, we want to go home and have some sleep!"

In answer the bride's escort refused and said, "I was under the impression that all of you here are Wakerewe! If so, what don't you understand here? Do you need to be reminded of what the Wakerewe do before they can ferry a bride across a river? If so, then we'll stay here this way forever."

A woman in the wedding procession, whose name was Murwa, came forward and said, "You have indeed to listen to what the bride's escort is saying, because she is right. That is what we all see done in this Ukerewe of ours, and you all know that in our case we will have to cross three rivers. So if you have one new iron hoe give it to the bride, as her reward for our crossing her over all the three rivers which lie in our way, so that we can take our newlywed home. That's all."

Katetwanfune pulled from under his robe a hoe and threw it on the ground. Munegera then helped her niece stand up and made her step over the hoe lying on the ground and then Katetwanfune picked it up and gave it to Munegera. That done, the wedding procession carried high their bride amidst shouts of jubilation and resumed their journey. On arriving at the second and third rivers they forded the rivers with their bride high on their shoulders, with her escort saying nothing more, since she had been satisfied with how Murwa had pleaded her case for her. As they approached Myombekere's home, they hollered really loud their jubilation shouts so as to be heard by the people at home: "*Ya! hooyee! hooyee*! We've come with her, yeees! We didn't leave her behind, *eee*!" and their chorus answered: "*Hooyee! hooyee*!" and their women ululated: "*Keye! keye! keye*!"

People in Ntulanalwo's parents' home heard their shouts of jubilation and the women in the home began drumming rolls of rawhides by the door of Bugonoka's house to welcome the newlyweds and their procession home.

At the gate of Myombekere's household Munegera once more detained her niece and wouldn't let her go any further and thus halted the entire procession outside the gate, and on seeing that Myombekere asked the people gathered in his home: "And what on earth does this woman want?" to which the people answered, "Can't you see she wants her child's reward! At the gate of the household too an article of value has to be thrown on the ground for the bride to step over before she can be brought into the bridegroom's home." At once Myombekere dived into his house and emerged with a new iron hoe, which he personally carried to the gate of his household and threw down in the middle of the gate. Once again Munegera made the bride step over the hoe and that hoe too was picked up and given to the bride's escort and she received it. That over the wedding procession lifted high their bride once more, but before they got her to the porch of the house, there was Munegera again, already blocking the house door as if to make sure her niece would not be carried into the house until she had been given another reward. This time those present in Myombekere's home, Kanwaketa included, disagreed with her and said, "No, dear fellow parent-in-law, if you want an article of value like what you were given at the gate it won't be forthcoming, because, in our estimation, the hoe you were given covers the gate of the household and the threshold of the house, which is just another gate in the same home. What is more, these two crossings are usually counted collectively, as we count river and sea crossings together when a man marries in one of our kingdom's smaller islands[36] and brings the bride here on the main island. This is a similar situation, dear fellow parent-in-law, believe us!" Munegera, confronted that way by that noisy crowd, when she too knew the other side was right, got out of the way and the bride was carried into the house and taken into the inner-room.

In the sky it was already an afternoon sun.

Chapter XXXIII

NOTES

1. *Endumya*:   The newlywed's "food-tasting" maid in the *kurumya* ceremony below.
2. *Ensendekelezya*: See note 29 of Chapter XXIX.
3. *Ekitukuru*:   See note 16 of Chapter V.
4. Wazinza hoe: See note 18 of Chapter V.
5. *Ekitala* (plural *ebitala*): See note 18 of Chapter I.
6. For the custom which forbad a son-in-law to mention his mother-in-law's name and a daughter-in-law her father-in-law and mother-in-law's names see note 23 of Chapter XVI. The son-in-law however called his mother-in-law by her title and not by her substitute name, since use of substitute vocabulary, *kusinda*, was for women only.
7. *Emitaho*, plural for *omutaho*: See note 9 of Chapter I.
8. *Olugali*:   See note 6 of Chapter I.
9. *Omusimbe:*   See note 24 of Chapter II.
10. *Kurumya* Literally "to give a bite of food to", food-tasting rite for the bride and bridegroom, first in the home of the bride's parents and then at bridegroom's, with a woman, usually a young girl from the bridegroom's family, acting as the officiant, *endumya* of note 1 above.
11. *Omulindi*:   See note 8 of Chapter XXI.
12. *Obwita*: See note 14 of Chapter I.
13. *Enkole*: See note 25 of Chapter XII.
14. *Endwero*: See note 8 of Chapter XII.
15. *Embozu*: See note 8 of Chapter XIX.
16. Under normal circumstances women would have formed their separate meal circle some distance away from the male meal circle, since Wakerewe women and men usually ate separately.
17. *Amasabuzyo* or *ensabuzyo*, plural for *olusabuzyo:* See note 12 of Chapter I.
18. *Enanga*, plural for *olunaga*: Se note 16 of Chapter I.
19. *Emamba*: See note 17 of Chapter II.
20. *Ekikome*: See note 1 of Chapter II.
21. *Lwakalera*, commonly called *enkanda:* The traditional Wakerewe women's wedding dance, in which rolled cow hides (*enkanda*) are used as drums. For the other meaning of *enkanda* as material for wear, see note 22 of Chapter VI.
22. *Akahira*: See note 11 of Chapter IX.

23.   Polygamous Kikerewe society in which, as we hear on a number of occasions in the story, husbands were at liberty to have extramarital affairs as they pleased, was likewise very accommodating to adulterous wives and   not only was jealousy deemed contemptible behavior in a man, but even proven cases of adultery, of which only the wife could be guilty, were normally resolved through the elders' counseling, with husbands rarely accepting reparation, which was usually a goat or a cow, for their wives' transgression. Above all adultery would not be grounds for divorce, unless it had become a "bad habit" of the wife, which was then seen as potentially dangerous to all involved, besides being a disgrace to her husband's home and family. For that reason Wakerewe husbands usually did not accompany their wives to their parents' or other relatives' homes when they went there for a number of days to celebrate occasions like weddings and other family festivities, since it was assumed that women on such occasions tend "to forget themselves" a bit. Hence the significance of this adulterous incident in the story, as well as of the later reprimand of Myombekere and Bugonoka to their newly married son when they felt he was carrying the manifestation of his love for his wife to the point where it could be mistaken for jealousy.

24.   *Enerere* or *obunerere:* See note 23 of Chapter VI.

25.   For fish and meat eaten by Wakerewe men only, see note 17 of Chapter II. Since women ate these men-only fishes and meats when they were still young and stopped only when they reached an age when custom judged they had become women, that is on reaching their puberty, it is quite likely that those who retained a taste for them continued eating them even as adult women whenever they could get away with it, and may be that is what Kitereza is driving at here. It could also be that Kitereza is as early as 1945 suggesting that this was a Kikerewe custom unfair to women and should be dropped, as it eventually was.

26.   See also note notes 14 of Chapter XVII and 5 of XVIII for this Kikerewe saying in praise of a woman's full and well-rounded buttocks.

27.   The mother's child-nursing present. For *engozi* see note 9 of Chapter XXI.

28.   For hoes as bride-price items, see also note 18 of Chapter V.

29.   *Omwonki*: "A sucking child", a young male or female relative of the bride chosen by her family for their daughter's new husband to "nourish", by giving the child a present, before their daughter becomes the nourisher and caretaker of her husband and his people.

30.   Omurongo (plural Abarongo): Member of Abarongo clan of ironsmiths of Uzinza kingdom, the main suppliers of ironwares and other metal objects for

Ukerewe and the entire southern part of the lake region. Matale is the name of one of the localities where Aborongo lived in Uzinza. See note 18 of Chapter V.

31.   *Ebyeyela*: Wedge-marks shaved into the foreheads of the newlyweds and some of their female attendants. See note 7 of Chapter XXVIII.

32.   *Olukoba* (plural *enkoba*): Band-and-veil of beads worn by the bride on her forehead both as an ornament and facial cover. *Enkoba* also means bead-decorated costumes worn by singers and dancers in certain dances.

33.   *Omugazu*:   See note 23 of Chapter VIII.

34.   Since their weapons had been received and kept for them on their arrival the previous evening, we assume they had been returned to them before this part of the wedding ceremonies. The custom of depriving the bridegroom and his male companions of their arrows, considered as a bride-price item, is no longer practiced, probably because men no longer carry bows and arrows whenever they go on a journey. Nowadays on that wedding day (which has been kept even in Christian marriages, which normally take place in church following that traditional giving away of the bride by her parents) only the bridegroom carries a symbolic bow, with or without arrows, on a much shorter version of this ceremony, in which his party no longer spend the night at the bride's home, and in which in the case of Christian marriages the bride remains in the home of her parents, from where she goes to join her husband at church for the church ceremony.

35.   A paternal aunt is treated like the bride's father, her brother. See also note 20 of Chapter VII and note 9 of Chapter XXXIV.

36.   For the minor islands of Ukerewe see Introduction.

Chapter XXXIV

CEREMONIES OF NTULANALWO'S WEDDING AT THE HOMES OF THE NEWLYWEDS' PARENTS

As soon as the bride was taken inside the house, Ntulanalwo too was told to go inside at once for their newlyweds' food-testing rite,[1] where he found her sister Bulihwali, who had been chosen as their food tasting maid,[2] already waiting, wearing strings of waist beads and a white *ekirungo*[3] medallion hanging on a string slung across her shoulder. After the food-tasting rite, the bridegroom's wedding companions left to go to their homes and have some sleep, since they had passed a sleepless night, leaving in Myombekere's home only the people who had gathered there to stay for days and help prepare the marriage feast and Munegera, the bride's escort.[4] Inside the house Barongo, the designated cook for the newlyweds, put a pot of *obwita*[5] on the fire. A thick layer of soft grass had been spread on the floor over a large area of the inner-room of Bugonoka's house, and the bride, together with her escort and the newlyweds' food-tasting maid and Ntulanalwo were made to sit on that bridal-spread.[6] Then it was time for Ntulanalwo to wear his wedding amulet and the cumbersome ritual article was put around his neck, as was the custom in those olden days, and then his face was trimmed and wedge-marks[7] shaved in his short hair, but only slightly at the front, without forming the wedges fully.

The newlyweds were served food at their bridal-seat in the company of small children, the girls and boys who had accompanied their mothers to the wedding celebrations. Next to the bride sat her escort, their shoulders touching, the bride sitting to the left of her escort, the bride's lovely neck bent, her face turned away from the food, her eyes closed all the time, not uttering a word, and her demeanor completely subdued.[8] The newlyweds were given water to wash their hands before eating and Ntulanalwo put the water near his bride's escort and told her, in parables, the way he had been instructed: "Please do touch a bit of this water, my father-in-law,[9] so that we can see what has thus invaded us."

Munegera answered back her son-in-law: "Thank you, son, we have seen the water." As a visitor, she preferred her son-in-law to wash his hands first, lest   people gossiped about her before her niece had even left the bridal-seat and said: "Was there nothing to eat where she came from, for her, a visitor, to rush to wash her hands that way, before her hosts had done so?"

And so an impasse developed and Barongo had to tell Ntulanalwo, "It is you, the man, who should wash your hands first, before passing the water to our visitors. Then after our visitors have washed their hands you will pass them leaves to dry their hands with."

Ntulanalwo washed his hands and then passed the water to his bride and her escort and they too did the same and then he gave some soft tree leaves to the bride's escort, who dried her hands first and then wiping dry her niece's hands. That done, a dish of *obwita*, really big, was put before them, followed by another equally big pot of *ensato*[10] and an equally huge plate[11] on which to serve the fish and a number of small-size bowls[12] in which to put *obwita* for the boys and girls. Ntulanalwo dished fish onto the plate, put *obwita* in the bowls for the children and put fish into the hands of each one of the little boys and girls and then welcomed his bride's escort as he had been told by his parent's to do: "Please welcome, my father-in-law."

Munegera cut off a piece of *obwita* with her hand, the women way,[13] and held the food in her left hand and then cut off from that piece in her hand a morsel of the right size and gave it her niece. However the bride on her part did not receive it and at once Munegera told his son-in-law, in whispers: "It appears the bride has boycotted eating."

Immediately Ntulanalwo called his mother and when she came he told her, "The bride has boycotted eating," and Bugonoka in turn at once called out to her husband seated outside and told him, "I appears here inside the house the bride has boycotted eating."

Myombekere answered back in a big and loud voice to end the bride's boycott: "Let her eat, there is already a black cow in the kraal as her reward."14

After that promise by the bridegroom's father, Munegera again gave her niece the morsel of food the bride had at first refused and this time she received it and, like her escort, she too kept the morsel of *obwita* held in her left hand, and then her escort put into her right hand a piece of fish fillet and they ate. All this while the bride still kept her little neck bent, never even once lifting her head. From time to time her escort would put out her hand and feel in her niece's hand, only to find the morsel of *obwita* she had given her still intact: she had been just holding it in her hand all the time. After a while she returned the morsel of *obwita* and the piece of fish to her aunt, without having as much as tasted a bit of either. Munegera took back the food and ate it herself. In no time the newlyweds had stopped eating. When Barongo came to take away the food utensils and found *obwita* hardly touched, she told the bride's escort, "You didn't eat, my fellow parent-in-law! What happened? Was *obwita* uncooked?"

Munegera responded, "No, that isn't the case indeed, my fellow parent-in-law, for we did eat."

Barongo, pretending to apologize to her in-law for her bad food, insisted, "No, you did not eat the food. What happened? Could it be the taste of our *obwita* of bare millet flour, without enough cassava flour mixed with it the way you are used to doing in your part of the country?"

And Munegera in turn said, "You are better off here, since you have such excellent millet. With us this year millet harvest was a thing known only to the usual few lucky homes, but for the rest of us the unfortunate ones we harvested nothing as usual, proving our ancestors right when they said: 'The river always flows through its old bed,' my dear co-parent-in-law."

Bugonoka then chased away from the bridal-seat the children, among them Bulihwali, who looked as if they were going to eat forever and told them, "Get up and move to the door and give room to the newlyweds, so that they can stretch out a bit, lest they develop chest pain." The children moved away and went to eat with the women of the wedding celebrations by the house door. However, when young Bulihwali finished eating she was told to go back and rejoined the newlyweds at their bridal grass-spread and did so.

Then Ntulanalwo was called aside and his face was once more trimmed and the *ebyerera* wedge-marks in his forehead fully shaved.

In the evening again *obwita* was prepared for the newly-weds. Again the bride, as at the first meal, didn't eat: from the morsel of *obwita* her aunt placed in her hand she cut off with her fingers one very tiny bit and that was the only thing she put into her mouth. After eating, the bride's escort called her co-parent Bugonoka and told her in whispers: "We want to go and relieve ourselves." It was already dark night and Bugonoka led the way and took the bride and her escort behind the house and they passed water and returned to their bridal-seat. Shortly after that, Bugonoka called Barongo and told her, "Go and make beds for Ntulanalwo and his wife and for their escort in his bachelor house. You the rest of the women celebrating the wedding with us will sleep in our house here." And at once Barongo with a few other women went and made beds in Ntulanalwo's bachelor's hut:[15] for the bride and bridegroom they made a bed on the floor of the front room of the house and put the bride's escort on Ntulanalwo's bed in the inner-room.

Then dancers began dancing, but since they had come without their lead singers they danced only for a little while and then left.[16] As for Ntulanalwo in his bachelor's hut, he was a bit like what our people mean when they say a sentinel never sleeps. However, dear friends, we've better leave that alone. Let the one who has been there know what there is to know and the one who hasn't stay that way, because, even if I could tell it all, I've seen isn't the same as I've tasted!

The following morning, at the time of the women's pre-dawn which ushers in daybreak, Bugonoka with Barongo and Myombekere's sisters woke up and went to Ntulanalwo's house and asked him, "Ntulanalwo, are you bathing or not?"

Ntulanalwo answered them, "Yes," and they all understood the marriage had been consummated.

Ntulanalwo's mother then went to her husband Myombekere, the word ready to drop from her mouth, and told him the good news. And at once she got busy and gave instructions to those who were to draw water and those who were to collect cow urine and when everything was ready the women went and told Ntulanalwo, "Get up and take a bath: your water is waiting for you behind your house." Ntulanalwo woke up and went out to where his bathing water was waiting for him in a huge pot. Then his little sister, their newlyweds' food-tasting maid, came and poured cow urine on the soles of his feet before withdrawing and going to the bride inside his bachelor's hut and Ntulanalwo bathed. As soon as he finished, he was told to come away at once, so that bride's escort could bathe the bride before the sun came out and he did so and went into his father's house. He was about to go to the cooking-stones to warm himself at the fire when the women in the house stopped him: "No, stay where you are and wait for your partner, because you are about to be incensed. Why should you feel so cold anyway!"

In the meanwhile the bride's escort with a few other women took the bride from her husband's bachelor house and escorted her to the bathing place and once there the newlyweds' food-tasting maid, the bridegroom's little sister Bulihwali, poured cow urine on the soles of her feet as she had done with her brother. The bride's escort then bathed the bride and after that took her to join her husband in his parents' house. Then some women put embers on a piece of a broken pot and smeared pieces of *emigazu*[17] with oil ready for incensing the newlyweds. At once all the children, male and female, were chased from the house.[18] That done, the pieces of *emigazu* smeared with oil were thrown on the embers and the fire fanned by some women blowing on it and a cloud of incense smoke rose from the fire. That ready, *enkanda*[19] sheet was thrown over Ntulanalwo and his wife covering them completely, right up to the hair on their heads: *vuu*! and immediately the potsherd with smoking *omugazu* was slipped under their legs and they were incensed, at the same time as the entire house was pervaded by *omugazu* wedding smell.

After that Ntulanalwo and Netoga with their escort and Bulihwali resumed their places on their bridal-seat.

Bugonoka then went and told her husband, "We women are today like you men who never cook: we can't cook anything for our visitors for lack of relish." Myombekere sent for one of Kanwaketa's sons so that they could slaughter a cow for the newlyweds, and when the young man came he told his wife, "Go and tell our fellow parent-in-law to come so that we can present her her relish." Bugonoka went and took Munegera into the banana plantation, where the young man had already taken a bull, brown and white in color, for slaughtering. Myombekere presented the bull to his co-parent-in-law: "Please, fellow parent-in-law, accept your relish: here it is."

Munegera replied: "It is adequate," and then went back to her niece in the house.

The cow was slaughtered and its meat cut in all the different cuts, after which Myombekere selected and put aside choice pieces of steak, soft and boneless meat fit for serving the newlyweds at their bridal-seat. A plate was brought him and he put the meat on the plate and said, "Take this meat to the women quickly and let them cook food for the newlyweds." Then he cut into smaller pieces some of the meat cuts as relish for the people of his home and their visitors of the wedding celebrations. The men who slaughtered the cow then divided among themselves their customary share for butchers, what is called the slaughtering share, before carrying the rest of the large cuts of meat into Myombekere's house. Inside the house Myombekere took out two large cuts of meat and hang them separately: the rump, which is the customary share for the parents of the bride, and a fore-limb, the bride's escort's share, the meat she goes back to her home with after the newlyweds' days at the bridal-seat are over. From then on, *obwita* with meat was to be cooked and served to the newlyweds five times a day, with the evening serving, the one after their evening incensing, as the sixth, the meals themselves being served at the following times: in the morning after their morning incensing they would eat their first bridal meal; at the morning sun at which milk curdles they would get their second meal; at the boiling-hot noon sun their third; during the afternoon sun their fourth one; when the sun is about to set their fifth; and in the evening, after they had bathed and had been incensed and perfumed for the night, their sixth.

On that day, when it got cool enough in the afternoon, the dancers of the previous night came back to dance for the bride, and since this time their lead singers were with them their performance was simply great, and from that day on they danced in Myombekere's home day and night, going back to their homes just before cockcrow, daily, until the wedding celebrations were over. During daytime Ntulanalwo danced too, but at night he did so only for a little while and then retired to join his wife in his house, leaving his friends still dancing outside.

The following day Myombekere sent an envoy to the father of his daughter-in-law to take to him his present of the rump of the slaughtered bull. That day again Ntulanalwo and his wife took their very early morning baths, after which once more they went to their bridal-seat to be fumigated with *omugazu* perfume. That perfuming of the newlyweds went on for two days, morning and evening, and on the third day the bride and bridegroom left their bridal-seat. The bride's escort, however, did not go away on that very third day but stayed on for one more day at Myombekere's home to see her niece settling down in her new home.

On the day Netoga left their newlyweds' bridal-seat, her mother in-law

Bugonoka first gave her a tiny bit of millet and she ground it into flour on the grinding-stone. Then, accompanied by her sister-in-law Bulihwali and some other women, she went to the lake to bathe, carrying a really tiny calabash in which to draw water, as if she were going to draw water for some ritual. That's when everybody saw what she looked like for the first time and everyone agreed she was a really desirable woman, as her name signified![20] She was of a very light complexion and whoever looked at her said: "Yes, the parents of the wife of Ntulanalwo the son of Myombekere did indeed beget a beauty!"

The day following that, in the afternoon, the meat of the fore-limb of a cow, the bride's escort's present, was loaded in *ekitukuru*[21] basket and given to Ntulanalwo to carry and Ntulanalwo and another young man took their bows and arrows and escorted the bride's escort back to the home of the bride's parents. She carried back with her some pieces of *omugazu* incense, taken from those which were used to perfume the newlyweds during their days at the bridal-seat, which she was going to mix with other *emugazu* pieces which had been kept aside for the purpose in the bride's parents' home. Ntulanalwo and his companion got to the home of Ntulanalwo's father-in-law and just handed the parents of their bride her escort's basket of meat and immediately left and returned home.

Back in Kalibata's home for some days Kalibata prepared himself as well as he judged fit for the celebration of the first visit of his newly married daughter Netoga and her husband to his home, and when he was ready he sent to Myombekere, as his invitation for the newlyweds to come to his home, a delegation of several people carrying with them to his daughter's new home one pot of banana beer, one cooking pot full of cooked fish and a huge bowl loaded really heavy with flour. The invitation delegation arrived in Myombekere's home and food was prepared for them and they ate and then left.

Immediately Ntulanalwo got busy again and summoned people to accompany him to his wife's homecoming ceremony. This time he gathered more people than he got together for his wedding journey: as many as fifty-eight. The following day when all the people invited assembled, Myombekere gave Ntulanalwo and his companions a goat for *ameko*[22] sacrifice and the rawhide of a calf, which his son received and carried held under his arm. With that he took his bow and arrows and his male companions also took their weapons and their party set out, with their bride Netoga leading the way. When they had been traveling for quite a while and were some distance on their way, Katetwanfune said to rest of his companions, "I must admit, ladies and gentlemen, that I find the behavior of brides puzzling!"

"Puzzling in which way?"

"On the wedding day, when you bring the bride from her parents' home to the bridegroom's home, she comes crying, and then on her first homecoming, she goes to her parents' home all happiness, unable to contain her laughter, overflowing with joy, retracing without difficult from beginning to end the way which brought her from there carried high on people's shoulders, as if it was a way she had frequented her entire life!"

Immediately a woman answered Katetwanfune and said, "We women as brides cry on account of our sadness at parting from our parents and due to our apprehension at the prospect of going to pass our entire lives in other people's homes, since, for anything you know, that man you have married may have this or that terrible habit, for human beings, whether male or female, are capable of any behavior. And so when we think of that, of the prospect of going to live forever with strangers, we cannot but cry. On the other hand, on our way to our first homecoming, yes, we are all cheerful and jubilant, because we are going back home, to meet our parents and our other relatives. That's why we behave that way."

Some of the men responded to her and said, "Why then is it that even when we marry you when you are already divorced women[23] you still leave your husbands and go back to your parents' homes? No, what you are telling us is not the whole truth.   You women are simply incomprehensible."

And the woman who had spoken said, "Dear me, what's wrong with these men! I better leave you alone, because I see you are something else! What has a wife leaving a husband got to do with what we are talking about? That's a matter of incompatibility of character between the wife and her husband. And in most cases it is you men who usually don't want us anymore and as a result falsely accuse us of all sorts of terrible things: `My wife practices witchcraft, she has I don't know done what and what and is this and that and that and that.'  And when we too realized that you have closed us out of your love that way, we decide to cut off all ties  with our husbands in time and say to ourselves: `It's time to grow up and stop behaving like a child. Even if I continue forcing myself on this monster of a man who doesn't want to see any more of me, there is no more marriage between us worth the name.' And so, rather than drag on an impossible situation, it is much better to get out of his way so that he can breathe relief and you too can be free to look for another caretaker, since, as our ancestors said: 'A contest in which no one yields destroys the contestants.'"

And the men said, "I see! So that's you women's lot!" and the woman answered, "Yes."

When the newlyweds and their companions got near the home of Netoga's parents, they sent forth shouts of wedding jubilations. On hearing them, the women in Kalibata's home began drumming rolls of rawhides as at the same time some men in the home fetched the skin of a cow and came to stretch it across the household gate, so as to prevent the homecoming procession from entering the home before performing the sacrifice for lifting *ameko* sex prohibition.

The homecoming visitors on arriving at the gate stopped and grouped there, Ntulanalwo and his wife in front, their goat crying beside them. The people from the bride's parents' home then came to the gate and stood next to the cow-hide stretched across the household entrance and, from their side and over the cow-hide, began pouring liquid butter from *enchuma*[24] calabash on Ntulanalwo and his wife and their companions on the other side of the gate, making them oily all over.

That over, Ntulanalwo and his wife were told to strangle together to death their goat, right there in the middle of the gate of Kalibata's home, after which they were given a knife and, again husband and wife holding the knife together, they stabbed the dead goat. As the goat's blood streamed from the animal's neck where they had been instructed to stab it, Kalibata and his wife gave the couple leaves of *amabingo*[25] canes held together with those of *olusombwa* shrub, an aspergillum which the couple received together and dipped into the goat's blood. Then, again the two of them holding the bundle of *olubingo* and *olusombwa* leaves, they lifted together that aspergillum full of animal blood and struck with it the cow-hide stretched across the gate once, accompanying the blow with the words: "We are immune to *ameko* death." They then passed the aspergillum of animal blood to those inside the home by passing it under the rawhide across the gate and those on the other side too repeated the action of striking the rawhide at the gate with it. Then those inside the home passed back the bundle of leaves to the newlyweds by passing it over the rawhide at the gate and that action was repeated three times and the rite was completed.

The bundle of *olubingo* and *olusombwa* leaves was then placed on the dead goat, after which Kalibata removed the cow-hide from across the gate of his home. He was wearing on his head a crown of *olwihura*[26] grass made in the form of a ringed head pad[27] and holding in his right hand a wooden rake[28] for raking together ears of corn or grass. He then welcomed Ntulanalwo and Netoga to his home and the couple and their party entered the compound of the home of the bride's father. Behind them, some men skinned the goat at the very spot at the gate where the couple left the strangled goat.

When all the homecoming visitors were inside the home, the women dance *lwakalera*[29] was erected in the very middle of the compound of the homestead and the drumming of cowhides rumbled on and the women with beautiful voices sang and other women ululated.[30] The first dancer to enter the dance arena was Kalibata, the crown of *olwihura*[31] on his head and the rake in his hand. Then his newly married daughter too stepped into the arena, and father and daughter, all alone, danced and moved and danced! *Aa*! I am telling you, it was some performance to behold! With Netoga over there saying to herself, "See me dance, you who have never seen me do so!" and moving her body as if she had no bones, making rapid movements with her legs as if intending to go to her father's end of the arena and yet without ever getting there! *We*! In response to which then Kalibata would take up the dance and with the wooden rake in his hands would pretend to be raking his daughter towards him! *Aa*! Everybody had to admit and say : `Age takes its toll indeed, because certainly when this man was still in the prime of his youth he had no peer as a dancer!' As to their spectators, on seeing father and daughter capering and play-acting that way in the dance arena, they all burst out in endless peels of laughter, their hearts full of merriment! Kalibata and his daughter danced for a while only and then came out of the arena and only then did the other people too enter the dance arena and begin to dance.

Tibwenigirwa then made a mark with butter on the face of her husband and marked in the same way the face of her daughter. Immediately after that Ntulanalwo and Netoga were called inside the house for ritual food-tasting, and they chewed the same foods they tasted in the home of Ntulanalwo's parents. Then they sat at what had been Netoga's bridal-spread and were given water for washing their hands and served *obwita* with, for relish, *enkole*[32] beans, wonderfully well prepared but cooked whole and not mashed as *enkole* taken with *obwita* normally are. How sweet *enkole* can taste! No wonder our ancestors gave us the expression:

"to die and leave behind *obwita* with *enkole*!" When they finished eating, the couple came outside again and sat down for a while. Shortly after that many dishes of *obwita* and pots of fish and meat were brought outside and placed in front of the homecoming visitors, together with plates on which to dish out that great food and each and everyone in the homecoming party ate all his or her appetite allowed and his or her stomach could take and still they all ate their fill and left the food almost untouched! For what could they do to so much food except scratch at it just a little bit! true to the saying of our ancestors: "The stomach can make you still though no bigger than the gizzard of a chicken",   or again: "Except for the childbearing stomach of a woman, the human stomach is a good for nothing ingrate."

After that the visitors were taken to a resting house in Kalibata's home, to relax a bit after their heavy meal, where they found a big dugout used for brewing banana beer, whose top was covered with green banana leaves. It so happened that under that cover was banana beer full to the brim, and on realizing that those greedy for beer began inching their seat under them with their bodies towards the beer dugout. Beer for the bride's homecoming celebration is never drawn from its container and served to people. And so, beginning with their male visitors, people in Kalibata's home provided each one of their guests with a long straw of *amasekeseke*[33] twigs and the men lined up around the dugout of beer. The male visitors drank for all they were worth and then gave room to the line of their female companions and their women too drank their turn and when they had taken enough withdrew to the rear and their men returned and fell to the beer again, and among the women too those with the stamina went back for some more. By and by, the other people present saw that their visitors could hardly drink any more and so they too joined, fighting over each other to get their straws into the dugout of beer.

When the beer was finished another dance was announced. It was already nighttime.

Finally the homecoming visitors felt it was time to leave, for the night had really advanced, and asked for their weapons and took their bride and left, to go and pass the night somewhere else, leaving behind in Kalibata's home the dancers, many of whom were now fairly drunk, still dancing as if the visitors they were honoring with their dance hadn't left at all! Ntulanalwo and his new wife went to pass the night in the home of Bugonoka's grandmother's female relative, because it was taboo for the newlyweds as well as their companions to pass the homecoming night in the home of the bride's parents.

The following day, first thing in the morning, as soon as they got back home, the bride and her husband went to the lake to bathe. When they came back from the lake both of them had their faces trimmed again and decorated with new wedge-marks. That done, they went back to the home of the bride's parents, Kalibata's home, to breathe relief.[34] On that breathing-relief visit nothing out of the ordinary happened. All there was for the visitors and their hosts was to chat and relax and eat, and Ntulanalwo and his wife went with only two companions: a woman, to keep Netoga company, and, as company for Ntulanalwo, a brother of his, a son of a relative of his father. They were served food twice at Kalibata's home that day, and when they were about to leave they were given *enchuma* calabash in whose butter was placed *empindu*[35] needle. Back in the home of Ntulanalwo's parents the newlyweds had left behind the same objects: *enchuma* calabash with *empindu* needle in its liquid butter. On top of that the newlyweds were also given, as presents, a large bowl full of flour and a pot of cooked meat and they left, with Bulihwali, their newlywed's food-tasting maid, who had also come with them, carrying the small *enchuma* calabash, Netoga carrying the pot of meat and the other woman, her companion, the bowl of flour, and arrived back home, where they were received and relieved of their presents. The food the newlyweds bring home as presents from their breathing-relief visit is never eaten by the bride or her husband or their food-tasting maid. It is taboo to them. And so Bugonoka went to invite some neighbors of hers and they came to eat those presents with her and her husband while Netoga and Bulihwali and Ntulanalwo were given something else to eat, whatever other relish there was in Myombekere's home that day.

After that Netoga and her food-tasting maid Bulihwali spent one day at home and on the next day, the two of them, accompanied by another woman, went back to Kalibata's home: to return *enchuma* butter calabash. Bulihwali was the one who carried the two *enchuma* containers, the one brought from the bride's parents' home and the one from the Myombekere's home. Netoga was still wearing her bride's band-and-veil[36] of beads over her face and the bride's amulet around her neck. The bride and her companions got to the home of Netoga's parent's and Netoga's mother received from Bulihwali the two *enchuma* calabashes, each with *empindu* needle inside its oil, and hang them in straps on the wall of the outer-room of her house. Shortly after that food was prepared for the visitors and they were served a meal. After eating Netoga's bride's band-and-veil of beads was taken from her face and her bride's amulet from her neck, thereby ending Ntulanalwo and Netoga's wedding ceremony and all its rituals.

Finally it was time to go back and the visitors were escorted and returned home, where Netoga arrived to find her husband Ntulanalwo too was no longer wearing his bridegroom's amulet around his neck: like her, he was back to normal life.

Chapter XXXIV

NOTES

1. *Kurumya*: See note 10 of Chapter XXXIII.
2. *Endumya*: Se note 1 Chapter XXXIII.
3. *Ekirungo*: Round white ornament the size of a large wrist watch with a hole in the middle made of sea shells, ivory or the bone of an animal.
4. *Ensendekelezya*: See note 29 of Chapter XXIX.
5. *Obwita:* See note 14 of Chapter I.
6. *Omukugiro*: Here the newlyweds resting bed-spread on the house floor of their parents' houses during their wedding ceremonies. Normally the word meant the inner room of the two-room Kikerewe house (see note 10 of Chapter I).
7. *Ebyeyera*: See notes 7 of Chapter XXVIII and 31 of Chapter XXXIII.
8. This subdued demeanor called *kubonzya,* literally "to look without opening eyes", was required of the bride throughout the two days she spent on *omukugiro* of note 6 above. Speaking or looking or in any way breaking out of that perfectly subdued appearance was a sign she was badly brought up. Even relieving a long call was not allowed her: she could only go out to pass water, in the company of her escort, as Netoga does here.
9. Sons-in-law treated the paternal aunts (called in Kikerewe "female fathers") of their wives like they were male and their real fathers-in-law. See notes 20 of Chapter VII and 35 of Chapter XXXIII.
10. *Ensato:* See note 2 of Chapter VI.
11. *Olunanga*: See note 16 of Chapter I.
12. *Ebibo*, plural for *ekibo*: See note 15 of Chapter I.
13. That was the correct way for the Wakerewe women to eat *obwita:* they never took morsels of *obwita* from the dish directly to their mouths as men did. See beginning of Chapter XIX.
14. The bride did not eat food in the home of her husband's parents, that is in her new home, until she had been promised a present to break her boycott. Her boycott-lifting present was always announced by her father-in-law or the elder representing him as "a black cow already in the kraal", although it did not have to be black, the cow customary slaughtered in her honor the morning after her arrival in the home, subject to her new husband having consummated their marriage during the night. When the new wife made her first round of visits to the members of her husband's extended family, heads of the households she visits had also to break her boycott with presents, of

their choice, before she could eat in their homes.

15. *Endaro*: See note 8 of Chapter II.

16. There can't be any real celebration of the wedding until the marriage has been consummated, and so there can't be any serious dancing the night of the wedding day. Likewise, as stated in note 14 above, no cow could be slaughtered in honor of the newlyweds until the following morning when consummation of the marriage has been confirmed by the relatives of the bridegroom asking him the customary phrase (the custom is still current): "Are you bathing or not?" and getting a positive answer from him.

17. *Emigazu*, plural for *omugazu*: See note 23 of Chapter VIII.

18. To avoid bad luck in their adult lives of love and marriage.

19. *Enkanda*: See note 22 of Chapter VI.

20. Netoga: See note 1 of Chapter XXVIII. Also see meaning of names at the end of the translation.

21. *Ekitukuru*: See note 16 of Chapter V.

22. *Ameko*: Kitereza in his note for his Swahili translation of his novel says: "Breaking a sex prohibition by a married couple, a transgression the cleansing of which calls for the offenders sacrificing a goat."

23. *Abasimbe*, plural for *omusimbe*: See note 24 of Chapter II.

24. *Enchuma* or *oluchuma*: Kitereza' in his note for his Swahili translation says: "Liquid butter used in a wedding rite performed during the newlyweds homecoming at the bride's parents' home; also the name of the calabash container from which the liquid butter is poured on the newlyweds and their companions."

25. *Olubingo*: Slender sugarcane-like cane; *olusombwa*: name of a grass-like shrub. The leaves of the two plants are also what are used as an aspergillum in the rite of the first outing of the child after birth. See note 7 of Chapter XXI.

26. *Olwihura*: Kitereza in his note for his Swahili translation of his novel says: "Hat made of the grass of that name worn during the sacrifice of *ameko* in the home of the bride's parents."

27. *Engata*: See note 13 of Chapter I.

28. *Enkokobyo*: A (wooden) rake.

29. *Lwakalera*, also called *enkanda*: See note 21 of Chapter XXXIII.

30. *Akahira*: See note 11 of Chapter IX.

31. In the text of his Swahili translation Kitereza has two grasses as the material of which the crown is made, *olwihura* mentioned above and *akabindizi*, though this latter is not in the original text, suggesting that the Kikerewe author remembered it when writing the translation.

32.   *Enkole:* See note 25 of Chapter XII.

33.   *Amasekeseke*, plural for *isekeseke*: Shrub with long jointless hollow twigs used as drinking straws called *enseke* (singular *oluseke*), from the name of the shrub.

34.   *Kwich'omwoyo*: Literally "to breathe relief". Kitereza in his note for his Swahili translation of his novel says: "A rite performed in the home of the bride's parents to mark the conclusion of wedding celebrations." However, as we see in the story, the celebrations are actually not concluded until the bride returns the *enchuma* of note 24 above to her parents' home following this ceremony.

35.   *Empindu:* See note 17 of Chapter X.

36.   *Olukoba*: See note 32 of Chapter XXXIII.

Chapter XXXV

MASAI CATTLE RAIDERS, A PLAGUE OF BOILS, NTULANALWO MARRIES A SECOND WIFE

In the days following Ntulanalwo's marriage, the days when the Wakerewe speaking of the newlyweds would say, "Their soles are still wet with the water of their wedding baths," Myombekere and Bugonoka were to the newlyweds like the foster parent who said: "I am a foster parent, let what goes wrong with this child be only what can be blamed on its real parents." Bulihwali stayed on in her parents home, where she found great pleasure in keeping her sister-in-law company. Netoga herself lost no time in getting used to how things were done in the home of her husband's parents and adjusting accordingly. She too now ground flour like her mother-in-law, before dawn, at the second cockcrow, and went to draw water too at Bugonoka's early morning hour of drawing water. Myombekere, on seeing his daughter-in-law prove herself such an ardent worker, became really fond of her, and likewise Bugonoka loved her daughter-in-law without reservation. And so did Ntulanalwo. In fact we cannot even begin to describe how much Ntulanalwo loved his wife. Yes, maybe we could try to give you an idea of his love for her by describing what we saw him do for her with our own eyes, otherwise nothing else would do! Here you are then: when our Ntulanalwo saw that his wife was taking rather long to come back from an errand on which she was sent, he went looking for her. When Netoga went to dig sweet potatoes from the lakeside crop fields and did not come back quickly, again he went for her. In the end some people began to say: with Ntulanalwo this isn't love for his wife! He's being consumed by jealousy, that's all!"

His parents too felt that way and strongly reprimanded him and told him to put an end to that habit of his of following his wife everywhere she went and said to him: "If you don't put an end to that kind of behavior, your father-in-law will take your wife away from you and you'll become a man without a wife, because following your wife everywhere that way breeds jealousy. Such behavior can also lead to your killing your wife or to some people harming you or even killing you the husband. For jealousy is a really bad thing: it can send you spying on your wife when she goes to her parents' home or to visit her other relatives. And once you do that, you are bound to end up harming somebody or being harmed. You have therefore to put an end once and for all to this behavior of yours. It looks bad in people's eyes and it is something you should be ashamed of. That's not how to be a good husband; you've got it all wrong!"

Ntulanalwo listened to his parents and dropped that habit of his of following his wife everywhere she went. From now on he kept to himself his feelings for her. The day his wife went to her parent's home and stayed overnight, that day Ntulanalwo until sunset would not take his eyes from the road his wife took, then during the night he would seek consolation in music by playing his *enanga*,[1] since he was such a consummate *enanga* player. And when he wasn't feeling like playing *enanga* he would go to a dance while saying to himself, "Let me go and seek sleep," or he would do one thing or another of that kind, like looking for an unmarried woman[2] for a sleeping-mate and indulging in the many other amusements of the young. But we know all that, for, as the Mkerewe of yore put it: "The green banana leaf shakes in the wind above and boasts: *bagabaga*! and the dry one down below on the ground answers: that's where I came from."

In the dry season of that same year the Masai invaded the Wakerewe. It is true this time they did not cross the Lugezi[3] ferry and come into Ukerewe Island itself, but they entered Ukerewe Mainland[4] and killed multitudes of people and took their livestock and torched their houses before withdrawing back to their country. When rumors about the invasion began to spread, Myombekere asked his friend Kanwaketa, "Have you heard the news? The Masai mowed down people in Butimba and all the way to Kibara in our mainland!"

Kanwaketa said, "There is no doubt then that when they invade us here in the island we'll all die right to our little babies strapped on their mothers' backs. The Masai's sword is a terrible thing, according to what our fathers, who fought against them, used to tell us. It is the worst thing imaginable, because a Masai knows no child or woman, he kills indiscriminately!"

Myombekere said, "How can the Masai know woman or child as if their war takes hostages like ours! Yes, even with me my father used to tell me of that when he was still alive, adding: `The Masai war you hear of is a thing of wonders, because the Masai have charms for making enemy weapons miss their targets. It is very unlikely that in this Ukerewe of ours there is any medicine man whose charm can equal that of the Masai in its power to deflect enemy arrows and spears. It is true there are people in this country too with weapon-deflection medicine, but not as potent as that of the Masai. That is another thing altogether!' He would say: `Look! Even if you are however big a crowd of people attacking one single Masai enemy, you will shoot all your arrows at him until you have no more left with the Masai dodging all the time or deflecting your arrows with his shield and sending them straying into the ground, without a single one of your weapons ever touching him! And in the meanwhile he with his sword would be cutting down your people by the piles like a man clearing brush with a billhook from his wife's water-side crop field ready for tilling and planting. And a Masai doesn't run, he blows by like a stormy wind: the legs of a Masai are thin like straws the Waruri, Abakwaya[5] and Wakara people use to drink their *enkongo*[6] beer. And his tall head gear with its feathers together with the jingles on his legs make him a really frightening sight! To say the truth, the only Masai you can look into the face long enough to make out his features is a dead one.' And how can people of such wonders, who also happened to be extremely rash, not be frightening? All the same, let's prepare. Let's sharpen our barbed arrows and our spear-headed ones and wait to hear what *omukama's*[7] call will be, for what else can we do? But, even so, we are under impending doom, my dear brother! It is true we won't die like women, without putting up a fight, but even then, I'm telling you, it looks like time to say good-bye and lament: `We've eaten our last meal!'"

Then after sometime Myombekere and his friend heard people saying: "The invading Masai killed a whole lot of people in the areas of Butimba and Kibara, torched houses and grain stores, took away countless cattle and goats and sheep and then drove away their loot of livestock and went back and now they must be celebrating in their homeland, if they made it back." Only then were people's fears laid to rest and calm returned to the country and people resumed their daily preoccupations, after living for days on end under the terrible scare of the threat of a Masai invasion.

One day Ntulanalwo asked his father, "What are the Masai really after when they invade and attack people like that and take away their livestock?"

"What they want is this livestock of so many beautiful colors you see in front of you, because that is their only food. All they live on is meat; they never eat *obwita*9 like us. When there is famine in their land, that's when they take to invading and attacking us. I am sure you have heard here too people say: `A starving person hears no reason.' When he begs all he can to no avail, then he resorts to the use of force, come life or death. And there is war for you. For how can you take away another man's animal wealth with him just looking on, without your having to fight him first?"

"Even if you are a weakling on that day you too will try to confront that invader and make sure he takes your property only after he has overcome or killed you."

"That's the way to talk! I was afraid you might say you wouldn't fight him. Let's face it, if you are a real man and not a living-dead, can you sit back and simply watch another man, to whom you don't owe a thing, come here and take away say that multicolored cow of ours tethered over there?"

"*Aa*! I'll die for my property before he takes it! I mean it. When he has completely killed me only then will he take it, but not before."

A short while after the Masai invaded the mainland part of the kingdom, an epidemic fell on Ukerewe. Everybody wondered what was happening to their country for people to be all of a sudden invaded by such a terrible disease of smallpox combined with an eruption of minute boils. And so smallpox killed people as had never been heard of, and the boils likewise. Every elder who was head of a household gave very strict orders to the children of his home to stop going to play in other people's homes lest they fished out of those homes the terrible epidemic. People who were parents of grown up and married male children gave their sons strict injunctions requiring them to discipline themselves and not only desist completely from any mischief and unbecoming behavior with outside women but also to strictly observe the spousal sex prohibition with their wives. And so during those days of the epidemic, as a measure of precaution, the marriage act became a thing strictly forbidden, lest the epidemic should fall on a home which was also afflicted with *amakire*10 disease, for when that happens the epidemic really rages wild until everybody in that home has danced to its macabre tune. And indeed in a home where the epidemic struck while there was *amakire* affliction in the household the plague hit really hard and ravaged the entire homestead. All over the country people cried until they had no more tears in their heads, until finally they cried out: "Dear brothers and sisters, we'll all perish! This disease must have been brought here by the Masai. They must have been the ones who sprayed it on our people." In their desperation, they finally went all the way to Bukindo[II] to see their *omukama* and told him: "Power to you, Great-giver! We are here in front of you to pay our homage to you and to pray you, Builder-of-homes, to lift this pestilence from us, because you are the Final-action, son of a king!"

The king answered them, "Go over there and sit down; I heard your words." The men withdrew, went aside and sat down.

Omukama then first asked the gray-hairs among his gathering of courtiers: "What do you say to the important words you have just heard, gentlemen."

Among his courtiers a man, rather old, whose name was Lubezi, stood up and came in front of *omukama*, folded a knee and sat down and, speaking with full voice, said, "We have understood their important words, Great-giver, because we too grew up seeing kings reprimand pestilences and put an end to them. It may very well be that those present here are all young people, with no one among them as old as I am, so that they have never seen the like of what is facing us. But I cannot claim to be that young, for I cannot go back into the womb of that great woman who gave birth to me."

Omukama said, "*Aa*! Will you just go on!"

Courtier Lubezi said, "You are right, Great-builder, since I have already started talking I should finish what I am saying. And so, Great-giver, what I saw I saw, and it is that at the end of a war in a country there always follows an epidemic and a great and frightening famine, those evils following on each other that way, like urine and shit."

Those present burst out laughing, like really happy people.

Lubezi said, "You are laughing, gentlemen, I am wrong? You wait until the planting season comes. Even if I am already dead, you'll see and remember what I am telling you. And that's all I have to say, my sovereign."

Omukama said, "Go and sit down." The king then contemplated the matter alone inside his being for just a short while and then told those come to supplicate him: "You go back, and we'll see what we can do." And the men answered, "Power to you, the Sun, power to you the Lion! May you live long, son of a line of kings!" Then they said good-bye to the king and went home. Myombekere was among them.

Two or three days after that, towards evening, Myombekere was down with high fever and had to take to his bed. When Bugonoka saw her husband down with such high fever, all sorts of things went through her mind. She gave strict orders to Ntulanalwo and Netoga, over and over and at every occasion saying to them, "Children, you shouldn't take this lightly and think it is a joke and forget yourselves and give in to mischief in your house. He is really sick and as an ancestor of our people said: `What eats hair on the head is after the brain.' For you too see for yourselves, my dear children, that great affliction has befallen the land in the days we are living through!"

Ntulanalwo responded to his mother and said, "Even without your telling us, dear mother, that's something we too have seen and of which we hear people talk all the time. Therefore we too dare not transgress in such a grievous way and risk harming ourselves and harming you our parents. We simply can't."

When Bugonoka rejoined her husband in the house Myombekere asked her, his jaws knocking against each other as if chattering from cold due to his sickness, "By the way, what were you saying outside there?" Bugonoka repeated to him what she told Ntulanalwo and her daughter-in-law. Her husband said, "And so you think that what you told them alone is enough to make them abide by your injunction? You women are indeed something else! That's why people say you never grow up! For, my dear wife, what can I say since I can't say you womenfolk are all children! You my wife too should know how it is with young people! Why don't you just try and remember how you too used to be? Because if you do that you will understand why mere words cannot hold back a person in his or her adolescence and keep him or her from the mischief I have heard you talk to them about. My wife, do you want me to tell you what you'd better do? Please make for me two *amakire* amulets from the medicinal stick which is in that *ekitwaro*[12] box and put them on my hand here." And so quickly Bugonoka fashioned with a knife two amulets for the prevention of *amakire* disease and put them on her husband's hand. That was better protection, because with it even if a person who has transgressed *amakire* sex prohibition were to invade the place where a sick person is the patient would not be in danger catching the *amakire* disease in addition to his sickness; not at all. But if a sick person is without such protection and a person guilty of breaking *amakire* sex prohibition goes near him or her, the sick person would become critically sick and possibly die, for we don't want to hide from you the truth of the matter.

After some time that fever died down and left Myombekere's body, but with that those with him saw his entire body completely covered with smallpox: from his head, his nose, his chest and right to the soles of his feet. Myombekere's relatives, who had gathered in his home to be with him in his sickness, sharpened splinters with which to open the smallpox rashes and drain pus from them all the time, the whole day long. Your Myombekere became a really terrible sight: the entire skin of his body peeled off, completely, from his head right to the soles of his feet, and left him looking like a skinned carcass of an animal. Whoever chanced to look at him if he or she happened to be a person with a weak stomach like mine, that one couldn't eat meat again for many days. I am telling you![13] At the same time *omukama* sent men throughout the country to vaccinate people against smallpox and they vaccinated each and every person who hadn't caught the disease, including babies still sucking their mother's breasts, in each and every village. And so in that home of Myombekere too Bugonoka, Bulihwali, Ntulanalwo and Netoga were all vaccinated before they caught the disease.

Vaccinating of people came and went and the inmates of Myombekere's home were left nursing Myombekere and waiting. And with him too after a few more days the wounds of his peeled off skin became less sore. With that, those nursing him began taking him into the cold water of the lake very early in the morning, before sunrise. Once in water, they would massage his body with sand and cold lake water while stretching out his hands and legs by jerking and pulling them with force, so that he wouldn't become lame on healing. All poor Myombekere could do at such moments was to cry out loud with pain and for the rest just submit. Finally a time came when he asked his nurses to give him a stick of *omulindi*[14] cork tree to use as a crutch on his way alone to his daily early morning cold lake water baths. When he resumed eating with his son outside, his son talked cheerfully again and felt happy and said to himself, "I can see! I think father is healing now!" Finally he healed, but the scars of smallpox had given him a different appearance. Now I see! No wonder smallpox is such a terrifying killer disease! *Ahee*! It can turn a person of brown complexion like Myombekere was into somebody pitch black he became!

Then after a few more days went by, the epidemic of smallpox and likewise the disease of tiny boils ended. But then in no time people everywhere were suffering from body eruptions which looked like large rashes. Each and every former smallpox patient caught the new disease. When the elders who had suffered from smallpox were asked about the new disease they said: "That is chickenpox." And after a few more days passed the eruption of chickenpox too ended and people were well again.

And the people of Ukerewe said, "We are fortunate we have a good *omukama*. He is the one who reprimanded the two epidemics and made them leave us quickly. But without that we wouldn't have survived, we would all have perished!"

Myombekere's smallpox scars finally healed completely and only pockmarks remained dotting his face and nose, and when he saw that he began a second courtship for his son Ntulanalwo so that he could have two wives. That way even when he himself died he would leave behind him a real household, big and strong. But above all he wanted to make sure his son would leave his posterity on earth, have many children, to one of whom he could give his father's name, to continue carrying it on earth after he Myombekere was gone. The woman Myombekere courted this time too was a maid and so he courted and courted, days on end, since as you too know the courtship of a maid cannot be rushed, it moves on slowly like the heavy giant boat of hippopotamus hunters until it eventually reaches its destination, since, as seafarers say: "The slow boat also lands."

At that very time the country was experiencing a really great and terrible famine, which, like the two epidemics before it, also killed lots and lots of people. Just to give you an idea of how terrible such a great famine is, our ancestors found it such a disaster they coined for it the saying: "A great famine has no succor." In the end the people whose daughter Myombekere was courting told him, "You have better just go home and rest, dear brother, and let's first wait and see whether we'll survive this death and destruction ravaging our country and we'll take up the matter again later. For in the situation we are in now we are in no position to sort out things and come to a sensible conclusion; not in the least." Myombekere also debated the matter in his mind and admitted to himself: "*Aa*! That's true, indeed. Really, gentlemen, the way we are dying from this famine, even if your in-laws give your son a wife, what kind of wedding celebrations will you hold for him when your home is starving, when every day, daytime and nighttime alike, your people are still hungry after a meal?

Aa! No, that won't do. I am an adult and I can see how all of a sudden almost everybody has become a thief and steals other people's food. As soon as it is the dead of night, their day begins and out they go to steal other people's foods, by piercing holes into their stores of grains with pegs. I see how some of these thieves die, speared to death when caught, how others get so badly beaten with sticks and clubs. This is no ordinary famine, it knows no nobility of character, and neither can one laugh at another person and blame that person's plight on his own laziness; not in the least. See how really hard working farmers are also among those badly hit, their homes the ones in which there are so many people dying of starvation! No, really, I shouldn't insist on something I can't handle and be like the character the Abakwaya women sing in their songs: `You want many wives when your chest has no ribs!' meaning `You want many wives when you don't have what it takes to support a home with many wives!'" And so Myombekere concentrated on how to succor from famine the people of his home.

And days passed, with people desperately doing whatever it took to get something to eat, others having turned into apes and climbing *amakunu*[15] trees in search of their fruits for food! Then as days continued to pass, the famine relented, as people say when speaking of heavy rains, and slowly the situation improved until there was no more famine.

When people in the country recovered enough to begin going about their normal preoccupations, Myombekere too resumed his courtship for his son. On the day he resumed courting, on arriving at the home of the father of the girl he was courting for his son people told him, "The master of the home has died. This is the fourth day since the day he died and today the mourners will bathe his death and lift the mourning.[16] However, the man didn't die of a disease, he died of starvation." Myombekere exclaimed loudly: "*Yu*! And what am I to do! What an ugly turn of events!" The dead man's mourners in the home responded to him and said, "That shouldn't discourage you and make you stop courting. Yes, it is true the master of the home has died, but he has left behind him a household on its feet, because he has left behind a married son. In fact his son too has already brought into the world his own posterity: his wife is suckling a baby-boy. And so the dead man's son will do, because our elders of yore said: `You work wood with the chisel at hand.' And Myombekere responded and said: "Yes indeed. I too agree with what you say." He stayed with the mourners for only a bit and then said good-bye to them: "I wish you a good day in your time of grief, my brothers and sisters," and they answered, "Thank you. You too have a good day and a safe journey." And since in a mourning visitors are never escorted out the home in grief, Myombekere was given his bow and left alone and returned to his home.

After some days passed, Myombekere resumed vigorous courting. In no time the courtship matured and he was sent to court the consent of the relatives of his in-laws, as in the meanwhile both his in-laws as well as himself were waiting to see what type of harvest the millet they planted following the end of the great famine would yield them. By the time people finished threshing the millet of that harvest, Myombekere had completed courting among the relatives of his in-laws and had completed whatever task his in-laws had told him to do for them and so he went back to find out what they now had to say about his son's courtship. He was told to go and fetch the bride's escort,[17] and two days after that the bridegroom and his party went to the girl's parents' home for the wedding and the bride was duly brought into Myombekere's home. And Ntulanalwo became a husband with two wives: the elder wife, the one called Netoga, and the second wife, the junior wife, whose name was Mbonabibi, daughter of Kongwa. On the day he brought Mbonabibi into his parents' home he took a new iron hoe and went into the house of his first wife and gave her the hoe for lifting the spousal sex prohibition attendant on a husband marrying another wife. Netoga was delighted and jumped about with happiness while holding her hoe in her hands.

And so Myombekere's home now became a real household, a home with three houses. And when Netoga and Mbonabibi both began to cook in their own kitchens of their separate houses, in Myombekere's home a meal became a serving of many dishes and Myombekere and his people no longer felt apprehensive at the prospects of receiving many visitors as the inmates of a one house home, the home of a husband with his poor lonely single wife, usually are. Before they knew it, people saw the belly of Kalibata's daughter swell, and she carried her pregnancy and the days passed until she delivered her first-born child, a baby-boy. Myombekere and his son named the child Galibondoka, the name of Ntulanalwo's grandfather, Myombekere's father. When Ntulanalwo's little son became a darling little baby, when it began smiling at its baby-sitters, his other wife, Mbonabibi, also became pregnant.

Chapter XXXV

NOTES

1. *Enanga*: See note 9 of Chapter IX.
2. *Omusimbe*: See note 24 of Chapter II.
3. Lugezi (sometimes Rugezi): Ferry, name of the   water canal between Ukerewe Island and Mwibara or Ukerewe mainland.   See Introduction.
4. For the Ukerewe Mainland and the other regions of Ukerewe kingdom see Introduction.
5. Abakwaya: See note 5 of Chapter I.
6. *Enkongo*: Fermented beer of foreign origin made from *endwero* millet, to which warm water is added at the time of drinking and which is drunk with straws called *enseke*. For *enseke* see note 33 of Chapter XXXIV.
7. *Omukama*:   See note 26 of Chapter II.
8. *Ebitala*, plural for *ekitala*:   See note 18 of Chapter I.
9. *Obwita*:   See note 14 of Chapter I.
10. *Amakire*: See note 4 of Chapter XII.
11. Bukindo: See note 8 of Chapter IV.
12. *Ekitwaro*:   See note 19 of Chapter VIII.
13 Kitereza's father died of smallpox when the author was five years old (see Introduction) and this detailed account of the devastations of the affliction on a patient may be from personal childhood memories of his father's sickness and death.
14 *Omulindi*: See note 8 of Chapter XXI.
15. *Amakunu*, plural for *ikunu*: Large tree which bears an abundance of fleshy fruits ordinarily eaten only by birds and monkeys and baboons, and not by human beings.
16. For the way the Wakerewe mourned their dead see Chapter XXXVI.
17. *Ensendekelezya*: See note 9 of Chapter XXIX.

Chapter XXXVI

MYOMBEKERE'S SICKNESS AND DEATH

That day Myombekere had been weeding undergrowth in his now large banana plantation when on coming back home he told his wife, "As I was working in the banana plantation, I felt sudden pain shoot through my spinal column like lightening, and immediately I felt very cold all over, as at the same time my arms and legs became completely drained of their strength. Something inside me is telling me that this cold which has overwhelmed me this way doesn't por tend well for me. I am in for what looks like a fatal sickness, certainly not ordinary sickness."

"No, don't say that! You must survive it, dear man! You must fall sick and then be well again the way all of us everyday fall sick and recover."

"Yes, you are right indeed. However, our elders once said: 'Pregnancy which begins with complications kills the mother.'"

At dinner time Bugonoka cooked *obwita*[1] and served her husband and her son food. Myombekere cut off with his hand a morsel of *obwita* and forced himself to eat and swallowed it, but when he put a second morsel into his mouth and struggled to swallow that one too saliva filled his mouth and he felt like vomiting and spit it out. He washed his hands and went into his house. During the night the situation became really bad and he couldn't sleep a wink. When Bugonoka saw her husband in that condition, muttering things to himself, tossing in bed this way and that way and at the same time boiling hot with fever, sick to the extent of not knowing whether he was naked or covered, she became terribly afraid and went to wake up his son in one of the houses of his two wives in which he was passing the night that day. She called him with alarm, twice, and the third time Ntulanalwo answered, rather startled: "What has happened, mother?"

"You have better wake up and come and help me look after your father. I no longer know what to do in the house; the sickness he was complaining of in the evening has apparently become worse."

"Mother, what did you say?"

"I am calling you because of your father. His sickness has apparently become serious. Come and see him first and then go to call his relatives."

Ntulanalwo woke up, and so did both his wives, and they too came and saw that the condition of the patient was really bad. Bugonoka sent Ntulanalwo to call Kanwaketa: "Go and call Kanwaketa for me, to come and help me see what kind of disease this is, because I have never seen your father this way since he married me." In no time Kanwaketa arrived and found: "*Aa*! Yes indeed, this is a seriously sick person!" He quickly left and returned to his home, where he sent one of his sons to fetch Myombekere's relatives, so that they too could come and witness the frenetic dance they were facing, as people say, and on coming back he told Bugonoka, "We are nursing our patient the stupid way, because we are just looking at him, without taking an oracle to seers or even trying to gather for him some herbs with which to try and bring down a bit this fever. Isn't that being stupid?"

Bugonoka and her son and two daughters-in-law all agreed with him and said at the same time, "That's stupidity indeed. Even livestock, mere animals, are given medicines and treated whenever they fall sick, leave alone a human being!"

Kanwaketa asked Bugonoka to give him an bowl[2] in which to gather medicinal herbs for trying to treat his friend, and, accompanied by Ntulanalwo, left and went to procure medicine in that middle of the night. The two men brought medicine, whatever herbs they had managed to gather, that is, and cooked it in a small-size pot. When it boiled once, they took it off the fire and placed it on the ground to cool and when it cooled sufficiently Bugonoka bathed the entire body of their patient with the medicine. However, the fever showed no sign of relenting; if anything that medicine seemed only to have poured oil on fire. Finally it dawned.

It was not until sometime in the morning that Myombekere's relatives began to arrive in all their numbers. They found their patient already overcome by his disease, and poured millet into a calabash[3] to go and have his oracle[4] told so that they would know the origin of his sickness.

Myombekere was asked to spit saliva into the millet and some male relatives of his, accompanied by Ntulanalwo, went to seek a seer.

The seer they went to told them in no uncertain terms how their patient had been hit by a magic stroke when he was in a banana plantation, how those who hit him with that witchcraft were two old women, and how their patient could not recover from his illness, because the witchcraft stroke the two women hit him with was fatal.

The men returned and told those who remained at home what the diviner told them and immediately all Myombekere's relatives in their hearts knew at once the two women mentioned by the seer. With that, a clan brother of Myombekere spoke and sent out many and loud threats alluding to the two women: "We have found that there are two women in this neighborhood who want to engage in their evil mischief and take to his grave our all great son here, because they envy him his wealth. But let them be warned, because we too are real men like our son himself. Even if they succeed in killing him, they will still have to deal with us and it won't be easy. Wherever other people go for magic to deal with their like, we too will get there and make them regret their evil mischief."

When Myombekere's relatives took his oracle to another diviner, that other seer divined for them and said: "What I see is that this man is suffering from a very grievous sickness, which you must confront with all it takes. If you take the matter lightly, you will lose him before you know it. But, above all, what I have seen in this oracle of yours is this: your patient is sick because he needs to offer to his ancestors the sacrifice of a cow and a goat. And so go and offer the sacrifices so that your patient can become well again."

Those relatives of Myombekere came back ready to share with the rest of their kith and kin that divination too, but with their spirits very low. Still on their way back home an elderly man among them told the others: "We may now be acting out of sheer desperation, my dear brothers. I am saying so because I once saw a sick man, who was head of a family like our patient, for whom similar sacrifices were offered, but as soon as the sacrifices were offered instead of getting well he died. And so it is with us, and until we have saved our brother from this disease we won't know what to believe." To which the other men responded by telling the old man, "We have indeed heard your words and, yes, you are right. However, we too would like to respond to what you have said with what our ancestors once said: 'The sinking boat goes down those in it still singing songs of hope.'"

And the old man responded: " I too do agree with that; because a sick person who has some relatives is never just looked at. His or her relatives will keep on trying to find out from seers the truth about their patient's sickness and look for amulets and medicines with which to treat him or her so that, if his or her end has not yet come, their patient would be cured."

And the others said: "Yes, that's much better said."

On getting back home the men turned to looking for yet another medicine man, the one who would preside over the offering of their sacrifice and tell what the entrails of the two sacrificial animals would reveal.

The medicine man for the sacrifice came and told Myombekere's relatives he would come back the following day to preside over their offerings, and on the following day, very early in the morning, he came. He found people in Myombekere's home still asleep and woke them up, went and greeted the patient and found that his condition hadn't improved. Then he told Myombekere's relatives they should start on the job he came to do and they got up and did so, slaughtering a cow first, a sizable young bull, and one of Myombekere's relatives with the authority to offer sacrifice to their ancestors made the offering. The offering of the cow over, the goat was brought, slaughtered and offered too in sacrifice as the cow had been offered: "Our ancestors *bananka, basunga, banyonyo*[5] (but by the officiant actually mentioning their ancestors by their real names), please accept your sacrifice of a cow and a goat, which we have offered you today to restore the health of our patient. And if he is sick because he owed you this sacrifice, deign to accept it: here it is! We are offering it to you so that you may remove his affliction from him, so that tomorrow will find him completely cured. Let that be, so that we your children can be happy again as people were created to be." Offering sacrifice over, the work of butchering the cow and the goat was carried on and completed. Then the seer turned to telling the signs the sacrificed animals revealed, by looking in their entrails and in all the other relevant parts of the meat,[6] beginning with *ibigo*[7] of the cow's intestines, which as soon as he examined people present saw him silently shaking his head and asked him, "What is the matter?" He said, "Nothing." Then he examined the entrails of the goat and he found its *ibigo* propitious and his audience saw him smile. Then he said aloud to the women, "Women, I want to hear ululation!"[8] and on hearing that Bugonoka ululated in peels like a woman whose husband had landed from a sea journey or who had seen this or that relative of his return from a foreign country or from some other similar distant journey across the sea.

Following that meat of the sacrificial animals was cooked and *obwita* prepared. The diviner told Myombekere's relatives, "Try and have the patient too taste a bit of *obwita* and meat of his sacrifice," and everybody agreed, "Yes, that's right." Women sliced off a bit of obwita of *endwero*9 millet flour and selected a small piece of soft meat and took the food to their patient and said, "Wake up and taste this morsel of *obwita* and this tiny bit of sacrificial meat."

Myombekere said, "My dear brothers and sisters, even if this is the medicine which will restore my good health, I still must say you just go ahead and eat your meal, because I am simply in on position to eat, for I simply don't have as yet the appetite for all the different things you are trying so hard to make me eat. Will you please take them away quickly, lest I vomit. Maybe just give me some water, water to drink is the only thing I want." He was given some water, but not much, and he drank it all and asked for some more but those present said, "No more! You must not give him too much water with such a high fever."

Myombekere said, "I see, I am keeping you from your meal and that's why you don't want to give me water! Never mind then, you just go and eat your meal."

His relatives said, "Indeed sickness is a terrible thing: it make us act like children again! It prevents us from eating even our favorite food and makes us talk like children!" And others rejoined: "And what did you take it for? There is nothing like sickness. So you think it is a joke! Sickness knows no child nor adult!"

After the sacrificial meal the seer reexamined the entrails of both the cow and goat and this time those present insisted on wanting to know what he saw and told the seer, "No, please don't do that: you must reveal to us what you saw in the entrails of the cow, so that we too can be enlightened. Please!"

"I see. So that's what you want."

"Yes, for didn't you see how satisfied we were when you examined the goat's entrails?"

"I shook my head that way because what I saw in my divination made no sense to me; not at all."

"And what did you see?"

"I tried all I could to no avail. I looked again carefully, the way I divine everyday, to see how our omen stood, still, *aa*! my brothers and sisters, it remained prostrate, as if I have never divined! So, may the relatives of the patient come aside so that we are alone, with no outsiders around, and I will speak to you more clearly." The relatives of the patient got up and followed the seer and when they had separated themselves he said, "Sit down here." They all sat down and the seer told them: "Since the patient isn't eating, try and bring him the organ of a cow's gluttony[10] and make him wear it around his neck and wait and see what will happen. It is obvious this sickness of his is aggravated by his not eating anything and if he eats he will in no time recover." And he added, "And yes, that cow's gluttony organ is something you have to find urgently, say if possible this very day, and put it on him. Doesn't any of you have it?"

Ntulanalwo said, "I think I have seen it somewhere here, so if it hasn't got lost we have it. Let me go and ask mother." He was gone for a while and then came back and said, "Yes, it appears we have it all right. I asked her and she confirmed we have it."

Then the diviner went on to say, "But what I saw as the proper and fitting thing to do is this: You must move your patient, take him away from his home and go and nurse him while he is staying somewhere else. If you do that, he will definitely recover. That's why I couldn't tell you this in front of outsiders, lest they know our secret," and after that he left.

In Myombekere's home people gathered together the meat bones and the animals' stomach refuse and the green banana leaves on which their sacrificial animals had been slaughtered and hauled off everything to a crossroads.[11]

That day, at night, Myombekere's relatives held counsel and considered the matter carefully, so as to select from among them the person who would remain behind in Myombekere's home to take care of his livestock and the rest of his property, and finally they said, "Katoliro and Ntulanalwo are the ones who will remain in this home. The rest of us will take our patient to Mwebeya's. And the two of you who will remain here will be only coming to visit him there and returning home. Bugonoka will be among those going with the patient, because she is his wife, the person who will be making gruel for him and, above all, consoling him."

And so they took their patient, on whom they had already put the cow's gluttony organ the seer had prescribed, all the way to Mwebeya's home, in a different village.

Once in that place, the patient was able to drink a bit of gruel. Then Mwebeya sent away the rest of their relatives who had gathered: "The rest of you too must go back to your homes; you too will just be coming to see how the patient is doing and then going away, because the heads and footsteps of so many people around him would only make his condition deteriorate."

His fever too had subsided a bit, and so his relatives who went back to their homes left with some hope.

However, after just a few days passed, their hopes were all gone. Myombekere was again really boiling hot with fever and that fever in turn led to another disease: he developed a slight but endless cough and was coughing all the time, unable to sleep a wink. The day Ntulanalwo and Katoliro came to see how their patient was doing, Mwebeya and Bugonoka told them, "Last night and the night before that we didn't sleep at all, to say nothing of what the patient himself was going through, for he was coughing nonstop the whole night long. During daytime we would say, `Yes, this is much better,' but as soon as night fell it would become simply terrible! We have tried all we can, given him every medicine known to cure coughs, in the hope that his cough would thicken so that he could cough it up and spit it out, but to no avail. *Aa*!" Katoliro said, "Try to peel cords of *omusindayaga*[12] bark and let him chew it and swallow its sap, because I too once suffered a similar cough and that was the medicine which cured me."

Mwebeya took a chisel and went off into the woods to collect the medicine, brought it, and gave it to their patient. The patient chewed the medicine and when he swallowed the thick saliva of its sap once he said, "No, please, the stuff you have given me this time is simply too bitter! Can't you give me medicines which are at least palatable! *Ahee*! my friends!"

"In that case try your best and swallow at least some three mouthfuls and then let's see how you'll pass the night." Myombekere forced himself and managed to swallow three mouthfuls of the medicine as he was told. He also drank a bit of gruel, but not with any appetite, not by noisily sucking in the thin gruel the way patients who can't eat anything else normally do.

On the day following that, Kanwaketa came to visit his sick friend and when he got there those with the patient told him, "At night your friend didn't sleep a wink. And then it appears his cough has led to a stabbing pain in the side of his chest. We have made him wear all the amulets known to treat that kind of pain but to no avail, the patient is simply groaning with the pain all the time. Some people have even fashioned for us amulets to be worn with rabbit hair, which is what he is wearing at this very moment, but again to no avail. We have tried every know amulet, from the bones of *engonge*[13] to the rib of a dog. *Aa*! What can I tell you! But all that to no avail!"

The patient on his part, as soon as he saw Kanwaketa he told him, "Today, dear friend, you have come to say good-bye to me. This is no pain from which I can recover. I will die of this disease."

Kanwaketa said, "May that never come to pass, friend! What we wish for you is that you recover, be on your feet again, so that we can be happy together once more." When he was about to leave, Mwebeya and Bugonoka told him, "Tell Ntulanalwo and Katoliro to come here tomorrow. We want them. But tell them we don't want only one of them, we want the two of them to come together, if they are both well."

Kanwaketa did not even pass by his home before going to his friend's home, to deliver his message to Ntulanalwo and Katoliro and to report to them the condition of the patient, and the two men listened to him with drooping heads, saddened beyond words by what they heard.

And so early the following morning, at cockcrow, Ntulanalwo and Katoliro set off to see their patient and found he was in a really critical condition. They spent the whole day with him and then when it was evening, together with all their other relatives who had come to visit the patient that day, they took him and returned him to his own home.

He stayed in that home of his three days and then his condition deteriorated beyond hope and continued to get worse with each passing moment. Finally it reached the point when people usually say: "Listen!" expecting to hear mourning cries any time.

On the fourth day, at nighttime, the patient fainted, water was poured on him, and only then did he revive, but not before some of his relatives had cried out mourning him and stopped crying only when he revived. However, the patient himself on regaining his senses had caught some of them still crying and heard them and so he told his relatives, "You are mourning me when I am still alive!" Some of them said, "Whatever the case, his tongue is only trying to hoodwink us when the truth is that he is already beyond hope, for, as you know, the human tongue is like the leaf of a tree, which drops down suddenly and unannounced!"

Shortly after that, they heard their patient, as he struggled with the last breath of his life, the poor man, tell them, "Call my children for me, so that I can say good-bye to them, because I now feel I am dying."

At once Ntulanalwo and Bulihwali were called. Their father stared at them for some time, then he felt them both with his hands and said, "My children, I am dying. Share your property nicely between you." Then he turned and stared at his wife Bugonoka, against whom he lay supported, and kept on staring at her and then closed his eyes again. Not long after that he asked for water to drink and swallowed some two mouthfuls of water. Then immediately after that he said, "I am hungry. Please give me a bit of *obwita* and meat."

Bugonoka quickly cooked some rather soft *obwita*, cooked with milk instead of water, with, for relish, a bit of the meat of the goat Ntulanalwo had slaughtered for their relatives gathered there to be with his father during his sickness, and when the food was ready she served him. The sick person pinched off with his fingers some two morsels of *obwita* and took one really tiny piece of the meat and stopped eating and said, "I would have eaten a bit more, but the taste of this meat simply made me feel bad. Maybe let me try some milk." With the milk too he simply sipped at it and said, "I wanted milk but this milk doesn't taste good." A person was sent to bring some milk from Kanwaketa's home but, before that person had even left, the patient asked again for water to drink, "Give me some water to drink, my throat is parched." He was given water and he drank it in a single breath, rather wildly, and finished it, completely emptying the small cup.[14] Those present, on seeing him drink water wildly like that, waited with apprehension to see how his stomach would receive that water, and, indeed, hardly any time passed before he broke out in hiccups and then asked again for water. People told Bugonoka, "This time give him just a little, not much more than what is needed to stop his hiccups." Bugonoka drew in the cup just a little bit of water and gave it to her husband, who now lay supported by one of his sisters. Then shortly after that they heard some big stomach worm move as if coming from the patient's stomach and going towards his throat with a heavy sound: *gugugugu*! followed by: *choroloroloro*! Immediately after he dropped his head from the middle of the chest of his sister, who was supporting his upper body, so that his head now hung drooping and turned sideways like this. Then he opened his eyes again and glance upward once, this way, and closed them again and now hiccupped rapidly and nonstop.

Mwebeya said, "*Aaye*! Hear that! That huge worm which rumbled:

gugugugu! that way is what came to finish off our brother!" And those present agreed with him: "Yes indeed, it is that monster which came to cut off his soul." In that very instant they saw our Myombekere pour out of his mouth the water he had drank and the sips of milk he had taken followed by the morsels of *obwita* he had eaten, all of them just as he had taken them, you would think he hadn't even chewed the morsels! *Yu*! And at once he shitted death's knell! His body became cold, starting with his legs and arms, so that the fever he had remained in his chest only, and the man himself could no longer utter a word. And from there on he silently fought on with his soul, the poor man, now it is ending now it isn't!

Inside the house everybody was now with a drooping head asking himself or herself how he or she would die when his or her turn came. Among the women whoever tried to burst out in a mourning cry, her companions would restrain her and say to her: "Be quiet and let's take good care of a human being, lest he departs seeing (meaning with his eyes wide open) or open-mouthed and we become the laughing stock of the entire world! As you see he is already dead, so why can't you wait? What if we see you dry-eyed at his funeral?"[15]

As Myombekere continued to struggle between life and death, the only people now left attending him in the house were the womenfolk who bring us all into this world, since folding the dead is also their exclusive responsibility. Whenever the patient was short of breath and tried to open his mouth gasping for breath the women present would hold his mouth shut, as if to actually strangle him, and likewise when he tried to open wide his eyes they would hold them shut and keep them forcibly closed. On that day people even saw some women go the extent of holding Myombekere's nose, as if to prevent him from breathing through the nose as well. (I see! So that's it! It is women who give us our finishing stroke!) And when it was early morning, at the women's pre-dawn, just before sunrise, by which time the women had already finished folding their dying patient (tying him up with ropes well and tight), his legs and arms firmly bound together as if he were a bundle of some inanimate matter, his heart finally stopped beating inside his chest and he became cold like cold water and Myombekere said to himself: "There you are! I leave you your world!"

Outside the men, some of whom were sitting at the courtyard fireplace[16] and others by the door of the house, heard the mourning cry of Myombekere's sister, against whom his body lay propped, announcing to the entire world that at that very moment a human being had departed from the earth and all of them, some of them jumping over the courtyard fire, rushed into the house and went straight to Myombekere's body and touched it, and when they found that their relative was indeed already cold like cold water, only then were they convinced that he was indeed gone and they all dropped their heads, bent their necks and held the back of their drooping heads between the palms of their hands.[17]

At once loud mourning cries burst open the sky, female ones and male ones mixed together, and those cries of human sadness went on unbroken until sunrise. When a person wanted to go out to pass water, he or she left the house crying and also re-entered crying, and on getting back to the dead body when he or she blew his or her nose he or she would touch and feel their dead his hands or her hands full of the muck of his or her running nose. Oh yes indeed, that's why the Mkerewe of yore said: "In a house of mourners you see wonders!" Among the mourners, Bugonoka's sisters-in-law were crying out as if alluding to Bugonoka in what they were saying, implying that she was the one who had actually killed her husband and saying as they cried: "I have killed him, yes; now the home is all mine; my child is taking care of me; we will inherit his property; his paternal relatives will see none of it!" Bugonoka on her part in the words accompanying her crying was just bewailing her plight, her lot of not knowing what the future now held for her and her fatherless children.

At daylight the dead man's neighbors came in all their numbers to keep the relatives of the dead person company and to wait for the digging of the grave and the burial of the deceased. As the number of women increased, since women always mourn a dead person from inside houses, the men left the house in which the dead body was and gathered outside, and once outside they selected reliable messengers from among their midst and dispatched them to announce Myombekere's death to his absent relatives in nearby villages who had to be informed at once, people who should be present before he could be buried. In the meanwhile the women from the neighborhood fetched strips of dry banana fiber from the dead man's banana plantation and tied mourning bands[18] around the heads and waists of all the bereaved women and did the same to Ntulanalwo and to all the clan brothers of his dead father.

As the morning sun advanced in the sky, men outside talked about digging the grave. Since their deceased was male and head of a household, his grave was dug right in the middle of the compound of his home, near his homestead's courtyard fireplace. The man who buried the dead was

Ntulanalwo, he was the one who cut the burial ground with his hoe first, wearing across his shoulders *ensembe*[19] his late father wore when making sacrificial offerings to his ancestors, before being seconded by Katoliro, after which the other men present dug the grave. By the time all the people to whom messages of Myombekere's death had been dispatched to summon them to his burial arrived, it was already about noon. Some men among the neighbors and relatives of the deceased were then instructed to slaughter a cow for the skin in which to bury the dead person and some of the young men present were told to slaughter a goat whose skin would serve for what is called underclothing *ensembe*, the underwear for the body of a man who was head of a household. That work done and finished, some of the men who had come to keep the bereaved people company took the skin of the cow, raw as it was, into the house where the dead man's body was, and the women now came out of the house.

Inside the house the men lifted Myombekere's dead body and wrapped it in the cow skin. When they delayed in bringing the body outside, because they were disputing the correct way of positioning the body in the grave, outside the other men asked them, "And what could you be doing in that house? Please bring him out quickly, lest he begins to turn bad. It is quite some time since daybreak and he died before that!" Hearing that the men in the house brought the dead man's body out carried over their arms stretched out from both sides of the body and joined together in the middle. They were about to bring the body feet out first when somebody stopped them and said, "No, don't! That's wrong. You have carried the body of the deceased facing the wrong way. That's never done. The head is always carried out first." Then yet another person burst out loudly in the midst of that big gathering of people and said, "You are right, indeed. This situation is similar to the way a woman gives birth: the normal human being comes out head first. In which kingdom did these men grow up! You want to bring him out feet first, who told you he was nature's freak!" Many people, men and women alike, burst out laughing on hearing that man, an adult, being funny in such a situation! In fact even those who didn't laugh had to bite their teeth together to prevent themselves from laughing. I now see why our people said: "A stifled laugh is a pain!"

As soon as the men bearing the dead body on their arms emerged from the house, the loud mourning cries now burst open the entire sky, and from everybody present, the only exception perhaps being the dead man's burial officiants, Ntulanalwo and Katoliro, who were now inside the grave and so couldn't cry, because it is taboo to cry while inside a grave. Inside the grave, Ntulanalwo positioned himself on the east end of the grave, where the legs of the dead man's body would lie, and Katoliro on the west end, where his head would be, both men standing erect in the grave, ready to receive the dead man's body from those above and carefully and correctly place it at the bottom of the grave. Before the men above lowered Myombekere's body into the grave, the mourners were told to stop crying, because the moment of silence had come, the moment of burying their dead, and all the mourners dropped completely silent: *di*! and there was not a sound to be heard anymore from anywhere. The two men in the grave placed the dead man's body at the bottom of the grave, and then the men above told them, "Uncover his body so that we can see whether he is lying correctly." The two men did as they were told and the body was found to be lying a bit face downwards and those above again told the two men below, "Raise up his face a bit or you'll bury him wrongly!" And the men in the grave now made the body lie completely face upwards and on seeing that Mwebeya from above told them, "You men, what have you done to the dead man's body now?" Still the burial officiants in the grave kept their silence, listening and carrying out the instructions of those above without uttering a word. And since we men tend to be forgetful of the correct way to bury the dead when it comes to which way a dead person's body faces in the grave depending on whether the deceased is male or female, after Myombekere's body had been correctly placed in the grave lying on its side Mwebeya too found himself needing to consult the women and so he asked them, "Women, we want to ask you something. On which side of his body does a male deceased lie?"

All the women remained completely quiet, until   a woman of fairly advanced age, whose name was Kalihanza, said, "What we see daily among our people is that we women are buried lying on our right-hand side, facing south, and you men are buried lying on your left-hand side this way, facing north."

On hearing that the men said, "Indeed, the women are the authority in burial matters. Just imagine what could have happened if we men had acted alone! We could have broken a taboo and created a potential danger, and when ravaged by a curse later on on seeking divination we would have been told: `In your clan you buried a person wrong, he is the one who cursed you.'"

With that the men inside the grave turned the dead man's body and made it lie on its left-hand side, the way in life a woman lies in bed when facing her husband.[20] The body was then moved right into the head-end corner of the grave, with its face looking northward, the back of its head to the south, the head pointing west and the legs pointing eastwards. That done, those above passed onto Katoliro the skin of the slaughtered goat, that is the underclothing *ensembe*, and he received it and was told to put it on the dead man's body by passing it in between his legs with the meat of the skin sticking to the dead man's body and its hair on the outside. Mwebeya knew that Myombekere belonged to a society of initiates, that of the hippopotamus hunters,[21] whose secrets he had inherited from his father and forefathers, that Myombekere's father was a famous hippopotamus hunter and that even though Myombekere himself had not hunted hippopotamuses during his life he nevertheless knew the herbs, that is the medicines, of their society. And so when the men in the grave finished putting underneath *ensembe* on the dead man Mwebeya at once brought the medicinal herbs for hippopotamus hunting and gave the medicine to Katoliro to place in the hands of the dead man.

The men above then told the two men below, "We have finished everything now, replace the cow skin nicely again all around the dead man's body." Those in the grave did so, and immediately after the men above told them, addressing Ntulanalwo, the man who cut the burial ground first in digging the grave, "Start west at the head and finish at the east-end of the grave, dropping the soil into the grave using both your elbows this way."[22] After that the other people present too performed the burial ritual by throwing soil into the dead man's grave. Bugonoka too stood up and did the same, and likewise her daughter Bulihwali and every person present, relatives and non-relatives alike, each one of them throwing soil into the grave, until everybody present had done so. That done and finished, men began filling the grave with hoes, by at first dropping in the soil slowly until the two men in he grave had supported the dead man's body with enough soil so that it would not fall flat but remained lying sideways. Then those filling the grave dropped soil into the grave continuously, with the men inside the grave working their way up by all the time pressing down well the soil with their feet all along the walls of the grave so that the grave wouldn't afterwards collapse and fall in, and on and on until they finished burying the dead man.

Bugonoka was then told to bring her men's meal bowl[23] and some water, and Mwebeya and some other male relatives of the dead man brought *omwitango*[24] and *emboga*,[25] the herbs for burial cleansing, poured water into the men's meal bowl and then put in the ritual herbs and mixed them with water.　The first to cleanse their hands were the two burial officiants, the two of them together washing their hands at the same time on top of the grave and rubbing their hands clean with the medicines, before the other men present followed suit and then the women cleansed their hands last. That done, Ntulanalwo was instructed to break on top of the grave a handle of a Wazinza hoe,[26] the worn-out one he had used to bury his father, that is the hoe he used to initiate the digging of the grave, and was given a stone to do it on, after he had knocked the hoe out of its handle and then put it back in such a way that if used it would cut the ground as if it were an ax splitting wood. He raised the hoe in his hands with all his manly strength and struck the handle against the stone. It proved to be some tough piece of wood and he had to strike some four blows before those around him saw the head of the handle split into two pieces at the fifth blow, the bigger piece, with the hoe in it, falling on the grave while another fairly sizable piece of the handle head remained on the handle stick Ntulanalwo was still holding in his hands. He was then told to pierce a hole through the men's bowl, the one in which his late father used to be served food, and he did so using that piece of the broken handle he remained holding in his hands and the medicinal water which was still in the bowl dripped through the hole onto the grave. With that he left everything he had used for the rite on top of the grave and the burial ceremony was concluded.

The men now ordered the women in the dead man's home to look for food, because the day was already fairly advanced. You know, nothing in your mouth, not as much as a morsel of sweet potato the whole day, since morning, is no joke! And the women got busy, some going to dig sweet potatoes in lake side fields others to draw water from the lake. Katoliro supervised the cutting up of meat for cooking. Since women don't eat goat meat,[27] all the meat of the goat to the last bit of it was put into one huge pot and the men erected their own cooking-stones outside on which to cook their meat. Outside too was where they would do their own cooking of the rest of their men's meat relish for all the days of the mourning period. Only women would cook from inside houses, and even with the women, since too many of them would be needed to cook for that big crowd of mourners, some would have to cook outside.

Some time in the evening that same day Bugonoka began her widow's *lutindi*[28] seclusion to mourn the man who married her when she was still a maid. *Obunerere* [29] she was wearing as ornaments were taken off her and put away for the duration of the rite, because she had lost forever the pillow on which she rested her head for support and comfort in life.

Ntulanalwo's fathers-in-law and mothers-in-law, together with their relatives, came to the mourning of their late co-parent-in-law, and so did all the relatives of the deceased who would when he was still alive avenge for him a wrong done him by an outsider. All of them assembled to mourn his death. Some of them, especially since cows were slaughtered in countless numbers, not to mention the fact that there was also banana beer to drink, saw their huge gathering as a dance instead of a funeral. Oh yes! What! Don't say it can't be, because I was there and saw it. What's wrong with you, man? I think I've better leave you alone. Oh, dear me, you must be crazy no to believe me!

As usual the mourning of the death of Ntulanalwo's father lasted four days and on the fifth day the mourners bathed his death and the funeral ended. After that people kept on coming in small numbers to pay their condolences, this day some five of six mourners would come and pass a night of mourning in the home, and so on, until they came no more. Then after many days had passed, Bugonoka, the widow of the deceased, purified herself from her husband's death the way widows in this country of Ukerewe purify themselves.[30]

When the mourning of their dead became a thing of the past, Myombekere's relatives received their shares of the property he bequeathed them. But since Myombekere had children, there wasn't really much to do by way of sharing out his inheritance, because most of his property had its rightful owner, that is his son Ntulanalwo. However, since we human beings will never be all satisfied whatever the case, yes, some relatives of the deceased still resented that and envied Ntulanalwo and felt bitter towards him, even though all their tears of bitterness could avail them nothing: how could they when the property had its indisputable owner!

Chapter XXXVI

NOTES

1. *Obwita:* See note 14 of Chapter I.
2. *Ekibo*:   See note 15 of Chapter I.
3. *Ekisusi:* See also note 20 Chapter II.
4. *Ekisano:* See note 9 of Chapter XXIII.
5. *Bananka, basunga, banyonyo*: See note 17 Chapter XXI.
6. For divination by telling signs in the entrails of a sacrificial animal, see also Chapter XXI.
7. *Ibigo:* In his Swahili translation of his novel Kitereza has inserted in the text this explanation for *ibigo*: "The fore part of the intestines where they begin to fold and coil."
8. *Akahira*: See note 11 of Chapter IX.
9. *Endwero:* See note 8 of Chapter XII.
10. *Enamba*: Gluttony. The Wakerewe believed that some animal, as well as some human beings, have an organ in them which makes them gluttonous. Kitereza in his note to his Swahili translation of his novel says: "The gluttony of a cow is a round object found inside a slaughtered cow deemed to be the organ of its appetite, which is used as an amulet for the treatment of lack of appetite in a patient by making him or her wear the animal organ around his or her neck."
11. For the offering of a sacrificial animal see   Chapter XXI.
12. *Omusindayaga*: A tree whose bark peels off easily and can be made into cords. Kitereza in his note for his Swahili translation   of his novel says: "Omusindayaga bark is cough medicine. It is also pounded and made into sieving material used by women to filter skimmed milk when decanting churned milk into containers."
13. *Engonge*: A small fish-eating aquatic animal with very beautiful skin. Kitereza in his notes to his Swahili translation of his novel writes: "The animals have a very beautiful black skin and very sharp teeth and are excellent divers and roam the waters of the lake in herds looking for fish".
14. *Omutaho*: See also 9 of Chapter I.
15. Failing to shed tears at the mourning of a relative was a thing of great shame on the part of a Mkerewe woman, so much so that women were known to put a pinch of snuff (later on onions) into their eyes to start off the tears, after which apparently they flow on readily!

16. *Ekikome*: See note 1 Chapter II.

17. Holding one's head that way, called *empunge*, is a sign of mourning. Up to this day every Mkerewe child grows up knowing that gesture to be very serious matter and never to be done in jest.

18. *Ebikamba*, plural for *ekikamba*: Band of dry banana stem fiber tied around the head and waist of a bereaved person as a sign of grieving during the period of mourning. See also note 12 of Chapter IX.

19. *Ensembe*: See note 24 of Chapter XXI.

20. For the relative positions of a man and his woman in bed see note 25 of Chapter VI.

21. *Abanyaga:* See note 9 of Chapter II.

22. Hence the graves were rather narrow and shallow.

23. For men's *ekibo* see note 16 of Chapter VI.

24. *Omwitango*: Name of a herb.

25. *Emboga*: Kitereza in his note to his Swahili translation of his novel has three meanings for the word: an eye disease, a type of green vegetable, and, as used here, "medicine people wash their hands with for purification after a burial". See note 11 of Chapter XXV.

26. Wazinza hoe: See note 18 of Chapter V.

27. For relishes the Wakerewe women did not eat see note 17 of Chapter II.

28. *Lutindi*: Kitereza in his note for his Swahili translation of his novel says: "Widow's mourning rite for her husband who married her when she was a maid, in which, from the day her husband is buried and throughout the days of the mourning wake, the widow is covered with a soft cow skin sheet from head to foot and observes complete silence, does not speak or even greet people and neither are other people allowed to greet her, the only exception being that the relatives of her dead husband may speak to her in whispers, until the morning of the fifth day when the period of mourning ends".

29. *Obunerere*: See note 23 of Chapter VI.

30. *Kuyera*: Widow's and widower's "purification" from her husband's or wife's death. The widow, after an appropriate period of grieving, several months to a year or so, purified herself of the death of her spouse by having sex with a man with whom she had never had sex before and will never have sex with again for the rest of her life. Only after that could she resume her normal sexual life and remarry, if she so chose. The same applied to widowers. Since a strong stigma is attached to men who are used as *abezya*, "death purifiers", by widows, widowed women often have to travel to distant places where they are not known, often under the escort of their former sisters-in-law or other

female relatives of their late husbands, and quietly perform the rite, in which many people still believe. The practice is now under attack by women rights groups and other human rights activists for demeaning human beings, as well as by public health officials and medical practitioners for its role in the spread of sexual transmitted diseases, especially the AIDS epidemic, in a situation where, with changing times and widespread economic hardship the country has been experiencing for decades, *abezya* "for hire", male and female, have appeared on the scene.

Chapter XXXVII

NTULANLWO BECOMES HEAD OF A HOUSEHOLD AND GIVES AWAY HIS SISTER BULIHWALI IN MARRIAGE

After the death of Myombekere, Ntulanalwo lived on in his late father's home with his mother Bugonoka, his two wives, Netoga and Mbonabibi, and his sister Bulihwali. Young Ntulanalwo therefore became what the Mkerewe elder of yore meant when he said: "You work wood with the chisel at hand."

Two months after the death of his father, Ntulanalwo's wife Mbonabibi too gave birth to a baby boy and Ntulanalwo named the child after his father: "Grow up, your name is Myombekere."

Shortly after that Ntulanalwo's grandmother, Nkwanzi, Bugonoka's mother, also died. Ntulanalwo and the people of his home went to mourn her. On coming back, Bugonoka returned with the children of her brother Lweganwa and brought them to live with her in that home of her son Ntulanalwo. Bugonoka herself was devastated by the loss of her husband and her mother, following on each other so closely in that same year like deaths caused by the deadly magic of *ekitego*[1] we hear of. But there she was, with her family, and, dear friends, such misfortune is the destiny of all human beings and never befalls trees and stones. And so eventually she and her children put behind them that past of theirs, the way we all do. For, ladies and gentlemen, where in the world did you ever see a bereaved person who remains weighed down by the sad memory of his or her dead forever? Well, maybe you have, but that would still be something rare!

And so days passed and soon people saw that sister of Ntulanalwo, that same baby girl Bulihwali, reach adolescence. Breasts were forming on her chest and Bulihwali herself too could be seen casting glances now and then at that very chest of hers in an amateurish way, with girlish coquetry. What with the fact that her mother took great care of her appearance and cleanliness, by making her take a bath daily and anoint her skin with oil all the time the way clean women keep themselves looking, wear her hair trimmed short and done well and formed into neatly patterned naps[2] and never leaving it unattended until it became long and bushy on her head, because that is nothing but being dirty, and by making her keep her fingernails and toenails always pared, shave the hair off the hidden parts of her body which should be kept clean-shaved, brush well her teeth. Suitors could not but point her out to their people and flock to court her. When suitors began coming to Ntulanalwo to court his sister and kept on coming, he said to himself: "I can see that these are real suitors and no joke!" He therefore consulted his mother: "By the way, what am I to do with these suitors?"

His mother told him, "My son, the Mkerewe of old said: `A shoulder is always below the head.'   And so since you have junior fathers, the brothers of your father, alive, when those suitors of your sister come again speak to them like an elder and tell them: 'Go and court her before my father Mwebeya, because he is the head of our family. I don't want to usurp a function which is not mine, because the shoulder is always below the head,'" and Ntulanalwo did so. The suitors then courted Bulihwali before Mwebeya and kept on courting until finally out of the many one was preferred to the others and chosen to be her future husband and his courtship accepted. At that point Mwebeya consulted with his sister-in-law Bugonoka as to whether it was all right with her if within a few days he would send the suitor they had selected to court their daughter before the rest of their relatives.

Shortly after that one day Mwebeya went to graze cattle on his turn of duty in their neighborhood grazing round[3] and while bringing back home his own cattle in the evening after his neighbors had taken away theirs from the communal herd he realized that a cow he happened to have in the stock of that home of his, a thief inveterate, forever running off to graze in people's crops, was missing. And so after herding the rest of the cattle into his kraal he retraced his steps to look for it on the way leading to his home, and hopefully find it before it had strayed off to graze in people's crops as usual and put him into trouble again. When he saw the cow, it left the way and run into some empty fields. He was seized with anger at the trouble it was causing him and chased it everywhere through the brush until he caught up with it and punished it with some painful blows of a stick, and when he finally got it into the fenced cow-trail leading to his home he walked slowly behind the cow, while still boiling with anger and throwing all sorts of curses at it. As he got to the gate of his home from nowhere the flying snake *nabuzumiro*[4] shot through the air whistling like a stone released from a sling and struck him on his right leg. His wife was untethering calves of his milk cows by the fence of their household compound nearby and heard her husband exclaim really loud and say: "*Aaye*! dear me, a snake has struck me!" She left the calves and came running to see what had happened to her husband and found him looking for the snake which had bit him, before he started to feel the effect of its venom. She was about to bend and examine her husband's leg when, lo! her eyes fell on the snake, which was none other than *nabuzumiro*, wriggling on the ground and she said, "Here it is, kind of shortish. I think it is trying to get away." Mwebeya too spotted it and beat and killed it. Then at once he told his wife to call one of his sons and tell him to bring him a papyrus cord[5] without delay, and his eldest son did so and, with great anxiety, tied his father's leg as tight as he could to prevent snake poison from climbing up his body and getting into his heart, and then called his younger brother, and the two of them, one holding his head and the other one his legs, carried their father into his house. Immediately after that, their mother sent her oldest son to call their father's brother, that is Katoliro. Then, addressing his wife, Mwebeya said, "Could you mix for me chicken dung in a calabash bowl of water and let me drink that, maybe it will make me vomit." His wife brought the revolting mixture and gave it to him and Mwebeya drank it all, to the last drop, and they waited and waited, but he didn't vomit. His brother finally came and found him already groaning and agonizing with pain, but still he hadn't vomited. Katoliro said, "The venom of that snake is usually very bad indeed. If we are not lucky and obtain for him really strong medicine we are likely to be in real trouble, to face real danger. But let me too all the same try this medicine of mine and let's see what happens." Quickly Katoliro mixed the medicine in question with water and at once added very strong tobacco into it and when the solution was ready and strong enough, he made his brother drink it until he finished it all. And again they waited and waited for him to vomit and once again nothing happened. In the end they ran off to call another snake poison healer, although it was already nighttime. That healer too came and tried his medicines to no avail. Mwebeya's condition now became really critical.

At about the middle of the night, the man died. And so Katoliro and his sister-in-law sounded the mourning cry, joined in by the sons of the deceased. Their neighbors were at a loss as to who could have died in that home of Mwebeya, and in the morning when first thing on waking up they went there and found that it was Mwebeya himself who had died they all exclaimed, greatly surprised, and said, "Yes, indeed the death of a human being is always nearby! The man who yesterday was the whole day long running all over our neighborhood with our cattle is now dead! *Yu!* We must admit we have never seen the like of this! No, this wasn't an ordinary snake, it was a snake on an errand of some evil people! If it wasn't on such a wicked errand he would have survived. Haven't snakes been biting people for as long as we can remember, who would then be treated for snake venom and recover?"

Ntulanalwo was informed of the death and he came to the mourning, accompanied by his sister and their mother Bugonoka. After the mourning wake the three of them went back to their home.

Bulihwali's suitors resumed their courtship by now coming to Ntulanalwo, but he sent them to his remaining junior father, that is Katoliro. Katoliro then sent the suitors to court among the girl's clan relatives and when they completed that phase of courtship too the suitors came to him and reported on it. Katoliro on his part swore his self-praise, the man he was, and said, "*Aaye*! My name is Katoliro, the man who loves to eat with his visitors! Yes indeed, I must admit you have completed all the required courting and I am the only one now delaying the wedding. And that is because I don't want the daughter of my late brother to be married off like some unfortunate girl who has no relatives or like the daughter of some destitute people, and neither do I want to burden her brother at his young age with the responsibility of giving his sister away in marriage; no, I don't. Since, thank heavens, I am still alive, I want to honor the daughter of my deceased brother, to give her a proper wedding, the way people should celebrate the marriage of their daughters. And so my wish is that, since I am *omugonzo*[6] fisherman and happen to have in this home of mine my poor man's succorer, my *omugonzo*, which unfortunately has lost some of its hooks, I would first like to have replacement hooks made for me so that I can repair it as needed, then I will throw it into the waters of the sea for some four or five days and see whether Mugasa[7] will smile favorably at us, which would give you too some time to better prepare yourselves. Because, with us poor men, the only thing which can save us in times of functions like this one is the sea."

The suitor too agreed and went along with his co-parent-in-law's wish. Anyway, Katoliro was the parent of the girl he wanted, the decision maker, so that even if he the suitor had wanted things hurried up, until Katoliro was ready to give his daughter to his son there was nothing he could do.

The following morning Katoliro on his part tied together scraps of metal consisting of worn-out hoes and took them to the forge of an ironsmith to have the hooks he wanted made for him and the ironsmith made the fish hooks for him and he gave him his due fees and took his property and returned home. The day after that he made strings for attaching hooks to the center-piece rope, attached the strings to the rope and replaced the missing hooks of his *omugonzo*, finished, and then took his mended fishing gear and left it soaking in the lake overnight. Then on the third day he went to cast his fishing gear and left it out at sea being tossed about by the waters and the winds and lying in wait for a catch. By the way, lest we forget, the day before the one on which he cast his fishing gear was the day on which Katoliro sent his daughter Tibwomo to fetch Bulihwali from her mother and bring her to his home, since her wedding was approaching, and Tibwomo did so and brought Bulihwali to Katoliro's home the following day. The two women had just come when Katoliro too arrived form casting his *omugonzo*, carrying with him hanging from a string a rather large size *embozu*[8] catfish, about which he said, "I found this fish dead in the water in time before it was eaten up by *enkunga*[9] and said to myself: `Since it isn't too spoilt as yet I've better take it home and we'll eat it, lucky me!'"

The day after he cast his *omugonzo*, early in the morning Katoliro took his oar and his fishing spear – he would have taken his bail[10] too but he usually left it in his fishing boat – and off he went, passing by the home of a neighbor of his to fetch a rowing-mate. The two men got to the lake, sat in their fishing boat and went to fish their *omugonzo* which had been in the sea overnight. They finished retrieving their *omugonzo* from the waters at the time of the morning sun at which milk curdles and then rowed back their boat and landed their catch. They pulled their boat ashore and stringed their fish through the gills for easy carrying and ascended back to their homes. Once home, on counting all the fish he caught, which were a mixture of *embozu, emumi*[11] and *emamba*,[12] Katolilo found he had altogether fifty-three fish. He was not satisfied with his catch and said, "I had a poor catch; I should have caught at least a hundred, if not more." He took three fish, the three in excess of fifty, and gave them to his rowing-mate. The following day when he went to retrieve his *omugonzo* he caught sixty-seven *embozu*, twenty-three *emamba*, sixteen *emumi*, ten *embete*,[13] four *enzegere*[14] and two *enkuyu*,[15] that is altogether one hundred and twenty-two fish. That day the man congratulated himself and said, "Yes, today you can say I caught a bit of fish." Also on that day some of *embozu* catfish he caught were so huge you needed an ax to cut them up. Yes indeed, a poor man's bounty is in the sea! On Katoliro's third fishing day, early in the morning, before he left for the sea, Bulihwali's suitor called. As Katoliro was escorting him he told the suitor, "Gentleman, go and take a rest tomorrow, then come back again the day after tomorrow, and we'll know what to do." That day when he went to fish his hooks out of the water he caught altogether ninety-six fish, of which he gave the six in excess of ninety to his rowing-mate.

On his fifth day[16] of casting his *omugonzo*, it took Katoliro some time before he put together the baits for his hooks and as a result he went to cast his fishing gear late in the day. He had cast into the water only some few tens of the hooks when accidentally one of them caught him in the thigh and at once into the water he went and, as it happened, so did his rowing-mate. By that time the sun had already sunk below the horizon and darkness had set in and so with both of them no one knew how to save the other, each one simply struggled to save himself. On his part, Katoliro found he couldn't pull the hook out of his body without help, and at the same time he was already deep under water. He tried to come up by pulling with him to the surface the fishing gear to which he was hooked and found he simply couldn't and died! His rowing-mate on his part kept on swimming towards the shore, only he couldn't make their usual landing place because it was already dark night and out of fright after seeing his companion thus snatched out of the boat, for what he thought was: "My companion was certainly snatched from the boat by a crocodile. It simply couldn't be anything else," and that's why he too capsized and swam without knowing where he was going and landed on the peninsula of rocks and stones. It was from there that he went home uphill and informed the people of Katoliro's home of what happened to the two of them while out at sea fishing. Katoliro's wife sent out a cry of death and mourning cries filled the man's home!

The suitor came back the following morning only to find Katoliro's home in mourning and he was shocked! He was told how the master of that home was snatched out of the boat while at sea fishing and how the search for his body and his boat had not yet started. Finally people assembled and Ntulanalwo also arrived and men took their oars and went to the lake to search for Katoliro's body as well as for his boat, carrying with them harpoons with which to attack the crocodile, in case they saw it, Bulihwali's suitor among them. They searched everywhere along the shore without sighting a dead body or a crocodile eating a human being or seeing the dead man's fishing boat. In the end Bulihwali's suitor told the other men, "Gentlemen, it is true we are searching and doing our best, but all the same I am of the opinion that we are doing it the stupid way. If you share my opinion, come and let's get into this boat here and go out to sea, to the very spot where the two men were casting their *omugonzo*, and take a look at the fishing gear they left in the water. If it is still there, we'll retrieve it and by its lay in the water we'll know how the wind was blowing when they were out at sea and continue our search with that knowledge." The majority agreed with him and said, "Yes, what you say makes sense too. Let's try and do that, out of our desperation." The men go into a boat and when they got out there in the sea where the two men were fishing they saw the buoys of their *omugonzo* and redoubled their rowing, got to the spot, and began retrieving *omugonzo* from the water. They could feel that, yes, it had a good catch of fish on it, only it appeared too heavy. The man who was pulling the fishing gear out of the lake finally said, "This isn't right! Gentleman, it looks as if this *omugonzo* is stuck. It can't be otherwise, because it is too heavy."

His companions told him, "Just keep on pulling it out, when we come to where it is stuck we'll unhook it out of the obstacle and if we can't we'll cut it loose." The man continued fishing *omugonzo* out of the sea and before he knew it he was pulling out a colossus of *embozu*: "What a huge fish!" everybody exclaimed and added, "We have never seen any fish grow so big ever since we were born! Maybe this is one of those fish of which we are told: `There are fish which swallow human beings whole.'" The rope of *omugonzo* remained taut even after that giant fish was pulled into the boat, really taut. The man holding it jerked on the rope as he pulled, and gave it another jerk, this way, and then he felt it become lighter in his hands, though still feeling as if something continued to weigh it down the way a big fish would, and so he told his companions again, "Now it feels as if I have come to the end of *omugonzo*, only it looks as if there is still one more big fish on it, possibly bigger than the one we have just fished out. Pass me that big fishing spear so that I have it at hand to make sure the fish doesn't escape me and disappear back into the water." The other men put the spear near him and told him, "There you are, may the stronger of you two win!" And when the man pulled some more *omugonzo* rope out and pulled again, the body of a human being surfaced, completely intact, except *omugonzo* which hadn't been cast into water when the man went down was now coiled all around his body. Every single one of the men in the boat jumped out of his seat instinctively! The man holding *omugonzo* rope looked as if he wanted to let go of it and on seeing that his companions urged him to continue pulling and told him, "We have finally found what we are looking for and you want to let go your hold on *omugonzo*! Gentleman, pull it out like a man and bring a human being out of water so that we can get out of the sea and go home." He pulled and got the dead man's body to the side of the boat and the other men mastered their courage and got on their knees in the boat, bent over the side of the boat and together got hold of the body and pulled it into the boat. And then, silently, they dug into the sea with their oars and made for land and landed at the women's bathing shore strip. The dead body of Katoliro had swollen beyond recognition and was oozing deep red blood from the mouth and nose. Yes, I now agree, if you are not a man of real courage you can't go near the dead body of your beloved one recovered from the waters! No, you can't.

As soon as the men landed, they sent Ntulanalwo to inform the women in the dead man's home that they had found the body and to bring a door shutter[17] on which to carry the body. Ntulanalwo came back to the lake shore with the women and the dead man's body was carried uphill to his home amidst a crowd of mourners crying out their sorrow.

When the days of mourning were over, Ntulanalwo returned to his home, taking his sister Bulihwali with him. That is when people started saying all sorts of things about Ntulanalwo and his relatives meant to malign them and tarnish their name in the eyes of Bulihwali's suitor and his relatives, to whom they said: "Stop courting the daughter of Myombekere, because her people are under the curse of the deadly *ekitego* magic. Didn't you see how all her fathers disappeared in a single day, all of them dying one after the other? It is obvious that the man who marries her will also die."

However the suitor in question completely ignored all that, because he was determined to find his son a wife and because when he debated with himself the matter he found that dying is for us all, that even if his son didn't marry that daughter of Myombekere all the same he too would one day die. And so, when he saw that Katoliro's mourning was over, the man went to Ntulanalwo to find out how matters now stood with his courtship. On getting to Ntulanalwo, the man told him that he was now the person in charge of his sister's courtship, since all his fathers had died. And indeed Ntulanalwo took charge! He sent his sister's suitor that very day to go and fetch the bride's escort[18] and when the suitor came back to inquire about the wedding Ntulanalwo told him, "Go and tell the bridegroom and his party to come tomorrow." The bridegroom and his companions came as told and he gave them his sister in marriage as people do in this Ukerewe and was done with it and the bride came out of her parents' house and the bridegroom and his party took her to the home of the bridegroom's parents.

Ntulanalwo's brother-in-law, the man who married his sister Bulihwali, was called Ngundamugali, the son of Kasankara. When he was still a child his baby-sitters had found his rather unusual name difficult to get used to and ended up calling him by a shortened form of it and he become just Mugali.

Our Bulihwali stayed with her husband for just two years, as seasons come and go out of this sea, and in the third year she resented her husband and said he was I don't know what and what. She therefore left him and came back to her parents', her brother Ntulanalwo's home. When Ntulanalwo on his part realized that his sister wanted to leave her husband, he became raging mad, the son of Bugonoka! And so he tried all he could to make her go back while his sister Bulihwali remained as determined as ever never to return there and told him, "If you want to kill me, come and kill me and be done with it so that I can join my father where he went. That's much better than your forcing me on a creature my heart has no affection for. And if your problem is his bride-price you ate, *he!* you can be sure you've had it! You'll have to sell your teeth to pay it back!" Ntulanalwo tried every ingenious way of punishing her and forcing her into complying with his wish, including beating her really severely, tying her with ropes to the trunk of *omulumba*[19] tree in the compound of their homestead and leaving her tied there overnight, *aa!* but all that to no avail at all. Ntulanalwo got so frustrated that he vented his anger on his mother and told her, "If you are the one encouraging your useless daughter in her wretched behavior, I will expel both of you from my home here and let you go and live with your other relatives wherever you choose to go! I can't live with you when you don't want to listen to me!" Oh yes! It must indeed be true that you can beat into submission the skin but never the heart!

When Ntulanalwo tried all that without getting anywhere with his sister, Kanwaketa, who at that time was still alive, told him, "You simply must stop beating your sister this way, lest you end up beating her where her life nerve happens to be and kill her and make yourself the poorest of the poor. If her heart resents her husband, let them part from each other. She will find another man she likes and he will marry her." Ntulanalwo heeded that advice and took his sister back to her husband's home to divorce her and returned to the man everything he gave him as bride-price for his sister, the only exception perhaps being the one hoe he gave as recompense for her mother's baby-carrying *engozi*[20] straps, the baby-sitting reward of the bride's mother, which is never returned, that's all. Bulihwali then lived her life of a free woman[21] in that very home of her brother Ntulanalwo. She hadn't been divorced for a year when suitors flocked in the home, men of every kind, from white ones to red ones, as we say, and our Bulihwali from morning till sunset was escorting out of her brother's home one suitor after another.[22] What with the fact that she was a perfect copy of her mother's great beauty you would think Bugonoka herself entered her own womb and them came out again! To add to that, she on her part was not of the smooth and marvelous deep-black complexion of *entundu*[23] banana stem like her mother and neither was she all-out light skinned but right in-between the two hues, with just enough light skin showing through her blackness, the complexion people find so lovely, you know!

After a while she selected from among her suitors the man between whom and her there was mutual agreement, a man she felt would be a good husband for her. Ntulanalwo told his sister's chosen suitor to bring him one house screen[24] and three hoe handles. He was determined to take from his sister's second husband as little bride-price as possible, and so he told the man to bring him, in addition, nothing else but six pots of banana beer. His sister's suitor brought what he was told to bring and Ntulanalwo told him to come for the wedding and gave him her sister in marriage.[25] That second husband of Bulihwali who married her when she was still a maiden-divorcée[26] was called Nemba. When Bulihwali had been in Nemba's home for one year she became pregnant and gave birth to her first-born, a baby girl. The second time she gave birth it was to a boy. And when that child became a lovely baby, who laughed to his baby-sitters, Bulihwali's maternal grandmother, that is Nkwanzi, died.[27]   A messenger came to inform Bulihwali and her husband and they went to her mourning. About a year after that her maternal grandfather, that is Nanwero, also died and Bulihwali and her husband went to mourn him and when the mourning period was over they came back to their home.

In that home of Nemba our Bulihwali said: "See me bear children and multiply!" No sooner had she dropped onto the ground a baby-girl than she followed her with a male child! Finally, when her youth wore out and she married off a daughter of hers and that first-born of hers too bore a child of her own, she settled down and became the solid foundation of her marriage. And before long her son too got married and gave her another grandchild and with that she had nothing to complain of in life anymore.

Shortly after that the mother of Ntulanalwo and Bulihwali, that is Bugonoka, died and her children mourned her appropriately and finished.

Chapter XXXVII

NOTES

1. *Ekitego*: Powerful magic whose owners were supposed to live in Uzinza (the country of Wazinza), which could be hired for a fee to avenge a wronged person and instructed to kill everybody and everything in the household, family or clan of the wrongdoer, including domestic animals and chickens. It was also believed that if a person stole property protected by *ekitego* he or she also risked such ruthless punishment.

2. The Wakerewe admired African hair which grew in hard naps, called *kaheke*, and a woman's most admired hair-do was *kusyonga*, which consisted in trimming her *kaheke* hair very short and then breaking it into patterns of separate hair grains by washing it with the foaming leaves of *oluzingwa* herb or an equivalent and giving the neat patterns of hair dots formed on her head a shining finish by rubbing them with oil. See note 3 of Chapter XXIII.

3. For the Wakerewe neighborhood grazing rounds of duty see note 7 Chapter XII.

4. *Nabuzumiro*: Literally "the zooming (snake)". Kitereza in his note for his Swahili translation of his novel says: "Very poisonous snake the color of an adder, which prepares to strike a person by contracting its length into a short thick mass and then springing at its target zooming like a stone released from a sling flying through air."

5. *Omuhotora*, plural *emihotora*: See note 2 of Chapter XXX.

6. *Omugonzo*: See note 4 of Chapter VI.

7. Mugasa: See note 27 of Chapter VII.

8. *Embozu*: See note 8 of Chapter XIX.

9. *Enkunga*: Kitereza in his note for his Swahili translation of his novel says: "Bird, white in color, which feeds on dead fish in the sea. The fishermen always see the birds from far because of their white color and know there is a dead fish at the spot and make for it. The birds would fly off when the men approach and if the dead fish is still in good condition the men would take it. If a group of men are involved, it is the one who sighted the birds first and said so to his companions who takes the fish."

10. *Olusabuzyo*: Here a wooden container for baling a water vessel. See note 12 of Chapter I.

11. *Emumi*: See note 34 of Chapter XXV.

12. *Emamba*: See note 17 of Chapter II.

13. *Embete*: See note 17 of Chapter II.

14.   *Enzegere*:   See note 17 of Chapter II.

15.   *Enkuyu*:   See note 17 of Chapter II.

16.   This is the fifth day of casting his *omugonzo,* even though it is his fourth day of fishing.

17.   *Ihara*:   See note 6 of Chapter III.

18.   *Ensendekelezya*: See note 29 of Chapter XXIX.

19.   *Omulumba*:   See note 16 of Chapter II.

20.   *Engozi*: See note 9 of Chapter XXI. For the Wakerewe bride-price items and their distribution, see   Chapter XXXIII.

21.   *Omusimbe*:   See note 24 of Chapter II.

22.   Among the Wakerewe, a divorced woman or a widow or spinster, that is *omusimbe* or free woman, unlike a maiden,   receives her suitors in her parents' or relatives' home and escorts them out as she pleases and she personally, and not her parents, picks her husband out of her many suitors.

23.   *Entundu*:   See also note 12 of Chapter IX.

24.   *Olusika*:   See note 25 of Chapter XXIX.

25.   Subsequent marriages of a divorced women are usually less formal and celebrated without much fanfare.

26.   See note 5 of Chapter XIV.

27.   Here again Kitereza forgets a detail of his long story: at the beginning of this chapter we learn that Nkwanzi, Bugonoka's mother and Bulihwali's "maternal grandmother", died shortly after the death of Myombekere and in the same year.

Chapter XXXVIII

NTULANALWO'S DAILY OCCUPATION UNTIL HIS DEATH, THE DEATH OF BULIHWALI

At the time his mother died, Ntulanalwo was already an adult and a man of responsibility, no longer afraid of heading a household, about which he always heard people in Ukerewe say: "A household is not a beast of prey to be afraid of!" His two wives, Netoga and Mbonabibi, were bearing children all the time and by the time his mother Bugonoka died his first born son Galibondoka was already married man   with children of his own. Of the other children of Netoga born after Galibondoka, the boys were grown up young men, already of the age to get married. We won't say much about Ntulanalwo's female children with that first wife of his, Netoga, since women were created to leave their parents' homesteads and go to found other people's households. Likewise Ntulanalwo's first son by his second wife Mbonabibi, the one he named after his father Myombekere, was already a married man and he too already with children of his own.

Sometime later Ntulanalwo married another wife, whose name was Masale, a divorced woman who already had children of her own with her former husband, so that Ntulanalwo's household become a real homestead, big and strong. With three wives, Ntulanalwo's home now was his poor man's kingdom, where he was a real sovereign, where every wish of his was at once a command, where his three wives were forever outdoing each other to win his favor. And not only that, each one of them was determined to be his favorite wife and so each and everyone of them was daily looking for love potions. Well, you all know the saying of the Wakerewe: "The people of Nafuba Island[1] destroyed each other over a newcomer!" And so that newcomer, Masale, became the real favorite of the master of the home, the woman Ntulanalwo really loved dearly, whose house became the place where Ntulanalwo kept every work tool of his and where he sent people to look for it. Netoga and Mbonabibi, on seeing their husband lose interest in them that way, forged an alliance and became very close friends and banded together determined to poison their husband's affection for Masale, inventing all sorts of untruths about her and reporting them to their husband so that he would stop loving her and divorce her, for nothing short of that would satisfy them. But because when it came to that wife of his Ntulanalwo had become like a crocodile, which once it seizes a prey never lets go, he heard all what his two other wives told him as if he had no ears, as if all that was no concern of his. When his two other wives had said to him all the bad things they could think of against Masale with no sign of their husband listening to them and sending her away, in their frustration and anger they now went about telling anybody who cared to listen that their husband hated them. Whenever they were in their houses and chanced to hear Masale while talking with their husband inside her house burst out laughing and sending out a loud hilarious cry, they would feel a pang as if she were maliciously stabbing them with a knife through the heart and really enjoying it! "Now the creature is backbiting us to her husband!"

That situation continued for a long time until finally the parents of Ntulanalwo's two other wives heard of it and became very angry with their son-in-law. Netoga at that time had just given birth to yet another child and was still nursing it, and so with her her parents told her, "You pretend to be a fool who doesn't see or know anything and stay and nurse your child, and as soon as you wean your child leave him. Come back here and live your freedom as an unattached woman[2] and you'll find other men who want to marry you, if your husband doesn't want you any more. What's more, he must be a very stupid man to want you to leave in spite of all those children you have born him! Yes indeed, men are monsters! And so it's up to you: if you find you don't want to leave your children, stay, but then be prepared to really suffer!" To which Netoga replied, "My children don't worry me, because they are in their home; for where do maternal half-brother and half-sisters come from?" Her mother answered her, "They come from their mothers getting married to several husbands, to men other than their first husbands and having children with those other men too. However, leave that alone, my dear child. I too will try to fortify you as parents fortify their daughters in a marriage when the need arises. If with that so-called Masale her mother was able to obtain for her medicine for attracting men's love so powerfully, we too will try our best to look for such a love potion until we find one. And so you just go back and wait, and in the meanwhile we'll inquire among people and we'll see! Listen, another woman just like you shouldn't keep worrying you so much as if she has I don't know what you don't have!"

And so Netoga went back and continued to live at her husbands home with her children, until one day all of a sudden her mother sent her a messenger to tell her that she wanted to see her on such and such a day without fail and on time. During all that time Ntulanalwo himself was completely unaware of it all, for, as the elder of old said: "A conspiracy in which you have no relative kills you before you know it." At her parents' home her mother put into Netoga's hands the medicines for attracting her husband's love she was calling her for: from the medicines she was to put in the food she cooked for him to those with which she was to fumigate his *obwita*[3] before serving him the food. And Netoga went back and did what her mother told her to do, but always when the children and Masale herself were not at home, only then did she give Ntulanalwo that medicated food, thus making sure he was always eating it all alone.

Mbonabibi on her part too obtained from her mother love medicines for charming her husband into loving her as well as those for repelling his love for Masale, some kind of bad luck charms she smeared on bed sheets on Masale's bed. And once Netoga and Mbonabibi resorted to the use of those love antidotes, they began to see Ntulanalwo's heart turn again towards them, their husband begin to love them again as he used to, at the same time as they witnessed their co-wife Masale became an object of their husband's real resentment. What with the fact that Masale had no child with Ntulanalwo, she became really miserable!

Once Masale on her part too realized how unwanted she had become to her husband, so much so that he now sometimes even skipped the nights he was due to sleep in her house, she said to herself, "Better get up and clear from here your baggage of bad feelings! It's time to go again, you poor woman, destined to be for ever on the move: you no longer have a husband here!" And so that woman Masale became like the person fabled by the old ones of yore: Leave-taker whose belongings are forever in the custody of

Chance, and she left. And after staying at her parent's home for just a few months her people brought her back to Ntulanalwo's home for divorce and Ntulanalwo divorced her and that became the end of that. Masale went into her house and took from its hanging place in the roof by the house door her ritual *enkorongo*[4] horn, took out of the house her tray,[5] took down the hangers of her few kitchen utensils and pots and said good-bye to her husband and his other wives and, *ei* ! she was gone forever!

And from there on Netoga and Mbonabibi began casting oblique glances at each other in their life of two women married to the same man. There was a day you would pass through Ntulanalwo's home and find those two wives of his happy together, and then on another day you would find one or the other of the two her throat swollen to bursting with anger like she were the flying snake *nabuzumiro*[6] tensed to spring and strike a person. And on yet another day the two women would be seated side by side but completely oblivious to each others presence, like some two *bukoko*[7] birds stealing side by side, as people say, so that if you were a visitor stopping for the night in their home you became apprehensive and said to yourself: "Is it really safe here!" And there were also days you would find them seriously quarreling with each other in the presence of their husband out of that co-wives' rivalry of theirs to the extent that you the visitor would say to yourself: "These two will certainly never share a meal again!" And then, when their husband went away, you would see those same two wives of his not only eating together but each one insisting on the other one eating a bit of *obwita* from her bowl[8] or tray and the two all the time saying to each other: "Now dear, what is it with you today! You are taking *obwita* only from your dish and eating none at all from mine! Is my food perhaps uncooked? Please, dear, don't be like that, try and eat some of my food too. Do you want mine to be the only food returned to the kitchen? *Yu!* my dear woman, don't do that!" sharing with each other even their relish and exchanging peels of hilarious cries amidst endless laughter, both in really good mood. But as soon as their husband's footstep would be heard stepping back into their home: *tini!* at once you would see their mood change, as if they had moods in plenty like the shades of the red goat *kasya*.[9] That was when you'd hear them vent their anger on their children with all sorts of allusions meant for the other woman, each one of them noisily reprimanding and insulting a child of hers: "Go away, you oversize-head creature! you freak! your chest so dirty and full of scratches like a *ninga*[10] bird forced to nurse a co-wife!" with the other woman perhaps answering that by throwing other innuendoes at a child of hers: "Go away, you big-headed monster! always up and restless like a chicken laying eggs!"

Then as days went by, all of a sudden livestock disease rinderpest[11] descended on the country and fell on people's cows and goats and struck them fatal blows: *pupu! pupu*! and rained complete ruin and destruction on the wealth of the households of herdsmen. In his home, Ntulanalwo was left only with a miserable two cows, both heifers.

Ntulanalwo found himself saying to himself, "I now see that inherited wealth, like stolen property, brings no good luck! And what I am going to do now, brothers and sisters, so that I can continue to feed the mouths of this large household of mine? We were people used to washing down our food with sips of milk and overnight we find all that gone!   What resourceful occupation shall I turn to for succor so that I can have some cattle again in my home quickly?" He debated the matter with himself and arrived at a number of possibilities, out of which he settled for the making of boats. So he went into the forest to look for trees which could yield a boat large enough to barter for a cow. That day he was gone into the forest the entire day, coming back home only late in the evening, after cows had already folded a knee for the night. You just imagine! The people of his home were about to mourn him, convinced that he surely must have been killed by elephants in the forest! And please don't be surprised by what I have just said about elephants, because in olden times elephants abounded in this forest of ours and people being trampled to death by them was a daily occurrence. Especially the Wakara,[12] who used to come to this Ukerewe of ours to look for wood for making the wooden hoes they used, called *amahaya*.[13] They could get the right wood for their *amahaya* only from our forest, where they usually looked for trees with really hard wood and a big core like *amameya*[14] and ebony already fully grown and seasoned. And so sometimes groups of Wakara looking for hoe wood would all of a sudden find an elephant already on them, huge and pervasive like the dawn of a new day. You too know how the elephant though such a huge animal moves without making noise! And on seeing the elephant the Wakara, in their cleverness -- for I can't say in their stupidity as if I have ever cheated them out of some property of theirs --, even if the elephant had yet to scent them, would at once break out jabbering in their incomprehensible language: *tokoli! tokoli*! kind of shouting, jokingly pointing out the elephant to each other, amused, and even laughing, their rags of skins no longer around their waists where they normally tie them but hanging loose from their haunches and leaving them virtually naked, with the Wakara men themselves even more oblivious to their nakedness than they usually are,[15] being in all male company and in the middle of the forest like that. At that point you would hear your Mkara fellow howling to call his friend's name and telling him in their Kikara language, "Mabere! Shee shis bull of Muswaga of shis Emulambo. Here, it ish coming! Ever sheen it?" that is, in our Kikerewe, "Mabere! This is Muswaga's bull which he keeps in this Omulambo land of Ukerewe. Look, it is coming. Have you ever seen it?" With that the Wakara would then stand all together and jabber, excitedly exclaiming their amazement at the huge size of the elephant, and before they knew it the elephant would blow its trumpet on their account, obviously having finally scented their presence, and then head for them and attack them, picking them up as a child picks up *ensungwa*[16] fruits from the ground before trampling them and flattening them out. Many times when elephant hunters[17] went hunting they would come across bundles of *amahaya* wood and Wakara men's skin rags on the ground, some already eaten by termites, and on looking more closely they would then see even the remains of human skeletons, hardly recognizable, because when an elephant tramples a human being it breaks to bits the victim's bones. Indeed, dear brothers and sisters, when death has decided to take you away it has better get you while in your bed any day rather than wait to end your life by giving you such a death, with this bit of your body here and that part of your liver on the other side!

Ntulanalwo finally came back from the forest and he told his sons, "Sons, I found the trees for making boats: one *omukimbwi*[18] and one *omugege*.[19] And so tomorrow I will go to an ironsmith to have made for me three axes and three *ebihoso*[20] for working wood." And on that following day Ntulanalwo took some scrap metal, used-up hoes, to a ironsmith and the tools he needed were made for him, including some chisels, which, together with *ebihoso*, he needed for hollowing a tree trunk and shaping the keel of a boat and making the frame boards. In the meanwhile people in Ntulanalwo's home had now been reduced to living on greens cooked with nothing but water and salt, the unpalatable greens the Mkerewe calls cooked "on and off the fire", without a single drop of butter or milk in them. He made two trips to the ironsmith's home to have his iron tools made and on the second trip he come back with three axes, two *ebihoso*, four chisels, about five billhooks, more than ten iron rods for boring holes in boards and seven fishing spears. Once back home, he told his wives and the wives of his sons to dig for him and his sons sweet potatoes to take with them to the forest during the time they would be making their boat and the women brought the sweet potatoes and his sons wrapped them in grass and tied them in bundles. Then the following day, early in the morning, he emptied his home of six grown up sons of his, with himself as the seventh man, and they took each and everything they needed for their work, their weapons included, and off they went, so that in that home of his there remained only young children and the women. Those who came across him and his sons on the way all loaded that way could not but ask him: "Dear man, where can you be going? What are you going to do? And what are you carrying in there?" You all know how the people of this country of ours are! The fact that they can never just look at another person's thing without also feeling it with their hands and pinching and squeezing it goes to show what an impossible people they are! And when Ntulanalwo answered them by telling them that he was going into the forest to make a boat, as soon as he left they at once began backbiting him and saying: "He must have nothing else to do! We live here with this Ntulanalwo all these years and not once have we ever seen him make boats and all of a sudden today he wakes up and drags along his children and says, `I am going to make a boat!' *Hee*! Does he take a boat for *enanga*[21] and hoe handles and the shapeless chairs he is all the time toying at chiseling in that home of his? *Hii*! Making a boat calls for really skilled workmanship! Anyway, he is welcome to it: since we live together here we'll see his boat!" And so those men would go their ways and keep in their minds what they had said: "We'll wait and see his boat!" putting aside their business to concern themselves with other people's business! I am telling you, our people are simply impossible!

Ntulanalwo and his sons finally got to the forest and decided to work on *omugege* tree first. When they got to the tree, Ntulanalwo told his sons, "Put down your loads and let's first clear a place for our sleeping site. You Galibondoka and Myombekere and Galikika, take each a billhook, here they are, and let's clear the bush. The remaining three of you, you will be removing from here the trees we are cutting down and putting them over there. And after that we'll work our wood flint with an iron rod and start a fire for roasting our sweet potatoes."

And the men set to work as directed by their father and finished clearing a camp site. Then their father showed them how men work a piece of wood with an iron rod to start a fire when in the wilderness, worked the piece of wood with their iron rod until fire appeared and produced smoke in the wood and burst into a flame, on which they put dry firewood and got going a real bonfire. They let the wood burn down to a pile of embers and then put inside the heap of embers a number of sweet potatoes they judged would be enough for their lunch. After that three of them turned to selecting and cutting trees and sticks of the right wood with which the rest of them got busy making handles for their new axes and chisels and billhooks and fishing spears. When the young men had been working for some time, they told their father, "Father, we are dying of thirst."

Their father answered them, "Well, you are men, aren't you? Take your weapons and a billhook for clearing undergrowth obstacles in your path and take three calabashes and go and bring water quickly, for the lake isn't far away."

Some of them went and brought water and some took from the fire sweet potatoes and they ate their lunch. After that they all rested for a little while to let food settle down a bit in their stomachs before resuming their work, now by cutting down the tree for their boat. When night fell, they slept there in the forest by their tree, near their forest bonfire,[22] on which they kept piling logs of dry wood so that the fire burned bright all night long. Whoever among them on waking up from sleep found himself feeling cold would go and warm himself by the fire first before going back to sleep. At daybreak they resumed their work and in no time *omugege* tree fell down, and at once they cut off its branches. That done, Ntulanalwo felt really pleased and he and his children began the important work of shaping the tree into a boat. And now they toiled in earnest. Whoever of his sons appeared to play about, Ntulanalwo would deliver him a blow with a stick, accompanying it with words of sharp reprimand: "We came here for important manly work, didn't we? And now you want to step aside and leave it to others! Don't those others get tired like you? Will what we are making here not be of use to you too, you freak? You'll come to no good with this laziness of your mother! What type of a fool do I have for a son? Quick, take up an ax and work like your brothers!" Whenever their food provisions were about to get finished the young men would go home for more, but Ntulanalwo himself was never to bee seen again in his home, no even once, all the time they worked on their boat in the forest.

He spent in the forest an entire month working before he completed the keel of a fairly large boat for eight rowers, nine including the pilot, that is a large boat with four passenger thwarts, together with the boards for constructing its frame. Then Ntulanalwo and his sons hauled the bottom of their boat and its side boards from their work site to the lakeshore and constructed the frame of the boat and completed their vessel, for which Ntulanalwo also made a bail[23] as well as nine oars, eight for the rowers and the ninth one for the pilot.

Their work completely finished, they put their boat on the lake and boarded it with all their belongings and rounded the coast to go back home and made for the lakeshore strip where the women of Ntulanalwo's home drew water, with Ntulanalwo himself piloting the boat so as to get a feel of how steady and fast it sailed. As they started on of their journey and Ntulanalwo sat in his boat and witnessed how it flowed on the sea, as swiftly as a water-snake, he gave it a name: Water-current,[24] and when he approached their landing place he burst out singing. What with the fact that the man had the beautiful singing voice of his late father, it was at once something to behold! His sons answered his song as they redoubled opening and closing their armpits digging deep into the water of the lake with their oars. On hearing people singing on the lake, his neighbors poured to the lakeshore in all their numbers, men and women alike, to witness what was landing and when they landed the people saw that it was Ntulanalwo and his sons. Everybody was amazed to see that Ntulanalwo could make such a beautiful boat, with such a well-crafted frame! And so people told him: "Really! Can this be true! Ntulanalwo all these years we see you here all quiet and unassuming and thought there wasn't anything extraordinary about you when actually you are such a great boat builder! Yes indeed! the old ones of yore were right when they said: `To underrate another person is to betray your own insignificance!'"

Ntulanalwo responded, "I see! Then it must be true that public opinion is impossible to predict, and also maybe that's why we have among us people named Disparagement! Did you then think: `The boat he will make will never float!' or perhaps: `It will be a boat sailing backwards, the stern in front and the bow at the back!' I acquired my skill of making boats from my maternal grandfather, with whom I was staying when I was a young boy, for, as people say, our knowledge comes form others. That's why I decided to try. And you all know the saying: `Tasting is eating.'"

The other men fell to examining his boat, over and over, every part of it, feeling it all with their hands as if caressing it! Ntulanalwo told them,

"It is for sale, so find me whoever wants it out there and let him come and buy the boat."

"What do you sell it for?"

"I want to exchange it for a heifer of a cow which is already pregnant plus a female young of a goat, that's all."

"We hear you."

Those who got word of the sale began pouring into Ntulanalwo's home to see the boat and ask him the price, and on finding that he wanted a cow plus a goat for the boat they gave up and left. Ntulanalwo said to himself, "Let them go, because: `A cow-skin in the house never lacks a needy sleeper.'" After only a few more days passed, one day Ntulanalwo had just returned home from renting his boat to *emigonzo* [25] fishermen for use on that day when Omururi[26] man from the distant land of Bururi came into his home. He had come from his country all the way to this Ukerewe of ours precisely to look for boats to buy. When they discussed the price of the boat and Ntulanalwo told the man what he wanted for his vessel the man agreed. He happened to have some cattle belonging to him in this country and so he told Ntulanalwo, "Don't send the boat anywhere again and don't sell it to anybody else, even if another buyer comes along. I am leaving to go and bring you your property, the price items you have mentioned, and I'll be back in no time. So please, gentleman, don't sell this boat to somebody else."

Ntulanalwo answered him, "You just go and come back; the boat will be here waiting for you. But please, gentleman, don't keep me waiting for you here and stop me from attending to my other matters for nothing and end by not showing up!"

Quite some time passed and again some more time went by and then back the Omururi came into Ntulanalwo's home, with a companion of his, having with them a cow and a goat, the two animals both overflowing with fat like bullocks on account of their good health. The animals were tethered in what used to be the kraal of Ntulanalwo's household before his cattle all died off, now an empty enclosure overgrown with *oluchwamba*[27] creeping grass. Ntulanalwo sent for people to come and witness their barter and the people gathered. Everybody present was satisfied with the cow and praised it: "It is good enough; what is more, it is pregnant" and people were likewise satisfied with the goat. Ntulanalwo took out a new iron hoe come all the way from Uzinza[28] and gave it to the barter witnesses as their reward[29] and said, "Here is a new iron hoe, my thanks to you for helping us conclude this bargain; go and buy some banana beer with it," and likewise the Omururi man rewarded the witnesses of their barter with a hoe. And so the man took his boat and its nine oars and bail and left to go back to his country of Bururi with whoever he had come with. Ntulanalwo gave that cow a name: Luzwelere, the name of his boat, and was out of himself with happiness and congratulated himself: "Lucky me!" like a person who had chanced on some treasure-trove.

After a few days passed, Ntulanalwo set off on a second journey to the forest with his sons to make another boat. This second time he cut down *omukimbwi* tree. When the tree fell down, its branches remained caught in *amakamira*[30] vines, which happened to be leaden with ripe *amakamira* fruits, and so, before clearing the vines away, the men fell to bursting open the fruits into their mouths, casting away fruit skins as they swallowed the rest, fruit-stone included, and savored their great sweetness. All of a sudden they heard in the thickets of the forest a sound of something: *tukutukutuku*! Ntulanalwo said, "My dear children, beware, we are in great danger, an elephant has invaded us! Take up your arms quickly and let it find us prepared like men. And should any of you prove a coward, we'll see! I myself will kill him here on this very spot and leave his body buried in a porcupine hole! Here it comes, face it like men."

The elephant in question on its side said: "Say no more, here I am!" announcing it had scented their presence by trumpeting its trunk. Ntulanalwo, his spear to which he had given the name Bonecrusher in hand, stood upright and dead-stiff like the tall *omuhama*[31] palm tree of Kahama reputed to have swallowed a Mkara. Looking really furious and deadly, he held that Bonecrusher of his in his right hand and in his left hand his bow, together with five poison arrows, two *amasagwe*[32] arrows with arrowheads as long as the span of the fingers of an open hand as well as two barbed ones. He had given that bow of his too a name: Savior-of-the-dying. And on came the elephant. When it was about to get within the distance of from here to there and was getting ready to pick up Ntulanalwo with its trunk, he released his Bonecrusher from his hand and swore a self-praise: "I have pierced you! I am the son of Bugonoka, in case you want to know!" And when the elephant tried again to reach for him and whisk him off the ground, Ntulanalwo dodged and passed under its belly and got to the other side at the same time as he heard from that other side his son Galibondoka utter an oath: "I have stuck you one! I am the son of Netoga." Immediately his other son Myombekere too swore: "I have fixed you one: I am the son of Mbonabibi,"33 and form yet another side his son Galikika too swore: *"Peki*! Yes, that iron was from me: I am the son of Netoga." When Ntulanalwo dived under the elephant's legs to the other side he at once shot a poisoned arrow into the animal's trunk and then struck it with yet another poisoned arrow in its flank. Now a real battle ensued: whenever the elephant tried to catch this one of its hunters, that one would pass under it belly and jump to the other side. Finally when the elephant lost too much blood and the poison shot into its body took effect, its hunters saw it sway on its feet ready to fall and then: *ligiti*! it tumbled down.

Ntulanalwo saw the elephant was finally dead and told two of his sons, Galibondoka and Myombekere, "Go and call for me the following elephant hunters: Kurundugara, Kamese, and Matebya. Tell them to come and help me handle this beast, because I am afraid of doing anything on my own lest I damage the king's tusks. But make sure you go home first and inform my wives that I have killed an elephant." And off went his sons, walking as fast as they could. When they informed their mothers at home, their mothers became the fabled bad-hearing woman who was told her husband had been killed by a rhinoceros and she cried out in jubilation: "May he kill them all!" and asked their children again, "Is it a real elephant, and have you really killed it, is it really, completely dead, you children?" Their sons answered, "It is indeed a real elephant, and a huge one at that, the famed colossus of an elephant, which at this very moment is lying dead where we left it, a mass this big, piled on the ground higher than a house by far." On hearing that, Netoga and Mbonabibi began making ready to strap their children on their backs and go to their husband in the forest, to congratulate him and to see the elephant, because they had never seen a dead elephant, nor a living one for that matter, for all they had seen of elephants was their footprints and their dung they saw whenever they went into the forest to cut thatch grass for roofing houses. When Galibondoka and Myombekere saw their mothers put their children on their backs, hurriedly, not even taking time to strap them secure and safe, they stopped them and said, "No, not now. Wait until tomorrow, when you can come with our wives, because it is now too late for you to get there and come back home traveling while carrying children this way."

The young men then left to go and fetch the elephant hunters, got there and conveyed their father's message to the men and   immediately the famous hunters, as if they had received a message they had been eagerly awaiting, got all worked up, took their special drums *ebipumpuli*[34] and: *hoho*! off they went, carrying their sword-like big knives and already accompanied by a huge crowd of people, attracted from everywhere by the sound of their *ebipumpuli* dance.

In the forest the elephant hunters found our man Ntulanalwo with his other sons seated aside, away form the dead elephant, as if reliving what the Mkerewe meant when he said: "He who knows how to step aside is the one who kills his prey." And since, as people say: "Prevention is better than cure, " the elephant hunters at once got busy looking for their medicines for the purification of the place on which the elephant died and for killing winds so that living elephants won't scent their dead one and come there and attack people furiously, but would instead remain immobilized in their encampment. And indeed they needed to take that precaution because the elephant is not an animal to play with, especially when it comes to how it reacts when it sees the dead body of a fellow elephant like that one. A whole herd of elephants would have flocked there to try and carry off the dead body of one of their own and take it to whatever place they would have chosen, where they would have placed it on the ground and then brought huge trees and piled them on top of it until the carcass was well covered, and only after covering their dead that way would they have returned to their base. That is their elephant way of burying their dead, according to the elephant hunters, who used to witness those animals burying each other that way all the time.

The following morning Kurundugara, the leader of the elephant hunters who had come, carefully looked at the dead elephant and examined every part of it and told Ntulanalwo, "What you have killed here is a giant elephant, the one which gives us our saying: `The tiny bird *enfunzi*[35] wants to compare footprints with the giant elephant!' meaning that a commoner who wants to confront his sovereign[36] is out of his mind." The men were still chatting and the elephant hunters hadn't even started removing the elephant tusks from the carcass of the dead animal when Ntulanalwo's two sons he had sent on errand arrived, accompanied by his wives and daughters-in-law as well as many other people. His wives were simply amazed at the size of the dead animal, but when they tried to come nearer and take a good look while carrying children on their backs that way the elephant hunters stopped them and told them, "First break off from trees some leaves or collect some grass and come and throw that on the carcass, in the manner of a burial ritual, before coming nearer to take a good look at it. This is a dead animal, and so we are afraid you mothers, and especially your children, may fall sick from *enkirabuzi.*"37 The other people present agreed with the elephant hunters and said, "The women wanted to err on that point, because what you say is our usual way of doing things in this country since the beginning of time. Even with an adult, if you are waking on the road and you come across a carcass, be it that of a dog, a wildcat or a snake, you cannot pass it without throwing on it some leaves of a tree or some grass for fear of the evil of the dead animal harming you, and with regard to children on the backs of their mothers our fear for them is lest they fall sick with *enkirabuzi* disease. And so we have to say that these women were about to do something seriously wrong. Honestly, not to tell them that would mean we don't wish them well; and, no, we can't do that to them as if we don't know them." The women of Ntulanalwo's home did as they were told and then took a good look at the carcass of the elephant and ululated38 for joy and came forward and congratulated their men: "Congratulations! Congratulations! our men! Yes indeed! You are men among men, you will rescue us from drowning in our deep waters! *Aaaye*! Our father of fathers!" Those present who didn't know Ntulanalwo and his sons began pointing him out to each other over and over and saying: "I see! So that's Ntulanalwo, the man who has accomplished this feat! I see! He is a real masculine figure all right and some firebrand of a man, and likewise his sons are men to whom fear is a foreign thing. Oh yes! Were they not bold men but a bunch of tremblers could they have fought and killed this giant of an elephant without the beast making short work of them?"

That over, the elephant hunters turned to removing the tusks from the carcass of the elephant, culling tusks, as people say. They removed the two tusks from the carcass nicely and carefully and put them aside and stuffed and closed with dry grass their openings at the end. Since they were really heavy, people cut shoulder poles on which to tie and carry them and   tied each tusk across four poles so that it would be carried by eight people, making a total of sixteen carriers for the two tusks. After that they cut from the carcass of the animal those parts of elephant meat they do eat39 and then told carriers to carry the tusks as well all their elephant meat and everybody left to go to *omukama's* palace to present the king with the tusks, leaving behind the rest of the mass of the elephant carcass piled high on the ground. There hyenas would come and dwell inside the huge carcass and eat it up while laughing really loud until they have leveled the entire mass to the ground, after which its bones would become the dwelling place of the big "I've-found-the-stench" flies ever so fond of stench and rot together with all sorts of other flies and a farm of the tiny black ants, determined as usual to always have their share of everything.

And so the elephant hunters and their procession went to Bukindo[40] singing, with the head of their group as the lead singer of their elephant hunters' songs while some of them played their *ebipumpuli* drums as was never heard before, amidst women's peels of ululation: *keyekeye*!

In Bukindo they were received by the sound of the king's palace drums[41] and then everybody in the palace was entertained by the elephant hunters' fantastic dance and play-acting, I am telling you! When our Kurundugara sang really loud, since he happened to have a stentorian voice, it was some spectacle! Finally it got to the time of the day when the king rests and takes his bath and *omukama* sent a courtier to tell *emilango* players to stop playing and all the drums and all dancing stopped. The elephant hunters and Ntulanalwo and his sons went to take a rest in the home of the courtier where their village headman[42] was normally received whenever he came with presents to pay his village's homage to *omukama*, where they found the king had already sent for slaughtering in their honor a huge bull, so big and fat it could hardly move! In the afternoon of a descending sun, *omukama* sent to the elephant hunters and their companions a courtier who came and told them: "I have been sent to tell you that you should go back to the palace compound and resume your performance. *Omukama* would like to see a bit of your show when it is still daylight."

The men took up their elephant trophies at the same time as our Karundugara went and painted and changed his face in the most incredible way! To mask himself, he painted his face with soot and red earth and white mud and looked so terrible that every child and woman who saw him was frightened, taking him for a zombie! The elephant hunters returned to the palace compound and *emilango* sounded again and thundered and rumbled in the palace of rain-makers, and Kurundugara, on realizing that *omukama* had not yet come to the palace compound, to entreat their sovereign to come to their show put all his being in his song and sang: "We are in the palace, the palace of the Rain-maker, in palace of the Bee, of the Honey-maker, the palace of hundreds-of-conversations, of the Great-giver, of the Generous-one, of the one Born-bathed-clean, the palace of the Muhaya of Goziba[43]; we are not in the home of the Miserly-one, of the

Born-alone-eagle, of *namuku*,44 the bird which calls for her children and gives them nothing; we are in the house of Generous-giving, my dear men and women." He was then answered by a prolonged: *hoo*! in the midst of peels of ululation from women. Kurundugara then spoke to himself and said: "Oh, I see! If you think I'm done, you have never witnessed people present trophies of a giant elephant like this one to their king!" and took up his song again and ended with the refrain: "Who of you here eats in far off Nafuba?45 Who eats in far off Gwanengo? Who eats in far off Gemitaro? Who eats in far off Sozihe? Who eats in far off Busyengere? Who eats in far off Songe? Who eats in far off Irugwa? Who eats in far off Lyamonde? Who eats in far off Lyamagunga? Who eats in far off Kamasi? Who eats in far off Kalwenge? Tell me, dear men and women, who of you here eats in far off Mafunke? I'll tell you: only the worms and maggots of the earth when they feed on the dead of those far off places." His spectators: "*Hooo!*" Ululation: "*Keye keye*" This time when he took up his song again the lead singer of the elephant hunters made for the finale and opened fully his great voice and sang: "So I say: it is in the Palace of Great-deeds where we all eat! in the palace of Great-deeds of the rain-makers! the palace of Great-deeds of Prince Kankombya! the palace of Great-deeds of King Katobaha! the palace of Great-deeds of King Kahana! The palace of Great-deeds of Princess Kogire and Nansato! the palace of Great-deeds of Princess Namugonzibwa and Bilekero! the palace of Great-deeds of Princess Mutaye and Bwizura! where when they throw your way what to them is some wretched piece of cooked rawhide you receive a great treat! where when they throw your way what to them is a bare bone you receive a great delicacy! Ladies and Gentlemen, the feet of a slave are covered with dust and ashes and smell bad! We embrace only the feet of *omukama*!" And the crowd: "Hooo!"

With that he concluded his singing and the king came out of his house and took his place in the palace compound. *Abagunda* together with Ntulanalwo and his sons then went to pay their homage to the king and presented him with the tusks of the elephant Ntulanalwo killed. The king asked Ntulanalwo how the elephant attacked them, how he killed it, and what he was doing in the forest and Ntulanalwo recounted to him each and everything to the end. *Omukama* was very pleased with the tusks and a number of his courtiers carried the trophies away and went to keep them for the king. Again the king congratulated Ntulanalwo and his sons and said, "Yes, you are indeed a real man, son of Myombekere! And your sons too are truly real men, sons you will always be able to count on." Then the king rewarded your Ntulanalwo with three heifers of cows, one of them pregnant, together with a bullock, for slaughtering in his home to feast the people who would come to congratulate him. Ntulanalwo embraced the feet of the king and hailed him and said: "Long live the son of a king, long live the Giver-of-habiliments!" Ntulanalwo's son Galibondoka, the one who seconded his father in hitting the elephant with his weapon, and Myombekere, who came third, were both given a heifer of a goat and a new iron hoe and likewise his son Galikika, the fourth person to hit the elephant, was also awarded a young female goat. The three elephant hunters, that is Kurundugara, Kamese and Matebya, were given a huge bull, so big it could no longer turn round its neck, a real mountain of a bull, the "terror of anthills", as we say, because when such a bull gets angry it attacks anthills for lack of other bulls daring to fight it. Ntulanalwo then said good-bye to *omukama* and he and his sons and their company went back to their homes amidst endless shouts of jubilation, bringing with them their rewards of livestock. Once back home, Ntulanalwo and his companions first slaughtered his bullock before ending their feasting and celebrations by slaughtering the elephant hunters' "terror of anthills."

Then that was that and people were left exclaiming with much wonder at Ntulanalwo's great luck in being able to possess livestock again in such a short time! He now had altogether six cows and four goats in that home of his.

When those celebrations were over, Ntulanalwo went into the forest again with his sons, to make a boat out of *omukimbwi* tree they had just felled when the elephant they killed attacked them, which they found where they left it and got ready to work. Only they did not find a trace of the carcass of the elephant anywhere in sight and what they saw only increased their wonder, because instead of the carcass they found footprints of other elephants indicating that several of them had trampled all over that ground! Ntulanalwo said, "It appears other elephants took away the body of their dead and went to bury it. Don't you see how this place is all roughed up with their footprints? Look, here is the trail of their way out. If you are real men, let's go and find out where they took it." His sons agreed and they all took up their weapons and followed the trail until they came to the elephant's burial place, a spot on the ground piled high with lots of big trees, some of which had been uprooted whole from the earth and brought there and thrown on the pile. Then they heard growling sounds coming from under that very pile of trees supposed to be recovering the carcass of an elephant and they all asked each other, "What can be making so many growling noises in there? Let's throw in sticks and lumps of soil and see what will come out.   If it is a dangerous beast, we'll fight it." Ntulanalwo told his sons, "If that's what you want, you must be prepared for the worst, for it could be leopards fighting in there, for anything we know." The men positioned themselves ready for battle and threw into the pile of trees sticks and hard lumps of soil. *Ehe*! lo and behold! Giant hyenas[46] in countless numbers dashed out, others passing under the men's legs with their jaws open and their teeth set and yet others running out with chunks of elephant meat hanging from their mouths! As to our men, there was nothing they could say, for they were the ones who had chosen to provoke the beasts. They attacked the fleeing beasts and killed twelve of them. Ntulanalwo told his sons, 'Skin them and keep their skins and also cut off their noses, because medicine men and medicine women, especially those who deal in magic, have some use for them." The young men did as their father bid them and then they all went back to their work.

From that *omukumbwi* tree Ntulanalwo and his sons made one single-piece boat of average size, with no additional framework and no interior joints for support.

While still in the forest, before they had finished making their *omukimbwi* wood boat, one day the sons of Myombekere all of a sudden had a dispute among themselves on how the indigenous Wakerewe women, the Abaseskazi,[47] swear in self-praise, until finally they asked their father, "Please, father, help us here! We want to know whether the oaths we hear all the time Wakerewe women swear by have any particular meaning?"

Their father said, "I see! So that's what I hear you noisily disputing about with each other while I am cutting this tree here for a hoe handle. I was wondering what it was you were discussing; so that's it! In that case let me explain it to you. The women usually swear by their clan oaths, and here are the oaths of just a few of those clans, some of them famous clans and others not so well known. You all know when, let's say, Wakerewe women are having a palaver and one of them accidentally drops something to the ground or a baby she is carrying urinates on her or she tells a child of hers to do something for her and the child dilly-dallies or appears reluctant to go on the errand, how at once you will hear a Mkerewe woman reprimand such a child and then slap the side of her own thigh and swear. Well, she swears by her clan oath. That clan oath sometimes simply identifies her clan or recalls the great cattle wealth of her ancestors or tells of the origin of her particular people."

"Tell us those oaths of the clans of the Wakerewe, father."

"All right, let me tell you the oaths of the following clans, which are just some of our clans:

Abasilanga women swear by: My father the Mhaya! My father of Goziba.[48]

Abayango women swear by: My father of Bwera! *Aaye*! the Erect-one!

Abakura women swear by: My father of Kwimba! My father of Nambuye!

Ababwarumi women swear by: My father of countless-cows! *Aaye*! the Promised-one!

Abamiro women swear by: My father the Jaluo! *Ee*! Ntana!

Abasegena women swear by: My father Man-of-plenty! *Ee*! Walu!

Abagwe (or Absita)[49] swear by: My father of Kitale! *Ee*! water current Kimiza, who urinates rivers like Kaboza rain![50]

Abagabo[51] women swear by: Butwaga!

Abahindi women swear by: My father of Mwanza!

Abazubwa women swear by: *Ee*! Bayondo!

Abaguza women swear by: My father of Bwandege!

Abahira women swear by: My father of Bwiru! Ee! Bwengoro! (or Bwenfunzi!)

Abaruhu women swear by: My father of Chanda!

Abatimba women swear by: My father of Kelango! *Ee*! the Seeing-eye which saw both the herder and his cattle!

Abazigaba women swear by: My father of Luguru! (our) Bwezya!

Abagembe women swear by: My father Masale! *Ee*! Garongo!

Abachamba women swear by: My father of Rubya!

"And so if you happened to be near a group of Wakerewe women holding a palaver and one of them swears you should be able to tell her clan from her oath. Or if, let's say, you want to know the clan of a Mkerewe woman or what is taboo to her and the people of her clan without asking her directly you can know by asking her her clan oath. And that is how it is, my children. And doesn't that settle your dispute?"

"Now we know, father, what the oaths are and what they mean."

Ntulanalwo and his sons finished making that one-piece boat of theirs and dragged it down to the lake and went back home.

And so Ntulanalwo's home once again became a household with

cattle, especially once the cows calved and the herd multiplied. Greens once more in that home were seasoned with butter and its people watered down their mouthfuls of sweet potatoes with sips of milk so that the morsels of potatoes simply slipped down their throats and people no longer had to strain before they could swallow their food.

After restoring the cattle wealth of his home Ntulanalwo now looked for an occupation to which he could devote his entire life: "Milk to sip with food is once more back into my home after is had disappeared from it, but still it would be better to satisfy both the desires of the woman in the proverb who said: `If you don't have relish broth for your morsel of food you should at least have milk to sip with it.' With me too, to be able to feed this home of mine really well I need to provide it with fish for relish broth, because already here is a fishing boat, and it is my very own property."

And so he told his sons to help him cut reeds for building in the waters of the lakeshore *olubigo*[52] fish trap. When they cut enough reeds, Ntulanalwo built in the floor of the shallow waters of the lake *olubigo* with four catching chambers. On his first fishing trip to the trap his maiden catch was twelve *ensato*.[53] Since that was fish of the maiden catch, all of it was cooked in one large pot with no salt: that saltless and tasteless fish was eaten by Ntulanalwo alone. On his second trip to his *olubigo*, Ntulanalwo caught one *emamba*[54] and on his third trip he caught twenty *ensato* and in the subsequent fishing trips he now caught sometimes ten or thirty or forty fish and the like, during that dry season in which he erected his *olubigo*. And since in those days there was plenty of fish in the sea, during the rain season he would catch fish in the hundreds, seven or nine hundred, sometimes even topping the one thousand mark, bringing home as many as one thousand *ensato* in one single day. And besides *ensato* he also caught all kinds of fish in that *olubigo* of his, including *emumi*[55] (which in those days were so plentiful that during the season of heavy rains they spilled over form the lake onto dry land), *emamba*, *eningu* [56] and *engere*.[57]

Seeing how well he had managed to supply his home with fish for relish broth, Ntulanalwo was encourage to try yet another way of doing so even better. He cut tall and slender twigs and sticks from forest vines and tree climbers and trellised them and made larger and stronger *emigono*[58] fish traps called *amahongora*.[59] When the number of *amahongora* he wanted was ready, he put them into his boat and went to sea. And from there on his daily occupation became fishing in his *olubigo* and with his *amahongora*.

One day he went fishing in his *olubigo* and on coming to one of its four catching chambers he found *emambagwe*[60] catfish in it. The big fish had seen the heel of Ntulanalwo's foot flash in the water as he stepped into the catch chamber and just as he was turning around to grab his *ekisanzo*[61] basket and draw it out of the water all of a sudden he felt the fish bite his heel: *kakacha*! and he instantly exclaimed aloud: "*Yu*! a fish has bitten me!" Immediately one of his sons, with whom he had gone to *olubigo* that day, his fishing spear in hand, had waded through the water to where his father was and asked him, "What kind of fish has bitten you?

"It is *emamba* and it is still clinging onto the heel of my left foot."

"Don't move so that I can strike it with my fishing spear."

"No, don't! Because if you try you can miss the fish and strike my foot instead and wound me, or get both the fish and my foot as well. I think the best thing is for me to try and get out of the water with the fish still on my foot, because I know that once *emamba* bites it never lets go easily." And so Ntulanalwo got out of the water and onto the sand of the beach with the fish still dug into his heel. It was once he was out of the water that he and his son saw that the fish in question was actually *emambagwe* and killed it, and only then did it drop off Ntulanalwo's foot. Ntulanalwo examined his foot and found he had a terrible wound and told his son to fetch him a strip of dry banana stem fiber and bandaged his wound with it to try and stop the bleeding. Once home his sons and his wives on examining his leg found he had indeed been seriously injured. That was the day when Ntulanalwo told those of his sons who tended to dodge going to fish in his *olubigo* or with his *amahongora* when their turns came: "Today none of you will eat this fish, because you don't want to go fishing. I am not your slave who will continue to bring you fish to eat while you don't even have an idea of the hazards of fishing!" And from that day those of his sons who used to find all sort of excuses to avoid going to sea became sensible and dutiful sons who willingly fished their father's *olubigo* and *amahongora*.

As soon as his wound got better he resumed his work, and on the first day of going to sea again he caught in his *amahongora* a huge *ensonzi*[62] catfish, a real *bush-rock-water-shitter*. When the fish was brought home and Ntulanalwo cut it up fish fat he got from it filled a huge pot to the brim. And the person in his home who ate that sweet "*bush-rock-water-shitter*" of a fish without moderation indeed that night didn't sleep a wink but was in the bush the whole night purging terribly! And for days after whoever passed through Ntulanalwo's home was at once swamped by the strong *ensonzi* catfish smell. In fact the people of Ntulanalwo's home themselves for days on end carried with them wherever they went that overpowering fish smell of *ensonzi*! No wonder some of them from that day for the rest of their lives could never eat that fish again!

From his fishing occupation Ntulanalwo was able to buy some more cows, five female cows and two bulls, by first bartering the fish he caught for millet and then buying cows and goats with the millet. That was how once more his home became the home of great cattle wealth, how his homestead which had been impoverished once more became a really prosperous home, the home people call: Somebody's home. And Ntulanalwo himself was to grow old until his head was all gray still pursuing that sea occupation of his, to tell you the truth. In his *olubigo* he narrowly escaped from being killed by crocodiles three times and he capsized as many as four times while fishing his *amahongora*, and regarding one of those accidents he would live tell his children and grandchildren: "My children, I once capsized in the middle of the sea and swam the entire night, arriving home the following day with nothing but my oar held in my hand. My whole catch of fish went down into the water when my boat overturned and I recovered the boat itself only after it had landed ashore on its own!"

Whenever the many children of Ntulanalwo fell sick, he went to consult oracles on their account and they recovered and when they didn't recover but died he gave them appropriate burials. As his age continued to advance his male member was eventually exhausted and he was left only with the pleasure of eating food and savoring his dear *ekilangi*[63] tobacco. He even stopped sharing a bed with his wives and instead slept on a separate bed of his own, which he shared with his little male grandchildren.

And lo and behold how afflicted with all sorts of old age diseases and aches and pains in his bones and all over his body he now became! Today it would be: "My back is paining," tomorrow: "My head is killing me," the day after tomorrow: "There is sharp pain shooting throughout my teeth," or "The shooting pain is now in my ear," or "It is now in my molar." His eyesight too was failing and to look at a person who was only a short distance away he had first to shield his eyes with a hand, like this! And so he lived on until finally he caught death, for only affliction from which a patient recovers should be called a disease.

His disease this time was a very high fever. His sons Galibondoka and Myombekere as well as the others went to consult seers and healers of every reputation and without respite over that illness of their father, taking to them oracles without end, from the roots of trees to the rest.[64] One of the diviners told them," This patient of yours won't recover. No, he won't. He'll die from witchcraft. And the evil people who have bewitched him have done so because they envy him his cattle wealth, the innocent and good man, and because he knows how to feed well his home, the man among men!" Which indeed he was, because the people of Ntulanalwo's home ate their fill, unlike the inmates of homes of men where the wife insults her husband: "What type of a man do you call yourself when you are another Cuddle-the-safe-lakeshore-sand like we women!"

Ntulanalwo's children were so determined to find seers and healers who would cure their father that the day he died they were all away from home on their daily search. It happened sometime in the afternoon and the only people at home were Ntulanalwo's wives and daughters and daughters-in-law and his young grandchildren, and from that time of day until sunset his sons were still all gone to consult diviners and find a cure for their father. It was not until late in evening when dark had already set in, at the time women put on the fire *obwita* pots for the night meal, that they streamed back, only to find their patient himself already departed, already as cold as cold water, as dead as a stone, and the men cried and mourned their father throughout the night, this one uttering his own words of sorrow as he bewailed his loss and that other one yet uttering his different sorrowful dole.

And since there has never been a magician powerful enough to keep a new day from dawning, it finally dawned and when it dawned and enough people gathered, Ntulanalwo's grave was dug. When the grave was ready and the cow for the skin in which the dead man would be buried had been slaughtered, the first officiant of his father's burial became Galibondoka, the son of Netoga. He was the one who cut the first hoe on their father's grave, seconded by Myombekere, the son of Mbonabibi. The mourning wake of the death of Ntulanalwo lasted the customary four days and on the fifth day mourners bathed his death and the mourning was lifted.[65]

On that day of lifting the mourning a certain man came to the home of the deceased and said that the deceased owed him one cow. The man was given the cow owed him, because the dead man's sons as well as both his two wives knew very well of the debt in question. Then yet another man also came into the home and said that the deceased owed him a young female goat and claimed: "He incurred the debt when we were in my home drinking banana beer." On hearing that everybody present questioned the man and asked for some explanation and when he failed to support his claim by naming the people who witnessed how the deceased came to owe him a goat he was jeered at by the entire mourning crowd in the home. He was huge person but in an instant he became a very tiny fellow indeed: so tiny that he slipped out of that home and disappeared without anybody at all seeing him!

That was how Ntulanalwo the son of Myombekere lived his life on this earth until he died and was buried gloriously, as we say in this Ukerewe of ours, since when he died he was buried by his sons and he left behind him his household standing strong on its feet and possessing cattle wealth and prospering.

As to Ntulanalwo's sister Bulihwali, she also lived a long life on this earth: she held in her hands her grandchildren of the fourth generation, the grandchildren of her great grandchildren. She left this earth because of what people call "days", which, as we say, finally triumph over even the longest living wild animal, and not due to any other cause. In fact, by the time she died her sons and their wives together with her grandchildren had become completely fed up with her: they had found her disgusting because she had become a person who played with her own shit and urine like a baby. She had reached a point where whoever came into that home of hers and saw her renounced completely his or her desire for long life on this earth! Let's say that she lived on only because a human being is never killed off when he or she gets too old the way we kill off old livestock, otherwise she would have been killed off long before, and also because a human being is never buried alive, otherwise her people would have buried her alive long before, to tell you the truth. She could no longer walk upright but moved by crawling on all fours. And when her daughters-in-law left sweet potatoes in an bowl for her, she instead would remove the food from the bowl and throw it in sand on the ground and then urinate in the bowl and the dogs, which had learnt her habits well, would always be there to eat the food she had thrown away.

And on and on her days dragged on until one day she wondered out of her house in the middle of the night and then could not make her way back. When she was found, she was already stiff dead! It was in fact her grandchildren who were playing by throwing stones at birds in the trees and shrubs of their homestead fence who found her and told the adults, who then came and took her from there and went and buried her.

But since a dead person is always dear, listen and hear how her mourners bewailed her loss, her dying and leaving them so lonely! To see them you wouldn't believe they had even stopped passing by to greet her in her tiny house in the home. Once she began putting filth in their food they found her repulsive and completely avoided her and often only sent into her tiny house her grandchildren to make some fire in it for her and that's all. But on the day she died she all of a sudden became very dear to them all again and they felt the pang of her loss to the very center of their being.

As to her burial, since she was a woman, she was buried lying on her right-hand side facing south and the back of her head pointing north, her head pointing west and her legs eastward. In her long life the dead woman had been an initiated healer and so her fellow women initiates danced *lwakalera*[66] at her grave and she was buried with a countless number of *enkorongo* horns, so many that, before her grave was completely filled with soil and covered over, the top of the grave was completely overlaid with them and still there were many more left and had to be stuck in the sides of the grave, bearing testimony to her very long life and to her life of a great healer.[67]

And now to make a long story short: Good-bye, ladies and gentlemen, keep on with your palaver. As for us, we are leaving: we had come to rest for a night and not to stay for good. All we wanted was to bear testimony to the truth of the names of the people of this country. Ask: "Who are they?" Answer: "The-people-of-this-country: Myombekere and Bugonoka and Ntulanalwo and Bulihwali." Ask again: "And what is their growing up name?"[68]   Answer: "Split-opener-of-truth, thunderbolt, where there's smoke there's fire, the son of Bugonoka! Misfortune-is-never-by-choice! the famous woman Frankness, the mother of all children, the caring layer-chicken of many colors, the daughter of every Myombekere, Lifestyle-of-all-households!" Can you tell me who is the older of these two: I've-always-been-here and I-was-found-here?   You all know the children game: "Narubengeya[69] in tatters and rags! Narubengeya in tatters and rags! You behind jump to the front lest you become Narubengeya in tatters and rags! Narubengeya in tatters and rags! Narubengeya in tatters and rags!" Yes: you at the rear must jump to the front lest you remain engulfed in your old ignorance. Good-bye and good luck! Just remember my story: Love's labor for an ingrate breaks the back for nothing!!!

Chapter XXXVIII

NOTES

1.   *Nafuba*: One of the minor islands of Ukerewe kingdom. See Introduction.
2.   *Omusimbe*: See note 24 of Chapter II.
3.   *Obwita*: . See note 14 of Chapter I.
4.   *Enkorongo*: Here a ritual horn. See note 20 of Chapter I.
5.   *Olugali*: See note 6 of Chapter I for the significance of *olugali* and a woman's ritual horn of note 4 above in her divorce.
6.   *Nabuzumiro*:   See note 4 of Chapter XXXVII.
7.   *Bukoko*: Name of a bird.
8.   *Ekibo*:   See note 15 of Chapter I.
9.   *Kasya*: Red goat, supposed to exist in numerous shades of the color.
10.   *Ninga:* Name of a bird.
11.   *Sotoka*: The livestock disease rinderpest.
12.   Wakara (singular Mkara): See Introduction.
14.   *Amahaya*: Wooden hoes. Kitereza in his note for his Swahili translation of his novel says: "Hoes made of very hard wood used by people of Ukara Island.
14.   *Amameya* (singular *imea*): See note 18 of Chapter XXX.
15.   The Wakara used to dress by putting over their private parts the barest of covers, *ensembe*. For the other meaning of *ensembe* see note 19 of Chapter XXXVI and note 24 of Chapter XXI.
16.   *Ensungwa*: Name of a wild edible fruit with a sweet-sour taste.
17.   *Abagunda*: Elephant hunters, a society of initiates. Kitereza in his note for his Swahili translation of his novel writes: "*Abugunda* were great hunters and very well known to the king because every time they killed an elephant they had to take the elephants tusks to the king as presents. *Abagunda* were the only people in Ukerewe who ate elephant meat and they too ate only the meat from around the animal's tusks, and the rest of the carcass would be left to the hyenas."
18.   *Omukimbwi:* Name of a tree.
19.   *Omugege*: Name of a tree. See also note 23 of Chapter VIII on *omugazu,* the incense perfume the bark of the tree yields.
20.   *Ebihoso,* plural for *ekihoso*: Chisel with a circular edge.
21.   *Enanga*: See note 9 of Chapter IX.
22.   *Ekikome*: See note 1 of Chapter II.
23.   *Olusabuzyo*: Here a wooden bail for a water-vessel. See also note 12 of Chapter I.

24. Luzwelere: "Water current".

25. *Emigonzo,* plural for *omugonzo:* See note 4 of Chapter VI.

26. Omururi: See note 15 of Chapter IX.

27. *Oluchwamba:* Type of creeping grass.

28. Iron hoes and other ironwares used in Ukerewe and surrounding areas were mostly made in Uziza by a clan of Wazinza people called Abarongo. See note 18 of Chapter V and note 30 of Chapter XXXIII..

29. The reward for witnessing a bargain, given to the witnesses by both the seller and the buyer. See the barter of a goat for tobacco in Chapter XXIX.

30. *Amakamira:* A forest climbing plant with sweet edible fruits.

31. *Omuhama:* A very tall palm tree with a swelling in the middle (see note 13 of Chapter XIII). When the Wakerewe children ask their parents why the *omuhama* tree has that swelling in the middle of its trunk, their parents answer back by telling them that the tree swallowed a Mkara (see note 12 above), the Wakara being usually short and thickset people like the swelling in the middle of *omuhama* tree. Kahama is the name of a country not so far away the Wakerewe knew which happens to rhyme with *omuhama*, hence the expression "*omuhama* of Kahama", for the sound of it.

32. *Amasagwe,* plural *for isagwe:* Arrow with a long arrowhead like the head of a fishing spear, the *isagwe* proper from which the arrow takes its name.

33.   In spite of the fact that Kikerewe children belong paternally in terms of clans and families, the Wakerewe swear by their mothers as often as they swear by their fathers and are likewise as often identified by their mothers' names as by their fathers'.

34. *Ebipumpuli:* Elongated drums used by elephant hunters in their dance.

35. *Enfunzi:* Here a tiny red bird of lonely habits, the totem of Abasilanga, the ruling clan of Ukerewe. See note 2 of Chapter XXIV and note 5 of Chapter XXX.

36. *Omukama:*   See note 26 of Chapter II.

37. *Enkirabuzi:* Kitereza in his note for his Swahili translation of his novel says: "A disease a child catches from looking at and smelling the carcass of a dead wild animal or of a snake, especially the python. In a case involving a dead python, when pregnant women see it, to avoid harming her child with *enkirabuzi* disease, when the child is born if it is female it is named *Nansato* and if male it is called Lusato," from *ensato*, a python, pronounced *ensáto*, as different from *énsaato* for *ensato* the fish tilapia.

38. *Akahira:* See note 11 of Chapter IX.

39. See note 17 above.

40. Bukindo: See note 8 of Chapter IV.

41. *Emilango*: See note 11 Chapter XIII.

42. *Omukungu*: See note 3 of Chapter III.

43. Abasilanga, the ruling clan of Ukerewe (see Introduction), claim to have come to Ukerewe from Ihangiro by way of the tiny island of Goziba, by which they still swear one of their clan oaths.

44. *Namuku*: According to Kitereza's note for his Swahili translation of his novel, the bird of that name is believed to behave that way towards its children and hence it is the symbol of greed.

45. The names in this song here are names of some of the minor islands of Ukerewe kingdom. See Introduction.

46. *Entana*: Kitereza in his note for his Swahili translation of his novel says: "Very large species of a hyena, which not only attacks other wild animals and livestock but can even attack human beings," and, by extension, general name for predators and other dangerous wild animals.

47. *Abasesekazi*: Wakerewe women, from *Abasese* for Wakerewe and the suffix *kazi* for *abakazi*, "women". See note 21 of Chapter XX.

48. See note 43 above.

49. Abagwe or Abasita: Clan of the king makers of Ukerewe, who were also the guardians of the tombs of the kings of Ukerewe. See Introduction and note 2 of Chapter XXII.

50. Kaboza: Interminable light rains of the month of May. The kings of Ukerewe were deemed to be the greatest rain-makers of the kingdom and possibly this oath of the clan of king-makers was meant to convey that they were also the origin of the kings' rain-making power.

51. Abagabo: This appears to be a misspelling for Abagabe, one of the clans of Wakerewe, since there is no Abagabo clan in Ukerewe. Unfortunately this particular clan oath is also the only one which is omitted in the author's Swahili translation of his novel.

52. *Olubigo*: See note 3 of Chapter II.

53. *Ensato*: See note 2 of Chapter VI.

54. *Emamba*: See note 17 of Chapter II.

55. *Emumi*: See note 34 of Chapter XXV.

56. *Eningu*: Name of a medium size fish with small bones all over its flesh.

57. *Engere*: See notes 17 and 18 of Chapter XVI.

58. *Emigono*, plural for *omugono*: See note 6 of Chapter II.

59. *Amahongora*: Large *emigono* above, made of trellised twigs and sticks instead of splits of canes or papyruses, the usual material for *emigono*. See note 6 of

Chapter II.

60   *Emambagwe*: Kitereza in his note for his Swahili translation of his novel says: "Type of *emamba* catfish (see note 54 above) reddish in color and a very fierce fish".

61.   *Ekisanzo*: Small basket of trellised splits of canes or papyruses. See note 3 of Chapter VI.

62.   *Ensonzi*: Extremely fatty and rare type of the *emumi* catfish of note 55 above. In his note for his Swahili translation of his novel Kitereza writes: "Anybody who eats this fish immoderately is bound to purge the terrible stench of the rot of overeating, hence its nickname 'shitter-of-water-on-the-rocks-of-the-bushes.'" See note 19 of Chapter XXVII.

63.   *Ekilangi*: See note 7 of Chapter VII.

64.   For the oracles of the Wakerewe see note 9 of Chapter XXIII.

65.   For the period of mourning see the death of Myombekere at the end of Chapter XXXVI.

66.   *Lwakalera*, also called *enkanda*: See note 21 of Chapter XXXIII.

67.   See note 4 above. Kitereza does not explain these horns or hint at their being special, so they could only be the horns of Bulihwali's personal charms, of which every Mkerewe had at least one, and the containers and drinking cups of her medicinal herbs accumulated over her very long life of a famous healer.

68.   For this Kikerewe way of posing riddles, see notes 13 of Chapter IX and 8 of Chapter XXVIII.

69.   "Narubengeya *nsasa*": "Narubengeya (female name) in tatters and rags", song of a game by children traveling in single file, in which the one who falls at the end of the line is at once taunted by his or her companions to run to the front lest he or she gets branded with that name of ridicule, with the result that the children keep on racing to wherever they are going while playing and having fun.

Cited Works

Ashton, E.O. *Swahili Grammar (Including Intonation)*. Harlow: Longman, 1947.

Betbeder, Paul. "The Kingdom of Buzinza". *UNESCO Journal of World History* Vol. 13.4 (1971).

Biebuyck, Daniel and Kahondo C. Mateene, ed. and trans. *The Mwindo Epic*. Berkeley & Los Angeles: University of California Press, 1971.

Blue Book Statistics. "Ukerewe Sub-District 1948 Census". Tanganyika Territory File No. 679. Tanzania Government National Archives, Dar es Salaam.

Bryan, M. A. *The Bantu Languages of Africa*. Oxford: Oxford University Press, 1959.

Harwig, Gerald W. and Charlotte Hartwig. "How Men and Women Came to Live Together: A Kerebe Tale" by Aniceti Kitereza. in *Natural History* Vol. 79 (1970).

Harwig, Gerald W. *The Art of Survival in East Africa: The Kerebe and Long Distance Trade, 1800-1895*. New York: Africana Publishing   Company, 1976.

Hurel, Eugene P. *"Religion et Vie Domestique des Bakerewe."* In *Anthropos* 6 (1911).

Johnston, Sir Harry H. *A Comparative Study of the Bantu and Semi-Bantu Languages*, London: Oxford University Press, 1919.

Kitereza, Aniceti. *Bwana Myombekere na Bibi Bugonoka na Ntulanalwo na Bulihwali.* Dar es Salaam: Tanzania Publishing House, 1980.

Lattimore, Richmond. "Introduction." Homer. *The Iliad*. Trans. Richmond Lattimore. Chicago: University of Chicago Press, 1951.

Lwanga-Lunyiigo and J. Vansina. "The Bantu-speaking People and Their Expansion". In *UNESCO General History of Africa. Vol. 3. Africa From the Seventh to the Eleventh Century*. Paris and Berkeley: UNESCO   & the University of California Press, 1988.

Machunda, John B. *Ukerewe: Leo na Kesho*. Dar es Salaam: Kituo cha Utoaji Vitabu   vya Elimu ya Watu Wazima, 1988.

Mkama II, Alphonce Golita. Records of Important Events in the History of Ukerewe and the Lives of the Kings of Ukerewe. Basilanga Family Records. Ukerewe, Tanzania.

Möhlig, Wilhelm J. G. *"Nachwort des Übersetzers"*. Kitereza, Aniceti. *Die Kinder der Regenmacher: Herr Myombekere und Frau   Bugonoka*. Trans. Wilhelm J. G. Möhlig. Wuppertal: Peter Hammer Verlag, 1991.

Mulokozi, M. M. " Book Review: An Extraordinary Novel Out of Africa." In
    Development Dialogue Vol. 1 (1985), Dag Hammarskjold Foundation,
    Uppsala, Sweden

Ogot, B. .A. "The Great Lakes Region." In *UNESCO General History of Africa,*
    Vol. 4 .

Africa from the Twelfth to the Sixteenth Century. Paris & Berkeley: UNESCO
    & University of California Press, 1984.

Okpewho, Isidore. *African Oral Literature: Background, Character and Continuity*.

Bloomington and Indianapolis: Indiana University Press, 1992.

Prinz, Manfred. "*Die Kinder der Regenmacher: Eine Familiensaga von* Aniceti

Kitereza". *Research in African Literatures* 24.2 (1993). (English translation from
    German   by Richard Bjornson).

Ruhumbika, Gabriel. "The African Language Policy of Development:
    African National

Languages." In *Research in African Literatures* 23.1 (1992).

Scheub, Harold. "A Review of African Oral Traditions and Literature." In *The*
    African Studies Review Vol. 20. 2/3 (1985).

Simard, Fr. Almas. "Préface du Traducteur". Kitereza, Aniceti. *Myombekere et*
    Bugonoka. Trans. Fr. Almas Simard. Société des Missionaires d'Afrique

(Pères Blancs), Montreal, c. 1952.

Stanley, Henry M. *Through the Dark Continent*. New York: Harper and Brothers,
    1879.

Werner, Alice. *Introductory Sketch of the Bantu Languages*. London & New York:

Kegan Paul, Trench, Trubner & Co. & E. P. Dutton, 1919.

Appendix to the introduction I

The Bahinda Kings of Uzinza and the Dynasty of Ukerewe
(Bahinda: "Descendants of Ruhinda").

1. Ruhinda rwa Njunaki, died c. 1447.
   |
2. Ntare Mganga-nzara.
   |
3. Nyarulenzi.
   |
4. Katobaha I of Uzinza.
   |
5. Kabura aka Nyangole (Nyamuha-ente-oturo).
   |
6. Kabambo Nyarugenda (Rubambura-engoma)

7. Chinwa cha Kabambo   Katobaha I of Ukerewe

After Betbeder (1971), 742-743)

Appendix to the introduction II

Dynasty of Basilanga-Bahinda Kings of Ukerewe
(Dates are for periods of reign)

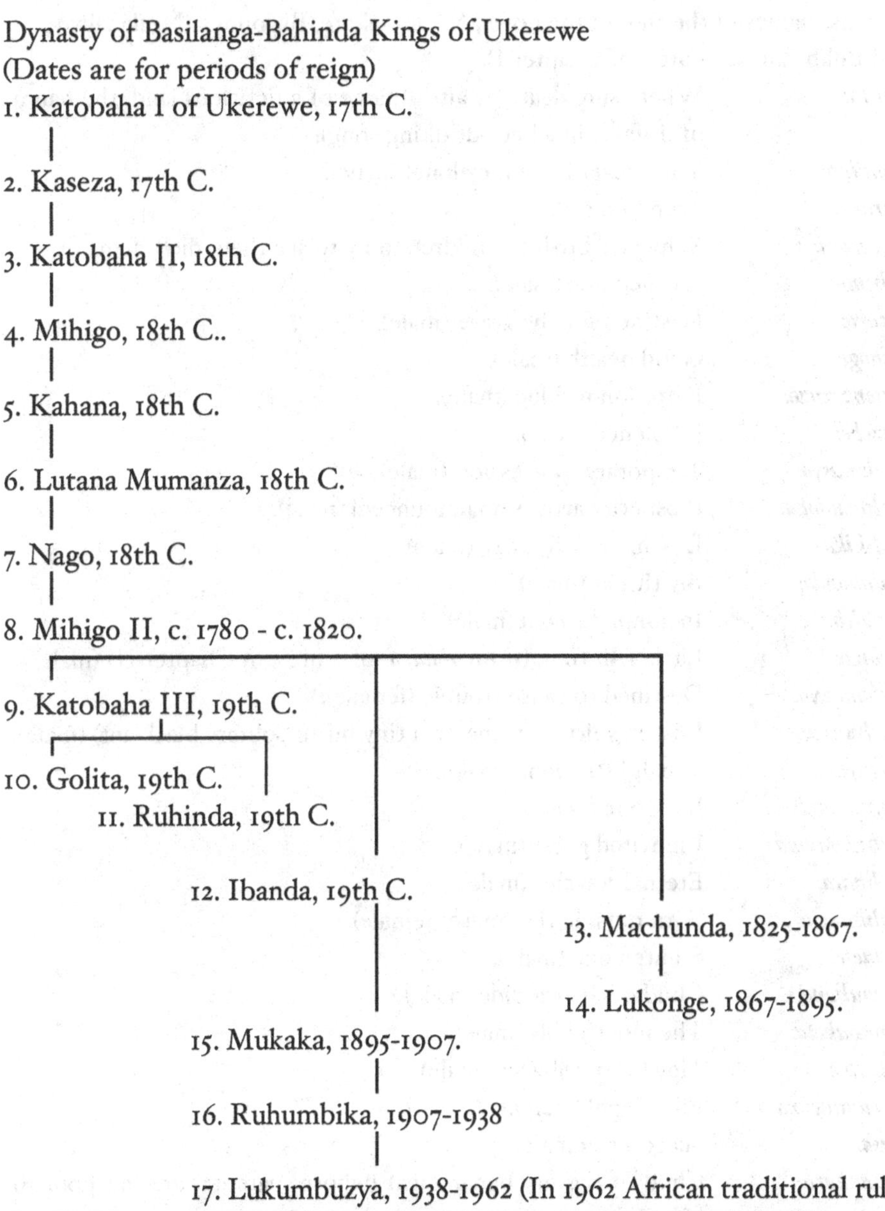

17. Lukumbuzya, 1938-1962 (In 1962 African traditional rule
    in newly independent Tanganyika was abolished by
    Presidential Decree).

From Hartwig (1976, 243) and the annals of Ukerewe as recorded by
Alphonce Mkama II son of *Omukama* Mukaka (Mkama II).

KIKEREWE NAMES IN THE NOVEL WITH THEIR MEANINGS

(For the names of the title of the novel, Myombekere, Bugonoka, Ntulanalwo and Bulihwali, see note 1 of Chapter I).

Balita:	Where sure death awaits! (name of a fictitious land, the haunt of drunks, in a beer-drinking song).
Bandiho:	They never leave me alone! (male).
Barongo:	Twin (female).
Bazaraki:	Why give birth to children (only to see them die!) (female).
Bihemo:	Scorned one (male).
Bituro:	Destined for the grave (male).
Bunoge:	Good health (male).
Busengezuzo:	Filtration residue (male).
Buzebe:	Indolence (male).
Byekwasyo:	Temporary possession (male).
Galibondoka:	Prosperity arrives unannounced! (male).
Galikika:	Destined to go awry (male).
Galubondo:	Big throat (male).
Gwaleba:	Incomplete soul (male).
Kabigo:	Little fish trap, (from *olubigo* of note 3 of Chapter II) (male).
Kabunazya:	Destined to cause trouble (female).
Kachwera:	Unseen spitter (name of a tiny biting solitary black ant) (male).
Kagufwa:	Tough little bone (male).
Kahwagizi:	Rash one (male).
Kahwamama:	Uninvited guest (male).
Kalibata:	Eternal traveler (male).
Kalihanza:	Born outside the house (female).
Kamese:	Stunted one (male).
Kamuhanda:	Child of the wayside (male).
Kanwakcta:	The mouth kills (male).
Kapapo:	Tiny bit of tobacco (male).
Karundugara:	Piled high! (male).
Kasaka:	Succorer (female).
Kasankara:	Child of the dry banana leaf (whose parents are too poor to afford proper swaddling for their newborn), also child of mourning times (when people use dry banana leaves as bedding for mourners during funeral wakes) (male).
Kasigwa:	Abandoned child (whose parent or parents died shortly after its birth (female).

Katetwanfune:	Too tough to kill by a fist (male).
Katoliro:	Eternity (male).
Kawherela:	Child with disappearing (skinny) body (male).
Kayobyo:	Child of the *omuyobyo* greens (born in hard times with no fish or meat for the mother's relish) (male).
Kazoba:	Tiny sun (male).
Kazoka:	Tiny snake (male).
Kazolika:	Child of drizzling rain (female).
Kibuguma:	The flaming one (male).
Kikunami:	Easily toppled (male).
Kongwa:	Rainbow (male).
Kurobone:	Staring eyes (male).
Lubezi:	Flame (male).
Lubona:	Destined for prosperity (male).
Lukonge:	The over-seasoned one (male).
Lumezya:	Germination (male).
Lusalira:	Bitter taste (male).
Lwakarege:	Blabber (male).
Lwambicho:	Bearer of tidings of death (male).
Lweganwa:	The longed-for one (male).
Mafwere:	Death's way (male).
Mahendeka:	Aches and pains (male).
Malyalya:	Indiscriminate appetite (male).
Masale:	Body incisions (clan name of the Abagembe clan of Chapter XXXVIII) (female).
Matebya:	The wily one (male).
Matogo:	Mention of the forbidden word (male).
Matulire:	Life without purpose (male).
Mbali:	Cunning (male).
Mbaliro:	Guessing (male).
Mbarwa:	One to count on (male).
Mbonabibi:	Destined for misfortunes (female).
Mbulamugani:	Pitied by nobody (male).
Mfwanabwo:	Destined to die in misery (female).
Mpazi:	"Safari" ant (name of big black biting ant often found in interminable columns) (male).
Mpigi:	Brave one (name of a big ant with a very hard body) (male).
Mpongano:	Grumbler (female).

Mpugayani: Unruly one (male).

Mugeniwalwo: Guest of death (male).

Mugimba: Rain-maker (male).

Mukingira: Locked-door miser (male).

Mukweru: Child of Kweru minor island of Ukerewe (male).

Munegera: Welcome visitor (female).

Murwa: Clear-minded one (female).

Mwebeya: Self-accuser (male).

Mwizanalwo: Born with death (substitute name for Ntulanalwo, "Death is my eternal companion", in the Kikerewe substitute vocabulary of note 33 of Chapter XXV) (male).

Nabutuma: Commanding one! (female).

Nabutwema: Child of morning dew (female).

Nakazenze: Woman of legendary beauty (female).

Nakiro: Born at nighttime (female).

Nakulinga: Lead singer (male).

Nakutuga: One who struts (euphemism for "one who limps") (male).

Nakuyenga: Wanderer (female).

Namiti: Born of the healer's herbs (female).

Namugambage: One who speaks his own mind (male).

Namuhani: Admonisher (name of a big ant with a painful bite)(male).

Namusya: Snuff grinder (male).

Namwero: Child of harvest (male).

Nanzala: Child of famine (female).

Nawanchuma: Hopper (name of a type of grasshopper) (male).

Nemba: Name of the bird of ill-fame (see Chapter XXV) (male).

Netoga: The heart's desire (female).

Ngundamugali: Huge calabash of banana beer, said to be an unusual name even in the novel (male).

Ngwebe: Starving-lean one (male).

Nkarani: Noisy one (male).

Nkubitizi: Garrulous one (male).

Nkwanzi: Beads (female).

Nkwesi: Person of attractive character (male).

Nsyana: Grinder (male).

Ntamba: The martin (a bird with a myth attached to it we find in Chapter XXV) (male).

Tibwenigirwa: One doesn't commit suicide on account of barrenness (female).

Tibwomo:	Misery is for us all (female).
Tilumanywa or	
Tirumanywa:	Death the unknowable (male).
Waburuza:	Child of Buruza minor island of Ukerewe (female).
Walyoba:	Foreign name which in in Kikerewe means "child of the sun" (male).
Weroba:	Child of the days of angling fish (female).